VAMPIRES IN VERSAILLES

THE COMPLETE SERIES

LILY RILEY

THE ASSASSIN AND THE LIBERTINE

BOOK ONE

PROLOGUE
DAPHNE

January 17, 1765
Paris

I WATCHED HIM, PATIENTLY, FROM BEHIND MY CARVED IVORY FAN. HE appeared to be a capable servant—unobtrusive, almost preternaturally aware of the needs of the duc's guests, and just on the attractive side of plain in his dark gray livery. When he finally flicked his gaze to me, I lowered my lashes flirtatiously and drew my fan across my lips—an open invitation for a clandestine dalliance. The corner of his mouth twitched, and he nodded almost imperceptibly.

From the edge of the stifling ballroom, a gong sounded, announcing dinner. Gentlemen paired off with ladies, making their way into the dining room.

"Madame, shall we go in?"

The fat, thick-headed, wealthy lout at my elbow held out his arm. He'd been trying to monopolize my attentions all evening, despite my thinly concealed distaste. He reminded me of an overfed leech, pawing at me with his slimy, limp appendages and grinning with his yellow, toothy mouth. I covered my grimace with a wan smile.

"Monsieur le Vicomte," I answered. "Please, do go in and find your seat. I need a moment to refresh myself. I'll be along shortly."

The leech eyed me up and down, offering a prurient wink. Unable to suppress my disgust much longer, I turned from him before he could see my expression.

The smell of food wafted in through the open doors. I hadn't eaten all day, but truthfully, I was not hungry—for *dinner*.

I left the gilt opulence of the ballroom and made my way down a candlelit corridor, discreetly checking the rooms for errant partygoers and trysting courtiers. I required absolute solitude, and fortune appeared to be on my side tonight. The duc's Parisian townhouse was impressive—if a little dated with all its *baroque* enthusiasm—and seldom in use. Like some members of court, he lived almost year-round at Versailles. Years before, King Louis XIV's paranoia had set that precedent for the aristocracy. *If you wish to feel the warmth of the Sun King, you must remain within his orbit.*

How suffocating. I was almost glad my husband had fled to Italy in disgrace, despite him leaving me to the absent mercy of the wolves of Versailles. At least I was free to maintain my own residence—and more importantly, I was free of him. The thought of my vile, abusive husband soured my stomach.

It seemed that King Louis XV, the Beloved, had a more relaxed view of things. *But for how long,* I wondered. France was changing at the speed of infection. The king could not continue to ignore *la peste du sang* that was starting to seep through the streets of Paris. The blood plague was upon us and I feared what was happening to the people of France.

Several doors down, I found what I was looking for—the duc's empty study. A few candles flickered inside, casting dancing shadows upon the gold brocade of the walls. Hopefully, young Giles had accepted my invitation and I wouldn't have to wait long.

I perched on the edge of the large desk, careful not to bend my panniers, and adjusted my navy skirts around me. The dark color was somewhat unfashionable this season, but I wasn't at Versailles and tonight I favored a gown that was a touch more utilitarian. The pastel palette of the court was hellacious for us more *active* members of the nobility. The stains could be murder.

Movement outside caught my eye, and I went to the window to observe. Snow had started to fall in soft, downy clumps. I watched the flakes drift gently onto the balcony terrace and smiled to myself. I flung the doors open, letting in a flurry of frigid air.

I almost didn't hear the soft click of the door closing behind me, but I'd been waiting.

Without turning, I spoke out to the snowy balcony.

"I'm so glad you came, darling Giles. I've been waiting all evening to get you alone."

Strong arms circled my waist, turning me to him and pulling me back inside the study. His eyes glittered fiercely, hungrily.

Without a word, he crushed his mouth to mine. His hands roamed my body, seeking the softness of skin beneath the silken layers of my gown.

"I don't have long," he grunted. He pushed me roughly against the wall, attempting to lift my heavy skirts.

"*Oui*, I know, *ma cher*. Neither do I," I murmured. He'd found my legs beneath the copious underskirts and ran a cold hand up my thigh. I grabbed him by the shoulders and reversed our positions, pressing his body to the wall with my hips. He gasped in excitement and fumbled for the buttons of his breeches. I kissed him softly.

Dispassionately.

With him distracted, it was almost too easy for me to stab him through the heart.

He pushed me away—bewildered, pained—as smoke curled from the small wound in his chest. I slid the thin wooden stake out, wiped the blood on his livery, and tucked it back in my garter for my next assignment.

Only then did his fangs distend.

"*Putain de salope*," he hissed. His skin turned a mottled grey and he slumped to the floor.

I *tsked*. "Oh, Giles. How long did you think you could carry on like this —feeding your way through the duc's housemaids? Six young girls are dead already, Giles. Six! Did you think we wouldn't notice a rotten little *sanguisuge* in our midst?"

He groaned in pain and glared at me.

"You're with them, then. *The Order*. Didn't think they allowed women in."

"Yes, well, what a lesson for you to learn today. *We are everywhere*. Too bad you won't be able to share that news with your filthy parasite friends, eh?"

The dying footman rasped a laugh, coughing up a trickle of black blood that steamed in the cold room.

"It won't matter if you're *everywhere*. It won't matter how many you are, how much money the aristocracy has or how good The Order's spies are. None of it will save you from what's coming."

A chill went up my spine that had nothing to do with the snow blowing in through the open terrace doors.

"What's coming?" I demanded, leaning in.

"*La mort.*"

His eyes dulled on a final exhale, and the young vampire Giles sagged against the wall. I dragged his body to the balcony and heaved it over, leaving it in the snow-dusted bushes for another agent to find and dispose of. I never asked anyone at The Order what they did with the bodies of all the vampires we dispatched. Truthfully, I couldn't bring myself to care.

After setting the room and my gown to rights, I exited the study and made my way to the dining room. I passed a note to a footman—a coded message for The Order that read *assignment complete, target retrieval requested*—and sat next to the Leech, who would no doubt boast about spending the entirety of the evening flirting with the Duchesse de Duras, thus providing me with an unattractive, dim-witted, but unquestionable alibi.

The remainder of the evening passed as planned. Giles likely wouldn't be discovered missing until the morning and, even then, people would suspect he'd run off with one of the "missing" housemaids. Even though the job was done, a whisper of unease went through me at his dying words. I tried to dismiss it as a final attempt to frighten me, or swear some kind of undead vengeance, but I didn't really believe that. Giles knew something.

Death. Death was coming.

ÉTIENNE

That Same Evening
Palace of Versailles

Just before her pleasure crested, my fangs lengthened and I nipped firmly at her thigh, drawing the blood I needed to survive. I'd waited too long to feed again, and the hunger clawed at my insides. I forced myself to take only what she could give without suffering. Fortunately, it was enough. *Barely.*

"*Très magnifique,*" she panted, reaching for me. "Now I understand what Yvette meant when she said you were a delightful beast."

The marquise giggled and sighed. I lifted my head from beneath her hideous orange skirts and grinned wolfishly at her, but the words had stung.

A delightful beast.

"What would the marquis say if he found you in bed with such a beast?"

The marquise snorted and stood from the chaise we'd been enjoying. She adjusted the bodice of her unfashionable gown and straightened the powdered mass of curls atop her head.

"He stupidly thinks I don't know about his penchant for the servant girls. If I were interested in catching his eye, I'd just have to don some depressing brown wool and bow gracelessly before bringing him dinner."

The Marquise de Balay was a dangerous conquest. She was fiercely intelligent, wealthy as sin, and, because she was a distant relation to the king, her witless husband enjoyed an impressive set of privileges at court. Her opinions formed his, and so if I needed help to sway the king's mind, I needed her manipulations at my disposal. Despite her unfortunate taste in clothing, the marquise was a powerful influence.

"He wouldn't be offended to find his wife *fraternizing* with a vampire?" I pressed.

She cut me a disdainful look and arched a supercilious brow.

"Possibly. But you're not like the rest of them, are you? Your father was the former Vicomte de Noailles. Even if he was disgraced, you come from noble blood. The rest of those plague bloodsuckers are all peasants, aren't they? Farmers. The *poor.* You're the king's appointed emissary and advisor on how to deal with the *sanguisuge* menace. You aren't really one of them," she sniffed.

She left off, *you aren't really one of us, either,* but the words seemed to hang in the air, nonetheless.

Anger burned through me at her distaste toward my family and my kind. With a flare of disappointment, I realized she wouldn't be willing to join my cause. *Vampire rights* were a joke to the over-primped peacocks mincing through the halls of Versailles. She didn't see the tension stretching between the classes—the danger we were all in as the impoverished vampire populace grew. She, like the rest of the court, was blind to the true threats to France. Terror would not come from the battles fought on foreign soil. It would come from within.

And nobody would heed my warnings.

"Besides, The Order will certainly stop them," she offered casually. She was replacing her diamond chandelier earrings—fat, colorless stones that winked in the candlelight.

I stilled.

"What do you know of The Order? I always heard they were a myth." I laughed. I knew they were *not* a myth, but it surprised me to hear the marquise discuss them so openly.

She shrugged. "Only the gossip, I suppose. Surely you've heard?"

"I haven't." I *had.* They'd sent two assassins after me already—one disguised as a cut-purse, and the other masquerading as a drunken brawler in one of my favorite taverns. I'd smelled the lies on their clothes before they'd had the chance to stake me. At least their blood had sustained me for a while. The intervening years of poverty between my

father's disgrace and my royal appointment had taught me that much—
waste not, want not.

The marquise waved her hand dismissively. "You know, they've finally
gotten sensible about the plague and excommunicated the members of
The Order from the lower classes. I mean, if it's only the weakest peasants
that suffer the infection, it's right that the stronger elites should decide
what to do about it. We have the intelligence, the funds, the breeding.
Don't expect me to listen to some dirt farmer about how to save my noble
soul."

She giggled venomously. My stomach churned with her snobbish
blood. I swallowed my disgust and nodded.

"We should return to the party," I said. "I believe I'm wanted for a card
game."

The marquise smiled, but it didn't quite reach her eyes.

"Thank you for the distraction," she said as she turned for the door. "It
was rather...*animal.*"

Instead of following her back to the party, I summoned my carriage
and returned to my château. Only when I was safely ensconced in my
familial home did I allow myself the pleasure of venting my rage by
smashing my fist through the wall.

She didn't care. None of them did. Despite my attempts to stop it—to
prevent it from happening, nobody else could see what was coming. And
many of them would pay with their lives.

1

DAPHNE

September 22, 1765
Palace of Versailles

I HURRIED THROUGH THE HALL OF MIRRORS AS FAST AS I COULD, WHICH WAS —unfortunately—not *at all* fast. It wasn't the formal court dress that hindered my progress—I could run from one end of Paris to the other in stays and panniers, if I needed to. Nor was it the flintlock pistol, wooden stakes, and throwing knives strapped to my thighs. My stilted pace was all for the sake of propriety. My need to blend in with the other titled ladies of court was distinctly at odds with my real reason for attending the king's party tonight. Running through the palace was not exactly the kind of behavior one would expect from one of the most notable duchesses of the *tonne.*

Since I wanted to avoid unnecessary notice, *hurrying* was well out of the question and the best I could manage was an ambitious glide— possibly an assertive shuffle. I regretted the decision to delay my arrival until after sunset. I should have given myself more time to make a proper appearance, circulate with the other members of court, and then ready myself to lay my deadly trap.

I paused in front of my reflection in the mirrored wall that led to the courtyard outside, frowning at the beads of sweat on my forehead. Darting a look at the stoic footmen in the room, I blotted my face with my handkerchief and opened my fan to cool myself.

Breathe, Daphne. It's almost over. Soon, there will be justice for Jeanne—and vengeance for Michel.

I caught the eye of one of the servants and raised my chin haughtily, as if to say, *Of course I wasn't sweating! Duchesses do not sweat. They glow with the pleasure and privilege of nobility*—even though none would dare make such a comment to me, particularly the footmen in the palace of Louis the Beloved.

As I made my way into the courtyard, a squeal erupted from behind a tower of champagne glasses.

"Daphne, *chérie*! You're finally here! I've been waiting for over an hour already."

I smiled at the mass of swirling blue silk careening toward me. My cousin, Charlotte, did not have the same issues moving in haste, though she had never been one to care much for propriety.

She kissed my cheeks and I embraced her tightly. After my brother Michel was murdered, Charlotte was my only remaining blood relative. She'd stayed with me for a time after his death, fussing over me in a way that helped to distract me from the abyss of my grief. She had become like a sister to me.

"*Bon soir*, Charlotte! I see you have swindled your husband for another new gown."

"That's not all," Charlotte giggled, gesturing gracefully at the diamond choker around her neck.

I furrowed my brow. "Oh, no! What's Philippe done now?"

Charlotte snorted with laughter, attracting the attention of several courtiers. Clearly, she'd had one too many glasses of champagne while waiting for my arrival.

"It's an 'I miss you' gift he brought back from Venice. It's beautiful, no?"

She twirled around, stumbling slightly. My arm shot out swiftly to steady her.

"Why, Duchesse de Duras, what *exceptional* reflexes you have," came a silky voice at my ear. I dropped Charlotte's arm and whirled around. The man seemed to have materialized from a pool of darkness at the edge of the garden. Despite the unseasonable warmth of the evening, I shivered.

He was clad in a rich, emerald green coat that made his striking hazel eyes appear strangely golden—almost wolf-like. They burned with heated intensity beneath long, feathery lashes. His sharp cheekbones, chiseled jaw, and elegant patrician nose looked like they'd inspired features of Michelangelo's *David*, but his full lips hinted at something much less divine and far more sinful. Unlike the other nobles, he wore no wig, but had powdered his own dark locks in a soft grey and had tied them back at the nape of his neck with a ribbon. Beneath the well-cut coat, expertly tied cravat, and indecently tight breeches, I knew he was a powerfully built man. His laid-back elegance and rakish charm did little to disguise the coiled tension and corded muscle of a predator.

I schooled my features in a mask of bland entitlement to cover my apprehension.

I'd been shadowing him whenever he turned up at court, usually when he was waiting for his weekly audiences with the king. Most of the *dames* and *demoiselles* at Versailles refused to acknowledge him publicly, but their lustful gazes followed his every move. I suppose I could admit—entirely dispassionately, of course—that he was attractive in an obvious sort of way. It didn't change the fact that beneath the seductive exterior lurked a bloodsucking villain—a selfish parasite of sheer malevolence. In fact, it made his allure that much more disturbing.

He bowed stiffly and smiled, his eyes never leaving mine. Despite my outward detachment, my heart pounded. Tonight was the night I'd been waiting for—the assignment that I hoped would further my position within The Order. I'd had to work twice as hard as the male agents—first, to prove I was worthy to join The Order in the first place, and then to be taken seriously enough to earn assignments that were more than just gossip-collecting intelligence work. Tonight, I'd banish any lingering doubts for good.

Realizing I'd yet to formally acknowledge the man before me, I inclined my head.

"I don't believe we've been introduced, Monsieur."

His strange eyes glittered, assessing.

"Oh, but I'm sure we have, Madame. You do not remember? It was perhaps a year ago, but I remember you, of course." One corner of his mouth kicked up in a suggestive grin.

I did not return his smile.

"Étienne de Noailles, vampire emissary to His Majesty," he said, executing another bow.

He left out *disgraced former vicomte, legendary rake, outspoken bourgeoisie sympathizer,* and—if my sources within The Order were correct—*cold-blooded murderer of Jeanne Antoinette, Madame de Pompadour.*

"Monsieur de Noailles," I returned. A tense moment passed between us, like a bowstring pulled taut.

Then, unfazed by my cold address, he turned to greet Charlotte. The flirtatious greeting he issued my cousin was nauseating in its effusiveness. I watched him carefully, trying to decide if he really was as dangerous as The Order affirmed, or if he was simply the rutting beast the women of court believed, driven entirely by his libido. Either way, his very presence unsettled me.

"Comtesse de Brionne, you look resplendent this evening! Did you know that sapphire blue is my second favorite color?"

"And what, Monsieur l'Émissaire, is your first favorite color?" Charlotte tittered.

"Perhaps it is a mystery," he said with a wink. "Or perhaps it is the lovely pink of your blush."

I suppressed a gag at Charlotte's breathy giggle and playful slap. I had strict orders to dispense with Noailles covertly, so I couldn't just stake him here in the middle of the party—despite being sorely tempted. I'd lure him away from everyone—particularly Charlotte. The hedge maze in the back of the grounds was the perfect spot.

In the corner of my eye, I caught Charlotte's husband, Philippe, Comte de Brionne, beckoning me over to a large potted palm. He'd helped convince The Order to train me as an agent—their first and only woman, I might add—in exchange for my permission to let him court Charlotte. The arrangement suited all three of us. Philippe was tall and plain, but he had always been friendly to me and kind to Charlotte. At any rate, he was less of a scoundrel than my own villainous husband, which meant Charlotte would be protected from the things I'd already had to endure. If I could shield her, at least, I might be able to convince myself that my marriage to the Duc de Duras had been worth something.

I frowned at my melancholy memories and then at Charlotte's outrageous flirtation with Noailles. Not bothering to make my excuses, I turned on my heel and made for Philippe.

"An 'I miss you' gift of diamonds? Really, Philippe?" I teased.

Philippe winced. "The Order is sending me to London for another three months. I haven't told her yet. I meant to tell her when I gave her the necklace, but she assumed it was for my last trip to Venice."

He pulled me back behind the large palms, safely obscuring us from the view of the other guests.

I looked back at Charlotte and Noailles, still engrossed in each other's company. "Perhaps she needs some looking after, or your company, at least. You could take her with you."

Philippe shook his head. "No. It will be difficult enough for me and soon it will be nearly impossible. The king is considering closing the borders to stop the spread of the blood plague."

"Close the borders! Around all of France?"

He motioned for me to keep my voice down and looked around.

"Be silent, Daphne. Very few at court know, and the king harbors no delusions that the act will go over well."

"But the plague is already here!" I argued. "What good will closing the borders do? And how will he enforce it with most of the army and resources depleted by his petty foreign skirmishes?"

Philippe shrugged. "The king is—shall we say—concerned. The latest reports indicate that it's more than just grubbing peasants being infected. The plague is starting to sweep through the bourgeoisie. Vampire numbers keep growing, Daphne, and no one knows what to do about it."

"Other than The Order," I said dutifully. The Order—a long-shadowed assembly of powerful individuals (some say descended from Templar Knights) had been convening on the matter since the first cases of plague appeared in France a few years ago. They'd taken a stand against the virulent disease, determined to protect the people of France at any cost.

"Yes, naturally," Philippe nodded. "The emissary isn't really helping matters, either. Instead of trying to find ways to safeguard the uninfected, he keeps insisting that we address the needs of the *sanguisuges* first. As if *vampire rights* would save the rest of us from such damnation. It'll be better for all of us when his influence has been tempered." At his last words, he eyed me meaningfully.

The news was grim. I looked toward the hedge maze, trying to find my focus.

"I'm sorry to tell you all of this tonight. I know you've other important things on your mind," Philippe said, taking my hand and holding it between his. I flinched and pulled away.

He frowned behind a pink wash of embarrassment.

"I'm sorry. I didn't mean—it's just that ever since Henri, you know…" I faltered.

He held up his hand to stay my explanation. "Please. Don't think on it. We all knew what kind of a man Henri was when you married him. For that matter, we all knew you were fragile—in a delicate position—"

My cheeks reddened with the unintended insult, but he blustered on.

"And, of course, I don't fault you for that. I only wish you would've let me—us—help you more. But I suppose now his absence is something of a blessing, is it not?"

Le Duc Dépravé," I spit. "From the Depraved Duke to the Departed Duke, even when he's gone his scandal blackens me."

Philippe stirred the gravel with the tip of his shoe and coughed uncomfortably.

"Do you know how you're going to do it tonight?" His icy blue eyes were fixed rigidly upon Noailles, who was whispering something in Charlotte's ear. A muscle ticked in Philippe's jaw.

I exhaled uneasily. "Yes. I've got it all worked out."

Philippe looked skeptical. "This isn't like dispatching some infected peasant, you know. Noailles is older than most of the other infected in Paris, and you mustn't underestimate his cunning. He is *dangerous,* darling. You know I adore you, but I just don't think you're up to this kind of assignment." He made a peculiar noise of frustration and I almost laughed. He glared.

"I am ready. I'm certainly more prepared than anyone else," I argued.

"Perhaps, but you just don't have the same physical capabilities as the other men. You lack their edge. Now, don't get upset, Daphne. I'm not saying you don't possess other exceptional qualities. I mean, you're certainly the best intelligence gatherer we have. It's only that I want you safe. The Order should have assigned another agent. I hate that you're mixed up in all of this, and I don't mind telling you I don't fancy you being alone with him."

"Jeanne wasn't just the king's mistress, Philippe," I whispered, ignoring the irritation I felt at his slights. "She was a friend. When I heard that she'd been attacked and left to die, I couldn't help but think of my brother, Michel. If Noailles is the bastard that killed her, then I'll happily dust him."

At that moment, Noailles looked directly at me and our eyes locked across the courtyard. I wondered if he'd heard our whispered conversation. I cursed my carelessness. I knew the creatures had supernatural hearing and sight, as well as accelerated reflexes. Something in his golden eyes made every nerve in my body crackle with energy. His otherworldly beauty was too much for something straight from the depths of Hell. Had Jeanne felt the same way? Entranced by the hypnotic eroticism of a predator? Had she left the king's bed one night to steal away with the irresistible libertine, only to be ruthlessly savaged while the rogue took his pleasure?

I closed my eyes against that disturbing vision and took a glass of champagne from a passing footman. Draining it in one swallow, I forced myself to face him, but he was gone.

Charlotte approached and threw her arms around Philippe's neck.

"*Mon cher,* everyone loves my new bauble! You are truly the best husband in France. Perhaps in all the world," she said. She swayed a bit as she spoke.

"Charlotte, darling, what did Monsieur de Noailles want?" Philippe asked with a touch of irritation.

She waved her hand airily. "Nothing of consequence, really. He mostly wanted to know about Daphne. I didn't tell him anything worthwhile, of course."

Philippe and I exchanged a look.

"You know, I think perhaps the good emissary fancies you. You should give him a whirl! All the ladies at court say that he's the most accomplished lover they've ever had," Charlotte whispered, though none too quietly.

Philippe sputtered a bit and wrapped a possessive hand around Charlotte's arm.

"Well," he huffed. "I believe on that note, we'll take our leave. Good night, Daphne, and good luck." He ushered his wife back through the palace, casting a meaningful glance at me.

"Come for tea tomorrow, *chérie*!" Charlotte called. I smiled and waved at the retreating pair.

"Your cousin is a charming creature."

I jumped at the vampire's voice near my ear again. Instinct had my fist at his throat before I could stop myself. He easily blocked the strike, grabbing my hand and using it to pull me in close to him. His iron grip didn't loosen when I tried to pull away, so I clenched my other hand and punched him in the stomach, only to connect with a wall of hard, tense muscle. He barely flinched—merely arched one dark brow and *tsked*.

"I think, *ma chère Duchesse*, we have a few things we need to discuss."

2

ÉTIENNE

September 22, 1765
Palace of Versailles

SHE WAS MUCH STRONGER THAN SHE APPEARED. NO MATCH FOR THE supernatural strength the plague had bestowed on me, certainly, but still, much stronger than I expected. While I didn't put much stock in the usefulness of the women of the court beyond slaking certain appetites and exerting occasional influence upon their more dim-witted husbands, I could at least acknowledge when some ornamental ninny possessed something outside the ordinary. I'd seen the duchesse watching me over the last several months but hadn't considered her a proper threat until recently. I realized now, clutching her arm, I had miscalculated—an oversight I soundly regretted. As my father had often warned, *"Never underestimate a woman."*

Especially one sent to assassinate you.

I had to hand it to The Order—of all the ways they'd tried to deliver me unto Death, this was the most…*enticing.*

Her soft peaches-and-cream complexion, wide violet eyes, and pert rosebud lips set in a furious pout gave her the appearance of a wrathful angel boiling over with self-righteousness. She was unable to free herself from my grip, so I allowed myself the luxury of an intimate perusal of her full form—partly because it unsettled her, but partly because I found her *fascinating.* My gaze raked lazily over her, from the top of her powdered curls, down the graceful column of her neck, to her luscious breasts straining at the top of her neckline. I tracked down the crimson silk of her bodice to her trim waist, ensconced in those unseen stays, and wondered what her undergarments might look like. Would they be silk? Would they be adorned with ribbons, rosettes, or lace? Would they match this daring, provocative gown? I hardened at the thought.

"If you wish to speak with me, Monsieur," she spat. "Then perhaps you might release my arm so that we can converse properly."

"Perhaps I don't want to release you," I murmured in her ear. "Perhaps I don't feel like being staked tonight, despite your *orders*." I breathed in her scent—orange blossom and vanilla. I wondered what she'd taste like.

I saw her eyes widen momentarily. So, now she knew that I knew her allegiance to The Order. When the moment of shock wore off, she huffed in irritation and gritted her teeth.

"Then go on and break it."

I stepped back, stunned. She hadn't offered it as a careless challenge. Her expression was determined, not daring.

"I beg your pardon?" I relaxed my grip on her arm but did not let her go. A quick glance across the courtyard told me we were beginning to attract attention. The disappointed moue of the Marquise de Balay told me that people would be gossiping already.

The beast has found his next diversion.

Cursing silently, I tugged her into the king's ridiculous hedge maze, away from the prying eyes and wagging tongues of the idiotic aristocracy. After so many clandestine trysts out here, I knew the ins and outs of the garden labyrinth almost as well as my own château.

She practically growled at me in response, exciting something embarrassingly primal in my blood. I was trying to sort out whether I wanted to feed on her or fuck her. *Probably both, provided she doesn't plunge a stake into my heart.*

"Break it, then," she repeated, steel in her gaze. She struggled and I tightened my hold on her.

She hissed at me in disgust and tried to pull away again.

"If you know that I'm with The Order, Monsieur, then you'll know why they sent me. You may break my arm to escape death at my hands tonight, but I assure you, I have had worse and it will only buy you a few hours reprieve."

I enjoyed that the spoiled little minx had spirit, but her comment ignited a spark of dread and anger. *She'd had worse than a broken arm? She was a beautiful woman, and a duchesse, for God's sake.*

Infuriated, she continued.

"Allow me to tell you how this will go. You will break my arm, I shall scream, the guards will come running, and even with your monstrous strength and speed, they will catch up to you—probably in the daylight hours when you need your rest. And because you'll have brutally injured the Duchesse de Duras—when you are *not*, in fact, her husband—our beloved king will have your head cut off and my task will be accomplished regardless of the function of one arm. So, either let me go or break my arm. It matters little which."

I tugged her further into the maze, impressed by her vivid imagination and the speed at which her mind worked. Yet again, her words gave me pause.

"When I am not, in fact, your husband—what do you mean by that, Madame?"

"None of your damn business, you brute!" Her cheeks flamed near the color of her gown. In her fury, she'd obviously admitted more than she would have liked. She kicked at my shin, but I sidestepped it. I twisted her arm behind her back and pushed her forward. She let fly a string of curses that I hadn't heard many ladies use. With her free hand, she produced a wooden stake from one of her pockets, which I knocked away. She uttered a muffled scream of frustration.

"Let me go, you oversexed bloodsucker!"

I couldn't help but laugh at the insult. *This is too much fun.*

Finally, we neared a stone bench at the center of the maze. Few other revelers would make it in this far, which guaranteed us a modicum of privacy.

"I'll offer you a trade then," I said. "I'll return your arm to you in exchange for the opportunity to *enlighten* you."

She narrowed her eyes and her lips twisted in derision. "If you think to *enlighten* me carnally, know that I would rather fuck Lucifer himself than willingly let you defile me."

My cock twitched at her profanity and I chuckled again. "What a wicked mind and sharp tongue you have, Madame. But no, rest assured I prefer my bedmates' dispositions to be much more amiable and, more importantly, willing. No, *ma chère Duchesse*, I mean only to enlighten you with the truth. With several truths, in fact."

"And you'll let me go unharmed? If I merely listen to you?" Suspicion darkened her tone.

"Of course. But you'll have to promise the same. We'll both leave this meeting alive—well, alive or undead."

"You'll just be postponing the inevitable," she sneered.

"Perhaps, but if that is the case, you have nothing to lose," I pointed out.

She considered this. Testing my grip on her arm once more as if to confirm her predicament, she groaned in irritation and relented. "Very well. You have my word. I will hear you out."

"And?"

"And I will not attempt to kill you tonight. I cannot promise the same for tomorrow."

I nodded, satisfied, and released my hold on her arm. She pulled away and sat on the stone bench, rubbing her hand. When I was sure she wasn't going to stake me or run, I sat on the opposite end of the bench and faced her.

"I wouldn't have broken it, you know," I said. "I do *not* hurt women."

She scoffed at me—her disbelief needling me more than it should have. *Irritating harpy.*

"...unless they ask me to," I purred. She attempted that imperious glare again, but it faded with her impatience.

"Plead your case, *Noailles*," she demanded.

"Étienne."

"Your Christian name will not soften me to you," she chided. "But in the spirit of *détente*, you may address me as Daphne."

Daphne. The beautiful nymph who begged to be turned into a laurel tree, rather than love the sun god, Apollo. A fitting myth of one woman's pride in the face of love.

"It suits you," I chortled.

She tapped her foot expectantly. I sighed.

"I did not kill Madame de Pompadour," I said. "I'm sure that's what The Order has told you and I'm sure that's why you're here tonight, but it isn't true."

"And I'll just take your word for it, shall I? You'll have to do better than that if you are to convince me."

"Were you at court that day? The day they found her body?" I asked.

She shook her head and glared at me accusingly. "No, but I heard the report and the stories. Her throat had been bitten, almost all of her blood drained. You are the only vampire allowed inside the palace. There are guards posted everywhere. If any other *sanguisuge* had come in, they would have been found and executed."

At her use of the elitist slur for the vampire peasants, I could not stifle my disgust. I whirled on her, enraged. My fangs lengthened and my eyes darkened. A predator ready to strike.

"Take care with your words, Duchesse."

She leaned back, eyes wide.

"Do you know why there are so many vampires in Paris?"

"The plague," she said. "Most say it came over from the East. There is no treatment or cure. It spread through the city because of the deplorable conditions the peasants live in." She spoke slowly —guardedly.

Waiting for me to attack her, I suspected. Most of the nobles thought vampires were little better than slavering dogs, unable to master their baser instincts. *The fools.* I leaned into her, forcing her back against the barrier of greenery.

"Wrong. Oh, yes, it's true enough that it came from the East. From somewhere around the Carpathian Mountains, in fact. And it's true that there are no treatments and no cure. But it didn't spread because of the *filthy peasants* and their *deplorable* homes. It spread because they are deliberately infecting themselves."

"What utter nonsense! No one would willingly choose such a life."

I stared into her lovely violet eyes, so blind to the struggles of a country—a world—outside Versailles. Frustration clawed at me, loosening the tether of my self-control.

"You might if you were starving! If you had too many mouths to feed and not enough bread because of the grain blight, and your beloved king had nothing to offer you but empty promises. No help, no charity, just taxes to pay for his foreign wars and the champagne at his garden parties, while he remains safely ensconced in his walled palace of decadence. How fortunate you are, Duchesse, that you've never had to put yourself in a position risking your very soul for a full belly."

"You know nothing of my life," she hissed, her eyes suddenly wild with emotion.

I seethed in silence for a moment, too afraid I'd given away my own secrets—my family's secrets. Anger, desperation, and a sense of solitary forlornness flowed through me. I was fighting a losing battle with the king and the court, and this damned woman represented every part of my struggle—the ignorance, the entitlement, and every backwards aristocratic ideal. The beauty, the glitter, and the wealth were everything I'd once been promised that had been ripped away from me, only to be dangled in front of my face like some kind of poisoned apple when the king needed a vampire to control.

"I can't believe you," she breathed. "That cannot be true. I know they are struggling because of the grain blight, but surely they can find other ways to—"

"To eat? Yes, they have found another way. Many of them have reasoned that it is easier, *more economical*, to sustain themselves on blood instead of bread. And I'll tell you something else, Duchesse—they have not forgotten who has forced their fangs. A day of reckoning is on the horizon for Louis, for all of us. And damned if we don't deserve it when it comes."

Daphne gasped. "You speak of treason!"

Defeat weighed down my shoulders as I shook my head. My fangs retracted.

"I speak the truth."

Unnerved by my emotional outburst and melancholy tone, she shifted uncomfortably on the bench and toyed with a ruffle on her skirt. After a moment, she recovered.

"And is this why you killed Jeanne? To visit some kind of twisted revenge on the king who has supposedly condemned your kind?" She shot to her feet with the allegation, but I saw the beginnings of doubt clouding her violet eyes.

I moved toward her slowly, stalking her. To her credit, she didn't back away or flinch. She stood her ground, staring up at me defiantly. I heard her pulse quicken and smelled the anticipation in her blood. *Exquisite.*

"Madame de Pompadour's throat was not bitten, Daphne," I said softly. "It was ripped out."

"What?" she uttered, horrified.

"I saw her body when they took her away that night. Her head had almost been severed."

Daphne paled. "But why would you—you could have—"

I rolled my eyes, my temper ebbing.

"In theory, yes, I could have. I possess the physical strength it would take to do such a thing to a body, but as I told you, I do *not* hurt women. I only drink from them with their permission, and almost never from the throat."

She stared at me in confusion. "Then, where…?"

"There are so many more delicious places where the blood flows. Would you like me to show you?" I offered, my voice a low rumble of desire.

I grinned lasciviously at her, loving the sound of her gasp. I was inches away from her, mesmerized by the blush blooming across her chest and cheeks. Suddenly, I was ravenous with hunger—but not for blood. Her lips parted on an intake of breath and my cock hardened to granite. *Damn it, man. Get ahold of yourself.*

I stepped back. Daphne blinked and straightened, and I felt a rush of pleasure at the thought that she, too, had been stirred by our encounter. That pleasure was swiftly followed by a jolt of panic—in the space of a few minutes, this woman had obliterated my carefully crafted sense of self-control. I'd have to be on my guard in the future. Clearly, she was much more dangerous than I'd anticipated.

She glowered at me.

"Are you so sure I'm to blame for Jeanne's death? Why do you think

Louis has not ordered my arrest, then? If everyone is so certain I killed his beloved mistress, why is it left to The Order to be responsible for my punishment?"

She turned from me and I knew I had her.

"Assuming you're telling the truth—which, I'm still not certain of—you must have some idea who killed Jeanne."

"I'm at a loss, I'm afraid," I admitted. "But that's why I have a proposal for you tonight, Duchesse."

She folded her arms in front of her chest, likely to signal her displeasure, but it merely served to squeeze her breasts tighter against her bodice. I forced myself to meet her eyes.

"You are charged with killing the murderer of Madame de Pompadour, no? I am in agreement, because *of course* I didn't do it. Furthermore, I don't believe it was any vampire. I don't want The Order to send some other assassin after me, so it's imperative I clear my name before they do. Ergo, I propose you and I work together to find the killer and bring the bastard to justice."

"Absolutely not," she scoffed. "Perhaps you are telling the truth. If that's the case, I'll discover the murderer myself and deal with him as The Order commands."

"And how will you eliminate the possibility of vampire involvement? Just stroll through the streets of Paris and knock on the nearest coffin for questioning?"

"Why not? I am the Duchesse de Duras," she said with a haughty sniff. "The title is good for something."

"No one will talk to you, Duchesse. You represent the cause of their misery. You'll be lucky if you return to Versailles unmolested and unbitten."

She frowned, uncertainty creeping into her lovely visage again.

"If only you had some sort of intermediary who could help you—an emissary, if you will! Someone who had connections all throughout the city, in both high places and low. Someone else with a stake—no pun intended—in the truth. But where would you find such a humble, handsome ally?"

A look of sheer loathing twisted Daphne's face and I preened.

"If I agree to a temporary alliance with you, it's just that—*temporary*. We will not become friends, or lovers, or anything more than a means to an end—the end, in this case, being the truth. And if I find out that you really are responsible for what happened to Jeanne, I will take great pleasure in cutting out your heart and feeding it to my dogs."

I arched a brow at the violent rage simmering beneath her soft curves.

"And they say that *I'm* the monster!"

3

DAPHNE

September 28, 1765
Château de Champs-sur-Marne

I MADE A DEAL WITH THE DEVIL. *DAMN HIM.*

Monsieur de Noailles or, as he preferred, *Étienne* swore he didn't kill Jeanne. Did I believe him? I hadn't decided. It was true that Étienne was a vampire, and in my estimation, a worthless *roué*, but I felt I owed it to Jeanne to be absolutely certain about his guilt as her murderer. He had, after all, alleged some rather shocking things that I felt compelled to disprove.

Tonight I hoped to do just that.

"Daphne, must we keep drinking this filth?" Charlotte whined, interrupting my thoughts. She wrinkled her nose at her teacup.

"Filth? I'll have you know this is one of the finest teas from China."

"Yes, it's fine and all, but couldn't we have something a bit more fortifying? Some champagne, perhaps, or even a glass of sherry? I mean, what's the good of being married to *le Duc Dépravé* if you can't enjoy a little debauchery yourself once in a while," she said.

"It's ten o'clock in the morning, *chérie*. Doesn't Philippe object to you drinking this early?" I laughed.

She narrowed her gaze at me. "We agreed we weren't going to discuss Philippe, remember? Otherwise, I shall have to plead with you to respond to his messages, and we were having *such* a good time by ourselves."

I winced at her veiled chiding. I'd been avoiding Philippe and the numerous missives he'd sent on behalf of The Order. I knew they'd be furious with me for failing my assignment, but I needed to know if there was even a remote possibility of Étienne speaking the truth—not just about Jeanne, but about the unfortunate people of Paris. Thinking of them offering themselves up to the horrible blood-drinking plague just because they had no alternative turned my stomach. It couldn't be true, could it?

"Incidentally," she carried on, oblivious to my wandering worries. "What he doesn't know won't hurt him, and I pay my servants assiduously to ensure that he *doesn't* know." She lifted her periwinkle-colored skirts and slipped a flask from her garter. She poured a healthy measure of brandy into her teacup and, with a saucy wink, into mine as well.

"Is he horribly cross with me?" I asked her.

Charlotte raised her eyes heavenward. "Philippe is cross about everything these days. The war, the grain blight, our estate, *les sanguisuges*—"

"Oh, don't call them that," I admonished, thinking back to my words with Étienne. I'd felt a curious sort of shame at his reprimand.

Charlotte's eyebrows rose with interest and her mouth split into a wide grin. "Ah! So, you've been entertaining our handsome royal emissary, have you? Lucky thing! If I were the type of woman to have a lover, he would *definitely* be at the top of my list. That naughty smile, that muscled body…" she opened her fan and cooled the blush reddening her face. "You must tell me everything, darling. What's it like with a vampire? Is he —you know—*well-graced?* Do his fangs get in the way when he's licking your—"

I nearly choked on my brandy. "Charlotte, I am *not* 'entertaining' him. We had a conversation at the ball the other night and that's it."

"Daphne, when he approached us, you were so rude to him I find it hard to believe you're not secretly in love with him. I don't blame you, of course. You deserve a little fun, especially after everything with Henri." Her tone was light, but her eyes were full of sympathy.

I shook my head. "No, *chérie*. I'm afraid that the romantic part of me is simply gone."

"So is he," she added with levity. The room started to close in on me and I forced a wry laugh.

"Étienne isn't my type, anyway! He is, perhaps, *too* handsome, and he struts around like he knows it. I hear he's had so many women—well, one mistress wouldn't be enough to slake his appetite. Henri was just like that. One wife and one mistress were never enough. He had to screw half of Paris with that pathetic little worm of his. If I were to involve myself with another man—which is unlikely, so don't get any of your matchmaking ideas—he would be sweet, soulful, and sensitive."

"And hung like an ox," Charlotte added.

I dissolved in a fit of laughter and threw a cushion at her. She dodged it and drained her teacup. My lady's maid, Eve, came forward to refill it. Charlotte shook her head but placed a hand on her arm before she could leave.

"Eve, darling, do you hear anything from the other servants about the emissary's household? What do we know of him?"

Eve shifted, casting her eyes in my direction. "Madame?"

"Come now, surely you'd be obliged to report anything that might have some bearing on Daphne taking him as a lover," Charlotte pressed.

"Charlotte," I warned.

"Any unnatural proclivities? Any madness or cruelty poisoning his mind and his household?"

An awkward silence settled over the room. Charlotte's light manner belied her penetrating gaze, and Eve finally looked at me thoughtfully.

"*Non, vraiment.* I don't know any dark secrets—he is a good master. I heard that much from my *maman*, who knew the cook in the vicomte's employ."

Charlotte seized upon this like a cat on a mouse. "The former vicomte, you mean? The emissary's father?"

Eve nodded.

"Why does the cook no longer work for the family?" Charlotte continued, then slapped her forehead. "Ah! I guess the emissary does not need to employ a cook. He let her go; I suppose."

"*Mais non!* That was not the case. When Monsieur returned to Paris, he offered the staff a choice. They could stay and work for him, or leave with full references and a small stipend."

"Why would they leave if they didn't have to?" Charlotte asked.

Eve's brows shot up. "*Madame,* he is a vampire! Most self-respecting servants would not want to serve such a master."

"But the vicomte had already lost his title by then. Isn't that more of a disgrace than succumbing to the blood plague?" I asked in astonishment.

Eve raised a shoulder. "The vicomte was beloved by his servants. The emissary did not expect that loyalty to extend to him after he was turned."

I nodded, lost in thought. "*Merci,* Eve. As always, I am grateful for your candor. Go on and take your tea, *chérie.* Charlotte and I will be fine alone."

She turned to go, just as Charlotte called after her.

"Eve, one more question before you depart. How many of the servants stayed on?"

"All but one or two, I believe," Eve said. She curtsied and at my nod, left the room.

Charlotte turned a self-satisfied smile on me.

"You see? I am *always* right, *chérie*. Now you can be assured that he isn't some kind of rotten scoundrel. Well, perhaps a bit of a scoundrel, but only in the best way."

"I fail to see how you've come to that conclusion," I argued.

"He had the grace to offer an out to his father's employees, but they all chose to remain with him. He cannot be a monster."

Not a monster, only a possible murderer, I thought.

"That doesn't mean anything. I understand employment is scarce, Charlotte, and lots of people are hungry. The servants probably didn't want to leave a sure thing for some unknown misery."

Charlotte rolled her eyes.

I sighed. "Besides, you don't know how much a person will endure in order to keep a roof over her head."

Charlotte's eyes snapped to mine, but her expression was soft as she considered my meaning. "Your servants stay for you, *chérie*. You bore the brunt of Henri's temper and shielded them from the worst of his torments. They aren't likely to forget it," she said quietly.

I finished the tea and brandy in my cup, briefly thinking about another stiff drink to hold back the sickening memories. Before I could sink into despair, Charlotte slapped her fan against my knee with a cheerful giggle.

"Well, *ma chère amie*, I should be on my way. I promised Lisette I'd look in on her since she turned her ankle. She says it was during her dancing lessons, but the rumor is that she tripped over her lover's breeches when the comte came home early. I shall let you know what I uncover!"

She kissed my cheeks and made for the door. For all her inappropriate behavior, Charlotte had a soft heart and a comforting nature. She was unfailingly devoted to Philippe and to me. Her loyalty inspired me to be honest with Philippe, but I needed to find the truth of the matter before I addressed him.

Later that evening, I dressed without Eve's help—I didn't need her worrying over my inappropriate attire. I needed freedom and a degree of anonymity tonight, so I'd donned some of Henri's old clothes—the ones he used to wear when he sought what he called *companionship* with the unfortunate prostitutes in the direst circumstances. *The ones who would not fight back against his demands,* I thought bitterly.

I donned the plain woolen breeches and hose, simple linen shirt, dingy brown waistcoat, thick black overcoat, and tattered tricorne hat. I'd taken care to bind my breasts beneath the shirt and hoped that no one would notice the ill-fitting wig, but as I surveyed my appearance in the mirror, I reasoned it would probably be acceptable given the late hour. In darkness, or even dim lighting, I would pass for a man.

In the pockets of my coat, I stashed a dagger, several small wooden stakes, my flintlock pistol, and a vial of holy water. While the holy water wouldn't do much good against vampires, The Order had instructed its agents to carry it for other potential supernatural threats. Since vampires were a reality now, the door to the impossible had been flung open. Monsters, ghouls, demons—it seemed only natural that other unholy creatures lurked in the shadows.

A soft knock at my door made me jump.

"Madame."

Eve poked her head in and blanched when she saw me. I offered her a sheepish grin.

"It's necessary, Eve. Trust me."

"Of course, Madame. Monsieur de Noailles has arrived. He's waiting for you downstairs."

"*Merci.*" I tucked an errant curl beneath my wig and took a steadying breath.

"Are you...Madame, are you sure you will be safe? Perhaps you should take one of the footmen, or Gaston, with you tonight," Eve whispered. She twisted her fingers in her skirts.

"*Non, chérie,*" I replied. "Grim business tonight. I'll be fine. I promise."

I smiled encouragingly at her, but she looked at me skeptically before nodding and hurrying back down the hall. Making my way downstairs, I paused by the table in the hall to put an apple in my coat pocket, as well. I'd declined dinner, too anxious to have much of an appetite, and now my stomach churned with hunger and nerves.

"Midnight snack?" Étienne's voice carried up the grand staircase from the front hall.

I cursed him softly, but his mouth quirked up in a smile and I knew he'd heard. He was dressed simply, and it seemed at odds with his ethereal beauty. He hadn't powdered his hair but had tied the thick waves back in a simple ribbon. In the candlelight, his locks shimmered like a raven's wing in the sun. Alarmingly, my fingers suddenly itched to touch them.

"I apologize if you've been kept waiting," I grumbled. "Have you been offered refreshment?"

The words flowed out of me reflexively, but it was impossible for me to keep the irritation from my voice. It wouldn't do for the Duchesse de Duras to have an inhospitable household, even if she'd rather tear her beloved château down brick by brick than have a lecherous vampire ruining its serenity.

"No, Duchesse, but I doubt your household was prepared to offer me *refreshment,*" he drawled. "Unless you'd care to do so yourself?"

Realizing my mistake, I felt my face burn in embarrassment. *Damn it, Daphne, you imbecile.*

"I meant water or wine. Perhaps a glass of something stronger. I have seen you drink, Monsieur le Vicomte," I said airily, trying to regain the upper hand.

He winced at my use of his lost title and turned his back to me, marching toward the front door.

"I am no longer Monsieur le Vicomte, Duchesse, and you would do well to remember that. You will call me Étienne. And no, I do not require refreshment. We must be on our way—my man at the graveyard will not wait for us indefinitely," he said, ushering us outside.

I nodded. "I—"

He turned; an impatient look etched on his handsome face.

"I'm sorry," I said. Flustered, my voice faltered. "For using your former title. I hope I did not offend."

He raised a brow at me. A slow smile spread across his lips. *The smug bastard.*

"What I meant to say was that while I do not mind offending you in many other, justifiable ways, that particular barb was not meant as offense. Just a force of habit. I'm not used to interacting with people who don't hold a title, you see," I said with acid-laced sweetness.

The pompous grin on his face didn't waver an inch, but he bowed politely and helped me into his carriage. I sat as far away from him as possible and stared resolutely out the window. How did he manage to come out on top of every interaction we had? Probably some kind of infuriating supernatural trick. It soured my mood even further, which I would've thought impossible considering we were on our way to the graveyard to dig up the body of my friend.

"Are you certain this is truly necessary?"

"Mais oui, ma chère Duchesse." His low voice was like velvet across my skin. Goosebumps rose on my flesh.

"You do not believe me," he stated matter-of-factly. "But you will. I will prove it to you, and to do that, you must first see Madame de Pompadour for yourself."

I shut my eyes and leaned back against the plush seat. The carriage pitched roughly over a hole in the road.

"It will be difficult," he continued. "I know she was your friend, but this is essential. We must begin our investigation in the right place, however gruesome it may be."

"I do not faint at the sight of blood, Étienne. I will do what must be done in order to bring justice to Jeanne's killer." I stared hard at him—at least, I thought it was him. In the gloom of the carriage, it was hard to tell.

"Is it that you are uncommonly brave, Madame? Or is it that you are used to such brutality?"

"Perhaps it is both," I replied. He didn't respond, but I had the distinct impression he was studying me. I felt at a disadvantage yet again.

We rode on in silence, until about a quarter of an hour had passed and the carriage slowed.

"We've arrived," he said. He'd moved in close to my ear and I caught his scent. Surprisingly, he did not smell of blood and death. He smelled of soap, cedar, and peppermint—putting me in mind of winter gardens and snow-covered pine trees.

"I'm well aware you find my company distasteful, Madame, but for your own safety, I must insist you stay close to me. Your disguise may fool drunkards and blind men, but anyone with two functional eyes and a brain will quickly recognize your—ahem—*charms*. Keep your hat low, your head down, your hands in your pockets, and let me do the talking."

As he spoke, his breath on my ear encouraged a blush that I felt creep all over my body. My nipples hardened beneath the painful linen bindings. Disgusted with him and with my body's instinctive response, I pushed him away and surged forward, nearly tripping on my way down from the carriage. With supernatural speed, he seized my coat to keep me from toppling into the street.

"Careful, Duchesse," he taunted, his golden eyes flashing. "We wouldn't want The Order to lose one of their talented hunters."

Chagrined, I followed him into the graveyard. Perhaps in another time, in another place, I would have delivered some kind of dressing down, but I found myself flustered by his presence, uncomfortable with my sudden ineptitude, and queasy at the thought of disturbing the resting place of my former friend. *Forgive me, Jeanne.*

Étienne led us further into the cemetery toward the only source of light—a dim lantern near a copse of trees. I'd been here back in the spring when they buried her and it had been beautiful, surrounded by flowers and greenery, flecked with dappled sunlight. Tonight, however, the clearing felt alien and malevolent. I tugged my coat close to me and fingered the pearl handle of my dagger. Its smooth warmth comforted me.

Étienne greeted his man, the gravedigger, who stood next to a pile of newly turned earth and poor Jeanne's waiting casket.

"Give us some privacy, will you?" Étienne commanded. He flipped the lanky gravedigger a coin. The man nodded and walked some distance away.

Étienne bent to pry the lid to the casket open and I braced myself. *God, help me. Please don't let it be like last time—like Michel.*

Étienne looked to me, waiting for my signal. I nodded and he pulled the lid away, letting it crash to the ground at my feet. I held my breath and opened my eyes. I was ill-prepared for the sight.

Oh, God, Jeanne Antoinette! What have they done to you?

4

ÉTIENNE

September 28, 1765
Cimetière Notre-Dame

BELATEDLY, I WONDERED IF I SHOULD HAVE BROUGHT SOME SMELLING SALTS. I knew this would be unpleasant for Daphne, but even I found my stomach souring at the grotesque scene before us. Having witnessed more than my fair share of deathly horrors, it still pained me to see a beautiful woman struck down in the prime of her life by something so unbearably savage.

I peered at my companion, ready to catch her if she swooned. Her breath came in shallow gasps and her pupils had dilated considerably, but she seemed steady enough. Assured that she wasn't about to keel over and fall into the open grave, I turned my attention to Madame de Pompadour's decaying body.

She was further gone from the last time I'd seen her, but her wounds remained pristine. I leaned in to inspect them. They weren't like anything I'd ever seen—they were certainly unlike any vampire bite I'd known.

"It looks like…" Daphne's whisper sounded unsettled. "It almost looks like she's been attacked by a wild animal—a wolf, perhaps. The edges of the wound are jagged and rough, as though the flesh has been ripped away. It would suggest fangs in the upper and lower jaw, as opposed to the neat insertion of a single pair of canines common in vampire bites."

I stared at her, unable to mask my astonishment. She was studying the body as intently as possible, though a sheen of sweat had broken out across her worryingly pale brow. Her voice shook as she continued.

"Étienne, her ring."

"She isn't wearing a ring, Daphne," I said, gently prodding the casket to feel for some misplaced jewelry.

"Exactly. Where is her ring? Most of her jewels were given back to the king after her death, all except for one ring that she never removed. It was a large pink pearl surrounded by diamonds—the first gift that Louis ever gave her. It was very precious to her, but I do not see it. Do you think grave robbers could have claimed it?" She wavered a bit on her feet. I needed more time to look around, but I wasn't sure how long Daphne's strength would hold out.

"Steady, Duchesse," I urged. "If you swoon now, I'll be forced to lay hands on you and carry you home."

That startled her enough. She snapped her eyes to mine and choked on an incensed huff.

"I am not going to swoon," she bit out.

"Too bad. I was rather looking forward to carrying you back."

I searched the rest of the coffin—no ring. She was right. It could have disappeared at any time, but I doubted grave robbers. They would have taken the simple burial shift—it was silk, after all—as well as the ribbons tying back the dead woman's hair. Daphne clearly suspected the killer had taken the ring and though I was loath to admit it, I agreed with her.

I'd hoped to find something else that would point toward a suspect, but other than convincing Daphne I hadn't killed the king's mistress, I was no better off than when we'd started this morbid little adventure. I scanned the body from head to toe looking for clues.

Something nagged at me—some peculiarity that I couldn't quite place. Closing my eyes, I inhaled deeply, allowing my heightened sense of smell to paint parts of the scene I could not see. I smelled death, of course, and rot. I smelled the decay before me but also something else. There was a bitter musk in the air that I'd never encountered. It wasn't quite an animal, I didn't think, but—

I leaned down next to the gaping wound in Jeanne's neck and breathed. Yes, this was where it was coming from. It must have been the scent of the killer. Bitter, sour, smoky, almost sulfuric. *Fantastic.* Now all I needed to do was walk around, sniffing everyone in Paris until I found the same odor. *No problem at all.*

Daphne was motionless, staring at me with revulsion.

"I think I know what the killer smells like," I explained. "There is something odd about her neck—the way it smells, even in death."

She nodded and crossed herself. I went to bring the gravedigger back to put Jeanne in the ground again and caught Daphne wiping a tear from her cheek. At my notice, she dropped her hand and straightened, her gaze turning instantly icy. My dead heart gave a curious little squeeze and I led her away.

When we reached the shadowy comfort of my carriage, I handed her my gold flask. She considered me a moment, her face inscrutable. I shrugged and started to pull away, but she finally reached for the flask. Without asking about its contents, she took a long pull on it. When she saw my surprised expression, she gave a tired half-shrug.

"I figured it was either blood or brandy, but you don't seem the type to carry around an expensive flask full of blood."

"I am fortunate enough to find willing sources when I require them," I admitted, taking a drink of the sweet brandy. I imagined I could taste her lips on the flask and heat spread through me.

She leaned back and closed her eyes, allowing me the time to drink in her lithe body, wrapped in those ridiculous masculine clothes. Who would've thought that a woman wearing breeches could be so *erotic*? The way they clung to her shapely legs and followed every sinful curve of her bottom—

"We should take you home," I said. I needed distance from her to clear my head and think. "I imagine your husband will be worried."

She barked a laugh and snatched the flask from me again, drinking deeply.

"I didn't realize you had such a scathing sense of humor," she seethed.

When she recognized the confusion in my face, she was taken aback.

"My apologies, Duchesse. Has he passed on?"

"You mean, you really don't know? How can that be? You worked out I was with The Order, but you managed to avoid the gossip about my marriage? It's all anyone's talked about for the last two years."

Frustration rose. "My presence at court is not the same as it once was. I am seldom privy to the gossip of the *tonne*. When I am around the ladies of the nobility, we usually aren't engaging in idle conversation."

I'd said it to shock her, but the night had taken its toll on her caustic façade. She had dimmed, somehow—softened beneath the weight of her own sadness.

"You are right, of course. Forgive my offense yet again. People do not often speak to me about my husband, preferring instead to delight in the scandalous rumors. No, Étienne. My husband does not worry for my safe return and he does not wait for me at home." She trailed off, a thousand miles away. Her manner made me uncomfortable, as if teasing her now would be like kicking a puppy. I tried for my courtly charm.

"Then he is either dead, or a fool," I said, taking the brandy from her for another drink.

A guarded smile broke upon her lips, like sunlight through storm clouds. *If only she weren't the Duchesse de Duras. Hang that. If only I weren't a vampire.* I noticed that the brandy had restored some color to her cheeks, and I imagined her warming all over—warming to me. *Damn it.* I hungered again. I would need to find a woman tomorrow, or tonight, if possible.

"*Alors,*" she said, stretching her legs out in front of her and eagerly changing the subject. "Where does our investigation take us now, Étienne? I am disturbed by the absence of the ring. I think we should try to eliminate the possibility that someone stole it between the palace and the cemetery for a quick sale."

"Sounds reasonable."

"As an underworld emissary to His Majesty, I don't suppose you'd know where to find a reputable fence for disreputably acquired jewelry?"

"I could certainly make some inquiries," I offered.

"*Bon,*" she said. "Shall we go, then?"

"Go where?"

She waved a hand dismissively. "To make the inquiries."

"I will do that on my own. I can't have you running amok in the streets of Paris inciting some kind of scandal that I'll be responsible for," I chastened. "For now, you must be patient. I'll have my driver take you home." I knocked on the roof of the carriage, signaling our departure.

"I assure you; I've weathered far worse scandals than you could possibly imagine, and I don't have a lot of time. My report to The Order is already long overdue and I need to give them a good reason why I haven't killed you yet. I would think haste would be a top priority for you, as well, Monsieur. As soon as your name is cleared, you're free to go back to your debauchery with your former impunity."

Her disdainful impression of me, like so many of the Versailles courtiers, stung more than it should have. She was right about one thing, though; time was of the essence. Despite my irritation, I still didn't want her out in the seedy underbelly of the city where the whispers of revolution were stirring. The vampires were becoming increasingly hostile to humans from every class—especially the aristocracy. My attempts to negotiate with Louis had slowed to the point of failure and there was a palpable restlessness across the city. I could protect Daphne from bodily harm, of course, but I knew I wouldn't be able to protect her from her world crashing down around her. To expose her to such brutal reality after forcing her to dig up her ghoulishly murdered friend all in one night seemed cruel, even for me.

"You're right, Duchesse, but I need some time to find out if my contacts are still in Paris. You should go home tonight. Send your report to The Order. I'd be obliged if you told them that you didn't think I was a murderer, but somehow I doubt it will make much of a difference in their minds."

"What do you mean by that?"

"You are not the first to make an attempt on my life on their behalf."

She stared at me in surprise.

"What else have they convicted you of? They do not kill arbitrarily. There is always a good reason. Protection of the king and country. Justice for those wronged," she defended.

I laughed bitterly. "They further their own aims, just like every other governing body. The Order protects its own power and its own interests, operating in shadow and serving as judge, jury, and executioner. It isn't right that so few should hold such sway over the lives and deaths of others—especially those who have no way to defend against their judgment. We already have a king, after all."

"What would you have, then? Anarchy in the streets? People left with no law and no moral guidance? Of course that's what you dream of—a city overrun with vice and depravity. You and your creatures of the night," she spat. "Your only aim is to bring your stain of darkness to the world around you. Well, you'll have to excuse me, but I for one do not wish to live in your realm of blood and filth and fear. I choose the light, Étienne, and I will always fight for it."

Rage ripped through me at her contempt and I leaped forward, pinning her back against the seat.

"You know nothing of my world," I hissed through my lengthening fangs. "And your privilege blinds you to the reality of light and dark."

Her heart beat a tattoo of fear and excitement in her chest—something I'd no doubt she'd deny.

"Release me," she said through gritted teeth. "I'm not going to stay here and allow you to insult me further."

I crowded in closer, the anger in my blood suddenly giving way to white-hot lust. I could see the rise and fall of her bound breasts beneath the coarse linen shirt. Her fragrance of orange blossom and vanilla surrounded me, and I was suddenly desperate to taste her. My hardening cock pressed against my breeches.

Time stood still—neither of us seemed willing to concede and back down. The delicate flare of her nostrils, the defiant tilt of her chin, and the wild look in her eyes nearly unmanned me. I briefly considered tearing those damn breeches from her, bending her over the seat and claiming her, but I reminded myself that I wasn't the animal she took me for.

The rasp of gravel beneath the carriage wheels signaled arrival at her impressive château, saving us both from God only knew what.

I sat back in my seat and let her descend on her own. As she climbed the stairs into her grand house, I called out to her.

"If we are to work together, Duchesse, I suggest you keep an open mind. In the world beyond Versailles, your pride will be your undoing."

And you will be mine.

5

DAPHNE

"Daphne, are you even listening to me?" Philippe complained. He seemed more ruffled than usual.

Truthfully, I was not. My mind had wandered back to the same place it had been for the last four days—Étienne's carriage. I'd tossed and turned for the last three nights, poring over his words. Had The Order really tried to kill him before? Why would they? What had he done?

Was he right about me?

He'd been right about Jeanne. I'd seen it for myself. The vicious tears in the flesh of her throat—no vampire would have done that. I'd seen real vampire bites firsthand. *My poor Michel.* I shut my eyes against the painful memories.

Philippe crossed the room and knelt before me. Concern marred his face.

"Daphne, please. Talk to me. You've got to tell me what's going on. I can't keep The Order at bay much longer. Why haven't you killed Noailles yet?"

"I do not believe he is Jeanne's killer," I finally said. Philippe rocked back on his heels and stood.

"Why not? You read the report. She was bitten. Her blood was drained."

"Who wrote the report?"

Philippe lifted one shoulder. "Another agent. I don't know who."

"Well, whoever it was either wasn't present and was putting it together from rumors, or is deliberately trying to accuse the emissary. That report is all wrong, Philippe. Her blood was not simply drained. Her throat was ripped open. She likely bled out. The wound was no vampire bite—it was too savage. Inhuman, even. It looked like some kind of animal attack."

He narrowed his eyes. "How do you know? Did *he* tell you that?"

I'd been debating telling Philippe the entirety of the situation. I knew he wouldn't approve, but up until now, I hadn't told anyone, and I needed someone I could trust within The Order. I faced him, mustering my courage.

"We exhumed her body. I inspected her myself. Étienne professes his innocence, Philippe, and I am starting to believe him."

He took the news like a physical blow. Eyes bulging, he gaped at me. "Daphne," he breathed. "That is—it's blasphemous! How could you?"

"Perhaps it is, but I wanted the truth, and now I have it. Well, part of it, anyway," I said, resigned.

Disappointment flowed off Philippe in waves and I found myself caught up in the tide. He stared at me in stunned silence.

"So, it's *Étienne* now, is it?" he asked, shaking his head. "If you don't believe he is guilty, why haven't you informed The Order?"

"I don't think they'll listen to me. They might listen to you, though," I hedged.

Philippe sighed deeply. "Have you any other evidence of his innocence?"

"Not yet," I admitted. "But I hope to soon."

"Darling, you know I can't just go to them armed with your unsubstantiated suspicions. You know what they'll say. They'll say he has bewitched you, just like he bewitches every other woman—that you think his handsome face and his charm excuse the horrible things he has done. They'll say you've been compromised by your emotions, and I'll have nothing to show them to prove otherwise."

"I'll get proof," I insisted. Philippe cast me a doubtful look. "One other thing—he mentioned that The Order had sent agents to assassinate him before. What do you know of that?"

Philippe shrugged. "Nothing, really."

"What else is he accused of?" I pressed.

Philippe looked at me like I'd gone mad.

"Well, murder, for one! And treasonous slander. And adultery!"

Suspicious, I approached Philippe and stared hard into his eyes.

"Adultery is the currency of Versailles, Philippe," I said. "That doesn't warrant a death threat from The Order. What has he done? Is it his politics? Does it have something to do with his title?"

"How should I know?" he blustered.

"You've been with The Order for eight years," I pushed. "You were with them before the blood plague came to Paris. You're one of their most trusted members."

Philippe's eyes flashed and his temper flared. "Not even I know everything, Daphne. Besides, why do you care? He's a *vampire*, just like the ones that killed your brother. Or have you forgotten? Do you need to be reminded of the fact that it was but five short years ago that Michel was found murdered—*drained*—right outside your family's home?" He threw his hands up and began to pace the room.

Pain at the memory rendered me speechless. But Phillipe wasn't done.

"You were *this close* to poverty, Daphne, when the title and lands passed to a distant relation with no provision for you. The only thing that saved you was an ill-advised marriage to a wealthy, titled man no better than the monsters who took your brother from you! And here you are! Throwing yourself in with their kind. I simply don't understand it."

The utter ass—bringing up my past in such a callous, judgmental manner and then refusing to help me.

"I have not thrown myself in with their kind!" I snarled, outraged at his scorn. "And I don't know why you don't understand my hesitation. Does the truth matter so little to you?"

"Does it matter that much to you?" he countered. "He's just some vampire!"

I gritted my teeth, trying to force down my rising temper. I recognized we were at an impasse, and alienating Phillipe seemed unproductive and unwise, even if he deserved a very thorough chastening. Despite the fact that I held a title above his in society, he was still senior to me in The Order and enjoyed all the undeserved privileges of the patriarchy.

I went to the front window and stared out at the drizzly, pewter afternoon.

He stopped pacing, then blew out a breath. "I'm sorry, Daphne. You know I'd do anything to help you, but with the Noailles assignment, I don't know if I can."

"Well, if I am on my own then, so be it," I replied in a wooden tone.

He made a noise of exasperation in his throat. "Even if I could, I doubt they'd listen to me any more than they would you. Noailles is on their list and I'm sure they have their reasons beyond Jeanne's death. I'm sorry, Daphne, but I can't protect you from The Order anymore. You wanted in, now you've got to figure your way of this mess. Find your proof, or find yourself facing their judgment."

With that, he picked up his hat and walked out of the room.

Frustrated, I stormed upstairs, my ire growing with every step. Certainly, he could refuse to help me, but how dare he shame me for Michel's death and for my marriage to Henri! I did what I had had to do to survive. I paced my bedchamber, punched my pillows, and threw a book across the room. The idea that The Order would suggest I'd developed feelings for Étienne enraged me even further. Of course I didn't care for the rogue! I cared about the truth—and so far, Étienne had been more honest with me than Philippe had. That was what mattered in all of this; *the truth.*

With renewed resolve, I went to my desk and drafted a missive to the vampire. It was time we continued our investigation.

WHEN I DRESSED THAT EVENING, I DONNED ONE OF EVE'S SIMPLE GRAY dresses and pinned my dark blonde curls beneath a cap. I wrapped my shoulders in a brown wool shawl and strapped my flintlock to my thigh. I kept my dagger and a thin wooden stake in my pockets, though I hoped I wouldn't need them tonight. I wasn't sure where Étienne was taking me, but I knew it wouldn't be anywhere near the world of Versailles.

He had responded promptly to my message, stating that he would be around after sundown to collect me. His terse response irked me. I wondered if he was still angry with me over our argument in the carriage. I hoped not. I only had the energy to deal with one intractable ass today and I'd already gotten my fill from Philippe.

Eve knocked at my door and informed me that Monsieur de Noailles had arrived. I braced myself for his broody temperament and went down to greet him.

He sat in the front parlor, staring fixedly into the fireplace. He was dressed in plain but well-tailored clothes, his hat resting idly on one knee. The warm firelight flickered across his sculpted features, casting him in a glow of amber heat. It struck me that he looked like one of Louis's golden statues come to life. I had the strange urge to reach out and run my fingertips across his lips to see if they really were as soft as the gossips said.

"If you're going to stand back there all night staring at me, Duchesse, perhaps you could make yourself useful and pour me a drink while you're at it," he said, his focus never leaving the flames.

I stiffened at his rudeness. "I can, if you require one. I was waiting for you to stand so that we may go."

"Go where?" he asked. "It is you who summoned me."

Still, he did not look at me. He seemed…strange, distant.

"Monsieur, are you well?"

He smiled cruelly and his tone dripped with sarcasm. "But of course, Madame. Why shouldn't I be well?"

"I'm sure I do not know, but you seem…not yourself tonight. I was under the impression that you had a lead for us to follow. Possibly related to Jeanne's missing ring?" I prodded.

I came further into the room and he finally looked up at me. I gasped when I saw his eyes—the honeyed hazel of his irises had changed to a deep, blood red.

Instinctively, I stepped back. "What happened to your eyes, Étienne? Are you ill?"

He laughed acidly. "I am dead, Duchesse! But do you mean, ill besides being a vampire?"

He stood suddenly, his movements erratic and supernaturally quick. He stalked toward me and backed me up against the wall. Caged between his hard, muscular arms, I took in the rest of his appearance—the stubble on his sallow-skinned jaw, the tendrils of dark hair escaping his queue, the shadows in the hollows of his cheeks and beneath his eyes. He looked like he hadn't slept in days.

He closed his eyes and buried his face in the crook of my neck. I froze like a rabbit before a fox. He wouldn't bite me, would he? What was wrong with him? I reached for the wooden stake in my pocket.

He inhaled deeply and growled. Panic started to build inside me. My heart thundered in my chest. *No, no, no. Please, no.*

Come back to your senses, Étienne.

"Shh," he whispered against my skin. "Calm your racing heart, little nymph."

I felt a hot, wet caress and realized he'd licked my neck. Unbidden desire ignited in my blood, warring with fear and shame.

"Étienne," I breathed. *I should stop him.*

Soft kisses danced up the column of my neck and a firm hand stroked my back. *When had it ever felt this good to be touched?* I wondered.

Never.

Something isn't right. He isn't well. You must stop this, Daphne.

"Étienne," I stammered, tears pricking at my eyes. "You are not yourself. Allow me to call a doctor for you."

"But I am myself, Duchesse," he drawled, dragging his lips up to my ear. "I don't need a doctor. You have everything I need."

He pressed his hips into me, and I felt the hard length of his arousal against my stomach. My knees nearly buckled and I grew wet with reflexive desire. *No! We mustn't!*

"Yes," he moaned, sucking on my earlobe and raining kisses across my jaw. "I can smell your passion, little nymph. I want you. Feel how desperately I want you. How I need—"

He stopped abruptly, pulling back. His eyes paled to hazel again and he stared at me in bewilderment.

"Daphne?" he questioned. His feeble voice sounded miles away. "What are you doing here?"

His unfocused gaze shifted to his surroundings and he blinked in confusion. As quickly as he'd returned to me, he vanished again—the blood-colored irises were back. He took a step in my direction, then stumbled and fell to his knees.

"Help me," he wheezed. "I need…" he trailed off, falling to the ground. Curling his knees to his chest, he gagged, vomiting black blood and bile across the carpet.

Angrily, I dashed the tears from my face. Warily, as if I was approaching a wounded animal, I leaned forward and pulled him up, gently shaking him.

"What do you need? What happened? What, Étienne?"

One of the footmen heard the commotion and came running into the parlor. He helped me attempt to rouse him, but it was no use.

Étienne slipped into unconsciousness.

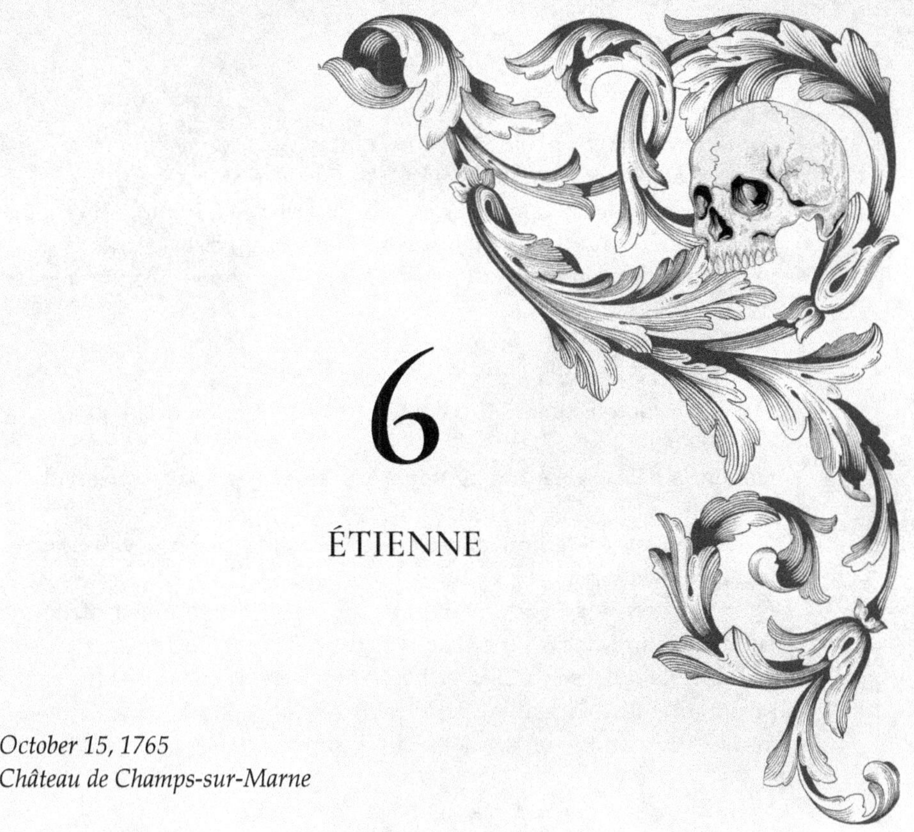

6

ÉTIENNE

IT WAS BETTER THAN THE DREAMS I WAS USED TO. SOFT PINK LIPS PARTED IN ecstasy—heavy-lidded violet eyes glazed with desire—my throbbing cock sliding into warm, wet silk. Attempting to hold onto the blissful vision, I kept my eyes closed and snaked a hand beneath the sheets, intent on alleviating my growing need. A rough moan escaped my lips when I grasped my erection.

"I see you're awake."

My eyes flew open and I jerked upright—*mistake*. Blinding pain rioted through my brain. I clutched my head and fell back on the bed with a curse.

"*Merde,*" came the voice again. "Don't try to get up yet. The doctor said you would be weak for some time."

I took stock of my surroundings and the confusion only made my head ache more.

"Daphne?" I rasped. My parched throat felt like sand.

"I'm here, Étienne," she said. "What do you remember?"

Things were fuzzy. I tried to piece together my remaining memories, but everything seemed unclear.

"Where am I?"

I closed my eyes to block out the pain. I was in a bed somewhere. The room was dark and cool, and smelled like damp earth and stone.

"You're in my wine cellar," she said. She came to the side of the bed and tipped a glass of water to my lips. I drank deeply.

"Should that mean something to me?" I grumped, wiping my mouth with the back of my hand. I felt several days' growth of beard. "I don't remember much right now, so I'd be much obliged if you filled in some of the blanks."

She busied herself at a small table by my bedside and returned with a shallow porcelain bowl filled with—*it couldn't be.*

"Whose blood is that?" I asked, surprisingly concerned given my weakened state.

Daphne's pale cheeks and tight lips expressed her disapproval without words.

"I haven't murdered anyone on your account, if that's what you're asking," she said tartly.

Questions formed in my brain, but the smell of the blood made me ravenous. I didn't know how long it had been since I'd fed, but considering I felt like I'd been run over by a stampede of horses, I assumed it had been a while. Normally I preferred to drink from the thigh veins of women in the throes of passion, but I supposed beggars couldn't be choosers.

"It's warm," I remarked, taking the bowl from her.

She sniffed haughtily. "Well, of course it is. My cook kept it at the proper temperature. I assume you don't eat it—drink it—cold."

My fangs distended and I drank from the bowl voraciously.

Never had I tasted anything so delicious. *Good God.* Rather than quenching my burning thirst and alleviating the painful hunger, I felt a bigger, more desperate need—lust. The desire for sexual release and more blood—no, more of *this* blood.

It must be because I haven't fed in so long, I thought, unsettled.

Already, I felt strength returning to my muscles. The ache in my head began to ebb.

Daphne took the empty bowl from me and set it back on the table. She crossed to one of the dusty crates, grabbed a bottle of wine, and uncorked it with practiced efficiency. She let out a shuddering breath and raised the bottle to her lips for a long swallow. She tilted the bottle in my direction, offering me a swig. I declined.

"Daphne, are you all right?"

With the sharpness of my supernatural senses coming back to me, I finally noticed her disheveled appearance. She wore a plain day dress of navy cotton that had smudges of dust and blood on it. Her eyes were red-rimmed, and several blonde curls escaped her lace cap. She'd been watching over me.

She cast me a withering look and chugged from the wine bottle again. When she was down a quarter of the bottle, her shoulders relaxed a bit and she came back to sit in the bedside chair.

Clearing her throat, she pointed at me accusingly.

"Now that you're not dead—or undead—re-dead?—you have quite a lot to answer for, Monsieur."

"I'm listening," I grumbled. Not like I had any choice in the matter. I was still too weak to leave and belatedly I realized I was naked beneath the covers.

She got up and strode anxiously around the room, like some kind of wildcat in a cage. I wondered how long it had been since she'd slept. She put the bottle to her lips again, but merely sipped at it this time.

"This is a fine Bordeaux."

Distracted, she offered me the bottle again. She obviously didn't want to drink alone. I took it from her and poured some into my empty water glass.

"*Santé*," I toasted. It really was a fine Bordeaux.

Heaving a great sigh, she sat once more.

"I have broken so many oaths these last few weeks, I fear the punishments awaiting me—in this life and the next." She scrubbed one hand across her face, trying to wipe away some of her fatigue.

"Did you ever know my brother, Michel? Before he died, he was... He would have enjoyed your company, I think."

I shook my head. "No, I did not have the privilege. I returned to Paris some time after he died."

"After he was murdered," she corrected. She sipped her wine. "He was the Duc de Lorraine for such a short time. Less than a year. He inherited the title after both of our parents died from consumption. He had such plans, Étienne. He was on his way to becoming a remarkable man and a dutiful steward of my family's title. His only worry was about siring an heir. He was never inclined to enjoy the company of women, even during his teenage years when all men are predisposed to—what is the phrase? —*sow their oats*. Not Michel. He was content with his books and his music and was dedicated to his duties. It never bothered me that he desired other men. I loved him so much—I didn't care. I only wanted his happiness. Things were simpler then, when we thought we had a lifetime ahead of us. But fate—she always has other plans for us, no?"

"Truer words were never spoken, Duchesse." Unease threaded through me. I worried where her recollection was going, and why she seemed compelled to share it with me now.

"Michel knew his duty. He did plan to marry and produce heirs. His predilections are not uncommon—he knew he could marry for duty and find a lover outside the marriage bed. He planned to provide for me, as well, because he did not want me to marry for anything less than love. *If I cannot marry for my happiness, chérie, at least you shall*, he said. My poor Michel! How I have dishonored his memory with my choices."

A tear spilled down her cheek and she swirled the wine in the bottle.

"When they found his body at the front gate of his château, he was naked—drained of every drop of blood. His lover—some vampire merchant, the gossips said—had killed him and tossed his body in the street like some piece of trash."

Christ. No wonder she harbored a grudge.

"I swore vengeance, of course. Against his lover—a man I still do not know the identity of—and against anyone who would prey on another's weakness. Against vampires. *All* vampires," she said with conviction. "It's one of the reasons I joined The Order. And yet, here you are. The most well-known vampire in all of Paris. Languishing in my wine cellar, drinking blood that I myself have served."

She said this last with only a slight hint of animosity, tilting her head at me curiously. She seemed struck by the absurdity of the situation. She chuckled to herself, but there was pain beneath it. Fresh pain, it seemed.

"Daphne." I reached for her, but she jerked her hand away. I cleared my throat again and ran my hand through my hair—unbound and tangled with the remnants of fevered sleep. "You could have staked me at any time, or allowed me to die, just like The Order commanded. Why didn't you?"

She was quiet for a long moment.

"I suppose…even though you are a vampire, it seems that perhaps you are the one being preyed on."

"Tell me what happened. How did I end up in your wine cellar, of all places?"

"You don't remember anything?"

I shook my head. Flashes returned to me—a young woman, a strange taste, then blackness. Anxiety knotted my stomach. I'd been unaware of any biological weaknesses brought on by the plague, save for the sensitivity to sunlight, garlic, and of course, wooden stakes. It seemed there was something else in this world that could wipe out my supernatural advantages—something unknown to me. The thought did not sit well. For someone who'd only just gotten used to the idea of immortality, I found myself remarkably concerned with it ending so soon.

"I sent you a message two weeks ago. You were to come here so that we could continue our investigation into Jeanne's death. Her missing ring. You arrived in the evening, but you were different—very unlike yourself.

Your eyes were red, and your behavior was…" she trailed off, sounding wounded.

I'd hurt her. My dead heart clenched at the thought.

"I was what?" I pressed.

"Ungentlemanly."

Hell. That could mean anything. I opened my mouth to find out more, but she hurried on.

"You were eventually overcome, and you fainted in my parlor. My staff helped me set up a bed here in the wine cellar—the only underground room in the château and the only place safe from the sunlight—and I sent for a doctor. I don't mind telling you that I had some time trying to find one who was familiar enough with vampire biology, but this doctor has proven to be very knowledgeable. She is staying upstairs in one of the guest rooms. I'm afraid I insisted that she remain on the grounds until you either expired or recovered."

I tried not to smile at her tyrannical tone. I was beginning to enjoy the high-handed way she managed her world.

At that moment, there was a knock on the heavy wooden door, and a curvy, dark-haired woman with spectacles entered. My brows rose in interest.

"Doctor Van Helsing," Daphne greeted. "Your patient appears to be recovering his faculties. I must congratulate you on your skill."

The doctor smiled and bustled over to me. She fussed about, examining my eyes and mouth, and pulled a red vial from her bag.

"Drink please, Monsieur," she instructed through a thick Dutch accent. "This should help."

"What is it?" I couldn't keep the suspicion from my voice.

"Virgin's blood. It will help restore much of your strength. Mind you, don't spill a drop—it's hard enough to find a virgin in Paris these days," she complained.

I tossed the vial back and felt a surge of euphoric power rush through my body. *Mon Dieu.* No wonder everyone was always banging on about drinking the blood of virgins. As restorative as it was, I still longed for more of the blood from the porcelain bowl.

"Now then," the doctor said. "Do you remember the last person you ate?"

Daphne was putting dishes on a tray, pretending not to listen. I felt strangely uncomfortable going into the details with her there, but I didn't think she'd respond well to my request that she leave. *Merde.*

"Vaguely," I hedged.

"Someone new?"

"Yes, why?"

"You were suffering from an acute attack of quicksilver poisoning. It enters the blood and affects the mind—usually resulting in brain fever and a kind of madness, which, when untreated, leads to a very unpleasant second death. Vampires seem to be more susceptible to its symptoms than humans, but not many people know that. The contaminated blood must be removed from the body of the infected, which is a very difficult procedure. You'll also feel weak, I imagine, for some time until you can feed enough to heal completely."

"How does one succumb to quicksilver poisoning?" Daphne asked.

The doctor handed me two more vials of blood.

"Take one vial just before sunrise for the next two days. You will recover entirely if you allow yourself the proper time to rest," she instructed. "As to the method of poisoning, I believe it was in the blood of the last person you ate, which means they deliberately ingested it before you fed on them. At the risk of sounding dire, Monsieur, I think you should make sure your affairs are in order. You seem to have a very formidable enemy who wants you dead."

7

DAPHNE

October 17, 1765
Château de Champs-sur-Marne

THE ORDER MUST HAVE SENT SOMEONE ELSE—ANOTHER ASSASSIN. I KNEW IT would happen eventually, but as usual, I'd miscalculated how much time I had, and Étienne had paid the price.

The two weeks that he'd been senseless had been some of the worst of my life. Not only had it delayed our investigation, but seeing a powerful man laid low and raving through unconscious delirium was disturbing, to say the least.

"After this, he should be well enough to travel," Doctor Van Helsing said. She expertly bandaged the small cut on the inside of my arm and carefully handed the porcelain bowl of my blood to the cook. "Keep it warm," she instructed, ignoring the cook's queasy expression.

"Thank you, Doctor. I appreciate the care you've bestowed on the emissary," I said. I tugged my sleeve down over the bandage.

Van Helsing cocked her head and studied me, her bright blue eyes made owlish by her thick spectacles.

"On the contrary, Your Grace. I merely treated the patient. He has you to thank for his care."

Uncomfortable with the insinuation that I cared for the vampire, I stood—somewhat unsteadily. Van Helsing caught my elbow and *tsked*.

"You've been feeding him for days now—you must take some time to recover your own strength. Red meat for your evening meal, and early to bed, I say. And this should be the *last* that you feed him. Understand?" She fussed over me, looking more like an aging governess than the voluptuous, vibrant woman of thirty that she was.

"Far be it from me to disagree with a doctor's orders," I smiled, steadying myself. "I'm fine, Doctor, I promise. Nicole, if you'll hand me that tray with the blood, and I'll see to our guest."

The cook nodded and handed me the tray, after half-heartedly offering to take it down herself. I brushed her off and descended the stairs to the wine cellar. Even though several of the household staff had offered their blood instead of mine, I'd refused. When Michel was found drained, it shocked and devastated our entire home—I did not grieve alone. I couldn't subject anyone else to something so unpleasant when I knew I had the strength to bear the burden. Besides, as long as Étienne was in my house, his care and feeding was my responsibility, though I preferred him being ignorant to that.

I knocked on the cellar door, and Étienne bade me enter. He looked vastly improved for a dead man. The hollows beneath his eyes had gone, and his gaunt features had evened out over the last several days, losing the sunken pallor of illness. He flashed me a grin and sat up straighter in bed, reaching for the tray in my hands.

"You must send my compliments to your chef—or whomever has kindly offered to sustain me. I must say, this is the best blood that I've ever had," he said, picking up the bowl eagerly.

I nodded and turned to leave, but he stopped me.

"Have you been in contact with your masters?"

I bristled. "My *what?*"

"The Order."

"They are *not* my masters. I simply work with them to address the more pressing threats to king and country," I said stiffly.

"Threats like vampires," he said, putting down the empty bowl. His fangs glinted in the candlelight as he dabbed at his mouth with a napkin.

"Yes. The blood plague is a threat to the country. People are dying, Étienne. Not every vampire leaves their victim alive after feeding."

"People are also dying of hunger, Duchesse. Certainly, the plague adds to the numbers, but I have a hard time agreeing with The Order when their policy is to simply stake all the infected to prevent the plague from spreading. You're a smart woman. You can't tell me that you think it makes sense to kill people in order to protect them." He picked up the wine glass from the tray and sipped at it.

"If the deaths of a few will protect the many, then yes, that makes sense to me."

"And you think The Order has the right to determine that? What if the plague had only struck the aristocracy? Would you feel the same way? Would you be willing to lay down your life as a possible disease spreader, in order to protect the lowly peasants?"

"I—well, yes, I would. If it was for the good for the many," I argued, folding my arms in front of me.

Étienne tutted. "Forgive me if I don't believe you. Trust me when I tell you that this condition—this burden—is not one to be taken lightly. The choice between infection and death is a near-impossible one, even for a disgraced wretch like me."

I narrowed my eyes. "At least you have an eternity to right your wrongs. To make amends."

"It's hard to make amends with the dead," he said quietly.

For the first time, I saw a flash of regret in his hazel eyes. I wondered who he thought of in that moment, and before I could catch myself, I felt a swell of sympathy for him. I knew what it was like to lose loved ones before you had the chance to tell them everything you wanted to. For a man who was surrounded by death, he must have felt that tenfold.

He cleared his throat and took a swig of wine.

"Besides, who told you vampires were the minority?"

I stilled. "But, they are! There cannot be so many. The Order—"

He cut me off with an arched brow. "We are more than you think, Duchesse."

His velvet tone implied he was referring to more than the number of vampires in France. I met his gaze and found myself thinking of his body pressed against mine, his kisses on my neck. I blushed. *I shouldn't have liked it—shouldn't have wanted it to continue.* I didn't trust him one whit, but that hadn't seemed to matter to my body.

Étienne stood from the bed, clad only in his loose linen shirt and breeches, and strode over to me. His eyes never left mine. When he was mere inches from me, he stopped.

"As am I," he murmured. He leaned forward and I closed my eyes reflexively, fearfully prepared—*no, shamefully hoping*—for the kiss to come. My breath quickened. My lips parted.

But the kiss never arrived.

Instead, I felt him gently lift my hand to his lips. My eyes flew open. He pressed a chaste kiss to the back of my hand and smiled up at me through his lashes.

"Thank you for keeping me company while I dined this evening. I'm deeply indebted to you for your hospitality. I'll bid you goodnight, Duchesse."

He opened the door for me, handed me the dinner tray, and bowed before retreating back inside the cellar. It took me some moments to recover my senses enough to make a rather incensed march back upstairs.

To distract myself from a whirlwind of confusing emotions—unspent lust, embarrassment, confusion, frustration, and no small amount of anger —I asked for dinner to be brought into the library and sat at my desk to tackle a mountain of correspondence that I'd been avoiding.

I put aside the apologetic missive from Philippe. I still didn't have any proof of Étienne's innocence, and I was loath to tell Philippe I was playing host, nursemaid, *and* dinner to the man I'd been sent to kill. Anxiety had rooted in my stomach at his suggestion that The Order would accuse me of having feelings for the vampire. Considering I'd been feeding him my own blood to keep him alive, that claim would be even more difficult to refute.

Days before, I'd finally gathered the courage to send a message to The Order and explain why I hadn't killed Étienne. I'd declined to tell them about digging up Jeanne's body and the recent events that brought Étienne to my doorstep—it made me uneasy to confront them about a second assassination attempt. Doing so would reveal that I was aware of it in the first place, and I didn't want to play my hand until I had all the cards.

I was surprised when they responded so quickly, but no better off than I had been. While they agreed to allow me time to find proof of Étienne's innocence, they made it clear that I would be doing so on my own. I wouldn't have access to the resources or contacts that The Order possessed. I suspected they did so to limit the impact of what they believed would be my likely failure. The clock was ticking, and I was alone in my quest for truth.

So be it.

The last letter I had was from Charlotte, keeping me updated on the latest gossip at court. My cousin had an almost supernatural ability to gather information—far better than my own, even when I was collecting intelligence for The Order. Her cheerful nature and sparkling wit made her a natural ally and confidante, and I relied on her observations heavily when I wasn't at court myself. Reading between the lines, I started to pick up on a worrisome trend. Despite the king's more relaxed attitude toward having the nobility in residence at the palace, more and more courtiers were leaving their private châteaux to move into vacant apartments within Versailles. I thought back to Étienne's words. Were the infected no longer the minority? Were these moves motivated by the fear of what was happening around Paris? If so, who else knew that we humans were in a more precarious position than the king—and The Order, for that matter— would have us believe?

Étienne believed a reckoning was coming. For the second time since I'd met him, I was starting to believe he was right.

8

ÉTIENNE

October 17, 1765
Château de Champs-sur-Marne

I FLIPPED THE PAGES OF MY BOOK IDLY, UNABLE TO FOCUS. MY THOUGHTS returned to Daphne and the expectant look on her face—the unmistakable desire I'd seen there. It had thrown me. She may not believe what I was telling her about the plague and the people of France, she may not believe I was innocent of involvement in Jeanne's murder, she may not trust me or my motives in the slightest—but I could sense that she was attracted to me.

It shouldn't excite me as much as it did.

Feeling like a caged animal, I threw the book onto the bed and paced my makeshift room. I was sorely tempted to work my way through the dozens of wines lining the walls, but I figured that would be a temporary solution at best. At worst, I'd get drunk enough to become senseless again, and I didn't want a repeat of whatever transgressions I'd managed while poisoned.

I sighed. Perhaps a different book. Knowing it was after midnight, I listened carefully for the sounds of the household, not wanting to startle some unsuspecting housemaid. After I was certain the rest of the château was abed, I crept out from the wine cellar and padded silently through the halls. I hadn't bothered with a candle—my unfortunate supernatural condition afforded me the ability to see well enough in the dark.

When I located the library, I was surprised to see a thin ray of light beneath the door. I knocked softly, and Daphne's voice sounded from within.

"Yes?"

I went in. She sat at a large desk, bent over a pile of papers. Her hair fell over her shoulder in a thick, golden braid and I glimpsed her white nightdress beneath her loose dressing gown. After a moment, she looked up, her eyebrows arching in bewilderment.

"Étienne! What are you doing out of bed? Are you well?" She stood to approach, but paused, suddenly embarrassed by her appearance. She tied the belt of her dressing gown around her and fidgeted with the knot. I'd never seen her look so unguarded—vulnerable, even. It was disturbingly appealing.

I grinned. "Forgive me for startling you. I thought everyone would be asleep by now. I merely came to find something new to read."

She nodded but did not sit back down. She gestured at the walls lined with books.

"You won't find a better selection of books anywhere—save, perhaps, Versailles. My father was a great collector and lover of the written word. Michel was, too. Help yourself," she said, turning back to her letters.

I strode over to the wall opposite her, nearest to the fireplace, and perused distractedly. "What about you?" I asked.

The light scratching of her pen stopped.

"What about me?"

"Do you share the same interests as your father and brother?"

The scratching resumed, then paused again. She sighed.

"I like books," she said evasively.

"The only books my father collected were about history, weaponry, and military strategy," I said. "I never appreciated them, but I had little else to read. My mother snuck some romances into our collection—which I enjoyed more than the lessons on combat—but not by much."

"What do you like to read?" Daphne asked.

"Adventures. Travel, art, music, culture. Essentially everything that my father despised," I replied, with more than a touch of bitterness.

She was next to me now, leaning against one of the high-backed chairs that faced the fireplace.

"He was a soldier," she said quietly, more observation than question.

"A highly-decorated general. A war hero, even," I replied, thinking back to the distant memories—and pain. "His last campaign was the battle at Dettingen in the war of Austrian succession. He was betrayed by two of his comrades, which led to his defeat. In the king's fury, my father was stripped of his title and most of our holdings. I'm sure you heard the rumors of our family's disgrace. *Vicomte* no longer. He died years later, broken and impoverished."

"I'm sorry," Daphne said, laying a hand on my arm. "I'd heard some of the gossip, but I didn't know the story. It was unjust for the king to punish your father so harshly—especially if it was the result of a betrayal."

"It matters little now. Louis knew exactly which strings to pull to coerce me into emissary service. My ancestral estate and holdings have been returned to me, at least. I don't care about the title. I shan't be having an issue to pass it on to, anyway." Frustrated and resentful, I turned from the bookshelves and sat heavily in one of the armchairs before the fire. It needled me, if I let it—the inability to sire an heir. In my boyhood, when I was to inherit a title and the responsibilities attached to it, my father worked tirelessly to drill a sense of duty and honor into my head. Even when I rebelled as a young man, I knew that I'd return to the fold eventually. Find a wealthy, well-connected wife—hopefully pretty—and get her with child after child. We would enjoy family holidays in the country and seasons in Paris; try not to squander the fortune my father had carefully amassed and invested; I'd find some way to serve France, whether on the battlefield or in court. *"Honor, duty, and responsibility, son. That's your lot in life. Do not waste it."*

And I almost had—but I was trying to make up for it now.

Daphne went to a sideboard, poured two generous glasses of cognac, and sat in the other armchair. She handed me a glass, which I took gratefully. I'd wanted company, but I hadn't expected to spill my life story. I swirled the cognac in the glass, unexpectedly self-conscious.

"Is that a…vampire problem?" she inquired awkwardly.

I nodded. "Hard to sire heirs when your body functions as a walking corpse. Did you and the duc never—"

"No," she cut in. "After a few months of marriage, I refused him. I would not consent to carry his bloodline." At this, she drank a sizable swallow of cognac. Her cheeks turned a fetching shade of pink.

"Was he—" I floundered for the right words, but she interrupted me again with an acerbic smile.

"He wasn't called *le Duc Dépravé* for nothing," she said.

Things started to fall into place, then—rumors I'd heard about the brutal, predatory aristocrat. I hadn't realized *le Duc Dépravé* was Daphne's husband. Horror filled me in a way I hadn't experienced in some years. The thought of her suffering the abuse of such a man made me see red. My fangs lengthened impulsively, and my muscles bunched, preparing to attack some unseen threat. Without warning, the cognac glass exploded in my hand.

"*Merde*," I swore. Daphne jumped up, grabbing a cloth and a pitcher of water from a nearby table. She reached for my hand—tentatively. "I'm not going to bite," I chuckled. My fangs retracted. Daphne eyed me cautiously and started wiping the blood from my palm.

An uncomfortable silence settled between us.

"I heard from The Order," she blurted.

I arched a brow. "Good news or bad?"

"Both, or neither, depending on your perspective," she said. "They seem open to considering your innocence in Jeanne's murder, but they require proof. They've allowed me some time, but no resources, to settle the matter."

"How magnanimous of them," I drawled. She'd finished cleaning my hand and was using a clean scrap of cloth to bind it. Her movements were firm, but tender.

"There's more," she said, gingerly picking up shards of glass from the floor. "I had a letter from Charlotte. It sounds like many of the nobles are relocating to the palace. I fear things are escalating. The aristocrats are worried."

This wasn't exactly surprising, but certainly more concerning.

"What will The Order do?" I wondered.

Daphne went to her desk to throw the broken glass and bloody rags away.

"I don't know," she admitted. "I don't know about all of their plans, and I'm afraid if I don't find Jeanne's killer and bring them proof soon, they'll kick me out and I'll know even less."

I agreed. "We must hurry. I'm well enough to carry on. I'll send a message to some of my contacts in Paris and let them know we'll be in the city tomorrow night. We'll start with the ring."

Some relief shone in Daphne's face.

"That would be best," she said. "I'm eager to see this through and move on with my life."

"As am I," I said. I stood to leave and she followed me to the door. "Tomorrow night, we'll need to play the parts of intimidating aristocrats. Prepare accordingly."

Daphne rolled her eyes. "I think I can manage that."

"I'll do what I can to keep you safe, but you should remain on your guard."

"I don't need you to keep me safe, Étienne," she snapped.

"Perhaps not," I conceded. "But I will try, all the same. Should things go awry, I mean."

We were standing at the threshold of the library, the dark hallway yawning behind me. Daphne appeared at a loss for words and stood at the door, hesitating. The tightness around her mouth relaxed and she mumbled a soft, "Thank you."

"I'll say goodnight, then," I said.

"Goodnight, Étienne."

I didn't go. I waited a beat—taking in the flickering candlelight on her golden hair, the worn linen of her nightdress, the perfume of cognac, blood, and orange blossoms. Here, in this quiet moment past midnight, I felt an alien sense of comfort. It was unlike the plush rooms at Versailles, unlike my own château, even—with its haunting memories and ghosts of failure. It filled me with a painful longing—a hollow ache in my chest that I knew would linger long after Daphne's orange blossom scent had faded.

Her eyes dropped to my lips, then, and her tongue darted out to lick her bottom lip. My restraint evaporated in an instant. Unable to stop myself, I pulled her to me and covered her lips with mine. Slanting my mouth over hers, I slid my tongue along the seam of her lips—a silent plea for her to open up to me. Almost straightaway, she melted into the kiss. When she opened her mouth and sighed, the sweetness of it overtook me, and I knew I was lost.

God help me—what have I done?

9

DAPHNE

October 17, 1765
Château de Champs-sur-Marne

Somewhere in the back of my mind, a voice called out to me, *Wrong. This is wrong. You cannot trust a vampire—especially this one.* I was dimly aware that I should be doing something—stopping this kiss. *This isn't kissing.* It was unlike the perfunctory and invasive attempts of Henri. It was *incredible.* Étienne brought his hand up to the back of my head and threaded his fingers through my hair, gently rubbing at the base of my neck. The pleasure of the touch rolled through me in waves. He tasted of cognac and something vaguely salty, but his lips felt so good against mine that I couldn't focus on much besides the feeling. *Dieu, how he felt.* My body craved more but there was something stopping me from seeking it…

Do not trust the vampire. Remember all his women. Remember the blood. Remember Michel.

Finally, the thought beat back the surge of lust and I realized my mistake. I pulled away immediately, stepping back into the library. Confused by my desire for the man who represented everything I stood against, I couldn't help the force of my response.

"You kissed me!" I exclaimed. My fingers reached up to my tender lips as if to confirm the truth of the matter.

Étienne cocked a satisfied brow at me. "You kissed me back," he said.

"I—I didn't mean to! The cognac—and I haven't been sleeping, and I forgot myself and *you* forgot *yourself!*" I stammered. *Damn it.* I didn't mean to sound so flustered. It made me even angrier. I fought for a steadying breath.

"It was a mistake," I gritted out. "It won't happen again."

Étienne's devilish grin slipped, and I could've sworn I saw a glimmer of hurt in his eyes. His face went blank. "A mistake. My apologies for being forward. As you say, it must have been the cognac."

I nodded, still not satisfied.

"We'll just forget it happened," I said, somewhat breathlessly. "And tomorrow, we'll resume our investigation. The sooner this is solved, the better."

Étienne bowed rigidly and turned down the hall. From the darkness, he called back to me.

"Sleep well, Duchesse."

I wondered if we both knew that was unlikely.

THE FOLLOWING DAY, I SLEPT IN MUCH LATER THAN USUAL. I FINALLY ROUSED myself in the afternoon, ate a belated breakfast, and hid in one of the front parlors. My mind returned to the kiss over and over—how my body wanted him, but my mind couldn't trust him. Even if something happened to change that—which I reasoned was unlikely given his scandalous reputation and supernatural state of being—I was not the kind of woman to take a lover, and as long as there were doubts about Henri's present whereabouts, I could not marry again. Besides, I was dedicated to The Order and in my experience, men didn't tend to share well when it came to their lady's attentions. *It doesn't matter!* I chided myself. *The kiss was a mistake—a weak moment. Do you want to end up another name on some libertine's endless list of conquests? Certainly not.* My pride wouldn't allow it.

Still, I worried over the possibility that I'd started to care for him. It seemed truer now than when Philippe had first presented the possibility. One doesn't aid in nursing a body back to health without forming some kind of attachment—an attachment that definitely needed severing.

I had to do it for the memory of Michel, for the sake of Philippe and Charlotte, for my duty to my king and to our dwindling human aristocracy. I had to admit that I felt less compelled to give him up for The Order now that they'd drawn a line in their support of my investigation.

I grunted. *Give him up.* As if you had him, Daphne. *As if I wanted him. Liar.*

The rest of the day, I tried—and failed—to distract myself with letters, estate business, menu planning, and books before I finally gave up and went to change for dinner.

Eve helped me into my most somber-looking gray dress—a late mourning gown from when my parents had died, and then Michel not long after. It was severity in thread—soft wool with an infinity of tiny buttons. Wearing it made me feel serious and sad and hardhearted all at once. It would be impossible for me to think of anything affectionate when it came to Étienne, and with the long sleeves and high neckline, I didn't think there would be anything that would remotely arouse his libidinous interests.

After I finished dressing, I twisted my hair in tight curls on top of my head, covered with a largely unflattering cap, and comforted myself by hiding an excess of stabbing implements in my pockets and sleeves.

If I came across anyone who meant me harm tonight, I'd take a great deal of pleasure in venting the maelstrom of destruction that seethed beneath my tightly reined exterior.

ÉTIENNE

I LAY IN MY WINE CELLAR BED FOR A WHILE THAT EVENING, GOING OVER THE events of the previous night in my mind. It was troubling to suddenly feel so unsure of myself; I'd thought the kiss was something we both wanted. While I knew Daphne had built an emotional fortress to protect herself, I'd sensed her desire and had felt it in her response. She'd wanted me as much as I'd wanted her.

…but what did that mean?

I hadn't been thinking about a future with her, or a future with any woman, for that matter. Women were delicious, wonderful playthings for me—food, pleasure, and tools to achieve what I needed to in court. With the disgrace to my name, the loss of my title, my inability to father children, and most importantly—the inevitable separation by time itself, if my paramour refused to infect herself with the plague—I had little to offer any woman beyond a few nights of passion. Frustratingly, I was beginning to feel that Daphne deserved more than that.

It didn't matter. I was recovering from a physical and mental shock, and I needed more than a few delicate porcelain bowls filled with donated blood. My lusty pursuit of this woman was likely the result of the euphoria I'd been experiencing from drinking virgin's blood. After our investigations ended, I'd go out and get something *properly* satisfying and leave the damned duchesse Daphne to her melancholy.

As I was contemplating the strange turn of events my life had taken, someone knocked at the door. The butler Gaston entered with a set of shaving implements and a pitcher of warm water. He offered to help me shave, but I declined his assistance. After everything that had happened, I felt decidedly less comfortable allowing a stranger to hold a blade to my throat. He stood patiently by the door while I washed, lathered, and dragged the sharp blade over the light growth of whiskers I'd accumulated in my convalescence. When I was finished, he spoke.

"Her Grace instructed me to assist you with your dress tonight. If you'll follow me to the duc's bedchamber, we'll find something appropriate for you in his wardrobe," he said.

"Do you think the duc would object to my use of his clothes?"

Gaston glanced at me, eyes wide in surprise.

"His Grace is…gone," he said, fumbling for the right word.

"Yes, so I heard. What *exactly* does that mean, I wonder?"

Gaston didn't answer. We reached a sumptuous bedchamber decked in dark wood and burgundy velvet. It reminded me of the color of Daphne's gown the first night we'd met. The room seemed a tad stale, as if it hadn't been opened in some months. There were strange, lingering scents in the air that I struggled to name: faint wisps of opium smoke, the cloying reek of vomited brandy, the musk of ancient lovemaking, and—disturbingly— the metallic tinge of old blood. I'd smelled rooms like this before—in the dank basements of brothels that specialized in pain over pleasure. I couldn't imagine Daphne willingly submitting to such debasements and I started to understand her fears. The hairs on the back of my neck stood on end and my fangs lengthened.

"What happened in here?" I growled. On some level, I already knew. A rush of protective indignity coursed through me when I imagined what Daphne had endured. *So, the gossip about le Duc Dépravé had been true.*

A deep sorrow filled Gaston's gaze.

"We do not discuss it, Monsieur." Shame and regret radiated from him.

"Just tell me this, then," I bit out. "Is the duc dead?"

If he isn't, I will amend that promptly.

A long-suffering sigh escaped him while he pulled ornate jackets, breeches, and matching waistcoats from a large ebony armoire.

"We do not know, Monsieur. But we do not think he will be coming back."

"Why not? He has one of the most influential duchies in all of France, a fortune almost as vast as the king's, this exceptional château, and a rather formidable wife. Even with the requisite carousing of the aristocracy, they're usually quite dedicated to at least some of the responsibilities of the peerage. Siring an heir is the most pressing one that comes to mind," I grumbled, then remembered Daphne's words from the night before. Her refusal to carry on the duc's bloodline. *Brave girl,* I thought. *Considering procreation was the only important preoccupation of titled women.*

I selected a charcoal-colored velvet coat adorned with silver embroidery. Despite the duc's obvious predilection for depravity, his taste in clothing was impeccable. He'd obviously enjoyed the slighter stature of the nobility and the coat was tight across my chest and shoulders, but I thought it would do for our outing tonight.

"You look very fine, Monsieur," Gaston said, offering me a selection of shoe buckles to choose from. "Most satisfactory for l'émissaire vampire."

I arched a brow at him. "You know who I am?"

"Bien sûr." His reply was tight with stifled affront. "You've been a guest with us for some time now, Monsieur."

"Ah, so Madame has told you about me?"

"No, of course not. Her Grace does not share everything with us. But we know—all the same. We've been with her since she came to this house and we are loyal to her," he said tersely. He finished tying back my hair in a silver ribbon.

He offered me a matching hat and shiny ebony walking stick, which I took with a nod.

"It is possible that you know my reputation," I said a touch more defensively than I would have liked. "But I assure you I'm not here to take advantage of your mistress."

"As you say, Monsieur."

I made to leave but stopped at the door.

"And I did not kill Madame de Pompadour."

"Oui. As you say, Monsieur," he said, his expression unreadable.

I didn't know why, but it bothered me immensely that Daphne's household thought ill of me. They likely believed I was as much of a villain as the duc. *As much as Daphne does.*

My mood was dark as I went downstairs. *Damn The Order. The sooner I can find Jeanne's murderer, the sooner I can put this mess behind me.* It might be time for me to take an extended trip abroad and leave Paris entirely. Perhaps ride out the winter months in the south of France, or even Italy. Even if I couldn't enjoy the sunshine, I could enjoy the warmth of an evening, or the smell of the sea. They were better substitutes for light than the stifling candlelit ballrooms of Versailles.

Daphne cleared her throat behind me.

"Are you ready?"

Even with her drawn expression and her severe gray attire, she was still the most luminous thing I'd seen since I'd been banished from the sunlight. Her self-assurance and confidence emanated from every curve of her body in a way that seemed positively magnetic. The determination in her violet eyes hid every other emotion I knew she kept contained, daring me to try to rile her—to remind her of our kiss. *I would not.* We had work to do—and she was not for me. I could not afford to let her presence distract me and keep turning me into some mindless, rutting beast. I was above that.

"Indeed. After you, Duchesse."

We got into her waiting carriage and crunched down the gravel drive. She stared out the window, avoiding conversation, until the feel of the street changed, and we rumbled into the louder, grittier neighborhoods around Paris. Sounds and smells changed to an earthiness that I doubted Daphne had experienced before.

"We're going to the jeweler first," I said. "Perhaps you should wait in the carriage for me."

"Why?" she asked.

"Because I don't want to worry about protecting you while I'm trying to focus on getting information from this man."

"Protecting me?" she scoffed. She stuck her hand in her pocket and I heard the unmistakable click of a pistol cocking.

I rolled my eyes. "Are you any good with that thing?"

She cut her gaze to me disdainfully, then flicked her wrist. A small silver dagger shot forth and embedded itself in the seat half an inch to the left of my head.

"Almost as good as I am with that thing," she said with a cheeky smile.

"Very well, then. I suppose I should have known better. No offense meant."

She lifted a shoulder in a shrug. "No offense taken. I am used to being underestimated."

The carriage stopped outside a small shop on the main street. We got down and knocked on the door, seeing only darkness inside. Some minutes passed with no one coming to let us in.

"Perhaps they're closed for the evening?" Daphne suggested. "It's very late."

"No, it isn't. Most of the shops and vendors have changed their hours to keep pace with their increasingly vampiric clientele. You'd be hard pressed to find an establishment that closes before midnight around here." I gestured to a sign by the door—a hastily scrawled, *We welcome our immortal brethren.*

Daphne's brows rose in surprise, but she said nothing. Finally, the bobbing light of a candle broke through the gloom and a corpulent man in a leather apron unlocked the door.

"Ah, Monsieur l'Émissaire! How fortunate to see you here this evening. And I see you brought a new—ah—friend!"

"*Bon soir*, Georges. Duchesse de Duras, allow me to introduce the finest jeweler in all of Paris—Versailles included," I wheedled. I hoped that Daphne would take my wink as instruction to follow my lead.

She did, indeed. Tilting her chin up haughtily, she sniffed.

"We shall see about that." She offered Georges her hand to kiss and I noticed him instantly eyeing the necklace of expensive black pearls at her throat. His piggy eyes sparked with hunger.

Georges led us into his shop and went around lighting all of the candles. Jewelry and unset gemstones glittered up at us from velvet-lined cases atop a counter.

"How may I be of assistance, Your Grace?"

When he turned to open another box of necklaces, she caught my eye and I nodded to her encouragingly. If she could get information out of him without me having to use force, so much the better. Besides, I was curious to see how well this lady agent handled herself.

"I'm looking for something special—very special. I have a new gown being made for an upcoming ball at Versailles and it's in the loveliest shade of pink. A soft pink, like the inside of a shell, you know. Normally I would pair a pink gown with my pink diamonds, but I feel as though I need something new and dazzling. Something to win the right amount of attention from His Majesty, you understand. I couldn't go to the court jeweler, of course—he is already designing pieces for several other ladies and I simply cannot wait. I thought I was forsaken! Then, as luck would have it, Monsieur l'Émissaire told me that he knew of just the man to accept such a commission." She blushed prettily and gently touched his arm. He reddened to an unflattering, mottled purple and stared up at her with pure adoration. *He was hooked.*

"Of course, Madame, of course! I am at your disposal. What sort of piece do you have in mind? A necklace? Some new earrings? A new brooch for your bodice, perhaps?" He licked his lips and stared at her breasts. Anger and a fierce possessiveness crept through my veins.

"Oh, la! No, I have all of those things. A ring, I think. A ring with a pink pearl at the center. I will be just like Madame de Pompadour; God rest her soul. Pearls—they come in pink, do they not? I have seen them in every other color at court. Have you ever done something like that before? With pink pearls, I mean?" She ran her fingertips along the black pearls of her necklace, drawing his attention—and mine.

"Pink pearls? Yes, yes. They come in pink. They are rare, though, Madame. It would take me some time to acquire the necessary—"

"Oh, but I don't have the time, Monsieur. I simply must have it as soon as possible. I will, of course, be happy to pay for any trouble you have in trying to find the very best materials. In fact, I will double your usual fee. My husband, the Duc de Duras, is rather generous with both his pocketbook and his oversight." She arched a brow suggestively and leaned forward. I'm certain both Georges and I cursed the high neckline of her dress.

"Perhaps, Georges, you might find the gems at a more ready source," I offered. "I know that Madame de Duras is—shall we say—less than particular about the provenance of her jewels."

Daphne nodded emphatically. "You must understand how important it is for me to present myself at court in the height of fashion. And I will do anything to get what I want." Her long lashes fluttered, and a coy smile spread across her lips. *God, she was magnificent.* My cock twitched in the duc's too-tight breeches.

Georges' attention was fixed on Daphne's mouth. I had a sudden urge to remove his eyes from his skull.

"I have employed such methods before, Madame," he oozed. "Don't you worry your pretty head over that. I understand you perfectly. I have—perhaps—heard of something that may help *expedite* the process. But it is not yet in my possession. Give me seventy-two hours to attempt to acquire it," he rasped, clutching at her hand. He was beginning to sweat, and his breath was coming in heated pants.

"You have thirty-six," Daphne snapped icily, breaking the spell of sensuality. "Or I shall take my custom to another jeweler. Oh—and this should go without saying, but this arrangement is entirely confidential. I shall remain anonymous. If I find out you've told anyone about this, I will deny everything and have your tongue cut out for slander. Do you understand?"

Georges nodded vigorously and bowed.

"Of course, Your Grace. Of course. You may trust Georges!"

Daphne smiled coldly at him and left. I tipped my hat to the quivering man and followed her out.

When we were alone in the carriage, I let out a bark of laughter.

"You did not need to be so rough with him at the end, Duchesse."

She bristled. "He does not have it, and yet he will try and sell it to me! The ring of my brutally murdered friend. Without a thought to her memory, he will try to find someone to dig her up and take it, and then sell me something that was once so precious to her. I do not regret dashing his ill-mannered hopes. Besides, he was entirely inappropriate to a lady in mourning attire."

I knocked on the carriage roof to signal our driver.

"He's just trying to earn a living, not an easy thing to do in these times. I'm sure if he had the meager luxury of not worrying about feeding himself or his family, he would leave a dead woman's jewelry alone."

"Perhaps," she said stiffly. "It's still wrong."

"So, in your estimation, it is wrong to take from a dead woman in order to feed oneself, and it is wrong for the peasants to become vampires so they do not need to eat. What do you suggest they do, Duchesse? Wait for the scraps from your table?"

"It cannot be so dire," she insisted. "I refuse to believe that there are no alternatives to surviving than to rob graves and drink the blood of the living. I myself have had to think laterally in order to avoid destitution."

I could not help but laugh.

"As the emissary between a largely impoverished vampire class and the declining human nobility, let me assure you, Duchesse, that the destitution of the aristocracy is very different from the destitution of everyone else."

"An empty belly is an empty belly regardless of the body's social status."

"The difference is that you had the opportunity to marry a wealthy, titled duc. Most other women do not."

She continued to stare out the window, but I saw a flash of anguish in her eyes. She was quiet for long moments, and when she spoke, it was so low I almost missed it beneath the noise of the street.

"Had I known what kind of man was saving me from hunger, I would have starved to death a thousand times."

10

DAPHNE

I DIDN'T HAVE MUCH HOPE FOR A LEAD FROM THE JEWELER, GEORGES. If Jeanne's ring had made its way to some black market jewelry merchant, I suspected we would have had some inclination about it by now. We were no closer to Jeanne's killer.

After our outing into Paris, we'd returned to my château to regroup. We decided our next move would be to hunt down the woman who'd poisoned Étienne. The more I thought about it, the more I wondered if she *had* been on assignment from The Order. As far as I knew, I was still the only female member, though I supposed she could have been hired or coerced by one of the other male agents. Either way, we needed to find her and question her.

In an effort to regain some of my lost influence with The Order, I'd also sent them a message about what I'd learned in Paris—the late hours of the merchants and their willingness to do business with the vampires—and told them I suspected a change in the attitudes of the people. *Were the other agents aware of this? If so, what was the plan to deal with it?* I left out several details, not wanting to damn the unfortunate Georges, but made it clear that my investigation was progressing regardless of their assistance. I hadn't received a reply, but I didn't really expect one, either.

Étienne had refused to tell me where our investigation would take us tonight and had become somewhat agitated in response to my questions, so we'd been careful to avoid each other for the rest of last night and the first part of this evening. While I didn't know what to expect, I was sure we would find ourselves in yet another dark and dangerous part of the city, so it seemed silly for me to be bathing now, but I didn't care. Relaxing in the hot water helped me shore up my courage—and I'd spent so much time worrying over Jeanne's murder, The Order's grand plan, and Étienne's recovery, this was my first opportunity to enjoy time to myself and let my swirling thoughts still.

At least, I *had been* enjoying it until my infuriating houseguest knocked on my door.

"*Go away!*" I shouted.

"I've come to apologize," he called. "I'll tell you where we're going tonight, but I'm not going to yell at you through this door."

"Well, it will have to wait," I replied.

"We're already losing evening hours—I don't believe it can," he said, and forced the door open.

I shrieked and ducked beneath the bubbles, covering as much of my nudity as possible. His face lit with a pleased grin.

"There had better be an exceptional reason why you're here," I growled. "Otherwise, I'm going to call Dr. Van Helsing again and have her put the quicksilver *back* in your blood."

Étienne chuckled and sat on a chaise opposite the tub. He stretched his long legs out before him and leaned back, making himself comfortable. His manner was no longer dark and brooding—rather, he seemed extraordinarily gleeful.

"We're off to the *Maison des Nymphes* on the Rue Saint-Denis," he said, his eyes never leaving me. "I'm sorry I didn't tell you sooner. I was…*uncertain* about allowing you to accompany me. You are, after all, a duchesse."

"Rue Saint-Denis? We're going to a house of ill-repute?"

"The finest in all of Paris," he winked.

"And you're worried that will offend my delicate aristocratic sensibilities?" I scoffed.

"Certainly not. I'm worried you'll offend the ladies within. I must insist you be on your best behavior," he drawled, eyeing me up and down.

If the water was warm before, I was set to bring it up to boiling in my ire.

"We're going to a bordello that you patronized, and you think *I'm* the offensive one?" I gritted out.

"Well, you do have a firm set of opinions and a rather sharp tongue, Daphne. Not that I'm complaining. In fact, I rather like your tongue."

Lust heated his gaze and he smiled wickedly.

The audacity of the man!

"I'm sure I don't know what you mean, Monsieur. If you're referring to that *mistake* in the library, I've quite forgotten it. And just because you had the misfortune of succumbing to your poisoning in my house does not give you leave to address me like one of your mistresses or your meals. Now, gather up your arrogance and get out."

"*My* arrogance?" he laughed. "Duchesse, you are quite possibly the most arrogant woman I've ever known."

"And yet—remarkably—still less arrogant than nearly every man on Earth."

"I can't argue that," he conceded, standing up. Just when I thought I'd won, he proved me wrong and started to disrobe.

"Did the poison damage your hearing, Étienne? I told you to leave."

His eyes sparked as he casually unbuttoned his cuffs. "Have you really forgotten it?"

"Of course. I remember the cognac and nothing more," I grumbled. *Liar.*

He took off his shoes and pulled his linen shirt up over his head. I opened my mouth to yell at him again, but froze, strangely mesmerized by his bare torso. Taught, sculpted muscles flexed beneath smooth, pale skin. A thin trail of dark hair descended from his bellybutton into his breeches, hinting at some dark, secretive virility. Infuriated with myself, I found it impossible to look away. Henri hadn't looked like this. There wasn't an ounce of softness to Étienne, merely hard planes and smooth angles. My fingers fidgeted with the desire to touch him.

Beneath the blood rushing through my ears, his voice carried like a devilish hymn.

"Do you like to watch, Duchesse?"

His movements slowed as he caressed his abdomen and stepped toward me. His hands were on the buttons of his breeches, undoing them one by one. I needed to leave—to put a stop to this, go get dressed, and find Jeanne's killer. Restore my place in The Order. Figure out what the blood plague was actually doing to my city.

Why wasn't I leaving?

Étienne's breeches slid down his hips and to the floor. My breath shuddered on an exhale as he stood before me, naked, sinfully handsome, visibly aroused. He grinned down at me, fangs extended, hazel eyes glowing. He stepped into the large copper tub facing me, and began a slow, predatory drift in my direction.

Get out, my brain screamed. *Get out of the tub, Daphne. This is wrong. He is a libertine and a rake. He will throw you over when he is done, and you will be just another one of his conquests.*

I stood abruptly, water sloshing down my naked body. Modesty forgotten in the face of my anger, I stepped from the tub and pulled a towel from the chaise. Instantly, Étienne was behind me again, pressing his hard body against my back. His arms snaked around my waist.

"Have you not come to care for me, Duchesse?" Étienne whispered against my neck. "At least a little?"

I squeezed my eyes shut.

"No," I breathed.

He chuckled at the lie. *Merde.*

Soft, wet lips pressed against the back of my neck. Desire and wild curiosity paralyzed me. I couldn't believe he'd had the temerity to enter my bedchamber in the first place, let alone the brazenness to strip before me and insinuate himself in my watery sanctuary. I fought to ignore the heady thrill I felt at the press of his hard cock against my backside. It was almost dizzying feeling how much he wanted me.

What would it be like? To be with a man who wasn't Henri, to feel intimacy without pain and humiliation, to have a man touch me with more than his own pleasure in mind, to be worshipped and caressed, and not used or brutalized.

His cool body sent little shockwaves of pleasure through me when he brushed against my skin. He ground his hips harder against me and he let out a guttural moan that made heat pool at my core. When my lips parted, the bridled tension between us snapped, and he whirled me around to crush his mouth to mine.

His kiss was rough with urgency, his soft lips covering mine entirely. He was a man dying of thirst in a desert and I was his only oasis. I'd never felt such passion before, having long believed that after Henri, that part of me was a cold hearth full of ashes. My desire rekindled, some distant joy erupted within. *Perhaps there is hope for me yet.*

My thoughts of protest seemed to dilute in the ocean of lust swirling between us. He shoved one hand into my hair, scattering pins across the floor. He pulled at my curls gently, massaging my scalp with his fingertips. I whimpered at the exquisite pleasure of it. His lips left mine and he kissed my jaw, working his way down. His other hand stroked my breast beneath the towel, lightly at first, then with more insistence. He rolled my puckered nipple between his fingers and I became a bottomless pit of sexual need.

Then, came that eerily familiar, warm wet stroke along my neck as he licked me.

Just like his night of madness—his poisoned mind. The shame of that night returned to me—the thought of wanting him even when he was sick and disturbed. *Dieu.* What did that say about me? *It says you will probably suffer the same fate as your brother — too easily seduced by a man who will turn you out when he's done with you.*

I flinched and froze. As quickly as it had come, my lust evaporated. He stopped immediately, pulling away with a question in his eyes.

"Daphne, what—?"

I pulled away and shoved him back—hard. His eyes widened with shock and offense.

"I cannot do this," I ground out through gritted teeth. Shame and guilt powered my anger and I stood before him, wrapping the towel tightly around me like some kind of armor against my own desires. "I will not do this. I will not be another woman who lines up before you to be fucked and feasted upon. I will not fall prey to your charms just so you can use me and take from me and then discard me like some forlorn, dried-up husk of a woman. I am more than food. I am more than a warm place to put your cock. I am more than some gossip-trading courtier looking for a tryst. My purpose on this Earth is greater than your base needs, Monsieur, and you shall remember that from now on or so help me God, I will stake you and not bother to brush your dust from my skirts."

"Daphne, wait! What happened?" he called, but I had already stormed from the room.

It occurred to me in some vague part of my mind that I was—perhaps—overreacting. Perhaps I was punishing Étienne for the sins of Henri and the tragedy of Michel's death, and that I was frightened—not because Étienne was a vampire, but because he'd awoken things in me that I'd long assumed dead or destroyed. Yes, all of these things whispered through me, but the most resounding thoughts were sheer instinct. *Protect, endure, survive.*

Eve helped me dress in a plain gown of lavender silk. Like last night, I pinned up my curls and comforted myself with a variety of weapons tucked against my body. When I met Étienne in the drawing room downstairs, he said nothing—simply nodded and escorted me to the waiting carriage. His expression was unreadable, but his manner was dark, as if he were being followed by a little black raincloud. It didn't do much for my own feelings of anxiety, and a whisper of regret went through me.

We drove down a street in a shabby neighborhood of Paris, lined with prostitutes calling out to men. Unbeknownst to Étienne, I was already familiar with the area, having had to come collect Henri from countless dens of iniquity when he'd rendered himself senseless from opium or alcohol. My stomach soured when I remembered it. I felt overwhelmed by regret and shame. When I'd refused to allow Henri to torture me and torment the ladies of my household, he inevitably wound up here, visiting his evil upon women too disadvantaged to say no. It broke my heart and made me feel sick at the same time. I only *just* managed to convince myself that my queasiness had nothing to do with the jealousy over Étienne coming here to be with other women.

"Why have we come here?" I demanded. "Is your would-be assassin a prostitute? Is that how you feed?"

He laughed at me then. A warm, full-throated chortle that crinkled his eyes and showed his dazzling white teeth. I would have felt abashed if some part of me wasn't charmed by how sweet and boyish he looked in a light mood.

"What an inappropriate question! Are you jealous, Duchesse?"

"Don't be absurd. I simply want to know why you've brought me here."

"If you're uncomfortable, you are free to wait in the carriage. In fact, perhaps that would be best. I don't need you upsetting the ladies with you in all your *state*," he said with a grin. The carriage pulled up to a large building at the end of the street—a once-grand home that had been turned into a modest hotel.

Étienne got out of the carriage. When I made to descend, he stopped me on the step.

"I meant what I said, Duchesse. I won't have you insulting or upsetting the women here." The good humor had left his face and his hazel eyes bored into mine.

Since I didn't trust myself to speak without some sharp retort, I merely nodded and followed him. Instead of approaching the front door, he went around to the side and entered through the kitchen.

"Étienne! You've come to visit me! And have you brought me sweets?" A blur of chestnut curls and matching brown wool hurled itself at him and jumped into his arms. The girl—likely no more than six—was covered in flour, which resulted in a soft puff of white enshrouding the two.

"Marie, *mon Dieu!* You are covered in enough flour to bake an entire loaf of bread," Étienne laughed, reaching in his pocket for a gold coin. He palmed it and made it appear behind her ear. She squealed a giggle.

"I don't have sweets on me today, but this will do—our little secret, okay? Where is your *maman?*" Étienne kissed the girl's cheek and stood.

"She is upstairs in the sewing room. Come, I'll take you—and your pretty friend!" Marie danced from foot to foot as if she had more energy than a swarming beehive.

"Manners, Marie! This is the Duchesse—"

I cut him off. I bent to the girl and stuck out my hand.

"Daphne, *chérie*. My friends call me Daphne." The girl beamed at me and shook my hand. Étienne eyed me warily, but he said nothing.

Still gripping my hand, Marie tugged me through the house, which was humbly furnished, but clean, warm, and comfortable. Up the small staircase lay several rooms on either side of the hallway. The lilt of feminine laughter sang from every closed door. If this was a brothel, it was unlike every brothel I'd ever entered. *What was this place?*

Marie paused before a large oak door, brushed some of the flour from her cheeks and dress, and knocked politely.

"*Entrez-vous!*"

"*Maman,* Étienne is here! And he has brought a Daphne!"

A round woman with soft red curls pinned on top of her head turned from her sewing. It looked like she was stitching a small repair in the skirt of a buttercup yellow dress. She smiled at Marie and Étienne, then stood to greet me with a polite curtsy. Marie scampered back through the hallway, closing the door behind her.

"I imagine, Madame, you should be addressed as more than just Daphne," she said. Warmth shone from her smile and she had startlingly familiar hazel eyes. *It couldn't be…*

"Perhaps elsewhere. But here, tonight, I am just Daphne."

"I am Josephine," she said. "Welcome to the *Maison des Nymphes.* But I'm sure Étienne has already told you that—if he has brought you here."

I glanced at Étienne, who was watching our interaction with guarded interest. When I didn't reply, she tutted and whacked Étienne's shoulder.

"This imbecile is my brother."

I gaped. Étienne rolled his eyes.

"Half-brother," he corrected.

Josephine tutted again and waved her hand. "Half, quarter, cousin, whatever. Half-brother by blood, but full brother indeed."

Seeing my confusion, she threw a withering glare at Étienne.

"You did not tell her, *mon frère?* Oh, you are *impossible!* Fine—I shall do so." She settled down on a chair in the corner and motioned for me to do the same.

"Josephine, please don't. We are in a bit of a hurry," he grumbled.

"So, you bring a woman of your own here for the first time and you tell her nothing? *Quel crétin!* What are you on about? Are you ashamed all of a sudden?"

"You know I'm not. We just don't have the time tonight and Daphne is not interested in our family dramatics—"

"Yes, I am." I interrupted and grinned at Josephine. "Tell me, please, Madame."

"Josephine!" Étienne cautioned.

She ignored him. "Our father, you see, was the Vicomte de Noailles. At least, he was born and raised as the vicomte. Étienne is the only legitimate heir, but we have at least six half-siblings, three of whom live abroad.

Papa had so many mistresses around the world, we are forever finding new relations. It wasn't as bad as it sounds, of course. He was not a bad father, really—not as bad as some men. We were always provided for, even if we were just his bastards. But then he suffered that humiliating loss at the Battle of Dettingen and the king was so angry…"

"Yes, Étienne told me. I'm so sorry," I said. Josephine patted my hand.

"Well, as you would imagine, funds became a little short. Étienne was off in Italy or England at the time—I don't remember which—so it was just me, Noelle, Anne, and Eve left here in the city. We'd never had much to begin with, but then we had even less. We had but one way to make ends meet—to start selling our company."

My jaw dropped. She spoke of prostitution openly, without shame or regret. Étienne, however, was less than pleased. His jaw clenched and he strode to look out the window.

"Well, we were doing okay—not great, but okay—and Étienne came home to find his identity seized, his entailment demolished, our father on his deathbed—the shock, you know, the poor thing—and his impoverished half-sisters running a brothel. You can imagine his temper!"

"Enough. She doesn't need your life story, Josephine," Étienne growled.

"You mean, you don't want her to know *your* life story, eh?" Josephine teased. "He must really fancy you then, *chérie.*"

He turned from the window to fix her with a glare. "*Josephine,*" he warned.

She sighed. "Another time, then. *Alors, mon frère.* Why are you here tonight? It cannot be good."

"The woman from earlier this month—the new arrival. Is she still here?"

"The blonde one? Brigitte? No, I'm afraid not. She packed up and left in the middle of the night a little over a week ago. No note or anything. Just picked at her dinner—didn't eat much, the little mouse—went to bed, and then *poof.* Gone the next morning."

"You didn't go look for her? What if she's in trouble?" I asked.

"It is a common thing, Madame. The young girls come here looking for a place to stay. Sometimes they want to work as a light-skirt or a bleeder—we give them a safe place to ply their trade—but many of them find other work. Laundry, sewing, even a few governesses. They come here to find a degree of comfort and security while they get on their feet. But many come and go, just as easily. It is their choice. We do not indenture them here. Brigitte was not the first—nor dare I say the last—to come and go so quickly."

"What's a bleeder?" I asked. Josephine turned disbelieving eyes on me. Étienne scoffed.

"You do not know, Madame? But they are all over the city—there are so many now. Perhaps even more than the light-skirts." She was baffled by my ignorance.

Embarrassment pinked my cheeks. "I'm afraid I don't get out much in the city."

Étienne threw the explanation over his shoulder at me as he began pacing. "A bleeder is a common term for a woman who sells her blood. A blood-whore, if you will." He glared at me in irritation, then turned back to Josephine. "You have no idea where she went? Did she have family? Where did she come from?" Seemingly unable to stand still, he resumed his pacing.

Josephine arched a brow at him. "You know as well as I that the women here are free from the shackles of their past, Étienne. I knew almost nothing of the girl, except that she was anxious to make your acquaintance."

"She was?" I asked. "Was she particularly interested in him?"

"Of course! All the ladies are, especially the new ones. They hear the stories from the older girls, and all have the same hopes that the dashing vampire emissary will one day come and fall madly in love with his meal," she chuckled. "The saps. Incurable romantics, the lot of them."

Étienne crossed his arms and harrumphed.

"Well, whose fault is it that these poor girls have such notions? I try to divest them of their false ideas that you are anything but a tried-and-true rogue, but they don't listen. Anyway, why are you asking after her? Has something happened?"

While Étienne stewed in frustration and embarrassment, my mind worked.

"That's what we're trying to ascertain. May we see her room, please?" I asked.

"Suit yourself. Lucky for you I have not had time to clean it and turn it out properly. We haven't had need of it yet, but inevitably, some new wretch will show up on our doorstep soon." Josephine put her sewing down and led us out to the hallway. At the far end was a smaller staircase that wound up to an attic with low ceilings and a small bed. A cacophony of noise erupted below, and Josephine excused herself to go determine the cause, leaving Étienne and I alone.

"Well?" he challenged tersely.

"Well, what?" I started opening drawers in a small bureau to see if Brigitte had left anything behind.

"Aren't you going to ask me a thousand insulting questions about my family? My past? My failings as a brother and as the heir of an unseated vicomte?" He sounded petulant. I recognized it as the irritation commensurate with a close sibling relationship. It lent him an air of vulnerability and—more than that—*humanity*.

"No."

The drawers were all empty. I went to the small writing desk to see if she'd left any papers or letters.

"No?" Étienne asked in an incredulous tone, and did I detect a hint of disappointment?

"Well, yes, actually. When you were here with Brigitte—"

He cut me off with a laugh.

"Oh no, Daphne. I didn't come *here* for her. I sent for her. She came to me. I wouldn't feed or…do anything else here. Certainly not in Josephine's home."

"What else do you know of her? Did you converse at all? Were there other clues to her identity or anything?" I felt the underside and the back panels of the writing desk. *Nothing.*

"We didn't speak much," he said. "We had other things to do."

My exasperation grew. Étienne smirked at me. Peevishly, I went to the small bed and felt around the sheets and pillow. *Still nothing.*

I swore. This was proving to be another dead end.

"Can you give me nothing that would help? This woman tried to kill you, Étienne. I'd think you'd be a little more interested in finding out more about her," I muttered.

He sat on the bed, thwarting my search of the sheets and blankets.

"Very well. She was blonde, her name was Brigitte, and she tasted strange," he said unhelpfully.

"That'll be the quicksilver, I wager. And she didn't say anything else? Nothing seemingly innocuous about a previous customer?"

"Daphne, there's nothing here. My interactions with her were minimal and professional. She obviously didn't live here long enough to leave anything behind."

"Get up," I said with a spark of inspiration. "Get off the bed. I want to check something."

He sighed and stood. I hefted the lumpy straw mattress off the bed frame.

"You're really not going to ask me anything about Josephine? About this place?"

My annoyance finally won out.

"Étienne, if you wish to tell me about your past—your father, your sisters, your turning, this home for wayward women—please do so. However, I will not pry. I believe in what Josephine said. One should be free from the shackles of one's past, if given the chance. My only interest right now is in the truth—in this woman Brigitte and her vendetta against you, in Jeanne's killer, and in the blood plague devastating our city. So, if asking you questions you do not wish to answer will only derail me with falsehoods, then I will not waste time for either of us."

Ignoring his piercing gaze, I studied the bottom of the mattress. There, in the lower corner was a small seam that did not belong. A three-inch long tear that had been hastily stitched back together. Hands shaking in near triumph, I took out my dagger and slit it open.

A small, black leather pouch fell out and landed on the floor.

Étienne picked it up and sniffed it.

"It's him," he said, stunned. "It smells of Jeanne's killer."

11

ÉTIENNE

October 19, 1765
Maison des Nymphes

DAPHNE TOOK THE POUCH FROM ME AND OPENED IT WITH THE EXCITEMENT OF a child opening a present. She removed a small glass vial and two squares of parchment. She passed me the vial and, as expected, there were minuscule droplets of quicksilver sliding around inside.

"*Drink two hours prior to bleeding,* says the first one. Instructions from someone. The handwriting doesn't seem familiar to me. Do you know it?" she asked.

I shook my head. Thick, black script ran jaggedly across the paper. It was either an ill-educated hand, or an educated hand trying to disguise itself.

"What does the second one say?"

"It's an address. I don't recognize it, do you?"

"I know the street. It's at the other end of the city in the plague district." Foreboding snaked through me.

"I thought that area was abandoned." Daphne frowned.

"It was, back when the plague first arrived and people still feared it. Now that the poor have embraced it, they've repopulated the deserted buildings and shops. They call it *le Quartier Sanglant.* It's the only neighborhood in the city that's inhabited entirely by vampires."

Daphne's mouth dropped open in astonishment.

"I had no idea," she breathed. "The people…the state of things. I wonder how many in Versailles know."

I laughed bitterly. "Many of them, I'd wager. The king certainly does, as well as his closest advisors. They just don't want to admit as much to the rest of the court because they fear a panic, or worse, an uprising."

"An uprising that you already believe is coming," she murmured.

I nodded. "It is inevitable."

She scrubbed her face with her hand and checked her pocket watch.

"We have three and a half hours before sunrise. Do you think that's enough time to make it across town?"

I looked at her warily. "I think I should go alone. If you walk in there, it would be like ringing the dinner bell and I cannot protect you from an entire district hungry for blood, literally *and* figuratively."

"Then we shall have to be quick and careful," she said. "Face it, Étienne, I'm not going to wait in the carriage while you walk into a dangerous situation. It would be easier on both of us if you just accepted that. I recognize the peril, though, so I promise to do exactly as you say."

A hint of desire flickered at the idea of Daphne submitting to me in more ways than one. I dashed it away before it could distract me. I folded my arms across my chest.

"Impossible woman," I sputtered. She was unmoved.

We made our way downstairs and found Josephine in the kitchen with Marie. I kissed them both and stuck a purse full of coins into Josephine's pocket.

"I'm afraid we made a bit of a mess in Brigitte's room," I said. "This should make up for it. Be careful, *ma sœur*. If anyone comes asking after me, or Daphne, for that matter, you have not seen us. Understand?"

Josephine nodded, worry etched on her face. I tried to smile.

"Unless it is a very beautiful woman," I said with a wink. "Then, please do send her my way."

Daphne snorted a laugh. "Isn't that how you got yourself into this mess?"

Josephine giggled and hugged her. Daphne left to give us some privacy and stepped out into the night.

"I like her," Josephine whispered. "Don't fuck it up, *d'accord?*"

I glared at her and followed Daphne to the carriage.

"*Quartier Sanglant*," I told the driver. "Quickly, please. We're in a bit of a hurry."

Daphne watched me in the darkness of the carriage, her expression unreadable.

"How long have you been a vampire?" she asked.

Her question took me by surprise. I didn't often speak to others about my turning. Despite appreciating my abilities and accepting my lonely fate, turning was one of my life's low points. I looked on it as a moment of weakness and shame, brought on by the stupidity and impetuousness of unruly youth. It was one evening's mistake that I would be paying back for a thousand lifetimes.

"Twenty years."

"That is before the plague swept Paris," she observed.

"Yes. I was not turned here. And before you ask, *no*, I did not bring the plague to the city. By the time I returned from my travels abroad, it had already taken hold."

"I did not think—" she defended.

I cut her off. "Yes, you did. I don't blame you. You're not the first to wonder such a thing, particularly because I'm the oldest vampire in the city as far as I know. I contracted the disease while traveling through Hungary. It took hold in that region long before and has been slowly spreading east for some time now. The wars that Louis has been fighting all over eastern Europe have advanced the spread faster than *la grande verole*, thanks to all the eager soldiers."

"*La grande verole?* The great pox?" Daphne sat forward. "Syphilis!"

I arched a brow. "...yes? What about it?"

"Quicksilver!" she said with excitement. "Don't you see? Quicksilver is a treatment for syphilis."

I could see where she was going with this, but it still wasn't enough.

"Yes, but anyone can get their hands on quicksilver these days, not just physicians. Any corner chemist will have it."

She sat back, defeated. "Yes, you're right. I was hoping we could match the handwriting on the instructions to a receipt—maybe a signature, or a prescription. Perhaps a chemist would recognize it. But that would take too much time—questioning every chemist and physician in the city. The quicksilver and the ring seem to be dead ends for us at the moment. So far, we know that someone murdered Jeanne and stole her ring. It's possible that same person is familiar with vampiric poisons, knows Josephine's *maison* is connected to you, and sent Brigitte after you. Oh, and that if it is the same person, they want you dead."

"You don't think it was The Order?"

She shook her head. "I considered it at first, but it doesn't fit. They might want you out of the way, but they wouldn't chance sending another agent into my assignment. It would be too messy. Much of their power lies in their ability to operate in shadow, so they only authorize operations that can be easily and thoroughly covered up. Besides, if they suspect that you're under my protection at the moment, they won't run the risk of antagonizing me."

I was taken aback by the matter-of-fact way she spoke about her abilities. Given her marriage, I was sure her confidence had been hard-won, and I felt a peculiar sense of pride in thinking that she didn't fear the men in The Order—rather, that they should be intimidated by her. That was the truth. I smiled.

"Am I under your protection?"

Her eyes narrowed. "When it comes to The Order, you are. *At the moment.* And I shouldn't need to remind you, but that doesn't mean you're safe from *me* indefinitely."

I chuckled. "Promises, promises."

We sat in companionable silence for a while. Finally, the carriage came to a stop across from a dark alley.

"Put on your cloak," I instructed. "Pull the hood up and do *not* remove it for any reason. Do not speak. Do not touch anything. Do not go anywhere without me. In fact, do *not* leave my side. If things should go wrong for any reason—well, let's just hope they don't."

Fear clawed at me. Certainly not for my own safety, but for Daphne's. This was a terrible idea.

"Are you ready?" I asked. *Last chance to wise up and back out, Duchesse.*

She nodded once, steel in her eyes. *I should have known.*

I sighed, resigned.

She pulled her hood up, obscuring her face. I was less concerned about her being seen and more concerned with her being smelled. Beneath the mouth-watering orange blossom and vanilla fragrance wafted the sweetness of her blood. At this time of night, I hoped most would have already found their food and entertainment. Dawn would soon approach.

We stepped from the carriage and hurried down the alley. Daphne clung to my arm and a thrill went through me, though I suspected it was less to do with any fear or desire she felt and more to do with the fact that she could not see as well as I in the near blackness of night. I could hear carousing down a few side streets and smelled blood, both fresh and stale. We passed by a knot of people outside a tavern and I picked up our pace. Just as we cleared the group, a man called out to me.

"Monsieur! Fancy sharing your bite?" He cackled drunkenly. A few others turned.

"Not tonight, my good man," I tried jovially. Daphne stiffed beside me.

"Aw, come on," he jeered. "Be a sport. She looks tasty and I haven't had anything this evening. I won't take too much, love."

"I'm afraid I'm too hungry to share and I've already paid for the privilege," I said. I moved Daphne along as quickly as I could without drawing more notice. Unfortunately, the man followed with two of his friends.

"That's not very brotherly," he sang. The others laughed.

Nearly jogging, Daphne and I made a sharp right down a narrow street. Only one window at the end of the street flickered with candlelight, casting a dim pool of dingy amber on a stone wall. *A dead end. Merde.*

I pushed Daphne behind me and faced the men. Two would be no problem. Three would be troublesome. I could smell their newly turned blood, which meant I had the advantage of increased speed and strength. They would probably fight recklessly, as most new vampires do, which made them dangerously unpredictable. I leaned casually on my walking stick, affecting an air of nonchalance.

"*Mes amis,*" I began, silk in my tone. "Surely you don't want to fight me for this old slip of a thing? She's an aging widow, too wizened to survive more than one bite in an evening. Come, take my advice—there are far better meals wandering around tonight."

"But she's already right here," one of them said. "That's dead convenient."

The three guffawed uproariously at the wordplay.

I sighed. "So, you aim to take her from me?"

"If you're too selfish to share, then we'll have to teach you some manners," the drunkest said. "Some brotherly love, if you will."

One of them lunged at me. I sidestepped his charge and tripped him with my walking stick. Before I could turn to him, the other two were upon me. One punched my stomach and the air left me. I doubled over with a wheeze. The other grabbed my hair and hauled me up, landing a punch on my jaw. I whirled around and grabbed one man's arm, breaking it easily. He screamed and fell to the ground. The second aimed another blow at my face, but I saw it coming and ducked. His fist smashed into the stone wall behind me and he shrieked. He got back up but froze, stunned by something behind us.

I turned to see Daphne pirouetting gracefully away from the first vampire, then bringing her fist up to smash him squarely in the nose. He grunted with the impact but reached out again, trying to grab the blonde curls that had come undone from beneath her hood. She leaned back, using his momentum against him, and dodged out of the way while he fell forward. Then, with a speed that rivaled any vampire I'd encountered, she jumped on his back, yanked one arm behind him and bent it upward in an immobilizing hold. She flicked her empty wrist and a thin wooden stake slid from her sleeve into her palm. She held it threateningly above the prone vampire's back—exactly above his heart. The whole fight was over in a matter of seconds.

"*Enough!*" she yelled. "Étienne, are you all right?"

"*Mais oui.*"

Fierce energy rolled off her crouched form. I'd never desired another woman more.

"You!"

She jutted her chin at the man standing next to me. He cradled his broken hand and looked at her fearfully.

"Pick up your friend with the broken arm over there and go *now,* or this one is dust."

She started to slowly sink the wooden stiletto into the vampire's flesh, and he yelled a stream of profanities that shocked even me.

They scrambled down the street at a dead run, not daring to look back.

"Now," she said to the man. "My friend and I have some questions and I think you're in an excellent position to answer."

"Get drained," he growled.

Daphne *tsked* and twisted the stake in further. The man howled in pain.

"First question: what do you know of Madame de Pompadour?"

"Who?"

"The king's mistress. The rumors say that she was killed by your kind."

"I don't know anything about that!" The man screamed again. Tendrils of smoke began to curl from his wound.

"No? Because we followed the trail of a bleeder to an address around here. *Rue des Oubliés.* What do you know of it?" Daphne leaned on the man's arm.

"It's nearby, but no one goes there!" he shouted. "Please, release me. It burns—*putain de merde*—it burns!"

"Why does no one go there?" she demanded.

"Ease up and I'll tell you. I swear, I'll tell you," he gritted out. By the look on his face, he seemed close to passing out.

She lessened the pressure on his arm and slid the stake partway out. The man panted.

"No one goes there because it's haunted," he gasped.

Daphne leaned forward again and hissed at him. "Do you think I'm stupid? *Haunted?* There's no such thing."

"Just like there's no such thing as vampires?" he wheezed with a laugh. "Look, lady, I don't know if it's real ghosts or not. People don't go there because they say it's haunted. Strange noises. Awful smells. Unnatural darkness. It's a bad place."

"How do we get there?"

"Three blocks down, then turn right. You'll know it when you come to it."

Daphne released the man's arm and pulled the stake from his back. Brandishing it in front of her, she stood and took her pistol out and held it aloft for good measure. The man got to his feet slowly, threw a curse at the both of us and hobbled away. As he turned the corner to the street, I heard him mutter.

"May the ghosts take you."

12

DAPHNE

October 20, 1765
Rue des Oubliés

"THAT WAS...*IMPRESSIVE*. YOU COULD HAVE KILLED HIM!" ÉTIENNE REMARKED as we followed the drunk's directions.

"Well, I should hope so, otherwise I'd be a poor excuse for an agent. You said The Order had tried to kill you before. Hasn't everyone you've met with fought with the same skill?" I clutched his arm to avoid stumbling over the uneven cobblestones.

"No," he said. "The way you fought was...well, Daphne, you were magnificent."

A blush warmed my cheeks and I was grateful he could not see my face beneath my hood. His appraisal gave me immense pleasure, but I feared dwelling on it.

"Thank you."

"How many—ah—*assignments* have you had?"

I sighed. "In the beginning, The Order used me for intel. I sent them reports on the happenings at Versailles. Nothing treasonous, mind you. They just wanted to know what people were saying; the state of the war, who was sleeping with whose wife or husband, who was spending what on clothes, jewels, properties, that sort of thing. The whole time I had tutors coming to my home to teach me various fighting arts. My first few assassinations were newly infected vampires who preyed on young women—draining them and leaving their bodies in the streets, or making them disappear altogether. Housemaids and other servants, prostitutes, tavern maids, and the like. Women too lowly to attract much notice."

I had to pause to calm my rising ire. Étienne's arm rose as if he were going to reach out and touch me. Right now I wouldn't be able to withstand his touch, so I went on.

"Those women deserved justice. The parasites I killed would've continued to murder and feed indiscriminately. Tell me, Étienne, how do you justify your fight for vampire rights when those you protect are, by their very nature, predators? How many young girls should die so that your vampires may live free?"

"I won't deny that some of the infected are corrupt," he said. "But to lay the blame at the blood plague itself is irresponsible. Murderers existed before vampires and will continue to exist after we've all been extinguished. I seek to bring education to the infected. If so many have been turned and are continuing to turn, they should know how to manage their supernatural state. Right now, the desperate feel they have no alternative and are forced into a choice that they're not prepared to make."

"Education. That's what you're after?" I said with surprise. "Not the total eradication of the nobility at the expense of your vampire majority?"

He laughed again, warm and genuine. "If that's what The Order has told you, I'm afraid I have far less respect for your sources of intel. I don't want to eradicate anyone. I have already seen more death than I care to. My efforts have been to *prevent* a revolution, not incite one."

I was quiet in the wake of this revelation, realizing again that I'd once again misjudged him.

"Why did you join in the first place?" he asked suddenly.

The cold seeped in through my clothes and I huddled against him. I thought we were getting close—the air had changed. I considered his question. He'd been so exposed by our trip to Josephine's, I felt like I owed him some of my own truth.

"Michel's death devastated me, and I did want revenge," I admitted. "But I suppose that's not the whole reason. I wanted to be...*useful*. I wanted to have purpose. I wanted to be able to defend myself from men like Henri. I only learned about The Order a couple of years ago—whispered rumors at court about an old religious sect that had been revived to combat the blood plague and save the city, and perhaps the world. They did not want me to join at first. They said they had no need of women. Ha! With Philippe's help, I convinced them to let me prove my usefulness."

"Did the duc know?"

"No, he was gone by then," I said. "Not that he would have known when he was here. We did not enjoy the same leisure pursuits and thus spent very little time together." Cold sliced through me at the thought of Henri. The wind picked up, and I bent against the frigid breeze, then pulled up short with a cry of pain. *The damn drunk vampire had probably cracked one of my ribs.* Before I could react, Étienne's strong arms encircled my waist and hauled me upright. I grunted in pain when he squeezed the tender spot on my abdomen.

He dropped his hands like he'd been scalded.

"Did I hurt you?" The concern in his voice startled me.

"No," I huffed. "That damned drunk landed a kick in my side. It's fine. I'll have to forgo stays for the next couple of days, but it'll heal well enough."

"Are you certain nothing is broken?" He ran his hands along my ribs, feeling for swelling. My heart hammered in my chest.

"Oh, *mon Dieu*! Don't fuss, Étienne. I've had worse before, I assure you." I batted his hands away and straightened my cloak.

"So you've said," he retorted, his voice dark and vaguely threatening.

"I'm fine," I insisted. "We can continue."

Suddenly, he turned me until my back was pressed against the wall of the alley. I gasped in surprise. I could feel the hardness of his muscles beneath the velvet of his clothes and my desire ignited instinctively. Gently, he tipped my chin up and I could just see the outline of his face in the moonlight.

"You are not indestructible, Duchesse," he whispered, his mouth inches from mine.

"Neither are you," I breathed. Conscious thought fled. The chill of the night air, the low temperature of his body, his clean, fresh smell—if I closed my eyes, it was like I was standing in a snow-blanketed forest. I didn't feel cold, though. My body blazed with heat.

Before I could talk myself out of it, I was setting my lips to his. Beneath my kiss, I felt him smile. Unlike the assertive ardor from earlier, his touch was tender and languid. His tongue played slowly against my lips until I parted for him. I stroked against him, tasting the metallic tang of blood. I pulled back, my breath coming in ragged pants.

"You're bleeding."

He traced delicate kisses across my cheek and my jaw, lingering at my ear. He tugged at my earlobe, sucking at it gingerly. My nipples tightened and desire spiraled through me to my core. I whimpered at the delicious torment.

"Shall I stop?" His words were punctuated with little licks along the outer edge of my ear.

"Bleeding? Yes, if you have the power to command that sort of thing."

A throaty chuckle escaped him, and he leaned his forehead against mine. Perhaps it was the waning aggression from the fight, but I realized with a jolt that I wanted him rather badly. I found myself cursing my earlier reluctance in my chamber. *He was naked before you, and you cruelly rejected him. Why? What are you so afraid of, Daphne?*

Losing him, came the reply. I pushed it aside.

"Should we continue?"

"Yes," I moaned, tilting up to meet him again. His breath caught and his tone became pleading.

"No, Daphne, I meant we should continue to the *Rue des Oubliés.*"

I froze.

"… Ah. Yes, of course."

I tried to pull away, stung by his words and embarrassed by my own behavior. *Idiot!*

"Damn it, Daphne, wait. Stop. This is *not* a rejection. You must know that. You must know how desperately I want you. I cannot even *think* without wanting you." He pressed his hips into me, and I felt the hard length of his arousal. I stifled a groan at the thought of him sliding into me.

"You see? I would give anything to have you. But not here—not like this. We are running out of time." He reached up to stroke my cheek and I looked up.

Merde. He was right. The pitch blackness of the sky had already begun to lighten to a deep sapphire. Dawn was coming. We needed to hurry.

I offered him a chagrinned smile.

"*Allons-y!*"

We took off at a rapid clip, closing the distance to the street we sought. Nearing it, a chill ran up my spine. The drunk had been right. There was something *off* about this part of the neighborhood. Our steps slowed as we approached.

"This is it," I said. "How far down is the address?"

"Not far," he replied, gripping his walking stick more tightly.

A thick silence blanketed us as we walked down the street. We saw no light from beyond and heard nothing but the sounds of our footsteps and our anxious breaths. Even the air seemed stagnant—like it, too, waited for something malevolent.

Étienne stopped before a storefront with a boarded-up door and broken windows. I squinted up at the sign above the door but couldn't make it out in the gloom.

"It's a bookshop," he offered. He lifted his nose in the air and inhaled.

"What is it?" I whispered.

"It smells of the murderer. Stay close and keep your pistol cocked."

He wrenched the boards from the doorframe, and they came away easily. He beckoned me to him, and we entered the shop together.

"What do you see?" I whispered. We stepped over broken glass and a few discarded books. Most of the shop's contents had been looted, it seemed. I picked up one of the remaining books from the floor and held it up to the moonlight to read the title.

"Étienne," I said, fear building in my gut. "This is a book of dark magic. I don't think this is a normal bookshop."

He sniffed the air again and tugged me to the back of the store. An open door—probably a storage room—gaped like a tall, dark mouth.

"There's something in there. I can't see it, but the smell is getting stronger from that direction."

"Should we light a candle? I won't be any help to you if I can't see what I'm fighting," I hissed. In that moment, I wished for supernatural abilities of my own.

"I don't want to give us away," he whispered back. "Just hold onto me."

I didn't need to be told twice. I held onto his coat and willed myself calm. I was trained for this, after all.

We crept forward to the doorway and Étienne paused, listening. I couldn't hear anything, but I was beginning to detect the smell Étienne had tried to describe to me. A stinking, burning, rotting smell, like a tannery on fire. It made my insides twist with nausea.

"Well?" I pressed. "What is inside?"

"A stairwell going down. I can't see all the way, though. The drunk was right. There is something unnatural about this darkness," Étienne said.

Navigating the stairs proved to be incredibly difficult. We were forced to move slowly. After an interminable amount of time, we finally reached the floor below. It felt like hard-packed earth beneath my feet. *Is it some kind of cellar?*

"Étienne, what do you see?"

He was quiet while he surveyed our surroundings.

"I can't be sure," he began. I sensed an undercurrent of unease from him and started to grow nervous. He pulled away from my grip momentarily and bent down, then straightened again. He struck a flint, lit a small stub of a candle, and handed it to me.

I held it aloft and looked around. I'd been right on one count—we appeared to be in some kind of root cellar beneath the bookstore. It was strangely empty, except for a few wooden crates stashed to one side. In front of us, drawn on the floor in something suspiciously blood-like, was a circle filled with a pentagram and numerous symbols. At each point of the pentagram sat a glass jar containing a different object. I picked up the jar closest to me and gasped.

"Étienne! It's Jeanne's ring!"

He stooped to look in the jar opposite and growled an oath. The jar contained a pink ribbon garter stained with fresh blood.

"It's Brigitte's," he said. "She was wearing it when we…her initials are stitched onto the side."

"Check the other jars," I ordered, trying to stem the tide of panic. "I'll see what else I can find."

I ran to the crates along the wall. At the bottom of one was a large, leather-bound book with the words *Pseudomonarchia Daemonum* written in black. Dread gathered inside me. I picked up the book and flipped it open to the middle, where a gold ribbon marked a page titled *The Demon Asmoday*. What did it all mean?

"Two of the jars are empty," Étienne said. "One of them contains a gaming piece from a casino in Venice. It, too, is bloody. I recognize it, but—"

Without warning, the door upstairs slammed shut. A dry, hot gust of wind rushed in, blowing the book closed and extinguishing the candle. The rotten, sulfuric smell grew worse until I could barely breathe. Étienne leaped for me across the room, but as soon as he stepped over the markings on the floor, an invisible force hurled him back against the wall. He slammed into it with a violence that would have killed any human.

"Étienne!" I screamed. He moaned shakily.

"Daphne," he coughed. "Run!"

From all around us—yet nowhere at all—a dry laugh echoed through the room.

"Run? Before introductions? How…impolite," the voice rasped, whispering like sand across stones.

"Who are you?" I yelled. Anger warred with my fear.

That bone-chilling laugh came again. I scanned the room frantically, but couldn't find the source of the voice.

"What do you want?" I shrieked, louder this time. The demonic wind was picking up in the cellar, lashing my hair against my face and whipping my skirts around. I edged along the wall toward Étienne, who was still slumped on the floor. When I reached him, I covered his body with mine protectively.

"Daphne, go! I'll be fine!" he mumbled.

"In the name of God, what are you?" I whispered, more to myself than to our invisible attacker. Abruptly, the wind ceased, and the foul odor disappeared. A heavy stillness pressed in upon us. I helped Étienne to his feet and just as we turned to the stairs, a familiar cloying perfume floated through the room. It was a scent I knew intimately, and it frightened me a thousand times more than any supernatural entity.

No longer rasping, the disembodied voice drawled in a frigid baritone.

"Oh, *ma petite Daphne*! Don't you recognize the voice of your own husband?"

13

ÉTIENNE

THE TERROR IN DAPHNE'S EYES WAS UNLIKE ANYTHING I'D EVER SEEN. THE blood drained from her face and she froze, too stunned to move. That cold, evil voice laughed again, and I didn't fancy waiting around to see what else it had in store for us. I tugged hard at Daphne's arm, yanking her forward up the stairs. I smashed the door at the top of the stairs with my foot, showering us in tiny wooden splinters. As I hauled Daphne through the streets toward my waiting carriage, I could still hear the dark laughter taunting us from a distance.

The sky was paling to a fair lavender by the time I reached the carriage and threw Daphne inside. Dawn was upon me and if I didn't get underground soon, things would become dire indeed.

"Daphne." I knelt before her in the carriage. Her face was still pale—her gaze unfocused and her teeth chattering. *She is in shock.*

"Daphne, we need shelter. You're going into shock and I need to get underground. My home is nearer to us than yours, so I'm having my driver take us there. When you're recovered, I'll send someone to escort you home. Do you understand?"

She didn't respond, merely stared ahead at a fixed point behind me. I stripped off my coat and wrapped her in it, laying her back against the carriage seats. The ride seemed to take ages, but we finally arrived at my château. I scooped her up and carried her inside.

My father's château was one of the few things left of my family's once grand legacy. When I returned to France after my travels abroad, much of the grandeur of my family home had fallen into disrepair—the result of my father's decimated fortune and his broken spirit. After his passing and my royal appointment, I labored tirelessly to restore the upper floors to their former magnificence and took the opportunity to renovate the cellars into a comfortable suite of apartments for my vampire needs. For my own safety and for my self-indulgent sense of privacy, few outside of my architect and household staff knew of my secret chambers. I usually entertained others—notably women—in the upper part of the house. *Not today.*

I carried Daphne to the door hidden behind a floor-length tapestry and opened it. Another set of stairs descended below ground, though this one was not so dark. Candlelight flooded the corridor from dozens of glass fixtures that I insisted remain lit while I was at home. Sometimes, if I closed my eyes, it almost felt like my memories of sunlight.

I brought Daphne into my bedchamber and set her on the bed. Her eyes had closed at some point, hopefully in a dreamless sleep. I tucked her in beneath the thick silk coverlet and went to my wardrobe to change. I washed quickly in the basin—tomorrow I would indulge in a long, hot bath. For now, I needed the healing power of sleep to mend my wounds and refresh my mind. I'd pulled off the borrowed jacket and waistcoat, as well as the shoes, when I heard Daphne stir. She sat bolt upright and let out a ragged, shattering scream.

She babbled incoherently, unable to form intelligible words in her panic. Tears streamed down her cheeks when she at last mouthed the name like an oath.

"Henri!"

I rushed over to her and seized her shoulders.

"Daphne, he's gone! You're safe now, understand? It's just us. We are here in my home, far away from *le Quartier Sanglant.* Be easy, Duchesse. You are safe."

Wild-eyed, she continued to sob.

"He isn't gone, Étienne. *He isn't gone.*"

Her body shook and she fisted her hands in her hair, then brought them down to hold herself. She rocked back and forth, whispering prayers I'd long since forgotten.

Cautiously, I put my hands on her tear-streaked cheeks.

"Daphne, look at me," I soothed.

With effort, her wide violet eyes met mine.

"You are safe," I repeated. "It's just us here. Safe."

"Safe," she whispered. The word slowly took root and she ceased rocking. I climbed into the bed next to her and put my arms around her, holding her as tightly as I dared. She drew a shaky breath and nuzzled against me, her eyes drifting closed again.

"Safe," I repeated. "I'm not going to let anything happen to you. You are safe here with me. With Étienne."

I rested my cheek atop her silky blonde curls and stroked her arms and her back. Eventually, her taut muscles loosened, and her breathing slowed to a deep, steady rhythm. I blew out all but one candle on my bedside table and leaned back against the downy pillows. Sleep claimed me almost immediately.

When I awoke some hours later, Daphne was curled against me. The candle had burned out at some point, but I could see well enough in the dark. Her eyelids fluttered in sleep and she murmured something unintelligible. I pushed her hair from her face and kissed her forehead. Startled, she opened her eyes and tensed, but relaxed when recognition dawned.

"Étienne."

She didn't pull away, but continued to stare at me.

"So, it was not a nightmare," she said.

"No."

She rolled away from me, wincing at her bruises, and stretched her arms above her head. Her panic appeared to have diminished slightly, and she blew out a breath.

"You know, I never really believed he was dead. I just hoped he was. After he fled to Italy, I hoped he'd debauch himself into oblivion. Yet, it seems the rotten bastard was too ill-tempered to simply lay down and die, and now his ghost will haunt me…just like his memory."

"Why did he leave?" *How could he leave you?*

"I'm surprised you don't know. The king offered him the emissary position—your position. This was a couple years ago, before the court was fully aware of your turning. No one wanted the emissary post, least of all my wastrel husband. Henri left the country before the king could order him to take the post. I haven't heard from him since. Well, until tonight."

I turned onto my side to face her. She continued to stare at the ceiling. Tears leaked from the corners of her eyes and I wiped them away with my thumb.

"What is he, Étienne? A ghost? A vampire? A demon?" she wondered, her voice barely a whisper.

"I do not know," I admitted.

"Whatever he is, I'm still married to him. He was a monster before, and now…"

The realization gutted me. *She is taken. She is not mine. She cannot be mine.*

She turned to look at me, the despair on her face devastating.

"You weren't injured in the cellar, were you?"

I pursed my lips to avoid lashing out. I was angry at her foolishness—she could have been killed and here she was worrying about me—but now was not the time to chastise her. I swallowed my ire and brushed a lock of hair from her face.

"No. Nothing lasting, at least."

"What is it like? Being able to heal so quickly. Is it painful?"

"No. It is…well, it's hard to describe. Would you like me to show you?" I'd never spoken of my abilities with anyone, but a thread of mutual vulnerability now stretched between us in the dark.

"I don't know; I do not want to be a vampire," she said.

"That is not what I'm offering, Duchesse."

"What do you offer, Étienne?"

"A taste." My fangs lengthened. "I cannot heal all wounds, but bruises are an easy feat. Show me your side where you were kicked."

I expected protests, denials, disdainful refusals—everything but compliance. Perhaps it was the blackness of the room that made her feel comfortable; perhaps it was the traumatic experience we'd just shared, or —as my anxious mind suggested—the eagerness for physical strength and power over her husband, our new enemy. Whatever it was, she nodded to me and sat up on her knees to begin disrobing. The slow, sure movements of her fingers on her buttons were a sweet torment that I found unbearably arousing. I would watch them play out over and over in my head when I thought of her, marveling at the sainted restraint I exercised in keeping myself from ripping her clothes off. She untied her skirts and petticoats, letting them fall to the floor beside the bed. At last, she knelt before me in her stays and chemise, and paused.

"Do you need help with your stays, my lady?" My voice sounded husky and strangled.

In response, she turned her back to me to allow me access to her laces, which I undid with trembling fingers. When the last lace had been loosened, she let out a small breath of relief as the garment fell away. I swallowed, my mouth suddenly dry.

I'd seen her nude form in her chambers, but here, now, in her sheer chemise, she was baring herself to me of her own free will. It was the single most erotic moment of my wretched life. I wanted to make her crest with pleasure—to bury myself in her in a thousand different ways. I bit the inside of my lip hard enough to draw blood, forcing myself to focus.

"Lie back down, Duchesse," I instructed. "Relax."

She did as I asked, but she was far from relaxed. She was on edge, ready to jump out of her skin at the first touch. To comfort her, I clasped her hand.

"This is something not many vampires learn until they've had the time and inclination to practice. It may feel a bit...*strange*, but I promise it will not hurt you. I would never hurt you, Daphne."

She took a deep breath and smiled tightly. I pulled her chemise up over her hips, fighting every instinct to dive between her legs and wring climax after climax from her. *Focus, Étienne.* The bruise was the size of a melon, covering much of her side down to the curve of her hip. It was already darkening to an angry purple. *The bastard.* I should have ripped his head from his body for daring to lay a hand on her.

I delicately ran my fingertips across the discolored skin, and she shivered.

"Relax," I murmured again. I leaned forward and licked the bruise. Her sharp inhale hinted at her pleasure and I smiled against her skin. I dropped wet kisses over her side and slid one hand up her thigh, then bent and lightly scored the tender area with my fangs. Daphne elicited a soft whimper, stoking my desire. I sucked at the small scrapes, tasting her blood. *Orange blossoms, vanilla, and—God help me—desire. And something familiar...*

"It was you," I said against her skin. "It was your blood in the porcelain bowl. You fed me from your own veins."

Her eyes searched for mine in the dark.

"Yes," she whispered.

Somewhere in the back of my mind, it seemed fitting that this woman —this vampire-hating, strong, beautiful, untouchable woman—would be the best I'd ever have. The thought drove me nearly mad with desire and terror. She'd sustained me in my weakness, tried to protect me from the evil we'd encountered, was the most delicious, and yet, she was not mine. *Could* not be mine. I'd be damned if I let her go back to that bastard husband of hers, but I'd at least have to let her go back to The Order and the life she wanted—while I wandered throughout eternity, hunting for some other woman just as good. Not just to feed from, but...*but what?* I didn't know. All I knew was that as delicious as she was, my need for her felt *different.* She was not food to me. She was the angel sent to drive me to utter madness with wanting.

When I'd finished sucking the damaged blood from her injury, I licked the top of the scrapes again and they healed over immediately. The bruise was gone completely, and her porcelain skin was once more unmarred. Daphne was panting when I lifted my head.

"Well, Duchesse? What does it feel like to heal in such a way?"

She stretched out on the bed and moaned her reply. "It feels warm, hot. I feel...peculiar."

I chuckled. "Yes, *peculiar* is one way to describe supernatural abilities." She twisted on top of the sheets, testing my strength and sanity.

"I feel rather good, actually," she said, trailing a hand up her torso. "Powerful. Exhilarated." Her hands moved across her body, lifting to her breasts. Her eyes met mine, hazy with desire.

Every frayed thread of my restraint snapped, and I could not bear it any longer.

"Allow me," I begged in a gruff whisper. When she moaned her assent, I ripped the chemise down the middle and stroked her body from thigh to neck. She slid her fingers into my hair and pulled my face down to hers for a desperate, searing kiss. She sucked at my tongue and tugged at my shirt, frantically trying to pull it over my head. I eased myself away from her to remove my shirt and breeches, then crawled back across the bed to her. I kissed my way up her legs, pausing just below the blonde curls covering her sex.

"Daphne," I said, my voice raw with need. "Are you sure you want this?"

Please say yes. Say you'll be mine—if only for tonight.

"You tried to save me," she murmured. "Back in the cellar."

"You tried to save me *first*," I argued, slowly caressing the inside of her thigh. Her breath hitched. "And you didn't need me to save you, anyway."

"No," she agreed. "But it was…nice. The thought, I mean."

I ran two fingers along her sex, dipping one into her slick folds. She whimpered.

"Will you allow me to demonstrate some more *nice thoughts* I have?" I begged.

In answer, she pulled my face to hers again and caught my lip in her teeth, then hooked one of her legs behind mine and arched her hips up, seeking friction from my hardness. At the feel of her wetness sliding across my cock, I abandoned my attempt at chivalry and uttered a string of oaths. *Dieu, I would give this woman anything.* Everything she asked for. *But she is not yours.* I shoved the thought away and turned my gaze back to her.

She is tonight.

Setting my lips to her breasts, I reached one hand down, trailing along her abdomen, back to the slick seam between her legs. She cried out when I circled one fingertip against the bud of her pleasure and dipped another finger inside her, stroking as she bucked against my hand.

"More," she moaned. "Étienne, give me all of you."

My self-control already past its breaking point, I positioned my cock at her entrance and stopped again, my thumb working her core with firmer and firmer caresses.

"Tell me you're certain. Tell me you want this."

Her eyes snapped open and a sultry smile crossed her lips.

"Yes," she cried. "I need you, Étienne." She wrapped her legs around my waist and arched her back again.

Thanking God, Lucifer, and the universe itself, I sank into her ready heat on a moan from us both. She felt tight and hot and wet around me, and I ached with the pleasure of it. I moved inside her slowly at first, trying to regain control of my sanity, all the while stroking that tight bud where her climax would peak. Her hands slid down my back, grasping my bottom and pulling me into her deeper, harder. Soon, her cries reached fever-pitch and I felt her orgasm crescendo and break, and she came apart around me. Unable to hold back, I followed her over the edge, letting wave after wave of bliss roll through me.

I collapsed on top of her, our bodies a tangle of sweat-slicked limbs. My fangs were slow to retract—I couldn't remember the last time I'd made love without feeding. Daphne tilted her head to me and smiled shyly.

"I can see why the ladies in court gossip so much about you," she said. "That was—well, I've never had—you know, with a man—and—" She covered her furious blush with her hands.

Daphne, I would pleasure you for every day of my eternity. The thought turned me cold with panic. *She is not yours,* that dark voice of reason echoed.

I gathered her up and pulled her in to my embrace, kissing her temple.

"I'd prefer they didn't, you know," I murmured. "Gossip, I mean."

She chuckled, and the vibrations from her mirth reverberated through me like a plucked harp string. A phantom ache started to build in my chest.

"It's scandalous, to be sure, but mostly good. You're forbidden fruit to them, even once they've had a taste," she said with a yawn.

"Forbidden fruit?" I laughed. "More like a shiny apple that's rotten at its core."

Daphne's eyes drifted closed. She snuggled closer into the crook of my arm and drowsily grunted at me.

"That's just what you want everyone to think," she mumbled. "I'm beginning to know better."

With that, her breathing slowed in the satisfied sleep that always followed intimacies and her muscles relaxed against me. As she slept in my arms, my thoughts took off like a bolting horse. Instinctive protectiveness pulsed through me—something I'd not experienced with a woman in a long time. A sense of sick dread began to take root and I cursed my carelessness. How had I allowed myself to become so attached to this woman? She'd said it herself—ours was a temporary truce. I remembered the loathing on her face the night she'd tried to kill me. Would that hatred return when our investigation concluded and she returned to the arms of The Order? Would she regret this intimate act later on and feel as though I'd pressed my advantage during a moment of weakness?

On top of all that, she was a pillar of the *tonne* and a married duchesse. Even with my position at court and the changing populace of Paris, I was still leagues beneath her. She'd be risking everything to be seen with me outside the bedroom. Sadness and doubt bloomed in my chest and refused to be uprooted.

You cannot have her. You don't deserve her. She is not for you.

I knew the truth of those thoughts. It did me no good to chase after one woman—a man in my position needed more. I needed to feed. I needed more aristocratic allies for my cause. Those were hard to get without the freedoms of bachelorhood.

Obviously, it had just been too long since I'd been with another woman. I needed distance from Daphne. *What I feel is not real.* At worst, it was some kind of temporary infatuation.

Even as we lay there together, naked and entwined, I felt the thread of vulnerability between us break. I eyed her sleeping form, so beautiful and still, and felt my resentment and frustration reach a crisis point. Things needed to go back to the way they were, but I couldn't move forward while I felt so bound to her. I needed her out of my arms and out of my bed. I needed her away from *me.*

I shifted myself from beneath her, gently but firmly, and she stirred from her sleep. She yawned and stretched, blinking up at me with wide, expectant eyes.

"It is getting late in the day, Duchesse. I need my rest," I said.

A flash of some imperceptible emotion crossed her face, but she nodded. "Of course. There is much I need to do today, as well." She paused, perhaps covering the sting of my dismissal.

Guilt surfaced, but I swallowed it. "I believe you'll be safe for the day, at least. I can't imagine Henri would endanger you so quickly after the events of last night. If he hasn't come for you before now, it seems there is some other endgame that he plots."

"I will be fine, Étienne. I can take care of myself," she returned stiffly, but I could tell from her manner that she was covering her fear.

"Still, you should not be alone. Perhaps you can call upon a friend, or family member. Maybe stay with the Comte and Comtesse de Brionne for a few days," I suggested.

"I said I'd be fine," she bit out, then sighed and rubbed at her temples. "Do you think The Order will believe me when I tell them about him? About Henri, I mean. I don't know what exactly to tell them, whether he's some monster or otherworldly spirit, but that he's back in some form and seems to be connected to all of this," she said, her brows knitting together.

I scoffed, irritated that she'd seemed to pluck one of my worries from my head. *Already she is thinking about The Order again.*

"Hardly. They'll probably accuse you of being hysterical. In fact, I don't think I'd tell them at all."

She sat up and the sheet fell away from her breasts. My body responded immediately, but I turned away and rose from the bed.

She stiffened. "I must, Étienne. Do you not wish to have someone attest to your innocence? To try and convince them there is something darker afoot than a rogue vampire?"

"I don't need your protection," I snapped. My temper had crept up on me, goaded on by the fear and mistrust of my own feelings. "I'm not a fool. The Order has wanted me out of the way since I took the emissary appointment—perhaps even since I first returned to Paris. We were enemies long before you showed up with your stake in hand."

She watched me guardedly. Her breath hitched slightly when she whispered, "Enemies?"

"Apologies, Duchesse. I don't know if there's a better word for people who want you dead."

Her eyes narrowed. "I am not your enemy, Étienne."

"Don't you understand? If you're with them, you will be."

"No. I'll tell them the truth. We'll figure things out and you will be exonerated. I swear it."

"And risk your life's purpose? *Please,*" I sneered. "What happened to revenge against all vampire-kind? You say I'm not your enemy, Daphne, but I represent them—all of them. I'm fighting for their rights, not the least of which is the right to exist. Your work with The Order sets you against me. Besides, it won't be long before they manage to convince you that we're to blame for every evil in Paris."

"You believe my mind can be changed so easily?"

I laughed cruelly and gestured at the rumpled sheets. "I believe you told me you'd rather fuck Lucifer himself than me."

Anger flashed in her eyes, chased by regret. Whether it was for her earlier words or our intimacies, I didn't know. Minutes of tense silence passed between us, until she finally stood and retrieved her clothes. The disappointment in her eyes made me feel a thousand kinds of wretched, but it was better this way. I half-hoped she would argue—hurl some acerbic insult that I rightly deserved, but she didn't. I watched mutely as she dressed, pinned her hair up, and left the room without a word.

14

DAPHNE

October 25, 1765
Château de Champs-sur-Marne

J*UST A LITTLE FURTHER…ALMOST THERE…GOT IT!* I SEIZED THE BOOK FROM THE top shelf in triumph, then promptly stumbled off the library ladder when a shrill voice startled me.

"*Mon Dieu*, Daphne, what the Hell are you doing?" Charlotte yelled from the doorway.

I righted myself and dropped the book to the floor, then stepped down from my perch.

"Nothing! Well, reading," I replied, feeling like a child caught misbehaving.

Charlotte strode into the library in a gown of vibrant chartreuse that glowed in the dim light of the rainy afternoon. She narrowed her eyes in suspicion at the pile of books I'd collected.

"Daphne, *none* of these appear to be salacious novels. In fact, these are all religious texts and—What's this? *Malleus Maleficarum!* Have you taken up an interest in the occult?" she said with a raised brow.

"No! Of course not." I rubbed at my temples, trying to ward off the ache building in my head. Charlotte folded her arms in front of her and waited expectantly.

"Well, perhaps a bit," I hedged. She gasped, her eyes sparking with excitement, and clapped her hands together.

"Fantastic! I've always wanted to learn how to cast a spell. What have you learned so far?"

I sighed as she fluffed her skirts out around her and sat upon the floor. She picked up one of the books and flipped through it. I collapsed to the floor beside her and closed my eyes. I couldn't remember the last time I'd had a decent night's sleep and I felt stretched and threadbare.

"Can we find a spell that will help my husband become a better lover? You know, help him keep it up longer." She tossed the first book aside and picked up the second one. "Or perhaps there's a spell that will help him be able to find my—"

"*Charlotte, please*," I begged. "I am not in the mood to hear of Philippe's failings in bed."

She set the book aside and studied me. "Darling, what's wrong? You look positively dreadful. Shall I call for some tea?"

I sat up on my elbows and grinned at her. "Fancy a proper fucking drink?"

She leaned over, her expression grave, and felt my forehead. "Well, you don't *feel* feverish. I can only deduce that you've well and truly cracked, and to that I say, *it's about fucking time*. What shall we drink, *ma chère amie?* Brandy? Cognac? Whisky?"

"Oh, Hell. Let's go drink some of my bastard husband's good wine." I grabbed the stack of books and we made our way downstairs through the kitchens to the wine cellar. I hadn't had the bed removed yet and Charlotte's eyes grew wide at the sight.

"Daphne, you know I'm one for a fair tipple most of the time, but if you're sleeping in your wine cellar, it occurs to me that you may have a drinking problem." She sat on the bed and leaned against the pillows. "Although this *is* damned comfortable."

I handed her a dusty bottle of champagne and she popped the cork with practiced efficiency. She took a swig from the bottle and passed it back to me as I sat down next to her.

"It's a long story," I said. I drank deeply. "Tell me, Charlotte, do you believe in ghosts? Demons? Otherwordly apparitions?"

"Of course I do," she said earnestly. "I believe in everything." She chugged a good deal of champagne and burped, then laughed at her own rudeness.

"Do you think it is possible to kill them?" I asked.

"Probably. Everything dies eventually. I assume demons and spirits do, too. Why?"

"I think Henri is alive. Or un-alive. Or he's a ghost. He exists, somehow." I took the bottle back from her and drank again.

"What, like a vampire?"

"I don't think so. More like a phantom."

She snorted. "Figures. He was so much of a fiend that even Satan didn't want him in Hell."

"I'm serious," I insisted.

She peered at me curiously. "Well, I don't think you kill a ghost, *chérie*. I believe they need to be crossed over. Demons certainly must be exorcised. Vampires need to be staked, and I'm fairly certain I've heard werewolves need to be killed with silver—somehow. Have you spoken to a priest?"

"No. I'm worried they'll think me mad, or a witch. I don't know who else to talk to."

She drained the last of the bottle and stood to choose another one from a rack on the wall.

"You know, if you're really interested in things supernatural, there is *one* person you could ask," she offered.

Her sing-song tone told me she was thinking of Étienne. I cringed inwardly. Since our night of passion, I hadn't been able to stop thinking of him. I couldn't settle my mind on what exactly had gone wrong. One minute, I was enjoying the most passionate time of my life, and the next, Étienne had completely shut down—gone cold. I was distraught that he thought I would so easily go back to being his enemy after everything we'd shared. Clearly, the connection I felt had not been mutual.

Even when I wrote to him inquiring about our investigation, his correspondence was taciturn and monosyllabic—as if I was inconveniencing him with every missive. *Had he heard from the jeweler?* No. *Was Josephine well? Yes. Had anyone seen Brigitte?* No. *What should we do next about the sudden and unnatural appearance of my evil husband, and how was he connected to Jeanne? Did the jars of objects in the basement mean Brigitte was dead? And what of the gaming piece from the casino?*

No reply. Every night I waited, either for Étienne to appear at my doorstep or for some foul wind bearing Henri's cruel voice to blow through my home. I needed to find out what was going on. What *was* Henri? How was he back? Was he dead or not? Was he alone responsible for Jeanne's death? If so, why? What did he have to gain? If he was working with someone else—someone who had a more intimate understanding of things supernatural, who was it? Why murder the king's mistress? And if Henri was back and taking part in some kind of nefarious plot or revenge scheme, why hadn't he come after me?

I found myself frustratingly desperate to speak to Étienne. I wanted to figure things out with him, but his silence and sudden indifference made my head spin even worse than my ceaseless questions about our investigation. Plus, as much as I didn't want to admit, I wanted some kind of reassurance that I hadn't acted like a complete fool with him. It appeared that was not an affirmation I was likely to get.

In hindsight, I reasoned that I must have ended up as one of his short-lived conquests after all—the very thing I'd been trying to avoid. I felt completely humiliated. To have behaved so wantonly, allowing myself to be touched by his dark powers and practically begging him to make love to me... I couldn't believe I'd let it happen. When my final message went unanswered, I cried a river of bitter shame and chalked my behavior up to the vulnerability I felt after such a horrifying evening. I'd learned the hard way that the rumors had indeed been true—he was a reckless libertine who used women for one thing or another. I was lucky to get out from under him when I could. If he didn't want to work with me to figure out our predicament, I would carry on alone. I didn't need The Order's help and I certainly didn't need Étienne de Noailles.

"I don't think so. Just because he is a vampire doesn't mean he knows about everything supernatural."

Charlotte pulled the cork from the bottle and sniffed it. She nodded to herself and sipped the dark burgundy liquid.

"He's the supernatural emissary to the king, Daphne. If *he* doesn't know about whatever metaphysical mystery you're dealing with, he probably knows *someone* who does."

"Perhaps he does. I'd much rather do it on my own. After all, if someone is going to get to the bottom of Henri's schemes, it will be me. He made my life miserable before he left, and I'll be damned if I'm going to let him make my life a misery again. No...ghost, demon, monster, or plain old murderer, I'm going to see that his reign of terror finds an end," I muttered.

"So, you will not ask Étienne for help?" Charlotte inquired, offering me the bottle.

"Certainly not," I huffed.

She leaned in close to my face and stared into my eyes. I backed away, alarmed.

"What?"

"I knew it! You slept with him! Of course you did! I'm so proud of you. What was it like? Was he as masterful as everyone says? Come now, you must tell me everything."

I almost denied it, but the champagne and Charlotte's comforting presence unlocked something within me. A tear slipped down my cheek and I sniffed.

"Oh no! Was it horrible? He didn't take advantage of you, did he? I will kill him myself if he did!" Charlotte gripped the wine bottle threateningly in her hand and burgundy droplets splashed out onto her skirts.

I took the bottle and drank, shaking my head.

"No, it was...oh, Charlotte, it was wonderful. I felt things I've never felt with any man. But I fear I did something wrong because afterwards...he just shut down on me. Now I'm afraid that I just became another name on his list of mistresses. Women of the court to use and toss aside."

The tears flowed more freely, and Charlotte tutted affectionately.

"You poor thing! Why do you feel like you did wrong?"

"I don't know!" I wailed. "All I know is that we made love and then he just went cold! What if he's lost interest in me because he finally succeeded in getting me into bed and the chase is over? Either that or... well, I've only ever been with Henri and his tastes were *unusual* to say the least—what if it's because I am horrible in bed? He was likely disappointed with me, otherwise he wouldn't be avoiding me, right? I'm so furious with myself, Charlotte, I could just explode! I was doing so well resisting him and his charms and in the midst of *one* weak moment..." I growled and gulped the wine. Charlotte patted my back.

"My darling, I'm certain you performed admirably. Men just behave this way sometimes—they don't have much experience dealing with anything beyond their own set of immediate needs. Goodness, if I want a bit of a cuddle after sex with Philippe, you'd think I was asking for the moon. He was probably overtired, or hungry! Men can be such strange creatures, to say nothing of *supernatural* men. Don't fret over it."

She took the bottle and drank. I blubbered a bit more and she leaned her head onto my shoulder.

"Do you want me to punish him? I could have him ousted from the *tonne* or spread vile rumors about him. I could tell the women at court that he has *la grande verole* and his manhood has become black and shriveled."

I wiped my face and giggled. "No, but thank you. I suppose I'm just embarrassed about it all. And it feels strange...being with a man who isn't Henri. And rather regretfully, there was nothing shriveled about him."

Charlotte cackled and nearly spilled the bottle of wine. We dissolved into drunken fits of laughter and my tears were soon forgotten.

On a sigh, Charlotte tossed the second empty bottle across the room.

"*Alors*, tell me about your ghost. Is it his room? Your château isn't haunted, is it?"

"No. Charlotte, you must never repeat what I'm about to tell you. Our very lives may depend on it."

"Cross my heart."

I took a deep breath. "I am investigating Jeanne's death."

"For The Order?"

My jaw dropped. "Charlotte! How did you—what do you know of The Order?"

She laughed. "If you think Philippe is smart enough to keep that big of a secret from me, you seriously underestimate me, *chérie*. I have known since we were married, and I know that you are also with them. Do not worry! I have kept it to myself for this long. Your secrets are safe with me. Now, go on. Tell me of the ghost."

My shock waning—*of course Charlotte would figure it out, Philippe has no talent for espionage and Charlotte has a mind like a whip*—I cleared my throat and continued.

"Right. After Jeanne was murdered, they believed Étienne was responsible—"

"What utter rot!" she interjected. "That man seduces women, he doesn't murder them. If he murdered women, there would be fewer pussies for him to—"

"Yes, well, there was a report of Jeanne's death and it said *vampire bite*. I was supposed to administer justice on their behalf, but—"

"You mean stake him?"

"Yes, Charlotte, *please* stop interrupting. I'm getting to that."

She selected another bottle of wine and sat primly at the foot of the bed. I told her everything about the investigation and about Étienne, from our first meeting in the hedge maze to the graveyard, to his poisoning, to our encounters with the jeweler, Josephine, and the drunks, and finally the black magic bookshop basement. I told her about making love to him, though I left out the part about his healing abilities. For some reason, divulging that felt like a betrayal of something strangely sacred. When I finished, the third bottle of wine sat abandoned on the bedside table and her face was a pale, inscrutable mask.

"Well?" My nerves crackled as I worried about how she would respond.

"I cannot believe you've been through all that in the last few weeks," she said. "Firstly, I retract my earlier defense of Étienne's behavior. He is certainly an ass. Secondly, this book you found in the basement—what was the title again?"

"*Pseudomonarchia Daemonum.*"

"You must be dealing with a demon of some kind," she said, her brows furrowing.

"*Dieu*, I know nothing about demons! The Order won't help me and it's been far too long since I've set foot in a church..." I groaned.

"I think I know where we may find a copy of that book," she said, her eyes sparkling with intrigue.

"No! Where?"

"The library at Versailles."

"That cannot be. King Louis would never have such a heretical text in his library," I said with a frown.

"You are right. It wouldn't be in *his* library, but it would be in Jeanne's."

"What? Charlotte, you aren't making any sense. Jeanne was a devoted Catholic, just like Louis."

"Yes, but she was also a grand patron of the arts. She attended salons with some of the most liberal thinkers in France. She was friends with Voltaire, for God's sake. The library in her apartments is said to have a much more *enlightened* and *progressive* catalogue of texts. Did you never hear the rumors of her interest in life beyond the grave? There were even whispers of her holding a séance at court."

My mind worked. I'd always thought Jeanne was an innocent victim in all of this. Was it possible she was caught up in something dangerous and otherworldly?

"But her apartments have been closed up," I said. "Even if she had a copy of the book, it would be nearly impossible for us to get inside that wing of the palace without attracting too much attention."

"Well, then, it's fortunate indeed that we have the perfect excuse to skulk around Versailles in the middle of the night next week!" Charlotte nearly fell off the bed in her excitement. Seeing my confused expression, she groaned in exasperation. "Oh, Daphne. Tell me you haven't forgotten about the midnight masquerade on All Hallow's Eve. You told me ages ago that you were thinking of the perfect costume."

Merde.

15

ÉTIENNE

"I think you've had enough this evening, Monsieur. Why don't you go home and sleep it off, eh?" The barkeep tugged the empty tankard from my clammy grip. My fangs extended and my eyes darkened.

"Another," I snarled at him. He sighed and waved to one of the curvy barmaids at the back of the tavern. Nervously, she brought me a fresh ale and hurried away before I could unleash my ire upon another undeserving person. A month ago, she would have been winking at me and refilling my drinks with overt displays of her impressive cleavage. I would have taken her to bed for pleasure and blood.

Not anymore, I thought sourly.

After Daphne took off into the afternoon, I fell into a restless sleep and promptly woke at sunset, tormented by growing fears that I'd been wrong, and somehow Henri or the thing bearing his voice had made its way to her. I rushed over to her château, but once there, refused to allow myself the pleasure of meeting her in person. Instead, I miserably patrolled her grounds, hunting and sniffing for any putrid whiff of the murderer's scent. When I was satisfied that he hadn't been there, and I'd caught a vexing glimpse of Daphne seated at her library desk, I turned from the estate and sulked all the way back to my own home.

I returned the next night and two nights hence to perform the same ridiculous ritual of ensuring her safety.

The evening of the fifth day, I decided to forgo my warped desire to prowl around her home and dressed instead to seek different company. I went to all of my favorite haunts—upper class gaming clubs, bourgeoisie taverns, even a few questionable brothels, but nothing appealed. Woman after woman solicited my attention, but each one left me feeling cold and uninspired. I sated myself with drink and went home hungry. The next night, I suffered the same disappointments.

Necessity forced me to find someone to feed upon. Shamefully, I found a bleeder with golden hair and light eyes, but even when I had her naked in front of me, I could not bear to pursue any carnal pleasure. Angry with myself, I told her to dress and drank what I needed from her wrist. Since then, I'd given up seeking pleasure with other women, at least until the damned duchesse Daphne was out of my system. I'd been enamored before. I knew it was only a matter of time and distance before she was forgotten.

Unfortunately, Daphne was not making it easy on me. She'd sent me several letters asking reasonable questions about our investigation. *Where should we go from here?* Damned if I knew. I suspected there was something much more demonic and less ghostly to *le Duc Dépravé*'s appearance, but I couldn't concentrate long enough to figure out my next steps. Every thought circled back to Daphne—to her strength and wit, her soft skin and shimmering hair, her beautiful violet eyes glittering with desire. It was infuriating. Trying to screw her out of my mind was supposed to work, to help, but then message after message arrived, smelling of orange blossoms and vanilla, and I'd inevitably lose an evening caressing myself with memories of her velvet heat.

It was pathetic.

So, I'd decided the only acceptable plan of action was to keep myself in the throes of a drunken stupor until enough time passed that I could think about anything other than Daphne. *Daphne.* Things were—it must be said —not going well, but I was immortal. I had all the time in the world.

"Monsieur, you look so hungry! Do you care for a bite?" The woman next to me stroked her neck seductively, showing off half a dozen bite marks in various states of healing. Her arms, too, were covered in scrapes and punctures. She grinned lasciviously with a mouth full of brown, rotten teeth. My gut churned and bile rose to my throat.

"Not tonight, my lady. Find another gentleman," I slurred. I stared into my ale.

"What's wrong, *mon cher*? My blood is as sweet as any aristo's! Just a taste, then, on the house." She pouted and shoved her wrist under my nose. I pulled away from her and slipped off my chair, falling to the floor. The bleeder laughed heartily and extended a hand to help me up, but I batted her away. I supposed that was enough humiliation for one evening. I stumbled out of the tavern, tossing a handful of coins at the barkeep and one to the bleeder. I bowed unsteadily amid guffaws of drunken laughter from the other patrons.

"My apologies for my unseemly behavior, good people." Their laughter followed me out the door and carried a good way down the street.

I wandered the streets for a while, not wanting to go home. I didn't know if it was worse to have my sheets smell like her and dream in torment, or if it was worse to feel the tightness in my chest when, each day, her scent lightened a bit more. I swore and ran my fingers through my hair, yanking it out of my customary queue. This was madness. My immortal life was in danger from some obscured threat and here I was— one of the greatest lovers of Paris—reduced to a simpering pup over some prissy courtier who was completely wrong for me. *No, you fool, you're the one who's wrong. Wrong for her!*

"Get ahold of yourself, Étienne!" I yelled. A few street urchins eyed me and backed away from my ravings. *Pity,* I thought. *I could do with a good fight.*

Unaware of the path my feet took, I found myself drifting aimlessly in the direction of Daphne's château yet again. I stopped to reorient myself, realizing I was near the *Faubourg Saint-Germain* and some of the wealthiest town homes in the city. I quickened my pace, worried that I'd be seen in my disgraceful state by some gossiping lord or lady out for a moonlit stroll. Because good fortune seemed to have abandoned me entirely, it wasn't long before I heard a familiar trill at my back.

"Monsieur de Noailles! Oh, Monsieur! Yoo-hoo!"

I stiffened and attempted to straighten my cravat, frowning at the spilled ale and blood on my waistcoat. My dark hair hung in loose waves around my face and I hadn't bothered to bathe or shave. I probably looked like some sort of wild man who'd only just found his way to civilization. *Well, nothing I can do about it now,* I thought with a grimace.

I turned and bowed to the Comtesse de Brionne and her petulant husband. He looked an impressive mix of haughty and irritated as his wife tugged him forward in my direction. She, however, seemed beyond delighted to see me, given my disheveled appearance. Her eyes flashed with humor and feminine conspiracies.

"Charlotte, it seems Monsieur de Noailles is having himself an unsavory evening. I suggest we continue on our way home and leave him to his debauchery."

"Nonsense, Philippe! One must always say hello to one's friends when out and about. Is that not so, Monsieur de Noailles?" She extended her hand to me to bow over, but her husband yanked her arm out of my grasp.

"Do not touch her," he hissed at me. "Carry on your way, Monsieur. Come along, Charlotte—*now.*"

The threat in his tone would have stayed many a woman, but Charlotte just whacked his shoulder with her folded fan.

"Philippe, *please.* I apologize for my husband's rudeness, Monsieur. He has just lost a tidy sum at the card game following the duc's dinner party and will be in an unbearable temper for the rest of the night." Philippe glowered murderously and I smothered my laugh.

"From whence do you come, Monsieur l'Émissaire? Working late in the evening? Maybe leaving a new paramour? Or perhaps as my husband says—a night of well-earned debauchery?" Charlotte's tone was light, but the scrutiny in her gaze sent a fresh wave of hot shame through me.

"The latter, I'm afraid, though it was hardly well-earned. How fare you on this fine October evening?" I tried for the smooth coolness of my courtly tone, but it came out gritty and flat.

"Oh, fine, fine! You seem somewhat out of sorts, Monsieur, are you certain nothing is the matter? You look a little sick—*or is it lovesick?*" Her piercing eyes took in my rumpled appearance with a hint of sympathy.

I bristled. "No, Madame. I assure you that is *not* the case."

She eyed me for a moment, unmoved by my protest. I hid a grimace when her lips split into a wide, self-satisfied grin.

"Well, I wish you the best with your mystery lover. As I said, we've just come from the duc's little get-together. It was lovely, of course, but they served *stewed fruit* for dessert—can you believe that? Really, what are we, *English*? I felt it was incredibly unpatriotic, don't you? I'm sure the other guests were scandalized, as well, don't you think, Philippe?" She laid a soothing hand on her husband's arm, but his icy glare did not stray from me. He gripped her arm tightly.

"Well, we've paid an acceptable call upon Monsieur de Noailles, darling, and it's time we let him return to his evening. Come along, Charlotte," he growled between gritted teeth.

"Philippe, *mon cher*, not so tight, please. You shall wrinkle my gown. *Alors*, Monsieur de Noailles, my husband is right! We must away, but do tell me, are you planning on attending the All Hallow's Eve masquerade next week? I understand it's meant to be a rather *spirited* evening," she said, giggling at her own joke. "I will be glad to have Philippe by my side, in case I become frightened. It is good, I think, to have one you love close by on such a night, don't you agree?" Her intense expression hinted at some secret meaning that the alcohol prevented me from understanding just then.

"I hadn't thought to," I answered. "I'm really quite busy at the moment. I don't know if I have time for—"

"Well, that's very nice, Monsieur. Thank you for your time. *Bon soir,*" Philippe muttered. Charlotte glared daggers at him and yanked her arm from his grip.

"*Philippe. Arrêtez!*"

"Damn it, Charlotte, go get in the carriage! We will discuss your behavior when we get home. *Let's go!*" Without a glance at his wife, he whipped around and stomped over to their waiting carriage.

Charlotte turned wide eyes on me and flicked open her fan. Her hands trembled—no doubt at her husband's outburst—and she dropped the ivory accessory on the ground. Reflexively, I bent to pick it up and nearly fell backward when she bent down to meet me.

"Gather up your courage, Monsieur," she whispered. "If you do not attend the masquerade, I daresay you will disappoint some very important people."

"*Mon Dieu,* Charlotte! Get in here, now!" Philippe yelled from the darkness of the carriage.

"Oh, la! Monsieur l'Émissaire was just retrieving my fan for me, darling!" Charlotte called back to him. "You know how clumsy I can be after champagne *and* sherry at dinner," she laughed. She gave me a dazzling smile and a saucy wink, then plucked her fan from my fingers and bustled away.

"*Bon soir, Monsieur, et bonne chance!*"

I swayed slightly and blinked at the retreating carriage. Already, my head was beginning to ache from the drink and Charlotte's unsettling insinuations. I turned around and walked back the way I'd come, seeking my waiting carriage back at the tavern. I tried to sort through the comtesse's words, but ale would not wear off until I fed. Forcing my despair down, I re-entered the tavern and beckoned to the bleeder from earlier. Without a word, she took me into a dingy room above the bar and sat on the bed. I stopped her from undressing and knelt before her, taking her wrist gently. When I'd drunk what I needed, I licked the wound closed and paid her handsomely. She smiled weakly and I made my way back out to my carriage, lost in thought.

The warm fingers of sunrise trailed across the sky and I felt painfully weary. One thought seemed to return over and over as I neared my home. Charlotte's teasing words were seared into my mind. *Lovesick.* What was she suggesting? That I was in love with Daphne? *Impossible.* She was a passing infatuation, that was all. Did it matter that I thought of her constantly, that I worried for her safety, that for the first time in my life, I found myself *unworthy* of a female? Of course not. Certainly, I wished for her safety and her happiness, but any gentleman with an ounce of chivalry in him would. Disappointment flared. I did want to protect her, but that job was not mine. She'd told me so many times that she could protect herself, no doubt because she'd been doing so from the moment she'd had to marry *le Duc Dépravé*. She'd had to guard herself against his cruelty and brutality before, and now she would have to do it all alone yet again because I couldn't bear to be near to her.

The memory of the scents in his awful bedchamber resurfaced in my mind. Henri, whatever he was, whatever he'd become, was dangerous. Just because he hadn't come for Daphne yet didn't mean that he wouldn't come for her still. The thought gripped me in a panic that I could not assuage. *Damn it all.*

If she'd been able to endure his cruelty for so long, surely I could endure the pain of being near her in order to help protect her, at least until we'd brought this whole horrible investigation to a close. She deserved that much.

I couldn't do that acting like an inebriated imbecile. It was time to straighten up and honor my responsibilities—to the country, to my reputation, and to Daphne. Then, when this investigation was finished and she was safe, I could well and truly move on.

Satisfied with myself for the first time in ages, I hurried inside my château and called for my butler and valet.

"François, Robert, have a bath prepared downstairs immediately. Then while I rest, send for my tailor. I'll need something appropriate to wear to the All Hallow's Eve masquerade at the palace. Spare no expense—just tell him to have something ready for me by sunset on the thirty-first."

"*Oui, Monsieur.*"

"*Bon. Merci, mes amis.*" I stripped off my soiled clothes on my way down to my apartments. I entered my bedchamber and tossed the clothes to the side. My men followed and, to their credit, did not bat an eye at my carelessness. I'd managed to retain most of the staff after I'd been turned. A few of them had chosen to leave, understandably, but many of them felt a sense of familial obligation. My father had been well-loved, even in his dour twilight years of failing health.

"Do you wish for us to change the bed linens now, Monsieur?"

"No!" I barked, startling them and myself. Daphne's scent still lingered, but it would be gone in a few more days. She'd be safe by then and I could let her go—orange blossoms and vanilla and all. "No, thank you. When I am ready for new linens, I shall strip the bed myself."

"As you wish, Monsieur."

I nodded gratefully. Two footmen appeared carrying the large copper tub and started the laborious process of filling it. Sinking into the hot, lavender-scented water, I allowed myself to revisit the memory of Daphne's bath. I hardened, fantasizing about the episode ending differently. I should've checked my need and moved more slowly—kissed her and stoked her and made love to her until her cries shattered the steamy silence.

What a fool I've been about her. I groaned, gripping my cock and thinking of her passionate words. *Étienne, give me all of you. I need you.* Desire arrowed through me, closely followed by the remembered pleasure. This was the last time, I told myself. It had to be the last time. I did not love her. I could not love her.

I should not love her.

16

DAPHNE

October 31, 1765
Palace of Versailles

"Daphne, you look absolutely gorgeous! Surprisingly virginal for Aphrodite," Charlotte laughed.

"*Mon Dieu*, do I look like I'm supposed to be Aphrodite?" I cursed. "I was going for Artemis."

"Oh, really? But you're covered in all those pearls."

"Well, yes, but they're supposed to symbolize the moon. Did the bow and arrows not give me away?"

I peered at my reflection in a back corner of the Hall of Mirrors. I'd decided on a shimmering silk gown in the palest blue, so light that it almost looked silver. I wore a spiked silver tiara to represent a crown of moonlight and had adorned a matching satin domino mask with several large pearls. I'd strapped a bow and golden arrows to my back, as well.

"It doesn't matter. You are breathtaking, *chérie!* I'm sure your dance card will be full in no time."

"*Merde!* I don't want to be the center of attention, Charlotte. We're supposed to be sneaking into Jeanne's library."

Charlotte rolled her eyes. She was dressed in a gown of fine plum silk that was almost dark enough to be black. She'd attached matching silk wings to the back of her gown and wore a black mask with high, pointed ears.

"Charlotte, I thought you were coming as a peacock," I said.

"Well, I was, but then I had this moment of divine inspiration! I changed my costume at the last minute and decided to come as a bat. Oh, Philippe was *furious* about the expense!" She chuckled and to illustrate her point, she held her arms out and the wings unfolded beautifully. She did, indeed, look like a lovely, mysterious bat.

"How clever you are! You look beautiful," I said with a smile.

Philippe joined us and held out two glasses of champagne. He'd come dressed as Apollo, resplendent in gold brocade with a glittering mask and crown. A papier-mâché lyre hung from a belt at his waist.

"Daphne, you are certainly the most beautiful Aphrodite—lovelier even than the goddess herself," he gushed.

I scowled at him.

"She's Artemis, *mon cher*," Charlotte said, nudging him with her elbow. "See her bow and arrows?"

"Yes, of course," Philippe said, though his mouth was twisted in confusion.

I sighed and sipped the champagne. I tried to avoid looking around the room nervously, but it was difficult considering the last several days had me in a tangle of raw nerves. Sleep had all but eluded me over the past week and I'd taken to prowling the moonlit halls of my château, gripping my pistol and a vial of holy water, waiting for Henri's return. Add to that the simmering resentment I felt at Étienne's abandonment, and it seemed that it would be a long time yet until I could drift off in some sense of peace.

I had no idea if Étienne would be coming tonight, but I hoped not. I didn't think I could restrain myself from issuing a very thorough dressing-down. I held onto the anger as best I could, mostly because it covered the hurt I couldn't seem to overcome. Besides, if he was here, I'd end up thinking of his dreamy, golden eyes and his hard, muscled body, and I wouldn't be able to properly focus on the task before Charlotte and I tonight.

If only I could focus now.

I'd thought of him ceaselessly since our night together and found myself squirming in bed, dreaming of his lips and hands on me. I reasoned that it was only natural, since the only physical love I'd ever known beyond my own explorations was with a man who couldn't climax without the sight of blood. Of course I would feel some sentimental attachment to Étienne. I wasn't made of stone. *Regrettably*, I thought.

"Might the humble Poseidon fill a slot on Aphrodite's dance card?" A courtier in sea-green silk bowed before me. He stroked his trident pruriently and winked behind his mask. I looked around for Charlotte, but she had wandered off.

"Oh, well, I—" Panic had me stuttering and backing away from the unpleasant overture, until I came up against a solid wall of man. I shut my eyes. My body knew him immediately.

"I'm afraid the lady Artemis has a full dance card tonight, Monsieur."

That voice—velvet across my skin. The smell of soap, cedar, and peppermint. Snow-covered pine trees. Cool, smooth skin and lean, hard muscle making me burn with desire.

Putain.

Poseidon prowled away, grumbling. I opened my eyes and spun around. For all the angry words I wished to lash against him, I was ill-prepared for the impact seeing him would have upon me. He was clad in a suit of deep burgundy velvet and wore a leather mask topped with a small pair of black antlers. His sensuous lips curved up in the hint of a smile and his warm hazel gaze scorched me in its intensity.

"Étienne." His name came out more breath than sound. Of its own volition, my body arched toward him, magnetically drawn to what it wanted most.

"Duchesse." He took my hand and bowed over it, then turned it over and pressed a lingering kiss to my wrist. Lust blazed through me, wild and urgent. I stared—gaping like a ninny at his seductive beauty. Try as I might, I could not form the sharp retorts I'd been clinging to for the past days.

Étienne smirked. "Perhaps we should make our way to the dance floor? I'd hate to have Poseidon accuse me of lying. I believe that's actually the Marquis de Balay beneath that hideous mask. I can't believe he adorned his wig with *real* seaweed. In an hour, this room is going to reek of low tide."

Despite myself, I chuckled. Étienne's hand found the small of my back, gently guiding me to the other dancing couples. I drew in a breath, fighting for calm—fighting to remember my anger and disappointment.

"I'm surprised you bothered," I managed.

"Pardon?"

"What do you care if the Marquis de Balay asks me to dance? You made it abundantly clear you want nothing to do with me—after *every-thing*," I sneered, hating the petulant tone of my voice and the undisguised hurt that bled through.

A look of pain flitted through his eyes but was gone quickly. He opened his mouth to reply, but the strains of an *allemande* began, and he grasped my hand to start the dance.

"Though I suppose you're not here for me," I goaded. "Probably just back to your regular hunting grounds now, eh? Isn't that how it is for you, Étienne? Use one up, then move onto the next—a little sex, a little blood, a little influence. The Order isn't sending another agent after you because of my interference, so I suppose that's all you needed from me, then."

The dance swirled us away from each other for a moment, and when we came together, he was white lipped with anger. When we clasped hands again for a turn, his grip was rough.

"What do you want from me?" he hissed. "By your own admission, our alliance was only ever meant to be temporary."

"That doesn't mean I appreciate being cast aside like another one of your conquests! For a moment, I thought you were… I thought I was… I thought *we* were—" I cut myself off, too afraid to say the words out loud. *I thought you were different. I thought I was special. I thought we were…something.*

Étienne paused, missing a step in the dance. He stared at me; his eyes unfathomable behind his demonic stag mask. Couples spun around us and I started to suffocate in the stifling room. I needed to get out and get some air. *Breathe, Daphne.*

Without another word to Étienne, I fled the room before the dance ended. I barreled through the other revelers, fighting my way to the doors that led out to the gardens. I was grateful for the sharp bite of late October chill. The bracing cold allowed me to regain the composure I seemed to misplace whenever Étienne was around. I stared out at the dark garden beyond, dotted with guttering torches. Had it only been five weeks since my encounter with him in the hedge maze? It felt like a lifetime ago.

"You never answered my question."

The words at my ear made me jump. Once again, I marveled at his stealth. He came up to stand next to me, looking out into the inky blackness.

I blew out a breath and watched it condense in a cloud of frost before me.

"I want what I've always wanted," I answered. "The truth."

He turned to face me, raising his fingertips to my cheek.

"Is that all?" he murmured.

"Yes," I whispered, leaning into the feel of him. *No. I don't want to live in fear of Henri's return. I want to be able to sleep at night without dreaming of your hands on me. I want to feel like I was something to you.*

He chuckled. "Liar."

I shut my eyes against the truth of his words.

"We will get to the truth," he said, taking a step closer to me. His legs brushed against my skirts. "Daphne…whatever happens, you will be safe from Henri. I swear it."

"And then?" I asked.

He swallowed. "And then you will go back to The Order and continue your life as an agent. I will go back to my duties as emissary, trying to convince the king to see reason, trying to convince the court to accept the blood plague as our new reality. We'll go back to work, Daphne, and Jeanne's spirit will be at peace."

His words formed an ache in my chest that spread through my entire body. *But why? Isn't that exactly what I wanted?* I knew it wasn't—not anymore.

"What if that's not enough?" I whispered.

Étienne sighed. "Daphne, it has to be. You're a smart woman. You understand what it would take for us to be together. I'm immortal—eternal. I will not watch you wither away with age and die, and I hardly think you're leaping at the chance to sacrifice a lifetime of sunrises on me. You must understand. It's better this way."

A sharp pain chased the ache away, followed by an overwhelming numbness. I swallowed back tears I didn't want him to see. He was right. Even entertaining the idea of there being something more between us made me feel foolish. What was I expecting? I didn't just want a passing fancy, but the reality was we couldn't be anything more.

I swallowed and nodded. The look of anguish in Étienne's face nearly unraveled me. I turned to head back inside, but he caught my arm and pulled me to him.

"Daphne, I wish it could be another way," he said, wrapping his arms around me. "I won't dishonor you by asking you for more, but you must know you were never just another conquest to me."

He tilted my chin up and set his lips to mine. There was no lightness to the kiss, just the untamed unleashing of need and a thousand shades of passion. His arms around my waist tightened and I clung to him, holding on as if I were adrift in a storm. I pressed him back against the stone balcony railing, painting my body against his.

He groaned against my lips. "Daphne, I can't—*mon Dieu*—I can't do this. I can't keep doing this. I have to let you go."

But his hold on me tightened, and his lips found mine again, and the only time he paused was to feather kisses against my cheeks, jaw, and neck. His arousal pressed against my belly, sending fire straight to my core.

"Why do you have to?" I panted against him, nearly faint with desire.

He pulled away to look at me, staring hard into my eyes. "Because, Duchesse, you are not mine."

He tilted his head down to resume the kiss, his lips inches from mine, when a rough voice called my name. The look in Étienne's eyes went cold. At the interruption, I froze, panic snapping my mouth shut. I straightened and backed away from him.

"Daphne!" Philippe called again. "Daphne, Charlotte needs you, darling. Over there. Now, please." He pulled me firmly away from Étienne. "She was most insistent."

The look in Philippe's eyes was murderous. I burned with embarrassment at being caught, but Étienne stood straight and narrowed his gaze at Philippe. A heavy silence descended upon the three of us.

"Daphne," Philippe prodded. "She said it was important."

I nodded and stepped back toward the ballroom. Étienne bowed stiffly at Philippe and followed me.

"I believe the ladies would like to be alone," Philippe said, staying Étienne with a hand on his arm. Étienne glared, but let me go.

Rather than get in the middle of whatever unpleasant altercation seemed about to take place between them, I hurried inside the palace, searching for Charlotte.

The candlelit corridors blurred as I careened forward, quietly calling for her. Finally, a door cracked open, revealing a thin stream of amber light. A familiar head poked out and beckoned to me.

"Daphne! Come here! I've found the library!" Charlotte ducked back inside the room and quickly closed the door behind me.

I ripped my mask off, throwing it onto a desk beside Charlotte's bat mask and crumpled into a nearby chair. Seeing my pink cheeks and breathless manner, Charlotte threw her head back and laughed.

"Oh, *chérie*! Tell me what happened with Étienne."

"*Mon Dieu*, Charlotte, I have no idea!" I shook my head in confusion as tears started to well in my eyes. "One moment, I was arguing with him on the dance floor, the next I was outside trying to get some air, and then I found myself before him again, wondering *what if we could be together?* But we can't because he will live forever and I can't become a vampire, and so we have no future—and then it was as if we were saying goodbye to each other, but then we were kissing, and then Philippe found us and he's just *furious*, Charlotte—I don't think I've ever seen him so angry!" The words rushed out of me as the tears started to fall, dropping onto my shiny, pale skirts.

"Hush now, *ma chère amie*! You are fine now, are you not? Philippe and his temper are out there, and we are safe in here. And as for you and Étienne—well, what do you really want?"

"I don't know!" I wailed.

She tutted and hugged me, but her tenderness only made me cry harder. I buried my face in her shoulder and sobbed almost as hard as I had when Michel had died. *What was wrong with me?*

"You must figure that out first, *chérie*. Otherwise, how will you know what to ask him for?" she soothed, pulling a flask of brandy from her garter. "Here. Have a drink of something medicinal."

I sipped at first, enjoying the sweet warmth of the liquid. Then at Charlotte's insistence, downed the rest of the flask.

"I don't know what I want. I don't understand my feelings for him, Charlotte. I want to hate him. He makes me so crazy! And he's a *vampire!* Just like the ones that killed Michel."

"But he did not kill Michel," Charlotte pointed out. "And you know, darling, I don't think he's really like *all* vampires, any more than one man is like *all* men. Why are you so confused by these feelings? You simply thought he was one thing, and then you got to know him and learned that you were wrong. And now you must figure out if you want him at all, if you love him and will make it work, or if you think it's best to part ways and move on with your life."

"It's not that simple," I argued.

"*L'amour* rarely is. But for now, we have work to do, so no more tears, *d'accord?*"

"Yes, yes, I know. *Merde.* It's fine. I'm fine, really."

"Good," she said, taking the empty flask. "Now that you are fortified, we shall look for the book. I would love to hear of your troubles and your heartache, *chérie*, but we don't have much time before the silly men come looking."

She was right. I stood and forced Étienne from my thoughts, intent on finding a copy of the book. I blew out a breath and took a candle from the desk.

"Thank you, *chérie*. As always, you are right." I offered her a wan smile. "You start over by those shelves and I'll start on this side."

We perused the bookshelves lining the walls, standing on chairs to reach the uppermost volumes. Unfortunately, they didn't seem to be in any kind of order, which meant we'd have to individually check every book. I groaned. This room wasn't as large as the formal library at Versailles, but it was big enough to take us all night.

"I should have brought more brandy," Charlotte muttered. "Do you think I should go and get us some?"

"No! It'll take us long enough to search together—it'll take twice as long if we're drunk."

A soft knock startled us both. Before I could climb down from the chair, the door opened. We froze.

A pair of antlers poked in, followed by the rest of the man I wanted to see the least.

"Étienne!" I gasped. "What are you doing here? Get out before someone sees you and finds us in here!"

I jumped down from the chair and hurried over to him.

"My, my," he drawled. "What have we here? Two sneaky little vixens hiding away in Madame de Pompadour's private library? What *will* the king say?"

I started to push him out the door, but it was like trying to move a block of solid stone. He chuckled at my feeble attempts and removed his mask. Charlotte narrowed her eyes at him, but suddenly gasped and pulled him further into the room.

"Charlotte, *what* are you doing?" I whispered.

"Daphne, he can help us look!"

I scowled.

"Look for what?" Étienne glanced from me to Charlotte, then back to me again.

"Nothing!" I whispered. "It's nothing. If you want to help, go keep watch and leave Charlotte and I to work. You haven't exactly been the best partner in this investigation lately, anyway."

He peered down at me, his expression unreadable.

"No," he said.

"No—what?"

"No, I don't want to leave. The Comtesse de Brionne has asked for my assistance. I will stay to help." He faced Charlotte and smiled charmingly at her. "What are we looking for, Madame?"

I seethed with anger. Charlotte raised her brows at me.

"*Pseudomonarchia Daemonum,*" she said.

"Traitor." I folded my arms against my chest.

Étienne's smile dropped.

"Daphne," he said in a warning tone. "This is extremely dangerous. You have no idea what you're getting into."

I raised my chin haughtily. "Oh, and you do? Well, by all means, share it with me. You forget, Étienne, I was in that cellar, too. I want to know what we're up against, be it ghost, supernatural beast, or demon. Whatever it is, I will defeat it. We have no other leads to follow, and I don't think I need to remind you that time—and The Order's patience—is running out."

"The Order's patience? Because it's not enough to simply find Jeanne's murderer—we have to do it so that your masters will welcome you back into their good graces," he scoffed.

"How dare you!" I growled. "If it wasn't for my intervention with The Order, you'd probably be returned to dust from some other assassin's stake."

Charlotte rolled her eyes. "Stop! Both of you. We're wasting time. Help us look for the book, Étienne, and then you two can spar all you want."

Chastened, I returned to my spot at the bookshelves. I resolved to ignore Étienne as best as I could, but it was difficult with him smiling smugly a few shelves over. I cut my eyes to him. He was scanning the titles with inhuman speed and I swallowed an oath. Charlotte had been right to ask him for help. I'd almost forgotten about his supernatural speed. I could only hope I found the book first, just so that he wouldn't have the satisfaction of—

"Found it," he called.

Merde.

He pulled a thick, leather-bound volume down and placed it on a table near the middle of the room. It looked almost identical to the one from the cellar. Without hesitation, I flipped through the pages, looking for the one that had been seared into my mind.

The Demon Asmoday.

Charlotte and Étienne stood on either side of me, reading over my shoulders. The page detailed horrifying rituals for summoning and controlling a demon. In exchange for sacrifices of blood, the demon Asmoday was said to bestow wealth, charm, power, and all-compelling allure upon his summoner, in addition to granting any number of requests. The demon could appear in his own form but had the power to both remain unseen and inhabit bodies. With the illicit gifts listed, I could suspect any number of people of summoning him—especially at court. Who didn't wish for wealth, power, and the lust of others? The only thing that didn't make sense to me was Henri's involvement. Why would he have summoned a demon to give him everything he already had?

"What does this mean?" Charlotte's humor had faded, replaced with a look of horror.

"We're dealing with a serious force of evil here," Étienne said, turning the page. "Someone has summoned the demon Asmoday and somehow, he is connected to Henri's body, or his spirit. I can't be sure which. We will need to petition the Vatican for an exorcism. That's the only way to defeat the demon."

"Are you certain? There has to be another way. Holy water, prayers, silver—something like that," I offered, desperate and starting to panic.

"Well, I don't know for certain about the holy water and prayers, but I believe silver only works on werewolves," he said thoughtfully.

"We don't have time to petition the Vatican," I said. My voice sounded on the verge of hysteria, even to my own ears. *Henri is connected to a powerful demon! As if he wasn't terrifying enough as a mere mortal man. What has he sought and gained in this new supernatural state? Strength? Immortality? Other unnamed dark powers?* Each prospect became more terrifying than the last, but I willed myself calm with a steadying breath. "You read the text.

There will be more deaths—more sacrifices until the summoner has what he wants. If we don't stop him, who knows what will follow? To stop Asmoday, we must stop the summoner."

"How do we do that?" Charlotte asked. Worry lines creased her forehead.

"We don't," Étienne said emphatically. "We must have help—someone who has performed an exorcism before. I've certainly never done one and I doubt either of you have. I do know that if it isn't done properly—*safely* —it can go very, very wrong."

I ignored his words. "Perhaps there's another book in here…a book about exorcising demons. Charlotte, help me look!"

"What the Hell is going on in here?" Philippe threw the library door open, knocking several books from their shelves. He tore his mask off and threw it aside, face purpling in anger. His eyes lit upon Étienne and he practically vibrated with violence.

"Philippe!" Charlotte laughed to cover her nerves, but her voice shook. "Nothing, *mon cher*, nothing! I was just having a quiet moment with Daphne when Monsieur de Noailles came in and—"

"Not another word, Charlotte. Not another lie shall cross your lips tonight. Get your things. We are leaving."

"Philippe, please, it was my fault. I—" I stepped toward him. He held up his hand to stay me.

"No, Daphne. I've had enough of this. It is your life—your decision—if you choose to remain under Noailles's influence, but I will not have you dragging my wife down with you. I feel like I can't trust you anymore, and if I cannot, then neither can The Order. I'll be writing to them this evening and telling them that you've been compromised. Do not send them any further messages."

Shock slammed into me. I felt rooted to the ground. My heart pounded with the speed of a runaway horse. I swallowed and opened my mouth, but no sound came out. *Out of The Order?* I couldn't believe it. Charlotte's worried gaze met mine and she shook her head, eyes warning me to be silent. She sighed deeply, picked up her mask from the table, then came to kiss my cheek.

"It will be all right, *chérie*. I will call on you in a few days when all of this has blown over. *D'accord?*"

Then, straightening with as much grace as the queen herself, she exited the room. As she passed Philippe, she looked at him and said in a voice more chilling than I'd ever heard from her, "Apollo always was a silly, jealous god."

A muscle in Philippe's jaw ticked and he slammed the door, leaving Étienne and I in devastated silence.

17

ÉTIENNE

October 31, 1765
Palace of Versailles

IT WAS SOME MOMENTS AFTER THE COMTE AND COMTESSE DE BRIONNE HAD left before Daphne finally exhaled. She sat heavily in one of the chairs and raised a hand to her forehead, rubbing a spot of tension between her brows. The defeat in her posture left a hollow ache in my chest and the mask of detached composure I'd been struggling to maintain began to fracture.

"Daphne…"

She closed her eyes and held up her hand to silence me.

"Please," she murmured. "I have lost much tonight. I do not wish to lose my temper, as well. Go away, Étienne. I cannot bear your presence just now."

Frustration tumbled through me. I was desperate to pull her into my arms, kiss away her sadness, and move heaven and Hell to right her world, but those promises would tie me to her and to a future I knew we could not have. A future she did not want. *No.* The best way to help her would be to deal with the demon and his summoner, and leave her to the luxurious life she rightly deserved. Emboldened by that sense of rightness and quelling the selfish wrongness I felt at letting her go, I knelt before her and cleared my throat.

When she opened her eyes, they were shimmering with unshed tears. For all her exquisite beauty in her angelic silk, there was something tragic lurking in the depths of those large violet pools. After a beat, I was able to find my voice again.

"Have you encountered demons before in your work with The Order?" She shook her head.

"We must find someone who knows how to perform an exorcism. The demon is the greatest threat to us now. If we remove him from the equation, the summoner is temporarily impotent. If we go after the summoner first, who knows what will happen. The demon may become untethered to Hell and be unleashed upon our world with nothing left to control him. Right now, he is bound by his ties to the summoner."

"We don't have time to wait on the Vatican. I don't suppose you know of someone who can help?" Her voice had lost its ragged edge and was frosty with irritation.

"Unfortunately, I do not often engage with men of the cloth," I said wryly.

She ignored my attempt at levity.

"I'm afraid I rather lost my faith after Michel died," she said. "I don't have many friends in the church. I would have sought assistance from The Order; they have several members familiar with some of the more indelicate religious practices, but I can't count on their help right now."

"Is there no one you could ask from The Order? Even if you do not petition the group as a whole..."

She looked at me murderously and gestured to the door. "Yes, there was! And there he goes! If you hadn't been here, Étienne... If you just would have gone when I first asked, I could have convinced Philippe that Charlotte and I had snuck away to be in each other's confidence. Why did you follow me?"

"My apologies," I said, more curtly than I intended. "I wanted to make sure you were all right after our little balcony *tête-à-tête*."

She stood and paced around the library, her skirts swirling in a soft rustle that sharply contrasted the resonance of her anger. I leaned against the desk, attempting to calm my own emotions.

"Yes, fine, thank you. Being caught kissing at a party is actually the least of my worries right now," she huffed.

"That's not what I was referring to," I said. I thought back to her words, *what if it's not enough?* Of course it wasn't enough—certainly not enough for me. But the possibility that the end of our investigation and return to our old lives was not enough for *her* filled me with a perverse kind of hope. It was the hope for a future neither one of us could have, and that I didn't deserve in the first place.

"Oh, that. Yes. You're right, of course. It doesn't make sense—the two of us. It was foolish of me to think…" She trailed off, her voice barely a whisper.

"Foolish to think what?" I pressed. *Foolish to think there was something more for us? That, perhaps, you wanted me as more than a throwaway lover like the rest of the women at court do? Foolish to think that you'd be willing to sacrifice so much to be with me?* I felt phantom beats from my dead heart in my chest, anticipating the rejection I knew would come.

"Nothing," she lied. "You were right, is all I'm saying. But we can't just give up on this investigation now. Especially not with…with Henri emerging. I've given almost everything to come this far and I won't stop until it's finished. If I do, I will have betrayed my friends, The Order, Michel's memory, and myself, in vain."

She turned her back to me and her shoulders slumped in fatigue.

"I don't know why you came tonight, Étienne. After everything I gave you, I left you to your solitude. I came here to finish things on my own. But you are back, wanting me to let you in again and to just pick up where we left off. I don't know if it's out of guilt, or self-preservation, or morbid curiosity, or perhaps so you can feel like you have some kind of strange sexual power over me. Whatever it is, *I do not know*," she stressed. "But…"

She faced me, tears gone, her face a study in fierce determination and exquisite beauty. Whether it was her pearlescent gown or the force of her will alone, she seemed to glow with an unnatural light. *She was magnificent.*

"What I do know, Étienne, is that I do not need your blessing or your approval to finish what we started. I will do it on my own—for Jeanne, for Michel, for the people of Paris, and most importantly, for me. Your involvement, or the lack of it, will not stand in my way. And if it becomes necessary, I will go through you."

She stepped toward me, eyes narrowed and chin raised in defiance. She squared her shoulders and crowded me back against the desk.

"Now, tell me, Étienne. Why are you here? Why did you come tonight? What do *you* want from *me*?"

Everything, Daphne. I want everything. I want your body, your mind, your heart. I want to make love to you every dawn before I sleep so that I will dream of you every day. I want to spend my nights finding ways to challenge your incomparable wit and trying to draw forth that small smile that makes my dead heart beat anew. I want to give you pleasure and happiness and all that my wretched body and damned soul has to offer. I came here tonight for you—to see you safe and to protect you so that I can let you go, but God help me, I don't think I'm strong enough.

I briefly considered prevaricating, but the bold frankness on her face prevented me from lying to her outright. I met her gaze unflinchingly, a cool smile on my lips. It was becoming harder for me to affect an air of detachment when every part of me felt like it was reaching for her. She waited for my answer, but because I couldn't lie and I wouldn't tell her the truth, I had no other alternative.

I pulled her to me and kissed her.

I could taste her conflict—torn between her body's desire for me and her mind's recoil at that need. I didn't give her time to think—to object. I licked her lips and she opened to me on a resigned sigh, meeting my tongue stroke for stroke. She tasted like brandy and fire, igniting every nerve in my body. I tugged at the neckline of her bodice, gently lifting her breast from the satin. I lightly caressed her pretty, pink nipple until it hardened beneath my touch. Breaking from the kiss, I bent and put my lips to it, sucking at it delicately until Daphne threw her head back and moaned in a rough tremor. I scraped my teeth across it and lifted her other breast from her gown, kneading it softly in my hand. She gasped and the sound went straight to my cock, already stiff and straining in my breeches. Mindless with want, I almost didn't hear her tortured, soft-spoken words.

"So, this is what you want from me. I hate you for it, Étienne, because —*damn us both*—I want it, too."

I ignored the guilt snaking through me, resolving to devote myself solely to her pleasure in this moment. I lowered my hands to her waist and pushed her back against the wall of bookshelves in the darkest corner of the library, then dropped to my knees. For once, it felt right for me to be here, kneeling before this powerful, luminous goddess.

"Étienne, what are you—?"

I bunched her gown and lifted it, gazing upon pale blue stockings and the leather garter that strapped her flintlock pistol to her upper thigh. A growl of desperate lust issued from my chest at the sight of the contrast. Delicate, proper undergarments topped with lethal practicality. If that didn't sum up Daphne as a woman, I didn't know what did.

Her hands had threaded their way through my hair, and I took them in my own. I handed her the bundle of skirts.

"Keep it there, Duchesse," I purred, sliding my hands up her legs. "I'm going to need both of my hands for this."

Her eyes danced with excitement, but her mouth was a tight line.

"You say I have some kind of sexual power over you?" I blew a stream of cool air against the thatch of blonde curls at the apex of her thighs. Her knees trembled.

"Perhaps you do," she gasped. "Perhaps it is this way for all of your women."

Pleasure thrummed through me at her ill-disguised jealousy and I slid my hands further up her thighs, caressing her curls with my thumbs.

"Perhaps you are afraid to admit that you desire me, Duchesse," I said, lightly rubbing my index fingers along the outer folds of her sex.

"I am not afraid." I watched a blush creep across her chest and cheeks.

"Then say it." The command was as much of a challenge to her pride as it was a need for me. I looked up at her, meeting her eyes above her gathered skirts. One long, languid stroke of my finger through the wet seam of her entrance and her eyes snapped shut, her mouth falling open on a whimper.

"I desire you," she breathed.

"Brave girl," I chuckled, rewarding her by finally setting my tongue to her, licking every sweet, perfect inch of her. I circled the peak of her pleasure and her soft cries became louder, more insistent. She fell back against the books and I held her hips to my face, worshipping her feminine perfection with lips and teeth and tongue. One of her hands dropped the bundle of satin and I felt her fingers wind through my hair again. She bucked against my mouth, driving for the friction against the places where her pleasure grew. Her instinctive pursuit of her own bliss made me wild.

"Am I the first man to touch you like this?" I panted, sliding a finger into her soft, wet heat.

"Oh, yes. Yes." She fisted her hand in my hair, pulling my lips back to her sex.

A primal sense of possessive triumph coursed through me as I pulled one of her legs over my shoulder. I dropped an airy kiss to her tight bud, then sucked it between my lips and worked it with firm strokes of my tongue.

"*Oh, mon Dieu. Putain de merde,*" Daphne swore, guttural and lewd. I nearly spent in my breeches.

Fighting the animal urgency to take her hard and fast, I focused instead on her—on the beautiful way she embraced her sensuality. The way she looked above me, eyes half-closed in hunger, yet watching me bring her to the brink. I slid a second finger inside her, and her other hand let loose her gown, draping me beneath the weight of her skirts. I did not mind. I wanted to watch her come apart from every angle, and soon I heard the escalation of her cries telling me that I was succeeding. Her pleasure crested and she screamed, clutching my head as her legs gave way. In a moment of selfishness, I let my fangs extend and nipped at the vein in her thigh—not to feed, but just to taste. *One last taste of perfection.* She cried out again as a second orgasm rolled through her—my favorite benefit of drinking from this part of the body.

Dieu, how could I live without this? You must, logic argued. *For her.*

I licked the wound closed and caught her as she fell, holding her tightly and laying her down on the thick Persian carpet.

For one satisfying moment, she lay sated and panting in my arms. I still ached with need, but it was a small price to pay for such a thorough distraction from her damaging line of questions. She sighed, slung one arm over my chest, and nuzzled into my shoulder. My chest tightened at the tenderness in the gesture. She looked up at me, eyes finding mine in the flickering candlelight.

"As enjoyable as that was, you never answered my question, Étienne. Why are you here tonight?"

Putain.

18

DAPHNE

October 31, 1765
Palace of Versailles

THE PANIC THAT FLASHED ACROSS ÉTIENNE'S FACE ALMOST MADE ME LAUGH. *Poor thing.* He'd really believed he could just kiss me into forgetting my questions. What kind of a simpering fool did he take me for?

He was quiet, staring fixedly at my bare breasts, eyes hazy with lust and his breathing still shallow. I knew he wasn't going to answer me—or if he was, it would be some kind of falsehood. It didn't matter. If he thought he could control me by using my lust as a weapon, he'd just learned that I am not so easily victimized.

I sighed and sat up, tugging my bodice back in place and smoothing the wrinkles from my gown. Étienne stood, helping me to my feet. I blushed at seeing his rather conspicuous excitement, and he smiled predatorily at me.

"How fitting that you would come dressed as vestal Artemis and I as the poor, hapless stag," he chuckled, his voice a low rumble that vibrated through me. "Actaeon stumbling upon his lovely goddess, only to be struck down and ripped to pieces by her hounds."

I smirked and tied my mask back on.

"Oh? And here I thought you showed up as a stag to engage in some mindless rutting with some poor, unsuspecting doe."

"It is never mindless, Duchesse," he purred.

"Well, it's lucky for you I left my hounds at home, then."

He came up behind me and kissed the back of my neck.

"What is your plan?"

"Why?"

"Because I'm going to help you. You cannot face Asmoday and the as-yet unknown summoner by yourself, Daphne, which is what I know you intend to do. It would be *ungentlemanly* for me to go back on our original agreement. Consider the last several days a temporary setback in our progress." He bowed with exaggerated gallantry.

Irritated, I adjusted my crown and re-pinned a few of the curls that had come loose during our tryst.

"*Our* progress? Forgive me if I'm misremembering, Étienne, but it's been by my wits alone that we've made *any* progress at all. Bringing Van Helsing to you was my idea, as was searching Brigitte's bedroom, as was seeking out the book that led us to Asmoday. Well, I had Charlotte's help for that, but my point is, Monsieur, that you overestimate your usefulness to me."

"Oh, you think so? I hate to disappoint you, Duchesse, but if I hadn't brought you to Jeanne's grave, you'd still be laboring under the false information supplied to you by The Order. And how would you have found Brigitte and the bookshop if not for me?" Étienne's temper flared as he straightened his hair in its queue.

"We were led to Brigitte because you fucked her and she tried to kill you, Étienne. Perhaps that's how we should proceed, then. You can hump your way to the truth and seduce Asmoday and his summoner all the way back to Hell. While you're at it, why not visit The Order, as well? You might find your way off their hit list, and then the whole useless lot of you can stand around and stroke each other's massive egos while Paris bleeds around you."

Hurt flashed in Étienne's eyes, but was gone almost as quickly as it had appeared. "You sound rather bitter for someone who seems to enjoy my seduction so well."

I bristled. "Yes, well, given my past, I'm sure I would have enjoyed myself with any man who didn't leave me bruised or bleeding after the act."

"Your low expectations of lovers don't insult me, Duchesse—what is it you so often say? 'I assure you, I've heard worse'. Especially here, at court. They call me 'a delightful beast', you know. Not a paramour. Not a vampire. Not a man." His cocksure manner slipped, and for the first time, I saw him radiate sadness, insecurity, and loneliness.

"Then, why do you do it?" I asked.

"You said it yourself, Duchesse. Food. Influence."

I knew exactly what that was like. I'd heard scant rumors of Henri's cruelty before I agreed to the match, but it was only after we were wed that I fully understood the depth of his depravity. My marriage had saved me from one kind of Hell, only to usher me into another. Étienne seemed to be in a similar Hell, though not necessarily one of his own making. I felt a swell of empathy for him and immediately regretted some of my words. Yes, I was angry and hurt, and incredibly tired of being underestimated by the men in my life, but that was no excuse to lash out at Étienne. Truthfully, I treasured our intimacies, but I was afraid of being strung along by a notorious rake who was only interested in saving his own skin.

Étienne leaned against the desk again, his handsome face inscrutable. I didn't like the hiccup in my pulse when I looked at him; all those taut muscles sheathed in sumptuous burgundy velvet, the antlers on his mask making him eerily demonic in the candlelight. He was a devil—born of fire, to be sure, but much of the fault lay within me for being so ready and willing to burn.

"So, Duchesse. Where do we go from here?"

I sighed and shook my head. An ache was building at the base of my neck and I needed quiet and clarity to think.

"I don't know," I said. "But I won't figure it out sitting in here."

I smoothed my skirts and left, casting the barest glance back at him. He remained motionless, obviously lost in thought—still so handsome, still so tempting, still so dangerous. I walked down the hall back toward the ball, though I knew I wouldn't stay long without Charlotte and Philippe to keep me company. Halfway there, I felt a cold draft of air blow through the hallway and I stopped. To my left was another narrow hall that led to the courtyard and gardens beyond. At the very end, I could see one long curtain swelling and fluttering with the breeze. *Curious.*

Why would someone leave a window open in the chill of October? I crossed slowly into the hall, the hairs on the back of my neck standing up.

This was wrong.

My shoes crunched over broken glass and I saw that the window hadn't been opened—it had been broken. Flecks of blood dotted pieces of glass that trailed outside into the frigid Paris night. Something bad had happened here.

Dread gathered in me when I realized that Philippe and Charlotte had been the only other people in this wing of the palace. Had there been some kind of accident?

"Étienne!" I called.

He was there in an instant, taking in the scene with a bright, intense gaze.

"Was it like this when you came through to the library?" I asked.

He shook his head. "No. It must have happened after I came through."

"Do you think—" I swallowed the lump in my throat and tried again. "Do you think it is Charlotte's or Philippe's blood?"

Étienne picked up one of the glass fragments and inhaled, then licked the droplet of blood staining it. His pupils dilated to black pools and his fangs extended.

"I do not know who the blood belongs to, but I can tell you that it is a man's." He sniffed the air again and cast his eyes about, looking for something unseen. He walked to the billowing curtain and bent to pick up something on the floor.

I gasped in horror when he held it up.

"Charlotte's mask!"

Étienne approached me, our argument forgotten, his face etched with concern. He took my hands in his and looked into my eyes.

"Daphne, there is something else," he hedged.

Frightened, mind racing, I braced myself for what I knew would be devastating information.

"I smell the murderer here. I don't know if it's the demon, or Henri, or the summoner, but I smell it on the glass."

The world spun on its axis and I shut my eyes tightly. *No, Daphne. You cannot faint. Keep it together! You must—for Charlotte.*

"What else do you detect?" I whispered.

"A few things I cannot place," he said. "Some things I recognize from the bookshop. But, Daphne, if he—it—took Charlotte and Philippe, they're probably still alive. Remember what the book said."

"We have to go after them now! Before it's too late!"

"We don't know what we're walking into and we don't have any way to fight a demon. If we go in there ill prepared, it'll be four corpses, not two. We have to come up with a plan."

I wracked my brain, wildly grasping for a solution. *How can you fight a demon?* The obvious answer seemed to be a priest, but Étienne didn't know any and the only ones I knew were in The Order. *When was the last time I was even inside a church?*

Suddenly, I remembered. I turned a half-crazed smile on Étienne.

"I know where to find a priest," I said.

He eyed me skeptically.

"Come on," I said, tugging at his arm. "This time, I'm leading the way."

He didn't argue or challenge me, and although his face was stern, I swore I saw the glint of amusement in his eyes.

THE CARRIAGE RIDE WAS SILENT WITH REPRESSED TENSION. ÉTIENNE WATCHED me from beneath long sweeps of lashes but did not speak.

Uncomfortable with the insults I'd hurled at him back at the palace, I cleared my throat.

"Étienne, I—" My voice rasped. "What I said back in the library, it was—"

Mon Dieu, why was this so hard? Out with it, Daphne!

Étienne's lip twitched. *"Unladylike?"*

"It was wrong. You were right. If it hadn't been for you, I would probably still believe the worst of you—that you murdered Jeanne. The progress we've made has been *ours*, not mine alone. On top of that, you saved my life back at the bookshop and I'm grateful to you for that. I said those things out of anger, and I shouldn't have. I am sorry."

He remained quiet, but nodded once. I held my hand out to him, hoping to put the awkward mess behind us.

He regarded my outstretched hand. Grinning wickedly, he took it and pulled me onto his lap.

"Étienne!"

"What? I was just going to tell you that I forgive you. Shall we seal it with a kiss?"

I wriggled against him, trying to extricate myself from his grip. I felt his arousal through my skirts. He tipped his head back and moaned.

"If you keep that up, Duchesse, I shall seal it with more than a kiss."

The carriage slowed and I looked out the window. We were near the abbey.

"We are here," I said.

Étienne swore. He brought my face down to his for a quick kiss, then released me. He looked out the window and swore again.

I hesitated. "Can you enter a house of God?"

He laughed. "Of course I can. I just try not to. With all of my sins, it's a wonder I'm not struck down the very moment I set foot on holy ground. I feel as though I'm tempting fate."

"We'll have our fair share of tempting fate tonight," I muttered. "No point in avoiding it now."

"As you say, Duchesse. *Alors*, shall we go in? I am yours to command tonight, *chérie*."

We approached the heavy oak doors and I stopped for a moment. Shoring up my courage, I knocked loudly. It wasn't long before the door swung open and we faced a young and somewhat rumpled-looking priest. His close-cropped brown hair stood out at odd angles and he had a shadow of whiskers on his face that badly needed a shave. He blinked blearily at us, but seeing our extravagant dress, straightened his robes and bowed.

"Madame. Monsieur. How may I assist you?"

Without waiting for an invitation, I swept past him into the nave. Candles flickered in the darkness, but it was still possible to be awestruck by the beauty and grandeur of the building.

"Do you know who I am?" I demanded of the priest, who was shutting the door behind us.

"No, Madame, I don't believe I've had the pleasure."

"I am the Duchesse de Duras. My husband and I were married here four years ago in a wedding presided over by Cardinal de Bernis."

The priest's eyes widened, and he looked at Étienne in confusion. Étienne grinned at him, showing a good deal of fang. The priest let out a noise somewhere between a squeak and a gulp. He bowed again.

"I've come here tonight to seek his help. It is a matter of grave importance and I'm afraid it is rather urgent. Would you be so kind as to direct me to him?"

The priest shook his head. "But, Madame, His Eminence is not here."

"No, I didn't expect he would be *here*. But I do expect that you'll be able to help me find him," I said, glaring at the quivering man.

"You do not understand. His Eminence has been retired for some time. He no longer resides in Paris—he is at his home in Soissons." The priest swallowed and darted his eyes over to Étienne.

"Retired," I huffed.

"Well, yes. For some time now…as I said."

Nervously, the priest shifted and wiped a droplet of sweat from his forehead. Not looking away from Étienne, he forced a laugh.

Blocking out the rest of the priest's stammering, I sat on a pew and sighed. *So much for my stroke of genius. How will I defeat the demon Asmoday now?*

Étienne sat down next to me and put his hand on my knee.

"I'm afraid we won't be able to make it all the way to Soissons tonight. Even if we could, the chances of Charlotte and Philippe being alive by the time we returned would be slim. I fear I've let them down," I said.

Étienne sighed. "It was a good idea."

The priest stepped forward, apparently taking pity on me.

"Madame, is there anything—I mean, I am certainly not as capable as His Eminence, but I am a man of God and—is there any way that I might assist you?" He produced a rosary from his pocket and toyed with the beads.

"What is your name, Monsieur?" I asked.

"Father Clarence."

"No, Father Clarence. I don't suppose you can be of assistance—unless, of course, you are somehow adept at performing exorcisms and banishing demonic entities from this earthly plain," I quipped humorlessly.

His eyes flicked to Étienne again, who growled at him.

"Not me," he said.

"No, of course not, Monsieur," he stuttered. "Well, what I mean to say is that I can, of course, perform an exorcism—it is one of the rites that we must all know, you see—but I would not dare to do such without the express permission and assistance of the Vatican. To do so would be dangerous and practically blasphemou—*erp!*"

Father Clarence's skittish ramblings abruptly ended, and I looked up to see Étienne holding him one-handed by the front of his robes. He lifted him easily until the priest's feet dangled above the ground. Eyes darkening, fangs extended, Étienne hissed an oath that made Father Clarence blanch.

"Monsieur! This is a house of God!"

"Do you think he will come home before I can separate your head from your body and drain the blood from your corpse?" Étienne thundered. Father Clarence whimpered.

"Étienne, I don't think that is necessary," I said. He ignored me.

"What happens if you perform an exorcism without the knowledge of the Vatican?" Étienne demanded. His voice was low and threatening.

"It is not done!" Father Clarence choked out. He kicked his legs futilely. "I could lose everything—be excommunicated! It could go all wrong!"

Étienne's eyes had blackened to solid pools of onyx. As I watched in horrified fascination, his handsome face started to morph into something monstrous—his gaping mouth expanded, showing off rows of needle-sharp teeth. His tongue snaked out, forked and flittering like a snake's. His cheekbones and jawline sharpened, and two horns started to protrude from his forehead. When his transformation stopped, he looked just as satanic as the pictures of Asmoday. Had I not known the man he was and admittedly enjoyed such sensual pleasure in his arms, I would have been paralyzed by fear.

"And what do you think you will lose if you do not help us now, priest?" Étienne said, his deep voice sounding like a legion of angry demons.

Father Clarence's white face wavered as if he were about to be sick. He whispered prayers and called upon saints I hadn't even heard of, until finally his eyes rolled back in his head and he passed out.

As quickly as Étienne had transformed, he snapped back to his ethereally handsome self. I glared at him, hands on my hips. He winked at me.

"Well, aren't we just full of surprises? And where was *that* when we were fighting vampire thugs in an alley?" I sniffed.

He chuckled. "Parlor tricks, Duchesse. But I do believe Father Clarence will help us now—just as soon as he comes to. In the meantime..." He shifted the limp priest over his shoulder. "I suggest we make him comfortable in your carriage and find our way to the bookshop. We're running short on time."

19

ÉTIENNE

FATHER CLARENCE ROUSED HIMSELF SHORTLY AFTER THE CARRIAGE TRUNDLED off from the abbey. I'd considered tying him up, but Daphne would hear none of it.

"He is a priest, Étienne! That would be incredibly undignified. Besides, we need his cooperation and he's already bound to be cross with us for abducting him in the middle of the night."

"Cross and confused," Father Clarence said. He rubbed his head. When he saw me sitting across from him, he paled and thrust himself back in his seat. He held his rosary up in front of him and started reciting a litany of prayers.

"Back, vile beast! Back to the depths of Hell with you!"

I arched a brow and looked to Daphne.

"Monsieur, *please*. That is uncalled for. We didn't have time for introductions back at the abbey, but may I present to you Monsieur Étienne de Noailles, vampire emissary to His Majesty," Daphne said.

I inclined my head.

"A pleasure," I said smoothly.

Father Clarence looked even more horrified. Briefly, he appeared to consider his surroundings and his options—possibly to try and make an escape. Daphne seemed to read the same from him because she tutted and lifted her gown up to her thigh, drawing forth her flintlock pistol. She held it steadily, aiming at his knee. I found her threatening self-assurance incredibly erotic.

"Father Clarence," she said in a bored, aristocratic tone. "I really am sorry for the manner and insistence upon which you were brought with us this evening, but I'm afraid I've run out of time to do things with more decorum. You say you are confused, and I aim to alleviate that. I will also promise you that you will not come to harm while you are here with us. Unfortunately, I cannot maintain that same assurance when we reach our destination. Humbly, I beg your patience while I explain everything to you."

She lowered her pistol and Father Clarence lowered his rosary. He nodded at her.

"My companion tonight has been wrongfully accused of the murder of Madame de Pompadour. We've been investigating the manner of her death for weeks and have been led to a particular establishment in *le Quartier Sanglant*. The last time we were there, we were attacked by an invisible force—a force with the voice of my husband. We found evidence of a summoning circle, as well as a copy of the *Pseudomonarchia Daemonum*. We believe someone has called forth the demon Asmoday and he is somehow tied to either the body or the soul of my husband. We need someone to perform an exorcism and banish the demon back to Hell."

"But Madame, what you ask is impossible," Father Clarence pleaded. "I cannot do it alone, and certainly not without permission from the Vatican. They require proof that these events are indeed demonic."

"I know," Daphne continued. "And under any other circumstances, we would petition the Vatican for help. But two of my friends have been taken tonight and I fear the worst. I have no more time to waste in seeking permissions. My cousin's and her husband's lives depend on our urgency."

Father Clarence's features softened. "Madame, my heart goes out to you, but I simply do not think I am qualified to be able to hold an exorcism without—"

"What will it take?" Daphne interrupted, her manner brittle and nearing panic. "Money? Or perhaps you desire something else? A title? I am friends with the king, you know. Or—what else? A lover?"

Father Clarence's mouth dropped open and he reddened in embarrassment. Seizing her moment, Daphne leaned forward.

"Is that it, Monsieur? You wish for something discreet and carnal? I will take you to bed myself, if you want."

I could not control the growl of displeasure that escaped from my chest.

"Perhaps you prefer a male companion? Monsieur de Noailles is one of the most legendary lovers in all of Paris. Do you not find him handsome, Father Clarence?" Daphne pushed forward, kneeling before him. Desperation shone in her angelic face. I wanted to break something. Father Clarence would be a start.

"Madame, please," Father Clarence shied away from her kneeling form. "I have forgone such earthly pleasures. I do not carry a price."

The carriage shuddered to a stop and I felt despair leech into Daphne. We'd arrived in *le Quartier Sanglant*. Cold and withdrawn, she sat back and opened a hidden drawer beneath her seat. She pulled out several small throwing knives, a handful of thin wooden stakes, and a small pouch of gunpowder and bullets. She started to unfasten some of her heavy petticoats and her panniers, slimming down to her silk gown. From a second hidden compartment inside the carriage, she brought forth a simple leather harness that buckled around her shoulders and beneath her breasts. In it, she stashed her throwing knives and her pistol, coolly detached from Father Clarence's and my astonishment. In her pared down Artemis costume and armaments she no longer bothered to conceal, she looked like a goddess preparing for battle.

In one final moment of despondency, I snarled and seized Father Clarence by the throat.

"Fuck the Vatican," I raged. "If you don't agree to help us, I'll kill you now and distribute your body parts to the impoverished vampires nearby."

Father Clarence quaked at my violence, but Daphne laid a hand on my arm.

"No, Étienne. Leave him be. There doesn't need to be any more unnecessary killing. This is not his fight, *mon cher*. If he cannot help us, we must face it on our own. If only there was time to get a message to The Order—"

"Wait—but The Order does not have female members," Father Clarence choked through my grip. I loosened my hold.

"What do you know of The Order?" I demanded.

"Well, I know them by reputation, as any priest does. They do the work of God where we cannot! But surely, Madame—" He eyed Daphne's leather harness full of weapons and his fear melted away. "You *are* with The Order, aren't you, Madame? Oh, I cannot believe it! You must tell me—what are they like? Since when do they allow women among their ranks? Never mind, never mind. That would be presumptuous of me to ask and I am sure you took some sort of holy vow to protect The Order's secrets. Oh! I cannot believe I am meeting a member of The Holy Order!"

His face split into a wide grin and he reached for her hand, presently curled around a small glass vial of what I guessed was holy water. Daphne cocked her brow, perplexed by his sudden change in demeanor.

"Madame, if I have offended in any way, I regretfully apologize. I will do whatever I can to aid you in your mission. I only ask that you speak well of me to your masters."

"You will help us?" I asked suspiciously. "Meaning, you will perform an unsanctioned exorcism?"

He nodded vigorously, his eyes wide and sweat condensing on his forehead. "Yes, yes. If that is what you require. I am bound to do as you ask." Father Clarence felt about his pockets and produced a small, yellowed bible and his rosary. He gestured to the vial of holy water in Daphne's hand and she tossed it to him.

"Very well, Father Clarence. I thank you for your change of heart. Étienne and I will do what we can to protect you, but understand that we face a cruel and extremely dangerous foe tonight."

Father Clarence nodded. "Asmoday."

Daphne shook her head. "I refer to my husband."

Vibrating with excitement and no small amount of fear, Father Clarence got out of the carriage. Daphne made to follow him, but I held her back.

"Are you certain about this?"

"Of course not. But we don't have a choice. I don't know what we're going to face in there, Étienne, but I would rather face it with a man of God than without," she said, frowning.

"You go in with a man of God and a beast from Hell," I said, lightly touching her cheek. She smiled and the sadness in it nearly undid me.

"You are no beast from Hell. Trust me. I know the type." She leaned forward and pressed a small, chaste kiss to my lips.

With that, we left the safety of the carriage and began our march to the bookshop.

FATHER CLARENCE BABBLED INCESSANTLY TO DAPHNE THE ENTIRE WAY TO THE *Rue des Oubliés*, asking her question after question about The Order. I rolled my eyes in annoyance. If this priest failed us tonight, I would happily drain him. Now that he knew of Daphne's allegiance to The Order, he looked at her with something like boyhood admiration. I could understand it, but it needled my irrational jealousy.

For her part, Daphne was quiet in between her terse, one-word responses to Father Clarence. Her eyes darted around, and her muscles twitched with the slightest noises, though there weren't many. Curiously, and perhaps inauspiciously, the district was silent. There were none of the customary sounds of a lively neighborhood—no raucous groups loitering around late-night taverns or brothels. In fact, I couldn't see a single lit candle or the glow of a hearth anywhere. *Le Quartier Sanglant* appeared to be deserted once again.

A couple of streets away from the bookshop, Daphne hauled up. She beckoned to Father Clarence and I and motioned for us to be quiet.

"Étienne, can you detect anything?"

I took a deep breath and reached out with my senses. I heard rats scurrying around piles of refuse and wind whispering through broken windows. I heard the heartbeats of Daphne and Father Clarence, one steady and the other racing. I smelled the grit and damp of the streets—stale blood and old sweat, sour ale, and the offal of animals and vampires. Beneath it all, there was an almost undetectable thread; silk, rosewater, fresh blood, and sulfur.

"They are here. Charlotte is, at least. I am less familiar with Philippe's scent. I'm afraid I cannot tell if she is dead or alive. There is fresh blood in the air, though it could be from the broken glass we found at the palace. I'm certain the blood is from small wounds—if there were a greater quantity, it would be a much stronger odor and a greater draw for me."

Father Clarence grimaced and crossed himself.

"Save your prayers for the exorcism, priest," I grumbled.

Daphne let out a sigh of relief. "There is still hope, then."

Father Clarence patted her arm. "There is always hope, my child."

Checking the powder and shot in her pistol, Daphne nodded and started forward again. Father Clarence followed closely behind her, now thankfully silent. I brought up the rear, pausing every few steps to listen for something—anything. As we neared the dilapidated storefront of the bookshop, the sulfur grew stronger—much stronger than it had been when we were here last. I took that to mean either Asmoday had been here more recently, or he had grown stronger since then. Possibly both.

"Be on your guard," I warned. Daphne flashed me a look that said, *Well, obviously.* Father Clarence wiped the sweat from his brow.

The shop looked exactly as it had when we'd been here the last time. I wasn't surprised. I didn't think anyone would be so foolish as to come here—except for us, of course. I stepped through the doorway and held up my hand to stay the others. I closed my eyes and listened carefully—there it was, the faint fluttering of another heartbeat.

"Someone is here," I whispered to Daphne. "But I only hear one."

Her lips tightened in a firm line. We crept forward slowly, me leading the way, followed by Father Clarence, with Daphne bringing up the rear.

This time, I picked up a small candle from a shelf and lit it, then passed it back to Father Clarence. I moved to the back room and the staircase beyond. Even with the wavering light of the candle, the darkness seemed to close in on us. Father Clarence's breaths came in shallow pants and the beads of his rosary clicked softly in his trembling hands.

The stairwell gaped before us and we began our descent.

Halfway down, I could make out Charlotte's pale skin on the floor, directly atop the pentagram. She was breathing but showed no signs of consciousness. I frantically searched the rest of the room for another presence but saw nothing. We appeared to be alone.

I hurried down the remainder of the stairs. At the bottom, Daphne caught sight of Charlotte and rushed forward, but I stopped her.

"Wait," I cautioned. "See where she lies. Remember what happened the last time."

"Charlotte!" Daphne hissed. "Charlotte, it's me, Daphne! Wake up, *chérie*."

Charlotte did not stir.

Father Clarence came forward and bent down, crossing himself again. He reached one hand out, but the moment his fingertips breached the summoning circle, the air in the cellar changed. Gusts of rank, rot-scented air swirled around us, carrying a languorous disembodied voice.

"Oh, I really wouldn't do that if I were you, Father."

I looked at Daphne, who had paled. Her features twisted in rage.

"*Henri!*" She snarled. "Or should I call you *Asmoday*?"

A deep, malicious laugh echoed off the walls.

"Very good, *ma pute*. We're a little bit of both at this point."

Father Clarence swallowed a squeak and began reciting from his bible. The laughter grew louder, drowning out the priest's prayers to a litany of saints, until he called upon Archangel Michael. Suddenly, the laughter became a roar and for a second, all was silent.

Daphne looked around wildly. She threw herself forward, reaching for Charlotte's limp arm. The moment she breached the circle, she was thrown backward with violent force.

"Daphne!" I ran to her. She was uninjured, but dazed.

Father Clarence's eyes widened, but he did not cease his prayers. The small candle shook in his hand when another gust of foul wind blew through the room. Our only light now extinguished, Father Clarence cried out in fear. Without the ability to read the correct passages, he whimpered and resorted to a furious repetition of the Lord's Prayer.

"What did I say?" the voice bellowed. "You never listened to me—never minded me. You dishonored our marriage vows then, just as you dishonor them now. Fucking that vampire! Oh, yes, *ma pute*, you think I don't know? I know *everything*. I can smell him all over you, little whore. You hear that, priest? You think I am the worst of your troubles? Turn your prayers to this sinner, you fool."

Daphne shook with fury. Her pallor brightened to a flush of anger.

"*Monster*," she spat. She fumbled in her pockets and produced another small candle and a flint. She struck at the flint unsuccessfully. The laughter resumed.

"Stupid woman. Must I do everything for you?"

At once, the room lit ablaze. Several torches along the walls glowed with a sickly yellow light, casting the cellar in a polluted incandescence. As soon as my eyes adjusted to the brightness, I saw Daphne was paralyzed in revulsion.

Across the room stood a very solid—very real—man. He had once been attractive, I thought, but now his skin stretched and bunched over his sagging flesh in an unnatural way. His clothes were stylish and expensive, and would have been impeccable if not for the splashes of blood that covered them. His face was unmarred except for the gaping black voids where his eyes should have been. He grinned cruelly at us, then adopted a tone of bored nonchalance.

"There now," the man said. "Is that better?"

"Henri." Daphne's voice broke through on a sob.

"In the flesh—well, sort of."

"What has happened to you?" Beneath Daphne's terror was a hint of pitied sadness.

"You did this to me!" Henri snarled at her. "If you'd only been a better wife, I would not have sought fulfillment elsewhere—all the way in Venice! If you'd just been compliant, I wouldn't have been driven into the arms of all those other women. I wouldn't have been there that night in Venice when *He* found me."

"When who found you?" I asked.

Henri ignored me, focusing on Daphne. "You did this to me, wife, but it's not half of what I'm going to do to you." Henri raised his hand in the air and to my horror, Daphne choked a constricted scream. Her body lifted from the ground and she clawed at her throat, losing her breath with every gasp. Henri cackled and watched her feet kick and twist midair.

Without thinking, I hurled myself at him, fangs extended, face already contorting into something monstrous. Henri saw my attack and sidestepped, but my shoulder caught him in the chest and we both went down. I heard Daphne fall to the ground and suck in air and I knew I'd temporarily hit my mark. Henri growled and shoved me with the force of ten men, throwing me into the wooden crates in the corner. I staggered up just in time to see him lunging for Daphne. With supernatural speed, I threw myself at him again, driving him against the stone wall. He grunted with the impact but recovered quickly, wrapping his hand around my throat. His grip tightened and I started to choke.

"Father Clarence!" Daphne shouted. "Help us bind the demon!"

Henri sliced his other hand through the air and Daphne shrieked and staggered back as if she'd been backhanded. Darkness began to encroach on me as I lost the ability to breathe, but as my world began to slip away, I was dimly aware of another presence joining the fray. Another man stepped out from the top of the stairwell.

"Philippe!" Daphne called. "Oh, thank God. Philippe, the demon—he has Charlotte!"

Henri tipped his face up toward Philippe and grinned savagely. When he spoke his voice lost the low, aristocratic drawl and reverted to the raspy, guttural demon tone. "At last, you're here!" he hissed with glee. "*Master.*"

20

DAPHNE

October 31, 1765
Rue des Oubliés

Master.

Henri had called Philippe *master*. Had I misheard him?

"Daphne! Are you all right?" Philippe bounded down the stairs, his eyes never leaving my face. He was still wearing his Apollo costume, minus the mask and lyre. His thin, blonde hair had come out of its queue and hung limply about his face. *I must have misheard.* There was no way Philippe was...

He reached me and grasped my shoulders. This close, I saw lines of rough scratches across his face and a cut on his lip.

"Daphne, you're certain you're uninjured? He hasn't hurt you?"

"No, I'm fine," I started, confusion preventing the pieces from coming together. "What happened to your face? Was it Henri—Asmoday? What... what are you doing here, Philippe?"

He touched the red mark on my throat from Henri's earlier attack and frowned.

"This wasn't supposed to happen," Philippe murmured, but it wasn't directed at me. He whirled around, teeth bared at Henri, who still held Étienne by the throat. I could see his eyes rolling back in his head—he was about to black out. "She wasn't supposed to be harmed!"

A look of cold resolve crossed Henri's face. When he replied, it wasn't in Henri's voice—it was the hellish growl of Asmoday.

"She was uncooperative," he said.

Uncooperative? What the Hell was going on? I looked around. Father Clarence was cowering behind the smashed wooden crates. I didn't think Philippe had even seen him.

"Daphne, my love, do not worry. We'll have this sorted out in no time." Philippe smiled at me and I wondered if there was a touch of madness in it. *My love?*

"What shall I do with the vampire?" Henri asked. Étienne was clawing at his hand, leaving deep, bloody gashes all up his arm. Henri did not seem to notice.

"Well, I think that depends on our lovely Daphne over here," Philippe said in a light tone. *Definitely mad.* "What do you think, darling? Have you gotten him out of your system? Only I don't want to kill him now and have him become a martyr for your affections. But I worry that if I let him live, you'll just go on mooning after him, and we *cannot* have that."

My mind worked, but nothing was making sense.

"Philippe, what the fuck are you talking about?"

He sighed and nodded to Henri, who dropped Étienne to the ground in a pile of limbs. Étienne gasped and coughed, and Henri stepped lightly on his chest, ready to bring his foot down and crush Étienne's heart.

"This never would have happened if you'd just done what I wanted in the first place," Philippe said. He laid a gentle hand on my cheek, but there was something tightly controlled in his eyes.

"I don't understand."

"Oh, my Daphne, don't you see? You were *always* mine. You've always been meant for me—since you first came out to society and started coming to Versailles. Don't you remember? Well, perhaps not. You always were the belle of the ball and I only ever watched from the fringes. Always there for you, my love, ready and waiting for you to notice me."

"Philippe, this cannot be. You don't know what you're saying. Has he gotten to you? Asmoday? Does he control you now, my friend?" Fear raced through my blood at these bizarre admissions. They simply couldn't be true. I would have known if Philippe had harbored feelings for me—wouldn't I?

"*My friend.* Yes, I'm afraid that's all I ever was to you. Even when you were supposed to marry me after Michel—well, I had to force your hand, didn't I? If you weren't under his protection anymore, you'd be forced to find a husband—to turn to me. I was there, Daphne! Right there. But you chose the wrong man—you chose this *thing* who abused and tortured you. For a time, I let him—you deserved it, you know, for choosing him over me—but then it just became too much."

My heart stopped at his words and a pained cry escaped my lips. "No!

You—you didn't. Oh, Philippe, tell me you didn't take my Michel from me."

He lifted a shoulder. "Well, *I* didn't kill him. I simply provided a few financial enticements to his lover to drink more than was necessary. Things just played out as they were meant to, after that."

The room started to close in on me and I fought for breath. Philippe looked at me with concern and shoved me toward one of the wooden crates. Father Clarence flinched at that, but Philippe took no notice of the priest, who was still clutching his tattered bible and rosary. As I grabbed the crate for balance, I felt the clammy hand of Father Clarence on my wrist. He slipped me the vial of holy water. I maintained eye contact with Philippe, trying not to give the priest away.

"You look so pale, darling, best sit down for a bit," Philippe said.

"I can't… I don't understand. You're married to Charlotte! You have one of the most enviable matches in the *tonne*! How can this be?" Tears sprung from my eyes as the weight of his words sank in.

"Yes, and she tried, the poor thing. But she just wasn't *you*, you know? She did allow me to remain close to you, which I'm grateful for." As if only just realizing she was in the room, Philippe tilted his head down at Charlotte's prone form. "And now she will serve an even greater purpose, bless her."

"What greater purpose?"

"She will die so that your love may live," he said triumphantly.

Unbidden, my gaze darted to Étienne. Philippe saw it and growled.

"No, Daphne. But that's a curious development." He frowned. "It used to eat me alive, you know, the fact that you didn't love me. I would lie awake at night wondering what I could do to earn your affection. After Michel, I had hoped you would turn to me, but when you didn't, I had to figure something else out. Then, along came Jeanne and her fascination with the occult! It didn't take much for me to convince her to let me into her private library—especially when she believed it was on behalf of The Order. *Mon Dieu*, but that woman could be dense. It took me ages, but I finally found what I was looking for—a power strong enough to bend your will to my own; Asmoday! A demon who rules by lust. Everything just fell into place perfectly."

"But if Jeanne helped you, why did you murder her?"

Philippe shrugged again, unaffected by the destruction he'd wrought. "Well, the first time I summoned Asmoday was in her library. She walked in on me. Summonings require some sort of sacrifice and I'm afraid Asmoday needed a bit more than blood in order to assent to help me."

Henri grinned, showing off monstrous rows of sharp teeth. Frighteningly, Philippe chuckled.

"Oh, the things he did to that poor woman before and after her death." He shook his head. "Then, of course, Asmoday informed me that he could sway your affections in my favor but that it would involve a handful of lives in order to work. What is it the English say? *In for a penny, in for a pound.* Naturally, I had to clear the way for you to become mine, so it made sense for me to remove your husband from the equation. I went all the way to Venice to track down Henri—you should truly thank me for that one. I walked in on him *in flagrante delicto*—sodomizing some unfortunate prostitute in the back room of a gaming hall. Asmoday rather liked your husband. It turns out he could withstand an abnormal amount of pain—it took him *hours* to die. Asmoday took possession of his body after that and we returned to Paris."

"If you've been after Daphne's heart this whole time, why have you been trying to kill me?" Étienne bit out.

"Truthfully, The Order did think you were Jeanne's murderer. I needed a scapegoat and you were convenient. They were more than happy to sign the death order. I'm afraid your rather liberal political views have put a target on your back. It would have been much easier if Daphne had done what The Order asked and killed you without issue. Unfortunately, you stuck around and the two of you started to become *close*. What was left for me but to deal with you, as well?"

"Asmoday never came for me," Étienne said.

"No. I didn't know how a vampire would fare against a demon. I certainly couldn't take the chance that you would win. Still, it should have been easy enough. Everyone knew your weakness for women, and I knew that quicksilver would poison a vampire. I sent Brigitte into your sister's brothel with a handsome payment and specific instructions. When she returned to me having failed her task, it was right that she would pay with her life. It was only fair."

"Philippe," I tried. "This is madness. You must know that Asmoday is using you. He will never give you what you want. He is a demon—full of lies."

Henri hissed at me. Philippe glared.

"No, darling, he *will*. Once I finish with Charlotte, I'll give him Noailles and then he'll work his magic. You *will* love me, Daphne, and we *will* be together." He shook with manic energy—his eyes bright with hysteria. I clasped the vial of holy water in one hand and frantically sought an exit. My flintlock was in my chest harness, but I didn't think I could reach it without Philippe noticing. I needed a distraction. I darted a gaze at Étienne, who watched us from beneath Henri's foot.

"Philippe, I had no idea you felt this way. Why did you never come to me yourself? Perhaps if you'd just told me of your feelings, things would have turned out differently. If only you'd spoken to me. I would certainly have chosen you instead of Henri," I said in a soothing voice. I stood and edged forward, deftly unstopping the vial in my hand.

"Hey!" Henri shouted. I froze in place. *Had he seen?* "Henri may be dead, but I still have access to his memories. That's rather unkind, Daphne."

"Silence!" Philippe yelled at him. "Do you really mean it, darling?"

I swallowed and nodded, then took another step forward. I was right in front of him.

"And what of Noailles?" Philippe asked.

I tried for casual. "He is a vampire."

Philippe's eyes narrowed and he slowly shook his head. "You must think I'm a damned fool."

Henri hissed a laugh. Dread gathered in my gut.

"It's not that easy, Daphne, but it doesn't matter, anyway. I will sacrifice Charlotte, and then when you say those words, you *will* mean them, and I *will* believe you. There's no turning back now." Philippe started to turn to Charlotte and panic propelled me forward.

I flung the holy water at Henri, praying The Order's teachings were right. It splashed across his face and he shrieked—an unholy, ear-splitting sound. Angry burns erupted on his ill-fitting skin. Étienne seized his moment and snatched at Henri's foot, wrenching it to the side with a sickening crack. Philippe turned to the noise and I reached for my pistol. *Too late.*

He whirled back to me, betrayal and rage written across his face. He backhanded me, knocking me off balance, and I lost my grip on the pistol. I tripped over the wooden crates and fell backward next to Father Clarence.

"Finish the exorcism!" I hissed. "We will keep them busy."

He nodded, his terrified eyes wide, and began shouting passages from his bible. I looked back over the crate. Henri was limping, the wounds on his face smoking, but he had otherwise recovered. He and Étienne were throwing punches and kicks in a blur of motion—his demonic strength against Étienne's vampire speed. I didn't have much time to watch, though. Philippe came for me and pulled me up by my hair. Tears stung and pain seared my scalp.

"I'm going to have you, Daphne, one way or another." He wrapped his hand around my neck and pushed me back against the wall. Holding me by my throat, he fumbled for the buttons of his breeches.

Blind rage ignited in me and I kicked at him, connecting with his shin. He swore but stayed his course, reaching for the hem of my skirts. I beat against his arms, which were surprisingly strong despite his wiry frame.

I heard a roar from the other side of the room and saw Henri stumble. Between Etienne's assault and Father Clarence's prayers, the demon was suffering. Étienne saw his opening, and hurled Henri against a wall. Henri grunted with the impact and slid to the ground. Étienne leaped over him and seized his throat, fangs bared.

Philippe, still struggling with my dress, swore in a high-pitched cry of despair. His eyes lifted to mine and I saw the full measure of his emotions. *Hate, sadness, regret, shame.* Suddenly his head jerked forward with a loud crack. He fell, slumped over. I coughed and wheezed a ragged breath, then looked up into the apoplectic visage of Charlotte. She held a large board wrested from one of the broken crates.

"Oh, Daphne!" Charlotte threw her arms around me and sobbed. "Are you okay?"

Philippe groaned at her feet.

"One moment, *chérie*," she said. She raised the board overhead and brought it down on Philippe with another violent *whump.*

"That's for hitting me and ruining the ball!" She kicked him in the stomach. "That's for murdering all those poor people!" She kicked him in the groin. "And that's for using me to get to Daphne!"

Eventually, Philippe floated away into unconsciousness. Charlotte continued to kick him, laying out sin after sin. I touched her arm and she collapsed into me, sobbing hysterically. I pulled her back to sit on the crates next to Father Clarence.

"Charlotte, if you have any God left in you, you will help Father Clarence pray," I said. I retrieved my pistol from the floor and gave it to her. "If he wakes, shoot him in the knee."

"What about the head?"

"No, *ma petite amie*. We need him alive to exonerate Étienne to The Order," I said.

Her eyes narrowed. "That's not the head I was talking about."

I managed a wry smile and made my way over to Étienne, who was covered in a thick, black liquid. Henri sputtered beneath his hands, his voice vacillating between Asmoday's and his former, human voice. There was a loose mass of flesh where his throat should have been.

"You bitch," the creature chuckled at me. "You weren't worth the blood I spilled. I'll be back on Earth before you know it. This world is filled with desperate, greedy men."

Étienne squeezed the creature's throat, and a choking, gurgling sound spewed out.

"If you harm so much as one hair on her head, I swear on Lucifer himself that I will follow you into Hell and torment you all over again."

Étienne's eyes were black as pitch and the threat in his voice frightened even me.

The creature turned its dead, empty eyes on him and laughed louder.

"Witless fool," it snarled. "She will never love you. Not in the way that you love and long for her. You will pine for her every day, just as Philippe did, except you have an eternity of misery to face without her, vampire."

A look of gut-wrenching sadness crossed Étienne's face and I knew the creature's words had struck true. *Was Étienne in love with me?* Then his face changed, the sadness replaced with cold anger. He lifted Henri's head from the ground, then smashed it back down. More black liquid sprayed forth—from the sound of the smack, I suspected Henri's skull had fractured.

Étienne glanced back at Father Clarence, who had fainted in the corner. Charlotte attempted to rouse him, but it was no use.

"How about we send this vile thing back to Hell?" Étienne said, grabbing the bible and rosary from the prone priest's hands.

I found the passage Father Clarence had been reading, whispered a silent prayer that this would work, and shouted at the top of my lungs.

"Depart, then, impious one, depart, accursed one, depart with all your deceits, for God has willed that man should be His temple!"

Henri's body lifted from the ground and a deafening roar filled the room. Just as suddenly, the body slammed back down to the ground and started to dissolve into the same viscous black liquid. The torches on the walls blew out in a rotten gust of wind and the room plunged into silent darkness.

21

ÉTIENNE

November 1, 1765
Rue des Oubliés

"Is everyone okay?" Daphne asked.

Murmured assent came from all except Philippe, who remained unconscious on the floor with several bleeding head wounds. I made my way to him and tore several strips of fabric from his absurd gold waistcoat, then used the ties to bind his hands and feet behind him.

With perfect timing, Father Clarence roused himself from the floor.

"Oh! Is it done? Is it over? Is the demon gone?" the priest queried.

"No thanks to you," I growled.

Daphne interceded before I could wring the scrawny priest's neck. "Father, if you would be so kind, please take the Comtesse de Brionne upstairs and back to my carriage. I need you to bring it here so we can move Philippe discreetly. Besides, I'm not sure how long we've been down here, and I can't chance us not making it to the carriage before dawn."

"I'm certainly not leaving you alone with *him*," Charlotte mumbled. "I cannot believe I married this monster."

"I will be fine, Charlotte. Étienne is here with me. Hurry now! I don't want to remain here a moment longer than we have to."

"Allow me," I offered, escorting Charlotte and Father Clarence up the stairs. They both clung to my arms as I navigated my way through the blackness. From the top of the landing, I could see a worrying pink blush through the open front window. A new day was upon us.

I rejoined Daphne in the cellar, and we hauled Philippe upstairs together. We sat in the bookshop, nervously aware of the uncomfortable silence that stretched between us. Finally, I could stand it no longer.

"Daphne, are you all right?"

She turned to me, but I doubted she could see much in the gloom of the shop. I, on the other hand, could see her as perfectly as in the light of day.

Her hair had tumbled out of the elaborate coiffure and her pale gown was stained with blood and filth. Her body sagged with exhaustion and her eyes glittered with unshed tears. She was staring out the window at the lightening sky, chewing on her bottom lip.

"How can I live with this?" Her voice was a whisper. "Everything that happened…all of these horrors…they were all my fault. People are dead because of me, Étienne. Charlotte's marriage is over, and her future is… I don't know if she can bear the scandal. Asmoday is gone and Philippe's capture will prove your innocence to The Order, but how much of a difference did it all make? Paris is still rife with plague and I fear for the people. If a solution isn't found—if the king doesn't do something, I believe your uprising will indeed come to pass."

I walked over and reached for her, then thought better of it and dropped my hand. Asmoday's cruel words rang through my head. She didn't need yet another man pining for her, especially after everything she'd been through. Unsure of myself, I cleared my throat.

"When I was turned, it was not by my choice," I began. "I was staying with a friend in Budapest and we went out one night—drinking, gambling, carousing. There was a beautiful woman who caught my eye and I followed her back to her home. She attacked me—bit my throat and nearly drained me. As I lay dying on the floor of her cottage, she offered me the choice; die there and face my eternal judgment, or drink from her and live forever. I could not speak. I was too weak to tell her, but I wished for death. I knew I would face demons eventually and it didn't matter that I would face them that night or a thousand nights hence. She took pity on me, though, believing someone of my roguish nature would consider an eternity of sin a blessing. She forced me to drink her blood and I became a vampire."

Daphne's tears spilled down her cheeks, but I did not reach to brush them away. I did not trust myself to touch her, fearing I would never be able to let her go.

"When I returned to Paris some time later, I'd become accustomed to my abilities, but I feared the judgment of my family and friends. I was in

Paris when my father died—not abroad, as Josephine believes. I'd come home but was too afraid to return to my old life. My father died alone while I hid myself in a basement eight blocks away. Not a day has passed that I don't regret my cowardice."

Daphne touched my arm and I stiffened. Immediately, she pulled away.

"I'm sorry," she said.

I sighed. "I tell you these things because I carried on. The things that haunt us never simply go away, Daphne, but we are made stronger as we learn to bear them. Philippe's actions are not your fault, but you will have to live with them. Lives may have been lost in the balance but think of all the lives you saved in your fight for truth; mine, Charlotte's. Hell, even Father Clarence's. The countless others who would have fallen prey to a weak man with a powerful weapon. Let that knowledge be your strength."

She considered my words and we watched the sky soften through the window.

"Étienne, what Asmoday said down there about you—about us..."

"Lies designed to provoke. Nothing more," I said, cutting her off. She nodded, but I could have sworn I saw a flash of something like disappointment in her eyes. It was gone in an instant. My heart clenched.

"I will ensure that your name is cleared of any charges within The Order," she said brusquely.

"You think they'll believe you?"

She shrugged. "I will present my case to them and request another assignment. I only hope that I can use my position to do what's right for Paris. I believe I have the power to affect some change for the better, even if it is small."

"Eradicating the vampire menace?" I said, a smile breaking through my melancholy.

She laughed. "More like...rethinking where the threats lie, seeking truth before administering justice, finding a cure for the plague and the grain blight, convincing the king to cease alienating the vampires and the bourgeoisie."

"Careful, Duchesse, lest the aristocracy hear your liberal words," I teased.

She beamed at me, eyes darting to my lips, and I would have faced a thousand demons to kiss her then. A muffled groan came from the bundle that was Philippe and I growled and kicked him. A low rumble echoed in the alley before us, heralding the arrival of the carriage. I hauled him up and slung him over my shoulder, then made a mad dash for the safety of its dark interior.

I threw Philippe on the floor and sat across from Father Clarence. Charlotte took the seat to my left and Daphne climbed in last.

"So," Charlotte said brightly. "Are we all going to recover at *Château de Champs-sur-Marne*?"

Daphne blushed. "Certainly, you are all most welcome if you wish to stay with me."

Father Clarence inclined his head. "Thank you, Madame, but I must decline. I have a congregation to attend to and a mass to prepare for. If you'd be so kind as to convey me back to the *Basilique Saint-Denis*, I would be most grateful."

Charlotte's piercing gaze bored into me. I shifted uncomfortably.

"Thank you, but I must also decline. My home is better suited to my uncommon needs."

"But the bed in the wine cellar!" Charlotte protested. Daphne elbowed her and glared.

"Hush, Charlotte!"

I cocked a brow. "You've kept the bed in the wine cellar?"

"I haven't had time to move it," Daphne defended. "I'll get around to it eventually."

My resolution to give her up wavered slightly. *Was there a reason she hadn't moved the bed?* I watched her cautiously, warming at the stubborn blush that stained her cheeks. She studiously avoided looking at me.

Quiet descended on the carriage until we reached the abbey. Father Clarence made the sign of the cross over Charlotte and Daphne, and kissed their hands. He eyed me warily, then smiled and shook my hand.

"May the Lord bless and keep you," he said as he stepped out. "Do remember me to The Order, Madame!"

Daphne promised to do so, and the carriage trundled on in silence, Daphne refusing to meet my gaze and Charlotte staring at me like a bug in a bell jar. When we neared my château, I coughed awkwardly.

"I dread the thought of leaving Philippe in your hands, Duchesse, as capable as they are. Would you permit me to hold him in custody at my own home until The Order can be informed? I assure you he will come to no other harm in my care."

Daphne's brow furrowed. "But in the daylight…"

"I have a very secure room and a number of able servants to stand guard. I would feel much better if you ladies were allowed to rest knowing that he was not under the same roof, at least until he stands before The Order."

Charlotte frowned at the unconscious man tied before us. Then, she hauled off and kicked him in the stomach again.

Seeing this, Daphne winced. "Yes, you're right, Étienne. He'd probably be safer in your care, anyway."

The carriage came to a full stop outside my home. A footman and my butler came out and helped me carry Philippe inside, taking care to avoid the early morning sunlight. As desperate as I was for Daphne, I did not spare a backward glance when I entered the hall.

I locked Philippe in a small, empty storage room in the lower level of the house. To ensure his confinement, I hefted a large bookcase in front of the door and instructed three men to stand guard at all times.

Finally able to be alone with my thoughts, I went to my room, stripped naked, and fell into a heavy, dreamless sleep.

When I awoke the next evening, it was to an exaggerated pounding on my door.

"Yes, yes—I'm awake, damn you!" I tripped out of bed and grabbed my dressing gown just as the door burst open.

My butler, Robert, stumbled in on the heels of Dr. Van Helsing, who pushed her way inside my bedchamber as if she'd been in my home a thousand times. I eyed the curvy, enigmatic doctor warily.

"Good evening, Monsieur l'Émissaire," she said with a polite curtsy.

"My apologies, Monsieur," Robert said. "The lady was most insistent that she see you immediately. She would not be detained."

I nodded and dismissed the suffering man. "Thank you, Robert. All is well. You may return to your duties."

"I am sorry to be so forceful, Monsieur, but I do have other patients to attend to." Van Helsing bustled over to my bureau and started removing a series of instruments from her reticule.

"There must be a misunderstanding, Doctor. I did not send for your services. As you can see, I'm perfectly healthy. I'm sure you are aware, but I'm able to heal from most injuries with rest and blood." I went to the wash basin and splashed some water on my face.

"Nevertheless, I have been retained with the express purpose of ensuring your physical health," Van Helsing said. "I aim to do my job to the best of my abilities."

"I don't recall offering you employ—"

She snorted a little laugh. "No, no, of course you did not! You wouldn't, would you? Now, hold out your arm, please. I need to examine your blood."

"Doctor, please. I've had a very taxing few weeks and I'm in no mood to play games. Who hired you to look after me, and to what end?" I held out my arm, anyway. Van Helsing took it and began turning it this way and that, finding a good place to draw blood.

She regarded me with an expression of pity. "Why, Madame de Duras, of course. As to what end, I'm sure I cannot say. I can only guess that she cares for you and wishes to ensure that you remain in rude health, and since I am the very best vampire doctor in all of Europe, she paid me a full year's wages to periodically drop in on you every month or so—for check-ups and the like."

"That is unnecessary," I said. "I don't need a nursemaid."

Van Helsing tutted. She poked and prodded me in what was a very thorough, and thoroughly embarrassing, examination. Unsurprisingly, she proclaimed me fit and packed up her bag with haste. As she made to leave, she handed me a vial of virgin blood.

"Just in case," she said.

"Wait. You...you said that she cares for me?" The supposition flustered me, but I didn't know why. *Of course she did.* She was a good person, and we'd become friends—of a sort. Forced proximity often had that effect on people. I knew she cared for me, but ever the narcissist, I wanted to hear Van Helsing admit it aloud.

"A great deal, I should think. My services do not come cheap, Monsieur, and she did not bat an eye at the continued cost of maintaining your well-being." She looked at me like I'd gone soft in the head. "Surely you knew all that, right?"

"Well, the Duchesse is a wealthy woman. Such sums are probably trivial to her," I reasoned.

Van Helsing laughed again, her gaze perceptive. "My, my! What a fool love has made you, Monsieur."

"It is not love," I said reflexively. "Merely infatuation. Or, at best, a friendship united by shared trauma."

"I did not examine your eyesight, Monsieur, but perhaps I should have. I did not think you were blind." Van Helsing inclined her head with a grin and promptly hurried from the room, leaving me alone with my astonishment.

22

DAPHNE

December 18, 1765
Château de Champs-sur-Marne

"*Mon Dieu*, are you really wearing that?" Charlotte gasped, referring to my plain dress. In the days since the affair in the bookshop cellar, I'd taken to wearing much more…simple attire. It wasn't that I was avoiding society at Versailles, per se, but ever since Étienne had come into my life, I found myself less and less thrilled by the glitter of the palace.

Most days I spent at home working for The Order again. Étienne's exoneration had been my first priority, and after that had been secured, I took advantage of their good favor to petition for some changes of my own. The Order had readily agreed; partly, I think, because of their embarrassment at being blind to Philippe's true motives. I'd forced my way into a leadership position—organizing missions and investigations, managing my own network of informants, occasionally donning a disguise to enjoy a little espionage on my own.

This style of dress made it so much easier and more comfortable to get around, especially without panniers. The gown was a deep, emerald green velvet, reminiscent of the color of Étienne's jacket at the garden party months ago. The memory of our first meeting sent a wave of sadness through me.

"I'm not going to court, Charlotte."

"Well, no, but don't you want to wear something with a bit more…you know…" She gestured expansively at my bodice.

"Elegance?" I finished for her.

"Cleavage," she replied.

I laughed. Despite everything that had happened, Charlotte's spirits had not suffered more than an occasional dip. Philippe had been carted off for a secret trial within The Order where the agents and other members vehemently condemned his actions and, while unwilling to sentence an aristocrat to death, stuck him in the worst of all possible places—a filthy *oubliette* in the island prison, *le Château d'If.* To avoid further embarrassment, The Order offered Charlotte a falsified death record for him, which allowed her to maintain her wealth, title, and property, as well as her reputation—and she was free to pursue any number of courtly love affairs. Most of the time, however, she could be found at my château, assisting me with my work for The Order. Once they realized what a valuable asset she could be, they had eagerly requested her participation. We'd been devising plans for a separate branch of women agents, *Les Dames Dangereuses*, or *DD* for short. Charlotte had proven herself an extremely capable co-conspirator.

So, now she was here in my bedchamber, helping me dress and get ready for one of the most nerve-wracking errands of my life.

"Are you going to invite him to your Christmas party?"

"I have an invitation ready, just in case. If it doesn't go well, he might not want to come. He might be cross with me for some reason." I chewed on my bottom lip.

"I'm sure it'll go well," she encouraged. "Unless he was offended that you sent Doctor Van Helsing to him to spy on him for the rest of the year."

"Not to spy!" I defended. "Just to, you know, look after him, make sure he's all right. Van Helsing doesn't report to me, Charlotte. I just wanted him to be safe."

"He's a vampire, Daphne. He doesn't need you mothering him," she said, rolling her eyes.

"Well, how else was I supposed to be able to sleep at night? Worrying about him constantly—always thinking about him. It's maddening! I had to give myself some peace of mind. Van Helsing's support allowed me to do just that." I fastened a strand of pearls around my neck.

Her brows lifted. "Has it? You are such a horrible liar, Daphne. The whole time since the cellar you've been moping around your château, anxiously checking for letters from him every morning, tying yourself up in knots and consequently forcing your attentions on work. If that's peace of mind, *mon Dieu*, I'd hate to see what you're like when you're distraught."

Peevishness crept into my tone. "Just what are you implying, Charlotte?"

"Implying? Nothing. Stating outright? That you're in love with the man and you're too much of a twit to go after him and tell him so."

I *tsked*. "Don't be ridiculous. I am *not* in love with him. And even if I were, it wouldn't matter because he told me himself that he does not love me."

"He did not! When was this?" She came to stand behind me, helping me with my hair.

I felt the pressure of tears behind my eyes. I squeezed them shut and swallowed.

"Back at the bookshop. Asmoday—before he was exorcised—told Étienne that I would never be able love him in the way that he wanted. I asked him about it afterward, but he brushed it off. Said it was a lie meant to provoke him."

Charlotte's eyes widened, then she broke into a fit of giggles. Irritated, I scowled at her.

"It's really not funny."

"No, no, you're right, darling. It's just—you're so oblivious! And you're the best intelligence agent in the country. It's not often you miss things, but when you do—*mon Dieu*—you really miss them!"

Anger surpassed my annoyance.

"What the Hell are you on about?" I balled my fists at my sides. Charlotte continued to cackle, until she was wiping tears from her eyes and gulping down air.

"I'm sorry, *chérie*," she sighed. "I just don't understand how you couldn't put it all together. Étienne is obviously in love with you, otherwise Asmoday would have offered up some other insult. He went for what he knew would hurt most."

"But he denied it!"

"Of course he did. We'd just battled your dead husband, a demon, and my own idiot husband who'd been murdering people across Europe to try and win your affections. I can't imagine he would have thought *then* was a good time to profess his undying love for you."

The realization slammed into me and I staggered back.

"You think Charlotte, do you really think he loves me?"

She threw me a pitying look and poured herself a large brandy from the decanter nearby.

"Please don't be dense with me, Daphne. You know he does. I suspect you've always known, you're just too stubborn to admit that you rather like the idea."

For the first time in weeks, I felt a sense of lightness. *Was it true?* If he had loved me before—did he still love me now? Had he moved on with other women? How did I truly feel about him? *Stupid question, Daphne.* The truth of it burned through me. *I was in love with him.*

Charlotte handed me her glass of brandy.

"Fortification? You appear to need something steadying."

I took the glass and downed it in one.

"So? What are you going to do about it?" she prodded. "He's still a vampire, after all."

I considered the question. It had taken me some time to accept that Michel's death was on Philippe's hands—to let go of the hatred of vampires that had sustained me through my grief and despair. But as my work with The Order took me out around the city more and more these days, I'd begun to see that Étienne had been right all along. Certainly, there were still vampires who deserved a stake through the heart, just as there were human aristocrats who deserved the same—or more, in some cases. I could no longer lay the blame at the feet of the blood plague. Evil needed to be rooted out, wherever and however it lay.

Reading my thoughts, Charlotte took the brandy glass from my trembling hands.

"Would you give it up, do you think? To be with him forever?"

The tough question. Would I—could I—give up my humanity for him? A lifetime of sunrises? The pleasures of a mortal life?

I would.

"Yes," I breathed. "Yes, Charlotte, I think I would sacrifice just about anything to be with him."

She nodded sagely. "Great love demands great sacrifice."

I blinked back the tears that welled in my eyes.

"Besides," she continued, refilling the brandy glass and sipping at it herself. "Think how much better of an agent you'll be with all those supernatural gifts!"

Would he accept me? I wasn't certain. Regardless, I had to tell him. I *would* tell him—as soon as I'd delivered my message to him from The Order. I kissed Charlotte's cheeks and ran out my bedroom door, straight into Gaston. We both crashed to the ground.

"Madame! Are you all right?" he said, helping me to my feet.

"Yes, yes. I'm sorry, Gaston. I was distracted. Were you coming to find me?"

"*Oui*, Madame. You have a visitor." He handed me a calling card. "He is waiting for you in the drawing room."

Étienne.

He is here? But I was on my way to see him! My stomach twisted. I inhaled shakily and straightened my dress.

"Thank you, Gaston."

I went downstairs and entered the drawing room. He stood at the fire-place, staring down into the flames. I hadn't seen him since All Hallow's Eve and my heart leaped at the sight. He was as uncommonly beautiful as I remembered—wavy black hair tied back, chiseled features, lean, muscular body wrapped in gilt-embroidered navy wool. His full lips were curved in a private smile that vanished when he saw me.

"Duchesse." He bowed formally and my chest tightened. His manner had me rattled.

I inclined my head. "I was on my way to you with a message from The Order, but I see you beat me to the punch. To what do I owe the pleasure of your visit, Monsieur?"

He coughed and fidgeted with his cuff. It comforted me that he, too, appeared to be nervous.

"Shall I call for some tea?" I offered. "Or perhaps something stronger?" I gestured to the sideboard with crystal decanters of brandy, sherry, and whisky.

"No, thank you. I…I came to call on you to…thank you for Doctor Van Helsing's care. And to, you know, see how you fared."

"Of course," I said. "I hope I didn't overstep. I mean, I'm sure I did, but I was worried about you and I wanted to ensure that you had access to the best possible care. I…I'm sorry. Thinking on it, it was probably quite overbearing. I should have asked." *Stop babbling, Daphne!* Awash with anxiety, I sat on the small couch across from the fireplace. I pulled a cushion onto my lap and toyed with the tassels.

"No, it was kind of you, really." He gestured to the empty space next to me and I nodded. He sat, maintaining an even distance from me.

"And how do you fare, Monsieur? Are you well?"

"Yes, of course, quite well. I saw Josephine recently. She sends her regards."

Warmth filled me at the thought of his resourceful, plucky sister. I smiled. "Ah. Yes. I hope she's well, too."

He nodded. An awkward silence settled between us.

This was interminable.

"I have been working with The Order quite a bit," I blurted suddenly —and a touch loudly. I winced, but carried on. "That's why I was coming to see you. I'm trying to get a task force together to work with the vampires—looking for a cure, discussing their rights and grievances… trying to prevent that revolution you're always on about. So far, The Order isn't entirely on board; neither are the nobility, for that matter. I could use your help."

"My help?" he repeated, looking stunned. "Yes, of course. You've taken up my cause?"

I nodded. "Oh, and Charlotte has joined, as well. We have been designing missions for other members. We're forming a group of primarily women agents. It's been quite thrilling."

"How is Charlotte? Well, I hope?" A pained smile crossed his face.

"Yes, quite well, now that everything's settled with her estate."

"Good. Good."

"Yes, it is good, isn't it?"

The clock on the mantle chimed nine o'clock. The fire crackled in the hearth. I was going to die of discomfort. *Tell him, Daphne. Tell him you're in love with him. Tell him you want to be his forever.*

Étienne studied me, his hazel eyes glittering like gold coins. He seemed to relax a fraction, then offered me the first genuine smile I'd seen all evening. The smile broke into a warm chuckle that turned into a full-throated laugh. I giggled along with him.

"It's bad, isn't it?" I sighed. "The tension between us."

"Yes," he smiled. "But I don't know why it should be." He took my hand in his and our eyes met. "I miss you, Daphne."

"You do?" I said somewhat breathlessly. "Why have you stayed away so long?" *Have you found another woman?*

"I wanted to give you a respectful distance after everything. For a time, I convinced myself that you would want to be rid of me—that there was nothing left for us. Our conversation at Versailles that night felt so final, I convinced myself that I'd have to let you go. That you deserved a long, happy, mortal life—a life without me. But I don't know if I can accept that, unless you tell me otherwise. If you say so, Daphne, I swear I'll leave you alone and never darken your doorstep again. But if there's hope—if you feel differently… I came here tonight to…to…"

"To find out?"

He nodded, his handsome face a study in angst. Desire gathered in me. *He was mine.*

"Shall we see, then?" I breathed. I didn't wait for him to respond, or for the confusion to fall from his face. I leaned forward and set my lips to his.

He melted into me immediately, returning the kiss with the full force of his passion. He brought his hands up to my head, lacing his fingers into my hair as he had before. Pins scattered across the couch and the floor. He sucked my lower lip into his mouth and stroked it with his tongue. Lust stormed through me, setting my skin ablaze, tightening my nipples, and heating my core. I bent over him, pushing him back against the cushions. He moaned against me at the feel of our bodies pressing against each other.

"God, Daphne," he growled, breaking away to drop tiny kisses along my jaw. "How I've missed you. You don't know how much. You're all I can think about. It makes every day without you feel like a hundred years." His fingers found the buttons of my bodice and he frantically tried to undo them, seeking the feel of my bare skin.

"Why the Hell do all your gowns have so many damn buttons?" On an oath, he wrenched the fabric in two, sending buttons flying in all directions.

"Étienne! I liked that dress," I protested. He dropped his head to tug one of my nipples into his mouth, and the dress was forgotten. I ground my hips against him, loving the feel of his arousal beneath my legs. He sucked in a breath.

"I missed you, Étienne. I was so worried that you didn't care for me, or that you'd found another lover since we—*Oh, yes, right there!* I cannot go back to my life the way it was, the way *I* was, before you. You were right about me—about everything. I don't want to be without you, Étienne." I fumbled with the buttons on his breeches and he reached for the hem of my skirts, lifting them up to my thighs. When he pushed them up to bare my sex, he bit back a groan.

"Perfection," he breathed, sliding a finger through my damp heat. He circled the bud of my pleasure and I cried out. "You're so wet—so ready for me. So responsive to my touch. It's one of the things I love most about you, darling. I'm afraid this won't last as long as I'd like. It's been a while since—"

I grasped his hard length and he huffed in torment.

"Drink from me," I murmured.

"What?" he gasped, growing harder in my hand. "Darling, no. I will not just use you for blood."

"I want to be yours, Étienne, completely. I want to be yours forever."

His eyes snapped open and found mine in the firelight.

"Daphne," he said, placing a hand on me to stop my explorations of his body. "You don't mean that. I can't ask you to give up your mortality, not for me. I don't deserve such a sacrifice."

"I'm in love with you," I blurted.

For a moment, we remained frozen. He stared at me, eyes wide. Panic started to build while I waited for him to respond.

"Étienne?"

His lips broke into a wide, beautiful smile and his eyes shimmered with emotion.

"Daphne, I've loved you since the very moment you tried to kill me and I'm going to love you until one or both of us is dust."

I bent to kiss him, shutting my eyes against the threatening tears. I slid my tongue into his mouth, gently testing the sharpness of his fangs. He slid his hands up my thighs and I sighed into him, stroking his hardness until he threw his head back with a guttural curse.

"*Putain de merde*, Daphne, that feels—"

I stroked him again, firmer this time. His eyes squeezed shut again and he whimpered.

"Daphne, please, you're killing me. I'm going to—"

I straddled him, shifting slightly to position him just at my entrance.

"Tell me again," I demanded. Once more, his gaze flew to mine. That devastating smile again. He let out a breath so deep, it seemed he had been holding it since he first arrived.

"I love you, Duchesse. In fact, I'm really quite mad for you."

I laughed and slid him inside me. He cursed a litany of smut that rushed through me. He pushed me back down on the couch, driving into me with fire. My pleasure built to its breaking point and Étienne sensed it. He reached between us and pressed his fingertip against my bud.

He pulled out and ducked between my legs, setting his tongue and fingers to work. In moments, I began to see stars. When I came apart, I felt his teeth on my thigh—a momentary prick of pain, and then another tidal wave of pleasure, unlike anything I'd ever experienced before. He moaned helplessly against my thigh, gently sucking while I twined my fingers in his hair. Too soon, he stopped, and I mourned the loss of his warm, wet lips.

"You are, without a doubt, the most delicious thing I've ever had," he grinned.

He collapsed above me and rolled off the couch, bringing me down to the floor with him. He wrapped his arms around me and nuzzled my neck.

"My love," he said again. His smile would have made angels weep.

We lay there for a few moments, temporarily sated.

"So," I hedged, breaking the silence. "Is that the only reason you came here tonight?"

Étienne kissed my temple and adjusted his clothing. He reached into his pocket and produced a small box. I gasped.

"It's not what you think," he said hurriedly. "That is—I visited Georges the jeweler after we questioned him. He didn't have any real information for me about the murders. He could not find Jeanne's ring, for obvious reasons." He chuckled. "He was incredibly worried about how you'd respond to his failure. I told him you'd changed your mind, and that I was there to acquire something else on your behalf."

I opened the box to find an exquisite amethyst and diamond choker. It sparkled in the glow of the fire and I blinked back tears.

"Étienne, it's beautiful. You didn't have to—I don't deserve—" He silenced me with a kiss.

"Yes, you do. I came here tonight to ask for your forgiveness—to tell you that I can't help myself. You're worth someone ten times the man that I am, but I'm too selfish to let that man come along and take you from me. If you let me, Daphne, I swear I'll endeavor every single day to deserve you."

Tears rolled down my cheeks and I kissed him again—this time slower and more gently.

"No, Étienne. I was wrong about so many things. I thought the world was divided into light and dark, but then you came along and showed me otherwise. If anything, I should be the one proving myself to you."

Étienne tightened his hold on me. "You have nothing to prove to me, but I'd be lying if I said I didn't want to hear it again."

I sat up and tugged at the rest of his clothes, eager to have his sculpted, naked body beneath me again.

"I could *tell* you," I teased. "But perhaps I should just *show* you instead."

He laughed, low and seductive. "Nymph and goddess no longer," he said.

"No?" I slipped out of my skirts and chemise, baring myself to him. "Then what am I now?"

A heady possessiveness that heated me all over again flashed in his gaze and he smiled.

"*Mine.*"

EPILOGUE
CHARLOTTE

October 31, 1767
Palace of Versailles

I watched Daphne and Étienne twirl around the ballroom, their eyes never straying from one another. Daphne—newly-turned vampire and soon to be the Duchesse de Noailles, thanks to Étienne's newly bestowed title—was still the main topic of courtly conversation tonight. As the first titled woman to willingly succumb to the blood plague, she had shocked the court to a dangerous degree, but had weathered their disapproval with grace and aplomb. While her decision to ally herself with the supernatural set pushed her firmly to the fringes of the *tonne*, she didn't seem to mind in the least. I wondered if Daphne had even *noticed*, honestly, considering how starry-eyed and in love my cousin seemed to be.

To both Daphne's and my surprise, the Order had handled the news of her turning with eager anticipation. As I'd suspected, her increased stealth, strength, and speed were extremely beneficial for her work with the organization, and Daphne's progressive influence on the attitudes of the upper circle had started to turn a few minds to her new vampire rights cause—gradually, but with conviction. The Order seemed to be undergoing a change of nature, as well, or so I hoped.

The *allemande* ended, and the band struck up a lively *minuet*. All the couples on the dance floor—save for Daphne and Étienne—changed partners and began anew. Unsurprisingly, they had enjoyed a scandalous courtship, even by Versailles standards, and they'd eschewed propriety yet again by attending this year's All Hallow's Eve masquerade in matching Persephone and Hades costumes.

Really, I thought with a smile. *Can't they keep their affections to themselves for an evening?*

The dance ended and I watched them kiss, oblivious to the whispers around them.

I didn't bother to hide my grimace. I was happy for them, truly, especially after everything they'd been through, but it didn't stop the pang of envy that shot through me. I thought I'd had love once. Well, not love, really, but at least affection. The lovers I'd had after Philippe's imprisonment had all been temporarily satisfactory but had proved wanting in the end. Observing Daphne and Étienne on the dance floor now made me realize that the thing I'd been missing—the thing I'd been longing for— was a love of my own. A love like Daphne and Étienne's, a love that would defy the laws of nature and humanity and…well, any other laws.

Sadly, as I looked around the luminous ballroom, I reasoned I wasn't likely to find a love like that within the walls of Versailles. That was fine. Really, it was. I had my duties to the DD to occupy my mind and my time.

Speaking of which, I should really get back to work. My target tonight made Philippe's crimes look like child's play, and I was determined to see him brought to justice. Multiple counts of rape and abuse—including children —had been levied against him, and the DD had gathered enough evidence to warrant action from The Order. I was that action. I saw Daphne flick her fan twice in my direction—the signal that my target had arrived.

I climbed down from the perch in the beech tree from which I'd been surveying the ball, grateful for the freedom that my costume allowed. I certainly didn't enjoy donning men's attire as often as Daphne did, but one had to admit, breeches did make it easier to skulk around in the dark. Initially, I was disappointed that I wouldn't get to attend the masquerade in an outrageously expensive gown, but once I'd received the details of my assignment, I'd sort of come around to my Cupid costume.

I brushed the dirt from my toga, adjusted my mask and wig, and sauntered into the hall through the open glass doors. It didn't take me long to find my target in the crush of people—the Marquis de Sade stood out like a sore thumb. I wound my way around the edges of the ballroom, making my way to the vile man. He was dressed as a wolf—something that felt uniquely perverse to me, given all the innocents he'd preyed upon. I approached him with a glass of champagne in hand.

"Monsieur," I said, lowering my voice in what I hoped was a masculine timbre. "You look like you could use a drink."

The marquis eyed me appreciatively. "Most gracious of you, dear boy. Have we been introduced?"

I smiled shyly. "No, Monsieur. But I am most anxious to remedy that. My name is Latour."

"Latour. I am Donatien." Sade's eyelids began to droop—a sure sign that the sedative I'd slipped him was already beginning to take effect.

"Donatien," I said, taking his arm. "Might we find a quiet place to better get acquainted? I find these ballrooms can be *most* stifling, don't you?"

Sade blinked slowly and murmured his assent, allowing me to steer him outside toward the hedge maze. Out of nowhere, Daphne intercepted me, shoving a square of parchment into my hand. As quickly as she'd been there, Daphne melted away into the crowd. I pulled the marquis hurriedly through the garden and darted a look at the note.

Someone else has been watching the target. Étienne spotted him and is on his trail. Guard yourself well!

"*Merde,*" I swore.

"What's that, Latour?" Sade tripped over his feet and I almost fell. "*Mon Dieu,* I *do* feel peculiar… Where are we going, my friend?"

I reached the hedge maze and thrust him forward. "How about a little game, Monsieur? I'm sure you'd enjoy that. I know how fond you are of games."

Sade chuckled and mumbled something unintelligible. I made a left, a right, then two more lefts inside the labyrinth until I was absolutely certain we were alone.

"All out here on our own, are we?" Sade slurred. He began to pluck at the falls of his breeches, unsuccessfully attempting to remove them. "Come on, then, boy, let's play that game of yours…"

I unclasped the thick black cord from my neck that would serve as my garrote, but before I could pounce on the man, I heard a high-pitched whistling, followed by a soft thump, and then a groaning wheeze. Sade collapsed forward on top of me and we crashed to the ground. I shoved the marquis off me and swallowed a scream—protruding from his chest was a long, thin arrow shaft. Blood seeped out from the wound, staining his brown velvet waistcoat.

Panicked, I ducked down behind one of the bushes and cast my gaze around wildly. *Where did the arrow come from? Who else is here? Who else wants Sade dead?*

I waited long minutes for any other sound but heard nothing. Satisfied that I probably wasn't in any danger—the arrow could have hit us both, but it hadn't—I crawled forward to check Sade's pulse. The arrow, it seemed, had pierced his heart. *He is dead.*

Suddenly, I heard a crashing noise behind me. Before I could escape, a man tumbled out of the bushes and stood over me, a crossbow raised to my chest. A long, black cloak obscured his face and his form, giving him an air of menace.

"Do not move, boy," came a voice from beneath the hood. "Or I shall kill you, as well."

Irrational anger replaced my fear. I stood, throwing my shoulders back and finding my haughtiest aristocratic tone.

"Who the Hell do you think you are?" I snarled. "Do you realize what you've just done?"

The man threw back his hood and glared at me. My jaw dropped open. He was the most beautiful man I'd ever seen. He didn't have the dark, seductive beauty of Étienne, but rather a rugged self-possession that bordered on dangerous. Waves of chestnut hair fell across his face, mussed from wearing his hood. Dark slashes of brows and long, gossamer lashes set off vibrant green eyes. His strong jaw hadn't seen a shave in several days, his nose had been broken and reset at least once, and he carried a thin, crescent-shaped scar from his brow to his cheek. I felt my knees wobble a bit when the man sneered at me, his full lips drawing back to reveal a set of perfect white teeth.

"Ungrateful fop," he hissed. "I just saved your life. Don't you know who this man is? He eats young lads like you for breakfast."

Finally coming to my senses, I remembered my disguise and pitched my voice low again, growling at him in fury. "He was *mine*. You have no idea what you've done."

Disgust twisted the man's face. "Yours? Well, I'm certain you'll be able to find another demon to entertain your desires. Now, if you'll excuse me, I'll be off. I don't want to be around when the guards find his body."

I couldn't help it; I snickered at the man's choice of words—a demon to entertain—*oh, if he only knew*. My irritation returned, however, when the man turned to leave out the back gate.

"So, you're just going to leave me here to clean up your mess? I don't think so! I had my own plans for dispensing with the body, but since you were so insistent that he be *your* kill, you deal with it."

The man cocked his head in confusion. "Dispensing with the body? Wait—are you… You were not his lover?"

I threw my head back and laughed. "Certainly not! I was here to see that he pays for his crimes. I had everything worked out until *you* arrived and mucked it all up. How am I supposed to explain an arrow to the chest, then? I can't, you idiot! If only you'd let me finish my job and strangle him properly, it would have been easily made to look like an accident. But no! Typical man, running into a situation without thinking it through and then leaving me to clean up. Well, not this time, Monsieur!"

"Wait—your job? 'Made to look like an accident?' What are you talking about, boy? Are you well?" He looked at me like I was mad.

"Yes, yes, and yes. Don't you know? He was particularly fond of throttling during sex. We have numerous statements testifying to that. One small slip and, oops! *Quel terrible accident!* No one would be the wiser."

I glared at the man, beyond irritated that he'd ruined my assignment and my evening, and had so unsettled me that I'd muttered on about my plot to kill the marquis. *Hopefully he's too thick-headed to pay much attention to me. Still, it's probably best to make use of this disguise and let him think I'm some mad dandy.*

I took in the man's impressive stature and form—purely to see what I was dealing with, of course, and not because I enjoyed looking at him—and reasoned he must be the man that Daphne and Étienne had gotten wind of, but that begged a much bigger question.

Who was he?

THE MAN

I CONTINUED TO STARE, TRYING TO MAKE SENSE OF THE LAD'S MUTTERINGS. Who was this fop? In the gloom of the hedge maze, all I could see was a small, lean figure clad in some kind of ridiculous Roman costume; a pleated silk toga, small, feathered wings, and a bow with a quiver of arrows. A wreath of golden flowers and hearts sat atop a queue of short brown hair. The lad had a sweet enough face—big brown eyes, mink-like lashes, rosy cheeks, and a cupid's bow smile—but that could have been the beauty of youth. Was he a bit off in the head? What was he doing out here? Was the boy a guest of the masquerade? Was he one of Sade's men?

I shuddered at the thought. If he was with Sade, he would need protection. I started to say so when we heard the crunch of footsteps along the gravel path.

Someone else is coming!

We could not be discovered here with the dead marquis—especially with the young man and his quiver of arrows. I swallowed an oath. I should have been more careful. If I didn't act now, the boy would likely be blamed for the marquis's death. *I cannot have another death on my hands.* I did the only thing I could think to do. I whacked the boy on the back of the head with my crossbow, knocking him out. I slung the boy's body over my shoulder—quite a sturdy young thing—and snuck back through the bushes to the drainage grate in the wall. Once I was through the wall, I picked up my pace, not bothering to stop when I heard the pair of voices discover the body of the dead marquis.

"*Mon Dieu, Étienne!* An arrow? It's not one of hers, is it? Where is she? What do you think happened?"

"I don't know, Daphne, but I smell someone else here. I think—I think she's been taken."

To be continued in book two of the *Vampires in Versailles* series, *The Agent and the Outlaw*

FEMME BRÛLÉE
A VAMPIRES IN VERSAILLES STORY

AUTHOR'S NOTE

This short story was originally published in a holiday-themed charity anthology some years ago. The events take place after the end of the first book, but before the epilogue that leads to Charlotte's book.

1

DAPHNE

December 22, 1765
Château de Maintenon

"Duchesse, you are absolutely forbidden to leave until I am done with you."

The languid words slid out from beneath a tangled pile of bed linens and pillows in the darkness.

I arched a brow. Even though the room was black as pitch, I knew he would be able to see my haughty expression. "You think you can command me to do as you wish, Monsieur?"

I'd managed to get half-dressed—in the dark with *no* lady's maid, I might add—before waking him, or so I thought.

I heard the grin in his voice when he uttered the short word. "Yes."

Before I could blink, I was naked again, wrapped up in iron-strong arms and the rumpled sheets from our evening of lovemaking. That was what it was like being engaged to a vampire—it made one glad to be on the right side of all that supernatural strength and speed. *And hunger.*

"You thought to sneak out of here while I slept, didn't you?" Étienne murmured, sowing kisses along the curve of my ear. "How many times must I tell you? There's no sneaking around me. I will *always* hear you. *And* see you. *And* smell you." He punctuated his last words with a deep inhale at the crook of my neck that ended in a satisfied little growl.

I sighed. "Well, you were sleeping like the dead—"

"I *am* dead," he chuckled.

"—and I have too much to do today," I finished, ignoring his quip. "I don't know what time it is, but I'm certain it's late. Or early. The point is, I cannot lounge around in bed with you all day. I have a Christmas Eve party to finish planning and a summons from The Order that I cannot ignore."

"You've only been here a few hours," Étienne said.

"Ha!"

"The sun isn't even up yet," he drawled. "You have *ages* of time before you have to leave," he pleaded, pressing his finely sculpted body against mine.

I laughed. "I arrived here at midnight. I'm certain it's long past sunrise."

"Perhaps you are right..." Cool fingers caressed my skin, sending shivers dancing along my body. "Perhaps I am deliberately misleading you to get what I want."

"That's no way to talk to your future wife," I retorted, a bit breathlessly.

"That's *exactly* how I should talk to my future wife," Étienne said lazily as his hands firmly grasped my bottom. I squealed and rolled away from him—if we kept up this playful banter, it would be another several sweat-soaked hours before I'd be able to drag myself away from his embrace.

Étienne sighed dramatically. "If you must, you must. Though you know I've also been summoned by The Order. Why don't we go together? We could make an evening of it—a midnight stroll through the *Jardin du Roi*, a stop at that late night *pâtisserie* for something sweet for you and then a *romantic* assignation with a cabal of dangerous men who will probably charge me with crimes against humanity and the crown and then assign you to kill me again. What do you think, pet?"

"We've already been through that, *pet*. Besides, I told you that they've changed their tune. Now, instead of systematically eliminating those poor souls suffering from the blood plague, they've agreed to try and help the vampires integrate with the remaining uninfected in France. And as the vampire emissary to the king, you're their most important ally for the cause. I wouldn't let a little thing like attempted murder get in the way of such a promising future."

Étienne chuckled again. "Well, I suppose if you put it like that...I wouldn't want to disappoint the most powerful duchesse of the *tonne*."

"Powerful? *Quelle romance!* Is that all you think of me?" I teased, lacing up my stays. Instantly, he was behind me, tugging at the ribbons again.

"Powerful, elegant, striking, quick—"

"All things that could be said of a horse."

"Only the most *exceptional* horse."

At that, I threw an elbow into his gut and smiled at the pained grunt and ensuing laughter that spilled forth. He nipped at my neck and turned away to light a candle so I could better dress.

"You still don't trust The Order after all that's happened?" I asked. "Even with my new...*position.*"

He cocked a dark brow at me. "No offense, darling, but you'd have a hard time trusting anyone who'd ordered your assassination at least three times in the last several years."

He had a point.

"Perhaps. Though if The Order hadn't mistakenly blamed you for Madame de Pompadour's death and despised your liberal vampire rights views, they'd never have sent me to stake you, and I wouldn't be sharing your bed today," I smiled.

Étienne cinched a velvet dressing gown around his waist and winked at me. "Don't be ridiculous," he mocked. "It would have only been a matter of time before I'd convinced you to abandon your entire life's work, upright principles, and unwavering desire for revenge to throw yourself at my carnal mercies."

I meant to laugh delicately, but it came out in an unladylike guffaw with a sardonic roll of my eyes. Étienne pretended offense.

"*Chérie,* please! My fragile ego! If you do not cease being horrible to me, I won't come to your Christmas Eve *réveillon.* You'll be left to entertain an entire party of snobbish, entitled aristocrats all by yourself."

"You wouldn't dare!" I challenged.

"I might reconsider...if you get back in this bed with me right now."

I gave him a quick peck on the cheek. "Much as I'd like to, *mon amour,* I really must be off."

"Very well. The consequences will be on your own head then," he said with a smirk.

"Threaten all you like, Étienne," I smiled at him mischievously. "By the way, I invited your sisters."

Étienne stilled, panic creeping into his face. All of his former mirth vanished.

"Daphne, you didn't."

"I certainly did. Christmas is a time for family."

"Yes, but not everyone's family is made up of Paris's better-known prostitutes. This is an awful idea, Daphne—you don't understand what you're risking by having them here with half of Versailles. You're paving your own road to ruin!" Étienne grasped my arms and stared hard into my eyes, his golden hazel irises sparkling in the candlelight. "I'm serious. You can't just expect the *tonne* to happily mingle with ladies of the night over champagne and hors d'oeuvres. The scandal could jeopardize your influence with King Louis *and* The Order."

I finished dressing and pinned my hair up under my lace cap.

"And they say women are the emotional sex," I tutted. "Étienne, one of the hard lessons I learned over the last few years is that it doesn't matter to me what the *tonne* thinks. I spent enough time being married to —and *widowed* from—*le Duc Dépravé* that I know rumors will circulate regardless of their veracity. Despite being trained from birth to be the most accomplished duchesse in court, I was a scandal soon after my debut. My brother was a scandal. My cousin Charlotte is a scandal. And you, my darling, are the vampire son of a disgraced vicomte and possibly the biggest scandal of all. Your sisters attending a Christmas Eve *réveillon* at my château would probably be the tamest thing any of us do this year."

Étienne scowled at me and crossed his arms over his chest. My stomach fluttered at the way his lean muscles bunched beneath the dressing gown. He really was a beautiful sort of rake.

"I won't be responsible for their behavior," he grumbled.

"You don't need to be," I finally admitted with a laugh. "They have a prior engagement and sent their regrets that they could not attend."

Étienne gave me a dark look and threw a pillow at me. "You torturous minx," he growled, and pulled me in for a passionate kiss.

"Get some rest today, *chéri*," I said. "I'll see you this evening."

"One last question before you leave," he said, putting his hand on my arm.

"If it's about The Order summoning you, I truly have no idea what it's about," I said earnestly. "But I did manage to send them a message stating you were willing and able to assist them with the other vampires. Perhaps it's to do with that."

He nodded and smiled at me, but I sensed the trepidation behind his eyes.

"If it's anything else, I promise I'll do everything in my power to protect you," I added.

"Imagine that," he mused. "One of the *tonne*'s most talked-about duchesses swearing to protect a *filthy sanguisuge* from harm."

"Will wonders never cease?" I grinned and turned to leave.

"*Au revoir, chérie*," he called after me.

I blew him one final kiss and left his bedchamber. Unsurprisingly, his butler, Robert, waited for me in the hallway. Despite being human, I would have sworn the loyal servant possessed supernatural abilities, as well. He seemed to have a sixth sense for anticipating the needs of his master.

"Your Grace," he bowed, handing me my thick fur-lined cloak and muff.

"*Merci,* Robert," I said. "Do you happen to know what time it is?"

"Just after seven o'clock."

He led me through the winding hallways in the below-ground apartments—a recent addition to Étienne's family château. Entering the main foyer at the top of the stairs, I saw the golden light of sunrise spilling across the marble floor.

"Do be careful on the steps," Robert said. "Last night's snow has frozen over, and everything is quite icy this morning."

"I will. Thank you, Robert."

I bundled up and braced myself for the cold of late December. Leaving the warmth of Étienne's château was as dreary as leaving his embrace. I picked my way through the piles of snow and patches of ice toward my waiting carriage and was grateful for the small warming pan the driver had tucked between the blankets on the seat. This winter seemed harsher than any in my memory, as though nature itself was fighting against the people of France—not hard to imagine, given the rampant spread of the blood plague turning common folk into vampires. Étienne and I had seen the truth of it a few months prior during a murder investigation that had brought us together in fierce—and what would soon be eternal—love.

The carriage pulled up to my estate, and I hurried inside, immediately calling for a pot of hot coffee and sizable breakfast to be sent up to the library, where I preferred to work during the day. Being engaged to Étienne meant he fed on me exclusively, and as happy as I was to feel that connection with him, it left me absolutely ravenous after our evenings together.

"Oh, *there* you are! It's about time you got back. I've been reading through this latest intelligence report and *mon Dieu,* it's an absolute scorcher. I mean, it was a stroke of genius to recruit several of the women from the *Maison des Nymphes* as intelligence agents for *Les Dames Dangereuses,* but this report reads like an erotic novel, and I have a hard time believing the other members of The Order will appreciate it as much as I do."

Charlotte, Comtesse de Brionne, bustled over to me with a sheaf of papers in her hand. The glossy brown curls that bounced around her face were much like her demeanor: exceptionally vivacious and impossible to tame. Not only was she the most brilliant and capable agent, but as my cousin, she was also the only other member of the Order who I trusted without reservation.

"Charlotte, how long have you been working? Were you at this all night?"

"All night? What time is it?"

She blinked at me and whirled around, only just noticing the morning sunlight streaming in the library windows.

"*Merde,*" she swore. "I only meant to stay until midnight. It's entirely your fault for staying out and enjoying endless hours of passionate love-making while I stay here and toil like some sort of...*toiler.*"

I laughed. "The report will have to wait. I've got to finish preparing for the Christmas Eve *réveillon,* and I've been summoned before The Order later this evening. As has Étienne," I added. I fidgeted with diamond and amethyst choker at my throat—a gift from him that I treasured above all my other jewels.

"You're nervous," Charlotte said, studying me. "Why? Do you think the Order has changed their minds about him? They can hardly go after him now—not with his recent efforts and the commendation of the king."

"No. I don't know. I don't think it will be *bad* news, exactly. It's just... with The Order, it's never *good* news, either."

"True. *Dieu,* Daphne, you don't think it has something to do with your party, do you? Surely, they won't make you cancel it, will they? I mean, I know you invited Étienne's sisters, but they're not even coming. And everyone knows that a scandalous guest list always makes for the most interesting dinner party."

"I don't know, Charlotte. I suppose we'll have to wait and see. I'm sure you're right. Everything will be fine," I replied, with a lot more confidence than I felt.

Later that evening, I stood in front of the mirror, considering my outfit. It had taken me ages to decide what to wear in front of The Order, but I was satisfied with my choice. The gown of deep purple velvet was thick enough to keep me warm in the snowy December night, simple enough to be practical in case there were any *physical* demands, but luxurious enough to convey a sense of power in the instance I needed to exert influence on Étienne's behalf. It was understated, elegant, and dangerous in its message—*do not cross me.*

My lady's maid, Eve, finished pinning my hair in an extravagant *coiffure* powdered with silver and decked with pearls. Lastly, I fastened a simple black domino mask over my face. As the first woman member of The Order and the leader of the faction of female agents—the DD—the mask was a mere formality. Everyone inside knew who I was, though the disguise would grant me a modicum of anonymity from any other aristocrats who chanced upon me sneaking through Paris to the underground tunnels beneath the city.

I had just made my way downstairs when Étienne arrived, clad in slate-colored silk and looking like the devil himself come to tempt me. He grinned wolfishly as I approached.

"You look as dangerous as you do delicious," he said with a quick kiss. "Shall we, Duchesse?"

I nodded, ignoring the flutter of nerves in my stomach.

"After you, *chéri.*"

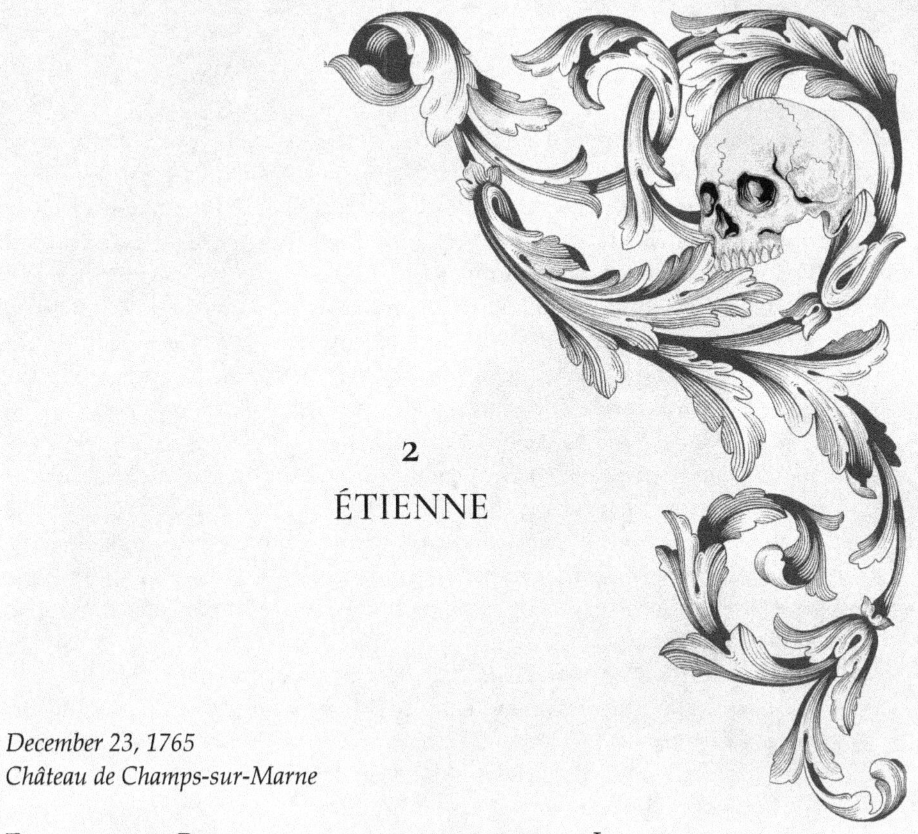

2

ÉTIENNE

December 23, 1765
Château de Champs-sur-Marne

THE STREETS OF PARIS WERE QUIETER THAN USUAL, BUT I SUSPECTED IT WAS A result of the dropping temperature and thick blanket of snow insulating the city. Daphne had tried to convince me it was because a frigid pall had settled over France after the arrival of the blood plague, but I had my doubts. I studied her in the darkness of the carriage—lips drawn in a tight line, brows narrowed, distracted violet gaze focused on some fixed point on the horizon.

"This is my first time in front of The Order," I said quietly. "I'm not sure what to expect. Are you always so nervous when you're summoned?"

"I'm not nervous," Daphne argued.

I scoffed.

"I'm not," she insisted. "I'm simply…on my guard. And yes. I'm always on my guard when I'm summoned."

Inwardly, I winced. That didn't fill me with confidence. Daphne seemed to notice my anxious manner and placed a reassuring hand on my knee. My stomach fluttered, as it did every time she touched me.

The carriage ride seemed interminably long, but we arrived at the grim locale within the hour. It was a forgotten cemetery on the outskirts of the city. If the pristine, undisturbed layer of snow was any indication, no one had visited these poor souls in some time. I made to open the carriage door, but Daphne's hand stayed me.

"Everything is going to be fine," she said, likely to convince herself as much as me. "Even if it doesn't seem so, I promise it will be. I will protect you from whatever comes our way."

The earnestness in her tone made my dead heart squeeze. Dieu, I loved her. I still marveled at how we'd ended up here, when less than a year ago, she'd sworn revenge against every blood-sucking vampire in France. Still, her words needled my male pride no small amount.

"Duchesse, *I* will be the one to protect *you*."

She smiled somewhat indulgently at me and adjusted her cloak. I heard several small noises, then the click of a flintlock pistol cocking, the snap of the leather harness she used for her throwing daggers, and the rattle of shot and powder in her tiny silver case. Anyone would think she was preparing for battle, but I knew this was a reflexive habit more than anything.

We alit from the carriage, and she led the way to a small mausoleum in the back of the cemetery. She took out a large iron key and unlocked the door, then pushed it open with a heave from her shoulder. With a creak and a groan, it opened, and we entered the tomb.

I'd expected darkness, but we found ourselves at the top of a staircase with candles and charcoal braziers lining the walls. Daphne picked up her skirts, and we descended, careful not to bump into the guttering flames. At the bottom of the stairs stretched a long corridor that smelled of damp earth and stone. Distantly, I heard the low hum of hushed voices.

Daphne took a steadying breath as we neared the end of the corridor, facing a large oak door. She reached back to squeeze my hand, then knocked firmly three times. A liveried servant opened the door and bowed, then took our cloaks.

The inside of the room looked like a cross between a well-appointed gentlemen's club and an impressive manor library. Maps of France lined the walls, alongside floor-to-ceiling bookshelves. Standing around a large oval table were twenty or so men, each dressed in dark clothes and wearing black domino masks. They greeted Daphne politely but eyed me with reservation.

One of the older gentlemen—*is that the Duc de Nevers?*—cleared his throat and motioned to the assembly to be seated.

"I'll get right to the point," he said, addressing Daphne and I. "Madame. Monsieur. Thank you for attending on such short notice."

Daphne nodded but did not speak.

"We have become aware of a rather delicate matter that requires our attention and utmost discretion. For several months now, we believe some of the courtiers at Versailles have been targeted by a thief."

"What has been taken?" Daphne asked.

"Jewels, primarily. Some…*significant* ones. Only items of great value and greater sentiment," the man replied. "The robberies are daring—some have happened in broad daylight—and always in the same milieu. Some party or aristocratic function takes place, then the items suddenly disappear in the hours that follow."

"Which would suggest a highly-placed individual. A trusted servant, or…"

Daphne's eyes flashed behind her mask.

"A member of the court," he finished.

"Hence the need for discretion," she continued, nodding again. "Is the king aware?"

"We do not believe so, and we'd like to keep it that way. His Majesty has other things to occupy his mind, of course."

"Are there suspects? Surely if the guest lists were cross-referenced, one would be able to find a common name," she said.

"We've managed to narrow it down, but that still leaves us with a handful of potential offenders. We *must* have this sorted quickly and quietly. There seems to be a dangerous pattern emerging."

"With each subsequent theft, the thief gets closer to the king," said another man.

"What do you mean?" I asked.

"At first, it was smaller items from less notable families. As time has passed, the thief has gotten bolder—larger items from families tied to the king. We are loath to name names, but I will say that the last theft was from the king's second cousin."

"Why has the *gendarmerie* not been involved? Jewel theft seems more their speed, as opposed to a group of agents with other, more important functions," I asked.

"We're not certain the *gendarmerie* can be trusted," the second man replied. "Having a thief in our midst has made us all jump at shadows, so to speak. We've decided to put the matter to bed ourselves."

"What do you want me—*us*—to do?" Daphne asked.

The first man smiled beatifically at her. My hackles rose a fraction.

"We've become aware of your Christmas Eve *réveillon*. It's possible the thief has, too. In fact, he or she may be on your guest list already," he said.

"And you want me to hunt for a thief at my own party?" Daphne sounded incensed.

"No, no," said the second man. "That's not what we're saying, exactly.

We simply want you to be on your guard. You may, in fact, be the next target."

"That's absurd," Daphne huffed.

The first man raised a placating hand. "You must admit you are uniquely positioned to help resolve this matter," he said. "Your holiday feast gives us a perfect opportunity to draw out the thief, and your impressive skills as an intelligence agent and field operative would make this particular assignment relatively easy for you, no?"

I could tell Daphne wanted to refuse, but whether the older man had appealed to her vanity or her sense of duty, she merely pursed her lips and nodded.

"I'll sort it out," she said tightly. "But I will want some things in return. Starting with your list of suspects, the previous victims, and the items that were taken."

"Of course. Naturally."

I scanned the other faces at the table, noting a mixture of relief and doubt beneath the other masks.

I cleared my throat. Several sets of disapproving eyes cut to me.

"I'm happy to help out here, but I must ask you, Messieurs, why did you send for me as well?" I wondered.

The second gentleman narrowed his eyes at me, and the smile of the first man dropped. The changes in their manners seemed to bode ill for me. My muscles tensed, waiting for what was surely bad news.

"As it happens, Monsieur, we thought you might be of assistance to Her Grace. You see, there is a name on this list of suspects that you will find familiar."

Ah, merde.

"Yes. We thought you would be able to help eliminate the Marquise de Balay from our inquiries, since previously you *knew* her so well," the first man said.

"Or perhaps persuade her to share her thoughts on the matter," the second man said. "We hear that's a specialty of yours."

My fangs lengthened reflexively at the challenge in the man's sneering tone, but I kept them covered. It was only recently these bastards had deigned to stop trying to kill me, and I didn't want my behavior to reflect badly on Daphne. Instead, I smiled at the men.

"*Bien sûr,*" I said in a silken tone. "I'm happy to help in whatever way I can."

"I'm sure you are," hissed the second man under his breath. Anger rose from within, and it was a Herculean effort for me to swallow my outraged reply. Daphne's hand on my knee beneath the table was the only thing that kept me calm. Her stormy eyes promised we'd discuss my past tryst with the wretched marquise, but I'd take a thousand jealous Daphnes over any discourse with these men.

She must have sensed my patience ebbing, because she stood abruptly, forcing the entire assembly to their feet, as well.

"If you'll excuse me," she said. "It's been a long night and I have much to do. The list, if you please."

She held out her hand expectantly. The older man took a folded piece of paper from his pocket and hesitantly handed it over.

"The utmost discretion," he repeated.

Daphne nodded once and took my arm. When we were back in the corridor with the door closed behind us, my supernatural hearing picked up the delightful things they had to say about me. *Bastards.*

We were both silent on the way back through the cemetery to the waiting carriage—me, lost in the fantasy of draining every member of The Order and then going home to Daphne's bed; her, predictably stewing in haughty jealousy over the mention of my former lover. I certainly didn't fault her. The thought of her dead and *quite evil* husband made me feel a jealous rage that usually led to splintered furniture.

"*Chérie,*" I tried. "That was practically a lifetime ago. And it was never for love—or even mutual regard, really. She was meant to be a means to an end."

"Oh, of course," Daphne said. She stared hard out the window. "It's fine, Étienne. I knew your reputation a long time ago."

"My reputation was widely exaggerated, Duchesse. And it wasn't some great love affair. It happened once, and I've regretted it since. I was merely trying to find some influence with the king, which didn't exactly work in my favor, considering she happens to be his *least* favorite cousin."

"Honestly, it's fine," she repeated. "We'll say no more about it, *d'accord?*"

I eyed her skeptically. She sniffed in irritation, and I couldn't help but laugh.

"Do *not* laugh at me," she growled. "I am still armed, you know."

"But it's just so sweet," I chuckled, dragging her into my lap. "I adore your jealousy. It makes me feel like you're just as possessive of me as I am over you." I pulled her head down to mine for a searing kiss. "It is the best kind of Christmas present."

Daphne sighed against me and melted into another kiss. Her lips parted and her tongue darted out, dragging lightly against my fangs. The sensation was like a bolt of lightning through my body, tightening every muscle and making my cock hard. The bouncing of her bottom on my lap as the carriage rolled over cobblestone streets did nothing to slake my building lust.

"You know," she murmured playfully at my ear. "I rather like this mask on you. It makes you seem like a charming, yet dangerous, highwayman."

"Stand and deliver," I growled. "Your money or your body!"

Daphne tilted back her head and laughed, and I took advantage of the pose to kiss her throat. She moaned softly and slid her hands beneath my waistcoat. It was like flinging a match into a tinderbox. I pushed her back against the opposite seat, diving for the pins and ties on her bodice. The carriage pitched roughly, and I lost my grip, then abandoned the quest in frustrated haste. An instinctive vampiric hiss emanated from my throat as I fumbled for her skirts.

"Daphne, *l'amour*, I need you," I demanded between kisses. I stared into her lust-glazed eyes in the darkness, feeling the blood pound through my body like a drum on a battlefield.

"You have me, *chéri*," she whispered. She pulled her skirts up to her waist and wrapped her legs around me, grinding her heat against my breeches. *Dieu, I will lose myself right here.*

One hand was at the falls of my breeches when the carriage came to a stop.

"*Putain!*" she swore. "What timing!"

I thought a thousand evil thoughts about the carriage driver, the roads, and the speed of our travel as we righted ourselves and stepped out onto the snowy drive in front of Daphne's château.

"Sunrise isn't for a few hours," she said in a low voice. "We don't have to say *aDieu* quite yet."

I needed no other encouragement. I picked her up and raced into the manor like Lucifer himself was on my heels.

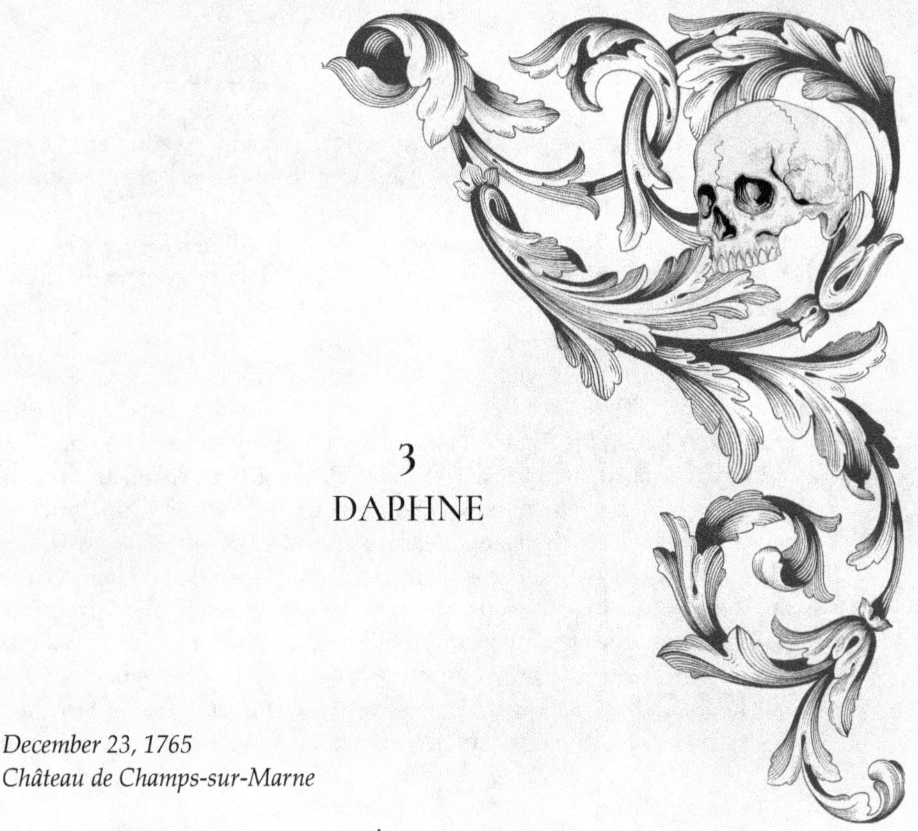

3
DAPHNE

December 23, 1765
Château de Champs-sur-Marne

I couldn't help but laugh as Étienne barreled through the house, heading straight for the wine cellar. Some months ago, he'd shown up at my home after a failed poisoning attempt, and I was compelled to set up a makeshift bedchamber underground where he could recover. In the following weeks, I had never quite gotten around to bringing the large bed back upstairs. It had worked out well for us—after our engagement, we'd made use of it more than a few times.

The entrance to the wine cellar was through the kitchen. Étienne plunked me down on the kitchen table to open the heavy door to the cellar but was disappointed to find it was locked.

"Merde! Daphne, why is this door locked? You never lock the wine cellar." His voice carried an edge of petulance.

"Oh no, I forgot! With the *réveillon* feast coming up, I had several cases of champagne delivered and my butler, Gaston, is keeping them under lock and key until Christmas Eve." I frowned.

Étienne's eyes flashed, and I knew exactly what he was thinking.

"Don't you dare break down that door," I warned. "There are beds in the rooms upstairs."

"But all those rooms have large windows, and it'll be sunrise in a few hours," he practically whined.

"We could go back to your place," I suggested.

The look he gave me was a cross between intense longing and sheer frustration. I pulled his face down to mine for a passionate kiss, reigniting the fire he'd stoked in the carriage.

"*Eh, laisse faire,*" he grunted, pushing me back on the kitchen table. He jumped up and rolled atop me, pinning me down beneath his lithe, muscular body.

"Étienne!" I laughed. "Please. I often eat at this table!"

"*Oui, chérie!* And so shall I." He tugged my skirts and chemise up to my waist and slid his cool hands up my thighs. Any thoughts of protestation died as he set his tongue to me, lapping at my sex until he had me writhing. My need for him was almost blinding. I threaded my hands through his thick, dark locks to keep him where I needed him, and he rewarded me by darting his tongue across the apex of my pleasure. Desire built in my body like the slow crescendo of an operatic symphony, and when he slid his fingers inside me, the cymbals crashed, and I sang my final aria. He nipped gently at my thigh and drank from me, as was our custom, which sent me down another valley of pleasure. When he was done, he licked the small wound closed and rolled over to lay next to me.

"Delicious," he said. His fangs had retracted again. "I'll never tire of that."

"I should hope not," I said with a faint smile.

"You haven't had dinner this evening, have you?" he asked, worry creasing his brow. "You look awfully pale."

"I'm fine," I said. "Perhaps a little hungry."

Étienne jumped off the table. "Say no more, Duchesse. Allow me to further satisfy you."

"I'm sure there's some leftover roast from the midday meal," I said. "Or perhaps some bread and cheese."

Étienne went to the pantry and returned with some of the day's leftovers, as well as an armload of other ingredients.

"Cream, sugar, eggs, vanilla, the oranges for the *réveillon* dessert table…what are you about, Étienne?" I asked.

He winked at me, took off his coat, and rolled up his shirtsleeves. "Sit and eat your meal. I'll make you dessert."

I tucked into the roast and cheese and watched him whisk his ingredients together over the stove. When he was done, he poured the mixture into two small dishes and took them to the kitchen door that led to the back garden. He stuck the two bowls of sweetened cream into the snow and came back inside. I raised a curious brow at him, but he merely smiled and cut into one of the oranges.

"*Mon Dieu!* These oranges are red!" he said upon seeing the crimson fruit.

"They're a new variety imported from Sicily," I said. "They're called blood oranges."

"Non. Vraiment?" He licked the juice from his fingers, spurring another wave of desire in me.

"Yes," I said, coming over to taste the fruit. "I thought you might like them."

"They are good," he said. "But not as delicious as you. Somehow, you always seem to taste of orange blossom and vanilla. That's why I'm making you this dessert; it's a treat inspired by you."

I finished my meal, and we sat in front of the kitchen hearth in companionable silence. The fire crackled and popped, and I brought out two glasses of brandy for us to enjoy. After a while, Étienne went out to the snow and brought the custards back in. I watched with fascination as he topped them with orange slices, sprinkled sugar over them, and held them under a red-hot pan plucked from the fire. The sugar melted and burned to a lovely caramel color.

"Where did you learn how to make this?" I asked.

"When I was a boy—before I turned—my family cook was renowned for her *pâtisseries.* I had such a sweet tooth when I was young! She made the most delicious desserts for me, but this one was always my favorite. *Crème brûlée,* she called it. Of course, I had to add my own twist just for you, *ma petite orange,"* he grinned.

He slid the dish toward me. I picked up a spoon.

"Wait," he whispered. "This is the best part."

He tapped the delicate sugar glaze on the top, cracking it and dipping his spoon in the orange-scented custard. He held it to my lips and my mouth watered—the fragrance of warm vanilla, tart orange, and creamy sweetness was too much to resist. He placed the spoonful on my tongue and I nearly swooned.

"It's unbelievable," I gasped. I reached for my own dish, but Étienne stopped me.

"It is *my* treat, Duchesse," he said. He dipped a finger in the dessert and held it up to my lips. I sucked it off and he stifled a growl. His fangs lengthened and his eyes flashed with that fire again. I smiled knowingly at him as he began to unbutton his waistcoat and then his breeches. I couldn't unlace my stays fast enough.

It was some time before we finished dessert.

The following morning, I woke to find myself tucked cozily in my own bed. Étienne must have brought me upstairs before returning to his château for his daytime rest. I yawned and rang for a bath. I was still covered in remnants of last night's *crème brûlée à l'orange*. While I was in the bath, I mulled over the list of names The Order had given me. I knew everyone on the list—not intimately, of course, but well enough. Of all the names, only a few hadn't been invited to my Christmas Eve party, and I called for Eve to send out invitations to them immediately.

Who would be foolish or greedy enough to steal such high-profile items? The stolen jewelry was well-known at court, so the thief wouldn't be able to sell it as-is; they'd most certainly have to break it down into singular stones. Would the average aristocrat be smart enough to figure that out?

I stared hard at the list. Right away, I was able to eliminate a few suspects I didn't think were imaginative or resourceful enough to carry out such bold crimes. Three names remained—all families that had recently suffered embarrassing financial losses, or so the gossips said. At the top of my list were the Marquis and Marquise de Balay. *Not for any personal reason or petty jealousy,* I thought to myself. I knew the marquis had serious gambling debts and that the marquise was unparalleled in her ability to navigate the politics of court with selfishness and malevolence. Her star had faded of late, partly because of her idiotic husband's gambling debts and partly to do with her outmoded attitude of disdain toward the growing vampire population in France. Embarrassing the court with a series of brazen jewel thefts was not beyond comprehension when it came to the devious couple.

Following the Balays were the Comte and Comtesse de Cagné, a pair of desperate aristocrats I knew would stop at nothing to improve their influence but didn't have the wealth required. Then there was Madame Catherine, the embittered wife of a lauded French war hero who did not return from his last battle. She was a ferocious and virulent gossip, who didn't let something as insignificant as the truth derail her from her aims.

They all had motives, as well as the intelligence and opportunity to carry out the thefts. Most disturbing was they all shared the same sense of disgust at the king's slowly changing attitude about the blood plague. They resented the shifting power dynamic and despised vampires—but not enough to ignore a coveted invitation to dine with one at my *réveillon*.

The Order wanted me to catch this criminal, and to do so I needed to set an impossible-to-resist trap.

I lay in the large copper bathtub devising my plan until the water had gone cold and most of the morning was over. I dressed plainly and went to the library, where I was unsurprised to find Charlotte bent over an account book. She had her own estate not far from mine, but after the recent fiasco with her husband, she preferred to spend her days with me. Even though I had Étienne now, it was lonely here during the day and I was glad for the company. She looked up when I entered.

"Daphne! I'm glad you're up. How did it go last night? What did The Order want?"

I poured myself a cup of chocolate from the still-warm pot on the sideboard and took a long, fortifying sip before answering her.

"It was only a little better than I expected," I sighed.

"So…no death threats, but an evening surrounded by irritating old men?"

"Precisely," I snickered.

"And the Christmas Eve party?" she prodded. "Are we still allowed to carry on?"

"Yes. In fact, it's *encouraged.* They summoned me about a jewel thief who seems to have some kind of set against the king. We're to uncover the culprit and keep everything as discreet as possible. The fewer people know about this, the better," I explained.

"What do you have in mind?"

"We're going to lay a trap. You and I will be the bait. I'll need you to wear your rubies tomorrow night. I'm going to wear my mother's diamonds."

Charlotte's eyes widened. "You're going to wear *l'Étoile d'Or?*"

I nodded. I'd only worn the necklace once in my life—during my first appearance before King Louis at Versailles a decade ago. The famous necklace was a chain of seventy-two perfectly cut white diamonds that encircled a 36-carat yellow diamond. It was an ostentatious display of wealth, which was why I normally kept it locked away in the family vault. It was also why I intended to bring it out to catch the attention of our burglar. No jewel thief worth his salt would be able to resist such a prize.

That afternoon, I filled Charlotte in on the rest of the plan's details. We would divide the suspects between us—Étienne would watch Madame Catherine, Charlotte would charm the Comte and Comtesse de Cagné, and I would keep my eyes on the Balays. Once we'd finished preparing ourselves for every eventuality, I sent word to Étienne.

I strolled to the large library window that overlooked the grounds. It should be about sunset, but a fierce snowstorm had rolled in, whiting out the sky and covering everything in thick, sparkling powder. Charlotte went over to the fireplace and poked idly at the blazing logs.

"I can't remember the last time we had a white Christmas," she mused. "Every one of them over the last few years has been wet, gray, and muddy. Not very festive, if you ask me."

"No," I agreed. "But we haven't had many festive holidays over the last few years."

"That's true. Perhaps we will now. You've still got me, and Étienne, of course."

I smiled at her. Charlotte could always cheer me out of my melancholy.

She shrugged nonchalantly. "And failing that, I suppose, you've still got your bastard dead husband's whole wine cellar to drink through. Should we go make a celebratory start on that?"

"That is, without a doubt, the best idea of the day."

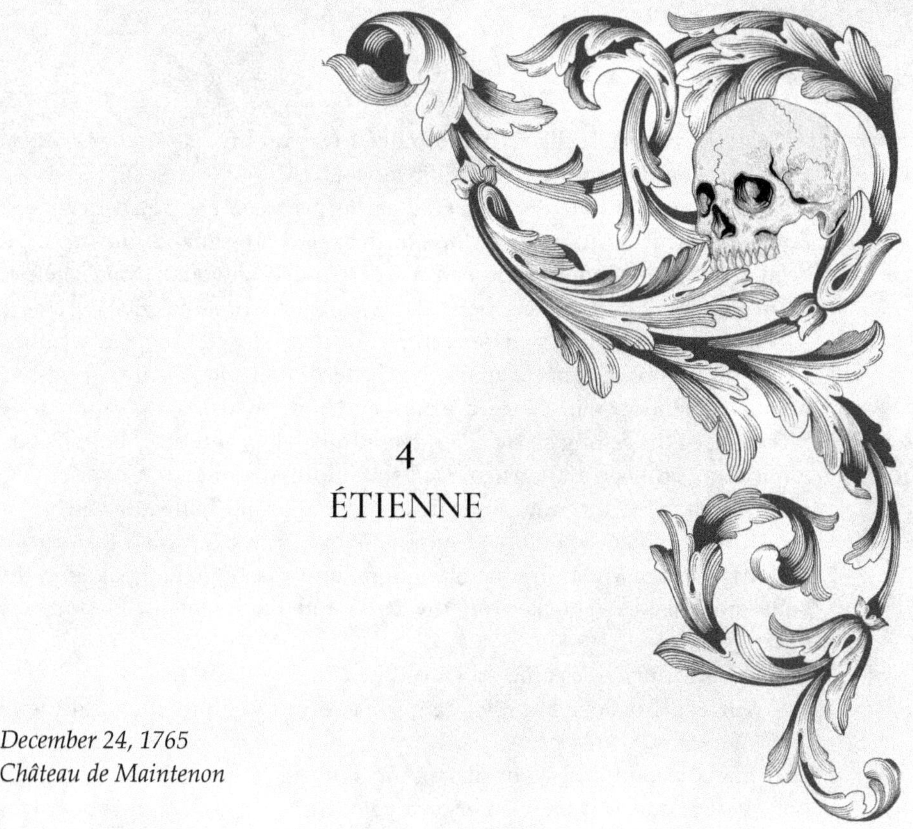

4
ÉTIENNE

December 24, 1765
Château de Maintenon

I REMEMBER THE LAST TIME I ATTENDED A *RÉVEILLON* ON CHRISTMAS EVE. I'D been a young man—not yet a vampire—and it was one of the last times I'd been in the room with my father without us having an argument. It had been a magical evening filled with family, food, and an exchange of small gifts. At midnight, we looked outside and saw huge, fluffy snowflakes falling, and my mother insisted on us going out to play in it. It remained one of my favorite memories of my life before everything changed…before my turning, my father's disgrace, then his death. In the years that followed, I wouldn't celebrate Christmas.

Until now. *Until Daphne.* The one woman who would consent to celebrate an eternity of Christmases with me. Hopefully, they wouldn't all involve parties of snobbish aristocrats and dangerous plots to capture jewel thieves.

Knowing Daphne, that's more likely than not.

I finished buttoning my gold brocade waistcoat and pulled on my overcoat. I wasn't looking forward to having to spend my night attending to Madame Catherine. I dreaded seeing the Marquise de Balay even more. If it wasn't for Daphne, I probably would've told the Order to find the missing jewels themselves and leave us alone to spend Christmas Eve the way we really wanted to, unwrapping presents—*and each other*—all evening long.

Alas, I thought. It didn't matter now. I was on my way to her château for what would certainly be a thrilling evening.

The snow that had started to fall earlier was coming down in earnest now—fat, white clumps that stuck to trees and streets and houses. If I'd been among the living, I probably would have shivered. Nevertheless, there was something quite special about snow on Christmas Eve.

I arrived at Daphne's château in record time, despite the bad weather. Everything looked spectacular. She'd decorated the estate in festive holiday splendor, with large braziers and torches along the front drive flickering in the falling snow. Evergreens, mistletoe, and holly boughs tied with large, crimson ribbons covered the impressive manor's façade. Two footmen escorted me from my carriage to the grand hallway, which was awash with the golden glow of hundreds of candles. Several other guests had arrived already. I saw them laughing and toasting champagne in the ballroom ahead. I shucked off my cape and handed it to Gaston, the butler.

"Has the duchesse come down yet?"

"Not yet. I believe she's waiting for you in the library," he said with a bow.

I thanked him and went upstairs to find her. I knocked at the closed library door and was bade enter by a voice that was not Daphne's—it was Charlotte's.

"Monsieur de Noailles!" she greeted with genuine enthusiasm. "I'm so glad you've arrived! Daphne is being dreadfully dull and will not cease working. You must entertain me while she finishes writing her letters."

"Of course! *Mon amie,* you look absolutely divine this evening," I said. "Pink is certainly your color."

She wore a shining gown of pink silk adorned with crimson ribbons. Her hair was swept up in a mass of powdered curls atop her head and pinned with jewels and feathers. As lovely as she looked, what caught my attention was the wreath of enormous red rubies wrapped around her neck, paired with matching ruby earrings. I hadn't seen jewels as fine on the queen herself.

She caught me eyeing the rubies and rolled her eyes. "They're quite obscene, are they not? I mean, certainly the stones are lovely, but the setting is so unfashionable. I've been meaning to have them reset but haven't gotten around to it. They were a wedding gift from my nefarious former husband—quite possibly the only thing he did right in our marriage."

"They're exquisite, but they pale in comparison to your beauty, dear Charlotte," I bowed over her hand and kissed it.

"Such flattery! If only you were not spoken for by the best of all possible women, I might think to steal you away," she joked. We had always had an easy flirtation, mostly because there was nothing behind it.

"You do realize I can hear you," came a voice from the hallway. "You're both so uncommonly loud in your philandering, you would make truly terrible adulterers."

Daphne stepped into the room, and I felt my knees wobble slightly. She was the most beautiful thing I'd ever seen. She wore a gown of pale lavender with gold embroidery that glittered when she moved. Her bright violet eyes flashed with laughter, and her luscious rosebud lips kicked up in a saucy smirk. A thrum of desire pulsed through my body, beating a tattoo—*mine…mine…mine.*

"Let's get this over with," she said. "This damn diamond is heavy."

Dieu! I hadn't even noticed. Around her neck was the biggest canary yellow diamond I'd ever seen, surrounded by dozens of smaller white diamonds. I let out a low whistle.

"That'll certainly attract the thief," I said. "But it'll be difficult to figure out who it is until they try to steal it tonight, since I'm sure *everyone* will be overly fascinated with it."

"Naturally," agreed Charlotte. "It doesn't hurt that it sits right above your cleavage, Daphne. I don't know if the lecherous Marquis de Balay will be more fascinated with the jewels or your breasts."

I felt an immediate and irrational desire to break something. "If the marquis can't keep his bloody eyes in his own head, I'll pull them out," I growled.

"That's sweet, *chéri,* but wait until he tries to take the necklace," Daphne said, patting my arm. "We must catch the thief in the act. *D'accord, allons-y!*"

We went down to the ballroom, Daphne on one side of me and Charlotte on the other. Most of the other guests had arrived in our absence, including Madame Catherine, the Cagnés, and the Marquise de Balay. I did not see her husband, though.

Charlotte and Daphne nodded at each other and peeled off to shadow their respective targets. I made for Madame Catherine, who was scowling over by a potted palm. I bowed before her.

"Madame! Such a pleasure to see you this evening. It's been some time since we've conversed, no?" I tried in my most charming voice.

She regarded me suspiciously. "Monsieur de Noailles," she said with a slight incline of her head.

"How do you fare this evening? Not too chilled by the snow, I hope?"

"No," she said.

"Ah, good, good. And do you have plans for Christmas?"

"No," she bit out again.

"No trips to the country, or…"

Dieu, I was dying here. Madame Catherine regarded me like some kind of pest, which wasn't something I was used to. Most of the women at court adored me—at least, they did before Daphne came into my life and I lost the desire to flirt with anyone else.

"No. I'm staying in Paris for the holiday with my aunt. She is in poor health and may pass on at any moment, if you must know," she grumbled.

"Oh, I am sorry to hear that," I said with a frown. Her aunt, a cranky, old duchesse, was well-known for her poor temperament and her obscene wealth. It was also well-known that she had no other living relations, which meant her entire estate would pass to Madame Catherine. There was no reason for her to steal anything.

I gave up trying to charm the widow and made my excuses. I was just looking for Daphne when I heard a familiar cutting voice.

"Bonsoir, ma bête."

I turned and found myself face-to-face with the Marquise de Balay.

"Good evening, Henriette," I said, returning her cold smile.

"I'm pleased to see you here tonight," she continued. "Though a little surprised. I thought you would have tired of the duchesse by now. You've never been one for lengthy romantic pursuits."

I opened my mouth to reply, but Daphne swirled to my side.

"Oh, Madame! I'm so glad you could join us this evening. But I'm afraid I don't see your husband. Not out at the gaming tables again, is he?" she said with false sweetness.

The marquise looked like she wanted to strangle Daphne, but the look was gone in an instant. Her eyes darted to the necklace at Daphne's throat, then back up.

"Madame," she said, inclining her head. "He sends his apologies. I'm afraid he's at home with a fearful attack of the gout."

"That's terrible news," Daphne replied. "You must send him well wishes from my fiancé and I." She wrapped a possessive hand around my arm, and I fought to keep the smirk from my lips.

A muscle in the marquise's eye ticked.

"Of course," she said. "I think I see the Cardinal over there. If you'll excuse me." She made a hasty retreat, and I could no longer keep my laughter in.

"I dare say you've made a powerful enemy there," I murmured in Daphne's ear.

"Tant pis," she said with a shrug. "Did you see how she eyed the necklace? If she is the thief, I'm certain she'll try to steal it tonight. If not for money, for revenge."

The gong sounded for dinner, and we went through to the dining room. Each course smelled more delicious than the last, but I abstained from eating any of it. I would drink from Daphne later. I could eat regular food, but the flavors were diminished to my palate—despite enjoying the aroma, everything tasted like bland mush to me.

Every now and then, I caught the Marquise de Balay scowling at me, but I didn't see her look at Daphne or Charlotte's jewels. *Could she be the thief? She certainly doesn't seem interested in either necklace. She seems angry, of course, but she always seems rather splenetic.*

I turned to watch Charlotte and the Cagnés. She seemed to be having a terrible time trying to keep the Comte de Cagné from groping her leg beneath the table. The comtesse seemed oblivious—in fact, she seemed rather drunk. I didn't think the thief would be so focused on sex or so unprofessional as to become intoxicated before a robbery. No one here seemed to be a criminal mastermind. Was there something or someone we'd missed? Maybe the thief wasn't here after all. Maybe The Order had been wrong about their suspects.

Suddenly, there was a shriek from Charlotte's end of the table. She had dumped an entire decanter of wine into the lap of the Comte de Cagné. The comtesse was screeching with drunken laughter and Charlotte pretended ineptitude.

"Oh, Monsieur, I am *so* sorry! How unbelievably clumsy of me! I hope I did not ruin your lovely breeches," she pouted. The comte narrowed his eyes at her and without a word, yanked his wife up from the table and stormed from the room. There were some scandalized gasps and a few snickers, but for the most part, everyone carried on with their meal. *Would they go straight home?* I wondered. *Or hide and wait for the chance to steal something?*

The rest of the evening passed in relative peace. By the time the last of the after-dinner drinks had been polished off, it was well after one o'clock in the morning and only a few guests remained. The Marquise de Balay had disappeared, and I wondered if she was off plotting somewhere or if she'd slunk back home to her gout-riddled husband.

As Daphne waved at the last departing couple, I came up behind her and planted a kiss on her neck.

"What do you think?" she asked. She stifled a yawn.

Charlotte approached us. "To be honest," she said. "I have a hard time imagining any one of them as a brazen jewel thief."

"Yes," I frowned. "I must agree."

"Well, all we can do now is wait," Daphne said. "Our trap is baited and set."

"I'm going to have some coffee," Charlotte said. "I have a feeling tonight will be a long night."

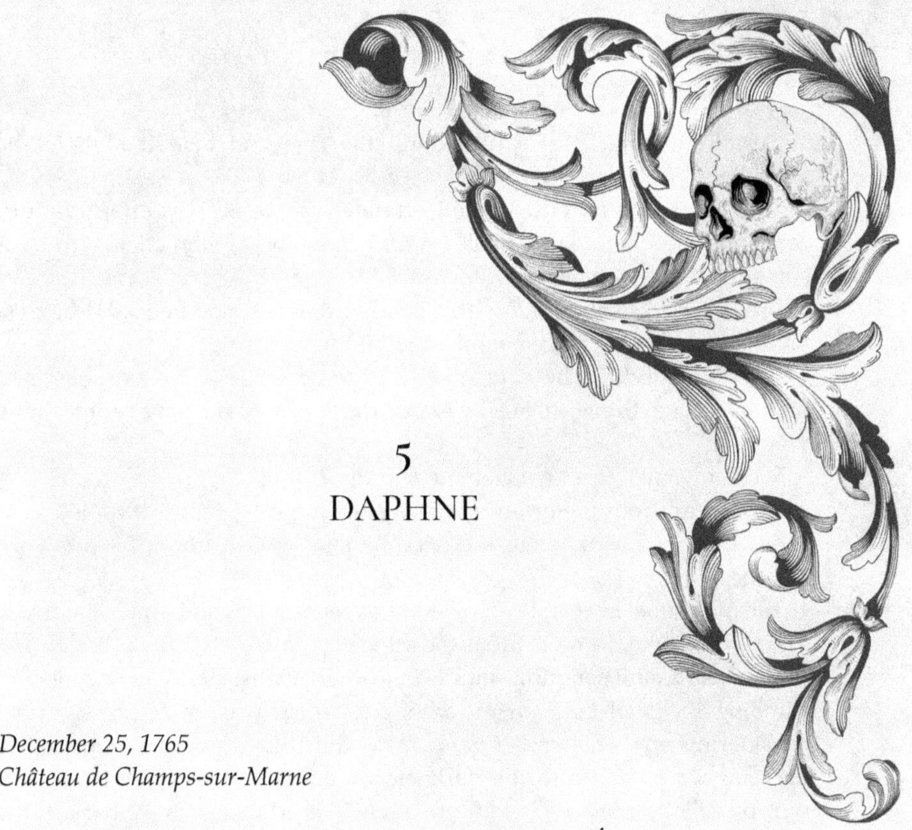

5

DAPHNE

December 25, 1765
Château de Champs-sur-Marne

I LAY IN BED THAT NIGHT, TRYING NOT TO DOZE OFF. ÉTIENNE AND I HAD occupied ourselves for over an hour with spirited lovemaking, but now we were spent. After the day I'd had, I could feel the exhaustion creeping in. I wasn't sure how much longer I could wait for the jewel thief to strike.

I got up and went to the window of my bedchamber. Snowflakes were still falling, but much slower than the frenzied blizzard from earlier. The sliver of moon made the snow on the ground glow a pale blue. I opened the window and inhaled. There was a faint whiff of smoke from the hearths of distant houses, but everything else smelled cold and new and wet.

"I forgot how beautiful winter can be," murmured Étienne. He'd snuck up behind me, padding silently across the carpet on stealthy feet. He wrapped his arms around my waist and leaned his chin on my shoulder. We continued to watch the snow fall in silence.

"It's long after midnight," I realized. "Merry Christmas, *chéri*. Do you want your present now?"

"Absolutely," he said. "But truthfully, Daphne, you're the only thing I need."

I tutted. "Don't be silly. This is important."

I went to my dresser and pulled out a small velvet box. Étienne took it and eyed me curiously. He opened it slowly and exhaled.

"Daphne, what…" He picked up the ring and held it aloft in the moonlight.

"I know, it's a bit odd," I said, strangely nervous. "But after you turn me, you won't be able to drink from me anymore. I wanted you to have something to remember how it was."

The ring was solid gold with a small droplet of blood encased in crystal. In any light, it would look like a stunning ruby ring.

"It's wonderful," he said quietly. "I'm speechless. No one has ever offered me anything so precious. But darling, I could never forget how you taste."

"I just wanted to—shh! Do you hear that?"

Rising up from the ground below came the soft crunch of footsteps in snow. I stepped away from the window and looked around. I didn't see anyone.

Étienne inhaled deeply. "Someone is near, but I can't smell them yet. The woodsmoke from the fire is too strong."

We heard faint scraping sounds of leather against stone—someone was climbing the wall beneath my window, which was an impressive feat considering my bedchamber was on the third floor. Étienne motioned to me, and we melted into the darkness on either side of the window. I'd purposely left *l'Étoile d'Or* out on a table instead of putting it back in the vault. The necklace glittered temptingly.

Two hands reached over the railing and hefted a body inside. Just as fingers closed around the jewel, Étienne and I launched ourselves on top of the thief, knocking us all onto the ground.

"Unhand me!" cried a rough male voice.

I lit a candle and held it in front of the intruder.

"Robert!" Étienne and I said at once.

Étienne's butler grimaced at us.

"Robert," Étienne repeated. "Oh, *mon ami*, how could you?" The sadness and betrayal in his face was almost too much to bear. I tied his hands behind him with one of my hair ribbons, cinching the knot a tad tighter than was necessary.

"It is not as it seems," Robert cried. Tears started to leak from the corners of his eyes. "Monsieur de Noailles, forgive me, please! Forgive me!"

"You're going before The Order, Robert. You'll have to ask them for forgiveness," Étienne replied bitterly.

"Wait," I said. "What do you mean, 'it's not as it seems'?"

"I still have the jewels!" he said. "All of them! I didn't want to steal them, Your Grace, I swear I didn't. They told me to take them. They said if I didn't, they'd tell Monsieur about my past."

"Your past?" Étienne repeated, confused.

"Forgive me, Monsieur. I...I used to pick pockets, but it was a long time ago—before I found a job in service with the old Vicomte de Noailles. I'll admit I was a thief, but no longer, I swear to you! They told me if you found out the truth, you'd turn me over to the *gendarmerie*, or The Order. I don't want to leave your service, Monsieur, I don't! Please don't send me before The Order. I can return everything!"

Robert choked out a sob and my heart clenched. Étienne looked less convinced.

"Who's blackmailing you, Robert?" I asked.

"I can't," he cried. "They'll ruin me."

Étienne's expression softened a touch. "If what you say is true, I promise we'll keep you safe."

Robert considered us and blew out a miserable sigh.

"The Balays."

"I knew it!" I exclaimed, unable to stop myself. Étienne and Robert looked at me in surprise. "Sorry," I whispered. "It's just that I suspected them. Do go on."

Robert continued. "I don't know how they found out about my past, but somehow, they did. Every few weeks, they give me a name and a jewel to steal. I'm supposed to give them everything next week— including your necklace, Your Grace. The marquise sent word to me this evening when she returned from the party."

"How were you supposed to deliver the jewels to them?" I asked.

"I was supposed to put them in a box on the back of their carriage when they leave for their country estate next week," he sniffed. Étienne handed him a handkerchief.

Suddenly, Charlotte burst into the room wielding a fireplace poker.

"I'm here! Have you apprehended the—oh, *merde.* It seems I have missed out."

"Robert, Étienne's butler, is the thief, but he is being blackmailed into it by the Balays," I summarized for her.

"I knew it!" she crowed. "I knew it had to be them, the rotten snakes."

"What are you going to do with me, Monsieur?" Robert asked.

"It's up to the duchesse. She's the one you tried to rob," Étienne said. Robert let out a tortured wail.

"Calm yourself, Robert," I said, untying him. "I'm not going to turn you over to the *gendarmerie* or The Order, and it's very likely that Monsieur de Noailles is not going to terminate your employment. As for me, I'm going to see that the marquis and the marquise receive exactly what they're supposed to."

"You want me to give them the jewels?" Robert asked, astonished.

"Precisely," I said.

SEVERAL DAYS LATER, ÉTIENNE AND I DECIDED TO TAKE A LEISURELY EVENING stroll through the streets of Paris. We took our time, ambling along the sidewalk next to some of the more expensive townhouses in Paris. We watched people come and go, ducking the cold, snowy weather. A commotion in the distance attracted our attention.

"You know," Étienne began. "I never gave you your Christmas present. After Robert broke into your home, time just seemed to get away from us."

"Oh?"

A group of eight uniformed men with the *gendarmerie* had stopped a carriage and were swiftly emptying trunks and chests right into the street. Fine gowns and suits of clothing spilled across the mud, as well as folios of paper, hatboxes, boxes of cigars and cases of brandy. We heard the loud screech of a woman nearby, as well as the booming voice of a man who believed himself to be in charge of the situation. We strolled closer.

"Yes," he said, handing me an envelope. I opened it and unfolded the paper within.

"It's…an architectural plan?"

"For a new set of apartments in your château. All underground—designed for us after your turning. I didn't want you to have to give up your family home as well as your humanity," Étienne explained. He seemed anxious.

We neared the excitement in the street just in time to see an officer open a small wooden case with several priceless pieces of jewelry inside—some of which were strikingly familiar.

"I've never seen those before in my life!" The Marquise de Balay shrieked.

"Who the Hell do you think you're addressing? Do you realize we are related to the king?" The marquis shouted at the *gendarmerie*.

The officer shook his head in disgust. "I doubt His Majesty will be pleased with anyone that steals jewels from his courtiers, whether they're a relative or not." He shoved them both into a much *less* comfortable carriage—destined for the Bastille, I'd expect—just as Étienne and I walked past. I caught the eye of the enraged marquise through the barred window. The look she gave me was sharper than any of my daggers.

I blew her a kiss.

Étienne and I stood and watched as the carriage trundled away.

"Good riddance," Étienne muttered.

I smiled to myself and sighed. "I'm glad that's over with."

"Daphne, if you don't like the plans, you can always change them," Étienne said suddenly. "It's entirely up to you. I didn't want to overstep because it *is* your home, after all. I just thought that you might…"

"Étienne, stop!" I laughed. "I love it. It's a wonderfully thoughtful gift. We'll begin construction immediately."

Relief washed over his face, and I leaned in to kiss him. He smiled against my lips and wrapped an arm around my waist. His tongue slipped out and caressed mine. Heat coursed through me until I was certain the snow was melting around me. I pulled away.

"You know, I didn't have any dessert this evening," I drawled. "And I believe I still have some blood oranges at home…"

RECIPE

Crème Brûlée à l'Orange
Makes 4 servings

INGREDIENTS:
For the custard:
1/2 cup heavy cream
1/4 cup granulated sugar
1 vanilla bean
4 egg yolks
1 tbsp Grand Marnier
Pinch of salt
For the topping:
1 blood orange, peeled and sliced
4 tbsp granulated sugar

DIRECTIONS:
Preheat the oven to 300°F.

In a saucepan, stir together the cream, granulated sugar, and salt. Split the vanilla bean and scrape the seeds into the cream. Toss the vanilla pod in, as well. Bring to a very gentle boil (over medium heat), stirring constantly. Turn off the heat and add the Grand Marnier. Cover and let stand for about 20 minutes.

Meanwhile, in a bowl, whisk the egg yolks. While whisking constantly, slowly add the cream mixture to the yolks. Pour through a fine-mesh sieve into another bowl. Divide the mixture among 4 ramekins, each about a cup. Place the ramekins in a 9x13 baking pan and carefully pour hot water into the pan to reach about halfway up the sides of the cups. Bake until the custards are just set but still jiggly, 30 to 35 minutes.

Remove the custards from the water bath, place on a wire rack and let cool to room temperature. Cover with plastic wrap and refrigerate until the custards are thoroughly chilled, at least 2 hours or overnight.

Just before serving, place a blood orange slice on top of each custard and sprinkle evenly with about a tablespoon of granulated sugar. Using a chef's torch, melt the sugar until caramelized. If you don't have a chef's torch, put the custards on a baking sheet under the broiler 2-3 inches from the heating element. The sugar will melt quickly; watch them carefully so they don't burn.

Allow the sugar to cool and harden before serving.

ONE GOOD TURN
A VAMPIRES IN VERSAILLES STORY

AUTHOR'S NOTE

Hi, me again. This extra spicy little bonus epilogue takes place after the events of Femme Brûlée, but before the events in the original epilogue. Initially, the first book was just supposed to flow right into the second book, but I guess I couldn't leave Daphne and Étienne alone for too long.

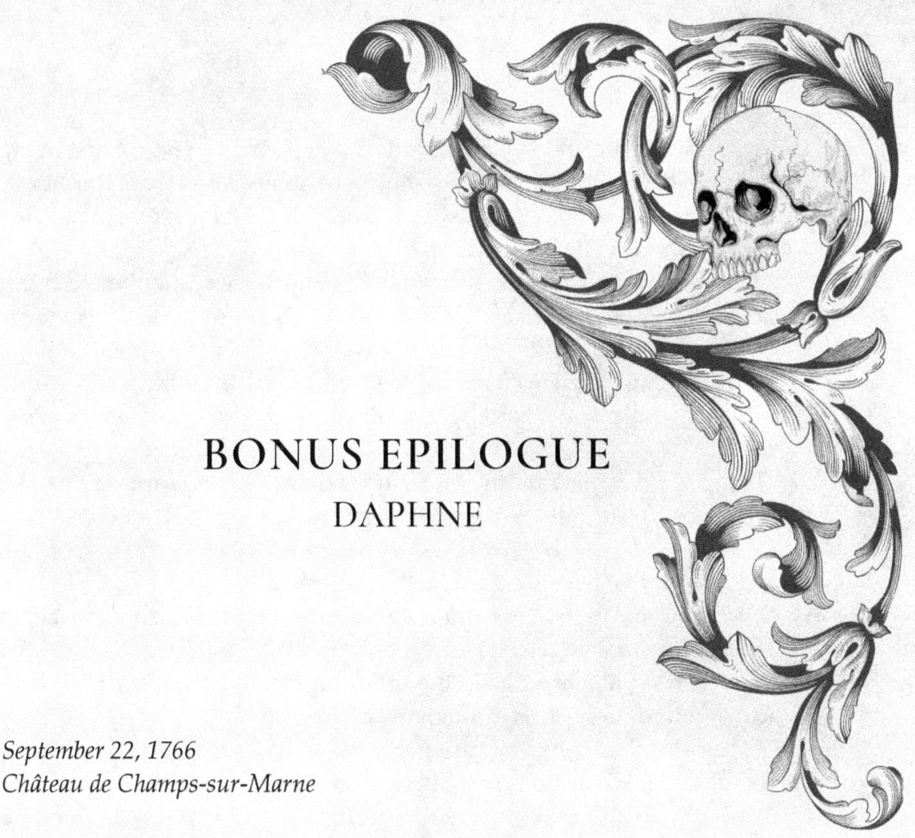

BONUS EPILOGUE
DAPHNE

September 22, 1766
Château de Champs-sur-Marne

DEATH CAME FOR ME WHILE I WAS DRIFTING BACK TO THE WORLD IN THE glittering wake of a bone-melting orgasm.

It had been Étienne's idea, of course, to give me the best end to my mortal life as we could imagine. Despite the lingering guilt he expressed over the fact that I'd long since committed my heart, my soul, and my eternity to him, he'd insisted on the immortal turning that he hadn't had—wrapped in the arms of true love, with as little pain as possible, and a few rooms away from the finest supernatural physician in all of France in the event that things went awry.

The day had been beautiful, and I'd spent the bright autumn afternoon outside, basking in the sun that I knew I would soon forgo for the rest of my years. Charlotte had prepared a lakeside picnic of all my favorite foods, and we'd loosened our stays before burying ourselves in roast chicken in truffle cream sauce, sage buttered turnips, rich and fragrant cheeses, delicate chocolate pastries, blood orange *pots de crème*, and bottles of champagne. With a full belly and pink freckled complexion, I'd bid my final adieu to the golden orange of sunset and the soft trill of birdsong. It would be a lie to say I wasn't melancholy over it, but I knew I'd give up the pleasures of daytime a hundred times over to be with my Étienne.

When I came home just after sundown, he was waiting for me clad in thigh-hugging black breeches and a loose linen shirt, his hair unbound and wild. Before I could say a word, he'd swept me up and carried me to our favorite bed in the wine cellar—now a permanent fixture in our home. He'd exhausted us both with exceptionally thorough lovemaking, then woke me a short while before dawn.

"Tasting you is like tasting the sun," he'd groaned from between my legs. "Are you absolutely certain you wish to give it up, *l'amour?* I would stay with you regardless, you know. I would love every softening limb, every deepening wrinkle. I would love you until they buried you and even then I would crawl through the dirt to sleep with your bones every morning."

"I know," I'd replied for the thousandth time. "But I want this, Étienne. I want to be yours fully. And I want you to be mine for an eternity of starry nights."

"Ah, *chérie,* I've been yours from the beginning."

"Oh? You mean when I tried to lure you into a hedge maze in Versailles to stake you? You loved me even then?"

There'd been a sharp nip at the artery in my thigh as he drank, and pleasure wound its tendrils through my core again.

"Especially then," he'd murmured against my skin. "Are you ready, my love? There will be no turning back after this."

"Yes, I'm ready. Make me yours, Étienne. Make me your vampire bride," I'd consented.

A robust groan of satisfaction punctuated his bite as he'd drunk more deeply than he ever had before. The warmth and sensual bliss that usually accompanied his feeding had faded slowly, like the last wisps of smoke from a dying fire. Cold seeped in like a silvery fog, moving from the tips of my fingers and toes, taking root in my chest. When Étienne crawled up my body from beneath the sheets, tears of blood pooled in the corners of his eyes. He pressed his head between my breasts to listen to the slow stilling of my mortal heart.

Just before things went dark, he'd bit his wrist and bade me drink. Though my thoughts were muddled and my dying body was calm, fierce hunger had sliced through me the moment the coppery salt hit my tongue. The more I'd drunk, the more I'd craved—until Étienne pulled away, licked our wounds closed, and wrapped me in his arms.

"Rest now, Daphne," he'd said. "Let the change happen. Rest, *l'amour,* and we will have Dr. Van Helsing check on you tomorrow evening."

I'd snuggled deeper into his embrace and let the darkness in.

WHEN I WOKE, I DID SO WITH A RIOT OF PAIN IN MY SKULL AND THE WORST stomach cramps I'd ever experienced. My senses were assaulted by thundering sounds, pungent fragrances, and piercing lights that seemed to blind me even through my closed eyelids.

"Is this Hell?" I hissed. "Am I being tormented?"

"Let her go, Monsieur, if you wish her to recover. I have quantities of blood for her to consume, and then we'll need to give her a proper examination," came a familiar accent.

"Dr. Van Helsing?" I rasped.

"In the flesh, Madame. Now, open up, please. Your changed body needs to feed. The pains will subside once you do," she said, holding a glass vial to my lips.

This time when the blood hit my tongue, a symphony of delicate flavors exploded in my mouth. Immediately, the throbbing ache in my head dulled and the twisting in my guts ceased.

Too ravenous and irascible for propriety, I licked the glass clean and finally opened my eyes. Dr. Van Helsing stood next to my bed; spectacles low on her nose but otherwise entirely unmoved by the terror of my experience. The bed shifted slightly, and I realized Étienne was still with me, though at some point he'd tossed on a loose chemise. The worry and despair in his eyes was evident, dulling their normal luminous gold to a muted hazel.

"Daphne," he breathed. "Thank the stars. I was so afraid the change wouldn't take."

I ran my fingers along the smooth skin of his jaw, but a fierce rumble in my stomach drew my attention.

"More," I snarled, my voice sharper than any blade I'd ever wielded. Dr. Van Helsing's eyes widened a fraction, then she smiled and passed me two more vials. I dispatched them with supernatural speed.

Before I could beg for more, Étienne pulled a decanter of fresh blood from the sideboard and poured me a wine goblet.

"You've had three vials of virgin blood, Duchesse," Van Helsing said. "That will help your body process its new functions. You'll be fine with the regular donated blood that your fiancé has procured from now on. Once you have recovered your full faculties, you won't need human blood quite as often. Animal blood will keep you nourished."

By the time she finished her explanation, I'd drained the glass and snatched the decanter from Étienne's hand. With an unladylike moan, I tipped it back and drank until only smears of ruby liquid remained.

"Well, I can see that your appetite is as it should be. I'll leave you to your rest. Pay heed to the fact that your body is still undergoing quite a radical metamorphosis, Duchesse," Van Helsing cast a disapproving glance in Étienne's direction. "You must not overtax her, Monsieur. Even if she seems…*virile*. It will take some time for her to become accustomed to her new senses and appetites. I encourage patience on your behalf."

Étienne nodded. "Of course, Doctor. We will be cautious."

Dr. Van Helsing narrowed her eyes and *harrumphed* from the room.

"How do you feel, Daphne?" Étienne asked softly.

Now that the all-consuming hunger had been temporarily sated and the pains of my new state had ebbed, I was able to think. Sensations still pressed in on me in aggressive ways, but I felt more capable of blocking them out and focusing.

The blood Dr. Van Helsing had given me raced through my body, striking flints across my nerves and kindling little fires in my muscles.

"Peculiar," I answered. "The sights, the sounds, the smells—they are all too much, and not enough at the same time. I still feel such hunger, Étienne…is this what it is always like for you? How do you stand it?"

He chuckled. "It is worse when you are newly turned. It lessens after a few days. Then you become more adept at mastering it. I will teach you, *ma petite*. When you are new, you are ruled by baser instincts: feed, fight, fuck. But you will come to control them. Think of it as your adolescence."

At his words, heat crawled through my newly cold body and smoldered in my core. I grinned up at him and felt my needle-sharp fangs extend. *What an odd, thrilling sensation.* I ran my tongue over them to test their sharpness.

Étienne sucked in a breath. "If that isn't the most erotic sight I've ever seen…"

His desire immediately ignited my own.

"Make love to me, *l'amour*," I pleaded. "Let us usher in eternity properly."

"Daphne, you heard Dr. Van Helsing. We must exercise caution while you're in this period of transition. You need rest, *l'amour*."

"I have an entire immortality ahead of me to rest, Étienne. I need you," I said, reaching for his shirt. He rolled to the side, dodging just out of reach.

"I will not risk you falling ill when you've only just come back to me," he insisted. "You don't know what it was like for me to have you die in my arms, *chérie*. I never want to go through that again."

I crawled toward him on the bed, grinning lasciviously. The glow of his eyes burned with the familiar excitement of lust as he watched.

"Have you ever known a vampire to fall ill?" I argued. "One of my hungers has been sated. Would you leave the other starved?"

To emphasize my point, I sat up on my knees and let the sheets fall away, baring my nudity to Étienne's fervent gaze. He stood frozen, eyeing my fingers as I trailed them over my pale, cool skin. When my hands reached my breasts and plucked at my pebbling nipples, he hissed in frustration and leaped on top of me, pinning my hands to the mattress above my head.

"Do you think to torture me for trying to keep you safe?" he uttered. The hard length pressing against my hip made me delirious with want.

I grinned and ground my hips against him.

"Yes," I admitted. "How many times must I tell you before you'll understand? I'm not made of porcelain. I will not shatter."

On a resigned sigh, he buried his face in the crook of my neck and chuckled darkly.

"Oh darling, but you *will.*"

With a growl, he yanked off his shirt and tore the fabric into long strips. Crowding me back against the headboard, he tied my wrists firmly to the bedposts. The knots were tight but not painful, and with my new supernatural strength I could easily break free from the bindings—yet the heady thrill of my lust-fueled submission had me coming out of my skin with amorous anticipation.

"I shall be the one to torment you now, terrible minx," he said, sliding one finger through the wetness that had already gathered between my legs.

"Yes," I purred, lifting my hips to meet his touch. "Give me all of you, my love."

"Not yet, Duchesse," he said roughly, licking my arousal from his fingers. He reached for the bedside table and produced a long, thin velvet box. "I got you a small token of my love to celebrate your turning."

"You wish to exchange gifts now?" I panted, my tone snapping with sexual frustration.

That low, villainous laugh again.

"I think it's rather the perfect moment," he said, opening the box and holding it out for me to see. Inside was an exquisite necklace of fat, blueberry-sized pearls shimmering in a purplish-black hue. Never had I seen gems so beautiful before, and I certainly owned my fair share.

"Oh, *l'amour,* they're stunning," I breathed. "Thank you, *chéri.* If you wish me to wear them now, I will—clasp them around my throat and then, *Dieu,* make love to me."

Étienne plucked the necklace from the box and dragged the cool spheres across my hardened nipples, sending shocks of desire straight to my needy sex.

"That's not quite what I had in mind," he murmured, drawing the necklace down my abdomen and letting the pearls settle in a line from my bellybutton down the seam of my sex. His lips dropped open on a sigh and his gaze lifted to mine from beneath his long lashes, and it was all I could do not to rip my bonds to shreds and pounce like some feral beast. Étienne had always been a masterful lover, but with the increased sensations given to me by my new vampire blood, every soft touch was a crack of lightning skittering along my nerves, and his every repressed moan a rumble of thunder, whipping me into a world-ending storm of dark desires.

"So, your new jewels please you?" he asked, mouth kicking up in a devilish grin. Before I could reply, he slid one pearl through my dripping slit, rolling the bead against my aching clit. Words seemed to fail me, but a wild cry burst from my chest in response, ending on a rough tremor.

"I see your new supernatural state has unleashed this tightly coiled, animal side of you I'm so often eager to call upon. How utterly splendid. Sometimes it maddens me to see you hold yourself back—to be so restrained in polite company," he said, sliding the necklace against the apex of my pleasure in an ever-increasing rhythm. Just as my building orgasm began to take shape, he tugged the pearls aside and tossed them on the floor.

I couldn't help the growl that gave sound to my frustration, and before I could stop myself, I shredded the binds tying me down and leaped for him. Pushing him down with one newly clawed hand at his throat, I snarled at him in a voice I scarcely recognized.

"I'm done with your teasing, you devil," I said, straddling him and fitting the head of his cock at my entrance.

"Ah, *there she is.* Well, my vampire bride, I must be at your mercy," he rasped. "Do with me what you will."

"You think you can unleash some kind of bloodthirsty hellion in bed?" I demanded, taken aback by the ferocity of the anger at my denied pleasure. I sliced one sharp claw down his neck and inhaled shakily as dark blood welled to the surface of the injury. Étienne's pupils dilated—the glittering black of his pupils completely engulfing his golden irises. He smiled through lengthening fangs with an air of triumphant satisfaction.

"I know I have," he said, gaze pinned to my mouth as I sucked the blood from my fingertips. Pleasure arrowed through me once more, and I whimpered as the orgasm started to build again. I bent to lick his cut closed, tasting all his fire and adoration from the life-giving liquid seeping from his throat.

Instead of swallowing, I spit the mixture of blood and saliva onto his hard length and slid him through my folds. His arrogant manner evaporated and he swore, guttural and desperate. As much as I wanted to torment him for his teasing, I needed him too much. With one swift motion, I sank down onto him.

"*Dieu, je t'aime, Daphne—l'amour,*" he grunted, gripping my hips and thrusting up into me in a frenzied rhythm. "I will spend every night laying the world at your feet and every day worshipping you until the stars burn out."

"I love you, my darling Étienne, and I would give you my mortal heart over and over until you finally believe you are worthy of it," I panted, riding him as if we were bound for death at dawn. "I'm already so close— come with me."

On cue, he reached up and pressed a thumb to my clit, sending me tumbling headlong into the most powerful climax of my life. With another curse, he followed me over the edge, clinging to me like wreckage in a storm.

Sated and spent, I flopped down onto the bed next to him and snuggled into his embrace.

"*Mon Dieu*. Is this because of my newly turned state? Or is it always like that as a vampire?" I asked. "Ravenous hunger and a beastly chase towards pleasure?"

"No," Étienne replied, tucking an errant curl of hair behind my ear. "I've never had anything like that before. But I hope it will always be like that with us."

I sniffed in mock offense.

"I would never promise an eternity of such unladylike behavior," I said. The sharp bite of my hunger already returning, I reached for another decanter of blood on the side table. As I took a long pull from the bottle, Étienne picked up the discarded pearls and held them out.

"Not even if it is very, *very* enjoyable?" he challenged, pouting.

"Well, I suppose we must have some way to spend our endless days," I said with a laugh. "And this was a very, *very* good start."

THE AGENT AND THE OUTLAW

OUTLAW

BOOK TWO

PROLOGUE
CHARLOTTE

November 15, 1766
Château de Champs-sur-Marne

It wasn't often that I desired bloodshed. In fact, the only other time I truly *wanted* to murder someone had been a year ago, when my former husband summoned a demon to try to force my cousin to love him. It didn't quite work out for him, and needless to say, it made for a rather awkward evening.

"Do you ever wonder what they do with these reports?" I asked, stamping my seal into the molten wax on a thick sheaf of papers. "Sometimes I think they don't even look at them. They couldn't possibly read them all—every scrap of *occasionally* useful information from every agent. I've half a mind to test the theory and slip in some dirty words to see if anyone says anything."

Firelight flickered around the room, casting an amber glow upon the towering shelves of books that lined the library of my cousin's impressive château. Daphne, Duchesse de Duras, agent of The Order, leader of their women-only sect called *les Dames Dangereuses*, and my best friend, peered at me over the rim of her champagne glass.

"Charlotte, I've read your reports. There aren't any more filthy words than the ones you already use. I've seen seasoned agents blush beneath their masks while reading them. Perhaps you should consider a career as a writer of erotic novels."

"I would truly excel," I preened. "I know so many good synonyms for male anatomical features. *Quivering rod. Virility spear. Throbbing manhood.*"

Daphne rolled her eyes to cover a smirk.

"*Silent flute.*"

"Speaking of silent…" She looked at me pointedly.

I grinned and handed her the sealed folio—thirty-six pages of tightly scrawled script outlining an avalanche of evidence of the Marquis de Sade's crimes. Treason, blackmail, extortion, sexual abuses, violence against innocents…it had been months of grim and grueling work, and my biggest investigation since joining *les DD*. At court, all the aristocrats knew of the marquis's villainous tendencies, but no one had the temerity to bring charges against him. As a member of court, he was a titled aristocrat. *A peer.* At least, until Daphne and I had come along and forced the issue with The Order—the long-shadowed organization of powerful men in France who tasked themselves with the safety of king and country, but which operated in a sort of gray area just outside the law.

"What is to be done about his associates?" I asked.

She raised a brow at me and drained her glass. "I thought you handled that already." Her displeased tone implied she hadn't approved of my methods.

"Oh, *chérie*, just because I killed a vampire doesn't mean it was an indication of my feelings about the poor souls suffering from the blood plague. You know I'm all for integration of vampires and humans—I have been since the plague took hold of Paris years ago, really—and you know how much I love you and Étienne. Your hematic preferences don't bother me one whit. But truly, that bastard was evil. I mean, *really* evil. Quite possibly as evil as my former husband, may he rot in Hell," I said earnestly.

"Charlotte, he's imprisoned in the Château d'If," she replied. "Not technically dead. Probably mad, but still quite alive."

"Well, it's almost the same thing, isn't it? And The Order gave me his falsified death record after all that *unpleasantness* a year ago," I grumbled.

"Yes," she replied drolly. "'All that *unpleasantness*.' Summoning a demon and murdering several people—including my own awful husband, as well as the king's mistress—is what you would call *unpleasant*." She chuckled. "No, *chérie*, it's not that I disapprove of you staking a vampire who certainly deserved it, it's just that you killed him before he could tell us who Sade's other associate was. We know he had more than one highly placed individual feeding his depraved desires."

"Well, honestly, Daphne, it's not *my* fault a supernatural kidnapper ended up being so frail as to die when he was stabbed a few times—"

"Twenty-seven times."

"Twenty-seven times, then. But really, who's counting?"

"You did. It was in your report!"

"Because I'm nothing if not efficient. Not only did I dispatch a villainous bloodsucker—no offense—but I wrote a fully accurate report on the matter. You're lucky you have me as a lieutenant for *les DD*, you know, especially when I'm here working while you're out having glorious carnal fun with your dashing rake of a fiancé."

My words were meant to tease, but Daphne sensed the sadness behind them.

"Oh, Charlotte, I'm so sorry. I know this past year has been tough for you, what with Philippe's crimes, the devastation of the blood plague, and my engagement to Étienne. I know what it is to see another's happiness when you yourself are laid low by life's blows. But you know you are always welcome here. You will always have a home with Étienne and me. We both love you, darling," she said, putting a hand on mine.

"I know, Daphne," I said. "But I've been hiding out with you for far too long. You and Étienne have a life to start living. It's time I returned to Philippe's—to *my* estate. There are things there that I need to put to bed."

"Like François?" she teased, referring to the latest in my string of occasional lovers.

"*Non*, no longer. He was beautiful, certainly, but so self-absorbed. And you know, I think he was stealing my stockings. Every time he came around, I discovered I was missing one. He must have amassed quite a collection by now," I sighed. "Really, if he wants to wear them, fine, but at least he could buy them for himself and stop taking mine. Although, I suppose if the occasional errant stocking is the price I must pay for some thoroughly enjoyable bed sport, I should be grateful." I laughed, but it sounded hollow even to my own ears. Naturally, Daphne picked up on it right away.

"Someone will come along for you, Charlotte. I'm sure of it. Philippe was not your match, but you have one out there. You'll see. One day, true love will come right up to you and knock you senseless, and you'll be as much of a lost cause as I am," she smiled beatifically at me, and if I didn't love her immeasurably, I would have kicked her in the shin.

"If true love knocks you senseless, then *mon Dieu*, I am much happier with a string of wholly inadequate but temporarily sufficient lovers. After everything that happened last year, I'd much rather keep a firm hold of my senses."

Daphne grinned at me and stood. "Ah, well. You'll have to fall in and out of love on your own time. We'll be late for our meeting with The Order. Once they have this report in hand, they'll issue the formal execu-

tion order for Sade, then the real work begins. They'll most likely want
you to see it through."

"Good," I replied. "I don't often feel compelled to carry out assassinations, but after all of this," I gestured to the file, "I've never wanted to
deliver justice so much."

"Yes," she said, pulling on her cloak and picking up her domino mask.
"It will be good to see it through and put this whole case behind us."

"Of course," I said. "I think after this assignment, I'm going to take a
little rest. Perhaps spend some time in the country or go on a grand tour
around the continent. I've earned a bit of fun."

"I completely agree. And who knows? Perhaps you'll find your match
when this is all over," Daphne added hopefully.

I laughed. "I doubt that, Daphne. I very much doubt that."

ANTOINE

That same evening
Island of Menorca, Mediterranean

"What have you done?" I whispered, gripped by horror. I stared down
at the papers on his desk. *These cannot be right.* King Louis would never
stand for it. "*Général*, this is…*unthinkable*! You'll never get away with it."

He glared at me from across the room, face purpling with rage.

"Lieutenant, I don't recall giving you permission to enter my private
study, let alone read my correspondence. Do you desire a thrashing, boy?"

The threat was not idle bluster, but I pressed on. "Why would you—
why have you done such a thing? The war has ended. The treaty has been
signed. We're stuck here on this godforsaken island to oversee the last of
our withdrawal while the British drink their tea from the summit of our
defeat. We have lost, Général."

"We haven't lost until *I* say we've lost, Lieutenant," he snapped, his
eyes flashing with anger. He shook his head to regain control of his
temper, then, eerily calm, he continued. "*Les armées du roi* are weak—
inclined to *libertinage* and slothfulness. If we have been set back
temporarily, so be it. I will regain control and force these useless, witless,
spineless men in my command to embody the kind of strength and
ferocity that we need in order to turn the tide and beat back the British."

He's gone mad. There was no other explanation for it. "The treaty has
already been signed! King Louis—"

"King Louis doesn't care how I win, Lieutenant, only that I do. This is the way I will deliver a result. Something you know very little about," he hissed.

"You underestimate him," I argued. "He would not stand for such cruelty or treachery."

"Silence! You haven't the faintest notion of the king's true feelings. If we have faltered in this war, it is because the king is too distracted with domestic matters. The blood plague rages still, turning farmer, peasant, and *bourgeois* into filthy, soulless *sanguisuges*. He cannot control the vampires, so he must play at appeasing them until a cure can be discovered. That absurd emissary is as powerless as they come, and no one believes The Order is actually doing anything other than fueling rumors of revolution." He turned to face me, and I saw disconcerting wildness in his gaze. "I will save France at any cost—even if the threat is France herself."

"Sir, you cannot mean—"

"You are dismissed, Lieutenant," he snapped, pushing past me. He sat down at the desk and picked up the damning papers, then tossed them into the fire.

"No!" I reached for them, but strong arms hauled me back. Two other soldiers had entered the room and now pulled me toward the door. I stared at the burning evidence, quickly turning to ashes before my eyes. I hadn't thought far enough ahead—would I really have gone to the king with proof of such corruption? *It doesn't matter now.* Even if I did report it, no one would believe me without something substantial to back my claim. Général de Vaux had the reputation and influence to do as he pleased, like all powerful men.

Gritting my teeth and brushing the dirt from my uniform, I stormed back to my quarters. It wasn't long before the two soldiers showed up outside again. I frowned, already suspecting what was to come.

"A dozen lashings for insubordination and disorderly conduct," one of them said. "To be delivered at dawn."

A dozen. Those scars could join the others. "No dishonorable discharge for me then?"

The soldier narrowed his eyes at me. "Certainly not, *monsieur.*"

I went back inside and turned to my own correspondence. I knew I had a letter from my sister, Marie, waiting in the stack. My heart clenched at the thought. She'd been unwell since the murder of her son, Louis. My sister's family had been a bright spot in my otherwise gloomy existence, but with the loss of Louis, now everything seemed bleak. I prayed her grief would lessen with time, but it only seemed to consume her more, until I feared she would be swallowed by it. Young Louis had suffered brutal mistreatment at the hands of a corrupt aristocrat, the Marquis de

Sade. As soon as I was able, I would confront the monster and have my revenge.

Her letter gave me no comfort—rather, it stoked my temper to a boiling point. Marie had questions about the circumstances of Louis's death. The things she suggested were horrifying, but something about them took root in my heart. *The général must see this.* Crumpling it in my shaking fist, I rushed from the room and back to the général's study. The two soldiers from earlier were standing guard out front.

"He is busy," one of them said. "Come back later."

"No," I said, trying to push past them. "He will see me now!"

The guards tried to restrain me, but I fought them both off, taking one down with a fist to the gut and knocking the other one out with a punch to the temple. I kicked the door open and faced the outraged général at his desk.

"We need to talk."

1

CHARLOTTE

November 1, 1767
Somewhere outside Versailles

WHEN I CAME TO, SEVERAL SENSATIONS ASSAULTED ME. THE RHYTHMIC GALLOP of dull pain inside my skull. The roiling of this evening's oysters swirling inside my guts. The earthy scents of sweaty horseflesh, leather, and mud tangling in my nose. Then, the slow and damnable realization that my hands and feet had been bound and I'd been thrown—rather indecorously, I might add—facedown across the ass of some idiot's cantering horse. *The nerve!*

I opened my mouth to protest, but the horse pulled up short, dangerously shifting the oysters. I choked out a groan as the bile started to rise.

"For the love of God, let me off of this animal, or I shall cast up my accounts all over you!"

My captor slid off the horse and lifted me easily. He—yes, certainly it was a *he*, and a rather splendid specimen of *he*, as I started to recall—set me on my feet, and I unsteadily hopped to the side of the road to be sick. I heaved and, tied as I was, began to pitch forward over the frost-covered leaf litter.

Calloused hands grasped my wrists and pulled me upright. I attempted to get a look at his face, but the low hood of his cloak and the darkness of the late evening—or was it early morning?—prevented me from doing so. The only part of him I could see was a strong, stubbled jawline and some very fine lips set in a tight line of annoyance.

"Easy, lad," he said softly, his voice as rough as his work-hewn hands. Chills danced up my spine.

Lad?

Ah, yes. A jumble of memories began to unravel. I frowned down at my Cupid costume. The once-pristine toga and breeches beneath were rumpled and stained with—*mon Dieu, please let that be dirt.* The small, feathered wings and golden circlet were gone, but I noted with relief that my wig was still secure.

What happened?

I'd been at Versailles for the king's All Hallow's Eve masquerade. My cousin Daphne and her fiancé Étienne had been with me. I was on assignment for les Dames Dangereuses—The Order's cadre of female agents. *But what had I been doing?*

I furrowed my brows to try and recall but immediately regretted it. The steady beat of pain in my head became a symphony of agony, and I vomited. I was dimly aware of a humiliating dribble down the front of my toga.

"Hell, lad, how much did you have to drink? Did Sade slip you something? Or are you just in your cups?" The soothing tone was gone, replaced by one of clipped irritation.

"I'm never eating another oyster again," I wheezed, feebly trying to wipe my mouth with my shoulder. *Wait...he said—*

Sade. The Marquis de Sade. My target. Yes. *Yes.* That was right—I was at the masquerade, dressed as a young man so I could lure Sade out into the garden and dispatch him there. Strangle him. *It should look like an accident,* The Order had said. A lover getting too carried away during a tryst, an incident too scandalous to be thoroughly investigated. *Not that anyone would press for an investigation.* Between Sade's crimes, the rumors, and victims from every social class, few—if any—would mourn his loss.

I remembered seeing Sade in the ballroom at Versailles. I'd successfully attracted his attention and plied him with a glass of drugged champagne, which had made him docile and willing. He'd followed me into that absurd hedge maze in the gardens and had been fumbling with the buttons on his breeches, when...*thwip!* An arrow—straight to the heart. *That doesn't seem right. An arrow? Sade is supposed to be strangled to death. I'm supposed to be the one to do it. Wait, that's it...*

I hadn't been able to complete my assignment. *Someone* had intervened, shot an arrow through Sade with, what, a crossbow? Yes, that was it. And there it was, hanging from the side of my captor's saddle. *My captor.* I tensed. This man had interrupted my assassination attempt and had murdered the Marquis de Sade. Who was he? Why did he want Sade dead? *Why has he kidnapped me and what does he want with me? And mon Dieu, why does that last thought send a perverse shiver of pleasure through me?*

Putain. Now is not the time, Charlotte. Focus!

Sade's death wouldn't look like an accident now. It would look like murder. Perhaps it would look like a political statement—a thought that truly worried me given the escalating tensions between the vampires and the aristocracy. *Merde.* Were Daphne and Étienne still back at Versailles? Had they tried to follow? They must be worried to death!

Despite myself, I chuckled. *Can the undead be worried to death?*

An owl hooted in the distance and the man shifted toward the sound. It was still dark out, but I could tell that night was waning. How much time had passed?

"How long was I out?" I rasped. The ache at the back of my head throbbed insistently, and I remembered a more pressing indignity. "You knocked me out! How dare you! What a horrible thing to do to someone you just met. I mean, we haven't even been introduced!" I tried to turn and face my captor with righteous pique, but I lost my balance and nearly toppled over. Again, he grabbed my bound wrists to steady me. "Oh, for the love of—could you at least spare me some humiliation and untie my ankles? I'm hardly in a position to run for it," I grumbled. "Being this unsteady on my feet is only adding to my nausea and increasing the likelihood that I will purge myself again."

The lines around his mouth tightened, but he kept silent. His bulky shoulders tensed beneath the cloak, and I fought to keep my lustful interest at bay. *Have I ever seen a man with such a build before?* I didn't think so. *He's kidnapped you, Charlotte, and likely not for some bed sport.*

I frowned. I did not enjoy being ignored, so I added, "You see, Monsieur, I'm afraid you're close enough to bespatter."

The threat seemed to have an effect on him. Carefully, he bent to untie the rope at my feet. Thighs like tree trunks tested the seam limits on his breeches as he loosened the knot. I gritted my teeth. He stood slowly but made no move to untie my hands. Of course, I considered running, but after taking measure of the man before me, the sorry state of my footwear, and the remaining oysters, I thought better of that notion. *He obviously* reached the same conclusion. I seethed and scowled up into his obscured face.

I saw little of him outside of his cloak, which was well-made but plain black wool, as if he had money but not the desire to spend it. *How...odd.* He was quite a bit taller than me—I faced his expansive chest directly— and broad-shouldered in a very *un*aristocratic sort of way, which clashed with the idea of him having any sort of wealth. *Curious!*

I shivered. Studying his cloak made me realize I was bitterly cold in the late October evening—*or is that early November morning?*—and I was still in my silly costume. It was fine for disguising my sex, but not ideal for the onset of winter temperatures. My breath condensed in frosty puffs in front of my face.

More memories solidified. He had been handsome. Rather, he *was* handsome. I remembered seeing him burst through the hedge maze back at Versailles and fall into the torchlight. A queue of chestnut hair, dark sweeps of lashes, vibrant green eyes, a once-broken nose that had been set well, and a thin, crescent moon scar that crossed from his brow to his cheek, and those lips… *Mon Dieu, such lips! A woman would sell all her jewels to hear sweet nothings drop from them.*

Though sweet nothings hadn't dropped from them. I recalled our altercation in the garden earlier in the evening. He'd been flippant, rude even, and had clearly misunderstood my intentions. However, I was fortunate he hadn't seen through my disguise.

Despite his enigmatic appeal, my temper surged.

"Kidnapping is a hanging offense, you know," I said archly. "I'd hate to see a neck as fine as yours stretched because of some silly mistake. Release me and I assure you that no harm will come to you from my quarter."

The man said nothing.

"You don't even need to return me to Versailles. I can make my own way. Simply untie me and let me go. You've done a great deal of damage, you see, and it needs to be put right. Perhaps if I can get back soon, I can figure out a way to spin your interference. A robbery? No, that would be absurd. A religious zealot, maybe. Sade's sexual deviancy was well-known, and I doubt the church approved. That could work, you know. I've a friend in the church with a debt to repay…"

I trailed off, thinking. If I could get back to Versailles, I could fix it. I would simply present Daphne with an alternate course of action, and she would convince The Order that this could still work for us. Either way, Sade was dead, which was the one silver lining. He wouldn't be able to abuse any more innocents, and the vampire peasants and bourgeoisie who clamored for his blood—literally and figuratively—would be temporarily assuaged. *A peace offering of death.*

My captor studied me silently, seemingly frozen to the ground. He obviously didn't grasp the immediacy of my needs. When he had crashed through the hedge maze at the palace, he had stared at me incomprehensibly when I chastised him for his haste. Perhaps he wasn't the intelligent sort—a shame, really, since he was so thoroughly enjoyable to look at.

I spoke with a slow, deliberate pace.

"Monsieur? *Parlez-vous français?* Can you understand me? First, I need to be untied. Second, I need to return to the palace. Well, no—second, I need some kind of cloak or coat. It's bloody freezing out here. *Then* I need to return to Versailles, which hopefully isn't more than an hour or two's ride from where we currently stand."

He continued to regard me mutely, but his shoulders shifted slightly. *Ah, so he does understand me.*

"Where exactly are we?" I demanded. I had no idea how long I'd been unconscious. The navy sky was lightening to a lovely periwinkle, which meant the sun was soon to rise. Dread pooled when I realized Daphne and Étienne would not be able to find me now. They'd be beholden to their vampire schedules and would be below ground for the next day. My trail would probably be cold by the time they could reach me. *I am on my own.*

"Are you well enough to carry on?" His voice was like the dregs from a chocolate pot—deep, dark, and luscious. In another world, at another time, perhaps I would have tried to seduce him.

"I should think so," I nodded. "You don't need to worry, Monsieur. Untie me and I'll be perfectly able to make my way back from here."

He grunted and leaned forward to grab my wrists.

"Thank you, Monsieur. I appreciate your attempts to remove me from a dangerous situation at the masquerade, but I assure you, all will be well when I can get back and sort everything out. I say, that doesn't feel like the knot is loosening there—"

He hoisted me up onto the horse and swung himself up behind me. It seemed to take very little effort for him to lift me, which was both disconcerting and tempting. *Dieu, Charlotte. Stop thinking such things!*

"Forgive me, Monsieur, but we seem to have an error in communication. You aren't releasing me, which doesn't make any sense. I've already told you that you won't be in any danger from me for what happened at the palace, but you must let me go so that I can deal with things, *d'accord?* I mean, I don't really know what else you could possibly want with me. I'll only slow you down, and I'm sure you have lots of other lives to inconvenience."

"Silence," he hissed.

If there was one word I did *not* appreciate—especially from a man—it was that one. I'd certainly heard it enough from my former husband whenever he felt I was being inappropriate, which was to say, quite often.

"I—WILL—NOT!" I shouted, punctuating my words with fierce jabs from my elbows into his sides. I whipped my head back as hard as I could and felt it connect with his nose. He grunted, but I yelled.

Charlotte, you idiot! That's where the brute knocked you senseless.

I didn't have time to regret my mistake and the sharp pain radiating through my head—I acted as fast as my reflexes would allow. With my captor temporarily distracted, I leapt from the horse and tucked myself into a ball to cushion my fall. Quick as a flash, I jumped up and took off through the forest, running in a zigzag pattern. I wasn't sure if the bulge I'd felt at my back was his masculine endowments or a pistol, but I wasn't going to take any more chances.

When I'd run far enough to reach the limit of my breathing capacity, I paused behind a large oak tree and listened. I heard the chorus of early morning birdsong and the distant burble of a stream. I smiled to myself. I didn't hear a twig-breaking, leaf-crunching, crossbow-wielding madman giving chase. Perhaps he'd reasoned I was too much trouble—a fact I could heartily agree with—and rode on with his smelly, vomit-inducing horse.

When my breath returned to normal, I started moving again but stopped just as quickly. Some distance away, I heard a knot of low male voices creeping down the road. I strained to hear them. Had my captor persuaded a passerby to help seek me out? Crouching down beneath a thicket of greenery, I peered through the branches.

I could just make them out where they gathered along the road—there were five of them, all in identical burgundy coats. I squinted. They looked like soldiers, but I didn't recognize their uniforms. Were they English? They wore that gaudy red, didn't they? What would English soldiers be doing here?

Leaning forward, I tried to get a better look. If I could get a bit closer, I might be able to hear what they were saying. I prepared to make my move.

"Don't."

The word was a whispered command coming from somewhere just above my head. I looked up and nearly shrieked. My captor was perched on a limb in the large oak directly atop me, staring murderously at the group of soldiers. *Merde.* How long had he been there?

Sullenly accepting that my *great* escape had been anything but, I narrowed my eyes.

"Don't *what?*" I hissed back.

"Move."

"Ha!" I retorted. "Forgive me if I'm a bit loath to take your advice. You did, after all, bludgeon and abscond with me. I'm beginning to doubt your intentions to ensure my safety."

He didn't acknowledge my response, but I knew he'd heard. I could see the muscles work in his jaw as if he were gritting his teeth. My former husband, Philippe, used to do the same thing when he would tire of my cheek. I considered it one of my greatest virtues, to be so infuriating to the simpler sex.

To prove my utter unwillingness to listen to the crossbow-wielding madman, I snaked forward through the undergrowth to hide behind yet another bush. I could practically feel the fury emanating from the oak tree behind me. From this better angle, I could hear the soldiers more clearly.

They were speaking French! Two of them had thick foreign accents—Prussian, I guessed. The other three were clearly Parisian. *But why the burgundy uniforms?*

"We must turn back. We won't be able to find him now. It's too late," one of the Prussians was saying.

"We can't just leave! We know he's in the area. Fan out," said another.

"We won't find him here," said the tallest Parisian. "These woods stretch for hundreds of acres, and he's had more training than all of us."

"But we have the advantage," grinned the first Prussian.

I probably would have heard more, but at that moment, I leaned a *bit* too far forward and a twig snapped beneath my palm. I froze, praying the soldiers hadn't heard.

They had.

Within seconds, the soldiers were upon me.

The tall Parisian hauled me up by the back of my toga, lifting me well off the ground. His anger at uncovering a possible spy dissolved into guffaws of mirth as the group took in my admittedly bizarre ensemble.

"Thank heavens!" I enthused, pitching my voice low and hoping my disguise was still intact enough to fool them. "Gentlemen, you have certainly saved my life. I was traveling with my master on our way home from the masquerade at Versailles when we were set upon by highwaymen! They tied me up, tossed me out of the carriage, and rode away with my master to ransom him. I must get back to Versailles to get help. Can you aid me?"

The outrageousness of the lie seemed to fit with my strange dress. I could see the wheels turning in the Parisian's head.

"Who's your master, boy?"

"The Comte de Brionne."

Oh, Charlotte, you ninny. The name—my name—had slipped out. Now, I had to work with it. Something like recognition flashed in the Parisian's eyes, and I tried to mask my panic.

"I thought the Comte de Brionne was dead," he said, but he didn't sound certain.

"Of course not!" I argued with mock affront. "I've been serving the Brionne family for several years now—I think I would have noticed such a thing, Monsieur."

The Parisian set me on my feet. His cold gaze assessed me.

"Have you seen anyone else come through here? Anyone else on the road?"

It was my chance to rid myself of the crossbow-wielding madman, but something unknowable prevented me from doing so. I shrugged.

"*Non, Monsieur.* I've been too terrified to come out from behind the bushes to see anyone else. You fine gentlemen are the only men that I've come across. Now, please, will you help me? Do you have horses? Or perhaps you can tell me where the nearest town is?"

"The nearest town is about three miles down the road," he said with an unnerving smile. "But I'm afraid you won't make it there."

2

ANTOINE

November 1, 1767
Somewhere outside Versailles

I WATCHED IN HORRIFIED FASCINATION AS THE YOUNG MAN ATTEMPTED TO fight off all five of the soldiers at once, with his hands bound, no less. Granted, he didn't seem to be doing well, but that fact didn't appear to stop him or diminish his resolve. I had to hand it to the lad—he had spirit. What he didn't have, however, was the faintest idea who or what he was dealing with.

I cursed and leveled twin pistols at the two nearest soldiers. I knew it wouldn't stop them, but it could slow them down. I aimed and fired.

The two took bullets to their legs and went down. Jumping from the oak bough, I barreled toward the fray, tossing my pistols aside in favor of my short swords. In this chaos, I didn't want to risk hitting the young man —irritating though he was.

The other three turned in surprise when they heard the shots, which gave the lad the opportunity to deliver a devastating knee to one's groin, then duck and roll behind the other two. I managed to slash one across his arm, causing him to drop his sword. The lad caught it, cut the ropes binding his hands, and picked up one of the soldiers' dropped pistols. Holding it aloft, he aimed steadily at the last soldier's head.

"Who are you?" The boy snarled. I could've sworn his voice rose an octave.

The soldier smiled. I knew he would tell the lad nothing.

"Leave it," I said. I approached the lad and tried to wrest the gun from him, but he aimed it at me instead.

"Don't," he warned, echoing my instruction from earlier.

The soldier sensed his opportunity and reached for his sword, but without batting an eye, the lad turned the gun back to him and fired, hitting him in the stomach. The soldier crumpled to the dirt, black blood spreading across the golden brown leaves. The lad pocketed the pistol—the lethal barrel sticking absurdly out of his toga—and turned back toward the road at a rapid clip.

I stayed to tie the wounded soldiers together. My stomach soured at the notion that I'd have to use my short swords to dispatch the lot of them. *Grim, bloody business, but it needs to be done.* As I began to reconcile myself to the task at hand, the wet slap of hoofbeats in mud gave me pause.

He didn't. Dieu, tell me he didn't.

I made it to the road just in time to see the lad race past me on *my* horse.

Putain!

I ground my teeth together and started after him—my horse, Tartuffe, was more important to me than anything. I ran behind him for a while, eventually losing sight of him on the road toward the town. I'd passed through it on my way into the city and knew there was only one inn, which was the most likely place the young man would go. The sun was rising, and I was certain he was as exhausted as I was, so I didn't think he would try and head back toward Versailles yet. It would mean chancing upon the soldiers again, and I didn't think he was that foolish.

When I get my hands on him, I'm going to—

I heaved an exhausted sigh. *You're going to what, Antoine?* I had no idea what I was going to do with him. I'd been so stupid, so rash. I should have waited for a better moment to kill Sade. I'd been biding my time for the last year, what difference would a few more hours have made? But I hadn't been able to stay my hand—I couldn't have—and now there was another young man involved. A young man who likely cared for the rotten marquis and was probably riding to the nearest town to summon the *gendarmerie* and have them cart me off to the Bastille for the killer that I was.

No longer just a killer.

A murderer.

The word seemed to hang about me like a slack noose. Would the lad turn me in? I quickened my pace. Either way, he was dangerous, *and* he was in danger. If this had all happened but a couple short years ago, I probably would have killed him and been done with the whole thing.

Killing was what I'd been trained to do and had spent my life perfecting, all to impress a man I'd never accepted was impossible to impress.

Even now, I could hear his criticism in my ears. *Foolish boy! How could you be so stupid? All my influence, all that training, all your years of experience, and still you languish away as a mere lieutenant. Purchase your company command? Don't be an imbecile. You are an embarrassment to me and to our family name.*

I cringed, forcing my thoughts back to the present and the lad I should probably kill.

But I didn't want to kill him. I didn't even want to leave him to the mercy of the soldiers who'd surely hunt him down. I'd had far too much death for one lifetime. Sade had deserved it—had deserved much more than the swift death I'd delivered—but the lad didn't. He'd been in the wrong place at the wrong time and was probably the victim of a deviant predator, just like Louis had been.

My stomach churned as I hurried on and tried to figure out what to do with the lad when I reached him. Killing him, certainly, was the last resort. Could he be reasoned with? If he knew what kind of a man Sade was, would he find himself lucky to have only just escaped his clutches? I frowned at that thought—likely not. I didn't think he'd be grateful to me for saving him from the marquis *or* the soldiers, especially since it was my fault he'd been endangered in the first place.

Merde.

Perhaps he could be bribed. I certainly didn't think he could be terrorized into silence. I'd seen the look in his eyes when he shot the soldier in the stomach. *Oh, yes.* I'd seen it many times, usually on the faces of men who'd left the battlefield bodily but who remained there in their minds. The lad had known suffering in his life, of that I was sure. I was also sure of the fact that he wasn't the effeminate, garrulous fop I'd originally believed he was. Something darker lurked inside him. *Like recognizes like.* I would not underestimate him.

By the time I finally, *blessedly*, reached the edge of the town, my lungs burned, my feet ached, and despite the chill, I dripped with sweat. The sight of the inn made my knees nearly buckle with relief. Exhaustion, cold, and hunger clawed at me, fighting for dominance over my senses.

I staggered through the door into the tavern and sat hard on a wooden bench. The innkeeper—a corpulent, red-faced fellow—approached me warily. Most men did. The scar across my face seemed to suggest I was the troublesome sort.

"I'm looking for a young man," I said. "Slip of a thing—dressed in a toga. He took off with my horse a bit ago. I'd very much like to see him returned."

The innkeeper grunted and shrugged. "The horse or the boy?"

I did not answer.

"Haven't seen him."

I narrowed my eyes. I knew he was lying, but I didn't want to cause more trouble than was necessary. Glaring, I tossed a handful of coins onto the table. The innkeeper's eyes widened greedily.

"The horse is in the stables," he said.

"And the lad?"

The innkeeper chewed on his lip, apparently waiting for something. My fingers itched to throttle him, but I reached for more coin. *You'll catch more flies with honey than vinegar*, Marie had always said. *Well, who wants to catch flies, ma sœur?* I'd always replied. The memory brought on a throb of heartache, but I set it aside.

The innkeeper jutted his chin toward a staircase behind the bar, leading up to the rooms.

"First door on the right."

I nodded and crossed the room in long, purposeful strides. Still debating what to do with the lad, I reconsidered my options. *Protect him. Plead with him. Bribe him. Kill him.* I swallowed my frustration and despair. I'd just have to play things by ear.

Figuring it would be better for me to have the element of surprise—he still had the soldier's pistol, after all—I crept up to the door and kicked it open. The heavy wood crashed into the wall, and I heard shouts from downstairs at the disturbance. I ducked into the room and froze, confusion clouding my brain like fog.

Standing in a small washtub in front of the fire was the young man—only, *he* wasn't a *young man*. I tore my gaze away from the rivulets of water sliding down an exquisite feminine form and stared into those same outraged brown eyes. It was only when I heard the unmistakable *click* of a pistol cocking that I realized she had the gun trained on me.

I gaped. "You—you're—*Mon Dieu...*"

"Get out!" she bellowed.

I scrambled back to the hallway and tried to close the door behind me, but only served to yank the damn thing off its hinges. The innkeeper stomped up the stairs, swearing roundly and demanding I pay for the damages. I awkwardly leaned the broken door against the opening to the room and took a step back. All the while, my mind struggled to process what I'd seen.

He was a *she. Mon Dieu, the sight of her naked. Those full breasts, the curves of those hips, that dark triangle of hair covering her sex. Not a man.* My body responded before my brain even registered the implication, making me uncomfortably hard. I fought to focus on something more productive than my arousal's clamoring need.

She had been in disguise—why? Why had she been with the Marquis de Sade? Who was she? Unease rustled through me. If she'd been at Versailles, chances were she was a member of the aristocracy. Was she in hiding? Perhaps avoiding some brutish or unsuitable marriage—I'd read things like that in romantic novels. But then, how did she know how to fight? She'd either learned from life's harsh experiences or by training. She didn't fight like a street urchin, though, so I reasoned it had to be some kind of formal training. She must be a spy then, but for whom? *Damn it!* Who *was* she? What the Hell was going on?

The innkeeper continued shouting at me. He made a move for the broken door, but I stepped in front of him.

"I'll pay for the damages," I growled. "It was an accident. We won't disturb you further."

The innkeeper spat on the floor at my feet and sneered. He opened his mouth to hurl another insult, but I'd had enough. I pulled my cloak aside and placed my hand on the hilt of my short sword.

"Go," I said. Eyes wide, the innkeeper stormed off, grumbling the whole time.

Turning back to the room, I knocked on the broken door.

"Leave me alone!"

Her guise now revealed, she stopped lowering her voice. The smooth, velvety timbre wasn't too dissimilar from a young man's voice, but it seemed so obvious now, I kicked myself for believing in the ruse.

"We need to talk," I said calmly.

I heard a derisive snort from the other side of the door, then a muttered, "Do we?"

"Please. Keep the pistol if you like. I just…need some information," I stammered. I knew the innkeeper and several tavern patrons were listening to our shouted exchange through the door, and my discomfort only grew.

"I have no information to give," she said petulantly.

"I do," I replied, lowering my voice. "And it might save your life."

I heard an exasperated groan and the sound of water swishing about. A vision flashed—soft, heat-pinked skin dripping with water and soap suds. Full breasts, long auburn hair, and a scorching gaze that promised a deep well of passion. My heart pounded in my chest. It had been too long since I'd been with a woman. Hell, I couldn't remember the last time I'd spoken with one for longer than a brief, curt exchange.

From inside the room, I heard prolonged muttering, then a damp stomping over to the door. She glared at me through the gap between the warped hinges and the wall, then angrily pulled me into the room. With a kick of disappointment, I saw she'd finished bathing and had wrapped herself in a shabby blanket stolen from the bed. She crossed the room with the haughty poise of a noblewoman and sat in a chair in the farthest corner of the room. The pistol lay on a table at her side.

The morning sunlight was just beginning to warm the room, and the golden light coming in through the window spilled across her alert form. I cursed myself for failing to recognize that she'd been a woman in disguise —seeing her now, I couldn't believe I'd mistaken her for anything other than a creature of devastating beauty.

She twisted her hair into a knot atop her head, showing off her elegant neck and shoulders. Her exposed skin looked softer than silk, except for the angry welts across her wrists where I'd bound her hands. *You wretched monster! Those wounds are your fault!*

I frowned, but she seemed to take no notice.

"Who are you?" we both demanded in unison. I reddened. She laughed.

"No, no. You go first," she said. "You are trying to save my life, after all. It's only fair that I have a name to direct my gratitude."

I ignored the sarcasm.

"I… Well, you may call me Antoine," I said.

Silence descended. She waited.

"Antoine," she finally echoed.

I nodded, trying to hide the irrational surge of pleasure I felt at hearing my name on her rose petal lips. When I didn't offer anything more, she rolled her eyes and carried on.

"Very well, Antoine. What information do you possess that you believe will save my life?"

I shifted uncomfortably, feeling as though I was being interrogated by an enemy. *You are, you fool.*

"Who are you?" I asked.

"I suppose you can call me Charlotte," she said.

"Charlotte…have you a surname?"

"Certainly."

"What is it?"

She rolled her eyes again, apparently tired of our exchange.

"Charlotte None-Of-Your-Concern. The information, Monsieur. I'm afraid I'm in a bit of a hurry."

"Why?" I asked, unable to help myself. She looked at me like I was a complete idiot.

"Those soldiers know exactly where I—we've—gone. This is the closest town for some distance, apparently, and I don't imagine they're particularly thrilled to be burying their comrade. I'd like to get out of here as quickly as possible. If you do, indeed, have life-saving information you wish to impart, I suggest you do it while our lives are still able to be saved."

At this, a knock sounded. Charlotte picked up the pistol and I went to see who disturbed us. A young girl stood in the hallway, arms full of clothing. I opened the door a bit wider, and she entered the room.

"You are most fortunate, Madame! I was able to find something suitable at my aunt's house. It's not as fine as you're used to, I'm sure, but it'll be warm enough to see you on your journey," she said.

Charlotte's frigid manner melted away and she smiled brightly at the other woman.

"*Merci*, Hélène, you absolute angel!" Charlotte went to the discarded Roman costume on the floor and pulled out a staggering amount of money for the girl.

"Oh, no, Madame! That's too much—I couldn't!"

"Nonsense, *chérie*. Keep it close to you. Don't let that bastard downstairs wheedle one coin from you, *d'accord?*"

The girl nodded fervently.

"Good. Now, be so kind as to bring up some breakfast for my companion and I, would you? *Merci beaucoup*," Charlotte said in a generous lilt. She ushered the girl back out and began to lay the garments out on the bed.

"Woolen stockings, good…good…quilted stays, very good. The skirt isn't a particularly flattering color for me, but it'll be warm enough to see me back to Versailles. Hopefully the soldiers who were after you won't pay too much attention to a woman…" she trailed off, muttering to herself again.

Distracted by the nearly sheer chemise spread across the blankets, I swallowed hard. Blood was rapidly leaving my head and venturing south again, making me feel slow-witted and uncomfortable. Distantly, I heard myself arguing.

"After me?"

"Well, I would assume so," she stated matter-of-factly. "They certainly weren't after me, and I imagine if you go around murdering marquises and kidnapping young gentlemen, it makes sense that you'd have a posse of Prussians and petulant Parisians pursuing you." She chuckled at herself. "Ha! Try saying that five times fast."

She lifted the edge of her blanket and began to slide on a woolen stocking, apparently unconcerned that I was in the room. She was still talking, but all I could hear was the rushing of blood in my ears. The blanket lifted again, affording me another tortuous glimpse of graceful, shapely legs, and my tattered composure snapped.

"You can't go back," I almost shouted. "I won't allow it."

She paused, tying a ribbon garter around her stocking, her eyes narrowing in warning.

"Please," I said. "You don't know what you're dealing with. If you leave without my protection, you won't make it back to Versailles."

3

CHARLOTTE

November 1, 1767
Somewhere outside Versailles

"*Mon Dieu*," I said, exasperated. "Will you please just tell me what you're on about?"

My patience was wearing thin. I was cold, tired, sore, and hungry to the point of ill-humor, which was not often a state I found myself in. If this brooding beau didn't stop gawking at my calves and carry on with his message, I'd have to resort to *unladylike* behavior.

Still, his eyes followed my movements, captivated. Deep down—very deep, of course—I preened with the thought that I'd pulled one over on him and that my unabashed manner had him unsettled. *Good.* He *should* feel bad for walloping my skull and tossing me across his horse's rear.

"*Monsieur*," I prompted, hoisting the thick skirts in place and tying the last few ribbons. The garments were plain, but warm, and they would help me blend in with the common folk until I could get away. I sat back down to plait my hair to better hide it beneath a simple lace cap.

"You cannot leave," he said again. "They will find you."

"Your concern is noted," I said archly. "Was that your life-saving information? That those soldiers would be bent on revenge and scour the countryside hunting me to stretch my neck? *Please.* I expected that from the first. I doubt they'll bother a plain old maid, though."

"They'll find you anyway. They're not like normal men. They don't have to look for you. They'll be able to smell you from a mile away," he muttered darkly.

"I beg your pardon! How uncouth to comment upon my odor when you're the one who threw me across your foul beast and made me retch up last night's oysters. Besides, I've just had a bath."

That muscle in his jaw twitched—the one that indicated extreme displeasure. I smiled to myself.

"That's *not* what I meant," he growled.

"Then speak plainly, Antoine," I replied.

My use of his name seemed to unlock something inside him. Abruptly, he stood and started to pace the room.

"How do I know I can trust you?" He ran his hands through his hair, agitated. Loose waves escaped his tight queue, leaving him looking distressed and disheveled. It was adorable, really.

"You don't," I shrugged. "And honestly, I wouldn't advise it." I secured my cap and tilted my head toward the door. I could hear a slight creak outside—someone was eavesdropping. I motioned to Antoine to be silent, and he looked at me in confusion. I gestured to the door, grabbed the pistol, cocked it, and walked over as quietly as possible. I aimed forward while I threw the door open with my other hand.

The tavern girl, Hélène, shrieked and stumbled backward, nearly dropping the tray she held in front of her. I lowered the weapon and grabbed her arm, steadying her.

"*Pardon, Madame!*" she gasped. "You startled me. I was just coming up with your breakfast tray and to see if you needed any help with your hair, but I see you have managed."

I smiled sheepishly. "My apologies. I'm afraid I read too many Gothic novels and have my mother's nervous disposition. I startle at the slightest sound."

She eyed the pistol warily but was eventually disarmed by my vivacity.

"Is that food for me? *Mon Dieu*, Hélène! Everything looks positively delicious. I've never seen pastries look so perfectly flaky and golden, have you, Antoine? Come, *chérie*, bring in the tray and have a cup of tea with us."

"Oh, I don't think I should—Monsieur Rocher would be furious if I was found out."

"Nonsense! You may tell your employer that you stayed to help me dress."

I tugged her into the room and secured the door behind us. She placed the tray down and began to set the table for two.

"No need, *chérie*. Antoine and I will not stand on ceremony. Please, have a seat. I'm sure your poor feet could do with a bit of a rest," I said with a wink. Hélène blushed prettily and sat in the chair across from Antoine, who tracked her with a hooded gaze. I felt irrationally annoyed with him—and with sweet, pretty Hélène.

Don't be absurd, Charlotte. You're trying to get information from the girl and dispense with this crossbow-wielding madman as soon as possible.

Nodding to myself, I pasted a bright smile on my face and sat on the bed. Neither Antoine nor Hélène reached for the tray of food. The smell of buttery pastries, warm bread, strawberry jam, and a simple, soft cheese made my stomach rumble. Not wanting to wait any longer, I poured everyone a cup of tea and began to butter a roll for myself.

"Monsieur Antoine," I began, realizing I didn't know his surname. "This is Hélène. She's been working here for—what was it you said to me, *chérie?* —four years now?"

Hélène nodded.

Antoine tore at a chunk of bread and spread some of the cheese on it. His expression was grave, but I paid no attention. I'd dealt with surly gentlemen like him before—in fact, I'd been married to one. I knew the best way past their grumpy defenses was usually in some mix of infuriating femininity and good-natured teasing. Good food and copious spirits didn't hurt, either.

I sipped my tea and bit into the warm roll. It was soft and sweet—almost melting on my tongue. I moaned in satisfaction.

"Hélène, do you bake these yourself? They are *divine.* Simply the best rolls I think I've ever had. Don't you agree, Antoine? Oh, you *must* try yours with the strawberry jam. It's positively sinful!"

Hélène smiled and blushed again at my praise. She lowered her lashes in a fetching sort of way, and Antoine's bread paused in its journey to his lips. I found myself dreaming of strangling them both. *That would be one way out of your predicament, Charlotte,* I thought sourly.

"I imagine you work long hours here, as this is the only tavern and inn nearby. You must receive such fascinating patrons!" I gushed with false enthusiasm, taking another drink of my tea.

Antoine's eyes flicked to me as he chewed his bread.

"Oh, yes, I suppose so," Hélène agreed.

"Do tell, *chérie,*" I urged. "Has anyone particularly interesting come through the inn recently? Any exceedingly handsome men? Or perhaps someone from abroad? I do so love to hear thrilling tales from people who've come from other parts of the world. Here, Hélène, allow me to refill your cup."

The bewildered girl automatically held out the chipped china.

"*Oui, Madame!* We had some soldiers in here not two days ago. But, how did you know?"

"Well, of course I didn't! It was only a guess—my curiosity is insatiable, you see. My father always said that I got it from my mother, bless them. Do indulge me, *chérie*. Tell me of these soldiers. What were they like? Did they bring news from some foreign front? What kind of uniforms did they wear? Oh, I do *love* a man in a uniform. I'd wager they were handsome."

Antoine's teacup shattered in his hand, spilling scalding tea all over him. Hélène leapt up to help clean up the mess, but he waved her away. He mumbled oaths that made her blush even redder—*Dieu, has the chit never heard such language working in a tavern?*—and she rushed to the door.

"I'll bring another cup, Monsieur, and I'll fetch some more rags." With that, she was gone, as was my opportunity to discreetly learn what she'd observed about the soldiers who'd attacked us. *Merde.*

Antoine's hand was an angry red, nearly matching the hue of his furious face. I huffed and yanked at his arm, pulling him toward the pitcher of cool water on the bedside table. I dunked his palm in and scowled up at him.

"You have got to be the most infuriating, thick-headed, blundering lout I've ever crossed paths with, and that's saying something considering my former husband was the true king of prize idiots," I hissed.

Antoine glared at me and pulled his hand out of the water, flinging droplets about the room.

"You're one to talk! Why are you badgering that poor girl? Don't you realize how dangerous those soldiers are? If word gets round that some ridiculous woman was asking questions about them, she'll be in danger, too," he argued. "Besides, what do you mean by asking her if they were handsome? They're not handsome! They're horrible!"

I rolled my eyes at his petty male jealousy—if he had stirrings for Hélène, he could conquer her on his own time.

"I was trying to put her at ease so I could question her about them. I want to know when they came into town, what they said, why they're here—if she knew they were after you, in particular. I'm trying to find out more about them, since talking to *you* isn't getting me anywhere useful, and I need to know what I'm up against. I would have found out plenty from her if you hadn't behaved like a fool and sent her away when she was about to answer my questions."

"It doesn't matter. You don't need answers. All you need to know is that those soldiers are dangerous, they'll come for you, and I'm the only one who can protect you," he practically growled.

Reflexively, I made to protest but forced myself to pause and consider him. What did I know about this man? He'd snuck into Versailles, murdered Sade, abducted me for some unknown reason, and was trying to take me to—where, exactly?—when we were set upon by a group of soldiers he was obviously familiar with. That likely meant he was either a fugitive from justice even before his recent venture into aristocratic murder, or that he knew the soldiers personally and was possibly a soldier himself. He'd been armed to the teeth when he waded into the fray on the road and had handled himself well, so he was no stranger to violence, and he'd repeatedly professed his insistence at helping and protecting me. It could be a bluff, of course—he might be keeping a close eye on me merely because I was the only witness to his murder of Sade—but I didn't think so. His barely restrained emotions made me think he was unused to deceit. It felt chivalrous to me. *A soldier, then.*

That rationale gave me little comfort. Even if he was a valiant sort, I still didn't know what his intentions were toward me. If I'd been caught in the same kind of compromising position, I would've been compelled to do away with any witnesses. Instead, he'd abducted me. Why? To try and convince me that Sade deserved to die so I wouldn't turn him in? Lock me in some dungeon and torture me into forgetting I'd seen him with his absurd crossbow?

I snorted. His actions didn't make sense. Either I was missing something crucial, or he was operating on panicked instinct without sufficient forethought. *He's a man, and probably a soldier, so I'd wager the latter.*

I took a deep breath and changed tactics. If I was going to get back to Versailles safely, I needed to understand Antoine and find out just how much trouble he was in.

I tore a strip of fabric from my discarded toga and dipped it in the cool water. Motioning for his burned hand, I held it out in a gesture of truce.

He regarded me suspiciously.

"The cool water will help lessen the pain," I offered. "And it will prevent the burn from blistering. Allow me to wrap it for you."

"I'm fine," he gritted out, but extended his hand anyway.

I dabbed at it gently with the cloth. Antoine flinched at first but started to relax after a moment. When his shoulders began to sag—either from exhaustion or reprieve—I seized the chance to question him.

"Why did you kidnap me?"

"I didn't kidnap you," he grunted.

I quirked a brow. "What, exactly, would you call it then?"

He clenched his jaw. "Protecting you," he said.

I laughed. He scowled. When I finally recovered, I shook my head.

"Protecting *me*," I chuckled. After so much training and so much blood on my hands, the thought seemed ridiculous.

"Would you rather have been found by the guards at Versailles? With your stupid costume arrows and a dead marquis at your feet?" he grumped, frowning.

"Who was he to you?" I asked.

"A loose end that needed tying," he said. His voice cracked roughly.

"And is that what I am?" I prodded, eyes darting to the pistol on the table. "A loose end that needs tying?"

He shook his head. "No. I don't know. Who was Sade to *you*?"

Two could play at that game. "As you say, he was a loose end to tie."

He didn't seem to be any more interested in offering information than I was. Having reached a conversational stalemate, we were silent for a time. Eventually, I spoke up again.

"Those men back there—they were hunting you." It was a statement, not a question, so he did not answer. "Was it something to do with your reasons for killing the marquis? Are you a soldier?"

"Are you a spy?" he countered. "Seems you know how to fight."

"Seems you have an arsenal of weapons tucked away in that cloak of yours. Was Sade your *only* target?"

He heaved a sigh. I could tell this verbal jousting was starting to grate on his nerves, but I hadn't gleaned anything helpful. I tore another strip of fabric from the discarded costume and wrapped it gently, but firmly, around the burn.

"There," I said. "That will do until you can find some salve, or a poultice."

He didn't pull his hand away—not immediately. I caressed it softly. His gaze followed the movements of my fingers across the makeshift bandage.

"Will you at least tell me where you intended to take me for protection?" I asked, quietly this time.

His eyes met mine—fathomless pools of mossy green. There was a flash of something helpless in his gaze, which quickly shuttered. He turned away and lifted a shoulder in forced nonchalance.

"You ask too many questions," he said roughly.

"Yes, and you haven't answered any of them. Don't you think I'm somewhat entitled to even the smallest scrap of information, given how ferociously you behaved with me? *S'il vous plaît, Antoine.* Tell me something. Anything!"

His cheeks reddened again, but I wasn't sure if it was from frustrated apoplexy, or from shame. My entreaty worked, however, because he relented.

"I don't know. I needed time to think. I thought I might bribe you to forget what you saw. Failing that, I...I don't know. I did not want to kill you."

"That's comforting," I chuckled.

He suddenly looked rather miserable, and my heart dropped.

"It's my fault you're in danger," he said. "I was careless back at Versailles, and because you were with me, the *bêtes de sang* will come for you, too."

"The Beasts of Blood? What are you talking about? Were those the soldiers?"

Antoine nodded.

Unease took root in my gut. "I've never heard of them. Are they King Louis's men? What do you know of them?"

He stood and paced, darting glances back toward the door. Clearly, he was worried about them. I crossed over to him and put a hand on his shoulder.

"Tell me what you know of them," I said again.

He frowned.

"You fear them," I observed.

He nodded. "As should you," he said.

"Why should I? I managed to kill one of them already."

"No," he said slowly. "Bullets do not kill vampires."

4

ANTOINE

"Vampires," she exhaled.

Her breath stirred a lock of brown hair that had escaped her cap. I stared at it, transfixed.

"How is that possible?" she asked. "I know how the king feels about vampires. I can't believe he would allow his armies to be infiltrated. He does not trust them. Even with all the work the emissary has done, there's a difference between accepting the blood plague as an inevitability and throwing the full weight of his support behind the integration of vampires."

"Nevertheless," I hedged, dodging her questions. "It is so. Now do you understand why I cannot just allow you to traipse about the countryside alone?"

She narrowed her eyes. "I can take care of myself."

Before I could argue, she began tearing her discarded costume into large squares of fabric—fabric that probably cost more than the average Frenchman's annual wages—and packing up whatever she could find into little bundles. In went the rest of the bread and pastries from the breakfast tray, a candle and spare flint from the bedside table, the pistol and a small bag of powder and shot. When she'd finished scouring the room for anything else useful, she carefully tied the small bundles together and stashed them inside her skirts.

Clever girl.

"What are you doing?" I asked.

She looked at me with thinly veiled disdain. "Well, if your pursuers are vampires, that means we only have the rest of the day to make a head start. I must get back to Versailles."

She made for the door. I moved in front of her.

"Step aside, Antoine," she said forcefully.

I didn't move.

If she left now, it was possible she'd reach Versailles by nightfall. Then again, maybe not. The *bêtes de sang* would be fully recovered after going to ground today, and their speed would be increased—partly because they were supernaturally cursed, partly because of their penchant for cruelty and thirst for revenge. Besides, they knew I was here now. They'd be seeking vengeance upon this woman—Charlotte—but they'd certainly be coming for me. However I considered it, our chances of survival would be better if we stuck together.

I swore.

"I'm coming with you," I said.

Charlotte's eyes widened. "No, you're not!"

"I am. They'll be after us both now, and the least I can do is see you to safety. If that means taking you back to Versailles, so be it," I offered with grim determination.

"Don't be absurd. You murdered a marquis! I'll not have you risking your life unnecessarily because of some misplaced sense of obligation. I can look after myself. Now, I thank you for your assistance back on the road, and I assure you that your ruinous secrets are safe with me, but it's time for us to part company."

I stepped toward her, prepared to argue again, when the door exploded open behind us. I whirled around to see the innkeeper aiming a pistol straight at us. I groaned inwardly. This was the last thing we needed.

"Neither of you are going anywhere," the innkeeper smirked.

"What the devil do you think you're doing?" Charlotte exclaimed.

"Earning the reward," he said. "For him."

Damn. What a fool I'd been. Of course, he knew who I was.

Charlotte turned wide eyes on me. "There is a reward for your capture? *Mon Dieu*, Antoine, and that was before the events of last evening! Why is there a bounty on your head?"

I ignored her.

"Whatever they promised you—whatever the bounty—I'll double it," I said quietly.

The innkeeper's greedy eyes glittered with momentary interest, then wavered with doubt.

"I think not, Monsieur. Those men will return at nightfall, and I plan on handing you—both of you—over to them. I'd rather not find myself on their bad side," he said. He waved the pistol and gestured for us to precede him down the stairs.

"Just a minute, Monsieur," Charlotte said. "I'm not traveling with this man—might you be persuaded to let me go? I can assure you I'll make it worth your while."

The innkeeper and I exchanged a look. He seemed tempted but resolute.

"No, little bird, I'm afraid you both await the soldiers. Perhaps you can use your charms on them, no? They might let you go after all," he chuckled.

"You can't be serious," she said haughtily. "If it's money you want, I can *triple* what you're already getting."

The innkeeper's face twisted—he almost seemed to be regretting his decision—but eventually, he shook his head and pushed us out of the room.

Charlotte frowned but led the way down the stairs. She protested the entire way. The innkeeper guided us to the root cellar out back behind the inn. Hélène eyed us guiltily from behind the bar. *The traitorous wench.*

After flinging open the heavy wooden doors, the innkeeper shoved us both down a set of stone steps into the damp, earthen room. It was cramped and filthy. The walls were lined with shelves of dust-covered preserves and crates of junk. The room was barely high enough for me to stand up in.

"Make yourselves comfortable," he offered, his voice laced with sarcasm. "I'll be back for you with the soldiers when they return."

Then, he slammed the wooden doors shut and proceeded to lock us in. We both waited for the sounds of his footsteps to fade away before turning to each other. Shafts of sunlight streamed in through the weathered slats of the door, illuminating Charlotte's petulant scowl. She sat down on a wooden crate and sighed.

"This is all your fault," she grumbled. "If you hadn't shown up at Versailles in the first place, I'd be asleep in my delicious bed, awaiting a warm morning bath, a pot of chocolate, and a day of leisure pursuits."

"My apologies," I said gruffly. "But it was your fault for getting in my way and then not heeding my warnings back on the road. If you'd just come along willingly, we could have worked something out."

"Oh, yes, and then when you'd run into the *bêtes de sang* with me tied across your horse, they certainly would have let us both carry on our merry way unmolested! You'd probably be captured by now, and God only knows what they would've done with me. Probably drained me, or worse," she said bitterly. "And now we *are* in a bind, aren't we? That lousy innkeeper likely overheard our argument and—even as thick as he is— probably knows I was headed back to Versailles."

"Probably," I agreed.

She stood and went to the cellar door, testing the handle. The heavy iron padlock rattled on the outside. I joined her at the door and inspected the frame. Thick, solid oak blocked our way out.

Charlotte began to survey the room in much the same way that she'd surveyed the bedroom in the inn. It was deliberate, methodical, and thorough. It seemed at odds with the lifestyle that she'd described, unless my earlier supposition was indeed correct.

"Who do you work for?" I asked.

"What an absurd question!" she laughed. She'd uncovered a hammer beneath a length of canvas and hefted it in triumph. She continued to root around through the crates. "I don't *work*—I'm a member of the aristocracy."

She said it with such haughtiness that I believed her immediately, but her actions belied her protestations. What kind of a noblewoman knew how to fight and shoot and don disguises with practiced ease? I knew she was a spy—I just didn't know for whom.

She cried out in triumph when she found a small set of rusty tools, extracting a chisel. She moved for the door, and I realized quickly what she had in mind.

"Allow me," I offered, holding out my hands for the hammer and chisel. She raised a brow at me but handed them over.

"Why is there a bounty on your head?" she asked as I lined them up over the door handle.

"Tell me who you're working for," I countered. I brought them down hard, leaving a small dent just above the iron handle.

She *tsked*. "I told you, I don't work."

"Right. And the innkeeper was merely mistaken about me," I said, a smile tugging at my lips. I lifted the hammer again and brought it down with force. A greater chunk of wood dislodged and fell away. I needed to hurry, lest the innkeeper hear the racket and come to check on us.

"Fine," Charlotte huffed. "We both have secrets. But if we're going to get out of here, we need to trust each other at least a *little*."

A raspy chuckle escaped my throat. It had been a long time since I'd laughed.

"Certainly, Charlotte. Ladies first."

"Very well," she said arrogantly. "What's your plan for when we get out of here?"

My hammer paused mid-air. I hadn't considered that far ahead.

She smiled in mock sweetness. "How am I supposed to trust you if you don't know how you're going to keep us alive?"

I let the hammer fall on the chisel, and one of the boards in the door split. Not enough to break, but two or three more strikes ought to do it. All the while, my mind worked. We needed somewhere to hide out. A place the *bêtes de sang* wouldn't be able to follow. Somewhere we could stay until the likely uproar at the marquis's murder died down. Somewhere we could figure out what to do about each other and our precarious predicament. Away from Paris, away from Versailles, and far away from here.

Suddenly, I had it.

"Gévaudan," I said. "We'll go to Gévaudan."

Charlotte blinked in surprise. "Gévaudan? Down south? But it's so far away! It'll take us days—a week, probably—to reach it!"

I struck one final blow at the weakened wood, and it cracked along the split. I wiggled the iron lock and door handle and wrenched them away, then kicked the doors open.

"If we move quickly and rest only when necessary, we can make it in two and a half, three days," I said. I grabbed her arm and tugged her toward the stables.

She allowed me to pull her forward, then down behind the low bushes along the back of the inn. I knew we'd made a hell of a racket breaking out of the root cellar, and we needed to hurry. As soon as we ducked into the stables, Tartuffe's soft nickering drew my attention. He was in a back stall, perfectly content with a bucket of oats. Relief unknotted some of my muscles—if the innkeeper had mistreated my beloved black Andalusian, I would've had to break his arms, and I didn't think Charlotte and I had the time for that. Charlotte kept watch out the front while I saddled him, then led him around to the door.

"You're not going to toss me over your horse's ass again, are you?" she asked warily.

In answer, I swung myself up and held out my hand to her. She took it and pulled herself up like no aristocratic woman I'd ever known, sitting astride behind me.

"Ready?" I called back to her.

From outside, we heard a clatter followed by an enraged bellow. The innkeeper had discovered our absence. Charlotte started to respond, but I didn't wait for her words. I dug my heels into Tartuffe's sides and shouted him forward. He took off like a shot, weaving past the apoplectic innkeeper and making for the main road through town.

I heard Charlotte squeal in surprise at our abrupt departure, then felt her arms tighten around my waist as we galloped through the bustling street, attracting the angry shouts and incensed attentions of several villagers. We raced on, not daring to slow our breakneck speed until the town was well behind us and Tartuffe's sides heaved with exhaustion.

As we slowed to a trot, Charlotte's grip loosened, and she lifted her face from my back.

"What's in Gévaudan?"

"Shelter," I replied. I didn't want to go into details. If she wasn't going to trust me, I certainly wasn't going to trust her.

She made a noise of frustration I barely heard over the clop of Tartuffe's hooves.

She leaned closer, her breasts pressing into my back, and spoke in my ear. "But you think we'll be safe from the soldiers? The *bêtes de sang* won't find us or follow us? What's to stop them?"

"Nothing," I said, gritting my teeth to fight the rising tide of lust brought on by her excruciating closeness. The heat from her body sang through me like a siren's song. I swallowed hard. "I'm certain they will eventually catch up to us. This merely buys us some time."

She laughed. "How very soldier-like you think—or perhaps I should say *how very male you think.* You plan nothing out and wait for someone with more brains than you to provide guidance."

I stiffened.

"Now, I mean no offense. It's the fault of your sex to be creatures of action and, bless you all, sometimes you don't have enough blood in your brain because it finds its way to other extremities. Not that I'm complaining about male virility, of course," she carried on.

Irritation climbed up my spine. Not only had she insulted my intelligence and that of my fellow man, but she acted like I was some thick-headed soldier incapable of thinking for myself—a nerve too often struck by my father's harsh criticisms. Even more irritating was the kernel of truth in her words—she was in this mess because I'd acted rashly back at Versailles. It didn't mean I was some incompetent fool, though.

"It's just that more often than not, men don't think things through, and women must enter in some capacity to assist—yet you call *us* the more emotional sex!"

A barely restrained growl climbed out of my throat. She either didn't hear it or carried on as if she hadn't. *Probably the latter.*

"Well, you needn't worry, Antoine, I am perfectly capable of being the brains in this temporary outfit. We will travel as far as we can until late afternoon, take a small respite, then get back on the road as soon as the sun sets. If these soldiers are vampires, they will travel at night, and we cannot afford to let them catch up to us. We must stay on the move."

"You don't say," I muttered darkly.

"Unless, of course, we are able to find some suitable accommodation in which to hide tonight. Then, as you say, we will arrive in Gévaudan and apparently pray the *bêtes* do not follow, since you have no other course of action in mind."

My temper flared and I pulled Tartuffe up short.

"If you'd rather take them on by yourself, by all means, Madame, take your chances with their mercies—only I can assure you, mercy is not something you are likely to receive from them. You would be lucky and *singular* to escape their clutches with your life," I warned.

She huffed her indignation.

"As for my *simpleminded plan*," I continued. "I take it you have not heard the news from Gévaudan all the way up in Versailles lately—or perhaps you're too busy insulting everyone, or maybe too wrapped up in your own selfish affairs to bother paying attention—but the entire town is locked down. Completely closed off to supernatural outsiders. The *bêtes* may follow us to the border, but they will not be able to enter. We will be safe—for a time."

I'd felt her bristle at my insults, but her curiosity superseded her ire.

"Closed off? Because of the blood plague?"

"No," I bit out, spurring Tartuffe forward. "Not because of the vampires. It is another threat they fear."

Her shock was evident in her slight gasp and the pressure of her arms around my waist. Reflexively, my mind went back to the sight of her in the bath, then dressing in that slow, torturous manner. I wondered if she acted so passionately in bed. Quickly, my senses returned, and I drew several deep breaths to calm my racing heart and stiff cock. It had been *much* too long since I'd bedded a woman, but I'd consider myself desperate indeed to try and bed this hellion.

"What other threat?" she prodded quietly.

"A werewolf."

5

CHARLOTTE

November 1, 1767
The road to Gévaudan

"What an inappropriate time for you to develop a sense of humor, Antoine," I said with a laugh.

I could tell by the straight, hard line of his jaw he did not share my amusement.

"A werewolf," I repeated. "That would be preposterous."

"Is it? And yet, we so easily accepted that there is a strange disease turning normal men into immortal parasites. We execute witches for consorting with the devil. The church has us believe that demons may escape Hell and walk among us."

"Oh, demons *do* walk among us," I cut in. "Of that, you may be certain."

"But werewolves are beyond belief," he said sarcastically.

"Well, no," I answered. "But there must be some logical explanation."

He shrugged. "Perhaps there is. For our purposes, it does not matter whether the fear is based in fact. Their caution will allow us some sanctuary since no supernatural creature is allowed entry."

So, he does have a plan after all.

"How do they keep them out?" I wondered aloud.

"I've no idea. Walls. Armed guards. Prayers. Magical herbs and potions. Perhaps a battalion of forcefully opinionated aristocratic women who hurl unfounded insults all day. That would be enough to keep any man away," he grumbled.

I laughed again. "How unexpectedly amusing you are, Antoine! You must forgive me for offending you. My intent was to goad you into revealing your plans, and I'm afraid you fell rather well for my tactics. I would never believe you to be unintelligent. I hardly know anything about you."

I peered around him to see his face twist sourly and I stifled another giggle.

"Come now, we've quite a journey ahead of us. Surely, we can allow ourselves the small luxury of learning about each other. At least *something*. It will help us pass the time," I coaxed. "And, as an offering of peace, I'll start. Though I keep it closely guarded when I'm not at Versailles, my surname is Brionne. I am Comtesse Charlotte Nicole Louise de Brionne. There, now. Your turn."

Tartuffe's hooves thudded softly on the hard packed dirt, as steady as a metronome. Long moments of quiet passed before Antoine replied. So long, in fact, that I'd almost forgotten I'd asked him anything. I'd become lost in the world around us—the dull gray of the sky obscuring the November sun, the silvery bare trees and dead, fallen leaves lining the road, the distant fields of green and gold. It was beautiful, really. Like the scene of some salon landscape painting in a parlor of moderate good taste.

"De Valle," he said, somewhat suddenly. "Antoine François de Valle."

"Well done," I said warmly. "That's a lovely name. I'm sure I've heard it before, but I can't quite recall where."

He scoffed. "I'd appreciate it if you didn't bandy it about in public."

"Ah yes, because you're in hiding. The soldiers hunting you and all."

His posture had been rigid before, but now he turned to stone in front of me. It was impossible for me not to notice how he felt—the hard muscles beneath my arms. I'd wager he had a body like a Grecian marble of Zeus, or perhaps Ares. With that dashing scar, he would certainly be closer to the god of war. A pleasing shiver vibrated through me at the wicked imagery.

"Well, you needn't worry, Antoine. You've never met another who can keep a secret as well as I can."

"Because you're a spy?" he tested.

"A spy! What utter rot. I told you, I'm a comtesse. I live a life of leisure. Don't be so bourgeois, Antoine."

A lie. One of many.

"A lie," he echoed, his voice hinting at some dark humor beneath. "Don't bother lying to me, Comtesse. If you're going to pester me with your incessant prattling, at least have the courtesy to tell me the truth."

"I am a paragon of honesty! But if you're looking for other truths so you can better learn my impeccable character, I'll graciously oblige. My favorite food is asparagus."

"You're teasing me," he said. "Lying again. No one really enjoys asparagus."

"I do. I like it so much that sometimes I have my cook prepare it for me for breakfast. Gently steamed with a poached egg on top and toast points on the side."

My stomach rumbled at the thought. I reached into my pockets and pulled out one of the pilfered buns from breakfast, then offered one to Antoine. He took a bite and chewed slowly.

"*Civet de sanglier,*" he said.

"I beg your pardon?"

"It's a kind of stew. Wild boar, chestnuts, vegetables, red wine. When I was a boy, my father was stationed in Corsica for a time. He developed a taste for the cuisine there and brought a cook with him when he returned home. Lucia always made it for me on my birthday. It's my favorite food."

"So, you followed in your father's footsteps to become a soldier," I observed. Immediately, Antoine tensed beneath me. *Wrong line of questioning—his father is apparently a sore spot.* I returned to the more acceptable subject.

"When was the last time you had it?" I asked.

"A long time ago."

"I envy your worldliness, Antoine. All I've ever known is society. Paris, Versailles. I should like to see the world someday." I could not keep the wistfulness from my voice.

"Have you never ventured abroad?"

"No. My husband—former husband—used to travel often. He would bring me presents and stories from all over the continent, perhaps to appease me, but it only whetted my appetite for adventure," I said with no small hint of bitterness.

"Where is he now?" Antoine asked.

Oh, what a question! When last I checked, he was locked away in the Château d'If for the rest of his miserable life for summoning a demon and murdering several people because he was desperately in love with my cousin. Who really knows, though? Perhaps he has had the good sense to die.

Not something I wanted to get into with my secretive travel companion.

"He is…gone. Are you married?" I asked.

"No."

"Why not? Didn't you ever want to?"

He shrugged. "I spent long years abroad, fighting in battles that no one really wins. It's cruel to start a family and spend all your time away from them."

"You speak from experience."

I didn't expect him to answer, but he nodded once. I grinned at his back.

"Well, now I know I was right about you, Antoine. You *are* a soldier. My first impressions are seldom wrong."

"It's lucky for you that mine often are," he chuckled. It was a deep, warm sound, so low that I felt it vibrate like the string of a harp plucked between our bodies. Heat sparked low in my stomach.

"I'll take it as a compliment that you don't still think I'm a young lad besotted with a depraved marquis. Will you tell me why you killed him?"

Instantly, a wall of icy silence fell between us. Try as I might, I couldn't get him to respond to any more questions. It appeared I'd crossed the line and our friendly tête-à-tête had ended.

We rode for several more hours through the countryside. Antoine picked up the pace in the late afternoon, perhaps hoping to find a suitable spot for us to rest for a while. The clouds above began to darken to an ominous pewter and thunder heralded the onset of a winter storm, but we still hadn't come upon the next town. The trees had thinned out, which would leave us dangerously exposed—especially if we camped somewhere and had a fire.

"Have you been this way before? Do you think we're far from the next town?" I asked. The road showed precious few signs of frequent use— scraggly, bare weeds crept in from the nearby fields and flat stretches of unblemished mud lay before us. Obviously, it had been days since anyone had come through.

Antoine frowned as fat droplets of rain started to fall. In the gathering storm clouds, it had been difficult to determine the point of sunset, and I realized it was too late. Surely the sun had gone down now, and the *bêtes* would be waking up to begin their hunt.

"There's no point in resting if we can't find some decent shelter," I said. "We should carry on as long as we're able. At least the rain will help disperse our scent."

Antoine nodded and spurred Tartuffe forward in a gallop. The rain came down in earnest, then, as if the forces of nature sensed our resolve to find somewhere out of the elements. Ten minutes later, we were both soaked to the skin and shivering, but at last we spotted a light down the road ahead of us.

The village was smaller than the previous one, boasting a dilapidated church, a couple boarded-up shops, and an ancient-looking tavern and inn. We trotted up to one of the empty horse stalls beside the tavern and dismounted. Antoine turned to enter, but I laid a hand on his arm.

"We'll need a cover story," I said. "If we're to escape notice in a small town like this. Especially if we're to hide here tonight from the *bêtes*."

"Shall I follow your lead then, Madame Spy?" Antoine smirked.

"I'm *not* a spy, it's just common sense. But yes, you may follow my lead. Keep your head low and your scar covered—it makes you rather rakishly noticeable, and I don't have the energy to deal with some overzealous tavern maids tonight," I said brusquely.

Antoine pulled the hood of his cloak down, but I saw his lips kick up in a lopsided grin, showing off his perfect white teeth and—good heavens —was that a dimple? *Mon Dieu.*

"Take my arm," I said somewhat breathlessly. "We're a young married couple on our way to Provence for our honeymoon and we got caught in the storm."

Antoine's eyes widened and his mouth dropped open, but he held out his arm and guided me inside the tavern.

Warmth enveloped us as we entered, along with the smell of baking bread and some savory stew. My stomach rumbled again in demand. I cast my eyes around and breathed a small sigh of relief—thankfully, it was nearly empty. A few soggy travelers sat in a far corner, and a robust woman with silvering hair bustled over to us.

"Smile," I hissed at Antoine through gritted teeth. "We're newlyweds, remember."

He smiled and pulled me closer to him, wrapping his arm around my waist. My breath caught involuntarily, and I let out a nervous giggle that was only half faked.

"*Bon soir, Madame,*" Antoine said. "My new bride and I were on our way to Provence but I'm afraid we cannot make it much further in this weather. Have you any rooms available?"

The woman tutted and handed me a cloth to dry my dripping face.

"You poor lambs! I've just the one room upstairs. It's no honeymoon suite, mind, but it's warm, clean, and dry."

"Bless you, Madame!" I said. "We'll take it. Would it be possible to get some of that delicious-smelling food sent up to us? We're nearly dead on our feet from exhaustion, and I don't know that I could sit in the tavern here without falling over. We journeyed all the way from Poitiers this morning and had our things sent on after us, but I expect they're half a day's ride behind us."

"What a journey you've had," the woman exclaimed. "So, you've no other clothes or supplies to see you through to Provence?"

"We planned on stocking up here, if that's possible," Antoine chimed in with a charming smile. "My wife and I will need some dry clothes and food for another two days. And my horse is out in the stall—he'll need to be tended to."

"Of course, of course. Georges! See to the horse outside!" she called to a disgruntled, rail-thin man. "You two, follow me! Dry off and get settled, and I'll send some food up right away."

We followed her up a back set of stairs into a tiny gable bedroom. She'd been right. It was cramped to a ridiculous degree—Antoine had to duck down to enter—but there was a fire in the small hearth, and it was clean. She handed us some candles and promised to be back swiftly with a hot meal and some dry clothes.

Antoine went to the window and looked out. The rain lashed against the glass and made it impossible to see very far down the road.

I dragged the moth-eaten armchair in front of the fireplace and collapsed into it.

"Why newlyweds?"

Antoine's voice sounded soft and distant.

"We're traveling together without a chaperone, and we don't look like siblings. Besides, would *you* want to disturb a couple of newlyweds in a cozy bedroom of a roadside inn?"

That low, warm chuckle rumbled from directly behind me, and I looked up to see him leaning against the back of the armchair.

"Fair point," he conceded. "Why Poitiers?"

I shrugged. "It was the first place that popped into my head that's about a day's ride away. I didn't want them to know we'd come from Versailles—or anywhere near Paris, for that matter."

Antoine dragged another chair toward the fire and sat in it next to me. He stretched out long legs until his feet almost touched the hearth.

"But you say you are not a spy," he murmured.

I snorted.

"Perhaps you just haven't met that many quick-witted women in your lifetime. There are plenty of us out there, you know. It doesn't mean we are all spies."

"Perhaps," he said. The ghost of a smile played about his full lips.

They really are fine lips.

There was a loud knock at the door, and we both jumped.

"Only me!" The lady innkeeper said, bustling in with a bundle under her arm and a tray of food in front of her. Antoine jumped up to take the tray and set it on the small table by the window. The innkeeper nodded gratefully.

"I didn't have much luck finding clothing at this hour, but I found some clean nightclothes for you both. If you'll remove your own garments, I'll make sure they're cleaned and dried for you in the morning."

Antoine frowned but nodded. "We'll leave them out by the door, along with the dinner tray when we've finished. We're most grateful for your hospitality, but I'm afraid my wife is exhausted, so we'd like to be undisturbed for the rest of the evening."

"As you wish, Monsieur," the innkeeper winked at him, then bustled off with a giggle.

Despite the warmth of the room, I was still freezing. The rain had soaked the thick woolen dress and underclothes completely, making it waterlogged and heavy. I eyed the food hungrily but wished for the dry nightclothes with more immediacy.

"Turn around," I instructed Antoine. "I'd like to change."

"I thought we were meant to be newlyweds," he teased, that sly smile returning.

"Certainly not behind closed doors! Hurry up, I want to get changed and eat," I returned testily.

Antoine's eyes flashed in a curious way and suddenly my damp clothes and the winter chill were forgotten. My skin heated to a blush under his intent gaze.

"You didn't have an issue dressing in front of me before," he said, turning to face the opposite wall.

"Yes, well, I was in a hurry, and I didn't think we'd see each other again," I huffed, shucking the drenched skirts and petticoats as quickly as possible. My chilled fingers fumbled at the sodden knot securing my stays, but try as I might, I could not undo it.

"*Merde*," I swore under my breath.

"Everything all right? Can I turn around now?"

"No, I can't get—oh, *putain*—it's really stuck. Well, there's nothing for it now. Antoine, I may require your assistance. The lace on my stays is knotted and—"

Quick as a flash, he was behind me, his hands working at the delicate ribbon. He took to his task with infinite care and patience, slowly pulling this way and that. His breath was warm against the nape of my neck, tickling several strands of hair that had escaped my cap. I shivered with pleasure for the second time that day.

I felt his hands still, but neither of us moved. A pulse of instinctive lust whispered through my body. Visions flashed—his full lips on my skin, his eyes squeezed tight in ecstasy, his hard, muscular body bared before me. My heart pounded. If I turned around now, I could kiss him—taste him.

What could it hurt? Longing coursed through me. I shifted, but the air in the room changed. He'd stepped back and was returning to the other side of the room.

"There," he said in a gruff voice. "You are undone."

Mon Dieu, yes. In so many ways.

6

ANTOINE

November 1, 1767
The road to Gévaudan

I'D ENDURED COUNTLESS MISERIES IN MY LIFE, BUT I WAS STRUGGLING TO recall a more agonizing event than undressing a beautiful woman with no hope of bedding her. The softness of her skin, the rain-damp scent of her hair, the hitch in her breath at my nearness… I'd been moments away from ripping the blasted stays off her lithe body and sinking to my knees before her in a bid of sheer desperation. It had been so long since I'd enjoyed any kind of intimacy, I would've *begged*.

Fortunately, I'd recovered my senses in time. *Not now, Antoine. Not this woman. She is a spy, and she cannot be trusted. You do not want her.*

Don't I?

I listened to the soft rustle of fabric behind me, which invited torturous images of her naked again. My cock hardened uncomfortably in my breeches. *Dieu*, could she not hurry this along? It was maddening.

"Are you finished, Comtesse? Our food is probably cold by now," I grumbled.

"Yes, yes, *all right*. You may turn around. Only I shan't apologize for the indecency. If I'd stayed in those cold, wet clothes, I would have certainly gotten sick. Just…be a gentleman about it, would you?" she said, a touch of anxiety in her voice.

"I'm no blushing virgin nor slavering youth," I shot back. "I've seen plenty of women in various stages of undress. Yourself included,

Comtesse. I'm perfectly capable of maintaining my composure. In fact, you are not even the type of woman to tempt me."

"What a relief," she said acidly. "Since you are not the type of man to tempt me. It makes our arrangement much simpler."

I turned around, but my sharp retort died on my lips. *You've already seen the woman naked,* I foolishly thought to myself. *How much worse can it be?*

Much worse.

She'd loosened her hair from beneath her cap, and it cascaded down her back in thick, glossy waves. The nightdress that the tavern lady had provided her was worn to threadbare softness, affording me glimpses of dusky nipples and that sinful dark triangle at the apex of her thighs. One sleeve slipped down her shoulder as she sat down before the table of food. She tore a chunk of bread from the loaf and set it into the steaming bowl of stew. Her easy movements and the tranquil domesticity of the scene filled me with a hunger far beyond food. How many times had I waded through the mud and blood of the battlefield, longing for something so simple—so *pastoral?*

She realized I was staring—she'd probably known all along, really—and raised a brow at me.

"Are you just going to stand there dripping on the floor while your food gets cold? If so, I'll eat your share. This stew is *delicious,* and the bread is warm from the oven. The ale is subpar and, frankly, I'd prefer wine, but it'll do."

She dipped the bread in the stew and raised it to her lips, licking the drips from her fingers. My mouth went bone dry. Frustration pulled my nerves taut, and I hastily started shucking my own clothes. Under different circumstances, I would've slept in them or gone nude, but they were filthy and wet from the rain, and I was damned tired of being cold. I turned around again and tugged my shirt off, tossing it into a pile with my coat, cloak, and hose. I reached for the innkeeper's proffered nightshirt when I heard a coughing, choking sound behind me.

Charlotte's wide eyes were watering, and her cheeks were pink, but she waved away my concern when I made to help her.

"No, no, I'm fine, Antoine. Really fine. Some ale went down the wrong way. Just give me a sex—*second*—and I'll be all right again," she spluttered. Her cheeks reddened even more, and I grinned. *Well, at least I'm not the only one overset.* That realization was quickly chased by another more damning one—if we both felt physical stirrings, it was a short road to ruin for us, and I couldn't allow that. Partly because I didn't trust her, partly because I needed to protect her, and honestly, partly because I needed to protect myself.

I pulled off my breeches and donned the nightshirt. It was just long enough to be decent but was far too tight across my chest. I stretched my arms out to the sides and felt the seams along the sides split a little. *Ah, well. The innkeeper will have to forgive me.*

I crossed the room and sat opposite Charlotte. She offered me the other half of the bread and a full bowl of stew. I raised my mug of ale to her and dove in.

Already, I felt worlds better. She'd been right—the stew and bread were delicious, but the ale was inferior. Still, it swept through my veins and loosened my tight muscles. It had been some time since I'd been able to relax a little. I thought back to Charlotte's earlier questions and swallowed a mouthful of stew.

"Have you siblings?" I asked.

She smiled and swiped a hunk of bread in some butter. "No," she replied. "But my cousin Daphne is just like a sister to me."

"What of your parents?"

A look of melancholy passed over her face. "Mine died shortly after I married. A wave of illness took them both—not the blood plague, before you ask. Daphne's also passed on, as did her older brother. It was a difficult time for both of us. We clung together like wreckage in the storm. We'd been close as children, but grief has a way of hardening things—not just people, you understand, but relationships, too. With loss, love can become fiercer, just as hate can become more vitriolic. Our playful childhood bond cemented us together like drying mortar."

I was speechless for a moment, astonished by her ability to put into words something I'd so often felt myself. Marie and I had been cemented by my mother's passing and my father's cruelty, which was partly why her absence still felt so painful.

I swallowed hard. "Sisters are one of life's greatest joys—and miseries."

She laughed. "To be sure. I take it you have one?"

The bread turned to sand in my mouth. "I did, yes. Marie. She passed away a little less than a year ago. We were very close."

Charlotte reached forward and laid a hand on my arm. Heat bloomed beneath her touch.

"Antoine, I'm so sorry. How awful for you," she said, her face a study in sincerity. "It wasn't the blood plague, was it?"

"No," I said. I didn't want to go into details tonight. My mood turned black.

She sensed the change and withdrew her hand. She was quiet for a moment, searching for something to say, perhaps.

"My husband—Philippe—well, I don't actually know if he's alive or dead. The last time I saw him was as he boarded a boat for the Château d'If. He committed *terrible* crimes, Antoine, and was punished brutally for them. Rightly so, of course. But he was my husband, and I was devoted to him. He had been there when my parents died. Not in a supportive way, really, but he had been there. I've only recently learned to separate the truth of our marriage from my perception of what it was at the time. When I think back on it, I believe I grieved for him long before he went away, but that doesn't make it easier. It is a hard thing to lose someone. Their absences linger like nothing else in this life."

She drained the rest of her ale and popped the last chunk of bread in her mouth.

"What were his crimes?"

She sighed, a world weary, deeply sorrowful sound. "Antoine, you wouldn't believe me if I told you."

"Try me," I challenged.

She arched a brow. "I don't think that would be a good idea for either of us, do you?" She'd deliberately mistaken my meaning to avoid answering the question, a tactic I knew well enough, but for some reason, I found myself blushing beneath her heated gaze.

"Did you love him?" I asked, then immediately wished to take the words back. It wasn't my business whether she cared for him—he was her husband, after all. We were mere strangers. Still, I railed against the spark of jealousy that burned in my chest.

Charlotte tilted her head, thinking. "You know, I thought I did. But perhaps I just loved the idea of us. He was rich, titled, powerful, and not unattractive. He was a catch by the standards of the *tonne*. My parents were delighted at his offer. Alas, he fooled us all with his well-guarded villainy."

"Some people are masters of deception. They delight in hiding their true nature from the eyes of the world," I growled. My voice sounded rougher than I'd intended, but I was irritated by her memories of marriage and reminded again of my father's treachery. His betrayal felt as fresh now as it had been when I'd first discovered it.

Charlotte nodded. "I take it you have personal experience with that."

"Deception? Certainly. It's why I cannot abide dishonesty. The world would be a much better place if people didn't go around perpetuating falsehoods," I grumbled.

Charlotte covered a wince with a yawn—perhaps hoping I didn't notice. *As if I don't notice every damn thing about her.*

"Yes, of course. Well, Antoine, I'm exhausted. We should probably get some rest if we're to make an early start."

"You take the bed," I offered. "I'll sleep in the chair by the fire."

She snorted. "Don't be absurd. We can share the bed. You'll need to sleep if you're to be alert enough to get us to Gévaudan and keep an eye out for more soldiers."

I balked. "That's a horrible idea. I'll be fine."

"We're both adults, Antoine. I assure you that I have no interest in you carnally, and even if I did, I'm far too tired to attempt to seduce you. But if you're afraid that I'll attack you in the middle of the night..." She chuckled.

"I'm *not* afraid of you," I barked. "I was thinking of propriety and of *your* comfort."

She lifted her brows. "Well, I'm sure I've never been comfortable with propriety, but you may do as you wish."

She gathered up our damp clothes into a bundle and set them atop the empty dinner tray, then took it outside for the innkeeper. When she returned, she pulled one of the blankets off the bed and tossed it to me.

"I said I'll be fine," I protested.

"Yes, I'm sure you will. Do me a favor and take it anyway to spare me the guilt."

With that, she got into bed, pulled the remaining blankets up to her chin, and blew out the candle on the bedside table.

I sat down in the armchair in front of the fire, tucking the proffered cover around me. I was loath to admit that she'd been right about my level of comfort. Fortunately, the fatigue and ale had me dozing sooner than expected.

Some hours later, I woke with a start. The room was black as pitch, save for the dim glow of embers in the fireplace before me. Quietly, I listened, coming to full awareness. The storm had eased, and the rain had softened to a gentle tap upon the windows. What had woken me?

A distressed murmur rose from the bed where Charlotte lay. She mumbled something, then began thrashing violently in her sleep. *Nightmares.* I knew their sting all too well. Her cries grew louder, reaching a fevered pitch of sheer terror. I got up and went to the bed, trying to find her arm in the tangle of bed linens.

"Charlotte," I whispered. "Charlotte, wake up. You're having a nightmare."

I grabbed her shoulder and shook her gently. In an instant, she sat bolt upright, and her hand shot out to my throat. Before my shock could register, she'd started to squeeze my windpipe, cutting off my breath. I pulled at her arm, surprised at her strength, until she seemed to come to her senses and let go.

I coughed and sucked in air.

"Antoine! Forgive me. I thought… I think I was dreaming. Are you all right?"

"I'm fine. You were having a nightmare. I worried that you'd wake the whole inn. Are you well?" It was partially true. Mostly, I'd been thinking of her, wanting to end her torment, but I hated to admit that, even to myself.

"Yes, of course," she said.

I sat on the edge of the bed, and she shifted over. Despite her insistence, I could tell she was shaking.

"What was your dream about?" I asked.

"Needlepoint."

"Very funny."

"You know, I don't even remember." Her faint reply was not convincing.

"You were shouting something about demons."

She didn't answer. In the quiet, raindrops tapped a soft staccato against the windowpanes, and I strained to listen for a change in her breath to see if she'd fallen asleep again.

"Antoine, will you stay with me?" she asked.

The uncertainty in her voice elicited some primal, instinctive response in me. I knew she was dangerous, but here—now—in this dark room, she seemed so…*vulnerable*. It didn't sit well with my image of her as a devious hellcat.

"If you wish," I replied, knowing on every level that this was a horrible idea. She scooted over in the bed, and I grabbed the coverlet from the armchair. For the preservation of my own sanity, I did *not* get under the sheets with her. We lay down together, separated by a few worn layers of fabric and all the chivalrous strength I could muster, though it was beginning to fail.

"Thank you," she whispered. "I apologize if it's silly."

"I find that nightmares visit those who have known more than their share of earthly horrors, not those who have some weakness of character. You needn't apologize for it."

"You have them, too," she observed.

"Mmm." Too often I saw the faces of men I'd killed, friends I'd lost in battle, and always the faces of Marie and little Louis. If I had mountains of soap and oceans of water, I'd never be able to wash all the blood from my hands.

"One day, I'll find a way to banish them," she said with a yawn. "Perhaps with a magic spell of some kind. God knows wine and prayers haven't helped."

The warmth of her curves next to my wretched body and the sound of her sleepy murmurings squeezed my heart. In the darkness, I could just make out the outline of her face. In another time, in another place, I could have imagined myself pressing kisses to her cheeks, her forehead, her lips. Tangling my fingers in her glossy chestnut waves, running my hands all over her velvety skin, reaching between her thighs to explore her intimate secrets… *Merde.* I was hard as a rock again. I hadn't been this overruled by lust since I'd been a lad. I turned on my side, hoping Charlotte wouldn't notice my uncomfortable condition.

Her slow, steady breathing gave me some comfort—she'd obviously fallen back asleep. My relief was short-lived, however. Blissfully unaware, she rolled onto her side and snuggled back against my warmth. Despite the blankets between us, I felt the firm press of her lush ass cradling my insistent erection. I bit my lip to keep from groaning. Surely, this was what awaited me in Hell.

I gritted my teeth and tried to count backwards from one thousand, hoping for sleep. Given the softening of my feelings tonight, I could only pray that by light of day, my desire for the troublesome woman would wane.

One thousand. Nine hundred ninety-nine. Nine hundred ninety-eight.

7
CHARLOTTE

November 2, 1767
The road to Gévaudan

I woke slowly, blissfully warm beneath the comforting weight of a man's muscular arm. It was tossed over my ribs, gently cradled between my breasts. I smiled and reached behind me, snaking a hand down to playfully stroke my bedmate's morning erection. I couldn't remember the drunken dinner party that had brought this young stud from the halls of court to my bedchamber, but that wasn't going to stop me from getting one more good romp out of him before I sent him packing.

A low moan exhaled against my neck, and I felt soft lips kissing against my nape. I stroked him with more firmness, dimly trying to remember a name, a face, anything. I cracked my eyes open, taking in one of the shabbiest rooms I'd ever been in.

Horror gripped me as the realization dawned. I flung myself forward, falling to the floor as my feet tangled in the blankets. I followed the sound of my crash with a pained—*and furiously humiliated*—groan.

Antoine cried out and dove out of bed, reaching for his sword on the floor. He fumbled around wildly until, presumably, he also became aware of his surroundings. I heard him swear roughly and he leaned over the bed, taking in my indecorous state upon the floor. I disentangled my legs from the blankets and stood, shooting him an icy glare.

"Don't. Say. A. Word," I gritted out. "Nothing happened, but if anything *had* happened, it would have been a case of sleepy delirium and mistaken identity and nothing more. Understand?"

The expression on his face was stony, but I could have sworn a glint of laughter glittered in his eyes.

"I'm serious. If you bring it up, I'll kill you," I threatened.

He nodded. Then, from under his breath, I heard him mutter, "All due respect, Comtesse, but *you're* the one who brought it up."

My cheeks reddened at the innuendo, and I grimaced.

"Oh!" I shouted. "Well, I certainly wasn't the *only* one! You... you...*participated.*"

He shook his head and ran a hand through his loose brown locks. I was momentarily distracted by the flex of a bicep beneath the soft nightshirt.

"You said it yourself. It was a mistake. I was asleep and was merely reacting instinctively to a beautiful woman throwing herself at me." His face was set in its usual grave lines, but the humor hiding in his tone told me he found this whole thing *very* amusing.

"I didn't throw myself at you!" I stammered. I mustered as much indignation as I could, but it was difficult when my traitorous heart caught at the word *beautiful.* Antoine thought I was beautiful.

Oh, stop it, Charlotte! Don't be ridiculous.

"It doesn't matter. It *won't* happen again," I growled.

"Well, then you'll have to control yourself," he said smugly.

The bastard.

I was desperate to change the subject. "It's past dawn, and the rain has let up. We should hurry and be on our way."

My ploy, clumsy though it was, effectively distracted Antoine from my embarrassment. He went to the window and looked out.

As if on cue, we heard a knock on the door.

"No need to open the door, lovebirds, but I heard you stir and brought up your clothes and some breakfast! I'll leave the tray outside," the old woman called.

Dieu, if you're truly up there in Heaven, please heap blessings upon that creature, I thought as Antoine retrieved the food and clothes from the hall.

I refused to meet Antoine's eyes as he handed me the neatly folded pile of clean, dry garments, and sullenly retreated to the corner of the room to start dressing.

I forced myself to consider my predicament instead of my humiliation. I needed to try to get word to Daphne, but I didn't think Antoine would approve of me sending messages that might be intercepted by the *bêtes.* Never mind that as an agent of *les DD,* I'd been trained to send coded letters that were nearly impossible to decipher. He didn't need any more reason to convince himself of my secret profession.

After we finished dressing, I pinned my hair up beneath my lace cap and sat down to eat. The innkeeper had brought up a loaf of bread, a thick wedge of buttery cheese, and two apples. Without a word, Antoine and I polished off every crumb. Despite eating well last night and this morning, I still felt famished, as if my soul needed something other than simple bread and cheese. He stood to remove the tray, and I offered him a handful of coins.

"What's this?"

"Take it down to the innkeeper. It's my share of the food, laundry, and room cost," I said.

Antoine thrust the money back into my hands.

"Keep it. I've a purse of my own," he growled, strangely offended.

"I don't accept charity," I said, pushing the coins back toward him. "I can take care of myself, and I can pay my own way."

"If you think I'm going to let a woman—a *comtesse*, no less—pay our way out of a mess that I got us into, you're sorely mistaken. I always see to my own mistakes," he said sharply.

I could have continued to belabor the point, but my aim was more to get him to leave the room than to foot the bill. If he wanted to be a stubborn fool about finances, that was his pride-fueled prerogative.

I nodded. "Thank you. I'll be down in a moment—I have one or two things left to complete in my toilette."

He eyed me suspiciously but nodded and left. I went to the bedside table where I'd stashed my pilfered supplies the night before and withdrew a scrap of parchment, a small pot of ink, and a quill. After some thought, I decided against using our familiar code number cipher, since that would look even more suspicious than a silly letter to a family member.

D,

Hoping this missive finds you well. Sincerest apologies for dashing off early from the party—was called away unexpectedly. Hope the family isn't too cross with me. Promise to make it up to them as soon as I return home. Have decided to spend some time away to recover from this wretched rheumatism. I hear Gévaudan is nice this time of year. Will send you an update upon arrival. My love to E.

—C

It wasn't a lot of information, but I was being overly cautious. She'd at least understand that I was safe, the mission hadn't gone according to plan, that I was heading south and would write again soon.

I was preparing to seal the note when Antoine stomped in, startling me.

"What's that?"

"Nothing," I said, stuffing the letter in my pocket. He glared and strode forward, backing me up against the wall.

He *tsked.* "Hand it to me, or I shall forcibly retrieve it." His eyes glittered with the issued challenge.

Caged between his arms and the wall, my heart hammered in excitement. My gaze snagged on his mouth—those tempting lips stretched in a tight, frustrated line. Reflexively, my tongue darted out to wet my own lips. Antoine noticed.

The atmosphere between us changed, like the charged air in a thunderstorm right before the lightning strikes.

"Ha! You can certainly try," I challenged, but the bluster was gone from my tone. In its place was a throaty breathlessness I almost didn't recognize. *This man is rattling me, shaking my composure.* Heat blazed between our bodies.

One dark brow arched at my defiance, flexing the scar across his temple in a way I could only describe as *devastatingly handsome.* I tried to recover my senses—tried to stop staring at his strange, strong, handsome features long enough to ready myself for his *forcible retrieval* of my precious letter. I braced myself for the violence I suspected would come.

Instead, he kissed me.

His firm lips, so often set in that restrained frown, softened against mine. His tongue slid out, licking gently, tentatively, until I opened to meet him with the force of my unspent lust. *Dieu, he tastes delicious.* Like this morning's apples and mint tea, and the faintly salty taste of masculinity—nothing like the rank, perfumed sweets of my courtly lovers. His passion intensified and he pushed closer to me, crushing me against the wall. I felt his excitement press against my abdomen and it unleashed a new wave of desire in me.

I didn't hear choirs of angels singing. Rather, it sounded like legions of demons, moaning and writhing and goading me on, encouraging me to toss my skirts up and sink down to the floor on top of this glorious man.

I realized with a thrill that Antoine's hand was caressing me around the front of my skirt, reaching for the ties at the side and—

"*Ha!* You were saying?" he grinned, cheeks dimpling, holding my letter just out of reach.

He'd reached *right* into my skirt pockets and thieved it from me while I was lustfully compromised.

I gaped.

"You complete and utter cad! I cannot believe you did that!"

I was less embarrassed about the pursuit of my own carnal pleasure than I probably should have been. More than anything, I was angry at myself for letting him get the better of me, especially when I had to begrudgingly respect his unscrupulous tactics. I, myself, had often employed the same kinds of deception to extract information and influence. The rogue had beaten me at my own game.

There was also the possibility—as much as I didn't want to admit it—that I was disappointed he hadn't been as passionately moved as I'd been. My pride smarted.

He chuckled and stepped back, and I gritted my teeth at the sad loss of his warmth and the even sadder loss of the upper hand. I scowled at him and grabbed at the letter, which he held above my head as if I were a small, unruly child demanding sweets. Rather than embarrass myself further, I harrumphed and turned my back on him, hoping that even if he read the words I'd written to Daphne, he would merely think I was putting my cousin's worries at ease.

He frowned as he read, then handed the letter back to me.

"Why were you so protective of such drivel?"

I snatched the letter back from him. "Because a lady's personal correspondence is just that—personal. It's not for the eyes of every rapacious brute who doesn't respect a woman's privacy *or* personal boundaries."

"That's rich coming from the woman who crossed some very intimate boundaries early this morning," he snapped.

I put my hands on my hips and raised my chin haughtily. "It's really rather ungentlemanly of you to remind me."

"What does the letter *really* say?"

"You read it. It's familial drivel, as you say."

He snapped his fingers. "It must be some kind of coded message —*rheumatism*? You *are* a spy! Is she in on it, then? Your cousin? Of course, she must be. Who are you working for? The crown?"

"Don't be ridiculous. The idea of me—a comtesse!—working. You've clearly taken one battlefield blow to the head too many. I'm simply being cautious with what I reveal in the event the letter falls into the hands of the *bêtes de sang*. Really, it's common sense," I sniffed. I busied myself by packing my small parcels again, and once more looking for any supplies we might be able to use on our journey. Antoine stared at me, his characteristic frown tugging at his features once more.

"I told you last night, I can't abide deceit. Your actions may be putting us in further danger."

My temper was reaching volcanic proportions.

"How careless of me to put the both of us into great danger. If only *I* hadn't murdered a marquis in a palace, kidnapped an aristocrat, traipsed about the countryside with a bounty on my head, and run afoul of a murderous mercenary vampire death squad!" I snarled.

Antoine winced.

"But yes, you're right. A silly letter to my worried family with precious little traceable information is *surely* what will send us to our doom. Never mind the fact that we'd probably be in even more danger if Daphne *didn't* hear from me and sent a search party out after you. You think you have much to fear from the *bêtes de sang*? They'd be nothing compared to the wrath of my cousin if she knew you'd knocked me out and kidnapped me," I finished. I was breathless with anger and frustration.

Antoine folded his arms across his chest and stared hard at me.

"Fine," he conceded. "Keep your damn secrets."

I snorted. "As if I'm the only one keeping secrets! Why is there a bounty on your head? Why did you murder Sade? Why are there mercenaries after you? Why did you kiss me?"

I snapped my mouth shut. I hadn't meant to ask that last question. *Damn it, Charlotte!* No, damn this infuriating man. I'd never felt such a loss of control around anyone, and the fact that my life's work depended on my ability to maintain said control meant I needed to put as much distance as possible between us. The less I became untethered, the safer we would both be.

Antoine said nothing, his inscrutable gaze and hard frown hadn't even twitched when I'd fired my questions at him. *The horse's ass.*

I took a deep breath. "Forget it," I said. "Let's just get what supplies we can from this town and leave. We've already lingered longer than is wise."

He nodded once, picked up his things, and we headed downstairs. I smiled brightly at the innkeeper, jabbing Antoine with my elbow to remind him that we were undercover newlyweds. He flashed a grin at the elderly woman and inquired about the purchase of a second horse, some extra food, and additional warm clothes if possible. I handed her my sealed letter with a few coins, asking her to make sure it made its way to the next available mail coach.

We were successful with the extra food and warm clothes, but the innkeeper told us there weren't any spare horses to be had. I grumbled inwardly as I secured the thick woolen cloak around my shoulders. I was not looking forward to another day and a half of travel, pressed up against a thick wall of exasperating masculinity. By Antoine's sour expression, I surmised he felt the same way. He paid the woman handsomely, filled the saddlebags, and mounted his horse, then pulled me up in front of him.

Thankfully, the rain had let up, but the sky threatened more bad weather and the temperature had dropped considerably. Even with the additional warm clothes, we both shivered and sniffled, suffering each other's company in vexed silence. Antoine kept Tartuffe moving at a steady pace, and it was some hours after our departure before we paused to stop for lunch and allow the horse to rest. We found a dry log to sit on and dug into the bread, cheese, and apples the innkeeper had packed for us.

"They aren't mercenaries, you know," Antoine said quietly, as if I'd just asked him a question and we hadn't been riding for hours with nary a word between us.

I shrugged, still put out by our earlier argument. Surprisingly, he continued.

"They're soldiers. An elite squad of young vampires, newly turned to provide a strategic edge to the army, to be exact. With increased strength, speed, and an unquenchable bloodlust, they're the perfect warriors," he said, biting into an apple.

"Soldiers. For France?" I couldn't help it. My astonishment and curiosity overruled my hauteur.

He nodded.

I struggled to process this information. "How? Were they infected before or after they joined? It must've been after, but I can't imagine them retaining their posts once they'd succumbed to the blood plague. No commander would allow for infected troops. The prejudice against vampires is too great, though it's a silly prejudice, in my opinion. In fact, I could see how they'd be a huge asset to the war effort—what with them being mostly immortal and all. Wait—no! It cannot be that they were ordered to infect themselves?"

A shadow passed across his face. "Not quite. They volunteered for the post."

"That's preposterous. I know for a fact the king is unaware of any vampire troops. He wouldn't trust them at all, given what's been brewing in Paris. On whose orders were vampire soldiers created? And to what purpose?"

"The reasons are…complicated. As to whose orders, I'm afraid those come from Général de Vaux, the Lieutenant Général of the king's armies and the current governor of Thionville."

The name was familiar to me, as was his title, but I couldn't recall having ever met him at Versailles.

"Is he your commanding officer? Do you take your orders from him, then?" I asked.

Antoine sighed. It was the kind of bone-deep sigh that seemed to rise from his feet all the way up through his body.

"I've taken orders from him my whole life, Comtesse. Général de Vaux is my father."

8

ANTOINE

CHARLOTTE'S EYES WIDENED A FRACTION BEFORE SHE RECOVERED HER composure. Her brow furrowed as she studied the bread and cheese in her hands. She seemed to be puzzling things out, so I waited patiently for her to begin peppering me with the barrage of questions I knew would come.

"You told me your name was de Valle," she accused.

"De Valle comes from my mother's side. I have been traveling under that name since I left the front."

"I see. A half-truth, then," she sniffed. "The *bêtes* are your father's men?"

I nodded.

"Which means that he sent them after you. Is this because of some unresolved familial melodrama, or is this more to do with you being a deserter?"

My temper returned, quick as a flash. "I am *not* a deserter," I insisted.

"But there's a bounty on your head, and a group of your father's vampire soldiers after you," she mused. "It must be a particularly compelling family squabble for your father to seek you out with such industrious measures."

"It's complicated," I grumbled. I was already regretting my resolution to tell her some of my truths—an impulse that had struck when I'd seen the look of betrayal in her eyes after I'd kissed her and stolen her letter. *Trust a woman to twist the knife of guilt.*

"I'm sure it is," she replied, an edge of frustration creeping into her tone. "There's much I'd like to know about your relationship with your father, his motives in creating a superior soldier, his reasons for hiding those actions from the king, and why you feel the need to share this information with me now, but I suppose there are more pertinent questions first. Are there just the five of them? How skilled are these men? What will they do with you when they find you? Is the bounty for your capture or your death?"

The more she spoke, the more agitated she became, eventually abandoning her food and standing to pace in front of me. I tossed my apple core into the woods behind us.

"Yes, as far as I know, there are only five of them. They are a kind of… experiment, I suppose. They have been given more training than an average soldier, but they are newly turned and lack the experience of both seasoned vampires and seasoned soldiers. That makes them half as predictable and twice as dangerous as normal vampires and normal soldiers, which is why I cannot say for certain what they will do when they find us. My father would not have ordered my death, so I suspect he merely wants me to return to him, but whether the *bêtes* will obey that order is *questionable,* at best."

Charlotte paused her pacing and stared at me with those penetrating brown eyes. *Dieu,* she was beautiful. The early winter chill made her cheeks rosy in the same way that she blushed when she was flustered. I caught myself fantasizing about chasing that blush across her naked body but shook myself out of the vision. She was a spy. She probably used her beauty and charm to manipulate men with the detached precision of a clockmaker tending his cogs. *Do not fall for her, Antoine.*

She pursed her lips and nodded decisively, wrapping the food back up and putting it in her pocket.

"We shouldn't delay any further then," she said crisply. "You can tell me about the rest on our way to Gévaudan."

Her posture was stiff as she mounted Tartuffe, sliding forward on the saddle to allow me to heave myself up behind her.

"You're angry with me," I observed. "Is it because I got the better of you earlier or because of the danger I put you in?" I was unable to resist the temptation to tease her a little, though I kept my expression stoic as I guided us back to the southern road.

"You didn't get the better of me! And I'm not angry," she bit out.

I chuckled at the ironic denial.

"I'm *not* angry," she repeated. "I am *annoyed*. And it has nothing to do with the danger we are in. I can handle myself, thank you very much."

Of that, I had no doubt.

"Why are you annoyed with me then?" I prodded.

"It doesn't matter," she said curtly.

"It certainly seems to," I argued. "Whatever it is, I'm sorry. There, now. I've apologized. You can cease your petulance."

"Oh, for Heaven's sake! You are *such a man!*" she cried in exasperation. She turned halfway to glare at me from one eye, then opened her mouth to launch into what I could only assume would be a scathing, seething tirade, when she stopped and froze, as if she'd been struck. She craned her neck to squint behind us, coming up out of the saddle.

"What is it?" I asked.

"Hush!" she hissed. "Don't look now, but there is someone behind us on the road, traveling at quite a clip."

"On foot or horseback?"

"Horseback," she said warily. "It's a man on a lovely bay mare. He's dressed in dark green—looks bourgeois to me. I can't quite make out his face yet because his hat is pulled down rather low."

I made to turn but she stopped me with a firm hand on my arm.

"If you look now, it will be too obvious. Let's just continue on our way as the newlyweds we are and be prepared if it's trouble," she said, facing forward again.

I watched her slide her hand into one of her pockets and heard the sound of a pistol cocking. *So, she's kept the soldier's weapon this whole time!* I'd nearly forgotten about it. Reflexively, I felt for my own dual pistols and my short swords at my side. My crossbow hung from the saddle, though it would be useless in a roadside fray.

We were silent for the next several minutes, tensely waiting for the approaching man to either address us or ride on. As we listened to his horse trot up behind us, I felt the active tension gather in Charlotte's muscles, like a coiled snake ready to strike at a moment's notice. *Magnifique.*

"*Âllo!*" the man called. "*Bonjour, mes amis!* What fine weather we are having today! I only hope it doesn't rain later. Nothing worse than getting caught out in the rain, eh?"

I felt Charlotte relax a fraction, but I wasn't sure why. Looking up at the sky that almost certainly promised rain, I started to respond to the stranger, but Charlotte stopped me.

She didn't take her hand from her pocket. "It's worse to be caught out in the snow. Where are you headed, *mon ami*?"

"I go only where my masters send me," he said cryptically.

I stared down at her, perplexed. Her manner had me rattled. She almost spoke as if she knew this man, but that was impossible. She turned back to look at the stranger, darting a glance at me. She seemed more anxious about my presence than the man approaching.

She'd been right about him. He was dressed in dark green wool coat that was plain but well cut. He wasn't poor, but he wasn't an aristocrat, either. He'd obviously been traveling at some speed for some time, given how high the spattered mud reached on his clothes. I noted a few droplets of it on his cheek, as well—though with his dark eyes and placid expression, that was the only remarkable thing about his countenance. All in all, he was not unpleasant to look upon, but rather forgettable. He pulled up alongside us and I watched them greet each other with a guarded smile. *What the devil?*

"Bonjour, Monsieur," I said.

The stranger inclined his head at me but spoke again to her.

"Your companion?"

"Yes," Charlotte said, a touch anxiously. "I, too, go only where my masters send me. It's all right. He travels with me. Do you have news?"

The man reached into his coat. I laid my hand on my pistol, but Charlotte shook her head.

"It's okay, Antoine. This man is an…acquaintance," she said, fumbling for the right word.

So, she does know him. Irritation and irrational jealousy sparked, and I clenched my jaw.

"An acquaintance?" I echoed, incredulous. "Out here? Impossible. What the Hell is going on? Who are you?"

I wasn't sure if I directed that last question at the stranger or at Charlotte, but it didn't seem to matter as they both ignored me.

The man's expression didn't change as he handed her a letter. It was almost as if he wore a mask of humanity and it made me uneasy. Charlotte took the letter and nodded.

"Some miles back, there's an inn with a lovely innkeeper—she has a message for my cousin. Please see that she gets it. And tell her that I'll send a full report as soon as possible. We go to Gévaudan," she said, now focused on the letter in her hand.

"Charlotte!" I hissed. I couldn't believe she'd just revealed our plan.

Still, she ignored me. The stranger seemed to take this as his cue to leave, however, and he raised a gloved hand to his tricorn hat.

"In the darkness…"

"And in the light," Charlotte returned without looking up. She was engrossed in her letter, her brow furrowed.

The stranger winked at me, turned his horse around, and galloped back in the direction he'd come. Lucky for him that he'd managed it before I could yank him from his saddle and demand a rational explanation for this bizarre exchange. I reasoned, however, there was only one explanation—rational or not—and I'd known it since the very beginning of my encounter with this woman.

"You *are* a spy! You lied to me," I practically shouted.

She sighed, folding the letter carefully and tucking it into her bodice. The small action distracted me momentarily from my anger.

"Yes, yes. All right. I'll explain some things to you, but we must keep moving. Things are dire and we need to reach Gévaudan before nightfall, if possible."

The worry in her voice was genuine, but I didn't spur Tartuffe on just yet. The tangle of my emotions grew tighter and more knotted as I tried to sort things out in my head. *Charlotte lied to me. You lied to her, too, Antoine.* Had I? Not really. *Lies of omission are still lies, you fool, and it's your fault you're in this mess with her to begin with.* Anger surfaced again, but it was unclear if it was at myself or at this deceptive woman. I chose to direct it at the latter.

"Start talking," I growled.

"I'm not a spy," she said slowly, choosing her words carefully. "I am an agent of The Order. Not just The Order—*les Dames Dangereuses*, to be more specific."

I barked out a laugh. "Come now, you don't expect me to believe *that.*"

She tensed with affront. "And why not? You have been accusing me of as much since we met, you oaf."

"The Order is an absurd conspiracy—some portentous bedtime story to prevent people from rising up against the king. *Don't speak ill of His Majesty, lest The Order hear you! Stay away from the vampires, lest The Order come stake you! Don't forget to eat your vegetables, children, lest The Order find out!*"

Thunder rumbled in the distance, prompting me to kick Tartuffe into a trot.

I could feel Charlotte's frustration in her posture, but her tone was dismissive.

"Believe me or don't—you're the one who wanted an explanation."

"I want the truth, Comtesse," I countered.

"My explanation is no lie. Neither is The Order and my allegiance to it. Had I been able to find a way to speak with that messenger alone, I would have. Unfortunately, we're running short on time, and I'm forced to trust you with what you heard."

"Who was that man? And how the Hell did he find us?"

"I don't know him by name," she said. "But he is another agent of The

Order, too. I assume he found me the way any agent would—asking the right people the right questions and drawing the right conclusions. The first innkeeper and that tavern girl, Hélène, were not far from our point of origin. We are on the main road south. We've only had a short head start and were forced off the road by bad weather. It was only a matter of time before a person with an ounce of sense and a fast horse found us."

I scoffed. I wanted to believe that none of this made sense, but I knew deep down everything fit. The disguise, the training, the fighting, the manipulation… I just didn't want to admit that this beautiful, charming woman had the ability to wreak so much havoc. *Who are you kidding, Antoine? She's been wreaking havoc on you since you laid eyes on her.*

She must have interpreted my silence as a challenge, because she continued in a low, steely voice.

"I'm telling you the truth, Antoine. I was at Versailles to assassinate the Marquis de Sade on behalf of The Order. His execution had been finalized weeks before, but we had to wait for the right moment. I was to be that moment, you see. A lovers' tryst gone awry—a too shameful but entirely accidental death. The king never would have signed the death warrant—I mean, Sade *was* a marquis, after all—but it was decided that he needed to be stopped. His depravity could no longer be ignored or covered up. He deserved to die."

At her mention of Sade, I turned to stone, fighting the nausea and rage that blighted me every time I heard his name.

"He should have been dealt with properly, but you interfered. And so, help me, Antoine, if you breathe a word of any of this, or tell anyone about what you just saw on the road back there, I will not hesitate to use your interference to protect myself," she said icily.

I couldn't believe the audacity of the woman.

"First you lie to me, then you threaten me. *Tsk, tsk.* Is that any way for a comtesse to behave?"

"It's not a threat. It's my one and only attempt at setting terms. If you make trouble for me, rest assured, trouble will find you, too."

Rain started to fall—corpulent, nearly frozen droplets that hinted at becoming snow. I spurred Tartuffe on, now almost as worried about the weather as the skirted enigma in front of me.

"Trouble has already found us, Charlotte, with or without your lies."

"I'm sorry if you feel betrayed, Antoine, but you must understand that I was doing everything in my power to simultaneously protect you and extract myself from this situation," she called back. With Tartuffe's increased pace and the worsening weather, I could barely hear her words as they whipped past me on the wind.

"I told you I cannot abide deceit," I shouted in her ear. "Why didn't you admit as much to me when I first asked you?"

"I wouldn't be a very good covert agent—"

"You mean *spy!*"

"—if I admitted the truth about every aspect of my life to every random gentleman who asked," she said loudly. "Besides, you certainly have a lot of secrets for someone who professes to be such a paragon of honesty."

"I've never lied to you," I shot back. "Everything I've said has been the truth."

"Lying by omission is still dishonesty, Antoine. You can hardly think it's fair to expect me to divulge everything about myself when you won't even tell me why you were hunting the Marquis de Sade down in the first place."

Her words struck true, but I was still too angry to agree with her outwardly.

"I don't want to talk about it," I growled.

"Well, *I* don't want to talk about being an agent for The Order!" she shouted back at me. "But that doesn't seem to matter to *you!*"

"The Order is a myth! Just tell me who you're really working for, and I'll let it drop!"

We barreled on, our speed matching the rise of our tempers. I leaned forward into Charlotte's back, trying to ensure that she could hear my words over the wind and driving rain.

Mistake.

My blood boiled with exasperation, but the further I pressed against her in our rain-soaked clothes, the better I could feel her luscious curves jostling against me. The rhythmic pace of Tartuffe's feet striking the mud bounced Charlotte's ass against my hard cock, making me damn near feral with need.

"Why won't you believe me?" she barked, oblivious to my over-whelming desires. "Hell, I'll show you the damn letter he gave me—it's a report about Sade's associates. Signed and stamped with The Order's seal. I couldn't make that up or lie about it! I only lied about being an agent. Everything else has been the truth. Unlike *you.*"

"I already told you. Just because I haven't told you everything about my past doesn't mean I've told you any falsehoods!" *Dieu, help me.* I could see her chest heaving before me, her nipples puckered in the cold, wet fabric of her bodice. It nearly made me weep.

"Actions speak louder than words, Antoine," she shouted bitterly.

"What are you talking about?" I demanded, confused.

Suddenly, she recovered her composure and bit her lip, then shook her head. "Nothing. Never mind," she replied.

I slowed Tartuffe down, allowing him time to catch his breath and trying desperately to collect myself. I guided us off the road into a small grove of trees that provided a modicum of shelter from the rain. Despite the cold, I could see steam rising from our bodies. I dismounted to stretch my legs and, without waiting for her agreement, lifted Charlotte from the saddle.

"What do you mean?" I asked again, calmly this time—my gaze boring into the warm chocolate of her eyes.

She blushed. "I said it's nothing! I was angry. It doesn't matter."

Slowly, I reached up to brush a wet lock of hair from her cheek.

"It *does* matter."

She snorted in derision.

"Charlotte, I will not let it drop."

"Fine," she capitulated. She crossed her arms in front of her chest and threw me a withering glare. "Fine. For someone so opposed to deceit, you certainly had no problem using it on me this morning at the inn."

"Ah. When I stole your letter?"

She nodded once.

"And you're upset because I got the better of you?"

"No! Well, yes, but..."

"But that's not all," I finished. "How else did I deceive you, Comtesse?"

Charlotte twisted her face in agony, clearly embarrassed. She paced our secluded grove, muttering to herself beneath her breath. When I put my hand on her shoulder to stop her, she whirled on me.

"You made me believe!" she yelled. "You made me believe that you wanted me!"

Chagrinned, she covered her face with her hands and groaned.

"I will never forgive you for making me say that out loud," she muttered. "Now, can we be on our way? Night is falling and the *bêtes* will soon catch up to us if we don't keep moving. I don't suppose you know how much further we have to go before we reach Gévaudan—"

Whatever her last words were, she didn't have time to speak. Unwilling to resist any longer and unable to help myself, I grabbed her by the back of her neck and pulled her lips to mine.

9
CHARLOTTE

November 2, 1767
The road to Gévaudan

I'D NEVER PARTICULARLY ENJOYED BEING MANHANDLED IN SUCH AN aggressive fashion when it came to men, though I knew plenty of women who did. Antoine, however, was different. His touch wasn't an entitled drive to satisfy his own wants—rather, it was an outpouring of emotions he didn't seem to be able to express verbally.

The force of his passion was volcanic in its intensity, prompting me to step back and grab hold of him simultaneously.

One hand behind my neck, the other snaking around my waist to bring our bodies as close together as physics and anatomy would allow, he devoured my lips like a man going off to duel at dawn. Gone was the calculating sweetness of our kiss this morning—in its place, raw need and desperation.

His tongue tangled with mine as his hand slipped down to give my ass a firm squeeze, provoking a satisfied whimper from me and a groan of desire from him. He guided me back against one of the trees and pushed his arousal against my stomach, sucking in a harsh breath at the friction.

Pulling back slightly, he cupped my face in his hands and leveled his darkening green gaze at me. It stripped me bare and terrified me with its honesty. *The honesty of a man you do not deserve.*

"That was *not* deceit," he whispered. I shut my eyes, thrown utterly off balance by the impact of what had just happened. "Charlotte, look at me."

I forced myself to meet his eyes, fully intending to laugh off the awkwardness I started to feel, but found myself unable. My sharp retorts and witticisms died in my throat. I didn't want an uncomfortable silence or an indifferent conclusion to this strange encounter. I just wanted more of him. I reached up and set my lips to his again, half-expecting to meet some kind of resistance, but he yielded to me immediately. I threaded my fingers through his hair and sucked at his tongue, dizzy with lust. He dragged his lips from mine and licked the droplets of rainwater on my neck, then nuzzled his way back up to my ear.

"Oh, Antoine," I breathed.

"*Dieu*, Comtesse," he growled, tugging at my earlobe with his teeth. "I want you so badly I cannot think straight, but we should not continue. We cannot if we don't trust each other."

"Who says we cannot? Trust has nothing to do with sex."

He narrowed his eyes at me, his desire warring with his frustration. "You truly want me to continue?"

In response, I wrapped one leg around his waist and reached down to slide my hand along the impressive, hard length of him. He choked out a sound halfway between a cry and a moan, then yanked my hands away from his delicious body and pinned them down at my sides.

For a moment, my heart sank, interpreting the gesture as rejection. *He should reject you, Charlotte. He is everything that is honorable and straightforward, and you are more artifice than flesh.*

Afraid at what I might see reflected in his gaze, I tilted my face up to his, expecting to hear the censure I so often heard from my former husband. No such words came. Instead, he grinned wickedly, flashing a dimpled smile that made my knees wobble. Taking one hand and lifting my sodden skirts, he reached beneath the hem of my chemise and stroked cool fingers up my inner thighs.

"Your skin is like silk," he murmured. "Finer than anything a man like me should be allowed to touch."

He slid two fingers through the seam of my sex, pressing one fingertip against the bud of pleasure and prompting me to utter a stream of obscenities that made his breath quicken.

"From the first moment I saw you, Comtesse, I knew you would be this maddening. So passionate," he teased at my ear, rubbing firm circles with his fingertip and sliding his second finger inside me.

"*Putain de merde, oui, l'amour.* If you stop now, I will kill you!"

I grasped wildly for his breeches, but he stayed my hand and brought his lips to mine for a searing kiss.

"Not yet," he panted. "I've been wagering with myself that seeing you in ecstasy will be the most beautiful thing I've ever seen, and I plan to settle that bet first."

I whimpered something unintelligible—even to my own ears—and ground my hips against his hand.

"Now do you understand? My desire for you, Comtesse, is the most honest thing that has existed between us since we met days ago."

Faster and harder his skilled fingers worked until my bliss closed in around me and I began to see stars. His other hand came up to caress my breast through the drenched fabric of my dress. He sucked at my earlobe and pinched my nipple almost to the point of pain, sending me screaming over the edge. When my climax broke, Antoine held me through it, letting me ride the waves of pleasure in his arms. When I sighed in satisfaction, he dropped my skirts, swept another kiss across my lips and licked his fingertips.

"Perfection," he said with a smile.

I stared at him in wonder. Who *was* this man? He'd gone from gruff murderer to grumpy soldier to devastating rake in the time that I'd known him—a scant matter of days. *A man to keep you on your toes, Charlotte.* If I wasn't careful, I could fall for him, and that would most certainly complicate the life I'd worked very hard to craft for myself in the wake of Philippe's destruction. Suddenly self-conscious, I closed my eyes.

"Antoine, I'm sorry, I—"

A twig snapped behind our grove of trees and we both froze.

"Well, well, well, that *was* entertaining," came an accented voice from the darkness.

The darkness. What fools we'd been! In our sexual frustration, we'd completely abandoned good sense and had delayed too long. Night had fallen, and from the thick Prussian consonants emanating from the blackness beyond, the *bêtes* had found us.

Merde.

Antoine realized it, too, and stepped in front of me protectively. *The idiot.* Two of us could fight better than one.

From all around us, the five soldiers came forward slowly. They had our routes of escape blocked. Tartuffe whinnied as one of the *bêtes* seized his reins and grinned predatorily, showing off an impressive set of fangs.

"We have no quarrel with you, *petite.* It's the gentleman we're after," said one of the Parisians.

"Speak for yourself," grumbled the other Prussian. I recognized him as the one that I'd shot in the stomach. He kept his hand on the pistol at his side and narrowed his gaze at me.

My mind worked. On foot, we wouldn't stand a chance. If we could get to Tartuffe, we might be able to get away, but I wasn't certain how likely that would be. They had us surrounded and it was five on two. If I had more than the one pistol, I might be able to manage it, but between Antoine and I, a fight was doomed from the start. Perhaps I could negotiate.

"Why are you after him?" I asked the Parisian who'd addressed me.

Antoine's whole body tensed, as if he were preparing for the attack.

"That's none of your fucking business," snarled the angry Prussian.

"Well, at present, he's my escort, so I'd say that's entirely my business. I have a hard time believing that King Louis would approve of his men depriving a helpless woman of her travel companion and protection out in the middle of nowhere," I sniffed.

"Forgive me, lady, but your protection does not concern us at present. Perhaps when we've finished with Lieutenant de Vaux, we can come to some other arrangement with you," one of the other soldiers said with a smirk.

"Is it the bounty you're after?" I tried. "Whatever it is, I'll triple it." I didn't think the *bêtes* would go for it, but I was stalling—desperately trying to come up with a plan that didn't involve us getting drained and left to die in the woods outside Gévaudan.

"Charlotte," Antoine warned. "Please. I'll handle this."

I arched a brow at him. *Oh, really?* He didn't appear to be handling it at all. I pursed my lips.

"I'll come with you," Antoine told the *bêtes*. "But the lady leaves unharmed."

I rolled my eyes. Even if they did agree to that, I didn't trust them to uphold their end of that particular bargain. I'd known too many men in my life. Not everyone had Antoine's sense of honor.

The first Parisian smiled and inclined his head. "Of course, Lieutenant de Vaux. We can be civil, can't we, men?"

The group of men chuckled, sending the hairs on the back of my neck straight up.

"Please," I tried again, anxious at Antoine's misplaced chivalry. *Surely, he doesn't believe them, does he?* "Please. What is it you're after? Is it money? Influence? Say the words and I'll make sure you get whatever reward you desire. Eternity is such a long time, gentlemen—I can see to it that you have enough money to last you until the end of days."

That attracted the attention of the soldier to my left—the third Parisian.

"Oh, sure! You'll just run right up to the king and demand compensation for us, will you?" he snickered.

"Don't be ridiculous," I scoffed. "I would *never* run. A lady *glides.*"

The first Parisian barked a laugh. Antoine scowled at me.

"Who the Hell are you?" the Parisian asked, eyeing me up and down.

"No one," Antoine growled. "She's no one and none of your concern."

Bless him. I raised my chin haughtily and inclined my head at the vampire.

"Monsieur, you have the privilege of addressing the Marquise de Balay. You must forgive my state of dress and my earlier deception on the road. Monsieur de Vaux and I have had a very long and unbelievable journey. It's really quite a story," I said. I didn't want to give him my real name just yet, so the borrowed title would do for now. Antoine continued to glare at me, apparently finding refuge in playing the grumpy soldier again. *So much for my dashing rake.*

The Parisian considered me.

"I'm listening," he drawled.

"*Putain, Hugo,*" the grumpy Prussian swore. "We don't have time for this. Let's just take the lieutenant, drain the girl, and be on our way."

That familiar muscle in Antoine's jaw twitched—the one signaling extreme displeasure. The Parisian—Hugo, it seemed—frowned at the Prussian.

"I want to know who we're dealing with, Frederick. Don't you?" he said darkly. "Please, continue, *Madame la Marquise.*"

"Well, it started back at the All Hallow's Eve masquerade at Versailles," I said brightly. "I was there with my husband, the marquis, but he was *so* cross with me! You see, I thought it would be a riotous good time to come dressed as Cupid—which was how you gentlemen found me, remember?—and he certainly was less than pleased with my choice of costume, so he avoided me all evening, the cad!" Sighing heavily and willing blood to my cheeks, I looked down as if scandalized. "We had a rather public argument, I'm afraid. Oh, I cannot imagine what the gossips are saying right now! Anyway, I decided to leave the ball early and went out to meet my carriage, when Lieutenant de Vaux happened upon me. He's an old family friend, you see, and he valiantly agreed to escort me back to my château, but, oh, gentlemen, you know how a lady's temperament is, don't you?" I shot them beseeching looks and saw that I had their full attention. "I decided after the humiliating spectacle at Versailles, I wanted to spend some time alone, away from my fool of a husband, and I insisted on darling Antoine accompanying me to our country estate down south."

The lie became bigger and bigger as I prattled on, playing for time and hoping to come up with another plan of escape. *Think, Charlotte. We can't be that far from Gévaudan. Less than half a day's ride, if Antoine is right. Surely there are more people journeying this way, and it's only a matter of time before someone comes upon us and offers some kind of assistance, or, at the very least, a big enough distraction to allow us to escape.*

Eventually, however, I ran out of words. The long days and sleepless nights had caught up with me, and I fumbled over the end of my imaginary tale.

"And there you have it," I tried with false hope. "Now, will you gentlemen allow us to leave? What say you?"

"What say I? I say that was the most incredible work of fiction I think I've ever heard," Hugo chuckled.

Merde.

"Truly remarkable," laughed the less grumpy Prussian. "I haven't had entertainment like that since we left the front."

"You're quite the actress. I'm almost sorry that we'll probably kill you anyway," Hugo grinned, his fangs glinting in the moonlight.

"I'm not," hissed the grumpy Prussian.

Antoine tensed, prepared to leap forward at the soldier holding Tartuffe. Hugo caught the posture, naturally, and *tsked.*

"Please, Lieutenant. We've dallied enough. Just come with us and *maybe* we'll let your little tart live when we're done with her."

I heard a low growl then and turned bewildered eyes on Antoine. Was the noise coming from him? It seemed to emanate from every direction around us. Antoine reached for me protectively and I realized the noise was coming from just outside our grove—a realization that didn't *exactly* fill me with relief.

"What the Hell is that?" the grumpy Prussian hissed. "Hugo, do you smell that? What *is* that? Who's there?"

All five of the *bêtes* turned, sniffing the air, and listening with their supernatural senses. At once, they homed in on one direction—right behind me. Goosebumps rose along my skin as my dull human senses picked up on the thing they all stared at.

Once more, a low, feral growl vibrated through the frigid blackness of night.

Antoine twisted slowly, peering at something behind my left shoulder.

"Charlotte," he whispered. "Get ready to *run.*"

The fear in his eyes chilled my blood to ice, and it barely registered when he calmly slid his hands from my waist to the dual pistols at his sides.

Tartuffe whinnied in fear and bucked, yanking the reins from the vampire's grasp. He hissed and grabbed for them, which became the spark that our powder keg of a situation needed. The thing at my back snarled. I turned in time to see a dark shape leap forward, knocking me to the ground with a pair of savage claws. I felt the sting of them raking my shoulder—*merde, I hope those scratches are not too deep*—and braced for a second blow, but none came. The thing had fixed its attention on the vampires. Antoine dove down and rolled atop me protectively, then all Hell broke loose.

10

ANTOINE

November 3, 1767
The road to Gévaudan

CHARLOTTE AND I WATCHED, STUNNED, AS THE LARGE CREATURE WENT AFTER Frederick. In the darkness, it was almost impossible to see what it was, but it had the penetrating yellow eyes, ominous growl, and wild ferocity of an exceptionally large wolf. Moonlight glinted off fangs and claws and sketched an outline that was something *more* than canine—but I couldn't wrap my head around the idea that we were being attacked or saved by yet another supernatural creature. If, however, it *was* merely a wolf, I didn't want to stick around to find out where the rest of its pack lurked—now was the perfect time for Charlotte and me to escape the *bêtes de sang*.

Hugo aimed his pistol at the creature and fired, but the shot went wide, and the beast turned on him. Frederick hissed and pulled out his short sword, slashing wildly at the creature's back. The other soldiers rushed to Hugo's aid. He seemed to be having some trouble keeping the beast from closing its massive jaws around his neck.

"Now, Charlotte!" I urged. I grabbed her arm and hauled her up, running for Tartuffe.

I heard a snarl from behind us—whether it was the beast or the soldiers, I couldn't tell. Steps away from my horse, a great force yanked me back and I fell to the ground. I stared up into the vicious, grinning countenance of Hugo. Long, bloody gashes marred his face. He leveled his pistol at me.

"We're not done here, Lieutenant!" he shouted.

The vampires behind him had subdued the beast and were piling on top of it to hold it down, ready to shoot it at Hugo's word. The creature growled again and snapped at one of the soldiers, then pitched its head back and let out a guttural, unearthly howl. It sounded halfway between a wolf and a man in absolute agony. I shivered in fear.

Hugo turned toward the horrifying sound, and I reached for my sword but didn't move fast enough. From the darkness behind me, I heard Charlotte run forward. She kicked out at Hugo's knee with the full weight of her body, snapping his leg in two. Hugo screamed in pain as she fell on top of me, then rolled to the side in a predatory crouch. She snatched my short sword from my side and held it at Hugo's throat. He snarled at her and scraped his fangs across her arm, but she was too enraged to notice. She held him fast, aided by his sickeningly twisted broken leg.

"Let the beast go!" she yelled at the soldiers. "Or I will cut off your friend's head. I doubt that's a wound he will be able to recover from."

"Charlotte," I warned. "I don't think that's a good idea."

"I don't think it's after us," she said. "And I can't just leave it to the mercy of these monsters."

The soldiers eyed each other, frozen in fury. Charlotte pressed the blade into Hugo's neck, drawing forth a line of thick, black blood. Hugo choked and screeched at his men. "Do as she says!"

The soldiers flinched and loosened their hold on the beast, whose large yellow eyes fixed on the blood dripping from Hugo's throat.

"Antoine," she said steadily. "On the count of three, we're going to make for your horse and get the Hell out of here. One…two…three!"

The last vampire let go of the beast and Charlotte shoved Hugo forward, precipitating a sickening collision of bone, blood, and fangs. Instantly, Charlotte and I jumped on Tartuffe's back and kicked him into a furious gallop. Behind us, I heard the ferocious sounds of a grim battle being waged—the creature's teeth, claws, and massive size against the vampires' fangs, speed, and superior numbers. My gut twisted, but the only thing that mattered now was the fact that neither enemy gave chase.

I looked down at the torn sleeve and oozing gash in Charlotte's shoulder—a shoulder that had been perfect and unmarred before I'd let my desires carry us into disaster and *very nearly* death. How could I have been so foolish? I wasn't a brainless adolescent! I was a man—a man who'd long ago learned how to control his baser urges and set aside fanciful romantic notions in the face of duty. Then, suddenly, this woman —this *dangerous* woman—showed up, and in the space of a few days, turned my entire world upside down. *Damn it, Antoine. What has gotten into you?*

Charlotte was making me lose sight of things—my vengeful action against Sade and the very real repercussions of that action, my father's betrayal and the *bêtes de sang*, my future beyond the military...not to mention the fact that I barely knew Charlotte and trusted her even less. Especially now that I'd seen her in action more than once. What kind of a spy took on five supernatural soldiers at once, didn't bat an eye at shooting a man in the gut, and knew exactly how to snap a man's leg in two with a well-placed jump kick? No kind of intelligence agent I knew—to say nothing of the fact she was a *woman* and a damned comtesse.

That certainly didn't stop you from pushing her up against a tree and taking advantage of her, I thought darkly. But the way she'd responded to my touch had unleashed something inside me—something I now recognized as nothing less than utter damnation. Given that we'd only just escaped the clutches of the *bêtes* and some unknown creature with God-knew-what motives, it was distressing that I was still fixated on Charlotte and her effect on me. I should be trying to understand our predicament, but... Well, I'd thought myself a fool for less.

My bitter oaths died on the wind as we galloped on, Charlotte clutching Tartuffe's mane in a pained grip. I knew we were some distance away from Gévaudan, but I didn't dare stop until we reached either the city gates or sunrise. I only hoped we could hold on until then.

"How's your shoulder?" I said at Charlotte's ear.

"I'll be all right," she called back to me. "I can dress the wound when we get to Gévaudan, but I don't want to stop if I can help it."

Her face was pale, and her brow was damp, but I hoped that was from the earlier rain and not the onset of shock and fever. The tattered fabric at her shoulder was dark with her spreading blood, much more than had been there moments before. If we didn't find shelter soon... I didn't want to consider the alternatives.

We raced on, eventually slowing to a trot. Tartuffe's sides heaved and Charlotte's eyes occasionally fluttered closed. Right about the time I was considering a rest, the sky began to lighten, and I saw Gévaudan appear in the shallow valley before us. Encircled by a lazy, aquamarine river, the medieval town of stonework buildings was at once charming and ominous. Surrounding the township was a wall of thick timbers that looked like they'd been built in a hurry—as did the pikes along the road that were topped with fly-infested wolf heads in various states of decay.

I nudged Charlotte awake as we approached two guards flanking an iron-spiked gate. Her face was distressingly pale and there were dark purple shadows beneath her eyes, but she snapped to attention like a solder at inspection.

"Charlotte, we've arrived. Hold on just a bit longer," I murmured.

She nodded and adjusted her cloak to cover her wounded shoulder. In a flash, her weariness and discomfort evaporated, and she pasted a dazzling smile on her face. Her ability to transform her entire countenance in an instant both impressed and disquieted me. *Could she turn so easily on me?*

The guards nodded at us. *"Bonjour.* What's your business in Gévaudan?"

"Just passing through," I said in what I hoped was a charming manner. "My new wife and I are on our way south, but we've run into some troubles along the road. We're stopping in for supplies and a couple nights of lodging while our carriage catches up to us. Broke a wheel some miles back and didn't want to wait it out in the poor weather."

"Any supernatural incidents on your journey here? Or particular allegiances to vampires?" The guard queried.

"Mon Dieu, non!" Charlotte gasped. "Certainly not. That's why we went out of our way to come through your fine commune in the first place —we knew we'd be safe from *paranormal* influences."

The guard eyed her and flicked his gaze to the sunrise over his shoulder, apparently verifying our adherence to a daylight schedule.

"Very well. There's a curfew in effect. The gates are locked at sundown and unlocked at sunrise. Any wolf sightings or *unusual* behavior is to be reported."

"Goodness," Charlotte blinked. "That seems quite serious."

"Werewolf attacks, Madame. We've lost too many innocents not to take it seriously. But the beast only attacks at night and hasn't breached the wall yet. You'll be safe inside. There are three inns off the main street. You should be able to find lodging in one of them," he said. He stood to the side and pulled a massive lever, raising the iron-spiked gate. I dismounted and led Tartuffe and Charlotte through.

Once inside, with the *bêtes* and the creature behind us, I felt a flutter of relief, but it was fleeting. The early sun disappeared behind a blanket of clouds, casting a dim gray pall over everything. The hustle and bustle that I expected from an early market day was subdued and hurried, as if the town's residents were in a state of collective mourning—anxious to return to their homes as quickly as possible.

Off the main street, I noted a bakery and a couple of stalls of produce, as well as a modest-looking tailor and draper. As soon as we could find a room and I'd tended to Charlotte's shoulder, I'd head back out for supplies. I kept one eye on Charlotte, worried that she'd drop from Tartuffe, but though her face was strained and pale, she stared resolutely forward. It was hard not to admire her mettle, especially considering I'd seen soldiers in battle suffer lesser wounds and pass out in a dead faint.

There you go again, Antoine—mooning over this damn, dangerous woman that you swore to leave alone. Merde. I just needed some food, some rest, and some distance from her; that was all. *And the truth,* said a small voice in my head. *It bothers you that she's keeping secrets from you, even as you keep secrets from her, too.*

"What's the matter with you?" Charlotte asked, startling me. "We've made it to safety, and you look like you swallowed a lemon."

"I do not," I grumbled.

"Do so," she argued. "Besides, you weren't even injured. You don't see me scowling at a town full of grief-stricken countryfolk."

I exhaled wearily. "I'm just tired. It's been a long journey and I'm eager to find an inn."

Charlotte snorted.

"Well, we've already passed the one back there. Are you looking for a particular establishment or are you merely the persnickety sort?"

I swore under my breath. I'd been so distracted I'd completely missed the first of the three inns. Attempting to save face, I scanned the street ahead and saw a sign for one of the others, The Wild Rose.

"This one looks more comfortable. We'll stop in here," I said. Charlotte flashed a grin, but it quickly turned into a wince. I picked up our pace.

When we reached the inn, I helped Charlotte dismount, led Tartuffe around to the stables, and headed inside. Fortunately, it was empty, so we didn't attract too much attention. I repeated our now-familiar newlywed story, paid the dour innkeeper handsomely for the best room, a large meal, and a bath to be sent up, and practically collapsed with exhaustion and relief when I finally shut our door behind us.

Charlotte sank onto the bed and sighed. "Should we discuss what happened last night?"

I didn't know if she referred to our lustful entanglement, the *bêtes*, the horrifying creature, her saving me, or our lucky escape. I grimaced, knowing she likely meant all of it, but I didn't think either one of us had the energy to broach such overwhelming subjects just yet. I shucked off my damp coat and hung it next to the fire.

"We should, but I think it's best to wait until we've recovered a bit. Let's look at your shoulder, get some food and rest, and then figure things out."

Charlotte nodded, likely too tired to argue. "Antoine, might I prevail upon you to collect some supplies for my wound? I daresay I've had worse than this, and I know what's required to set it right."

I bristled at the idea that she'd had a worse wound than a lacerated shoulder, as well as at the idea that I couldn't—or wouldn't—tend to her.

"Will you let me look at it first, or does part of your treatment plan involve ordering capable men about?" I grumbled.

Her eyes widened in shock, then narrowed.

"You think you can care for me better than I can care for myself?"

"I didn't say that," I snapped. Fatigue was making me sharper than I wished to be.

"You certainly implied it! Are you a doctor as well as a soldier *as well as* an assassin? For all I know about you, Antoine, you may be since you've refused to tell me practically anything about yourself. Why should I trust you?" Her temper flared, catching me off guard. I had no desire to argue, but I was unable to stop myself from getting riled.

"Well, you obviously didn't have a problem trusting me to toss your skirts up and ravish you," I uttered darkly.

She gaped at me then and surprised me by tipping her head back and laughing.

"*'Ravish'* me! Oh, Antoine, the things you say sometimes. Positively delightful."

I scowled, reddening in embarrassment. "It shouldn't have happened. I…I apologize. I took liberties that I shouldn't have. I'm sorry."

"I'm not. Don't be ridiculous, Antoine. I'm hardly some blushing virgin. We both wanted it to happen, and we both participated, and I don't regret it. Of course, it makes things, what, complicated? Awkward? But we're adults, and as I told you, I've never been one for propriety." She flexed her arm and cringed again.

"We can discuss it later," I said quietly. "For now, please. You're obviously in pain. Allow me to assist you."

She sighed. "You are right, of course. I'm sure you've seen your fair share of battlefield trauma. It's not that I think you're incapable, it's just that I am rather used to looking after myself these days. The last time I allowed myself to be looked after, I'm afraid I was rather blindsided by a man who told me once too often not to worry—he'd take care of everything. And *Dieu*, he did take care of everything! Just not in a way that would have benefitted me at all." As she spoke, she began to disrobe, and I fought to keep my thoughts respectable.

"Was that your husband?" I asked, coming over to assist when she beckoned.

She fumbled with the ties on her bodice, a sign that her strength was wavering. The mark on her lower arm where Hugo had scratched her with his fangs seemed more superficial than serious, but it still infuriated me to think of him harming her. If he came after her again, I'd drive a stake through his heart and cut off his head, for good measure.

"Yes," she huffed. I peeled the blood-soaked fabric from her shoulder as gently as I could. She hissed in pain, and I frowned. Marring her perfect skin were three jagged cuts, just shallow enough to not need stitching. She kept perfectly still as I inspected them, flinching when I stood from the bed and accidentally jostled her.

"Well?" She gritted her teeth. She shivered slightly in her rain-damp chemise and stays. *Heaven help me.*

"You don't need stitches," I said. "But you'll probably have a scar."

"Lucky for me, exposed shoulders are out of fashion right now," she huffed with a forced laugh. "If you're going to treat me, please hurry. I'd rather not let it fester. I certainly hope you aren't a proponent of leeches and purgatives."

I shook my head. "I've seen too many men die from such ministrations. I'll wash and bandage it and see if the cook has any garlic and thyme oil for a poultice."

"Garlic and thyme oil? Do you plan on fashioning me into a stew?" she chuckled. The color had faded even more from her cheeks and lips, worrying me further. I stood and made for the door.

"I don't know why it works, but it does," I replied. "You'll just have to trust me."

"Trust is no small thing," she murmured.

I agreed. I offered her an encouraging smile, which she returned with an unfocused gaze.

She wavered slightly, then her eyes rolled white, and she passed out, falling backward onto the bed.

11

CHARLOTTE

I FELT SUNLIGHT STREAMING IN ABOVE ME. EVEN THOUGH I KEPT MY EYES tightly closed, its warmth was a comforting caress across my face. I was bombarded by a confusing array of scents—blood, herbs, flowers, freshly washed linen, leather, baking bread, burning wood.

I groaned. My throat burned from dehydration and disuse. *That can't be good. I wonder how long I've been in bed.*

Memories began to return to me, slowly, as if I could only see them from behind distorted glass—Sade's death, Antoine, vampire soldiers. The cold, rainy road to Gévaudan. A passionate embrace and brain-searing climax in a wooded glade, followed by a violent attack and a strange creature. Excruciating pain in my shoulder. Then the town and this inn.

But the sun was out now, and I sensed more than just Antoine nearby. How long had I been unconscious?

I cracked one eye open and looked around. Another cloak hung by the fire, but the room was otherwise empty. On the small table, I saw a tidy pile of bandages, small jars of medicines, and a set of severe-looking surgical instruments. Immediately, my hand went to my shoulder. It was wrapped in fresh bandages—as was the scrape on my arm from Hugo's teeth—but I didn't feel more than a dull ache from either injury. Whether it was Antoine or the mystery cloak owner, whoever had tended my arm had done a splendid job.

I rose, frowning down at my ragged chemise. I couldn't wait for a proper bath and some clean clothes. *Soon. Find Antoine first.* I went over to the cloak and felt around the pockets for any clue as to its wearer but came up empty. The garment was a lovely royal blue and was small and delicately cut, I suspected for a woman. I sniffed at the collar and sleeves and smelled faint odors of herbs, rain-damp wool, and something exotic, yet vaguely familiar—*lime blossom.*

"Van Helsing!" I exclaimed.

As if summoned, the curvy, dark-haired doctor bustled into the room carrying a cloth-covered tray. Lunch, perhaps. She regarded me with mild surprise, her deep blue eyes widening a fraction behind her spectacles.

"Ah, excellent! I had a feeling you'd be awake today," she said in her lilting Dutch accent.

"Where is Antoine?" I demanded. I flinched at the harshness of my tone. I hadn't meant to ask that, but the question had tumbled out of my mouth before any of the others. *What are you doing here? How long have I been in bed? What day is it? What of the vampires and that creature? Is there food on that tray? I'm ravenous.*

She cocked a brow at me and grinned. "After days at your bedside, the lieutenant was finally persuaded to get some much-needed food and rest. He's sound asleep next-door, in my bedroom."

At this, an unexpected flash of overheated anger and fierce possessiveness surged in my blood, screeching *"mine! He's mine,"* prompting me to practically growl at her.

"In *your* room?"

Van Helsing studied me intently over the rim of her spectacles, her eyes sparkling with curiosity.

"Very interesting," she murmured to herself. "Yes, Comtesse, he is resting in my chambers. It is nothing untoward, I assure you. In your comatose state, you thrashed about quite wildly, and he would not have been able to sleep in this room, let alone in that bed with you."

The explanation made sense, but I felt a tug of unease.

"Comatose state? What are you talking about? How long have I been here? How long have *you* been here? How did you even know to come here—and how did you get here in the first place?" The questions came on a rising tide of panic. *Something is certainly amiss.*

"Relax, please, before you overexert yourself. Here, sit on the bed and let me check your wounds. Yes, yes. Very good," she soothed as she led me back to the bed and started to unwrap my shoulder. "First, today is the 18th. You've been mostly unconscious for about two weeks now—"

"Two weeks!" I shrieked. "Tell me you're joking. It cannot have been so long."

"I'm afraid it has, Comtesse. You succumbed to a strange type of infection and a blood fever. Your friend, Lieutenant de Valle, did his best for you—and a fine job he did, I might add—but when you didn't recover after the first two days, he had the good sense to send an urgent message to your cousin. She, of course, had the *better* sense to send me to your aid, a wise move considering she and the duke would not be allowed to enter the city due to their supernatural condition."

Two years ago, Daphne introduced Doctor Van Helsing to me as the woman who'd saved her current husband's undead life. When Étienne, the vampire emissary to King Louis, had suffered an assassination attempt via quicksilver poisoning, Daphne had used her considerable influence and wealth to find the best vampire doctor in France—well, all of Europe, probably. Not only did Van Helsing heal Étienne, but she'd been instrumental in encouraging them to realize their love for one another.

After that, *les Dames Dangereuses* and even the men of The Order seldom used any other physician, and it became nearly impossible to secure her services due to the high demand for them. Fortunately for me, she and I had become friends of a sort, and she'd patched me up more times and in more ways than I cared to think about.

Her words whirled around in my head, giving rise to a new barrage of questions. *Strange type of infection?* I blanched. If the most eminent supernatural physician in Europe believed your illness *strange*, that certainly didn't bode well for you. And a blood fever? From a mere scratch? I reached for the shoulder she was still unwrapping, but she swatted my hand away.

"No, no," she tutted. "You're healing well now, but I won't have you corrupting the process. For once, Comtesse—*Charlotte*—do as I recommend and allow your body the proper time to recover. You are safe enough here for now. Lieutenant de Valle is helping to look after your needs, and Daphne and Étienne are in the next town over, waiting for you to be fit enough to meet with them. All is well. Simply rest. *Please.*"

Despite her making perfect sense, I scowled. "I've been *resting*. Now I feel rest*less*. At least give me leave to go check on Antoine. There are… things…we need to discuss."

Van Helsing regarded me for a moment, then went back to her examination of my shoulder. She pressed firmly into the tender flesh, and I expected to draw back in pain, but felt no more than a fleeting discomfort. *Strange, indeed.*

"Remarkable," the doctor muttered to herself.

"What's remarkable?" I replied, unable to see what she was marveling at beneath the mound of linen piled up on my shoulder.

Before she could answer, the door exploded open and Antoine barreled in, twin pistols drawn. Van Helsing and I jumped.

"You're awake!" Antoine said in a tone of stunned confusion. He lowered the pistols. "I'm sorry. I heard voices and I thought perhaps someone else had…" He trailed off and blushed. Taking a tentative step into the room, he cast accusing eyes upon Van Helsing. "Doctor, you promised to tell me the moment she awakened."

Van Helsing rolled her eyes. "Lieutenant, you needed sleep just as much as she did. Incidentally, she woke only a few minutes before you burst in here with your inappropriate weapons drawn." She shook her head. "You French, with all your hotblooded violence and passions. It's a wonder the entire country hasn't come down with apoplexy."

Antoine's jaw worked, clenching and unclenching as if he had a great deal to say to the doctor but was trying very hard to restrain himself.

"Comtesse," he coughed out awkwardly. "Are you well? I mean, how are you feeling?"

"I'm fine, Antoine, really. Remarkably well, even," I said with a smile. "With Doctor Van Helsing's care—and with your care, she tells me—and the rest of several days, I feel almost as good as new."

He nodded. "Excellent. Outstanding." He cleared his throat and fiddled with his loose cuff. Van Helsing watched his discomfort with growing amusement.

"Well, I've been up for some time. I do believe it is my turn to get some sleep now. Lieutenant, do keep an eye on our patient. Please try not to overexcite her or let her engage in any *vigorous* activity. I'll check in again later this evening," the doctor said, trying unsuccessfully to hide a smile.

Antoine looked murderous but nodded. "Thank you, Doctor."

Van Helsing winked at me, packed up her small valise of supplies, and headed for her room, leaving Antoine and I in what had become an uncomfortable silence. I took in his disheveled appearance and wondered how much of it was the result of prolonged stress at my illness and how much of it was because he'd obviously woken from sleep in a panicked state.

"We must talk," he said abruptly.

"Of course," I replied. I scooted over to make room for him, but he eyed the bed uneasily and dragged a chair over to sit directly in front of me.

"You were ill. Feverish. For days!" His manner was oddly accusatory.

I balked. "My apologies. Next time, I'll be sure to align my social calendar with yours before taking sick."

Antoine's green eyes sparked with irritation and barely restrained emotion. "I didn't know what to do when you wouldn't wake."

I was struggling to follow his line of overset inquiry.

"I can understand that," I said slowly, treading carefully. "But contacting my cousin was clearly the right choice."

"For *you*, perhaps!" he countered.

My brows rose in surprise. Suddenly very tired, I laid back against the pillows on the bed and waited. It was obvious he needed to get something off his chest, but what it was, I couldn't tell. After a few moments, he ran his fingers through his hair, tugging the dark waves from his queue. His scar flexed white, contrasting sharply against the tan of his skin and the dark stubble of beard on his cheeks.

"I put myself at great risk," he said finally. "Your cousin and her husband are more than just nobility. They're *dangerous*, Charlotte, and they know I'm involved with Sade's murder and your...your...disappearance."

"Is that what worries you? Honestly, Antoine, it will be fine. I'll explain everything to them. They're not like other aristocrats."

"That's not the point," he said in exasperation. He stood and paced the room.

"What is the point, then? You seem to be driving toward something, and I'll be damned if I can figure out what it is. If you're angry, then speak plainly and let us have it out."

"I cannot be around you, Charlotte!" he shouted. "Your very presence is a distraction and a danger to me. When you are recovered, we must part ways."

Shocked and stung by his outburst, I tried to quickly cover my hurt. "Fine. But you kidnapped *me*, remember. I've been trying to part ways with you since I regained consciousness."

"I've been trying to protect you," he grumbled.

"Well, I don't need your protection," I shot back.

He eyed my wounded shoulder and scoffed. "Yes, I forgot. You're some secret agent for a mysterious, mythical order of powerful zealots charged with protecting the people of France from supernatural threats."

"That's not entirely correct, but you're on the right track," I replied tartly.

"Ha!"

"At least I explained my reasons for attempting to kill Sade," I said. "You've been perfectly content to keep your own secrets and not offer me anything. You could be some escaped lunatic who hunts down noblemen with crossbows just to pass the time. Or maybe you're a social radical, trying to steadily eliminate the aristocracy...perhaps even a jealous, scorned lover of the torturous madman and you came out to settle a score."

Anger bloomed in his expression, turning his whole face red and his jade eyes wild. I sensed I'd touched a nerve, but I wasn't sure which one.

"Silence!" he bellowed. "For the love of God, can't you be anything other than aggravating?"

I glared at him. "Can't *you* be anything other than infuriating? If you're so aggravated and I'm such an inconvenient distraction and a danger to you, then *leave!* I didn't ask you to remain!" To emphasize my point, I threw one of the pillows at him. Despite the action startling him, he caught it mid-air. *The battle-hardened reflexes of a soldier.*

"I will," he fired back, but his tone had lost some of its edge. "As soon as you're well again."

"I'm fine," I sniffed. "How many times do I have to tell you? I don't need your protection."

"Maybe you don't," he said wearily. "But you have it anyway. I am honor-bound."

"Oh, *hang* your honor," I tossed back. I almost winced at how petulant I sounded.

"I won't," he said sullenly. "My honor is all I have left."

I snorted in derision. "This from a man who kills without reason."

His eyes snapped to mine. "Never. There is *always* a reason."

"What, your own perverse pleasure?"

He looked at me then, anger waning, and came to sit at the foot of the bed. He stared at his boots, or perhaps it was the floor, but either way, he could not meet my eyes. He was quiet for a time, thinking, and when he spoke, his voice was thick with emotion again. Not anger, this time, but a haunted sadness. My heart clenched and I suspected I would regret my words.

"I killed Sade for revenge," he said quietly. "Not for my own perverse pleasure, though I'd be lying if I said I didn't feel some satisfaction from watching him die."

"Who was he to you?" I asked.

He blew out a breath. "To me? A stranger, in fact."

I made a noise of frustration, and he finally looked up at me.

"He was not a stranger to my sister, Marie, or to her son, Louis. Marie's husband died some years ago, leaving them in dire circumstances. My nephew was still a boy then. Marie was utterly shattered. It had been a love match, you see. He'd been a tailor, exceptionally skilled but barely able to put bread on the table. My father never approved of the match and withheld his wealth and connections only until Marie was desperate. He only stepped in to offer assistance on the condition that he would be in charge of Louis's education and upbringing. Marie had no choice but to agree. She thought my father would send Louis to the elite military academy that he'd attended, but instead, my father wanted more for the boy. He wanted Louis to have better for himself—connections, a chance for a wealthy match, exposure to a world that was now beyond Marie's reach. To do this, my father reached out to an old friend from school— from the military academy."

"Sade," I breathed. "Your father and he were friends?"

Antoine's jaw tightened and he nodded once.

"My father is a brilliant general, Charlotte. He never loses in battle because he will sacrifice *anything* to get what he wants. The lives of others mean nothing to him. I can only imagine what he offered Sade in exchange for Louis's tutelage and introduction to court. I shudder to think."

I chewed on my lip. "You think your father offered Sade Louis's innocence in order to gain his aristocratic influence?"

He nodded. "Four and a half months after Louis was sent to Sade, we received word that he'd taken ill and died. Marie was inconsolable with grief, so I retrieved Louis's body myself to make the funeral preparations. If it was illness that took Louis's life, I'll throw myself into the Seine," he said bitterly.

"What do you mean? How did he die?"

"I recognize signs of torture when I see them, Charlotte. The marks on his body—it was unspeakable. He was only fourteen years old." A muscle below his eye ticked, and it struck me that perhaps he wanted to shed tears for his nephew and sister but simply refused. He clenched his fist. "Of course, most people didn't know about Sade's reputation for depravity at that point, but the rumors would soon follow. Louis became just one of a number of the marquis's victims."

"Do you really think your father knew? That he willingly sent his own grandson into the clutches of a vile predator?" I asked, astonished.

"At first, I didn't think so. But the more I grieved, the angrier I got. How could my father not have known about his friend's inclinations? Eventually, I confronted him. We were stationed on the island of Menorca in the Mediterranean then, after the treaty had been signed and the fighting had ended. I'd had a letter from Marie. She was...unwell. Alone and grief-stricken, I think her mind wandered to the same place that mine did. *Did Father know?"*

He paused, swallowing several times. I could see that he wanted to go on, that he needed to, but it was too hard for him. Compelled by the look of pain on his face, I grasped one of his hands. This seemed to steel him. Finally, he continued. "I cornered him one evening in his study. *'Of course,*

I knew, you fool!' He told me I was naive and weak for allowing my grief to get the better of me, that Louis should have been stronger, and that it was Marie's fault for birthing a whelp from such a disappointing match. *'Sade is a brute and a scoundrel, but the world is full of them, Antoine. You're just too stupid to learn how to use them to your advantage!'* I couldn't believe it. I lunged at him. I managed to get two good punches in before his guards dragged me away and beat me senseless."

"The *bêtes*, you mean?"

He nodded. "They hadn't been turned yet, but soon after. I wrote to Marie that night, but I didn't tell her the truth. I couldn't. I told her that Father hadn't known, but that I would set things right anyway. I thought I was sparing her emotions from any more blows, but I needn't have worried. She took her own life before we made it back home. I told my father it was all his fault—both her death and Louis's death were on his hands. He didn't care. *'I'm on my way to becoming the most formidable general in France, Antoine. There's more blood on my hands than you could possibly imagine.'* When we arrived home, I packed up and left, unable to think about anything other than making Sade pay for what he'd done."

"And your father?" I asked.

Antoine turned intense, emotion-filled eyes on me.

"He's next."

12

ANTOINE

November 18, 1767
The Wild Rose
Gévaudan

Charlotte sucked in a breath. "You're going after your father?"

I nodded.

"To kill him?"

"After taking out the *bêtes de sang,* that is my intent," I replied coolly.

Charlotte huffed out a breath. "Oh, certainly. Of course. Once you dispense with an elite vampire death squad—all *five* of them—it'll be no trouble at all to find and defeat one of the most formidable generals in France. I'm sure he *hasn't* connected you to Sade's death and surely *isn't* expecting you to do something so foolish in your anger and grief." Her voice dripped with sarcasm.

"He is too proud and too entitled to think of me as a serious threat," I argued.

"He is your *father,* Antoine! Even if you do manage to exact your revenge on him, have you thought nothing of the consequences? The danger you're already in for Sade's murder will be that much harder to escape when your own flesh and blood perishes by the same *mysterious* crossbow ailment. Those who know your family will make the connection. As glad as I am that the world is rid of a man like Sade, there will be repercussions for his death, which is why *I* was sent to take care of him.

Things were meant to go according to plan and now they are decidedly more...*sticky*."

"It's not just my personal vengeance, Charlotte. There are other things he has done that he must answer for. Of course, I've considered the consequences to my actions, but if hanging is the price to pay for justice and for the safety of all the innocents spared by Sade's depravity and my father's ambition, then so be it. Besides, as I told you before, I have every intention of parting ways with you as soon as you're out of danger," I said firmly.

"*Dieu* spare me from the misguided pride of men!"

Charlotte's stomach rumbled and she rubbed at her temples. She'd said she felt better when I first came into her room, but I could tell she was tiring, and I had no desire to argue with her, especially after I'd revealed so much about myself. Not only had I told her about my family's private trauma and my plans for killing my own father—dangerous enough, given that I was still trying to work out how much to trust her—but I'd practically admitted my desire for her was driving me to distraction. *You may as well just tell her she holds all the cards, you fool.*

The longer I stayed, the harder it was for me to maintain my distance. I'd been so devastated by her poor health, I thought I'd go mad. Every night, I watched her violent thrashing in bed, I prayed for her, calling out to a God that I'd long abandoned who had no reason to come to my aid. I watched her weaken in her fevered dreams and had curled myself around her protectively, deludedly hoping to impart some of my own strength through the merest touch of skin. I could only hope she had no memory of my weakness, my soft kisses on her damp brow and velvet caresses on her back, trying to hold her nightmares at bay. It certainly wasn't the behavior fitting the toughened, emotionally calloused man I'd fought to become.

I convinced myself that my desperate need to save her was because I'd failed so long ago to save Marie, but at this point, I had to admit that I'd grown...*fond* of her. It infuriated me beyond words. When I'd come into the room to see her conversing easily with the pretty Dutch doctor, I'd almost sunk to my knees in sheer gratitude that she'd made it through the worst of the illness and would soon return to her vivacious, exasperating self. Of course, it had been much easier for me to reach for my near constant anger than to throw myself at her, strip her bare, and kiss every inch of her skin.

I stood to go.

"Wait—where are you going? I still need to know what's happened these last two weeks. Have you seen or heard anything of the *bêtes* or that creature? Are we going to discuss what, exactly, we think we encountered that night?"

"Rest, Charlotte," I said. "I can tell your strength is waning. We'll discuss everything later."

"I feel fine! I've had just about enough of people telling me to rest. I've been resting for two weeks, and I want to know what the Hell is going on," she growled in frustration. She slammed her fist down on the bedside table.

It shattered into a jumble of splintered wood.

We both stared in shock at her fist, which looked none the worse for wear.

"How did you do that?" I demanded, coming over to inspect her hand.

"I...don't know," she replied in bewilderment. "Perhaps it was an exceptionally weak table, the cheaply made kind, you know? I didn't think I struck it that hard, but... I don't know, Antoine."

Her astonishment turned to concern.

"I'll fetch Doctor Van Helsing," I offered.

Charlotte nodded, dumbstruck.

"Don't bother," came a bleary voice at the door. "You two make so much noise, a person cannot sleep anyway." Van Helsing entered and rubbed at her eyes, then caught sight of the destroyed table. If she was surprised, it did not show. She regarded Charlotte carefully. "I take it you did this?"

Charlotte nodded again.

Van Helsing pulled Charlotte's hand from mine and turned it over. There wasn't a mark to be seen.

"Hmm," the doctor mused. She unwound the bandage from the smaller cut on Charlotte's forearm, where Hugo's teeth had found purchase. Beneath the linen wrappings, the skin appeared unblemished.

"That is interesting," Van Helsing murmured, more to herself than anyone else. Finally, she unwrapped Charlotte's shoulder and tossed the bandages aside, revealing unmarred, perfect skin.

"It appears you have healed," Van Helsing said simply.

"Healed?!" I exclaimed. "Doctor, no wound could have healed so fast. It looks like she was never in that attack to begin with. What the Hell is going on?"

"Van Helsing," Charlotte murmured, her voice barely a whisper. "I have only seen people recover from injuries this quickly because of one reason. Tell me, please. Have I succumbed to the blood plague? Am I a vampire?"

I could have sworn I saw a shadow of concern cross Van Helsing's face, but it faded so quickly, I might have imagined it.

"Vampire? No," Van Helsing said quietly. "Look, Charlotte. You're sitting quite peacefully in pure sunlight."

Charlotte tilted her face up toward the window and held her arms out before her, letting the late afternoon rays spill across her skin.

"Vampires cannot do so," Van Helsing continued. "Do you feel any ill effects?"

"No," Charlotte replied. "No, I feel rather good, actually. Quite hungry, though." Punctuating this statement was a rumble from her stomach. She chuckled. "Apologies."

"I'll get you something to eat," I offered. "There's a bakery just down the way."

"Are there any butcher shops in town?" Charlotte asked. "I'm ravenous for something more fortifying than bread. A joint of mutton, perhaps, or some beef? I've plenty of coin in my purse. In fact, that would be a delightful errand for me to get out and stretch my legs. Don't bother fetching me anything, Antoine. I shall go myself." She made to stand, but Van Helsing held her back.

"Relax, Charlotte," the doctor said. Her tone turned cryptic. "I have something here for you."

She went to a small wooden table with a cloth-covered tray and came forward. Charlotte sighed.

"Again, you attempt to imprison me here against my will. You're lucky I'm too famished to care and that whatever gastronomical delights you have on that tray smell too delicious for me to belabor the point. Is it stew? Bring it here, Van Helsing."

The destroyed table all but forgotten in the wake of Charlotte's hunger, the doctor brought the tray forward, a line of worry creasing her brow. She set it on the foot of Charlotte's bed and removed the cloth.

It was a thick slice of beef, so rare that I couldn't be certain it wasn't actually raw. Charlotte stared at the meat, then lifted her eyes to Van Helsing.

"I...I don't understand," she said, the fear and worry from earlier creeping back into her tone. She wrinkled her nose at the plate when Van Helsing pushed it toward her. "I can't eat that! It's practically mooing! Send it back, please, and have them cook it properly."

Van Helsing sighed. "Charlotte, listen to me. I have only seen something like this once before. I'm not even entirely sure that I'm right about it, but all your symptoms... Well, assuming this is the same thing, I fear you may have contracted a variation of the blood plague."

My jaw dropped. Charlotte paled.

"But you said I'm not a vampire! The sunlight—look!" Charlotte cried, flinging back the sheets and standing. "I don't have fangs!"

"No, you're not a vampire. To become a vampire means an exchange of blood has taken place—you must feed and have been fed on. But this...

this is something different. There is some other fluid exchange or combination that has taken place in your bodily humors. You were scratched by the *bête* and scratched by this mysterious creature out in the woods. Antoine said it was like a wolf, yes?"

Charlotte nodded in horror.

"This is preposterous," I exclaimed. "You can't be serious, Doctor. Two illnesses changing into something completely different in a person's body? Outrageous. There must be some other explanation."

"I'm not entirely certain myself, Lieutenant. It's just that all these symptoms fit. The rapid recovery and extraordinary healing, the inexplicable strength, the enhanced sense of smell, the desire for meat..." the doctor ticked these off on her fingers.

"I most certainly do *not* desire that bloody meat," Charlotte began, her voice rising in hysteria. Her eyes glittered as she looked at the plate of raw beef, and I doubted the validity of her refusal. "What are you suggesting, exactly? That I've become some vampire-like wolf creature?" The realization struck her like a blow. "I'm...I'm a damned werewolf?!"

Van Helsing's mouth twisted in a frown, and she shrugged helplessly. "As I said, I don't know for certain."

"There are several problems with your reasoning," I argued, finding this all utterly unbelievable. "Charlotte isn't sprouting fur all over her body and howling at the moon."

"Well, it *is* the afternoon. We don't know what will happen when the moon rises," Van Helsing reasoned. Then, upon seeing the frightened expression on Charlotte's face, tried to backtrack. "Allow me to run some small experiments. I could be wrong about all of this. I've only seen something like it once before, and that was a long time ago. It wasn't even the *same thing* exactly, but...*merde.* Charlotte, I'm sorry. We just don't know enough about this particular disease—the blood plague, I mean—to rule anything out. We've only just started to understand how it works, and even then, more by luck than any scientific triumph. I cannot tell you not to worry, but I can tell you that I will do everything in my power to help you. We will do our best to figure this out, all right?"

A tear spilled from Charlotte's eye, but she nodded. "Of course. Thank you, Van Helsing."

I couldn't believe she was accepting this ridiculous diagnosis. *What a notion!* It was only days ago that I was having to convince her of the possibility of werewolves existing, and here she was, suddenly accepting that she herself had become one. *It's absurd!* The doctor had to be wrong. There had to be another explanation.

I opened my mouth to speak, but Charlotte held up her hand in warning.

"Please," she said in a small voice. "I need some time to think. Doctor. Antoine. I'd like to be left alone for a little while."

Van Helsing nodded and gestured at the plate of meat. "Try to eat something. You're still recovering, and you'll need your strength to get through this."

I watched the doctor leave and turned back to Charlotte.

"Don't believe a word of it," I urged. "What she's suggesting…it's impossible."

"Please, Antoine. Leave me alone right now. I need to think."

"Fine. I'll go get you some *real* food. From the bakery! Bread, tarts, pastries, whatever you wish. Asparagus and poached eggs, if I can manage it. Don't worry, Charlotte. All is not lost." I stepped close to her, unable to resist running my fingers along her cheek. She turned away from me, and I frowned.

"I'm sorry, I—"

"Just go," she insisted.

Feeling hopeless, angry, confused, and a thousand kinds of foolish, I did as she asked. As I closed the door behind me, I caught a final glimpse of her burying her head in her hands. Suddenly, my earlier words came back to haunt me. *When you are recovered, we must part ways.* Oh, Antoine, you utter ass.

How can I leave her now?

13

CHARLOTTE

November 18, 1767
The Wild Rose
Gévaudan

I STARED IN DEFEATED DISGUST AT THE SLAB OF MEAT ON THE PLATE. My stomach rumbled shamefully. *It is like a steak,* I thought to myself. *Only it is quite rare. Just eat it, Charlotte. You have had worse before.* I picked up the silverware on the tray and cut into it, my vision blurring behind a veil of hot tears that gathered in my eyes.

How could this be? *A werewolf!* A kind of mutation of the insidious blood plague that had so challenged and changed our country. It didn't feel real. I glanced at the pile of splintered wood on the floor next to my bed and frowned. *I didn't hit it that hard, did I?*

Closing my eyes, I took a bite of the meat. The moment it touched my tongue, I gave up an involuntary sigh of relief. It tasted heavenly—like the best meal I'd ever had, multiplied by a thousand. I opened my eyes to look at the plate in a warped hope that it had somehow transformed into something else, but it hadn't. A tear slipped down my cheek as I took another bite. *No doubt about it now, Charlotte. You're eating raw meat and it's the best damn thing you've ever had.*

Grateful to be alone, I allowed the tears to fall as I devoured every scrap before me. Immediately, I felt strength return to my muscles and my senses sharpen to a previously unknown degree. Sounds became clearer, smells became more complex—even my eyesight intensified. I looked out the window at a tree some miles away and was able to count the leaves on one autumnal branch. *Seventy-two.* The distortion of the glass window-pane didn't hinder me a bit.

I took a deep breath and focused on the new feelings in my body. Physically, I felt the same as before, but with an added intensity and acuity. I simply felt *more.*

Was this what vampires felt when they turned?

Or werewolves? Or was this unique to me and my deviation?

I certainly didn't feel like a *wolf.* I still felt like a woman—like me, Charlotte. Did I look different? Would I behave differently? Was everything about me bound to change in the same way as my appetite? I grew melancholy at the thought. It had taken me a long time to recover from the disaster of a few years ago and my marriage to Philippe. I'd only just accepted myself in this new role as an agent of The Order and *les DD*, and because of one disastrous assignment, I now found myself having to accept a whole new identity. *Again.*

I didn't know how long I sat in bed staring out the window, but by the time I came to my senses, the warmth of the afternoon had cooled, and the sky had melted into a lovely sherbet sunset. I couldn't just sit here any longer. If I was what Van Helsing suggested—*a werewolf*—I needed to be certain. I needed to understand more about myself...more about this condition. Feeling stronger and having enhanced senses was a far cry from growing fur and running amok on all fours, baying for blood. *Or would that be howling for meat?* Who was to say that was how this blood plague variant would manifest?

Van Helsing said she wanted to run some tests on me.

Well, *I* wanted to run a few of my own.

Resolved, I threw back the covers and went to the corner wardrobe. *Finally, a spot of luck!* My borrowed wool gown and underclothes were clean and folded inside. I donned them quickly and tiptoed quietly from the room and down the stairs. I hoped Van Helsing and Antoine were resting and wouldn't hear me sneak out. I needed some time alone to figure things out before they showed up at my bedside fretting over something that none of us really understood. *Yet.*

I pulled the hood of my cloak over my bound hair and lace cap, hoping there wouldn't be any boisterous men around to trouble me. It was early enough in the evening that I didn't think there would be too many drunken louts about, especially in a somber town bracing for the next disaster, but one never knew. Trouble could find a lady anywhere.

Heading out the door, I turned in the opposite direction from the town's front gate. This way appeared less populated than the main streets. I pulled my cloak around me and tried to keep to the lengthening shadows. It would be dark soon, and then it'd be easier for me to stay hidden from prying eyes in a town of only humans. *A town of only humans!* I wrinkled my nose in distaste at the thought—as if I was already thinking myself better than human.

I furrowed my brows. *No, it is more than that.* Aside from the fact that Daphne and Étienne—my friends, nay, family—were vampires, I felt a sense of unsettling tension in a town that considered all supernatural beings evil. In Paris, all but the aristocracy had overwhelmingly accepted the inevitability of the blood plague. Certainly, that was out of necessity rather than widespread ill intent—it was better to drink blood than starve to death. Being in Gévaudan, a town that shut out the rest of the world because of fear, made me worry over the other parts of France. Étienne often said a revolution was coming—a war between vampires and humans. If he was right, I was sure the vampires would take Paris, but what would happen in all the small towns like Gévaudan? I dreaded to think.

I picked up my pace and found what I'd been hoping for—an unmanned back gate set into the town wall. Through the bars, I saw a rickety bridge set over the river and a dusty road disappearing into the dark forest beyond. The gate looked easy enough to scale, but because night hadn't fully descended, I reasoned it would be less noticeable to simply pick the large, iron padlock than to hoist my skirts and risk someone seeing me climb the wall.

I pulled out a hairpin and deftly picked the lock, being sure to close the gate behind me on my way out of town. I hoped I wasn't putting the people of Gévaudan at some great, unknown risk by defying their lockdown orders, but if I was to understand all that had happened to me, I needed a secluded space to do so.

Besides, if I *did* manage to transform into some kind of wolf creature, I didn't think a town as anti-supernatural as Gévaudan would approve of my doing so within one of their inns.

Once I crossed the bridge and reached the line of trees marking the edge of the forest, I allowed myself a sigh of relief. I'd managed a tidy little escape from the confines of the town. I walked along the road winding through the woods for what felt like hours, but as the dusky sunset faded and night gathered in around me, I marveled at the lack of exhaustion that would have normally overtaken me. Rather, I felt energized. I considered that was because I'd been cooped up in an inn for two weeks, but a small voice in my head suggested it was linked to the rise of the large, luminous moon.

Merde.

I stared up at it, wondering what one had to do to transform. If I were a werewolf—*you probably are a werewolf, Charlotte*—how would I change? Did it just happen? Did I have to do something? Did I need to be naked? Did it start with a growl or a howl?

Feeling a bit foolish, even though I was alone in a dark forest, I took a deep breath, tipped my head back, and let out a howl.

Nothing happened. It sounded nothing like a wolf, though… Perhaps I needed to practice? Should I be louder?

Maybe I needed to be deeper in the woods to really *feel* my "inner wolf." I shrugged and stepped off the road, weaving through the trees and bushes. At last, I came upon a small grassy hill that looked rather romantic in the moonlight. If I were a werewolf—*again, Charlotte, you probably are a werewolf*—this was where I would promenade.

I sat down on the grass, spread my skirts around me, and tried howling once more. Again, nothing happened. *Charlotte, you really have lost your mind.* I blew out a breath of frustration. The moon was high now, but I felt as normal as I ever had.

Perhaps Van Helsing was wrong. Maybe the infection had healed, and the table had been shoddy, and everything I'd been sensing had been the bodily culmination of an inordinate amount of stress. One could only hope.

Right, Charlotte, give this one more attempt, then if nothing happens, we'll return to the inn, tell Van Helsing she is wrong, and continue on our merry way, with or without Antoine.

Satisfied, resolute, I stripped my clothes off until I was completely bare. I folded them neatly, set them aside, and strolled to the top of the hill. It was remarkably freeing, being utterly naked out in a forest, and felt exceptionally sinful. I breathed deeply, inhaling the scents of frost-glittered grass, ancient trees, moss, and dirt. I closed my eyes and stilled my mind as much as possible, focusing on the sensations of the world around me. My stomach churned—*probably the raw meat disagreeing with me*—and I started to feel lightheaded. Oddly, it only now occurred to me that I didn't feel the cold at all.

Something inside me seemed to be gathering, drawing up, tightening. There was nothing for it now. I was going to try this one more time and then put the whole thing behind me.

Ignoring any remaining whispers of self-consciousness and shame, I dropped to all fours on top of the hill, tilted my head back, and howled with everything that vibrated through me. Blood rushed through my ears as distantly, the answering howl of another wolf pierced the night.

Merde.

Pain exploded in my body. I screamed and fell to the earth, writhing in agony. Every nerve was on fire, every bone breaking, every inch of skin scraping away from my flesh. I howled again, this time involuntarily, and only briefly registered the alien timbre of my voice. *What is happening to me?*

But I knew. Deep down, through the haze of torment, I knew what was happening. I sobbed my acceptance of it, and as I feared, the sound reverberated as a distinctly canine whimper.

Abruptly, the pain ceased. Dread like I'd never felt before pooled in my mind, and I was loath to open my eyes. Everything felt different. Everything *was* different. I didn't want this to be real. It needed to be a nightmare that I would wake up from soon, cuddled in bed with some courtly fop. *Or Antoine.*

I cracked one eye open and looked down. What I saw made my heart sink.

A mutant paw in place of a hand, tipped with long, sharp claws. An arm covered in glossy dark fur. Something brushed me from behind, and I whipped around to catch it—*mon Dieu, a tail!*

"I have a bloody tail!" I tried to scream, but of course it came out as a warped growl.

Mon Dieu. Yes, Charlotte, it's true. You're a werewolf.

Panic seized me. I needed to see just what I looked like. Was I an actual wolf? Or some kind of twisted monster? *If only I had my looking glass.* Then I remembered the river around the town. I could certainly see my reflection in that.

I attempted to stand, rather stupidly, and fell forward onto all fours. I took a few hesitant steps in this shortened creature form, gradually learning the muscle movements, and stumbled down the hill. It took a little bit of time, but eventually, I accustomed myself to walking with these strange, new limbs. One foot—*er, paw*—in front of the other. I traced my steps back toward the town, avoiding the road as much as possible. I didn't want to stumble upon any late-night travelers, and I certainly didn't want to be seen by the *bêtes* or found by Antoine.

Soon I came upon the river, black and glittering in the light of the moon. I padded down to the water and braced myself. I peered in.

What looked back at me wasn't simply a wolf. From a distance, perhaps, I might look like one, but I had a shorter muzzle, longer teeth, and loping gangly limbs. *I am a monster!* I tried to contain the cry of anguish but could not. I unleashed another chilling howl that—had I still been human—would have terrified me to hear in the distance.

I sat at the edge of the river, my awkward haunches folded beneath me. I stared into the water at my red-brown eyes for what felt like ages, contemplating my new aberrant existence, wondering how and why I'd been cursed, if there was a way back to a normal life, what it would mean for my future—if, indeed, I had a future. Were there others with this condition? Van Helsing had mentioned one other, but surely there were more. I couldn't be the only one with this horrifying variation of the blood plague, could I?

Gradually, the sky began to pale to a blueish purple, and I realized with a wave of anxiety that sunrise was coming, and I'd left my clothes at the top of the hill. More importantly, I needed to figure out how to change back into, well, *me*.

I started to run, digging my claws into the damp earth and pushing myself forward. I'd never moved so fast before. Trees became a blur of brown and silver as I raced past. I leaped over fallen logs and brambles, feeling like I was truly flying. For a moment, my cares were all but forgotten.

I reached the hill in no time and trotted up to my neatly folded pile of garments. I laid down on the ground and took a deep breath, reaching for that place inside that I'd found earlier this evening. I quieted my mind, thought of my human body, tilted my head back and howled.

Again, the answering howl of another far-off wolf, only this time, he seemed closer than before. Then came the fluttering in my stomach, the strange lightheadedness, and the gathering of something from within.

Then, the explosive pain. *Putain de merde!* It felt less intense than before, though still excruciating, and I wasn't sure if that was because I was going from monster to human, or perhaps because I was mentally prepared for the utter agony of changing shape.

I was momentarily dazed when it stopped, but was immediately overset with exhaustion and hunger. I donned my clothes quickly, certain I looked horribly disheveled. *Almost as if you spent the night romping about through the woods like a wild woman—or a werewolf,* I thought with a frown. *Dieu. How am I going to explain this to Antoine?*

My heart pounded as I made my way down the hill toward the road again. I couldn't tell him. He thought Van Helsing was mad to even consider this. Besides, he'd already told me he had every intention of going off on his own, on his stupid revenge mission to kill his father. *Imbecile.* He didn't want to carry on with me, anyway, so why *would* I have to tell him? Let him think the doctor was crazy, that I was healed and healthy from the accident thanks to my impeccable constitution, and that I was going back to my normal, happy life back in Paris. He could believe all the lies I was giving up on telling myself.

And that is that, I thought with a vague sense of loss.

"Excuse me, Madame, but are you in need of some assistance?"

Lost in my own misery, I hadn't noticed the approach of a figure from behind. Somewhat odd, considering my new supernatural senses took in everything all at once. I turned around to see a man on the road behind me, dressed in clothes so black they seemed to absorb every ray of light from the growing dawn.

The man removed his tricorne in a graceful sweep and bowed. His long black hair was pulled into a loose queue, and black eyes glittered beneath thick, dark brows. He was handsome, in an eerie sort of way.

"I heard you muttering to yourself," he said with a slight accent. "You seem distressed."

I felt my hackles rise—*wait, do I still have hackles?*

I surreptitiously rubbed a hand on the back of my neck. Nope. No fur. *Dieu, Charlotte, pull yourself together! Remember who you are! You are an agent of les Dames Dangereuses and a comtesse, for goodness sake!*

And…a werewolf?

I straightened.

"I wasn't muttering," I said firmly. "And it is improper for you to address me, as we haven't been introduced, but I'll forgive you this time, since you seem the chivalrous sort. Although…perhaps I shouldn't make that assumption, given you're suspiciously traipsing about through the countryside with no horse, carriage, or apparent aim."

The dark man chuckled. "Forgive any impropriety. Your French customs are unknown to me. I'm here to visit a friend in the area and figured I'd make an early start."

I arched a brow. Something about him was familiar, but I didn't think we'd met. He couldn't be with the *bêtes*, could he?

"Are you?" he took a careful step toward me. "In distress, I mean."

"No," I snapped, suddenly uneasy.

He nodded once and a small smile slowly tugged at the corners of his lips.

"I don't mean to frighten you," he said silkily. "I only wish to see you safely to your destination. Where I come from, it's dangerous for young ladies to be out on the roads alone."

"I'm fine," I said. "The town is not far, and I'd prefer my own company than that of a stranger."

"Ah," he said, taking another step to close the distance between us. "So, you are in distress."

"Whether or not I am in distress is *really* none of your concern," I replied. "I appreciate your noble intention, sir, but wish to continue on my way."

The haughtiness in my tone would have offended most men. The man in black, however, was unmoved. He continued to smile at me in a bland sort of way, but it was a strange mask on his intense face. I quickened my steps.

He followed.

"If you are distressed, Madame, perhaps I could help," he offered.

"Why are you so intent on helping me?" I shot back over my shoulder. I was hurrying now, practically running. "I told you, I'm fine!"

"I can sense that you are not," came a thrum at my ear. I whirled to see him next to me, when moments before he'd been a good distance behind me. I stood frozen in terrified fascination as he reached forward and plucked a leaf from my hair. He twirled it between long, pale fingers and his small smile became a grin.

A grin full of sharp, pointed teeth.

"In fact, I can sense that you are more than distressed, *petite louve.* You are almost wild with fear. It's a heady scent, you know. If you're a quick study, I can teach you to recognize it."

Who is this man? How does he know about me? Where has he come from?

Panic built in my muscles, urging me to flee. Before I turned to run, I caught a glimpse of his black eyes again—only they weren't black. They were yellow, rimmed with red.

The eyes of the beast.

14

ANTOINE

November 19, 1767
The Wild Rose
Gévaudan

Of course, she was gone. I expected her to be gone. What I didn't expect, though, was to see her out for a pre-dawn promenade with some unknown gentleman. *The absolute nerve of the woman!* Mere weeks ago, she was writhing in pleasure in my arms, and here she was having intense flirtations with some male passerby.

Antoine, you utter fool. You know she is not for you. Why do you care? She's a spy and a liar, and…quite possibly some kind of werewolf.

No. I wouldn't even think it. Doctor Van Helsing had to be wrong. There would be a logical explanation.

A logical explanation. Like Charlotte insisted when you mentioned the werewolf of Gévaudan.

I didn't know if I believed it then, and now I was determined to disbelieve it. Charlotte had simply been angry, and the table had been weak.

From my perch on the rooftop, I couldn't quite hear what the man in black was saying to Charlotte, but she suddenly stiffened. She looked frightened. Before I could make my way down from the roof, she bolted for the town gate, running faster than I'd ever seen a human run.

I jumped from the roof and ran toward the town gate as well, praying I would be able to reach her before any harm could come to her. Who was that man? What had he said or done that had frightened Charlotte? If he so much as *breathed* ill upon her, I would hunt him down and eviscerate him.

Not that Charlotte is yours to protect, said the annoying voice in my head. Still, I could be chivalrous, ensure that she was safe before we parted ways.

I dodged townsfolk as I wound through the alleys and streets. The sky was turning a lovely pink hue with the rising sun, which felt like a hopeful respite from the cold, melancholy gray that hung above Gévaudan.

Finally, I spied Charlotte on the road ahead. She saw me almost immediately—quickly enough for her to shuck her pallor of fear and school her features in an expression of haughty indifference. She slowed her pace and smiled at me when I reached her.

"Antoine! Good morning. It looks like it's going to be a fine day today, don't you think?"

Had this been a few weeks ago, I would have thought she was mad. Now, I'd come to recognize her expert deflections.

"Who the Hell was that?" I growled.

"Who?"

"That man! The one you were *flirting* with just outside the gate," I accused. I was in no mood for her outrageous denials.

"I have no idea what you're talking about," she shrugged. "Perhaps you're overtired, and your eyes are playing tricks on you. I'd recommend a nap and a light meal. I saw a bakery just down the street if you're feeling peckish. I certainly am! Ooh, do you think they'll have any meat pies?"

"Charlotte." I grabbed her arm and stared hard into her eyes.

She stared back at me, the very portrait of innocence. If I didn't know her better, I'd have thought she was right, and I'd been mistaken. The only thing that stopped me was a strange glint in her eyes—a flash of red I almost missed. Something was off and I felt a rising sense of panic.

"Where have you been? Who was that man? What were you doing outside the gate at this hour? It's barely sunrise! Do you realize you could have met the *bêtes* out there on your own?"

The forced innocence on her face twisted into irritation. Rather than answer my questions, she pushed past me and stormed down the street, muttering darkly.

"Honestly, Antoine, I don't have to answer a single one of your damn questions! Leave me in peace, for pity's sake!"

I stood in the middle of the street for a moment, staring at the bedraggled hem of her dress as it whipped around her feet.

That went well, I thought to myself. My anger spent, I felt a wash of acute embarrassment at my frustrated tirade. I contemplated my next move. *Should I go after her? Should I chase down the man outside the gate? Should I return to the inn, pack my things, jump on Tartuffe, and ride away, never to see the infuriating woman again?*

Probably.

Only I knew I wouldn't. Whatever complicated feelings I now harbored for Charlotte, I could at least acknowledge that my honor compelled me to ensure her safety—even if it was at the expense of my own. *But how can I if she won't let me? She won't even tell me the truth.* I frowned. I was no good with women—especially aristocratic women. In their company, I often found myself perplexed by their behavior and tongue-tied around their flirtations.

I groaned in exasperation and stomped after her, splattering mud everywhere in my ire.

"Watch what you're doing, you oaf!"

I turned to see a thick lout of a man wiping mud from his face and shirt. *Merde.* The last thing I wanted was trouble. We were meant to be laying low.

"Apologies," I grumbled. "I did not see you there."

"Like Hell," the man said. "You ruined my clothes!"

I gave him a once over. His clothes were so filthy, it was impossible to distinguish one patch of mud from another.

I gritted my teeth. "As I said," I repeated. "My apologies." I reached into my coat pocket and extracted a few coins, then tossed them at the man. He didn't reach for them, simply let them fall into a puddle at his feet.

"You don't seem very sorry," he said, pushing his sleeves up. He obviously wanted a fight. The stress of the last few weeks surged, and my temper flared.

"I've apologized and offered you fair compensation for my mistake. What more do you want?" I snapped.

"Retribution," he said with a wicked grin. Before I could answer, he let his fist fly, clipping my jaw as I dodged clumsily. I'd known the blow was coming but had underestimated his reflexes. I rubbed the spot he'd hit and nodded to him.

"So be it," I said. I shucked my coat and rolled up my own sleeves. *A fight might do me some good. Possibly release some of the tension I've been carrying around since I met Charlotte.* I feinted right and planted a fist into his stomach, but he came up swinging. I managed to duck the blow and threw my shoulder into him, knocking him to the ground. He grunted with the impact, and I got a few good punches in his sides, but he hooked his leg around mine and used the opportunity to flip me face-first into a sizable mud puddle. When I surfaced, I looked up and realized we'd attracted a crowd of eager onlookers.

"Five on the man with the scar," someone shouted.

"I'll take that bet," said another.

"Come on, lads! Ten on Jacques and his iron fists!"

Iron fists? Oh, Hell.

The man called Jacques landed a painful knee to my groin and an impressive uppercut sent me reeling. I tried to stand, but he kicked me as I rose, leaving me with a ringing in my ears and a bloodied lip.

As my thoughts began to cloud, a shabby hem swirled into view.

"I beg your pardon," came a fierce feminine voice. "But what do you think you are doing to my husband?"

Charlotte.

I lifted my face from the mud and saw her standing in front of me, facing "Iron Fist" Jacques.

"None of your concern, little miss. Just a private disagreement between gentlemen," he replied.

"Go back to the inn, Charlotte," I spit through the blood and filth streaming down my face.

"I certainly will not," she replied, never taking her eyes off Jacques. "Monsieur, my husband can be a complete and utter horse's ass, but he is *my* horse's ass. I must beg your pardon on his behalf. Might we not settle this dispute with a degree of civility? I wager you could use a warm meal and some fortifying spirits to start your day off on a better note. If you'll escort me to the best establishment, we can all breakfast at my husband's pleasure."

Dieu, she could charm the fleas off a stray. How I hated her in that moment. Embarrassment and anger welled up inside me at the thought that she'd intervened—probably thinking she'd rescued me from a sound thrashing. *One you likely deserve, you fool.*

"I don't need your help," I growled at her. She ignored me, spiking my temper again.

Jacques frowned, flexing his meaty fists. The crowd, disappointed with the interruption, booed and jeered, goading Jacques and me back into violence. I was definitely ready. Jacques seemed less sure.

I finally stood, wiping my dirty, bloodied face on my sleeve. I clenched my fists, moments away from venting all of my anger, frustration, and irritation on Jacques's ruddy face, but he raised his hands to the crowd and called for quiet. He nodded at Charlotte.

"Madame, I would be honored to breakfast with you. I reckon this town has seen enough bloodshed to last us a while anyway," he rumbled, extending his arm to her. She beamed at him in a way that made me want to rip his limbs off and beat him with them.

"So, I gather," she tutted sympathetically. "You must tell me all about it!" She took his arm, surreptitiously slipping her other hand in her skirts, where I heard a soft *click*. So, she'd had her pistol cocked and ready in her pockets.

Ready to defend me.

I stared after them in stupefied silence as they meandered down the road. The crowd dispersed, hurling a few insults at me as they did.

What the Hell had just happened? I tried to take stock of the situation, but my head throbbed, and my mouth tasted of blood, and I found it hard to focus. Surely, the comtesse-agent I'd accidentally kidnapped, dragged to the south of France, endangered countless times from natural and supernatural threats, and might harbor some flame of begrudging affection for, hadn't just saved me *again*?

I'd never felt so useless—so much a fool. My father's words rung true in my ears, as did Charlotte's early criticisms. *Always acting so rashly, too stupid to think things through, making a mess of everything and everyone. Antoine, the blundering imbecile languishing away as a mere lieutenant. Antoine, who could not save his nephew or his sister. Antoine, who could not save Charlotte, his...*

His what? What was she to me?

Before I could think too much on it, I heard her calling my name. She and Jacques were standing in the middle of the street some distance away, waving me over. As black as my mood was, I could not resist her bidding. I grabbed my coat—the only garment I possessed not covered in mud— and stalked over.

Charlotte cocked a brow at my brooding expression but tried gamely to make introductions. Jacques stuck his hand out and I eyed it suspiciously.

"Your good lady wife has explained some of your troubles," he said. His deep voice was like a wagon wheel over a rutted gravel road.

"Has she?" I was unable to keep the censure from my voice.

"It's nothing to be ashamed of, darling," Charlotte interjected. "The vampires who robbed us on the road were supernaturally strong and numerous. We were lucky to escape with our lives, despite your bravery."

"Indeed," I said, too exhausted to argue or keep up with her myriad stories—*or should I say*, lies.

"Jacques has forgiven your slights," she continued. "And wishes to make amends, and then we can all put this whole *memorable* experience behind us."

She eyed me pointedly. Her meaning was clear—we'd attracted too much attention and she wanted me to shake hands with the man and then disappear, just another typical brawl with some ill-behaved traveler. I wasn't *at all* an outlaw on the run from his father, a band of vampire soldiers, a possible werewolf, and the legal repercussions of murdering a marquis.

"I'm sorry for the, um…" Jacques gestured to my bleeding lip.

"Don't trouble yourself over it," I replied.

We were quiet for a moment, sizing each other up, until Charlotte rolled her eyes and cleared her throat.

"Well! That's settled. Jacques, you were telling me there was a lovely spot up ahead where we could get some meat pies and perhaps a pot of coffee or tea. Not to worry, *mon ami*, I always carry a little nip of brandy with me—the perfect way to warm up a morning in November! Now, you also mentioned some of the recent troubles you've all been having with some kind of local beast—pray, tell me over our meal," she trilled. "Your little town is *so* lovely, I hate to think of something so ominous marring its serenity."

Jacques smiled down at Charlotte. It seemed innocent enough, but it piqued my temper again and it took all I had to follow behind them without strangling them both. We stopped a short distance from the Wild Rose and went into a neighboring tavern.

"It's only a tavern at night, madame," Jacques said apologetically. "In the daytime, they serve tea when they can get it, and sometimes lemonade —perfectly respectable for ladies. I promise you the meat pies are the best you've ever had. My wife, Annette, is the best baker in Gévaudan. She runs the restaurant in the daytime, and I take over as publican in the evening. I'll introduce you, Madame."

"Why, Jacques! This is your establishment? *Mon Dieu*, you are clever, aren't you? My husband and I are absolutely overjoyed to sample the best that Gévaudan has to offer. Come along, Antoine, don't sulk back there. A nice hot meal and some good company is just what the doctor ordered. Go on, then, Jacques—Antoine and I will be right behind you. Choose for us the best table, *d'accord*?"

Charlotte pulled me aside and fixed me with a steely glare.

"You and I are going to have a *serious* discussion when we finish here. I cannot believe you would be so pig-headed as to start a fight at seven o'clock in the morning with the burliest man in town. We're trying to escape notice, Antoine!"

"He started it," I grumbled. "I tried to apologize but the fellow wanted a fight. If you think about it, I was actually being very obliging by offering him one. Would've been rude of me to refuse."

She raised her eyes heavenward. "*Dieu* save me from the hopelessness of men."

Needled by her lack of faith in my abilities—and me, in general—I tried to turn the tables.

"I'm willing to have this serious discussion," I began. "But you have a lot of explaining to do about your whereabouts last night and that man on the road."

"Don't be ridiculous," she sniffed, turning to join Jacques at the far end of the tavern. "I don't have to explain myself to you."

"Perhaps you don't," I admitted with a shrug. "But if you expect *me* to explain *myself*, it's tit for tat."

She threw a saucy glance over her shoulder.

"I'll bear that in mind if I'm in the mood for tat."

Blood rushed to my face in a furious blush, then surged south to my cock as her insinuation—obviously meant to unsettle me—landed with its intended effect. *Merde.* This woman would be the death of me.

Or you'll be the death of her, I thought miserably.

Every decision in the last few weeks had not only made me the fool, but they'd also put her in grave danger. Granted, she'd been more than capable of handling everything that had come her way, but the fact remained she would have been much better off if we'd never met. With a grave reluctance, I realized my honor and sense of obligation—all that I felt I had left—were causing more problems than they were solving. What was more, she'd protested so much that she hadn't needed my protection, and she was right. She *didn't* need my protection, but she certainly needed me to stop putting her in harm's way. Every moment we remained together was one more moment I was endangering her and clearly *not* protecting her.

I looked at her across the room, laughing easily with Jacques. Her warm brown eyes glinted with mirth and several curls escaped her cap with the movement. In that moment, she didn't look like a spy, or an agent, or a *comtesse*, for that matter. It was as if every part of her body felt every feeling, and she overflowed with joy like she overflowed with passion, or with frustration. As much artifice as there was to Charlotte, Comtesse de Brionne, there was even more that was genuine. The kind of genuine that men became hopeless around.

That I have become hopeless around.

With a knife-sharp sense of despair in my heart, I knew what I had to do. As much as I wanted Charlotte, I had to leave her.

15

CHARLOTTE

November 19, 1767
The Wild Rose
Gévaudan

As we made our way back to the inn, we were pursued by a black cloud that had nothing to do with the weather and everything to do with Antoine's surly countenance. Whether it was due to my exhaustion, our current circumstances, or the strange interaction I'd had with the "beast" this morning, I had no patience for his melancholy.

"That Jacques turned out to be a fine fellow," I said. "It's unfortunate you two got off on the wrong foot—or should I say, *fist*."

Antoine frowned but said nothing.

"Lucky for you, I was there to help handle the situation," I continued. "If I hadn't, I daresay you would've ended up with more than a black eye and a bloody lip."

Still, Antoine remained quiet. He simply refused to rise to my bait. The telltale muscle in his jaw flexed, though, proving that at the very least, he was listening.

"A simple *thank you* would suffice," I sniffed, playing my last card. He *had* to respond to that. We'd reached the Wild Rose and trudged our way up the stairs, plagued by fatigue. "Monsieur, would you send up a bath, please?" I called down to the innkeeper. I was cold, sore, and filthy from last night. I wanted to rest, but above that, I wanted to bathe.

"Thank you?" he practically choked on the words.

At last, he speaks.

We'd reached our room and he pushed me inside. I expected him to slam the door, but he closed it very slowly and quietly, which unnerved me more than his anger would have.

"Yes," I said, trying to recover my bluster. "If it hadn't been for me, you would've been beaten to a pulp by the Iron Fists of Gévaudan. Not only did I stop the assault, but I managed to sweet talk us into a lovely breakfast, as well."

Antoine's green eyes darkened. He opened his mouth to says something but thought better of it. He shook his head and began removing his mud-caked clothes, not caring that I was in the room and we were mid-conversation. Well, I was mid-conversation. He was silent, grumpy, and taciturn.

And suddenly shirtless.

Mon Dieu. I couldn't help but stare. I'd caught glimpses of him our first night in the inn but hadn't had the opportunity to give him a proper look. His unfashionably bronzed skin was crisscrossed with a roadmap of scars that pointed to a life of violence and pain. It made the scar on his face look like the least of his troubles. Soft, dark hair dusted his chest and narrowed to a thin line leading below his belly button—a different kind of road, and one that I found myself wanting to travel the most. He reached up to tug his hair from its customary queue, shaking the loose waves out and running his fingers through it. Muscles that I'd only seen in anatomy books bunched and flexed beneath his skin, unlike any man I'd ever been with. He moved to unbutton the falls of his breeches and paused, catching my eye.

"Perhaps it is ungentlemanly, but I hope you'll permit me to have the first bath. I'm certain you don't want our room to reek of blood and filth," he ground out. I'd almost forgotten that he was still annoyed with me. That fact didn't have any impact on the inferno of my desire.

"*Dieu,* Antoine," I breathed. "You're beautiful." *Did I mean to say that out loud?*

He blushed and turned away from me. "Comtesse, I'm sore and weary of your incessant teasing. If you've no wish to tell me about your night last night, so be it, but if you have any humanity in you, you'll grant me some peace."

I probably deserved that.

"As you wish," I replied quietly. "Though you must know that I am not teasing you."

He said nothing, but some of the stiffness in his back eased. I opened my mouth to speak again, but the innkeeper knocked then, bringing forth a wooden tub and two maids with steaming pitchers of hot water. After several trips back and forth to fill the tub, the bath was ready. I gestured to Antoine to go ahead.

"By all means, your needs are greater than mine," I said, though I doubted if anyone could presently surpass the strength of my need to touch him.

I went to the window to draw the curtains and offer him some privacy, listening to the sounds of him shucking his breeches and slipping into the water. His exhale of satisfaction made my heart race. My awareness of him in all his sullen, magnificent nudity was quickly becoming more than an inconvenience—it was becoming a torment.

Driven by lust, I turned to face him again. The sight was like a kick to my stomach. Water dripped from his wet locks and soap bubbles glided down his chest. I bit my lip but refused to hold back any longer.

"Of course, you'll need someone to help you wash your back," I said.

He quirked a brow at me. "What happened to giving me some peace?"

Embarrassed and angry at his rebuttal, I whirled around and snatched my cloak off the bed.

"Well, go on and wash it yourself then, but don't come crying to me about doing so with those bruised ribs," I snapped. My hand was on the doorknob when he called my name.

"Charlotte."

I stopped but didn't face him.

"*Charlotte,*" he said again, softer this time.

I peeked at him from the corner of my eye. He held out the bar of soap and I considered it. *Thank God I don't give a fig about my pride.*

"I will be the very personification of peace," I said. "As quiet as the second half of a sermon, when everyone has dozed off in church."

I grabbed the soap before he could object and threw my cloak back on the bed. Kneeling behind him, I dipped my hands into the warm water and started to lather the soap across his shoulders. They were warm and smooth, except for the scars, but the muscles beneath felt as hard as iron. I couldn't resist giving his biceps a little squeeze. He sighed again and smiled, then leaned back against the tub and looked up at me. This close to him, I could see flecks of brown and gold in his green eyes—the colors of sunlight filtering through a lush forest canopy. Under my intense scrutiny, he became self-conscious again and closed them.

I gently threaded my soapy fingers through his hair, though he'd already gotten the worst of the mud out. My nails scraped lightly along his scalp, and his full lips parted on a moan that made my nipples tighten and my skin prickle with heat. Tiny soap bubbles slipped down the path of his scar, tracing the moon-shaped curve from his brow to his cheek. I gently wiped them away with my fingertip, which drifted to his lips of its own accord. His rough, stubbled cheeks hadn't seen a razor in some days, but it didn't make him look unkempt as it often did on other men. It was almost as if his face needed the roughness of his cheeks and the long scar as armor against being *too* beautiful.

Too beautiful? Really, Charlotte? You've already committed to keeping Antoine in the dark about the truth of your new supernatural state, and here you are practically swooning over him just because he's ruggedly handsome and brooding. And infuriating. And certainly honorable but misguided in his feckless attempts at chivalry. Could he ever understand the life you lead? Poisoned by a failed marriage, accustomed to wealth and the entitlement of the aristocracy, surviving and thriving in a web of so many untruths and half-truths you've almost forgotten what it is to be honest—and that was before you transformed into some previously unknown supernatural abomination. No... I bet if you slice a bit off Antoine de Vaux, he will bleed honor all over you.

My thoughts heralded an onset of melancholy that stilled my hands. Antoine's eyes opened again.

"Have you finished your explorations, Comtesse?" he asked softly.

The hushed words were like a lover's caress. He was so unlike any of the men I'd been with, and I finally realized how dangerous my own feelings had become. I wanted him. Not just for the night, but for weeks. Months. Years, even. *Merde.* There was nothing for it now. I'd simply have to say goodbye to him and leave Gévaudan. As a newly turned werewolf, every minute I stayed in this anti-supernatural town was another minute I was putting everyone in jeopardy, not to mention the danger I found myself in with my feelings for Antoine.

I'll pack up tonight and leave while Antoine sleeps. Daphne and Étienne are in the next town over. With my new abilities, I fear crossing paths with the bêtes *considerably less. Perhaps they'll come for me, and I can dispatch them to protect Antoine.*

I pulled away and stood, determined to ignore his suddenly troubled expression.

"Charlotte, what's the matter? Are you unwell?"

"No, I...I'm fine, Antoine. Perhaps a little tired, that's all," I said, attempting to find my lighthearted tone again. "I'll leave you to your peace."

"Wait, Charlotte," he said. "Please. Don't go."

He rose from the bath and water sluiced down his body, dragging away the last of the dirt and soap suds. He stood before me completely naked, visibly aroused, with an entreaty on his face that I found myself precariously close to accepting.

"What of your peace?" I asked, taking a step toward the bed to retrieve my cloak. He wrapped a towel around his waist, and I failed to hide my disappointment. He got out of the bath and came toward me.

Staring deep into my eyes, he blew out a resigned sigh. "Because of you, I don't think I'll ever know peace again."

He brought his hand up to my cheek and caressed it with his thumb, then pulled me to him for a passionate kiss that felt like pleading, longing, and goodbye at the same time. His other hand let go of the towel and found my waist, expertly locating the ties of my skirt.

Just this once, my body cried. *Just this once before never again. But what of the blood plague? Am I putting him at risk of infection if we make love?* I hesitated.

"Antoine, the blood plague...the variant...I don't want to corrupt you. I won't take your choice from you," I whispered.

He pulled at the ribbon tying my skirts in place and brushed his lips across the skin of my neck.

"You were scratched by a werewolf *and* a vampire. Do you plan on scratching me that hard? Or biting me?"

I couldn't keep the teasing from my tone as I ran my hands over his hard body. "Perhaps. I make no promises."

He tilted my head up and dropped kisses along my jaw. "I accept the risks. Nothing you do will corrupt me beyond what my own sins have wrought."

Resolved, I wrapped my arms around him and my skirt tumbled to the floor in a heap. Without taking his lips from mine, he began to unpin my bodice and loosen my stays. Layer after layer fell away, until I was down to my stockings and chemise. He knelt to grasp the hem of the garment, looking up at me with heated intensity.

"Are you sure?" he whispered, his hands starting to tremble. "Do you wish me to continue?"

Emboldened by his uncertainty, I pulled the chemise over my head and sat on the edge of the bed, spreading my legs before him.

"Do continue," I managed, adoring the blush that spread from his face to his chest.

Smiling with relief, he leaned forward, pressing a kiss to the inside of my thigh. He slowly slid his hands up my calves to my knees, tugging them further apart, then ran them lightly over the tops of my thighs, around my waist and behind my ass. Pulling me forward on the bed, he found better access to all the places I longed for him to go. As his stubble scored the insides of my legs, I twitched in anticipation and heard his rough chuckle.

"Are you always so sure you'll get what you want?" he murmured, tracing the outer folds of my sex with his tongue. The effect was immediate and explosive, prompting me to throw my head back and swear. He repeated the move on the other side, then dragged a feather-light lick along the seam, ending it just below the apex of my pleasure.

"I asked you a question," he whispered, dropping kisses back down my thighs, moving away from where I needed him.

I wiggled forward, trying to make my preference known, but he only smiled up at me deviously.

"Yes," I blurted in frustration. "Yes, I am accustomed to getting what I want, but only because I have the guts to fight for it."

"We should all be so lucky," he said.

He set his tongue to me again, this time in the exact place of my torment. Moving in circles, he sucked at the bud of my pleasure and slipped his fingers inside me, working me to the peak of bliss. Before the orgasm could take form, he pulled away and pushed me back down onto the bed. I whimpered in disappointment. He grinned wolfishly, obviously quite pleased with himself and the torture he was wreaking upon my needy body.

"Perhaps I should be better about demanding what I want, secure in the knowledge that I would get it."

He crawled up my body, marking my skin with gentle, little bites on his way to my lips again.

"What is it that you want, Antoine?" I panted, nearly feral with lust. "It might be within my power to give it to you."

He nudged my legs apart with his knees and rubbed his hard cock against my sex, teasing a moan out of me that sounded alarmingly like a growl. *Dieu*, I needed him. *Now.* Libidinous to the point of madness, I grasped his cock and slid the tip inside me, cooing with satisfaction at his grunt of pleasure. He pulled back with what looked like great effort, gritting his teeth. Mischief sparkled in his eyes.

"I want your pleasure, as well as mine," he said.

"You have it," I moaned, arching up to meet him.

Again, he pulled back.

"I want to give you pleasure, Charlotte, without you having to take it for yourself. Just this once, let me take care of you."

The sincerity in his eyes nearly made me weep. For the second time, I didn't want to ruin our intimacy with sarcasm or wit. *This is goodbye, after all.* Embarrassed by the emotions caught in my throat, I merely nodded. He smiled down at me and leaned forward for a searing kiss.

"Tell me," he said, kissing my neck and trailing his fingers across my nipple. "No games, no lies, no deflections. What do you like, Charlotte? How do you like to be touched? What shall I do to you?"

"I…" Through the fog of passion, my brain stuttered to a halt. *What do I like?* I tried to consider the question. Each time I'd been with a man, or a woman, I'd found myself becoming what they wanted me to be. Submissive, dominant, silent, loud, loving to be punished or needing to exert some discipline… Even my husband had needed me to be someone else in bed. I'd found pleasure and passion with partners, but no one had ever asked me before.

What do I like?

The question overwhelmed me, and humiliating tears pooled in my eyes, blurring my vision. I squeezed them shut and tried to get ahold of myself, but Antoine noticed. He seemed to read my thoughts, because he kissed my forehead, then my cheek, then my neck again.

"Don't be embarrassed," he whispered. "We shall find out together."

He placed his hands on my breasts and lightly massaged them, then began rolling my nipples with his fingertips. My embarrassment now forgotten, I arched up again, seeking more of the exhilarating contact.

"Your breasts are flawless. Like beautiful vanilla cakes topped with rose petal nipples. They taste sweeter than any dessert I've ever had," he said, almost to himself. "I've dreamed of you so much, Charlotte. Of dining on the banquet of your body and sipping at the wine of your lips." His hand moved down to my sex again, which ached from unspent lust. "But here," he growled, dipping his fingers inside me again. "Here you taste like the nectar of the gods. I think I could die from the perfection of it."

All conscious thoughts fled. My entire body vibrated with need. He moved his fingers slowly at first, pressing his thumb to the pearl of my sex. It felt like hairline cracks were breaking all over me as my excitement mounted, until I was certain I was going to fracture and explode into millions of pieces.

Antoine withdrew his fingers before I could and I almost sobbed at the loss, but then he lifted himself above me and positioned his cock at my entrance.

"Have I given you pleasure, Charlotte?" The hopefulness in his face was cherubic, but as he slowly slid inside me, he swore enough to make Lucifer himself blush.

"Yes," I panted. "Yes, Antoine. You have given me pleasure."

He rocked forward, and we both moaned in a chorus of satisfaction.

"What more shall I do to you?" he asked, punctuating each word with a thrust of his hips. His hand was between us again, his thumb on my pearl once more.

Dieu, I am so close…so close…

"What more do you want of me?" he demanded, thrusting harder, faster. Stars began to twinkle in front of my eyes as I began the crescendo. Heat built to a fever pitch, and I came apart as he did, crying out into the passion-thick air.

"Love me."

16

ANTOINE

November 19, 1767
The Wild Rose
Gévaudan

Love me, she had said. Surely, she hadn't meant it. *Surely* it had just been the heat of the moment and the carnal excitability. We'd both been taut with sexual tension, and the release was what we'd both needed. I'd needed to have her before I said goodbye—to plunge myself into her wet heat and taste every part of her. I'd needed to hold her, so that I could let her go. *Hadn't I?*

Love me. She'd probably meant it in a sexual way. Perhaps she'd meant *fuck me.* Or *make love to me.* She couldn't have meant it the way I heard it. I could not—would not—allow my heart to trip over words carelessly shouted as a sexual climax.

She doesn't mean it, Antoine.

It didn't matter. I was leaving tonight. Firmly resolved to put distance between us for her safety, I would wait until she was asleep, pack my meager belongings, and leave. Tartuffe and I would be long gone by the time she awoke—hopefully drawing the *bêtes* away from her while avoiding the fallout from murdering Sade. Heading south was the best option. I could only hope she would find safety with her cousin and the emissary.

"Antoine," she said softly, placing her hand against my cheek. "That was wonderful."

Forcing myself to return to the present, I pulled her close and tucked the covers around us. I dropped a kiss on her forehead. Guilt whispered through me.

"I'm sorry about this morning," I said.

She leaned her head against my chest, and the intimacy of the gesture threatened to break my heart. *In another time, in another place, this would be enough for me. Here is the family you longed for—the family you lost.*

"Well, I'd say you more than made up for it," she said with a coy smile.

I swallowed. "Charlotte, why did you leave last night? Where did you go?"

She sighed and nuzzled into me, but I felt her muscles tense.

"I went for a walk, Antoine. I needed to clear my head and get out of this room. I've been stuck in here recovering and it was driving me mad."

I didn't think she was lying, but that wasn't the whole truth, either. I stroked her arm lazily.

"And the man in black?"

She smirked. "Jealous, Antoine?"

I frowned. That was part of it, to be sure, but I didn't want to admit it out loud to her. She looked up at me and laughed.

"Be at ease. I promise I'd never met him. He saw me on the road back to Gévaudan and asked if I needed any assistance, since it is odd for a woman to be out walking at night by herself," she said with a little shrug.

Again, not entirely a lie, but also not the full story. I decided not to press her any further, since I didn't think it would do me any good.

"It is odd," I admitted. "And dangerous. You could've come upon the beast, or the *bêtes*. I hate to think of you in danger, especially when I can't be there to help protect you."

"That is very sweet," she said, kissing my jawline. "But I can protect myself."

"I know you can. I just…wish you didn't have to. It is your choice to live a dangerous life—I would never take that choice from you. But I can't imagine it's easy for the people who care about you, seeing you so reckless with your safety."

I could tell by the hard set of her mouth that I'd overstepped. She pulled away and fixed me with a steely glare.

"Reckless? Antoine, look around you. The world is dangerous. I have worked hard to acquire the skills I need to survive. If I am in danger on occasion because of my work with The Order, it is for a good cause. As to my loved ones and their opinions on how I choose to live my life… Perhaps they have more faith in me than you do."

At that, she rose from the bed and collected her chemise from the floor.

The loss of her warm body next to mine was worse than the pain of starvation.

"Skills to survive?" I scoffed. "You're a comtesse, Charlotte, not a peasant. Is it really about survival? Or is it about something more? Something that you have to prove to everyone, or prove to yourself?"

"You know nothing about my circumstances," she shot back at me. "What I've had to overcome! Why I chose to learn what I did and why I do what I do—why I won't rely on anyone else to protect me. Why I have fought to learn how to protect myself. *You do not know.*"

"Why don't you tell me then?"

"That's not something I'm keen to go into with you right now, Antoine. Suffice it to say that you shouldn't be passing judgment on someone whose life you know nothing about," she snapped.

"I'm sorry. And it's not that I don't have faith in you," I said, rising to go after her. "It's just that I don't understand why you would willingly become a spy when you could be at home living a life of leisure. You shouldn't be worrying about the fate of France."

"Ah, and so, because I'm a woman and an aristocrat, I should just stick my head in the sand, keep my hem and my hands clean, and leave all the important work to the men in power? Because they're doing such a spectacular job of it," she snarled.

"Well, yes—I mean, no! What I mean is that you should be living a life of comfort, not having to worry about such political entanglements," I argued, already regretting my words. I reached for my breeches, watching her dress and grow increasingly frustrated with each subsequent layer she put on.

"Clearly, you've never been to court if you think the life of an aristocratic woman is anything but political entanglements," she scoffed.

"Charlotte, you can do anything you want. I know you are capable. I'm sorry that your circumstances have forced you to be so. I just wish you could live an easier life—a safer life." *Let me protect you. Be mine to protect.*

"That's rich coming from the soldier son of a decorated, wealthy, warmongering general. Why is it men are the only ones who should be allowed to choose their futures and their fates? Why can't I?"

"You can," I argued. "Who said you couldn't?"

"You did! You just can't accept that this life *is* my choice. Certainly, I should be allowed to control my life as long as it aligns with what you see for me—what society sees for me," she said bitterly.

"I just don't understand why you would choose such a hard path," I said, shaking my head.

"Oh?" she rounded on me. "Why did you follow in your father's footsteps, Antoine? Why aren't you at home managing the family estate? How many men did you kill on the battlefield in an attempt to secure your father's absent approval? Was that why you needed to murder Sade? Was it really about revenge, or was it to prove something to your father—maybe you need him to know that you're a man to be reckoned with," she sneered.

Her words sliced me to ribbons. I didn't know what was worse—her perception of shameful truths that whispered through me, or the fact that she'd fired them at me like bullets. I gaped at her, unsure of what my next words should be. I was angry and hurt and confused by how quickly things between us had escalated from bliss to battle. *At least it will be easier for me to leave.*

I finished dressing and strode to the door.

"You are right," I admitted quietly. "My troubled relationship with my father has caused me to make many decisions I'm not proud of. But after the deaths of my sister and my nephew, I realized I needed to set things right. I knew it would be ruinous for me—that, once I'd begun, I'd find myself hurtling toward my own judgment day." The words had poured out of me so fast I'd said them all in one breath. I had to pause to draw in another. "I used to have much to prove...to my father, to the world, to myself, but not anymore. Not to you, either, Charlotte. I've done too many things—killed too many men, made too many mistakes—to be a good man, but I've accepted that I don't need to be a good man to right my wrongs. I'm only sorry that you were another wrong along the way."

I opened the door, glancing back only once to see her staring at me with a mixture of anger and hurt on her face. Tears welled in her eyes, and she opened her mouth to speak, but I did not wish to hear the words. I closed the door behind me and descended into the tavern. In a sort of numb resignation, I paid the innkeeper the remainder of our bill, bought a bottle of cheap wine along with some additional food and supplies, and went out to the barn to saddle Tartuffe.

"You're going then, Lieutenant?"

Hand on my sword, I whirled to see Doctor Van Helsing brushing out her dapple-gray mare. I'd been so distracted when I came in, I hadn't noticed her in the shadowy back corner of the barn.

"I am," I replied. "Thank you for your services, Doctor. I appreciate you traveling all this way to help care for Charlotte."

Bright white teeth almost glowing in the gloom, she smiled. "I do not think you need my help to care for her."

I felt my face grow hot and I scowled. I repacked the saddle bags, trying to hurry away from the too perceptive woman. Tugging at Tartuffe's reins, I nodded to her by way of farewell.

"A moment, Lieutenant," she said, leading her horse out.

Merde. Is she leaving, too? Please don't be heading in my direction.

"I'm heading south to meet up with the duchesse and the emissary. They have some medical supplies for me but are not permitted to enter Gévaudan. Would you be so kind as to see me on my way?"

Oh, Hell.

"Forgive me, but I'd rather not, Doctor. I'm afraid I've delayed much too long here and I'm eager to get back on the road," I muttered. "Is there anyone else who can see you safely to your party?"

She shook her head. "I'm afraid not. It is far too treacherous on the roads around here for me to travel by myself. I must insist. It will be good for you, I think—I can tell you all about my experiments with the blood plague and my research. I'm sure you will find it all fascinating. Come along, Lieutenant!"

Unable to think of a way to extricate myself from the company of the commanding doctor, I frowned. The last thing I wanted was to ride for hours listening to some scientist prattle on about the plague, but she was right—the area around Gévaudan was exceedingly dangerous. I suspected the *bêtes* were still lurking around, and who knew what had happened to the beast.

"Very well," I grumbled. "I don't think I'll be good company, but I'll make sure you arrive at your destination safely. You're ready to leave now?"

"I am," she said, mounting her horse. "I packed while you were… otherwise occupied."

I reddened again and tried to hide my embarrassment by saddling Tartuffe.

"Do try to keep up," she called back to me as she turned down the main road toward the town gate. "I'm in something of a hurry."

"I'll do my best," I grumbled, spurring Tartuffe to match her horse's pace.

As the town gate came into view, I glanced back over my shoulder. I didn't know what I expected—or hoped—to see. Perhaps Charlotte running into the street, tearfully waving me down, shouting apologies out over the crowd. I'd jump down from my horse, run back to her, wrap her in my arms and kiss her, swearing that I'd never leave her again, and she'd tell me she was giving up The Order and any other dangerous pursuits so we could retire to her country estate and raise four precocious children. She would say we should go ahead and make plans for a spring wedding. She would insist on inviting my father, who would have given up his power-mad, bloodthirsty ways in the hope of repairing our relationship, then a messenger would arrive to say he's been tracking me down all this time to tell me Marie and Louis were, in fact, alive, and waiting for me back in Thionville. The *bêtes* would stop hunting us, the beast of Gévaudan would leave the town in peace, and all the sufferers of the blood plague would wake up human again, washed of their sins, and with tables groaning under the weight of food.

Despite my melancholy, I smiled at the absurdity of my imaginings. If only happy endings were as prevalent in real life as they were in novels.

"What is it that delights you so, Lieutenant? I am certain it is not my company," Van Helsing said, slowing to ride beside me.

"Nothing," I replied, chiding myself for losing focus. "It's nothing, Doctor. You mentioned that you had some new findings about the plague. Why don't you share them with me?"

Apparently, that was the right question. Her face lit up with excitement.

"It's really quite fascinating, Lieutenant..."

"Please, Doctor, just call me Antoine."

"Very well, Antoine. As I was saying, it's a fascinating disease. You see, the body *appears* to die when infected, but I don't believe that is actually the case. I would say it's more like the human part of the body goes into a kind of hibernation and the blood plague takes over the faculties of the infected," she began, growing more animated by the minute.

"How is that possible?"

"I have no idea!" she said excitedly. "But think of it like this: your body is a coach and four. When the plague comes upon you, it is as if the driver falls asleep at the reins. The horses continue to pull the carriage along without the driver steering, with often disastrous results."

I nodded grimly. "But the need for blood as sustenance?"

"I believe it is a property of the plague. Somehow, in order to reproduce itself, which must surely be the drive of everything on earth, a regular human diet is insufficient. It requires more blood to keep the body going. Isn't that amazing?"

I turned a skeptical face on her. "I wouldn't call it amazing. Apocalyptic, perhaps. Sinister, definitely. Hopeless, as well."

"Oh, but you're so wrong, Lieutenant—er, I mean, Antoine. I find it is anything but hopeless," she said earnestly.

"Are you suggesting that the vampires of the world may recover and become human again?"

She considered my question. "Truthfully, I do not know. Perhaps not. But after all, is it so bad for the infected to remain vampires?"

"Doctor, that's blasphemous! You really think it's permissible for people to live by feeding solely from another? Such a parasitic existence is frankly damnable."

She tipped her head back and laughed. "My friend," she chuckled. "I wonder if you only feel that way because it is the poor feeding off of each other, as opposed to the aristocracy feeding off of them?"

I opened my mouth to argue but reconsidered. She was right, of course, and the irony of it made me feel sick.

"I never thought of it that way," I said. "But still, think of what it means for humans overall. What happens when there is no blood left?"

"Ah, that *is* the question I hoped you would arrive at. What, indeed? What would happen if a vampire fed on another vampire? Or on another species, for example? These are all questions that must be answered. How can we understand the true nature of a malady if we do not understand all the variables?"

"You're speaking of Charlotte," I observed. "What do you know of her condition?"

She was quiet for a moment, peering down the road ahead of us. The afternoon had waned into a beautiful rose-colored dusk. As lovely as it was, I could not ignore the premonition of unease I felt at seeing the gathering night.

"As I said earlier, I have seen something similar before, but it was many years ago. It wasn't exactly the same circumstances, but the symptoms were very much alike."

I leaned forward in my saddle, trained on her every word. Her eyes flicked to me, as though she was nervous of how I would respond.

"You care for her, do you not?"

"It doesn't matter," I replied. "We lead different lives. It would be best if we stayed away from each other."

The words sounded false even to my own ears. Van Helsing quirked a smile at me and nodded knowingly.

"So you say. Well, then you should know of her fate. I believe Charlotte has become something entirely different. Perhaps she is unique—I cannot say for certain. She has a form of the plague, but it is not vampirism. She does not thirst for blood. I believe that when she was infected with the beast's claws and vampire's bite that night in the woods, somehow, the plague took on a new form. The supernatural essences in her body merged and shifted. We might call her a werewolf because that's a familiar mythology to us, but the reality is much different. She has mutated. She has become something altogether different from what we know. If we continue with my runaway coach metaphor, it would be like saying her coachman fell asleep and her carriage careened out of control, but then was suddenly hijacked by bloodthirsty highwaymen."

"That's a horrible prognosis," I said grimly, suddenly reconsidering my decision to leave her. Guilt and regret warred with my resolve. *I should turn around and get back to her—help her figure this out.* "What can be done for her? How do we regain control of her carriage?"

"I'm afraid that is up to her. She must learn. I do not think anyone else can do much for her, except to help and support her." She eyed me meaningfully. "And to love her."

"What you say sounds absurd," I argued, ignoring the tail of her comment. "And blasphemous—against God and science. Surely someone can help her—surely *you* can help her. There must be a treatment, or a ritual, or…or…something, dammit! How can you be so sure about these things? How do you know all this?"

The news settled on me with the heavy weight of despair and Tartuffe tensed. He nickered softly, and Van Helsing's mare responded, nudging closer.

"Shh, easy, Lucy," the doctor crooned. "Antoine, you're worrying the horses. Calm yourself."

The hairs on the back of my neck suddenly rose, and without thinking, I reached for my pistols.

"Tartuffe is a warhorse, Doctor," I said softly. "He does not care a whit about my anxiety. We are being watched. Do you have any weapons on you?"

Van Helsing's eyes widened in alarm. "Watched? Weapons? Certainly not! I'm a doctor; my entire purpose is to *save* lives, not to end them. Weapons, pah! Although, I suppose if you consider the surgical instruments that I keep in my medical bag, but they are…"

Before she could finish her sentence, we heard movement in the woods to the left of us. As if on cue, four of the *bêtes* materialized from the bushes and closed in on us. I did not see their leader, Hugo, and I wondered if the beast had made short work of him after Charlotte and I had made our escape. As they'd caught up with me again and Charlotte had been gravely wounded in the process, I ruminated that our escape had been for naught.

Van Helsing eyed the vampires apprehensively.

"I don't suppose you gentlemen are stopping us because one of you is in need of a doctor?"

Frederick grinned, showing a great deal of fang, and cast his gaze over me.

"All in good time."

17

CHARLOTTE

November 19, 1767
The Wild Rose
Gévaudan

AFTER ANTOINE LEFT, I STARED AT THE DOOR FOR A GOOD LONG WHILE AND let the tears fall. I cried for the cutting things Antoine had said to me. I cried for the guilt about the horrible things I had said to him. I cried for the loss of my normal, human life. I cried about the shame of my former husband. I cried because I felt like I was mourning the loss of something new and beautiful with Antoine, despite all the reasons why we shouldn't be anywhere near each other. I cried because for those precious moments in bed with him, I finally felt like I'd found what I'd been searching for with all the lovers I'd taken since my husband.

I'm only sorry that you were another wrong along the way. Was that what I was? Was that what we were? Would he only look back on our time together with regret? To my knowledge, I'd never been someone's mistake before. The revelation smarted.

In the midst of my glorious wallow, I felt acute pangs of hunger accompanied by an unladylike rumble from my stomach. Darkness had fallen, and I found myself ravenous with an appetite I didn't think would be easily sated. Deciding food was more important than my misery at present, I sniffed and wiped my eyes, straightened my shabby travel-worn dress, and made my way downstairs to the tavern.

The Wild Rose was busy, which suited me just fine. The din of drinkers and diners would help distract me from my ill humor. I approached the front and asked for whatever meat they had on offer, roasted if necessary but preferably rare, plus bread and vegetables. I also bought myself an entire bottle of wine, ignoring the disdainful look of the innkeeper. In times like these, I truly missed Daphne and her impressive wine cellar.

Daphne!

Dieu, I'd almost forgotten. She was just in the next town over! I needed to get to her and explain the situation. Perhaps she would know what to do about, well, *everything*.

When my food arrived, I ate as quickly as I could without attracting attention. I took a swig of the wine, then thought better of it and corked the bottle. I needed to figure out how to get out of town unnoticed and getting belligerently drunk—while amusing—would make that a degree more difficult. I paid the innkeeper, who continued to glare at me, and returned to my room to pack.

I didn't have much, but I was able to stash my meager belongings and remaining supplies in my pockets and bundle up in my cloak. Only then did I fully realize that my things were the only things that remained. I knew Antoine had left, but it struck me too late that Dr. Van Helsing had, as well.

I was disappointed that she had departed without at least saying good-bye, but knew it came with the territory of being the most formidable doctor for supernatural sufferers—she was constantly in demand.

As I left the inn, I debated my options for travel. Antoine had taken Tartuffe, and I didn't see any other horses available. The mail coach wouldn't arrive for another few days, and I could take my chances trying to hitch a ride along the road, but because of the infamous reputation for the beast and the dangers in the surrounding woods, other riders and travelers were scarce. Unless I wanted to walk the fifteen miles to the next town where Daphne and Étienne were lodging, it appeared I was stuck in Gévaudan.

Or was I?

Last night, I'd been able to run through the woods at breakneck speed and barely feel fatigue. Did I dare try again? Could I make the journey without being seen by anyone? If I could bundle and tie my clothes to my back, I could find a secluded spot to transform and dress before anyone would be the wiser. A thrill went through me at the thought—almost like I felt when I was a child sneaking sips of father's cognac. *Positively wicked!*

I reasoned I didn't have much of a choice. If I wanted to get to Daphne and Étienne, this would be it. I hurried down the main street to the gate, nodding at the two guards posted out front.

"My husband sent word that our carriage has been repaired," I said with a smile. "Do open the gate for me, gentlemen, so that I may depart."

One of them grumbled something about it not being safe for me to wander through the woods at night, but they raised the gate at my request. I warily eyed the rotting wolf heads on pikes outside the town wall. I didn't think it would be wise to tempt fate and come back to Gévaudan.

I walked quickly, pulling my cloak tightly around me, not because I felt particularly cold, but because it would seem odd to the guards out front if I didn't. The moon was high and full, casting a beautiful silvery light on the trees and road ahead. It hadn't rained in a couple of days, and with the winter chill setting in, I suspected the first snow of the season would soon fall. When I'd gone about a mile, I drifted away from the road and into a thicket of bushes. I undressed, bundled my clothes tightly and slung them over my shoulder, hoping my plan would work.

Taking a deep breath, I stilled my mind and reached for that place inside me—finding it at once peaceful and wild. Then came the explosion of pain. I screamed, but it came out as a howl, and despite the transformation being just as unbearable as before, it felt quicker this time.

I looked down at my claws and my chest, bundle of clothing still firmly tied, and took off at a gallop. The dark forest blurred past in streaks of green, silver, blue, and black. *Dieu, but it feels so good to run!* There was a freedom to it that I'd never experienced, and it was so satisfying, it felt absolutely sinful. Faster and faster I raced, reaching out with my enhanced senses to see and hear and smell everything around me. It was impossible to take it all in, and yet impossible for me not to.

All at once, I caught the scent of several familiar things that made me stop short. I guessed I'd gone about eight or nine miles south from Gévaudan, and through the undergrowth, it arose—death, rot, black powder. *The bêtes.* Also, herbs, wool, lime blossom. *Van Helsing.* More came at me—horse, leather, apples. *Antoine.* Then, just at the edge of my awareness—earth. Blood. Musk. *The beast—or rather, the man in black.*

My hackles raised of their own accord, and a low, angry growl emanated from my throat. Apparently, I'd just come upon a rather interesting little get-together. The animal part of me raged with a fierce need to protect my friend and my lover.

I listened closely and heard the distinct sounds of voices a little way off, deeper into the woods. Creeping silently toward them, I came upon a low hill, into which was set a cave. A fire crackled at the entrance and two of the *bêtes* stood guard out front. Further in, I could see two soldiers standing over Van Helsing, who was bound and gagged, seated up against the wall of the cave. After a moment, I spotted Antoine—unconscious, covered in blood, crumpled upon the floor. I sensed his slowing heartbeat; he was weakening. Panic and despair unleashed something primal in me, and I fought to maintain control of my senses.

"Easy now, *petite louve*. If you charge in there alone, they will surely kill you."

The words were a whisper at my ear, startling a yelp from me. I whirled to see the man in black standing next to me, glaring at the soldiers with his unnatural eyes. In this light, they looked more red than yellow, and despite my own frightening state, I shuddered in fear. My lips pulled back in an involuntary snarl, but he raised his hand to stay me.

"You have nothing to fear from me, Comtesse. On the contrary, I am here to protect you." His voice was deep and hypnotic, lulling me into a strange sense of comfort.

I would have scoffed had I been in human form, but it came out as a sniff. He chuckled.

"I have much to explain to you—not at this moment, but soon. For now, I think it's time we finished off these so-called *beasts of blood*. Don't you?"

I didn't trust him, but the soft *thump* of Antoine's heart sounded dangerously thready. What was the saying? *The enemy of my enemy is my friend.* I glared at the soldiers, then back at the man. He appeared to sense my resignation. He grinned, displaying two sets of fangs—teeth unlike any vampire I'd ever seen.

"Excellent. I'll take the two at the front. While I have them occupied, you sneak in and take out the two in the back," he directed, his tone suffused with ennui. He began to disrobe, and I looked away, embarrassed. Again, that dry chuckle. "Ah, and one more thing, *petite louve*. If you decide to eat them, I daresay you'll have a terrible stomachache afterward. Take it from me."

With that, he shifted into the wolf-like beast I'd seen before. It was a gruesome sight, watching the immediate restructuring of bone and skin and sinew. In wolf form, he nodded once to me, and we took off in opposite directions. The closer we got to the cave, the stronger the scent of blood.

Dieu, please let Antoine be okay.

"Frederick, do you smell that? I think it has returned—*ulp!*" Before the vampire could finish his sentence, the beast leaped atop him, clamping its jaws tightly around his throat.

The other soldier out front dove into the fray, hissing and screaming. I turned away to avoid witnessing the gory spectacle, praying that the wet crunching and yelping sounds meant things were going in our favor. The two soldiers inside saw the fight taking place out front and turned to help rescue their comrades, but they weren't expecting a second monster, which gave me the advantage. I jumped in before they could draw their weapons and knocked them both to the ground. I attempted to bite one around the neck but was clumsy and instead ripped open his shoulder. He screamed and pushed me off with impressive strength while the other soldier lunged at me with his sword. I dodged the attack, praising my balance on four legs instead of two, and clamped down on his arm, ripping his hand off. His sword clattered to the ground, and he screamed, clutching the bleeding stump where his hand had been. Before I could attack again, the first soldier slammed into me, knocking the wind from my lungs and pushing me back against the cave wall. He leaned forward, fangs bared in an attempt to bite my throat, but I twisted away in time, and he reeled back with a mouth full of brown-black fur.

"*Arrrgh!*" he spat. "What the Hell are you?"

His comrade moaned on the floor, attempting to staunch the flow of vital blood from his arm. I snapped at the vampire holding me, trying to force him off balance, until he stumbled backward and tripped over his prone companion. He rolled mere inches away from my unconscious Antoine, which elicited an automatic snarl from me. He raised a brow, apparently realizing my loyalty, and held his sword at Antoine's throat.

"One more step and I'll kill him," he threatened. I growled but backed off. He raised his other sword at me, preparing to strike. "*Stupid creature!*"

Before the lunge came, Antoine's eyes flew open, and he thrust his own sword upward, impaling the vampire from below. He crumpled to the floor on top of the other soldier, who was dangerously close to passing out.

Antoine looked at me, dazed and bleeding. To my utter dismay, his eyes filled with horror, and he gripped his sword until his knuckles turned white. He struggled to get to his feet and hobbled in front of Van Helsing protectively. She tried to speak around the gag in her mouth and her muffled cries echoed off the walls of the cave. Antoine's eyes darted to her before waving his sword threateningly at me.

"Antoine, calm yourself! It's me!" I tried to say, but it came out as a canine whimper.

I need to change back and let him know that he's safe—that I'm safe.

I closed my eyes and tried to find my humanity deep within, but the pain from my injuries was too distracting. Antoine picked up a stone from the cave floor and threw it at me, hissing and shooing.

"Be gone, foul beast!" he shouted. "Get back! We've no quarrel with you—leave us be!"

Van Helsing struggled some more, trying to attract Antoine's attention. I cowered against the wall of the cave, worried that, in his fear, Antoine would run me through with his sword. He took a step toward me, but in bounded the other creature, letting out a warning growl as he paced in front of me.

The shock at seeing two werewolves stopped Antoine in his tracks. He paled and stumbled to his knees, clutching at a bloody gash in his side. Again, I whined.

Thankfully, Van Helsing is here—she can patch him up.

I cut my eyes to her, but she was staring at my comrade with a mix of...*what?* It looked like disbelief, sadness, and...longing? *How odd.*

I heard the soft click of a pistol cocking and looked to see Antoine leveling his twin flintlocks at us.

How rude! I barked at him, but he gestured toward the mouth of the cave, indicating we needed to leave.

Again, the other beast growled, but I was not about to test Antoine's charity when he was gravely injured and near death at the hands of the *bêtes.* Tail tucked humiliatingly between my legs, I trotted outside. I would fetch my clothes, find a quiet place to shift, and come back to help Antoine and Van Helsing.

I thought I heard the other beast following me, but when I turned around, he was gone. *Merde.* I was unsettled by his sudden appearance and disappearance, and needed to ask him about a million questions that were racing through my mind, namely, *who are you, what are you, why are you here, how do you know me, what the devil did you do to me?*

The visceral remains of the two soldiers out front littered the grass and bushes. I wrinkled my nose, glad for the darkness. I didn't want to see any more blood tonight. The tally so far was at least three of the *bêtes* were dead—or, dispatched, as it were. That left the one called Frederick gravely injured and handless, and the one called Hugo... Well, I wasn't certain what had become of him.

I walked slowly back to the small glade where I'd stashed my bundle of clothes. My ribs hurt from smashing into the cave walls, and the bitter taste of plague blood lingered in my mouth. *Dieu,* I was tired. Had I really rested for two weeks during my transformation? It felt like I hadn't slept in a month. My stomach rumbled with hunger, despite having eaten a large meal just this evening. I suspected I needed to eat more often if I spent more time in this form, given that I'd just run several miles and fought a gruesome battle.

Enough, Charlotte. Relax. Take a deep breath. Find your center and shift.

I relaxed. I took a deep breath. I focused on my center.

Finally, I shifted. The pain of the transformation didn't ebb as quickly as it had previously, and I looked down at my naked body to see dark bruises and scrapes all over me. *Merde.* It appeared the fight had damaged me more than I'd thought. I dressed quickly and hurried back to the cave, calling for Antoine and Van Helsing. I was met with silence.

The cave was deserted, save for the bodies of the three *bêtes* who had met their respective ends. There was no trace of Antoine or Van Helsing, and only a thin trail of blood led away, which I knew to be from the remaining injured vampire. The sun would rise in a few hours—I suspected he would be going to ground.

Try as I might, I could not catch the scent of Antoine or Van Helsing. The area stank of blood and battle and of the other creature, and with the pain of my wounds, it was difficult for me to focus. Perhaps they'd rode on to meet with Daphne and Étienne, and I would come upon them in the next town.

I trudged slowly back up to the road and walked for a while, debating what I would say to Daphne and Étienne when I met them. I was certain they would immediately detect my transformation, so prevaricating was out of the question. Besides, I would need their help cleaning up after Sade's murder and exonerating Antoine.

Antoine. My heart stuttered and worry churned in my gut. He hadn't looked well when I'd seen him in the cave. I hoped he and Van Helsing had made it safely away, and that I'd soon reunite with them. I wasn't going betray my earlier resolution to part from Antoine. And while I didn't think I necessarily *had* to explain myself to him, I wouldn't soon forget the look of abject horror on his face when he saw me in my supernatural form. Perhaps it would be better if there was a little more honesty between us. He deserved that much.

The night lingered, but finally, I spotted a small town in the distance. Grandrieu! That must be where Daphne and Étienne were—and possibly Antoine and Van Helsing. I tugged the hood of my cloak over my head and hurried on, hoping against hope that we'd be able to sort everything out.

18

ANTOINE

I REMEMBERED VERY LITTLE ABOUT THE DAYS FOLLOWING OUR AMBUSH AND THE battle in the cave. I'd flitted in and out of consciousness, plagued by the horrors of what we'd just endured. I was dimly aware that Dr. Van Helsing had tied me to Tartuffe's saddle and led both of us, plus our horses, to the town of Grandrieu. It was smaller than Gévaudan but a bit more cheerful—though I'd been to funerals that had more cheer than Gévaudan, so that wasn't saying much.

We'd checked into another inn and Van Helsing, bruised and bedraggled as she was, insisted on tending to my wounds before seeing to her own comfort. After the painful poking and prodding, she informed me of three broken ribs, a stab wound to the side, numerous lacerations, a concussion, a dislocated shoulder, and two sprained fingers, but no vampire bites that she felt would cause infection of the blood plague. She stitched and bandaged what she could with her meager supplies and helped to set my fingers and shoulder, which brought on enough pain that I slipped back into unconsciousness for three entire days.

Dreams of Charlotte haunted my delirium. The sweetness of her lips, the angles of her face, the sparkle in her brown eyes when she teased me into—and out of—an ill humor. Damn, but I wanted her. I wanted to feel her again, wanted to taste her again. I wanted to make love to her endlessly and protect her from everything that would harm her or make her frown. I wanted to wake up with her every morning and share meals with her—even if it meant eating asparagus for breakfast. I envisioned a world where we could marry and have children—each one with wavy auburn hair and the glint of mischief in their gazes. My cracked lips formed a smile at the thought, until the fevered vision warped, and our children sprouted the fur, claws, and fanged teeth of the beasts we'd encountered in the cave.

Beasts. More than one. Was one of them the creature that had attacked Charlotte? What were they? Where had they come from? How many of them were there? Why hadn't they attacked Van Helsing and me? Did they have some particular distaste for vampires? Was Charlotte going to become like them? Then, a more frightening thought emerged—what if one of them *was* Charlotte?

I nearly vomited at the thought, just in time for Van Helsing to hobble into the room with a tray of food and her medical bag.

"Excellent timing," she said. "I'm glad you're awake. I would have hated to pull you from the rest you badly need. How are we feeling this evening, Lieutenant?"

"Restless. Injuries or not, I need to be on my way. Have you any news of Charlotte? Did you meet with your acquaintances here? Ouch! Would you stop poking at my ribs?" I twisted away from her, trying to ignore the pain from her ministrations.

"You are lucky," she muttered. "Even without supernatural assistance, you are healing quickly." She glared at me over the rim of her spectacles. "You heal because you have been unconscious, and you are here resting. If you leave now, all my good work will be for naught. Stay a few more days, eh?"

"A few days! Absolutely not. Out of the question," I barked.

"Yes, I did find my friends here," she continued, breezing past my retort. "They are most anxious to make your acquaintance. I told them I would be happy to introduce you once you were well enough."

I blanched at the thought. Charlotte's cousin was here and probably wanted to see me hanged. I'd heard rumors of the duchesse before, of course. Once a cherished jewel of the court of Versailles, then stuck in that awful marriage to the Depraved Duke, and then widowed in mysterious circumstances. All of this was followed by her engagement and turning at the hands of the most famous blood-drinker in France, the king's own vampire emissary. My stomach churned with anxiety.

"What news of Charlotte, Van Helsing?" I couldn't keep the pleading from my tone, and it annoyed me.

"You have nothing to fear," the doctor replied. "I'll not have you reopening that wound on your side when it is healing so well, so please do be still. Here. Eat something."

She pushed a tray of food into my lap, and before I could take a bite of some rather dubious-looking soup, the door crashed inward, and an impassioned vampire duchesse whirled in. She was dressed in a sapphire-colored silk gown and fur-trimmed cloak that probably cost more than several years of my lieutenant's salary.

"I know he is here and awake, Van Helsing, so stop trying to put me off!"

I made to stand and bow before her, but Van Helsing put her hand on my chest.

"Don't even think about trying to get up," she warned. "Duchesse de Duras understands that you are recuperating, doesn't she?" The doctor flashed an admonishing look at our intruder.

"You!" Her strange violet eyes pinned me back to my pillow. "You are the man who kidnapped my cousin after murdering the Marquis de Sade? The man who has apparently run afoul of Général de Vaux, the most formidable officer of His Majesty's army, who has demanded an absurd bounty for his capture?"

Merde. Well, I can't outrun the consequences of my actions forever. I may as well submit to the justice of The Order. It won't be any different from the justice of the crown. Both see me dangling at the end of a rope.

I swallowed and nodded.

"Yes, Your Grace."

I waited, ready for her to unleash a tirade that ended in an order for my execution. Instead, her lips parted in a grin.

"You can't imagine how pleased I am to finally meet you."

My mouth fell open in shock, but before I could reply, a man entered the room. He was fashionably dressed and unnervingly handsome, and I reasoned it must be the vampire emissary, Étienne de Noailles.

"*Mon amour*, I know you want to have a chat with the lieutenant, but don't you think it's prudent for us to wait until he is at least up and *not* eating?" He eyed me uneasily. "And when he is more appropriately dressed?"

I looked down and realized that Van Helsing must have removed my shirt to dress my wounds and had not bothered to offer me anything else to clothe myself. I reddened in embarrassment and tugged the blankets further up my body in a futile attempt at modesty.

The duchesse blinked at me, then back at her husband. "*Non.*"

Van Helsing let out an amused giggle and the duchesse winked at her.

The emissary scowled at both of them. Inwardly, I prayed the floor below me would open up and swallow me whole.

"Your Grace, Monsieur l'Emissaire, may I present Lieutenant Antoine de Valle. Do be gentle with him. I've only just put him back together," Van Helsing said with amusement.

I inclined my head in as deep a bow as I could manage without tearing the bandages from my shoulder and chest.

"Is it de Valle?" the duchesse asked, tilting her head. "Or de Vaux, I wonder."

I blanched.

"Lieutenant," the emissary said, nodding.

I cleared my throat. "Monsieur. Your Grace. Forgive me for not getting up. And, if you don't mind, I'd appreciate you calling me Antoine. I'd rather not use my family name in public when things are…the way they are."

"Certainly, only you must call me Daphne. Titles are for ballrooms and court, and my fiancé and I avoid those as much as we can," she said, taking the chair the emissary offered and sitting opposite me. "Antoine, it seems you have my cousin's knack for finding trouble. You must tell me everything that has happened."

I could no longer keep my curiosity at bay. "Please, Your Grace— Daphne. Where is Charlotte? Is she here? What has happened?"

Van Helsing cleared her throat and gave the duchesse a warning look.

"Has something happened to her? *Mon Dieu*, please tell me. Is she all right?" I leaned forward, felt a twinge of pain in my ribs, and fell back on the bed with an exhale of frustration.

"Rest easy, Antoine," Daphne said. "Charlotte is well. She arrived half a day before you and Van Helsing."

"Where is she? I must see her. We have things we need to discuss." I looked around frantically, trying to locate my clothes. I needed to get to Charlotte.

Daphne turned an apologetic face to me. "I'm sorry, Antoine, but she's gone."

"Gone? What do you mean? Where?" I looked at her, then at Van Helsing, who frowned sheepishly at me.

"She didn't want us to tell you she'd been here, Antoine. She wanted to make sure you were safe and well on your way to recovery, but she said she could not linger." Van Helsing pushed her spectacles up the bridge of her nose.

"She was here? And she just…left?" The disappointment I felt hurt more than my wounds.

Why did she leave without speaking to me?

I remembered our last words to each other had been in anger, but surely, she'd known it was the heat of the moment. She must have known my feelings for her were…different. *More.*

"She told us much of what happened over the last few weeks," Daphne said. "But I'd like to hear your side of things, as well."

"What did she tell you?" Panic edged into my voice.

The emissary smiled, his eyes glittering in the candlelight. "Some version of the truth, I expect. If you've spent much time in her presence, I'd wager you take my meaning."

I licked my parched lips and reached for the cup of watered-down wine on my tray.

"Why did you kidnap Charlotte from Versailles?" Daphne pressed. "Let's start there."

"I didn't kidnap her," I insisted. "I was protecting her. I thought she was a young man and that the marquis was going to take advantage of her. She was in the wrong place at the wrong time. We were about to be discovered, and at her feet was a dead marquis, shot through the chest, and her with a quiver of stupid costume arrows. I did not want her to be accused of the murder that I knowingly committed."

"Most honorable," Daphne said. "Why did you murder the marquis?"

"Didn't Charlotte tell you?"

She answered with a noncommittal shrug, which could have meant anything. I sighed, angry with the coy machinations of these women.

"My reasons are my own," I ground out.

"Your reasons must also be ours, if we are to protect Charlotte," Daphne replied. "And you."

"I do not need or want your protection," I snapped. "I just want to be left alone."

"*Mon Dieu,* man, you murdered a damned marquis! You cannot just be left alone," the emissary laughed. "We are beholden to the king and The Order, but we will do what is necessary to protect Charlotte and respond appropriately."

He had a point.

"Monsieur, we are very good at keeping secrets," Daphne said.

My mood darkened. "Sade abused, tortured, and murdered my nephew," I said, bile rising in my throat. "My beloved sister, Marie, killed herself from the grief and shame of it. My father knowingly placed young Louis in Sade's charge, likely offering the lad's innocence in exchange for Sade's tutelage and influence. Because of my father's need for power and control, my family is destroyed. I will not hide from the consequences of my actions, but if you are here to elicit some sort of apology and request for absolution, you will not get it. Sade deserved far worse than the quick death I gave him, and I regret nothing."

Daphne was quiet, but I recognized something like anguish flashing in her eyes. Her gaze shuttered before I could be certain. The emissary appeared to sense her feelings, though, and placed a gentle hand on her shoulder.

"We understand," he said. "More than you know."

"Sade's fate had already been decided by The Order," Daphne said, rising. "He was marked for death by Charlotte's hand, but it was to appear as an accident. Now that it looks like murder, there may be an investigation. Étienne and I will do what we can to settle things, but there are grave consequences to your actions, Antoine. The danger we are all in is very real. Sade certainly deserved death, but you should not have intervened."

"My vengeance is not your concern, nor is it The Order's or the king's. Sade was a deviant and a predator, and I've just saved everyone the trouble of figuring out what to do about a murderous aristocratic problem. You should be thanking me for doing your dirty work," I grumbled.

Daphne smiled, but there was something dangerous in it. "I do not shy from dirty work, Antoine. Neither does Charlotte. She is not simply a comtesse. She is not simply my cousin. She is not simply an agent of *les Dames Dangereuses* and The Order. Hell, Charlotte is not *simply* anything."

"I know that!" I shouted, angry that the duchesse was deigning to tell *me* about Charlotte.

She placed a hand on my arm. "Charlotte is not even *simply human* anymore."

My gaze flew to hers. "You know?"

Étienne chucked darkly. "Of course, we know. We're fucking vampires, Antoine, don't you think we'd recognize a werewolf in our midst?"

The sickness I felt had nothing to do with the pain of my injuries or the dread at spilling my secrets to these powerful and dangerous individuals. I looked at Van Helsing.

"The beasts in the cave," I said. "One of them was her."

She nodded.

Horror and despair washed over me. Even though Charlotte was still alive and was not mine to mourn, I felt a keen sense of loss. I had not protected her, and because of me, she'd become a monster. The forgotten self-loathing returned, and I attempted to quell my rising nausea.

"What now?" I whispered.

"Now, you rest," Van Helsing insisted. "If you don't allow yourself time to heal properly, it won't matter what happens with The Order or

Charlotte. You will die from festering wounds and not be alive to plead your case to either."

"You know what I meant," I growled at her. "I care not for my own future. Where is Charlotte? What happens to her? Can she be saved?"

"Saved?" Daphne inquired. "Why, Antoine, what *can* you mean?" She grinned, and the firelight glinted on her vampire fangs.

"*Pardon*, I meant no offense. I understand you may have chosen your fate, but Charlotte did not choose hers. She will have to live this cursed life for eternity."

The emissary lifted a shoulder in nonchalance but regarded me pointedly. "Eternity is not so bad as long as you have someone to share it with."

"My point is that she did not have the choice."

"Neither did I," Étienne replied. "*My* point is that even though I had no choice, I adjusted to life with the plague. Charlotte will do so, too. She is nothing if not resilient."

"You didn't see how devastated she was back in Gévaudan when she learned that she had contracted this new condition," I argued.

"Perhaps she is more accepting of it now," Étienne shot back. "I know where you're coming from, Antoine, but it is hardly the sentence you think it is."

I opened my mouth to argue further, but Daphne stepped between us. "Étienne, would you give us a moment, please? You, too, Doctor."

Looking rather murderous, Étienne bowed curtly and ushered Van Helsing from the room. Daphne sat back down and leaned forward to study me.

"What will you do if she cannot be, as you put it, *saved*?"

"What do you mean?"

"There is no cure for the blood plague," she said. "It is unlikely that there will be a cure for her. Her condition may not be unique, but it is rare. We know even less about it than we know about the blood plague. What then, Lieutenant? What will you do?"

Outraged that she was trying to draw so much out of me, I pursed my lips. I wanted nothing to do with this duchesse and her strangely accusatory questions.

"Nothing," I barked. "I only want to see that she is safe. It is my fault that she was endangered in the first place, and it is a mistake I mean to rectify. Once that is done, I will be on my way. I have things to settle with my father and I aim to ensure that the remaining *bêtes* are dispatched properly."

She tilted her head, eyeing me like a naturalist viewing a specimen under glass. "And then what?"

"Pardon?"

"After that, I mean. Where will you go? Assuming you go after your father—a wholly stupid idea, I might add—and dispatch the remaining *bêtes*, you will not be welcome back in the army. You would be on the run, I would think—trying to avoid the justice for Sade's murder, your father's, and potentially five French soldiers. Is that the life you're prepared to lead?"

"And what if it is?" I nearly shouted. "It isn't your concern!"

She raised a brow and stood again, making her way to the door. "It might not be mine, but it certainly seems to be Charlotte's."

19

CHARLOTTE

December 13, 1767
Château de Ruisseau Magdelaine

SNOW FELL IN SOFT, SLEEPY CLUMPS OUTSIDE, BLANKETING THE MANICURED grounds below. Since I'd arrived back home, autumn had ceased to hold back winter, and Paris had been frozen in an unending cycle of snowfall and freezing rain. It made everything in the city look as if it were plated in silver and dusted with powder.

My breath fogged the glass of the window and though I knew it was cold, I didn't feel it. I'd come to accept that part of my condition with some appreciation—no more freezing hands and feet during the winter, no more perspiring during thick, stagnant summers. My wardrobe could be more about fashion and less about function, which was one of the few things I truly wanted in life.

It had been weeks since I'd left Antoine at Grandrieu. Guilt gnawed at me, but I knew he was in the capable hands of Van Helsing, Daphne, and Étienne. Still, every day I wondered if I'd done the right thing. There was so much unresolved…so much unsaid between us. I'd started numerous letters trying to explain things—to admit that I was the grotesque beast in the cave, to tell him the truth about my former husband and divulge my secrets, to remind him that we were better off staying away from each other. To apologize for our last words and tell him I wished things were different—could be different. To confess my feelings for him had become something…*more.*

Every draft ended up in the fireplace. It was futile for me to say such things to him when several facts remained: Antoine was on a doomed revenge quest with his own demons to battle, and battling demons was something I'd already had my fill of. I had a duty to *les DD* and The Order, to Daphne, and to king and country. I was doing important work for the fate of France and wouldn't abandon my purpose to—what? Give up everything to marry again, have a litter of children, and set up residence in the countryside? While admittedly tempting, I rolled my eyes at the thought.

There was also—quite possibly—the fact that I might now be immortal. Daphne had given up sunlight for her love because she couldn't bear to spend a mortal life without him. I would never ask that of any man, let alone one I wasn't even sure could bear to be in the same room with me without argument. Plus, I'd seen the horror on his face in the cave. It was forever burned into my memory. There was no way on heaven or earth that Antoine would willingly offer himself up for the bite, be it vampire or a werewolf. And who was to say that was how the infection would be transmitted anyway? Van Helsing had been most evasive about the specifics of my supernatural state. Everything I'd learned about my condition had been through trial and error over the past weeks, and I suspected I had a long lifetime—if not eternity—to learn the rest. If only that man in black, the beast, hadn't run off after our battle in the cave. I hadn't seen hide nor hair of him anywhere, and I'd run the midnight miles in creature form to find him.

The Order had been thrilled, of course. When they learned of my new condition, they politely requested a demonstration of my lupine abilities, and so here I was tonight, dressed in a formal gown of dark purple-black silk and a domino mask, ready to go before them and perform like some kind of pet. My stomach twisted in disgust. I believed in The Order and wanted to ensure they were on the right side of things in France, but any time I had to appear for them, it soured my insides with distaste. *The dusty old prats.*

I'd considered declining, of course, but it would make things go a tad more smoothly when I explained what had allegedly gone wrong with the Marquis de Sade's death. Daphne and I had worked out a plan back in Grandrieu, and I hoped it would prove satisfactory for them. The cover story about Sade's death was already circulating by the gossip in court, which was the only opinion any aristocrat truly cared about. *Killed by one of his unwilling lovers in a fit of passion! Sade died as he lived—wretchedly.*

If The Order took us at our word, Antoine would be safe from one threat, at least. As to the remaining threats—his father and the *bêtes* who'd gone to ground since the attack outside Grandrieu—well, I feared he was on his own with them. Knowing he was a capable soldier did little to soothe the waves of dread plaguing me about it.

A knock at my bedchamber door startled me from my musings. My butler, Charles, inclined his head and informed me my carriage was ready to depart.

"*Merci*, Charles. I'll be down shortly."

I stashed a small dagger in my skirts and fastened my favorite bracelet, a ring of black pearls on an expanding cord that I had often employed as a garrote. I was as ready as I ever was. I picked my way carefully over the snow-covered stairs and stepped up into the carriage, but not before catching a whiff of orange blossoms.

"I didn't think you were coming tonight, as well," I said to the dark interior of my carriage.

"What, and miss the show? *Please*," Daphne said, the grin in her voice evident.

"The whole thing is absurd!" I complained. "Frankly, I'm annoyed I have to spend my entire evening with a bunch of obnoxious old men when I could be spending it drinking brandy in the tub with a roaring fire and a stack of erotic novels."

I signaled to the coachman to drive on, and we rumbled down the tree-lined drive of my estate.

"Charlotte, *chérie*, we both know that's not how you really want to spend your evening," Daphne said gently. Her supernatural eyes glowed in the dark like a predator. Did mine do the same?

"You're right," I sighed. "Drinking brandy in the tub is dangerous. Much too heady. Champagne, though—perfectly safe."

She laughed. "So, I see we're not discussing the tall, dark, brooding reason that *you* have gone all broody."

"I have not! How dare you suggest such a thing. I'm as silly and flippant as I ever was," I insisted, pulling a flask from my garter and taking a swig. I needed a little liquid courage to get through this evening. I offered it to Daphne, and she took a drink, as well.

"Charlotte," she said in a low voice. "It's *me*."

I frowned. "I know. I'm sorry. It's just...later, *d'accord?* We will talk later. I need to focus to get through this tonight."

She nodded and we sat in companionable silence for the remainder of the ride. The carriage wheels crunched wetly through the snowy ruts in the road. I peered out the window, saddened by what my enhanced vision could now see. Worsening poverty unfolded throughout the city—more poor souls lost to the blood plague than ever before. I wondered if there were any humans remaining outside of court. It had been a choice for Daphne, brought about by the luxury of love, but most of the other vampires had infected themselves as the only alternative to death by starvation. If this was partly due to the grain blight and the catastrophic absence of food, what would happen when France ran out of blood? Had The Order considered that?

Before long, we slowed to a stop in front of an abandoned cemetery on the outskirts of the city. The thick blanket of snow obscured many of the graves and I said a silent prayer for the forgotten inhabitants of this desolate place. Daphne and I descended from the carriage and walked to a shabby mausoleum at the back. She unlocked the heavy metal door and pulled it open, revealing an empty tomb lit by tall braziers and an ominous stairwell descending underground.

We both paused a moment, steeling ourselves for what we knew would be a trial, picked up our skirts, and went down the stairs. At the bottom stretched a long corridor lined with candles that flickered in the cold, damp air. Shadows danced along the black stone walls and, from a distance, my supernatural hearing picked up the hushed voices of men murmuring in secret conversations. Daphne adjusted her domino mask— mere formalities since we would be the only two women in attendance and our identities within The Order were well known—and we approached the large oak door at the end of the corridor.

I knocked three times and a liveried servant opened the door, bowing low before us. I'd been inside only twice before, mainly because I was used to conducting business through coded messages sent via other agents. The room was impressive, if a bit creepy. Lining the walls were massive bookshelves filled with years of filed intelligence reports. Large annotated maps of France hung like tapestries in between. Daphne adored the atmospheric chamber, but I felt like a bug in a bell jar surrounded by the twenty or so men who made up The Order's inner circle. Tonight, especially, they studied me with an intensity that put my previous discomfort to shame.

No sooner had we set foot inside the room than a masked gentleman approached me and smiled obsequiously.

"*Mes agents*," he purred. "Thank you for coming this evening. I think we have quite a bit to discuss, so let's take our seats and begin, shall we?"

Each person made their way to the large oval table in the center of the room. Two servants offered everyone glasses of wine or cognac, but they paused upon reaching Daphne and me. We were offered tea or sherry. I snorted in derision.

"Don't be ridiculous. We'll take cognac, as well. Lord knows I'm going to need it tonight," I grumbled.

The man to my left chuckled and winked at me from beneath his mask.

Is that the Duke of Nevers? The servant filled our glasses and melted into the background.

"Before we begin with the more *physical* aspect of tonight's meeting," the first man said, "we wanted to hear your version of the events leading up to the…ehm…infection."

"You've no doubt read my statement, as well as those from the duchesse and the emissary," I replied.

"Yes," said another man. "But we'd prefer to hear it from you, if you don't mind. Refresh our collective memories."

I narrowed my eyes in annoyance but smiled as sweetly as I could.

"Of course, gentlemen. I trust I don't need to remind you *why* we issued the death order for the Marquis de Sade, and since the beginning of the evening passed exactly as planned, I won't bore you with those details. I'll start, shall we say, with the moment when I led him into the garden for the fatal faux tryst. Perhaps the drugs were not as strong as we thought, or perhaps he had a much stronger constitution than I expected," I lied. "He came quietly enough, but he became rather overzealous in his attentions. He certainly would have discovered my identity in his feeble attempt to ravish me, had not a passing solder spied us through the garden gates at the back of Versailles. Thank God for Lieutenant Antoine de Vaux! I was knocked unconscious in the fray and the gentleman in question picked me up and took me to a nearby coaching inn to recover. It was there that I learned of the bounty on his head and that he was pursued by the *bêtes de sang*—a heretofore unheard of and thoroughly illegal group of private vampire soldiers under the command of Général de Vaux."

"Preposterous," came a disbelieving voice from the back. I glared but continued.

"The *bêtes* caught up with us on the road to Gévaudan—the town we headed for to try and escape their vigilante justice. During our confrontation outside the town, we were attacked by, presumably, the beast that had terrorized Gévaudan, and I was injured in the process. Dr. Van Helsing was summoned to see to my care, and I made my way home after that."

Daphne and I had discussed our version of events in detail, and we agreed to omit certain parts of the story unless absolutely necessary. *Stay as close to the truth as possible,* she'd said. *That will make the lies much more convincing.* As I looked around at the masked men seated around the table, most of them were nodding, thoughtful. In agreement that my story— while bizarre and fantastic—was at least plausible.

"And what of Lieutenant de Vaux?" came a voice at the other end of the table. It was one I didn't recognize.

"I haven't heard of him since I left and returned home. As his capture was not part of my assignment, I left him to his own fate," I replied, attempting an air of nonchalance. Outside of clearing his name with The Order, I wanted him to be beneath their notice. It was a gamble, to be sure, but one I needed to make to secure his safety.

"You didn't think to turn him in? Or inform any other authorities of his whereabouts?" That same voice at the end of the table. *Who is that man? Why don't I recognize him?* With my new powerful supernatural senses, I was just getting used to the scent of each man at the table. Hopefully it would help me to identify them later.

"Of course not. Doing so would have jeopardized everything," I snapped.

"How so?"

"He'd seen me with the Marquis de Sade. He saw me with another agent on the road to Gévaudan. He knows of my condition. If he's not a complete imbecile—and I daresay he isn't—he will put things together if he's properly motivated. I did not wish to give him that motivation. Our meeting was inconvenient at best and I was eager to part ways." I shrugged.

"Do you suspect treachery? Will he try to blackmail you, do you think? Perhaps we should do better to ensure he does not allow the puzzle pieces to fall into place..."

"Don't be absurd," Daphne spoke up. "Such rash action will only draw more attention and put him in a defensive position. He has his own troubles to worry about. Best to leave him be. Charlotte and I will task a detail of DD agents to keep an eye on him." She placed a surreptitious hand on mine beneath the table and gave it a little squeeze. She'd sensed that I would rise to Antoine's defense and stepped in to diffuse the situation.

"That's not good enough," said the man at the end of the table. "I say we bring him in."

I slowly began to remove my glove, attracting the attention of each man in the room. "I don't think that's a wise course of action," I stated. Continuing with my other glove, I started to shuck layers of my dress, boldly staring into the masked faces of each agent.

"Wh—why not?"

I was down to my chemise, stays, petticoat and stockings now. Confusion was thick in the room, but gazes were riveted.

"Lieutenant de Vaux saved my life," I said, affecting a bored tone. "As such, he is under my protection."

With the last word, I found my inner beast, called her forth, and shifted form. I'd been practicing every day, and while it still caused me great pain,

I was getting better at tucking it away. Through the rush of blood in my ears and the involuntary howls and growls that spilled from my muzzle, I heard the gasps and astonished murmurings of the men. When my transformation was complete, I sat back on my haunches and waited. A scent of fear hung in the room, which I found very satisfying.

"Remarkable!"

"Do you think she can understand us in this state? Is it capable of reason?"

"*Mon Dieu,* what a horrifying creature! It's as if Lucifer himself created a wolf. It certainly must be evil for how ugly it is."

I growled and bared my teeth at the prat who'd spoken the last comment. *The nerve of some men!*

"I daresay she can understand us, even in her current form," chuckled another. "I'd watch my tongue, if I were you."

"Very well then. She is a beast—that much of her story is true. But what can she *do*? We all know vampires possess supernatural strength and enhanced senses. Does she, as well?"

I nodded. The men were suitably impressed.

"Gentlemen," Daphne said, clearing her throat. "Charlotte has requested I answer your questions about her abilities to the best of mine. Allow me to elucidate more on her condition, based on what we know so far, which is—regrettably—very little. Van Helsing may shed more light on this new variation of the blood plague, but we do know it is rare indeed. Charlotte has the enhanced senses of a vampire, albeit with a more accurate and wider ranging sense of smell. She has the same speed and strength that we vampires do, and so far, we have been evenly matched in each contest. She does not hunger for blood but seems to prefer raw meat instead. She can transform at will and generally appears to be of a similar likeness to a wolf, with the notable exceptions of a human brain and consciousness."

"And what of her soul?" came the voice of the man in the back. "Is it lost to the fires of Hell, as yours is?"

Daphne narrowed her eyes at the insult. "I would not presume to judge her soul, nor its fate. As one of the supposedly soulless brethren, however, I might offer in defense that, in our line of work, we have met far more humans with no guiding religious light nor moral compass. Men, you would say, who are more certainly destined for Hell than many of the sufferers of the blood plague."

At this, the man in the back stepped forward and removed his mask. I was certain I'd never seen him before, but there was something about him that rang vaguely familiar. Unconsciously, my hackles rose, and a low rumble of warning sounded from my chest.

"Forgive me for not making introductions earlier, *mes agents*," one of the older gentlemen said. "This evening we have a guest in our midst. Duchesse, Comtesse, may I present Général de Vaux."

20

ANTOINE

December 13, 1767
Cimetière des Âmes Oubliées

IF I'D KNOWN HE WAS GOING TO BE TRAIPSING AROUND A GRAVEYARD, sneaking into tombs at night, I might have reconsidered my decision to follow my father. Yet here I was, crouched in a bush, soaked with melting snow and misery, still sore from my healing injuries, waiting in the worst place for the worst confrontation with the worst man. Things felt as hopeless and bleak as the weather.

I'd lost count of the nights since I'd left Grandrieu. They all seemed to blur together into one long stretch of frigid darkness. Sleep eluded me, and when I could shut my eyes for longer than a few hours, my mind conjured dreams of Charlotte. *Charlotte.* I still ached with her absence and the sadness I felt knowing she'd been in Grandrieu and had left without seeing me. When I decided to return to Paris to hunt down my father, I'd considered calling on her, but had thought better of it.

What would I have said? Would she even receive me? I could see it now—a shabby, damaged outlaw showing up on the steps of some grand estate, inquiring after a comtesse. Her servants would probably summon the authorities and I'd be carted off to the Bastille just for being a suspicious character—even without the murder charge and bounty on my head. I hated how much I needed her, as if every day since we'd parted had me living a sort of half-life. For the sake of my own sanity, I was determined to leave her alone. She had a life of passion and danger and…*werewolfishness* to return to and I had my vengeance. Neither of us wanted to watch the other go down in flames, so perhaps it was best if we simply turned our gazes away.

Another carriage arrived and the door opened. As soon as the woman descended from the interior, I knew her—masked or not. *Charlotte.* She appeared as if summoned from my very thoughts, not that she was ever far from them these days. As she stepped down onto the snowy ground, she was followed by the duchesse, who led her to the mausoleum where my father had disappeared. Fear pulled my nerves taut, and my stomach dropped. *No!* It couldn't be. *What the Hell was going on?*

I debated storming in after her, but every time I'd acted without thinking, it had ended badly for both of us. I needed to get her alone—to talk to her. *Nothing more.* What business would she have in this forlorn cemetery? Did it include my villain of a father?

The familiar dread and memories of trauma spurred me into action, and as soon as they were out of sight and her coachman was distracted, I crept through the bushes and discreetly climbed into her carriage. I wouldn't charge in after her, but I would wait for her here to ensure we had a chance to speak with one another.

Dieu, please let her be okay. Please protect her from my father. What could they be doing in there? It had to be the business of The Order, but I was certain that my father wasn't a member. *Why has he come?* My anxiety became almost too much to bear.

After an interminable amount of waiting, men started to file out of the dilapidated tomb, two or three at a time. I did not see my father, but after an eternity, Charlotte appeared with the duchesse following behind. They were having a somewhat frenzied conversation with each other until they both arrived a short distance away from the carriage. They stopped and turned to each other, bodies tense.

Damn! Of course, they can sense me. How stupid could I be?

"Charlotte, *chérie,* I do believe you have a visitor," Daphne said.

Charlotte's face tightened with emotion and—*is that longing?*—before she schooled her features in a mask of vexation. Her eyes narrowed on her carriage. "What is it about my carriage that seems to invite unannounced visitors? I must have the most unobservant coachman and footman in all of France."

"You know, it's such a beautiful winter night. I think I'll walk home," the duchesse said. I barely caught her wink. Charlotte's expression was drawn, and once again, I regretted the decisions that brought me here.

She stepped up into the carriage and sat on the seat opposite me. I waited with bated breath.

"So," she said. "Here we are."

"Charlotte," I said. I hated the way it sounded—like a whisper of hope.

"You look like you haven't eaten or slept in a week," she said.

I frowned and grunted, not wishing to lie to her or admit that I couldn't rest with thoughts of her haunting me.

She continued. "I'm only slightly surprised to see you, but I'm afraid to inform you that you're only the second person to ambush me in my own conveyance this evening. Daphne beat you to the punch earlier."

"It wasn't planned," I admitted.

"Of course, it wasn't! I assume you're here because of your father," she continued. "And not because you've just been out there paying your respects or going for a moonlit stroll through an abandoned cemetery."

I didn't trust myself to say much, so I grunted in assent. "What was he doing down there? He's not a member of The Order."

She leaned forward, and a shaft of moonlight spilled across her lovely face. "Perhaps you could tell me," she said. "After all, I'm sure you've been following him around. You know him better than most. What's his end game?"

"What did he tell you?"

She snorted. "He was a distinguished guest of The Order. He came under the guise of questioning me as to your whereabouts and to hear my testimony about Sade's botched assassination and my subsequent turning."

Panic crept into my voice. "He knows you're a werewolf. And that you were a match for the *bêtes*?"

"Well, he saw me change with his own eyes. But I'm uncertain how much he knows about our altercations with the *bêtes*. I didn't tell him anything that happened outside Grandrieu. I didn't think it would be prudent to tell The Order I was involved in the deaths of several vampire soldiers, which, by the way, you *never* thanked me for," she added with an air of petulance.

"Wait. He saw you change? What did you tell The Order? What did you tell *my father*?" I couldn't help the betrayal in my tone.

She signaled to her driver and the carriage pitched forward. "Oh, Antoine, don't get your hackles up. I didn't tell him or anyone else in The Order anything damning. I told them you killed Sade to protect me—not entirely a lie—and that we went to Gévaudan to escape the *bêtes* sent on your father's behalf. He denies it, of course. Says he sent human soldiers after you, and they must have been turned after they left his command. He says he only hopes for your safe return, so he can reunite with his beloved hero of a son."

I scoffed. "I'll bet."

"What's he really after, Antoine?"

"Truthfully, I do not know. But we can be sure it'll be about money, power, or any other self-serving greedy aim. I promise that's closer to the truth than any of that rot he's spouting to The Order."

She sat back against the cushions away from the moonlight, and I temporarily mourned the loss of her beauty.

"And what are you after?"

I shifted uncomfortably. The ache of how much I missed her hit me full force. *Dieu, why must this be so difficult?* "I told you before. I'm after him."

She was quiet, studying me. "Is that really all you want?"

"Yes. No! Damn it, it's all I can have, Charlotte. All I deserve," I said forcefully. *Seeing her is a mistake. Being this close to her is a mistake.*

"You're the only one who believes that, Antoine."

"What do you want me to say?"

"For pity's sake, Antoine, I want you to think about your life. Where it's going, what you want, what happens after you see your revenge mission completed—*if* it is completed. What would satisfy you? How would you find happiness?" She waved her hand in the air, exasperated. "What lies beyond the death of your father?"

"I...I don't know," I admitted. "I never felt I had the right to a future beyond his death. My life—my purpose—ends with him. I guess I always thought I'd hang for it, so I never allowed myself the luxury of dreaming about more."

"That can't be everything," she pressed. "You can't have *always* hoped for a suicide mission in your thirties. I know that's not what young Antoine dreamed of as a child."

I felt a blush creep up my cheeks. *Certainly not. Young Antoine dreamed of a pretty wife to embrace, children to spoil, winters throwing snowballs and summers eating strawberries beneath shady trees. A home overflowing with love and laughter, where death and disappointment dare not tread, with a partner like sunshine. Young Antoine dreamed of a woman like Charlotte, werewolf or not. Hell, Young Antoine probably would have loved the idea of a supernatural wife.*

"It doesn't matter now," I snapped. "My path is marked out, and my fate is sealed. Events have been set in motion."

"What utter horse shit," she laughed. "Why is it privileged men seem to have everything in the world laid at their feet and they still aren't satisfied? You may not be able to control the cards you're dealt in life, but you can certainly choose how to play them."

"So says the aristocrat born into a life of privilege."

"You're right," she admitted. "But at least I'm doing something with it that goes beyond my own selfish desires. And it doesn't mean I haven't had to adjust to less-than-ideal circumstances from time to time."

She had a point. "So, you transformed in front of all those men." Irrational jealousy bristled in me.

She stiffened. "They were far more receptive to my altered state than you were."

I could've choked on my shame and regret in that moment. "I didn't know that was you in the cave! I was half conscious at the time. And anyway, they were only receptive to it because they want to use your abilities to their advantage," I grumbled.

She crossed her arms in front of her chest. "You know, I've never pushed a man out of a moving carriage, but I think I might enjoy the experience."

I gritted my teeth. "Thank you for saving my wretched life. *Again.*" The words were hot and bitter in my mouth, but it was worth it to hear the slight smile in her voice when she answered.

"It's becoming a habit," she said. "Whatever will you do without me here to protect you?"

She'd meant the words in jest, but emotion seized my reply and tied it into a knot in my throat. The air between us became charged; the unsaid words hanging in the atmosphere like fog. I didn't know if or when I would get another chance to speak to her, so I said the one thing that had been weighing on my mind every day since we'd parted.

"Charlotte," I breathed. "I'm sorry."

"For what?"

"Christ, for everything. For the last words we spoke to each other in anger. For what happened in the cave. For being an insufferable ass in Gévaudan. For endangering you time and time again and getting you mixed up with the *bêtes* and now my father. For setting off the cascade of events that turned you into a fucking werewolf. For kidnapping you in the first place."

"You didn't kidnap me, you were protecting me," she said wryly.

Despite my misery, I chuckled. "If only I was. If only I could. Perhaps if I was better at protecting things, everything would be different."

She blew out a breath. "Antoine, if there's one thing I've learned in this life, it's that there are more than enough torments to go around. You needn't add to them yourself. Would my life be any better if I hadn't become infected? I don't know. Would it be any better if I wasn't an agent for The Order? Perhaps, but it would certainly be duller. Would it be any better if my husband hadn't summoned a demon to try and force Daphne to love him? Actually, yes, probably, but I would still be married to a man I did not truly love."

Horror gripped me. *Surely I'd misheard her.* "He did *what?*" White hot rage surged through me, quicker than lightning. "I'll kill him. Is he still alive? It doesn't matter. I'll drag him back from Hell and kill him again."

She smiled sadly. "My point is that we can speculate all we want. It doesn't change the way things are. Most of the time, it makes everything more painful because of failed expectations. We are where we are, we are *who* we are, and all we can do is make the best of it," she said.

I nodded. "It does not stop me from wishing things were different." *It does not stop me from wanting you. It does not stop me from needing you. It does not silence the part of me that wants to have a family and a safe haven with you; the part that dreams of walking away from everything to be yours forever.*

She seemed to take my meaning because her voice had lost its teasing edge when she replied. "Nor I."

We were silent for a beat, listening to the muted, snow-covered sounds of the street under the carriage wheels. I opened my mouth to say something—any one of the unspoken things that had been circling my head for the last few weeks—but words seemed to fail me. Desperation won out and I reached forward, pulling her to me and covering her lips with mine.

21

CHARLOTTE

HE CAME BACK. NOT FOR ME, EXACTLY, BUT HE CAME BACK, NONETHELESS. Was that enough for me? In this moment, I didn't care. The scent of him in my carriage elicited a primal response in my body—*my mate has returned.*

Ridiculous, Charlotte.

His kiss was fire and ice at once, and I met him with the full force of my desire, which only seemed to have grown in our time apart. I slid my hands up his neck and threaded my fingers through his hair. For a moment, everything between us other than this was forgotten. I tilted his head back and scraped my teeth along his jaw, drawing forth a deep growl that sent vibrations of need along every one of my nerves. A low moan escaped my throat, spurring his ardor. I nibbled at his ears while I hastily tugged at his coat, sliding cool palms beneath his shirt to his warm, bare chest. Every part of me was aflame. *Dieu*, I wanted him—this surly, complicated man. Now and forever.

"Charlotte." His voice came out in a rough tremor.

"Antoine?" *Why have you come for your father and not for me? What are your feelings for me? What are your feelings for my being a werewolf? What will happen to us?* I ignored the trepidation and the dark thoughts that circled my mind.

"I feel I must tell you…" he began, caressing my breasts through the bodice of my gown.

"If your words are anything but filthy ones right now, Antoine, keep them to yourself," I chuckled, until his hands slid to my thighs and he bunched my skirts in his fists. Straddling him on the seat of the carriage, I reached for the falls of his breeches, almost losing myself at the feel of his straining erection pressing against my sex. My composure, already frayed and failing, snapped. I gripped his hips and rocked against him, pulling forth from him a moan that was sweeter than any sound I'd ever heard on earth. *Fate be damned—I'm going to have this man.*

"Charlotte," he panted. His fingers fumbled with the bodice of my expensive gown. The silk was like water in his calloused fingers, making it difficult for him to untie, unlace, and unpin me. I struggled with the buttons on his breeches, eager as I was to bare him to me.

With a little growl of frustration—one that sounded alarmingly lupine—I ripped the front of his breeches, scattering the damned buttons across the carriage floor. I let out a triumphant laugh and saw the glaze of lust in his eyes sparkle. With a wolfish grin, he did the same to my dress, ripping it clear down the front. I squealed with laughter.

"This dress cost me a fortune," I huffed, ending with a whimper when he took my nipple into his mouth.

"Send me the bill," he murmured, sucking gently. I gasped and writhed on his lap, reaching down to wrap my hands around his hard cock. He swore, lewder and more guttural than I'd heard from him before. I slid my hands up and down, mimicking the movement of the carriage as the wheels jostled us back and forth. Already, I was close. *So close.*

"Charlotte, *putain de merde!* You must stop. I want you, my love—I need you." He slid a finger through the warm, wet folds of my sex and growled his desire. "You're so wet, *l'amour*…all for me. How I've dreamed of this perfect pussy since you left me. It's all I can think about. Late at night, alone, I fantasize about the pleasure that lives here." He pushed me back off his lap and against the wall of the carriage. Dropping to his knees, he licked at the insides of my thighs, working his way up to the pearl of my pleasure. I squirmed beneath his touch.

"This teasing will be the death of me, Antoine," I whimpered. "Kiss me like you mean it."

He grinned up at me and dove forward, sucking and licking at the apex of my sex until I was ready to come apart. He would have continued, but I pulled his face up to mine for a fervent kiss, then wrapped my legs around his waist.

"I need it all, Antoine," I demanded. "Give me everything." *What does that mean, Charlotte? What am I asking of him?*

"Everything," he agreed.

I grasped his cock and guided him inside my ready heat on a satisfied moan from us both. It was exquisite—magnificent. He moved slowly at first, seemingly unaware of the words as they fell from his lips. "I'll give you everything, Charlotte. Anything. *Putain, oui, chérie, juste comme ça.* My life, my heart, my soul—they are yours. *Yours.*" My cries cut through the night, and I pushed him back against the opposite wall of the carriage, grinding on top of him with boiling, out-of-control lust. He reached up to twine his fingers through my hair, sending a jolt of lightning from my scalp down to my sex.

"Harder, Antoine, *mon amour!*" I cried. He needed no more encouragement. He lifted me and turned me around, bending me over the seat in front of us. He stroked my breasts and pinched my nipples, and my knees buckled.

"How hard, *petite*?" He slapped my ass, and the sweet sting elicited a thrill and a curse from me. *I need him. I need him. I am his. He is mine. Mine.* I tried desperately to regain my sanity, then abandoned it entirely.

"My body mourns the loss of you, *chéri*," I pouted, wiggling back against him. "It would be cruel indeed to leave me so unsatisfied."

He slid into me again—*Dieu, I would never know another man like this*—and I moaned a litany of filth that made him groan. *It will never be this way again. There will never be another Antoine. Eventually, you will be parted by time itself.* Whispers of fear and regret echoed through me, but I chased them away with the explosive pleasure of each thrust. I would worry about everything when I wasn't joined with the man I loved.

The man I loved.

"I will never let anyone hurt you, *mon amour.* I will never let another man have you. You are mine. Your body is mine. Your heart is mine. All of it," he grunted, driving into me. He reached forward to find the peak of my pleasure and I almost screamed. "You are mine, Charlotte. *Mine.*"

"Yes," I panted. I felt my body draw up, as an archer draws a bow.

"Say it," he begged. His clever fingers had worked me to the point of combustion.

"I am *yours*," I shouted, coming apart beneath him, around him.

With a final thrust that nearly toppled the carriage and a roar that fractured the night, he joined me in *la petite mort.*

We stayed braced against each other for several minutes, trying to catch our breath and hopefully avoid the awkward words that often followed. Antoine kissed the back of my neck and slid out from me, and my body immediately protested. He'd given me pleasure unlike any I'd ever known, but my need for him was unmatched. As frightening as that thought was, I didn't want to face the consequences of our actions. I was not ready to return to the shaded reality of our world just yet.

The carriage slowed to a stop at my estate just as we were sheepishly attempting to right our clothes, and I stared at his grim, furrowed brow as he eyed his ripped breeches. I couldn't help but laugh.

"These were my favorite breeches," he said forlornly.

I wrapped my ripped dress around myself and took his hand. "I'll buy you a new pair. Now, come inside. I'm certain I have something appropriate you can wear—or not."

His green eyes flashed with hope and despair and lust like a promise, and he opened his mouth to say something rational. I stopped him with a finger to his lips.

"Tomorrow, Antoine. Just this tonight," I whispered. I dropped a kiss on his lips, and he nodded.

We exited the carriage and I winked at my driver's knowing smirk as we descended. I led Antoine upstairs to my bedchamber. He was quiet, as he always was, but I sensed a change in him. As soon as I shut the door, I was on him again, pressing my lips to his and meeting his eager tongue stroke for stroke.

Dieu, is this part of my supernatural state? Or is this something else entirely?

I pulled his shredded clothes off, casting them to the side. He really was beautiful—a study of hard muscles beneath golden skin and dark hair, staring at me with that mix of lust and possession that made my head spin.

"You realize at some point, we are going to have a conversation about Gévaudan, your turning, Grandrieu, and my father," he said, slowly tugging my skirts back down my hips. They fell to the floor in with a soft swish.

"Of course," I nodded, running my fingertips over his sculpted abdomen. "We obviously desire each other to the point of madness. We're just doing this to get it out of the way. When we're done, we'll be able to focus. Honestly, it would be irresponsible of us to try to settle things before we were satiated."

He grinned at the lie but made no argument. My hands trailed down the dusting of dark hair at his belly button and he sucked in a breath. He raised a hand to caress my cheek and tilted my face up to his.

"There are other things I want to discuss with you, Charlotte," he said in a low, deep voice. My belly flipped, and before I could remember every logical reason that separated us, I allowed myself a moment to entertain the idea of what he might say. A brief wave of warmth and happiness washed over me. I stepped backward to the bed and beckoned to him.

"Certainly," I smiled seductively as he devoured me with a heated gaze. "But if there are things you wish to say to me, you'll have to come whisper them in my ear."

He smiled that heart-achingly handsome smile, dimples and all, and crawled forward to me. His touch was tender, languid, not the frenzied need from earlier. The sweetness of it was at once too much and not enough.

My anger and frustration hadn't evaporated, but they waited in the corner of my mind. *Charlotte, you damned fool. You know you cannot have him. You cannot be with him. He is an outlaw and will probably go to prison if he murders his father. He will insist you leave les DD and The Order. Even if these things are surmountable, there is one thing remaining that is not: you are a werewolf, and he is human.*

Antoine noticed my distracted mind and pulled away instantly, worry etched on his handsome, scarred face. "Charlotte, are you well? Do you wish me to stop?"

I shook my head, squeezing my eyes shut against the tears that threatened to fall. "No, *chéri*. Not tonight. Do not stop for anything tonight."

He gave me a relieved smile and muttered a rough, "Thank *God*," and bent to kiss me. It was soft and sweet and promised a night of dark pleasures ahead.

If only that could be enough.

22

ANTOINE

December 14, 1767
Château de Ruisseau Magdelaine

I woke from what surely had been a dream. Cracking one eye open, I stared into Charlotte's slack, sleeping face and smiled. *Not a dream.* Tucked up in her massive bed, tangled in the softest sheets I'd ever felt, entwined with the only woman who alleviated as much suffering as she caused. She snored lightly and I swallowed a laugh. Her eyes fluttered open, and she gave me a slow smile.

"Any regrets?" she asked.

"Only that I didn't come round sooner," I said, pulling her into my arms.

"Mmm," she said through a yawn. "Why didn't you?"

Because I am an outlaw, you are a monster, and I am in love with you. Before I could answer, there was a soft knock at her door. I made to get up out of bed, but Charlotte put her hand on my chest.

"Stay," she instructed. "My servants are used to an *unusual* household. You need the rest and they'll have brought us breakfast."

I was embarrassed and uncomfortable, but I did as she asked. She bade her butler enter, and sure enough, he came in with a large tray covered with food.

"Good morning, my lady," he said. "I have your messages from yesterday."

"*Merci*, Charles," she said, reaching for the tray. "Ooh, poached eggs and asparagus!"

"And I'm afraid there is a gentleman here to see you," he continued, obviously anxious. "He has refused to come back at another time and prefers to wait."

I was instantly on edge. "Who?" I demanded.

To his credit, Charles didn't miss a beat.

"There is a Général de Vaux here to see you, my lady."

Blood drained from my face and my stomach twisted. I launched myself out of bed, scrambling for my breeches.

"I'm going to kill him!" I growled. "Why is he here, Charlotte?"

"I've no idea," she said with a shrug.

"He must be after you for the deaths of the *bêtes*. Or perhaps he suspects you'll lead him to me. Christ, once again, I've put you in grave danger!" I shoved one leg into my ripped breeches and frowned down at them. "I knew things would only get worse. I'm like an ill omen for you, Charlotte. I just didn't think he'd bring you into this... How dare he show up at your doorstep!"

Charlotte cocked a brow at my tirade and nodded to the butler. "Charles, would you mind finding some clothes for the lieutenant? And please inform Général de Vaux that I'll be down shortly. He may wait in the yellow drawing room." She swiped a piece of toast through egg yolk and popped it into her mouth in an unconcerned manner.

"You can't be serious," I said. "You can't receive him, Charlotte. He's incredibly dangerous and I'm certain he's not here for a social call."

She dabbed at her mouth with a napkin and uncovered a second dish on the breakfast tray—a plate heaped with raw meat. She began to tuck in unapologetically, as if she hadn't heard me in the first place.

"Charlotte," I warned.

"Antoine, do have some breakfast. You're clearly in need of rest and nourishment. The hollows in your cheeks and under your eyes look positively cadaverous." She pushed a plate across the bed toward me. "And please sit down. Charles will find you some clothes, but I'm afraid the rest of my staff may be somewhat alarmed by a naked man running through my household, despite my more liberal leanings."

My temper flared. "I don't feel like you truly appreciate the severity of the situation, Charlotte."

"Why do you say that?"

"You're calmly eating breakfast! And you're about to go meet with my father as if he isn't a traitor and the reason my family has been destroyed! I'm serious, Charlotte, I'm going to kill him." *Where are my short swords? And my pistols?*

She finished eating and stood, and it took me a moment to refocus after watching the sheets fall from her beautiful body. She pulled on a long silk robe and crossed to her dressing table, where she sat and started to comb through her glossy brown locks. Her eyes met mine in the mirror, and for a moment, the ever-present humor faded from her face.

"I'm going to meet him, Antoine, and I'm going to find out what he wants. My guess is he's here to try and get information from me about you—assuming he doesn't already know you're here. Have you considered the possibility that as long as you've been watching him, he's also had someone watching you?"

"I have." *I haven't.*

"Please, Antoine. Trust me this once. When he leaves, I'll come back and we'll talk, *d'accord?*"

"Absolutely not. You *cannot* meet with him. He's dangerous, Charlotte, and cunning, and—quite frankly—evil. I don't want you to have anything to do with him."

She sighed and turned around. "Do you trust me?"

I blinked.

She winced slightly. "I know I haven't given you a very good reason to, and I understand your hesitation, given your past and my present *hobby,* but if you could set those things aside and look into your heart."

I pursed my lips. "What are you asking of me?"

"Simply this: let me talk to him. Let me do what I'm best at and draw out his purpose."

"As charming as you are, he'll see right through you. He already knows you're a spy," I argued.

"An agent," she corrected. "Perhaps. But will you at least trust me to try? I want to protect you, Antoine, but I can't do that if I don't understand his aims," she stood in front of me, imploring. "Please. This is what I'm good at. This is why I became an agent. Stay here and wait for me."

I saw her now without any artifice, as bold and genuine as I'd ever seen. I had no choice but to agree. "But if he threatens you…"

"Yes, yes. If he threatens me, you may cut off his head, though I'd fancy doing it myself." She smiled and reached up to kiss me.

Before I could rethink my decision, another knock sounded at the door and her lady's maid entered to help her dress. Charles followed, handed me a robe, and escorted me to the next chamber down the hall, where a roaring fire and full, steaming bathtub awaited me.

Charles seemed to sense my distress. When the other servants had left, he leaned in close. "When you're finished, sir, you may wish to entertain yourself with a book. If you take the back stairs and turn left, you'll find the library at the end of the hallway. It's just next to the yellow drawing room. It may be a bit chilly in the winter, though. Such regrettably thin walls," he said.

Startled by his candor, I couldn't help but ask. "Does your mistress know you listen at keyholes?"

He smiled. "Lady Charlotte is a spy, sir. She pays us to listen at keyholes."

Well, then.

He laid out a jacket, waistcoat, breeches, hose, and shirt—fine enough to see me to court—and left me to my bath.

As I sank into the warm, perfumed water, my muscles clamored for the chance to relax and unknit their knots, but my mind raced with the knowledge that my father was downstairs and was here for Charlotte. I hurried to wash, shave, and dress, hoping Charlotte would take her time in going down to see him.

As Charles suggested, I crept down the back stairs and found the library just where he'd said it would be. My heart pounded. My father was in the next room. Did he know I was here? Was he here to threaten Charlotte? I'd kill him if he did.

Perhaps I should go next door and confront him.

It felt as if Charlotte was going off to fight my battles—again. *Dieu,* how many times had she done that? That was all she'd been doing since we first met, and I couldn't keep letting her fight for me just because I was too depleted to fight for myself.

I should be the one protecting her—even if I've done a poor job of it thus far.

Just as I was resolved to go next door and end things the way they should have ended ages ago, I heard the soft rustle of fabric down the hallway and the door to the drawing room opened. I scooted a chair close to the wall, but found it was unnecessary to press my ear directly against it—Charles had been right about the thinness of the walls. I could hear every word.

23

CHARLOTTE

December 14, 1767
Château de Ruisseau Magdelaine

"Général de Vaux! What an unexpected visit," I said, whirling into the room. Light filtered in through the front windows and illuminated the général's morose visage—quite different from my impression of him in the dark tunnels of the previous evening.

Mon Dieu, but he looks so much like Antoine! He was shorter and slimmer than Antoine, and was of course without the visible scars and marks, but they shared the same aquiline nose, full lips, and piercing green eyes. Antoine's had warmth to them, like a lovely green field on a hot summer's day. The général's were hard and cold, putting me in mind of oily seaweed washed up on a winter's shore.

He bowed smartly, dressed in his military uniform with his formal powdered wig. I inclined my head and gestured for him to sit.

"You've been kept waiting," I said. *Not an apology.*

"Forgive me," he said. "I called unannounced. I don't wish to take up much of your time. I simply had some questions for you following your testimony last night that may have been…*inappropriate* for the ears of The Order." He smiled like a predator.

"Well, Général, you know of my allegiance, so it seems like a fruitless journey considering the ears of The Order are right alongside my head. That *must* be disappointing. Would you care for some refreshment? Some tea, perhaps? You do look a bit bilious, and tea is *wonderful* for the digestion. Those English may yet have something right, *non*?" I tittered, waving for a footman.

He narrowed his eyes and frowned but carried on. "No tea, thank you. Comtesse de Brionne, I'm certain you don't share everything with your masters."

"My masters? My goodness, Général, who can you mean? My father and my husband are no longer with us, so I wouldn't—"

He cut me off, jawline flexing in that similar air of annoyance that he shared with Antoine. "Are you being purposely coy, my lady? It's just that it rings of obtuseness, and I cannot abide stupidity in any form."

"I certainly wouldn't take credit for being *accidentally* coy, Monsieur, but it is unfortunate that your patience seems so tested. Are you sure you wouldn't like some tea?" I smiled politely, pouring my own cup.

"I don't want any damn tea!" he spit out, then exhaled and composed himself. "I just need some answers."

"I daresay we *all* need answers, Général, but you haven't even asked me a single question yet. Imagine that! How can I be of help to you if you don't elucidate what you need in the first place? And to be sure, I am *most* eager to be of service to you. You do seem frightfully important." I nodded as earnestly as I could.

In addition to the tightening muscles in his jaw, a sizable vein on the side of his head began to throb. With my supernatural senses, I could hear the blood pumping through it. *He must have a splitting headache.*

"I came to ask where my son is," he said through gritted teeth.

"*Mon Dieu!* Have you truly lost him? You know, when I lose things, they're often in the last place that I look for them. When did you see him last? Oh, I offered you tea, but perhaps you'd like something to nibble on instead? My chef makes the most delicious pastries, but I think probably plain bread for you, *non*? You seem like a plain bread sort of man."

His face began to turn a mottled sort of red. The vein throbbed.

"Now, don't take offense, Général! I just meant that you seem the type to deny yourself certain pleasures in order to live a more ascetic lifestyle. Truly honorable. I imagine a life waging various wars would lead one to such simplistic tastes. Provincial, if you will. Forced to enjoy things that you could get on the frontlines of wherever the king sent you. If I were in such situations, of course I would develop a healthy resentment for the king, but as such, I haven't. He's such a dear, you know. I don't think I could stay mad at him for long." I prattled on, reaching for the tray of pastries in front of me. I looked up, expecting to see steam piping out of his ears, but instead, he was eerily quiet. He smiled coldly at me.

"Is he here?" he murmured quietly.

"His Majesty? Of course not. I imagine he's at Versailles. Why on earth would he be here?" I bent forward to pick up a tart, and his fingers clamped onto my wrist in a vice-like grip. He squeezed, which perhaps would have hurt without my supernatural strength. "Goodness, if you wanted a tart, you simply had to ask. Lemon or cream?"

His eyes flashed with rage and his voice was deadly calm when he spoke. Each word dripped with venom. "Listen to me, you damned, spoiled, ridiculous little slut. I know you lied to The Order. I know you were somehow responsible for what happened to my men. Antoine is too stupid and weak to have dispatched them. I'm certain you know what happened to him and quite possibly where he's hiding. It would be easier if you told me now," he said, twisting my wrist as if he would break it.

"Général," I sighed. While I could have easily pulled free of his grasp, I let him retain his grip, and his illusion of control, for a moment longer. "You must not be thinking clearly. You came into my home to threaten me for information? You're sitting before a comtesse, who you know to be connected with the most powerful people in all of France, who you *actually* witnessed transform into a werewolf—and you're going to break my wrist if I don't tell you what happened to the adult son who left your command? Forget the tea, do have yourself a brandy and a lie down."

I considered changing then and there, biting his arm off and then delivering it to Antoine as an early Christmas gift, but I restrained my more feral impulses. Obviously, the général was suffering from some kind of brain fever. One thing was clear, however—he knew far less than I suspected. I wondered how much information his remaining men had been able to impart to him before their demise.

Apoplectic, he released my arm and stood abruptly. "I know Antoine is responsible for the death of the Marquis de Sade. I know why, as I suspect you do. If he returns to me, we will work things out in our familial sort of way. If he doesn't return to me, I'll see him hanged for being a deserter. Perhaps when you see him, you will tell him that."

"As I told you before, after Gévaudan, we parted ways. If you wish to send your son to the gallows, I'm afraid that's your business. It would make for an awkward family reunion, since I'm sure you'll be joining him for treason."

"Treason? My only aim was to protect my country. I will do so at any cost and the king knows that. If you think he wouldn't sanction a few vampire soldiers to further his foreign ambitions, then I daresay you don't know him as well as you think." He straightened and brushed off his coat.

I smiled frostily. "We'll see about that. Charles will show you out. I would say that it's been a pleasure, but it hasn't, and I'm sure you wouldn't know pleasure if it slapped you across the face, so I'll just say *au revoir*."

His face twisted with anger, and he strode to the door, pausing with his hand on the knob.

"I know my son. Whatever happened between you, I'm certain he'll come here. I'll be waiting. You think you can protect him from me? You have no idea who you're dealing with," he threatened.

"Oh? Wait—you aren't a washed up, double dealing, traitorous blackguard who sacrifices his own family to further his warped political ambitions? Hm. I must've thought you were a wholly different Général de Vaux." I laughed.

His hand flew to the sword at his side and a low, wolflike growl vibrated from my chest.

"You could try it, you know, only I wouldn't. I'm still picking your pet vampires from between my teeth. Do you think you stand a better chance?"

His hand fisted but left the vicinity of his weapon. "I'll be watching you," he hissed.

"Of course, you will, Général!" I shot back. "But if I ever catch your scent around my home again, I will rip out your throat and eat every part of you but your black heart. *That* I will send to Antoine in a little box for him to bury with his sister. A life for a life—a heart for a heart."

He did not reply, but his posture tensed, and I knew my message had landed. He turned to go without another word, disappearing down the hall. I heard the front door close behind him.

I sat back down and reached for my abandoned tart. "Antoine," I called to the other room. "You may come out now. He is gone."

I waited, knowing full well he had been listening in the library next door.

"Antoine?"

I went across the hall to the library and peered in. It was empty. His scent lingered, so I knew he had been there for at least part of my conversation with the général, but at some point, he'd left. Looking around, I saw the wide-open French doors that faced the side of the estate, directly opposite the stables.

A small square of parchment fluttered from the top of a table to the ground. I stooped to pick it up.

Charlotte,

I know what I must do to lay my ghosts to rest. Do not follow me—I'll only endanger you further.

Yours,

Antoine

"Oh, Hell."

24

ANTOINE

December 17, 1767
Château de Sade
Condé-en-Brie

I'D HEARD ALL I NEEDED TO HEAR. THE LONGER I LISTENED TO THEM TALK, THE more things took shape in my own mind. Puzzle pieces fell into place, connecting Louis's death to the Marquis de Sade and the *bêtes de sang*. I may not have the evidence to support my suspicions, but hearing my father threaten Charlotte had brought about the clarity I needed to see the bigger picture.

He is here for me. Not because he wanted to see my safe return, but because I am one of the few people who could work out the truth of his crimes. I was the one in danger, after all. I knew exactly what my father intended—he would go through Charlotte to get to me. She might not fear him, but she didn't know how diabolical and cruel he could be. I couldn't let anything happen to her. *I wouldn't.*

He obviously suspected our connection, otherwise, he wouldn't have shown up at her doorstep to threaten her. The move was bold, but odd—it was reckless to ostracize a known member of The Order, especially when he knew her connections and her supernatural state. I'd seen her in wolf form. The vision still terrified me.

My father's actions were that of a desperate man: unpredictable, treacherous, selfish. He was like an animal caught in a trap, fearing the repercussions of the king discovering what he'd done. He would attempt to bury the evidence.

I pulled my cloak tighter around my body, leaning over the horse I'd stolen from Charlotte's stables. *She'll have to forgive me.* The frozen wind lashed against me. I had spared no time in setting off for the Marquis de Sade's estate outside Paris. Before confronting my father, I wanted to be certain my suspicions were correct.

I need proof! And I know just where to get it.

I couldn't believe I hadn't thought of it sooner, but my need for revenge had obscured more of my logic than I cared to admit. My father had burned the damning letters that would have seen him hanged, but that had only been *half* of the correspondence. Sade would have my father's letters, and I'd wager they were locked away in his study—assuming my father hadn't already sent his vampire guard dogs to destroy the evidence of his treachery.

It took me a day to reach the grand estate. Twice I'd gotten turned around on the snow-covered backroads, delaying me a frustrating amount. Despite Sade being dead only a short time, his grand residence appeared almost empty. There were fresh horse tracks marring the snow on the drive and one window glowing with muted gold light, but there was no domestic bustle around the building. *Perhaps it's one lowly house-keeper caring for the estate and the rest of the staff have already been dismissed.*

I guided my horse into a thicket of trees alongside the road and waited. My hands felt frostbitten and my cheeks were raw from the cold, but it was worth the discomfort to take the time to ensure I'd be alone. Finally satisfied, I circled the back of the manor and stabled the horse, taking great care to not be seen. The gardens were winter barren but looked a touch overgrown, making me wonder how long it had been since the marquis had been here. I peered in window after window but found no one.

The glow of firelight was visible from the windows lining the back balcony. If I could find some purchase, I could pull myself up and enter through the doors.

When I swung myself up over the balcony railing, shock stole my breath.

There, sitting at the large desk in the study, sat my father.

The lights hadn't been from a housekeeper or a servant. It had been him—*my father.* He must've passed me on the road when I'd gotten lost earlier. The sharp claws of anxiety seized my lungs and it took massive effort to will myself calm.

It was as if no time had passed. His face looked a bit more gaunt, but his eyes still glinted with the arrogance I remembered from childhood. I took advantage of his unawareness and kicked the doors in, which crashed open in an eruption of broken glass and fractured wood. He startled but recovered quickly, hands falling upon the pistol at his side. When recognition dawned, his face twisted in a grimace of disgust.

"Antoine! What in God's name do you think you're doing?" His hand did not leave his weapon.

"Général. I could ask you the same question."

"Don't be impertinent," he snarled. "Where have you been? Why have you come here?"

"I suspect you and I are here for the same reason—your letters to Sade," I growled.

"What the Hell are you talking about?" he shot back. His bluster didn't hide his twitching hand, however, and my gaze snagged on a thick stack of letters.

I chuckled humorlessly. "Well, for once, my timing has been fortunate. Hand them over, Father, or I shall shoot you and take them."

A sinister smile tugged at his lips. "It's a pity this is what it took for you to find the steel in your spine, boy. Yet you dare presume to threaten me after everything I've done for you. You must be stark raving mad," he shot back.

"Mad? Quite the contrary. For the first time in years, I feel an alien sense of clarity. It was a kind of madness that drove me forward after Marie and Louis's deaths, and truth be told, I've thought of little else but paying you back tenfold for what you did to them. I dreamed of Sade's death, and yours, for too many nights. *But no more, Father.* I have a new dream now, and your blood doesn't play a part in it."

His hand twitched on his pistol, and I pulled mine immediately, training the sights on his heart.

"I don't *wish* to kill you any longer, but I will if necessary. You made your bed with Fate, and now you'll lie in it. I'm going to take those letters and report your actions to the king. It will be his decision if you dangle at the end of a rope, or spend your life in prison."

He scoffed and rolled his eyes. "What are these *actions* you speak of?"

"Your *bêtes de sang*, for a start. That you had intentions of creating an entire army of vampire soldiers who would answer to you and only you. That I had the evidence, but that you destroyed it," I said.

"No one will believe you," he smirked. He picked up the stack of letters and I eyed him guardedly. "Least of all the king."

"They will believe me when I tell them you planned as much with the Marquis de Sade."

His smirk faltered and suspicion passed through his gaze. "What an absurd notion."

"Is it?" I accused. "Why else would you have sent Louis to him? What could you possibly have to gain by offering your only grandson to a known monster? It couldn't just be for influence. As power mad as you are, you have enough influence on your own. No, it had to be something else. The way the blood plague has alienated the human aristocracy—you saw the writing on the wall. What better way to protect yourself from vampires than to have your own militant force of the undead? It was never about protecting France. It was about saving yourself."

"Madness, indeed," he growled. "Perhaps you should be in an asylum."

"How did it first come about? Did you approach Sade with your plan? Or was he in on it from the very beginning? Let me guess—you knew in order to convince perfectly respectable Catholic soldiers to abandon their promise of Heaven in a blood-drinking bargain, you'd need the funds to secure their loyalty and their souls. You approached Sade then, didn't you? He could help finance your private army of the damned, and you would give him your own flesh and blood as payment." The words were ash in my mouth, and bile rose in my stomach. I felt sick as I laid the accusations before him, as if the truth was poison itself.

He stilled, wary. "That's ridiculous. And even if it were true, you don't have a scrap of proof. Everyone will think you're just the dimwitted, bitter son of a well-appointed and honorable général."

"I'm not leaving here without that proof," I threatened, cocking my pistol. My father's grip on the letters tightened and his eyes cut to the fireplace. "Even if you burn them," I continued. "I have the testimony from The Order and the word of two very powerful aristocrats. That's enough circumstantial evidence to rip your whole world away from you. In the court of public opinion, you'll be as good as gone," I said.

He frowned. "You know, Antoine, I am sorry to hear you say that. You always had such potential—not that I ever truly expected you to fulfill it, of course, but I did what I could to give you a promising start."

"You gave me nothing but cruelty and disdain," I hissed. "The only good thing you ever gave to me was Marie, and you took her away from me as certainly as you sent Louis to his death."

He narrowed his eyes and stomped twice on the floor. In an instant, there was someone else standing in the doorway.

Hugo.

"I believe you have some unfinished business with Lieutenant de Vaux," the général said. He turned to me; hatred written across his face. "He no longer has my protection. He is no longer my son."

Hugo's eyes darkened and he grinned viciously, showing off his fangs. He rushed toward me, grabbing me by the throat and pinning me back against the wall. He lifted me easily off the ground and I lost my grip on my weapons. As I struggled for air, I saw Hugo's fangs extend and he leaned forward, preparing to bite.

The général strode to the fireplace, casting a triumphant glare as he raised the letters in his hand. "You fool," he snarled. "You should have shot me when you had the chance. You'll never win against me. You never had it in you. You'll always be—"

An explosion of wood and glass sounded from below. I used the distraction to grab for my short sword, slashing wildly at Hugo's stomach. A gash appeared and he hissed in pain, but his grip on my throat only tightened. Distantly, I heard the général shouting. Darkness began to creep into my vision from the loss of precious air, just as I felt Hugo's fangs sink into my throat.

The pain was intense but fleeting. *Am I dead?* Hugo suddenly released me, dropping me to the floor. The pain that resounded throughout my body informed me I was still alive. *For now.* Shaking my head to clear it, I looked up to see why Hugo had dropped me. Across the room, he was entangled with the most terrifying, beautiful monster I'd ever seen.

Charlotte.

Gasping for breath, I watched them battle each other, almost evenly matched in strength and speed. Hugo grappled with Charlotte's massive form, twisting around to avoid her snarling jaws closing around his throat. The général shouted at Hugo as he skirted the fight, inching closer to the door to make his escape, the forgotten letters still clenched in his fist. Hugo shrieked as Charlotte's claws raked gashes along his chest, and he sank his teeth into her shoulder. She yelped in pain. The général shouted in triumph.

Desperate to be useful, I struggled helplessly on the floor. I tried to call to her, but only gasps came out. I reached up and felt blood gushing from the wound in my neck. *Merde.* I crawled across the floor to the fight, intent on reaching her. If this was to be my fate…my end…so be it. *Let me die close to the woman I love.*

I looked up to see the général shouting, screaming at Hugo to kill her. He had his pistol raised, taking aim at her enormous shoulders.

No!

A shot rang out. Time slowed to a crawl.

The général staggered backward, surprise written on his face. He stared at the smoking pistol in my hand, then down at the bullet wound in his chest—his bright blood staining the crisp blue and white of his uniform. With a solitary tear and a huff of astonishment, he fell to the ground.

Dead.

My pistol slipped from my blood-slick hand, and I fell back to the floor.

Charlotte froze, gripping Hugo's throat with her claws. She turned to me, red-brown eyes wide and howled an unearthly, terrifying howl. My strength began to wane. I closed my eyes, prepared to accept the end.

"Charlotte," I whispered to the gathering cold. "If only you would have loved me, I would have been yours for eternity."

25

CHARLOTTE

December 17, 1767
Château de Sade
Condé-en-Brie

No. No!

I'd spent too long searching for Antoine. It wasn't hard for me to pick up his trail at first, but I'd been thrown off by the snowstorm and it had been nearly impossible for me to track his scent. I'd lost precious time in finding Sade's estate, and by the time I came in, I'd only caught the tail end of his confrontation with the général. Then, Hugo had materialized, damaged and scarred from his encounter with the beast, but very much alive. *So, he hasn't been dead all this time.*

But I'd been too late. I broke down the door and raced upstairs just in time to see Hugo sink his teeth into Antoine's neck. Red-tinged fury descended as I launched myself at the vampire. He'd met me blow for blow, until I saw Antoine slump to the floor. No. *No! He is mine. Mine.*

I'd grabbed Hugo and lifted him from the ground. I would tear him limb from limb and spread his insides across the snow.

Antoine wheezed and I turned. *No!* I couldn't be too late! Blood leeched from his throat, spilling across the floor. I felt a rising wave of hysteria.

Hugo's brittle laugh choked out from between my claws as he attempted to free himself from my grasp.

"So much for your happy ending," he snarled.

Bastard. I squeezed until I heard a crack and black blood oozed down my arm. Hugo's body slumped to the floor, followed by his severed head.

How's that for a happy ending, you vile bloodsucker.

As quickly as possible, I shifted back to my human form and crawled over to Antoine.

"Antoine," I whispered fervently, trying to staunch the flow of blood from his neck. "Antoine, darling, you must hold on, do you hear me? It isn't your time yet."

He smiled weakly at me, his heartbeat slow and thready.

"Charlotte," he murmured. "You were magnificent. You saved me again. You're always doing that. I don't deserve it."

"Hush, Antoine. You must maintain your strength. I'm going to take you to Van Helsing—she'll put you right. Just hold on a little longer, *d'accord*?" Tears began to stream down my face, falling onto Antoine's forehead as I pulled him into my lap.

"I'm sorry for everything," he said. "Except for kidnapping you. If I hadn't, I would've never met you, my beautiful, infuriating spy."

I sobbed a laugh, trying desperately to figure out what to do. "You cannot leave me, Antoine. You've only just come into my life. We have so much more ahead of us."

His beautiful emerald eyes began to lose their luster. "Tell me," he whispered. "Tell me what we would have ahead of us."

I sniffed and wiped at the tears. "A spring wedding," I said. "We would have asparagus and poached eggs at the wedding breakfast, and *civet de sanglier* for lunch. You and I would sneak away to make love in a wooded glade, then we would jump on Tartuffe and ride for the first roadside inn we could find. It would be clean and comfortable, with a lovely old innkeeper who would keep the fire stoked and bring us wine and pastries."

He smiled and gazed up at me. "Perfect. I wish I could stay with you. I love you, Charlotte. More than anything. I love you more than any man has ever loved any werewolf."

A cry of anguish escaped my throat.

Wait. Any werewolf. A werewolf. I froze.

"Antoine," I said. "Werewolf!"

He was fading, slipping into unconsciousness, and I shook him awake.

"Antoine, let me scratch you. My werewolf claws—don't you see? That's how I was infected! You've already been bitten. *Please.* Please. Let me try. Will you let me try?"

His eyes were unfocused, and his smile was placid, resigned. He was ready to accept the death that I would not. "Anything for you."

Instantaneously, I transformed. *Pain be damned.* As soon as my claws formed, I dug them into Antoine's arm, silently praying and begging his forgiveness. He winced and whimpered, and I changed back to human form just as quickly.

"Do you feel any different?" I asked, shaking him. "Does it feel like you're changing?"

He looked up at me with a sad smile, closed his eyes, and slipped into unconsciousness.

26

CHARLOTTE

December 31, 1767
Château de Ruisseau Magdelaine

"No, Comtesse, there is still no change in his state. Please stop asking me. As soon as something happens, I will come inform you!" Van Helsing waved me off, exasperated.

"Charlotte, *chérie*, come and have a bite to eat. You're wasting away," Daphne ordered, pulling me toward the dinner table.

"I already told you—I'm not hungry. I want to go upstairs and sit with Antoine," I muttered petulantly, sounding very much like a spoiled child.

"Absolutely not," Van Helsing said. "You will disrupt his rest and the healing process."

"This is a fine domestic mutiny on New Year's Eve," I grumbled. "And in my own home, too!"

"It's for your own good," Van Helsing chastised. "And yes, do as the duchesse says—have a bite to eat. There's meat on the table for you."

I sat, scowling, but pulled the plate in front of me. It had been two weeks since the night in the manor house, and every hour had felt like a lifetime.

When Antoine had fallen into unconsciousness, I'd transformed back into my wolf form and carried him to my home. I tended his wounds as best as I could, then took off to bring Van Helsing here. She had no doubt been considerably perplexed by an aggressive werewolf trying to explain a somewhat complicated situation to her through barks and growls, but she eventually got my meaning well enough to get on my back and ride with me back to my château. Once there, she gave him the same tender care she had me, shooing me from the room while Antoine teetered on the precipice of mortality.

I paced the halls, driving her to the brink of madness before she finally convinced me to bring Daphne and Étienne here to keep me company. I'd done so and was immensely grateful for the comfort of family and the distraction, but truthfully, all I wanted was to crawl into bed with Antoine and hold him while his blood fever raged.

In the last few days, the fever had broken, but he had yet to wake. Van Helsing continued to minister to him most carefully, and she had proclaimed him to be in recovery but would give me no more information than that.

Blessedly, Daphne had helped me tidy things up for The Order. The damning letters Antoine had gone to retrieve were smeared with the général's blood, but fortunately, still legible. They outlined his corruption in detail and were more than enough evidence to put this grim matter to rest and prove Antoine the hero I already knew him to be. We presented the evidence to both The Order and the king, along with our account of the events that had led to the deaths of the *bêtes de sang* and Général de Vaux. Naturally, the truth was hidden from the rest of the court and the people of France—what an embarrassment for the king—and an official rumor was whispered in the right circles at court. *The général had taken ill in Menorca and died during the evacuation of French forces from the island. Such a tragedy!*

The Order had suggested a posthumous award for Antoine's bravery and loyalty, but I wouldn't hear of it. *Posthumous, my foot.* He still clung to life—perhaps by the tips of his fingers, but he would make a full recovery. I would see to it. If the Devil came to claim him, he would have to go through me first.

I finished the meat in front of me, and Charles came in to set down a plate of asparagus. I smiled, remembering my promise to Antoine.

Étienne saw the dish and wrinkled his nose. "Honestly, Charlotte, why do you bother with other food? If meat is enough to sustain you, isn't that rather superfluous?"

"Oh, I don't know, *mon amour*," Daphne smiled, eyeing him from beneath her lashes. "Food can be about more than sustenance. It can be about pleasure, too."

Étienne turned a heated gaze on her, and I half expected them to make love right there at the dinner table. He turned back to me, however, and grinned.

"Apologies, dear Charlotte. Sometimes I forget there are worldly pleasures other than my soon-to-be wife."

I stuck my tongue out at him and drenched the vegetable in a lovely lemon cream sauce. I was halfway through the plate when my supernatural hearing picked up movement from upstairs. *Antoine!* Quicker than quick, I rushed upstairs and into his chambers.

He sat up in bed, blinking blearily at me. A slow smile spread across his face. My heart stuttered and, rather embarrassingly, I choked out a sob. Immediately, his smile faltered.

"Charlotte," he said softly. "Please, don't cry. It's all right. I'm all right."

I ran to the bed and launched myself at him, burying my face in his chest. He stroked my back and whispered soothing things to me until I was finally able to compose myself. I tilted my tear-streaked face up at him and kissed him, then slapped him on the shoulder.

"Don't—you—*ever*—scare me like that again," I wailed. "You are not permitted to die unless *I* say so! Do you understand me?"

He chuckled and nuzzled my throat. "I'm sorry. Next time, I'll make sure I've cleared it with you."

"There won't be a next time," I grumbled. "How do you feel?"

"Hungry," he said. "Restless."

"Do you feel like a werewolf?"

"I don't know. What do werewolves feel like?"

I grinned. "Hungry and restless."

"Then yes."

Van Helsing entered the room carrying a plate of meat and her doctor's valise. She moved me to the side and unwrapped Antoine's bandages, gently palpating the places where his injuries had been. As I hoped, his skin was unblemished, and he looked as if he'd never been at death's door. The doctor performed a thorough examination and handed him the plate of meat, which he devoured and declared to be the best thing he'd ever eaten. Van Helsing nodded to me, confirming my suspicions.

He is alive. He is a werewolf. And he is mine.

"I'll leave you two to…ehm. *Discuss* things," she said, pushing her spectacles up and smiling at me. "Try to take it easy, Lieutenant. Or should I say *Capitaine*."

Antoine stared at me in confusion as Van Helsing closed the door behind her. I was already disrobing, eager to feel him alive and warm beneath me.

"*Capitaine?*" he asked.

"*Oui*," I said, tugging my skirts down over my hips. He smiled, his emerald eyes sparkling again and tracking me with green fire. "After the night at Sade's, Daphne and I made a full report to The Order and the king. They believed you would soon leave this mortal realm and offered a posthumous commendation. I refused on your behalf since, of course, I knew you would recover, and I told them when you were healed, you would return for your official promotion in rank. Congratulations, Capitaine de Vaux."

"De Valle," he corrected. "I've heard enough of *de Vaux* for this lifetime, I think."

"As you wish," I replied. He tugged his nightshirt over his head and tossed it to the floor. I stared at him hungrily, admiring the muscles moving beneath his bronzed skin.

"What else has happened since then?" he asked, rising from the bed to approach me.

I bit my lip and pretended to think. "Oh, not much. Your father is dead, and his estate has passed to you, Sade's crimes have become public knowledge, the *bêtes* are well and truly gone, Daphne and Étienne have finally set a wedding date, and Gévaudan has seen nothing of the beast since we left. There are rumors that it has made its way to Paris, but no one truly knows." I pulled my chemise over my head and threw it atop Antoine's. "Christmas was rather dull, but I did get you some wonderful gifts, and Van Helsing, Daphne, and Étienne are here to celebrate the new year with me—with *us*—and…"

Before I could finish, Antoine swooped me up and carried me over to the bed. He dropped me onto the soft blankets and smiled, his dimples flashing. I pulled his face to mine for a heart-stopping kiss.

"And?" he pressed, while I wrapped my legs around his waist and sat astride him.

"And I'm going to make love to you until you need another two weeks to recover," I said huskily, caressing his chest.

He sat up to kiss my breast and my breath caught in my throat.

"Marry me, Charlotte," he murmured, dropping kisses along my collarbone.

"I thought that was a given," I gasped, squirming with desire.

"It is for me, but I wanted to make sure. I love you. I don't want to spend eternity without you by my side. Stay with The Order if you must, but be mine. *Please*," he said.

Tears threatened again and I reasoned I'd cried enough lately, so I covered his lips with mine and slid him inside me. He moaned and gazed up at me, eyes bright with passion.

"So," I gasped, pleasure dancing along my whole body. "A spring wedding?"

EPILOGUE
VAN HELSING

April 13, 1768
Van Helsing's Clinic, Rue Ordener

"Take care of that scraped knee, little one! You must keep it clean. We don't want it to fester, now do we?" I handed the child, probably no more than five, an apple to soothe her tears. Her mother smiled gratefully, and I slipped a small loaf of bread in a bag and handed it to her. "No charge today, Madame. Just keep an eye on these children of yours and come see me if her knee doesn't look improved in a few days."

The woman ushered her three children out the door of my clinic and I sat down with a sigh. It had been a long day. Between my research into the blood plague, the house calls to newly turned vampires worrying over their bodily changes, and maintaining hours in the clinic for the less-fortunate families of Paris, I was exhausted. My days seemed to get longer and longer, and I felt stretched and threadbare. The lingering winter hadn't helped, either. I longed for the warmth and freshness of spring. *When was the last time I saw a field of wildflowers?*

The bell chimed on my door again, and I put down my cup of tea without taking a sip. Weariness settled over me, and I tried to shuck it like a coat. When I looked up, though, I smiled.

"Charlotte!" I grinned. "My friend, what a delight to see you. It's been a while, but I know you are busy with wedding preparations. You look well, Comtesse."

She smiled, and some of the fatigue dissipated. Charlotte had a smile like sunshine, and as a shy, austere foreigner, I gravitated to her friendship like a bee to a flower.

"Thank you, Mina! My goodness, you do look exhausted. You simply must stop overextending yourself. I worry for your health," she fussed, coming over to wrap me in a fierce hug.

I waved her concerns away. "You care for the people of France in your way, and I care for them in mine. Only, I think I got the better bargain. I don't have to kill anyone." I gestured for her to sit down and locked the front door for a moment of peace.

Comfortable in my clinic, she poured herself some tea, pulled a packet of pastries from her pockets, and placed them on the tea tray. *Trust her to come bearing food.*

"Little cakes for us, and I've a large basket of bread in the carriage for you to give your patients," she said.

I grinned and bit into a cake. "Almond! My favorite," I said, eyeing her suspiciously. "What do you want, Charlotte?"

"Whatever can you mean?" she asked sweetly.

"You only bring me almond cakes when you need something from me," I said. "Otherwise, it's lemon, raspberry, cream, chocolate..."

"What an exceptional agent you would make, Doctor. If only you would come and work with us at *les DD*!" She laughed.

I sighed. This wasn't the first time she'd come around to recruit me. "Charlotte, I told you before. I am happy in my role. I will help The Order as I can, but I like not having to answer to anyone but myself."

She pouted but winked at me. "Ah, well. They cannot say that I didn't try! Now tell me, my friend, what do you know of the beast of Gévaudan?"

The cake turned to sand in my mouth, and I coughed.

"Wh—what? Why?"

She eyed me perceptively. "Well, you see, there have been some sightings here in Paris and because of my state, I've been tasked with hunting him down. It's just that he doesn't seem to want to be found, and I've exhausted almost all my leads."

I paled but tried to keep my face a mask of indifference. "Oh?"

"Yes," she nodded, picking up another cake. "And I suddenly remembered that night in the cave outside Grandrieu...the way you looked at him. As if you'd seen him before—as if you knew him."

I took a sip of my tea, alarmed to see my hands shaking.

"Me? That...that's absurd!"

Charlotte cocked a brow, staring pointedly at my hands. "Darling, do me a favor and don't *ever* play cards. You do not possess the capacity to bluff."

I swallowed, not trusting myself to reply.

She sighed and placed her hands over mine. "Wilhelmina, I won't force it out of you. If you don't want to tell me now, that's all right. I'll keep your secret. But I know there is a connection between you, and if I know about it, someone else is sure to discover it. The Order is on his heels, and that means they'll soon be on yours, too."

My heart pounded. I'd run so far and so long from my past...I knew that it would catch up with me at some point. I just didn't think it would be today. *Here. Now.*

Charlotte seemed to take pity on me and leaned forward to give me another hug. When she pulled away, her effervescent manner had returned.

"Now, of course, I'll need your opinion on several *crucial* details about the wedding. Antoine tries so hard to be indulgent, you know, but every time I ask him about opinions on ivory silk versus cream silk versus eggshell silk, his eyes glaze over and he grunts something unintelligible. Do come over this evening, won't you? I'll have cook prepare your favorite foods if you'll help me decide on decor," she gushed.

Still reeling from her devastating news, I could only nod.

"*Parfait! Au revoir, chérie, et à bientôt!*" She hugged me a third time, kissed my cheeks, and whirled out the door of the clinic before I could find my tongue.

I blew out a breath. Lord, I needed something more fortifying than tea after that. I donned my cloak and closed up the clinic, fully intending on heading down the street to the nearby public house, *Le Raisin Perdu. A full dinner and several glasses of wine, I think.*

The sun had set, bathing the street in a soft seashell pink. This was my favorite time of day—when I gave myself permission to rest, relax, and try to prepare for the work that lay ahead. I closed and locked the door, and when my back was turned to the street, I froze. Something instinctive whispered through my body: *run.*

I whirled around, tripping clumsily over the hem of my skirts. I put my hands out, bracing for the fall, but it did not come. Strong arms saved me. When I opened my eyes, I found myself staring into the past I'd fought to forget.

Dark, pitch-black eyes bored into mine, and his frighteningly beautiful face softened into a devastating grin, displaying two full sets of fangs. He opened his lips to say something, and in that moment, I was certain my heart stopped.

"Good evening, Mina."

To be continued in book three of the *Vampires in Versailles* series, *The Doctor and the Devil.*

LONG LOST
A VAMPIRES IN VERSAILLES STORY

AUTHOR'S NOTE

This short story was originally published in a holiday-themed charity anthology some years ago. The events take place after the end of the first book, but before the epilogue that leads to Van Helsing's book.

1

CHARLOTTE

January 20, 1768
Versailles

"It's your turn, Mina, darling."

"I hate this game. I don't want to play," Doctor Van Helsing grumbled. She shifted from foot to foot, tugging at the front of her bodice and anxiously running her hands over the tops of her wide *panniers*.

"You look absolutely gorgeous, *chérie*," Daphne assured. "That powder blue silk brings out your eyes so well."

"I feel like an over-iced pastry," she huffed. "I should never have let you talk me into coming to this dreadful ball. What are we even celebrating? Christmas was a month ago and we had our New Year's *réveillon* already."

I looked around at the luxurious decorations—boughs of blue spruce wove around a pale blue silk-covered table, which practically groaned beneath the elaborate spread of decadent dishes. Spiced wine-drenched roast meats, delicate seafood bisques, beef and pork pies, an embarrassment of fine cheeses, tropical fruits from distant lands—*think of the expense!* —and pastries topped with edible sugar snowflakes glistened beneath glittering silver candelabras. Blue and silver draperies hung at the windows, putting me in mind of a snowy bluebird morning.

"The winter solstice?" I asked.

"That's in December, *chérie*," Daphne replied absently. "Perhaps His

Majesty is simply feeling festive and wishes to celebrate the beauty of winter."

I shrugged. "What does it matter? As long as we have an opportunity for the work at hand…"

"I'd much rather be back in my clinic," Van Helsing complained. "I have so much work to do."

I handed the petulant Dutch physician a glass of champagne.

"Take your medicine," I said with a wry smile. "You'll feel much better."

She wrinkled her nose at the glass. "Champagne gives me a sour stomach and a sore head."

"It's a requirement for socializing with the aristocracy," Daphne chuckled, candlelight glinting off her needle-sharp fangs. Despite being a wealthy and powerful duchesse, her engagement to the king's vampire emissary and her turning had left her on the outskirts of the *tonne*— though it was a consequence she heartily embraced. With the blood plague sweeping through France and the hungry peasants and *bourgeois* deliberately infecting themselves to avoid miserable starving deaths, the few humans of the aristocracy were becoming increasingly anxious. As recently turned supernatural beings, Daphne and I were working hard to try and force the king and court to see reason—to make peace and lend aid to those in need—but we were starting to lose hope. It seemed the more dire the need, the more ferociously the aristocrats clung to their power and wealth.

"The odious Vicomte de Malin has been eyeing you all evening," I teased. "That's fortuitous. If he asks you for a dance, you'll want the fortification. Besides, perhaps the effervescence will improve your mood."

Van Helsing cut her eyes to the vulgar aristocrat, who winked at her. She blanched and downed the glass of golden courage in one abundant swig.

"Don't worry, we'll protect you. If he's foolish enough to try anything untoward, I will take him out into the gardens and eat him," I giggled. My stomach growled, proving my willingness to shift into my werewolf form and dispatch anyone who laid a finger on my dear friend.

Daphne stifled a groan. "You'd have to save some for me, Charlotte. I haven't fed in two days. If I don't get some blood soon, it may affect my cheerful disposition."

Van Helsing and I looked at Daphne incredulously, then let out an unladylike eruption of laughter. Daphne was kind and loyal but known for her at-times *tenacious* character. She pretended to scowl, but her violet eyes glittered with mirth.

"Go on, then, Mina," I wheedled. "It's your turn."

"Pass. Daphne may go in my stead." Van Helsing plucked another glass of champagne from a passing tray. She hiccoughed and frowned at the leering vicomte.

Daphne sighed. "Very well. If I were not engaged to my handsome, charming Étienne—"

I rolled my eyes. "Yes, yes. We know. This is just a game, Daphne!"

"I would seduce Comtesse de Renarde, stab Monsieur Honoré, and sup on Malin," she finished.

"You wouldn't!" I cried, scandalized. "How could you stomach him?"

Her pupils dilated and her nostrils flared—I could sense her hunger. "Very fat. Lots of blood," she murmured, almost trance-like. I cleared my throat and she collected herself, opening her fan to disguise her embarrassment.

"That man is *awash* with garlic," I pointed out. "His blood would reek of it."

"That is a silly superstition, Charlotte. I quite enjoy garlic. The Italians are onto something, you know."

"Still, don't you think you'd want to bite someone else? He still believes bathing is ill for his health."

"Surely, but you dictated the rules of this game and you said they had to be in this ballroom. I challenge you to find a courtier who *does* bathe regularly."

"Fair point," I replied. "Honestly, I don't think I could sleep with *or* eat someone who believed such nonsense." I wrinkled my nose in disgust.

"Well, it's your turn, anyway, if you're so high and mighty about it," Daphne sniffed.

"Right. If I were not engaged to my precious, perfect pastry, Antoine—"

"*Urp.*" Van Helsing covered a burp, mortified. "Sincerest apologies, *mes amies.*"

"I would seduce that lovely lady-in-waiting—what's her name, Danielle? I would certainly stab Malin—though I don't think I'd stab him; I'd probably throttle him because I wouldn't want his poisonous blood all over my lovely gown. And I would sup on Monsieur Honoré."

"He beats his servants, you know," Van Helsing said quietly.

"Yes, we know," I replied, narrowing my eyes at the wealthy landowner. "It would be slow and rather painful for him, I'm afraid."

Daphne nodded sagely. Van Helsing began to look a tad green about the gills.

"Are you well, Mina? You do realize champagne is meant for sipping, not gulping, don't you?"

The doctor nodded, opening her fan with an unsteady hand. "Might we play a different game?"

I arched a brow. "It's not like you to be ill at the discussion of viscera. Do you need some air, *chérie*?"

She nodded vigorously. "It must be the champagne."

I reached for the jewel-studded *chatelaine* at my waist—an heirloom handed down from my mother. The delicate silver chains used to bear all the keys to the rooms of my family estate, but since my mother died, I'd taken to wearing the elaborate pin as a piece of sentimental, yet functional jewelry. Now, instead of the keys, at the end of each chain hung a tiny compartment disguised as a gemstone. The compartments held a set of small lock picks, a tightly coiled *pianoforte* wire I used as a garrote, and I still had enough space for secret messages, occasional poisons, and in this instance, smelling salts. I tugged at the ruby-covered box and offered it up to Van Helsing, who looked at me with the same disgust she would have displayed if I'd tried to hand her a beheaded snake—or an English pastry.

"Don't be ridiculous," she hissed, but her lips were pale and her complexion took on a waxy sheen.

Daphne and I led her through the sparkling gilt room, stuffed with over-important people all trying to catch the eye of His Majesty, King Louis XV. As soon as we made our way to the snow-covered courtyard, I breathed a sigh of relief. Van Helsing gripped the edge of the icy balcony and stared out into the torch-lit gardens.

"It was rather stifling in there," Daphne said, unsuccessfully hiding her concern. "Mina?"

"I'm fine," she said, closing her eyes. "I just detest these things."

"I've seen you face down supernatural terrors, amputate limbs, and stitch your own flesh wounds," I said. "Don't tell me you're overcome by a silly little party with a bunch of pompous wastrels?"

"Give me broken bones and septic wounds over an *allemande* any day," she mumbled. "Though…I don't attend to as many of those wounds as I once did. Lately, it all seems to be about helping new vampires through their transitions. I worry France will run out of blood before we see the end of the grain blight, and then who knows what will happen. We already know the blood plague has the power to mutate—" She looked at me pointedly. "—and I don't want to know what happens when vampires start to feed on each other. My research hasn't been as promising as I'd hoped." She wiped her damp brow with the back of her hand and frowned. "If only the king would do more to help feed his people. I truly fear what comes next."

"He will not," came a velvet voice through the snow-soft silence of the garden. Daphne's fiancé, Étienne, Duc de Noailles and vampire emissary to the king, materialized from the darkness and strode forward, sliding a possessive arm around his soon-to-be duchesse's waist and pulling her in for a ravishing kiss. Snowflakes dusted his raven-dark hair but wouldn't melt without the body heat of humanity. A small, unruly lock had escaped his queue, which—aside from his devilish beauty and rakish charm—was yet another thing that made him stand out at court. He never wore the powdered wigs or pastel colors that were fashionable, but was usually clad in rich, jewel-toned velvets and dark-as-sin silk brocades. His lean, muscular form and sharply angled face did nothing to discourage the notion that he was anything other than what he was—a predator, a *former* libertine, and ever hungry for the love of his eternal life, Daphne.

"Forgive me, *ma cher*, for taking so long. Antoine and I were trying to convince him to import more grain, but he won't hear of it. The prices of food will continue to rise, and so will the numbers of blood plague sufferers," his golden eyes flashed, matching the bite of his bitter tone. "He believes those that choose to turn are abandoning God and deserve to be punished. Not that he would say such things to us, of course. We only hear the rumors of what he says when he is alone with the other nobles."

"Choosing to survive on blood to avoid death by starvation isn't any kind of choice," came a second voice from the darkness. The low rumble of my beloved's tone raised goosebumps along my skin and sent my heart fluttering. Unlike Étienne, Antoine didn't appear to materialize from the gathered night—softly, he stepped forward like a cautious wild creature approaching from some dangerous, otherworldly woodland. Even dressed in his sharp captain's uniform, there was a touch of the primal about his tall, muscular form, his broad shoulders, and the moon-shaped scar that ran along his cheek. His chestnut hair was pulled back tightly, and his strong jaw sported a whisper of stubble that never seemed to leave his cheeks, no matter how often he shaved.

"Antoine!" I breathed, flinging myself at him and burying my face in his chest. He smelled as he always did—even before I turned him and saved his now-immortal life. Earth, leather, mint, apples, and horseflesh—he'd been out riding his favorite black Andalusian, Tartuffe, before coming here tonight. I stood on my toes to nip at his neck, a strange sort of *bon soir* between mates and a promise of lustful adventures ahead.

He blushed and dropped a soft kiss on my cheek. Unlike Daphne and Étienne, Antoine was still shy about public displays of intimacy and affection, which naturally propelled my ardor to white-hot intensity.

"Are you particularly fond of those breeches?" I said brazenly, sliding my hands over his firm ass. "Or will you give me leave to rip them to shreds when we get to the carriage?"

His blush spread from his cheeks to his ears and throat—my reward for being so bold. His moss green eyes darkened like night falling in a forest, and he leaned forward, brushing his stubble across my cheek.

"If you keep teasing me in public," he murmured in my ear. "I will be forced to punish you when we return home."

A satisfied growl emanated from my chest. "Tell me how," I breathed.

"Oh, do save it for the ride home," Daphne begged. "Those of us with supernatural senses can still hear you."

"Spoilsport," I pouted. Antoine winked at me, making me seriously consider leaving the ball early.

"Please," Van Helsing interjected. "Give me leave to return to my clinic. Or to go home. I'm too weary to be polite to the men whose servants I treat for various forms of abuse."

"But we only just arrived!" I complained. "And it's incredibly lucky that the Vicomte de Malin has been lusting after you—we're so close to finalizing a course of action for him and we could use your help in learning his whereabouts over the next few weeks."

"I do not work for The Order," Van Helsing replied. "I do not want to be involved in your organization's brand of punishing justice. I only care to heal people and to find a cure for the blood plague."

"Of course, *chérie*. We know how you feel about The Order, and we'd never ask you to betray your conscience. We only wish to know when he'll be leaving for his country estate. We just want to have a little…*exploratory adventure* in his private study. There are questions about some rather indelicate and potentially treasonous activities. We've asked his servants but they're too afraid to tell us anything," I explained, approaching to link arms with her.

"What will The Order do with the information?" she asked hesitantly.

The Order—a long-shadowed organization of the powerful and elite—often performed their own investigations into potential threats to king and country. They delivered justice that was, at times, beyond His Majesty's reach. Daphne and I had been working from within to curb their penchant for violence against impoverished vampire-kind, but it was getting harder to convince them to do what was necessary to support the middle and lower classes. Under the guise of establishing a group of women agents to serve The Order, we'd formed *les Dames Dangereuses* and were keeping a close eye on our male contemporaries. I didn't fault Van Helsing for being distrustful of them—I often felt that way myself. Still, I did what I could to help provide balance and ensure that the people being *punished* truly deserved what came their way. The Vicomte de Malin deserved more than most.

"Truly, *chérie*, I cannot say. But if we find the proof that we're looking for—that we are almost certain is there—I suspect he will meet an untimely end." I shrugged. "Given the number of servants from his household alone that you've patched up, I would think you'd consider that a fitting end."

"I can't have another man's death on my conscience," she said quietly. The phrasing struck me as odd, but I didn't press. It was likely she had seen death come too often in her line of work. I understood and respected her decision, but I couldn't hide my disappointment.

I nodded. "As you wish, *chérie*. I'll not press you again. Daphne, it looks like we're on with our original plan."

Suddenly Antoine, who stood furthest back from our little cabal and closest to the ballroom, hissed at us.

"Hush!" he whispered. He tipped his nose up to catch the scent of something on the wind. "He's coming, *mes amies*."

He and Étienne melted back into the darkness, leaving Daphne, Van Helsing, and I alone on the terrace. As predicted, Malin strode toward us with the equally distasteful Monsieur Honoré in tow.

Van Helsing flashed a pleading look at Daphne, undoubtedly hoping she would not address the men. As the highest ranking among us, Daphne could control the entire situation. If she did not acknowledge either man, they wouldn't speak to us. Unfortunately for Van Helsing, our plan dictated otherwise.

"*Bon soir*, Monsieur le Vicomte. Monsieur Honoré," she nodded briefly, her predatory smile looking polite and frightening all at once.

Both men bowed low. "Your Grace," they said in unison. Malin eyed Van Helsing with the same hunger as Daphne eyeing his pulsing neck vein. I didn't bother to hide my grin.

"Are you enjoying the wintry festivities, Monsieur Honoré?" I offered, reaching deep for my aristocratic charm.

"Indeed, Comtesse de Brionne, though I could enjoy it a bit more if you'd save a dance for me. Something vigorous, perhaps, to match your fertile temper." He smiled lasciviously at me, eyeing my breasts pressing against the low neckline of my bodice. *Disgusting. Perhaps I would simply eat him, after all.*

"Of course, Monsieur," I tittered. "I'd be delighted."

A disembodied growl punctuated the night air. The sound sent a thrill through me. *Ah, sweet Antoine seems a tad jealous. Poor thing. I'd much rather dance with him, but I must suffer through this to distract Honoré enough to let Daphne extract the information we need from Malin.*

Malin extended his hand to Van Helsing. Daphne attempted to redirect his gesture by ushering us back toward the ballroom again, but he remained unmoved.

"And you, Mademoiselle? I don't believe I've had the pleasure." The way he said *pleasure* made all three of us try not to grimace. Still—this was *the plan.*

"I'm afraid Doctor Van Helsing was just leaving, Malin," Daphne replied. "Perhaps you'd favor me with a turn about the room instead."

Something like shock lit in the vicomte's piggy eyes. "A physician! But she is a woman! How utterly absurd."

"I say, *Doctor,* I fear some of my humors may be out of balance. Perhaps we may find a quiet room where you might *examine* me," Honoré oozed, earning a mule-like guffaw from Malin.

"What a ridiculous liberal notion," Malin continued. "A *woman* in the sciences. If your spinsterhood has forced you into a profession, pet, perhaps we could come to some sort of arrangement? I've only just cut ties with my former mistress—an opera singer of some note. There's a ready vacancy to be filled. Or perhaps you'll allow me to fill *your* vacancy."

Fury rolled off Van Helsing like waves heralding a storm at sea. Another uproarious bout of drunken laughter came from the pair. My lip curled in disgust before I could school my expression in aristocratic blandness, and unfortunately Honoré noticed. His hand was on my wrist in a movement much quicker than I would have expected.

"Have you something to add, Comtesse de Brionne?" He glared at me, cruel eyes assessing my response through the sour fog of spirits. I felt my canine teeth lengthening.

Daphne kicked me from beneath her skirts—a clear direction to *stay the course. Remember the plan.*

I swallowed my rage and hunger, turning an absurd pout on the man.

"But Monsieur Honoré, you promised *me* a dance. Surely you haven't forgotten already?"

His grip relaxed—I almost mourned the opportunity to break his hand and rip his arm from its socket—and his oily grin returned.

"Certainly, Madame," he replied, tugging me forward. Though I was much stronger than he, I allowed him the luxury of believing he held the upper hand. Precious few aristocrats knew of Antoine and my supernatural state, and we aimed to keep it that way.

Daphne stepped forward as well, poised to offer Malin her hand for the dance no one wanted. Van Helsing cut her off, offering the vicomte a frosty smile to match the cold blue of her eyes. Even I shivered, and I'd long since stopped feeling the cold. Had the man an ounce of sense in him, he would have recognized the danger in her expression.

"Monsieur," she said, glacial eyes glittering. "I do have a vacancy on my dance card." She extended her arm to him and the delighted, disgusting ass led her inside. She glanced at Daphne and I with a look that said, *Leave him to me.*

I only hoped there would be enough of him left over when she was through with him.

2

CHARLOTTE

January 20, 1768
Versailles

Fat, wet globs of snow dripped through the trees and splattered on top of the frozen mud that crunched beneath the carriage wheels. If I were human, I would have been extremely put out by the frosty conditions, but they barely registered. The only temperature I felt anymore was usually in relation to Antoine, and it was only ever feverish.

Irritatingly, he sulked in the carriage as we ventured home, making it exceedingly difficult for me to peel his clothing from his brooding form. I made a noise of frustration as I attempted to yank the coat of his lovely blue and white formal uniform down over his impressively broad shoulders and expansive chest. He did not lift his arms to aid me, but held me firmly in his lap, jade eyes boring into mine.

"You are not listening to me, *mon amour*," he said in a low voice as I fiddled with the buttons on his breeches.

"Of course, I am! It's simply that I can hear you better when you are naked."

He didn't smile outright, but I could tell he wanted to by the way the edges of his lips twitched. He stayed my fervent touch with one hand and brought his other up to my cheek.

"I know your work is important, Charlotte, but you must understand how much I hate seeing other men paw at you."

"Jealous, Antoine? Or worried?" I teased.

"Neither. I trust you and I know you are more than capable of taking care of yourself. I just dislike how these titled men think they can press their advantage simply because you are a woman," he said softly, running his thumb across my lips. "Like you are a mere *plaything* to the likes of them. You're a comtesse, for fuck's sake, and my fiancée."

I leaned forward to press a gentle kiss to his forehead. "It's charades, *chéri*. That's all. When I flirt with them, it's never for pleasure. It's to give them the illusion of control. It's enough to be taken for granted, so that when I strike, they don't see it coming."

He harrumphed and frowned, flexing the moon-shaped scar across his brow.

"Besides, you are the only man for whom I would ever consent to be a *plaything*. I love you, Antoine—enough to spend eternity with you. But my work with *les DD* is for all the women in France who are at the mercy of powerful men. Not all of them are as lucky as I am."

My words unlocked him and he finally smiled, flashing dazzling white teeth in the darkness of the carriage. Hastily, he shucked his coat and slid one hand beneath the gold silk of my skirts.

"How much longer until we arrive home?" he murmured. "I want to hear more about your willingness to be my plaything."

I kissed him then, long and lush, sucking on his full bottom lip. Twining my fingers in his dark, wavy hair, I chuckled. "Darling, if you so wish it, I'll be your *anything*."

Supernatural eyes glowing, his hot gaze shot to mine. "You are my *everything*."

The carriage slowed, indicating that we'd approached the tree-lined drive of my family estate, where Antoine now resided with me. It was improper and scandalous, but we were engaged and since I was already a widow, I was allowed some latitude from the censure of the *tonne*.

"*Merde*," I swore. "Shall we send the carriage around again? We can be quick!"

His low laughter filled the space just as his clever fingers found the slick seam of my sex, already aching for him. Gently circling one fingertip at the apex of my pleasure, he growled in my ear. I bit back a moan.

"I do not *want* to be quick."

With that, he picked me up, kicked open the carriage door, and carried me up the icy steps to our home, still decorated for Christmas and New Year's *Réveillon* celebrations. Evergreen branches and holly boughs made the whole *château* smell like a wintry forest. Candles guttered in the chill wind, their light flickering on shining gold and red decorations. The scents of spices lingered in the air—ginger, cinnamon, and cloves—making my mouth water almost as much as Antoine did. When we reached the main bedroom on the second floor, he tossed me on the bed and dove down after me.

"I must make an early start tomorrow, *mon amour*," he huffed, tugging at the ties on my skirts. "I'm off to oversee the training of my new regiment." Before the heavy silk fell to the floor, he was already unpinning my bodice and nearly ripping the ribbon from my stays.

"I thought you said you didn't want to be quick," I teased. "I think this is the fastest you've ever undressed me."

He grinned and tugged his shirt over his head. I sucked in a breath. Even though we had eternity together, I didn't think I would ever get used to the raw beauty of him. Muscles like iron flexed beneath golden skin and dark hair sprayed across his chest and trailed below his belly button. The scars from a lifetime of battles decorated his too-perfect body, sharply contrasting his peaceful nature. He acknowledged my appraisal with a saucy wink, and I giggled and slipped out of my chemise.

"I can't help it," he retorted. "I've been thinking about you all evening." He pulled his breeches off and crawled up my body on the bed, dropping feather-light kisses up my legs and hips. "But I promise to take my time with your pleasure."

He nipped at my hipbone and spread my sex with his thumbs, baring my intimate secrets to him. He sighed in satisfaction, then drew one long, slow lick up my center, making me squirm and swear on an out breath. Pulling one of my legs over his shoulder, he nibbled at the inside of my thigh before returning his attentions to my desperate sex. Heat flared inside me like a bonfire of old tinder, and I knew it wouldn't take long for me to find my bliss. Again and again he licked, driving me toward some distant utopian galaxy that lay just beyond reach.

"Slow down, my love—I want you too badly," I pleaded. Chuckling at my torment, he found the peak of my need and sucked at it, then slid one long finger—then two—inside me. *Perfection.* "Please, Antoine, share with me *la petite mort*. I do not want it without you."

"As you wish, *chérie*," he growled, lowering my leg from his shoulder and moving up my body. Impatiently, I wrapped my legs around his waist and reached down to find him—glorious, hot, and hard. Gritting his teeth, he hissed a breath.

"I was going to take my time," he muttered, somewhat forlorn. "But I fear this will be quicker than I wish."

I slid him inside me on a gratifying moan from us both. He struggled valiantly to move slowly, trying to be noble and prolong my pleasure, but my love for Antoine would put Aphrodite to shame, and I could bear his slow romance no longer.

"Antoine," I huffed, slick with sweat and desire. "This is only the first bout. Fuck me like you mean it, damn it."

That heart-stopping, lop-sided grin again and he drove into me with enough force to crack the heavy oak bed. *Yes. Yes!* Harder and faster he moved, reaching the place inside me that I believed would let me see the face of God—or perhaps Lucifer. My back arched and he took my nipple into his mouth, but soon abandoned it with an uttered string of delicious obscenities. Stars danced around the edges of my vision, and that distant world spun into view, dancing closer and closer until we crashed into it together, orbiting as one perfect heavenly body. Waves of pleasure rocked through me, and Antoine held me as we came down, vibrating with exhausted joy.

"*Je t'aime, Charlotte,*" he whispered. "Now and forever."

"I love you, too, Antoine," I replied, nuzzling into his neck. "I'm going to miss you while you're away. What am I to do without you?"

His large hand swept over my stomach to rest gently on the swell of my hip, and I could hear the smile in his voice when he answered.

"You'll just have to think of all the things we can do upon my return."

"Oh, I have a few things in mind already," I sighed, tilting my head up to nip at his earlobe. "But it would be best if we tested a few of them out—just in case. What if you don't enjoy them?"

"Well, then," he conceded, pulling me on top of him. "I suppose we should try them out. *Just in case.*"

I was delighted to learn that Antoine enjoyed every single one.

THE FOLLOWING EVENING, I AWOKE IN A DISAPPOINTINGLY EMPTY BED, SAVE for the rose on the pillow next to me. From any other man, I would have scoffed at the saccharine gesture, but from Antoine, it was wonderful.

I'd hardly had time to throw on my dressing gown and call for some supper when Daphne whirled in, determined to yank me from my rest and relaxation.

"The sun has barely set, Daphne," I groaned. "What has you so vexed?"

"Have you spoken with her?"

"With whom, dearest?" I replied, stifling a yawn.

"Van Helsing!" she cried in exasperation.

"Not after last night, and not in detail. I lost track of her and Malin on the dance floor, and then after the dance ended, she handed me a note with some dates on it—presumably dates that he would be at his country estate—and left for the night. I assumed she simply danced with him, found out when he would be gone, and then went home for the evening," I shrugged. "Why? Has something happened?"

Daphne closed her eyes and pinched the bridge of her nose. "Malin never returned home last night."

Shock froze me in place. "You don't think..."

Daphne looked at me helplessly. "I don't know! I don't think she would do anything, but I certainly do not doubt her capacity to do so. She'd had a great deal of champagne and was absolutely furious about his advances."

"No," I stated firmly. "Certainly not. Van Helsing wouldn't have done anything to him. She has been so adamant about staying away from The Order and anything violent or nefarious. The bastard is probably with a mistress or sleeping off his drunkenness back at Versailles. I'm sure he'll turn up."

Daphne frowned. "Show me the note."

Unnerved by her manner, I went to my hastily discarded gown to get the note from its hiding place in my *chatelaine*. Antoine and I had been so distracted in our intimate attentions, I hadn't bothered to unpin the jewelry from its place on my bodice.

It was gone.

Panic edged into my chest, but I refused to let it take root. *It must be here!* Discarded in our hasty attempt to divest each other of our clothes— or perhaps it fell off in the carriage. I rang for my housekeeper, Madame Toussaint.

"Madame, have you seen my *chatelaine*? It is not here," I said, rifling through the mess of garments on the floor.

"*Non*, my lady," she replied, brows furrowing. "I have not seen it since you left for the ball last night. I'll assemble the staff and ask if it's been found."

"Check the carriage, as well, please," I said.

Daphne's eyes went wide as I hurried to dress.

"Do you think it is truly lost? Could it have fallen off your gown?" she whispered. "Or is it possible that someone stole it?"

"No—I don't know how they would have! Antoine and I came straight home after the ball. I had it when we went outside onto the terrace because I thought Van Helsing was going to faint, and then..."

No. Oh no. The fear I'd been holding at bay finally overwhelmed me as I considered the damning possibility.

"You don't think Monsieur Honoré took it, do you?" I choked out, incredulous. "Could he have? He was drunk! I don't understand why he would steal from me...it's only a mere bauble to him. He wouldn't know its true purpose or of my affiliation with The Order."

Daphne's brows knitted together and she blew out a breath. "It's possible that he's smarter than he looks. I don't know. What else did you have in the compartments? And what else was on the note from Van Helsing?"

I tried to remember. "I had smelling salts, my lock picks, my garrote, and a few other blank scraps of paper. And I only remember some dates on the note from Van Helsing, but we should probably check with her. Wait...did you go to her clinic already? What brought you here this evening?"

She sighed and came over to help me cinch my stays and pin my hair up. "I went by first thing this evening, but she did not answer. There were no lamps or candles lit and the door was locked."

Worry gathered in my stomach. "She is probably sleeping off the champagne," I said, but didn't feel entirely confident.

"With Van Helsing *and* Malin missing, plus your *chatelaine*, I fear there might be something more dangerous afoot," Daphne said.

"Well, first things first," I declared, putting on my favorite pair of gloves. "We must find Van Helsing and ensure that she is well. Let's go back to her clinic."

Daphne nodded. "Agreed. Let's take my carriage—it should still be out front and your footmen might be searching yours for your *chatelaine*."

We stepped out into the silvery night and I inhaled deeply. I'd loved the damp smell of freshly fallen snow before I was turned, but now with my supernatural abilities, I could sense a great deal more in the air. Woodsmoke from distant fireplaces, the domestic aromas of dinners being cooked, beeswax candles dripping, the earthy smell of horses and dogs, and skeletal winter trees—their bare branches bowing beneath the weight of the snow. I could even close my eyes and my nose would paint me a picture of all that lay before me—it was a wonderful boon to temper the excruciating pain that came with shifting form. I imagined Daphne and Étienne felt the same way about being vampires. The price of blood-drinking was a high one to pay for similar supernatural gifts.

Her footman ushered us into her well-appointed carriage and she settled back against the plush seats. She opened a small side panel next to her and pulled out a small champagne coupe and a crystal decanter filled with blood.

"Have you eaten, *chérie*?" she asked, filling her glass.

In answer, my stomach rumbled. Smiling, she pulled out a small basket covered with linen and handed it to me. Inside was a sizable cut of raw venison—one of my new favorites.

"Oh, thank you, darling! You're an absolute angel." I was *ravenous*. I pulled my gloves off and concentrated on extending one long claw from my fingertip. The dagger-sharp nail grew long enough for me to slice portions of the steak and I delicately dropped them into my watering mouth.

Heaven!

"So," I began after swallowing. "What do *you* truly think happened?"

She lifted one pale shoulder in a small shrug. "I have my suspicions, but I cannot be sure. To answer your next question, *no*, I do not think Van Helsing murdered Malin. I'm sure you're right and the blackguard will turn up—eventually. As to our other problem…I do not think it is past Monsieur Honoré to steal your *chatelaine*. Whether it was because he suspected you of hiding secrets, or because he is simply a greedy thief, I cannot say."

The venison churned in my stomach. The idea that I could have been thwarted by the evil man was disturbing at best and life-altering at worst. I'd only been bested by one man before, and I'd just spent the night in his arms. *Antoine.* I wondered where he was at this moment.

Sometime later, we arrived at Van Helsing's clinic on the *Rue Ordener*. She lived in a small apartment above the clinic and despite her success as a physician and notable scientist, she preferred to live a somewhat spartan lifestyle. I'd long ago offered to find her a larger estate, to help expand her clinic, to secure more funding for her research from the aristocracy, and *at the very least* gift her with a sizable wardrobe so that she might accompany Daphne and I to more parties. She'd laughed at several of the offers and scoffed at the rest, thanking me for my generosity but stalwartly refusing to live a life that didn't suit her. Daphne and I loved her for that.

I was heartened to see lamps lit upstairs and scent her familiar fragrance—wool, soap, herbs, almonds, lime blossom. I saw the relief in Daphne's face, as well.

Rather than enter through the clinic door, which was locked and bolted, we approached through a back stairwell off the side alley. When we knocked, she answered immediately, looking none the worse for wear.

"Bon soir!" she said, wiping her hands on an apron and ushering us inside a small study. "How are you, *mes amies?* You both look well."

"Where have you been? I was here only an hour ago," Daphne sighed in exasperation.

"I was out visiting patients," she replied, obviously perplexed by Daphne's manner. "Is everything all right?"

"Yes."

"No!"

Daphne and I spoke at the same time. Van Helsing's eyebrows shot up.

"Shall I make us some tea? I've got a lovely new herbal blend that will help settle your nerves," she said, busying herself around a shelf of small porcelain jars.

"Mina," I began, cutting Daphne off. "What exactly happened last night?"

"What do you mean? We were all there together the whole evening. What's going on?" she regarded the two of us suspiciously.

"No, *chérie*, I mean during that last dance and then afterward. I lost track of you while I was dancing with the vile Monsieur Honoré. Did something happen with Vicomte de Malin?" Daphne queried.

Her blue eyes turned frosty. "Such as?"

"We aren't accusing you of anything, Mina, but Malin happens to be missing. We simply want to know what you remember of him after the dance ended."

"Missing? When? How? *Mon Dieu…*" she sat down on a wooden stool and took a moment to compose herself.

"The gossip today was that he hasn't been seen since the end of the ball last night, and no one has come forward with any information. Not even Honoré has offered an explanation, and those two are thick as thieves," Daphne replied. "It's as if the man vanished into thin air after…after…"

"After we danced," Van Helsing finished. Her gaze snapped to ours. "I didn't kill him! We danced—that was all. I flattered him enough to merit an *unwelcome* invitation to his country estate, which he said he'd be leaving for in a fortnight. I scribbled the dates down and passed them to you as I left. I came home immediately after—I'm afraid I didn't see where he went after our dance. He was vile and certainly drunk, but I swear nothing else happened after that. Despite my distaste for the man, I would never have harmed him. I prefer he face justice in a lawful way."

I nodded. "Of course we believe you, darling. Did he say anything else to you that might indicate his current whereabouts?"

Van Helsing's face scrunched charmingly as she thought back. "I don't know. I don't think so, but I'm not a spy, so I wouldn't know what to listen for. He droned on about his former mistress—the opera singer—as if to convince me that he was fully done with her and that I would be a welcome addition to his nauseating, adulterous club."

Curiosity seized me. "What was her name?"

"She's Italian, I believe. Nadia something."

"Russo," Daphne and I replied in unison. We knew of the soprano—as famous for her violent temper as her vibrato. I couldn't believe that she'd let the awful vicomte even touch the hem of her skirts, let alone her person, but to each their own. It was a thin lead, but certainly a starting place.

"Well," I said with a smile. "You know what they say about a woman scorned."

Daphne grinned. "*Mes dames,* I believe we're headed to the opera."

3
CHARLOTTE

January 21, 1768
Versailles

THE *THÉÂTRE DES TUILERIES* WAS A SHORT DISTANCE FROM VAN HELSING'S clinic, so we piled back into Daphne's carriage and made haste. Despite the hour and the bitter weather, the streets bustled with sounds of vampire peasants adjusting to their new supernatural life. Raucous laughter poured out of a handful of vampire-friendly taverns and the wind carried scents of sizzling *boudin noir* and spiced wine fortified with blood.

The winter chill had started to seep in despite the carriage's plush interior, and since Daphne and I were no longer bothered by the cold, we bundled Van Helsing in every available blanket.

"By the way, Mina, I don't suppose you recall seeing my *chatelaine* after the last dance at the ball, do you? It seems to have disappeared," I asked, now that her teeth had stopped chattering.

"*Non,* I'm sorry," she replied. "I only remember seeing it when you offered me your smelling salts. Truthfully, I was still too put out by the vicomte to pay much mind to anything other than returning home. Is it important?"

It had been a long shot, but I was still disappointed.

"It was my mother's," I replied. "My father had it made for her when they married. She gave it to me when she—" I trailed off, emotion catching in my throat. Reaching for a light tone, I continued. "I would very much like to have it."

She frowned. "I wish I could be more help. Perhaps it will turn up."

I opened my mouth to reply again, but the carriage slowed, signaling our arrival at the opera house.

"Are you certain you don't want to wait in the carriage?" Daphne asked. "Charlotte and I can handle this. We just want to talk to Signora Russo and…you know. *Sniff around.*"

I chuckled at the jest, but Van Helsing's expression was grave. "It was my choice to get involved last night, and it will be on my conscience if something has happened to the man. If he's hurt or injured, I may be able to help." Her eyes darkened and she muttered, *"Not that he deserves it."*

"Very well," Daphne replied, then looked at me. "Do we have a plan?"

I lifted a shoulder in a shrug. "Not really. Go in, gain access to her dressing room, ask her enough questions to ascertain if she murdered her former lover, and take it from there."

Daphne sighed. "Normally, I have more time to plan these things, but I don't think we can afford to wait."

"I'm sure it will be fine," I said, though I felt a little less confident without my *chatelaine* at my side.

There didn't appear to be a performance tonight but there was a lot of activity at the theater as the company cleaned, dressed the set, and rehearsed for *Orfeo ed Euridice*. Van Helsing was somewhat anxious as we entered the grand hall, but I whispered to her to keep to the shadowy edges of the room and act as if we belonged there. I was prepared for someone to stop us, but as everyone seemed rather busy, no one paid much attention to us.

When we found the candlelit corridor behind the main stage, I breathed a small sigh of relief. We could hear the impressive trill of a high *c* coming from a room toward the end of the hall, which had to be Signora Russo.

Daphne knocked on the door and we heard a litany of profane Italian, followed by frantic shuffling.

"I said I didn't want to be disturbed until we're ready to rehearse!" she bellowed, pulling the door open with great force. Her beautiful brown eyes widened when she saw the three of us standing in the hallway, and before she had the chance to recover, I pushed forward into her dressing room.

"Madame Russo!" I cried, embracing her. "It is such an honor—truly! Please forgive my companions and I, but we are such great admirers of you that we were desperate to come meet you. We knew that you would be engaged on the night of a performance and decided to venture forth on an off night to make your acquaintance."

"Ah, *grazie,*" she replied, still quite stunned and confused. Not wanting to give her the chance to recover and shunt us to the door, I continued.

"Duchesse de Duras, may I present the esteemed Signora Nadia Russo. I am Comtesse de Brionne, and our companion is Doctor Van Helsing—another ardent lover of the opera."

The singer curtsied deeply to us and opened her mouth to speak, but I cut her off again.

"You are playing the lead in *Orfeo ed Euridice,* are you not? That is *so* thrilling. I simply adore a tragic love story. Actually, I adore *any* love story, but the tragic ones always have the better music, don't you find?" I whirled around her room, inhaling deeply, trying to scent the vicomte or anything else suspicious, but the dressing room was a riot of overpowering fragrances. Perfume, stage makeup, dust, wine, stale sweat from old costumes, and the heady aroma of a rose bouquet on top of her dressing table.

"Such lovely flowers," Daphne commented, seeing where my attention fell. "And so hard to find exceptional roses in the middle of winter. You *must* tell me who your florist is."

Signora Russo's eyes widened a fraction and I could hear the hitch in her pulse. Seizing the opportunity, I went to the table and plucked the card from the center of the bouquet before she could stop me.

Forgive me, mon petit chou, the card read. I brought it up to my nose and sniffed—it reeked of the vicomte.

"My, my," I drawled. "It seems you have quite the devotee."

Anger colored the singer's face, darkening her chocolate eyes and turning her cheeks as red as the roses on her table. She crossed her arms in front of her ample bosom and nodded at the door.

"I think perhaps you ladies have overstayed your welcome," she said haughtily. "It's rather uncouth of you to pry into my personal affairs—admirers or no."

At that moment, a soft thump sounded from somewhere in the room. No one moved. Daphne, Van Helsing, and I looked at each other.

"Go!" Signora Russo shouted. "Get out!"

Again, the dull sounds arose, a muted shuffling and light scraping. This time, I pinpointed it to a large armoire in the back of the room, which I'd assumed was filled with elaborate opera costumery and the singer's personal clothing.

Daphne must have heard it at the same time, for she crossed the room in swift strides and threw open the door. Out tumbled the villainous vicomte—blindfolded, bound, gagged, and apparently beginning to regain consciousness.

We all turned to stare at Signora Russo, whose fury remained frozen on her visage. After several moments of stunned silence, she arched a supercilious eyebrow and shrugged.

"I'll have you know, *he* started it," she snapped.

We continued to stare in astonishment. Finally, Daphne recovered enough to entreat, "Do explain."

"He came to my room late last night—or perhaps it was early in the morning, I don't know. It was dark out, and he was stinking drunk. He brought me flowers and told me that he'd made a mistake ending our arrangement. I refused him. *No one* humiliates la Signora Russo! He did not take kindly to my rejection," she said, venom in her voice.

Van Helsing went over to the man and removed the blindfold and gag, but kept him bound. She looked him over and nodded to me.

"He's had a terrible knock on the head and has been given opium, I'd wager, but he's otherwise unharmed," she said.

"Laudanum," Signora Russo offered, matter-of-factly. "When he made certain advances, I hit him over the head with a candlestick, which dazed him enough for me to drug him. I planned to have the doorman take him back to his home after our rehearsal ended and leave him in the care of his good lady wife."

"You…you mean, you weren't bitter about being scorned and sought to end your torment by kidnapping him? Or killing him?" I asked, somewhat disappointed.

Signora Russo tipped her head back and laughed until tears gathered in the corners of her eyes.

"Goodness no," she replied. "When our arrangement ended, I was able to find a much more agreeable patron. I was perfectly happy until he showed up again."

The vicomte moaned and slumped back down on the floor. No one approached him to help.

"She knocked out the vicomte and drugged him," Daphne whispered to me. "I'm a bit unsure about how we should proceed. What are we going to do with her?"

I grinned. "Recruit her."

TWO HOURS LATER, WE'D RETURNED THE INSENSATE VICOMTE TO HIS townhouse with a hasty explanation, but the Vicomtesse de Malin didn't seem overly concerned. She didn't even bother to inquire about the name of the woman he'd been with, leaving me to wonder if anyone actually cared for the bastard. His wife had simply wrinkled her nose at the bedraggled man and instructed the footmen to bathe him and lock him in his room.

As the carriage trundled back toward *Rue Ordener*, Daphne and I bickered about Signora Russo, who we agreed should be well compensated for her silence about the incident with the vicomte. I wanted to recruit her into *les Dames Dangereuses* immediately, but Daphne insisted we spend more time looking into her background and her politics before inviting her to join our covert agency. It made sense, I supposed.

As was her custom, Van Helsing grumbled the whole way back to her clinic, declaring that she never should have consented to help us in the first place. She swore roundly that she was done befriending vampires and werewolves, as we constantly made trouble for her. Naturally, I agreed, but reminded her that her life would likely be deadly dull without us, which she grudgingly acknowledged. Momentarily assuaged, she kissed us goodbye, and I promised to bring her a peace offering of her favorite almond cakes the following evening.

Daphne and I rested in companionable silence on our way back to my *château*.

"What are you going to tell The Order?" I asked.

"Most of the truth, I think," she replied. "Malin had a lover's quarrel and is now at home with his wife, safe and mostly sound…though I don't envy the recovery from a head wound and an ill-advised amount of laudanum. We'll still go ahead with the rest of our plans, assuming tonight's events don't impact his scheduled departure to the country."

"Of course," I agreed. "But running investigations into Malin and Monsieur Honoré's affairs will need to wait. I'm exhausted and starving. I long for justice, certainly, but first I wish to have a hot bath, a large meal, and a long sleep."

Daphne covered a yawn, which I took as tacit agreement. I noticed through the carriage's blacked out windows that the sun was rising and the dark sky was fading to a lovely periwinkle. When the carriage trundled up my drive, I gave her a brief embrace and dragged myself out and up the stairs to my front door.

I still found it difficult at times to keep to the nighttime schedule that the country increasingly favored, but I knew it would get easier with time.

"Madame Toussaint, please send up a hot bath and some dinner. Beef, if we have it, and some roasted carrots, bread and butter, cheese, and wine, please."

"Of course, my lady," she said. "Regretfully, no one was able to find your *chatelaine*. We checked the house, your wardrobe, the carriage—one of the footmen even went so far as to retrace the coachman's route to Versailles. It appears to be lost."

My heart sank, but I forced a smile. "Thank you, Madame. I appreciate everyone's efforts, nonetheless. I shall just have to have a new one, I suppose."

The disappointing news weighed me down with melancholy. I felt so careless, losing the one heirloom I truly cherished. A tear slipped down my cheek as I undressed, and with the fatigue, stress of the day, and hunger gnawing at me, I embraced the sadness and melancholy. By the time the large copper tub was filled with piping hot water, I was sobbing like a baby. I poured myself a large glass of wine, intent on drinking through my despair.

I was so wrapped up in my glorious wallow that I barely noticed Antoine until he rushed in, worry etched on his handsome face.

"Charlotte! What is it? Are you injured? What's happened?" He leaned forward to cradle my face between his hands.

"Darling!" I sniffed, surprised. "I thought you were away for training."

"I was—I am. But I missed you… I wanted to be with you. When the troops turned in after drills today, I shifted and ran here as fast as I could. Much faster than a carriage ride," he said, wiping my tears with his thumbs. "What has happened? Why are you crying?"

"It's nothing, *chéri*. I'm so glad you're home! How long do you have before you must return? How was it?"

Antoine pushed a damp lock of my hair from my face, the concern still heavy in his gaze.

"Charlotte," he murmured. "Tell me what troubles you."

Tears threatened to spill again and I swallowed.

"It will seem silly," I said quietly, swirling my hand through the water.

"If you truly do not wish to tell me, you don't need to," he said.

He pulled a chair over to the side of the tub, methodically removed his jacket and draped it over the back. He rolled the cuffs of his shirtsleeves up, slowly exposing his tanned forearms to the golden light of the candles and the crackling fire in the bedroom hearth. The corded muscles bunched and flexed, which was at once mesmerizing, soothing, and erotic. When he was through, he plucked my wine glass from my hand, refilled it, and handed it back to me.

"I promise I shall not laugh," he said.

He dropped to his knees behind me and tilted my head back, then started to pull pin after pin from my coiffure. I felt the soft weight of my hair fall around my shoulders as he worked, gently threading his fingers through my curls when he'd removed all the pins. The sensation was heavenly. I closed my eyes and relaxed into the pampering, exhaling much of my stress. He lightly massaged my scalp, then poured a bowl of the warm water over my head, careful to keep it off my face.

"I don't talk about them much," I heard myself saying. "My parents."

He picked up the lavender-scented soap and quietly worked up a lather, then spread it through my wet locks.

"They were wonderful, you know," I continued. "My father was kind and thoughtful, and my mother was warm and affectionate. They were lucky enough to have a love match—they wanted scores of children, but my mother couldn't have any more after I was born. Rather than resent me, like many aristocratic parents do without a son, my parents treasured me. I had a charmed childhood."

Antoine's large hands slowed, and he picked up the bowl to rinse the soap. He wrung out much of the water, then sprinkled a few drops of almond oil through my tresses and began to untangle the waves with my ivory comb. Comfortable in silence, he carried on his ministrations without interrupting.

"When my father first took ill, my mother would sit at his bedside for hours, reading to him, singing to him, helping him manage the estate— they were partners in love and in life. His death shook her deeply, and it wasn't long after that she..." Tears began to flow again, but I was compelled to continue. "Before she died, she gave me her *chatelaine* with all the keys to the house. Normally, the housekeeper would have it, but my mother was every inch the lady of the house. She worked to keep our servants comfortable and happy, and managed our family like a true queen. I've worn her *chatelaine* every day since she passed and now it is... gone. Lost, or stolen, I do not know. I know it's a mere bauble, but losing it feels like losing her all over again."

I breathed slowly, squeezing my eyes shut to keep the rest of my tears at bay.

"It isn't lost or stolen," Antoine said quietly.

My eyes snapped open and I whirled around to look at him, sloshing a good deal of water out of the tub.

"What?" I exclaimed.

He sighed. "Because I was ill—going through my turning over Christmas—I never got you a present. I knew the *chatelaine* was an heirloom from your mother, so I took it to a jeweler yesterday to have it cleaned, add a few more small compartments, and have some of the loose stones re-set. I was hoping to surprise you with it, but I didn't realize being without it would distress you so much. I'm sorry, Charlotte."

I blinked.

"It's not lost," I said simply, mind reeling, emotions condensing like clouds before rain.

"It is not."

"Monsieur Honoré didn't pilfer it while we were dancing, which would have made me the worst sort of spy," I confirmed.

"Spy? Or agent?" Antoine said, covering a smirk at our inside joke. "No, *mon amour,* he did not steal it from you."

"You took it—because you wanted me to have a Christmas present?"

He nodded, wincing slightly. "I'm sorry."

Relief, elation, and compassion washed over me and I leaped from the tub, toppling Antoine onto the plush carpet. I cried even harder than before, but they were tears of joy.

"You wonderful, wicked thing," I sobbed between kisses. "How could you torment me so?"

I felt the low vibrations of his laugh through the fine lawn of his shirt. "Next time, I'll try not to be at death's door for Christmas. Perhaps I'll have more time to come up with a better gift that doesn't involve driving you mad."

"I should get that in writing," I mumbled, tugging at the falls of his breeches, desperate to undress him. "But for now, it's only fair that I return the favor."

"You're going to give me a gift?" he teased. "Or you're going to drive me mad?"

I grinned. "Oh, *chéri*—isn't that the same thing?"

THE END

NIGHT OF THE HUNT
A VAMPIRES IN VERSAILLES STORY

AUTHOR'S NOTE

This extra spicy bonus epilogue takes place after the events of Long Lost, but before the events in the original epilogue.

BONUS EPILOGUE
CHARLOTTE

February 14, 1768
Château de Ruisseau Magdelaine

IF YOU'RE GOING TO TURN YOUR FIANCÉ INTO A WEREWOLF, YOU'LL WANT TO clear your social calendar.

There are countless changes in your body when you suffer from the blood plague, but perhaps the most unexpected is your advanced supernatural senses intensify when you're in proximity to those of your bloodline. And if you turn someone you're already quite enamored with, any kindling desire becomes a rather dangerous conflagration.

Actually, I turned Antoine before he proposed, but that was neither here nor there. And it had very little bearing on my current issue—the pervasive fitfulness that hung over our château like a miasma of ill humor. Since our supernatural condition was rather new, it was impossible to say whether it was due to our changed state of being, the approaching full moon, or the fact that it had been far too long since we'd satisfied our insatiable sexual appetites. I felt like I was going to crawl out of my skin with agitation, and it was making me a frightful dinner companion.

"You're certain you don't mind skipping the Saint Valentine's *fête* at Versailles this evening?" Antoine asked, frowning.

"I'm certain," I insisted, exasperation adding more bite to my tone than I'd intended. "We shall stay in tonight."

"Charlotte…" he began, setting his silverware down.

"You've asked me three times already, *l'amour*. This is always my least favorite ball, Daphne and Étienne won't be attending, and we've both been so busy lately, I feel as though I haven't spent more than an hour in your presence in weeks," I replied, devouring the last bite of raw mutton from the dish in front of me. It was the first meal we'd shared in far too long without one of us having to rush off for other obligations: wedding planning, Antoine's new conscription, my work with Daphne for *les DD* and social calls with Dr. Van Helsing. Considering our privileged, aristocratic life, our leisure time had been limited to frenzied bouts of lovemaking in the small hours of the dawn, and even that had waned in the face of our exhaustion. Anxiety had begun to needle me and grim thoughts sowed doubts in my mind. Antoine had only been turned in December. What if this wasn't the vision of immortality he'd agreed to?

"It's just…I don't think I've ever known you to turn down a party," he pointed out. "You'd tell me if something was amiss, wouldn't you, *petite*?"

"*Bien sûr*," I responded, not bothering to hide my petulance. "I just don't feel like going. Why are you so concerned? Do *you* wish to attend?"

Antoine snorted a laugh and rolled his glowing jade eyes. I watched the tendons in his neck stretch as he rolled out his shoulders. My teeth ached with the salacious urge to bite him there—*hard*.

"If I ever agree to prance around a ballroom with a court full of smelly aristocrats instead of bedding my delicious fiancée until she passes out from pleasure, you'll be obliged to cut off my head."

I sucked in a breath, lascivious excitement coiling deep in my gut. My skin felt too hot and stretched too tight over my flesh—sensations that often plagued me before I shifted into my lupine form. Despite my kindling desire, my concerns lingered in the front of my mind.

"So, truly, you have no regrets?" I asked, forcing levity into my tone. His gaze snapped to mine. Sharp as he was, he immediately sensed my question was about more than the declined ball.

"I have many regrets in my life, Charlotte. Loving you is not one of them. Perhaps the only regret is that we've both been so busy working to build our future that we haven't had as much time to enjoy our present. But everything is a season, my love. We'll weather it and more," he said, tilting his head contemplatively. "Is this what's been on your mind?"

I could've denied it, but my emotions stuck in my throat. I nodded, chagrinned.

"You've been like a caged animal these last weeks, and all because you fear I resent you for turning me? Or maybe you think I've changed my mind about committing my immortality to a beast—a monster?" he asked. Candlelight glinted off his lengthening fangs.

His ability to see through my artifice and bluster had always unmoored me, and even now I found myself regarding him with wide eyes and a trembling lip.

"Perhaps you need reminding that you are mine, Charlotte," he said in a low tone, laced with heat. "I chose you just as much as you chose me. You have a magnificent talent for engineering the world to be as you see fit, but you must give me some credit. You are my fiancée, my lover, my very heart. You brought me back from the grip of Death but I would not have come if you hadn't been waiting for me on the other side."

My heart stuttered—metaphorically speaking. *Dieu,* how I loved this man. I wiped the tears that had gathered in my eyes and sniffed.

"You wish to remind me, then?" I said with a small smile.

Carnal hunger sparked in Antoine's gaze and a dangerous smile danced upon his lush lips.

The remainder of our mid-evening meal lay forgotten between us, having become far less appealing than the handsome face and muscular body of my soon-to-be husband. His nostrils flared and his eyes darkened —he'd scented my arousal with his supernatural senses.

"It seems you have something in mind, Comtesse."

"You know," I began, slowly rising from my chair. "The full moon is only four nights away. I've been feeling a little restless. Haven't you?"

"I'm always restless in your company," he said, tracking my movements with tethered intensity.

I came around the shining oak table and perched atop his lap, twining my arms around his neck. His body went rigid beneath me, fingers gripping the arms of his chair. Long claws sprouted from his fingertips and left deep grooves in the wood of the chair.

"Do you remember our first night together?" I murmured, feathering kisses along his sculpted, shadowed jawline.

Antoine's brow rose, pulling at the white moon-shaped scar on his face as regarded me skeptically.

"When I kidnapped you?" he asked with sarcasm.

"You were protecting me," I said with a smirk. "But yes."

"What about it?" he uttered, inhaling at the crook of my neck. His hands trembled and his thick thighs flexed beneath me—he was losing our little game, the battle not to touch me despite how much I teased him.

"Would you have continued to chase me if the *bêtes* hadn't caught up to us?" I asked.

"Of course," he answered, confusion evident as he paused sowing small kisses along my throat. "*Dieu,* you smell so good—it's maddening."

I nipped at his ear and he moaned, the sound more erotic than a litany of prurient words.

If my heart could still beat, it would've been pounding.

"Do you think you could catch me?" I whispered.

"Well, I…"

Before Antoine could finish his sentence, I bolted for the front door. Once outside, I tugged at the belt of my dressing gown and let it fall to the ground, the white muslin landing like a puddle of pale moonlight on the gravel path. I didn't slow my stride as I tugged my chemise up over my head, and as I tossed it behind me, I heard the unmistakable sound of wood splintering and fabric tearing, followed by the blood-curdling, guttural howl of Antoine shifting into his werewolf form.

Like me and the man in black, Antoine wasn't a graceful natural wolf. The first time I'd seen him transform, I'd had to fight to keep my screams down, even though I'd been the one to turn him. With limbs longer than a wolf's, charcoal-colored fur, red eyes, and massive claws and teeth, he looked more like Hell's approximation of a wolf than the animals roaming the countryside. He was as horrifying as I was, and it was unbearably erotic.

Even without turning, I could sense he wasn't far behind me, so I banked quickly to the left toward the patch of woods skirting the estate. I could shift at any time and increase the distance between us, but the thrill of being chased ignited something primal in my blood—something other than fear. *Excitement. Heady lust. Possession. The need to be run down and claimed by my mate.*

I became the winsome young woman running for my life, determined to protect my soul and my chastity. *I snorted a laugh at that.* Threading my way through the dense undergrowth and towering trees, I looked back at the way I'd come. I was deep enough in the woods to block out the lights from the château. Bare branches stretched spindly black shadows against the nearly full moon above. The snow from last week's storm had all but melted, but the night was still clear, crisp, and laced with frost. It was a blessing I could not feel the chill.

Crouching low to the ground, I listened, waiting for the telltale sounds of panting, monstrous breaths and the crunch of decaying leaf litter beneath heavy paws. An owl hooted in the distance, and with my supernatural senses, I could hear the scurrying of rabbits and field mice beneath the ground, but I did not hear Antoine stalking me.

I tipped my nose up and inhaled deeply, trying to catch his scent in the frigid night air. In my haste and excitement, I'd foolishly run upwind and was unable to smell his telltale fragrance of apples, earth, leather, and horseflesh. Perhaps he was trying to wait me out and let me make a mistake that would give away my position.

After another two breaths, I sensed him just at the edge of my awareness. He was still some distance away, crawling through the forest on steps more silent than Death. In this position, I didn't think he could see me, but he certainly would be able to smell me. It wouldn't be long before he pinpointed my exact location, and I wasn't ready to give in just yet.

I hefted a melon-sized rock and threw it as far as I could in the opposite direction. Antoine was after it like a shot and I seized my chance to make for the folly at the other end of the grounds—the perfect place to hide with its massive stone columns and Grecian statues.

I hadn't had a chance to show the faux ruins to Antoine yet, but it was one of my favorite places in my family's estate. My father had constructed the reproduction of Aphrodite's temple for my mother, who spent ages coaxing pink roses and climbing vines around the chipped marble. Now that it was winter, the thick foliage had died back, leaving bare tendrils and sparse branches clinging to the walls. Fortunately, there was enough to conceal me for a few moments, and I hid in the small central courtyard encircling an ice-choked fountain, waiting for my dangerous wolf.

It wasn't long before I heard him coming—slow, deliberate steps in the soft mud. As he neared my hiding place, I saw he'd shifted back to an almost human form. He was so beautiful—completely naked, visibly aroused, his corded muscles flexing beneath delicious, scarred skin. Long claws tipped his fingers and his impressive fangs appeared to glow in the moonlight.

"Come out, come out, wherever you are," he growled in a half-human, half-monstrous voice. "I can scent your desire, *petite*. You've done very well keeping me at bay, but I know you're in here. Your body is mine to claim." He rolled his neck and sniffed the air, stalking toward me. If I didn't know him—hadn't turned him and promised him my eternity—I would've been terrified. As it happened, I was nearly mad with lust.

A flood of arousal gathered between my legs and as soon as it did, Antoine's head whipped in my direction. A predatory grin stretched across his lips.

"Bon soir, petite," he chuckled, meeting my gaze through the leafless vines.

I returned his smile and stepped around the low wall where I'd been crouching, crooking a finger in his direction. His eyes widened, his nostrils flared, and he pounced.

The fall wouldn't have hurt my supernatural body, but Antoine rolled me on top of him before we hit the ground, anyway.

"Did you enjoy the chase?" I asked, leaning down to press a scorching kiss to his lips.

"Mm," came his response. His claws dug into the soft flesh of my ass and I gasped—the pain sharpening the edges of my pleasure. "I always enjoy eating what I hunt."

He pulled my hips forward until my thighs bracketed his ears and my sex covered his mouth. There was no delicacy to his manner—his fangs scored the lips of my pussy and he sucked at the peak of my pleasure like the Devil come to devour my soul.

"This sweet cunt has been so neglected lately," he rumbled. "Poor thing. What a feast I'll make of you tonight."

My legs shook and I worried about crushing him, but the moment I tried to lift myself up off Antoine's face, he dug his claws in further and snarled.

"Don't you dare, Charlotte," he warned, eyes flashing. "You stole my breath long ago and I would drown in you if I could. Give me your weight, *l'amour.* Do not hold back—ever. I've come for your pleasure and now you'll come for mine."

Obediently, I leaned forward. When his hot tongue speared me, I swore and let out a sound between a scream and a wolf howl.

"I'm so close, *chéri,*" I panted, grinding against Antoine's ravenous mouth. On a satisfied groan, he slid his thumb forward to rub small circles at the apex of my sex—his claws gently pricking the lips of my pussy.

"*Oui, l'amour!* Don't stop—don't stop!"

He unleashed a growl that vibrated up through his throat and tipped me over the edge, hurtling headfirst into a brutal explosion of bliss. Waves of pleasure crashed over me, loosening some of the tension I'd been feeling over the last few weeks. Incandescent and temporarily satiated, I threw back my head and howled. Antoine answered with a rumbling growl and deftly lifted me to roll us onto our sides, cushioning my head from the damp ground with his substantial bicep.

"That was spectacular," I sighed.

"I wanted to do that to you ever since I saw you naked in that godforsaken inn outside Versailles," he admitted, pulling a twig from the snarled mass of my hair. "You spent so much time running from me—and then running circles around me, it was rather enjoyable to lead the chase for once."

"Well, I'd say I was the one leading the chase this time. After all, I led you right where I wanted you," I preened, running my hands down his muscular chest.

"If that's what you wanted all along, I beg you to simply ask me next time. I'm happy to hunt you down and claim your exquisite body over and over again," he chuckled.

My hands had drifted over the small line of dark hair trailing down his hard abdomen to his still hard cock. Already, my body burned for him again.

I quirked a brow at him. "Oh? I'd hardly call it a claiming."

Antoine narrowed his eyes and sucked on a fang. "Who said I was finished?"

"Well, I assumed since we're just lying on the ground here…"

"I'm giving you a moment to recover," he said darkly. "This is all the chivalry you'll have from me tonight. Once I start in again, I don't think I'll be able to stop."

The warning in his words sent a fresh wave of desire through my veins and I reached down to wrap my fingers around his thick length. He sucked in a breath and tensed beneath my touch.

"Charlotte, do not test me," he ground out. "I do not wish to hurt you."

I leaned forward to take his lips in an eager kiss, stroking his erection with a firm hand. His harsh breaths became deep whimpers, then morphed into feral growls as he found his beast form again.

"Come on, then, my love—I've been yours from the start. Let loose your monster and let it have its way with me," I breathed, heating the scant space between us.

No sooner had I issued the challenge than Antoine laughed—a dangerous, wild sound—and he whispered in my ear.

"Run."

Up I jumped, ducking through the bare trees and rushing past the folly. This time, I didn't make it far before he barreled into me, knocking me forward into the soft grass and slick mud. I hardly had time to catch my breath, and I shivered with lust-filled anticipation when his clawed fingertips parted the delicate folds between my legs.

"Still so wet for me, monster than I am," he grunted, the words sounding far less human than moments before.

My own claws and fangs lengthened in response and I lifted my hips to meet his explorations.

"Monsters that *we* are," I reminded him, digging my lengthening fingers into the dirt.

When he dragged the tip of his cock through my wet entrance, I howled, my humanity forgotten. In answer, he slid forward, pounding into me with the perfect exquisite, hellish rhythm. One fingertip circled the bud of my pleasure and stars danced along the edges of my vision.

"Mine," he demanded, repeating the word on each delicious thrust. "You will be my love, my wife, my monster. Every part of you—every shade of you—*mine*."

"Yes," I cried out, feeling my half-human, half-werewolf body draw up tightly with the onslaught of possessive words and unrelenting pleasure.

When my orgasm crested, this time Antoine followed me over the edge, clinging to my hips and slumping forward to drop kisses and fierce little nips up my spine toward my neck.

"Was that enough of a claiming for you?" he panted.

"For now," I chuckled. "That was a much more enjoyable chase than our first one outside Versailles."

"I would've much preferred our first encounter to end thusly," he said, finally catching his breath and shifting back to his human form.

"I would've preferred our first encounter to have *begun* so," I agreed. "Think of all the time and heartache we would've saved."

"Neither one of us were monsters then, though," he admitted, picking me up to carry back inside our home, where I knew he'd take infinite care in cleaning the mud from our naked bodies. For now, our beasts were sated, but the night was still young.

"How absurd!" I scoffed. "I've always been a monster. I'm only newly a werewolf. And you know, with an eternity of nights like that in our future, I've rather come around to the idea."

With a smile that would've tempted the Devil himself, Antoine winked at me.

"So have I."

THE END

THE DOCTOR AND THE DEVIL

BOOK THREE

PROLOGUE
MINA

October 25, 1747
Buda, Hungary

Since today is my 17th birthday, I asked the devil for a kiss. He winked at me and asked, "Where?"

"The library will do fine," I said.

He threw his head back and laughed at me, then tugged at my ringlets. Confused and embarrassed, I felt my cheeks burn and stormed up to my room to hide for a bit.

It wasn't until I persuaded the stable boy to explain the jest to me that I understood.

"I am happy to offer you a kiss in his stead," he said with a smirk.

I tried to hide my distaste at the thought of the stable boy's lips pressed against mine. "Thank you," I told him. "But I think I'd rather have a cup of tea and go read a book."

The sound of his laughter followed me out of the stables.

I find the male sex perplexing and annoying. It's a pity the devil is so handsome, since he is such a rogue—or so the housemaids say.

Later in the evening, I was in the library by myself. The cook had given me a spice cake as a treat and I was nibbling it while I read some of

Papa's anatomy books, and the devil came in. He sat on the chaise next to me and laughed at my book.

"Shouldn't you be reading something more appropriate for a young lady?"

I didn't understand, so I asked, "What is inappropriate about the vital organs of the human body?"

He looked somewhat stricken, and his eyes took on a strange light that made me feel oddly warm, but he did not answer me. Instead, he tilted his head in that infuriating way that made his dark hair swoop over his eyes and had all the housemaids sighing at him. Since he didn't reply, I assumed our conversation had ended, so I went back to my book and my spice cake. He did not depart, however.

"Didn't we have an appointment?" he asked, after a few quiet moments.

I was certain I looked confused, because he chuckled again. Oh, I didn't want to come off all silly over him, but his laugh makes me think of bitter coffee and too much sherry. It was low and dark and heady and sometimes I thought I could become intoxicated by it. I wished I were more charming or had a lighter temperament to draw it forth more often.

"You asked me for a birthday kiss in the library," he replied, moving closer. I knew I turned bright red at that—I thought he had forgotten my impetuous request.

I tried to calm my pounding heart and will the blush from my cheeks, but I knew it would do no good.

"Did I?" I lied. "I don't remember."

He shifted even closer, plucking the book from one hand and the cake from the other. He set them on a table at our side and licked the sweet crumbs from his fingers. A strange tightness began to build low in my abdomen as I watched him.

I had seen how quickly the devil can move—faster than anything on earth. Yet he drew my hands into his and leaned forward with such slow steadiness, I thought perhaps an hour could have passed. When his lips were but a breath from mine, he paused.

"Would you still like a kiss, little Mina?" he whispered.

I was entranced by his dark eyes. They had always looked black to me, but this close, I could see flecks of chocolate brown and warm copper in them. It made me curiously hungry, but I didn't think it was for food.

"Yes, if you please," I replied, suddenly shy.

He moved a hair's breadth closer.

"Why?"

I blinked, startled by my peculiar feelings.

"I haven't had one before, and I'd like to see what all the fuss is about,"

I said. It was an awkward, unladylike answer, but it was honest. I expected him to laugh at me again, as he always did, but he didn't.

"Are you ready?" he asked.

I sucked in a breath. "As I'll ever be."

His lovely lips turned up at the corners in a genuine smile and, finally, he pressed them to mine.

It was...odd. It was warm, gentle yet firm, and a little wet, but not in an unpleasant way, and it was over in half a second. I pulled away from him with what I was sure was an unflattering expression, because his brows pinched together in consternation.

"Is that...all?" I asked. I couldn't help it—it just seemed so underwhelming given how everyone spoke of kissing as a riotously pleasurable activity.

He raised one of those devilish black brows at me as if I'd challenged him to another game of chess.

"Spare not my feelings, little Mina." He laughed again. "I'd hate for you to end your birthday on such a disappointing note."

He leaned forward once more and—oh. *Oh.*

Oh.

His mouth sought mine again, and this time he sucked gently at my bottom lip. When I gasped in surprise, his tongue slipped in, slowly caressing mine in the most pleasurable way. Not wanting to waste the opportunity for a lesson, I attempted to mimic some of his movements, licking and sucking in a determined manner, unsure of whether I was performing adequately.

When his hands came up to the back of my neck and threaded through my hair, a deep growl rose from his chest. I pulled away, perplexed. *Was he angry that I was doing it badly?* We both stared at each other for a heartbeat, eyes wide in shock. He opened his mouth to say something, then seemed to think better of it and snapped it shut. He stood abruptly and bowed stiffly.

"I hope you had an enjoyable birthday, Wilhelmina," he said in a clipped manner.

"Did I do something wrong?" I asked, concerned by his sudden change in demeanor. "I am sorry, only...you know I have not tried this before. I apologize for any ineptitude on my part."

Some of his tension abated because that false, teasing devil was back.

"Think nothing of it, little Mina," he grinned, showing off his fangs. "We were all beginners at one time. I can scarcely recall that time myself, but you understand that was long ago."

His response made me churlish, and I frowned at him, hoping to hide the hurt in my expression.

"Thank you for your indulgence," I replied. "It was most instructive."

I picked up the remains of my cake and my book and left the library. When I cast a glance back at him, he was scowling and pouring a hefty glass of something from the crystal decanter on the sideboard. It appeared he was about to enjoy a fine old sulk.

Yes, I *did* find men perplexing and annoying.

1

MINA

April 13, 1768
Van Helsing's Clinic, Rue Ordener

The devil does not age.

The thought struck me like a bolt of lightning as I stared into the onyx eyes I longed to forget but would always remember. I'd just finished locking up my clinic for the evening, intent on getting a much-needed bite of supper and a moment's respite from work, but had tripped over my skirts. I braced myself for the pain the fall would undoubtably bring, but it didn't come. Strong arms righted me, capturing my body in a painfully familiar embrace that afforded me flashes of something much worse than the sting of a scraped palm. With that, two decades of scar tissue ripped open the wounds on my long-broken heart.

"Good evening, Mina."

The words were deep and low, soft and guttural—an elegant growl wrapped in velvet. My heart pounded against my ribs, a mixture of panicked fear and dusty memories of aching pleasure. He looked exactly the same—of course he would. Still beautiful, still magnetic, still powerful, still untouched by time itself.

"Rafael!" His name was a furious whisper on my lips. I felt the blood drain from my face. I recognized the signs of shock accumulating in my body, and I forced myself to inhale slow, deep breaths.

"Mina," he repeated. *Lord, how many nights had I dreamed of that hypnotic voice murmuring my name?* Even though it had been twenty years, I still couldn't comprehend the way it stirred my soul.

No! He made his choices, you silly woman, and they were never for you—or about you. Gather your wits and do not let him in.

It would have been easier if he wasn't holding me upright in the middle of the street. How long had I been clutching at him? Seconds? Minutes? *Oh, Mina!*

I pushed him away, nearly tumbling again. Attempting to recover from the surprise and embarrassment, I brushed off my skirts and fixed my askew spectacles.

"That's Dr. Van Helsing," I snapped.

He arched a brow. I hated that he was as handsome as I remembered. Lean muscle wrapped in moon-pale skin; dark eyes that felt both hot and cold when they raked over me; those high cheekbones and patrician nose that spoke of his family's royal lineage. His full lips parted over those frightening white teeth—two gleaming sets of fangs I'd never seen on another vampire—and he spoke again.

"So, your father finally allowed you to study," he said. It sounded like he was smiling, but his lips were set in a firm line. "I should have expected you'd wear him down eventually. Congratulations on becoming a physician, Mina."

The words stabbed at painful memories, and I flinched. *Is it possible that he doesn't know about Papa?*

"What are you doing here, Rafael?" The shock at seeing this ghost from my past had faded some, and now I found myself looking nervously over my shoulders. People—powerful people—were looking for him and had been unable to find him. *Yet here he is.*

I hadn't seen him in twenty years, except for the brief moments outside Gévaudan when he and Charlotte had come to free Antoine and me from the clutches of the *bêtes de sang*, a dangerous group of vampire soldiers under the command of a corrupt general. He hadn't looked like this, though—dressed in a gently worn black silk coat and leg-hugging black breeches. He'd been in his beast form—a massive creature resembling a wolf, if wolves had crawled their way up to earth from the bowels of Hell.

Is he here for me? Has he come for me? Sadness bloomed in my chest, chasing away the reflexive hope. *Don't be stupid, Mina. It must be some horrifying coincidence. And anyway, you don't want him here.*

"Is that any way to great an old friend?" he purred. "A friend who has very recently saved your life."

He was teasing me, trying to goad me into a spat, but I was too fatigued to play his lofty mind games.

"I haven't seen you in twenty years," I lied. "I don't know what you're talking about. Perhaps you have me confused with someone else."

Breathe, Mina. Air—yes, I need air. And…something else that starts with an A. Ale! Yes, back to what I was doing. Walk away. Get away from him. Calmly. Slowly. Do not run—he would only give chase.

Without waiting for his response, I turned back up the road, desperate to get to the warm, heady din of *Le Raisin Perdu* and to safety—if one could call a shady tavern in the poor end of Paris *safe*. Fortunately, having treated most of the patrons for one thing or another, I could. The tavern would be full, and I longed to have my supper and drown away this unfortunate encounter with several pints of ale. I wanted the company of people, even if I did not partake in the conversation. As a foreigner, it made me feel less alone.

"Oh?" His voice was in my ear as he kept pace with me. "You always were a terrible liar, little Mina."

"Don't call me *little Mina*. Don't call me Mina! I am Dr. Van Helsing! And you…you are…you are *unwelcome!*"

"*Unwelcome?* After all we have been through? After all this time?" He tutted, lips twitching as if he were covering a laugh. "Very well. If you insist on formalities, I will oblige. It has been an age, *Dr. Van Helsing*. How have you been keeping? I'm in town for only a short time—you must come to dine."

'*All this time? Come to dine?*' I stared at him, angry and perplexed. As much as I didn't want to rise to his teasing, my temper flared, and I stopped a few steps away from the tavern door.

"I'm afraid my calendar is quite full," I bit out. "But if you're short on dining companions, I know several people who would dearly love the pleasure of your company. Though, I am not certain you'd enjoy the dinner conversation with The Order."

He stilled, the expression on his face grave.

"Stay away from them, Mina," he warned. "They are not what they seem. And you are not prepared for what is to come."

Unable to control my anger any longer, I exploded.

"You unleashed this plague upon the world, Rafael!" I hissed. "And every day, I try to help hold back the tide of destruction. Do not offer me warnings or advice or inconsequential opinions while I am the one atoning for *your* sins." Rage and disgust leeched into my words. "I should stake you where you stand."

Betrayal and pain flitted across his face, along with a thousand unsaid words. He looked like he was about to speak, but his gaze snagged on something behind my shoulder. I turned to watch a drunk man stumble out of the tavern, recognizing him as one of the farmers from just outside the city. I'd treated his son for a broken arm last summer, one which I suspected had more to do with a drunken ass of a father and less to do with a tumble from an apple tree.

I scowled. *What a trying day this is turning out to be.* I would simply have to convince Rafael to leave me alone and return to whatever rock—or castle—he'd crawled out from. Steeling myself for another calm, cold tirade, I turned back toward him, only to discover that he'd disappeared. I tried to ignore the throb in my heart that always seemed to accompany his absence—rather, it had…twenty years ago.

Wonderful. Now he would be off lurking in the shadows again, waiting for yet another inopportune moment to risk putting me in danger once more.

Or would he?

It doesn't matter, I thought to myself. *He is here and you've been in danger since he showed up in France.*

I stomped into *Le Raisin Perdu* and sat down at my usual table—tucked into a back corner, cloaked in the gloom of the dingy establishment. As soon as I entered, the warmth of the room fogged my spectacles, and I pulled them off to clean them on my handkerchief. Tonight was busy but strangely subdued, as if the patrons bent their heads and muttered in hushed voices against some unknown, ominous portent.

Now, Mina! You're just being dramatic. Rafael's sudden reappearance has unsettled you. I frowned, lost in memories that I'd been fighting to repress for far too long. Perhaps it was time to simply let them go. *If only I could…*

"*Ça va, Mademoiselle Mina?*"

A plump woman with a halo of wild gray hair approached and handed me a mug of ale. Unlike my French friends, I preferred the bitter, golden liquid to the standard fare of wine—it reminded me of home.

"Yes, Madame Bénard, all is well, thank you," I said, trying for a smile. The sharp innkeeper narrowed her eyes at my feigned positivity and harrumphed.

"You need to eat," she said brusquely. "Our stew tonight is turnip and lentil, but for you, I'll put in some bacon, *d'accord?*"

I opened my mouth to argue—meat was expensive and in short supply —but she waved away my protest and bustled off to shout at a drunken patron. I smiled at her retreating form. Madame Bénard had been one of the first people in the city to show me kindness before she knew of my profession and my skills. I'd been coming to the dank tavern weekly since I'd arrived in the city years ago and now, it felt as much like my home as my small apartment atop my medical clinic. It certainly felt more like home than anywhere else I'd lived, except perhaps…

No! I shook myself from what promised to be some sort of lamentable reverie and took a large swig of ale. I would not allow myself to dwell on Rafael's unwelcome presence, nor the fact that he'd clearly been haunting France for some time now, *nor* the fact that our history was likely to be revealed when The Order finally got their hands on him—which would jeopardize everything I'd worked so hard to leave behind. I massaged the scowl from my brows and tried to lift my spirits with the ambient chatter of the crowd, but their conversations only saddened me further.

"...not enough bread. Never enough food. And with another babe on the way, why *shouldn't* we get bitten and make the change? Plenty of blood to go around, right?"

"...the blood plague already took my family—all but Jeanette, and she's run off and become a blood whore, now, hasn't she?"

"We can't pay the new tax! Who can? What with the blight wiping out last year's crop and soiling the land, there aren't even enough fields left to plough. Not that *they* care, mind you. Sitting up in that damn palace drinking champagne and eating cake."

"Well, I heard that the Beast of Gévaudan is here now—roaming the streets, feeding on all those pour souls, human and vampire alike. Do you think *The Order* will catch it?"

My ears perked up at the last words, and I swung my head around to find the source. Before I could locate the man, Madame Bénard returned and plonked a heavy bowl of stew on my table.

"Every bite, *d'accord?* You must eat every bite, Doctor. You need your strength, and I can tell when something is vexing you. Besides, you would not want to waste my good bacon!" She set down a thick chunk of dark rye bread and another tankard of ale, then winked at me and hurried off again.

The stew was thick and hearty, and the savory, smoky sweetness did more for my mood than I'd expected. Often when I was working, I would completely forget—or forgo—my afternoon meals. It was hard to think of eating when so many of my patients were starving. Still, Madame Bénard was right. If I wanted to continue my work, I would need my strength.

And if I intend to run and hide from the past that Rafael is here to dredge up.

I pushed the thought aside and swiped a piece of bread through the meaty broth, willing myself calm and praying the ale would soon temper my racing heart. Unfortunately, it wasn't long before my mind returned to Rafael. Why had he come? Where had he been? What was he doing? Why did he still look at me with those same penetrating obsidian eyes—like no time had passed? As if we hadn't been separated by half a lifetime and too many broken promises and too much cruelty.

I downed the last of the ale and stared at the foam swirling around the bottom of my empty tankard. I grimly contemplated alerting The Order.

I knew I should. I knew I wouldn't.

Dieu, Rafael, I hate you.

"Doctor?"

A sallow-skinned man who looked more skeletal than the anatomy etchings in my medical texts stood at my table, clutching a filthy cap in his hands. I recognized him as a young farmer who'd come into the city looking for work after the grain blight decimated his fields last year. He looked like he'd had a much harder winter than the other men here, though that was an unfortunate contest to win.

"Pierre, is it?" I offered a smile.

He nodded. "I'm told you can help…that is, I don't mean to interrupt your dinner, but my wife…" He trailed off, swallowing hard. His eyes flicked to my half-eaten bowl of stew and the bread.

"Won't you join me?" I said, gesturing for him to sit. "Madame Bénard makes lovely food, but I'm afraid it's always too much for me."

He sat but refused to meet my eyes. I pushed the food across the table to him, but he blushed and stammered a half-hearted protest.

"Please," I encouraged. "I was finished anyway, and if I leave anything but an empty bowl, Madame Bénard will gripe at me until the end of days."

Mollified, Pierre grabbed the bowl and began slurping down the delicious stew. Once he'd all but licked the bowl clean, I cleared my throat.

"Your wife?" I asked. "Is she ill?"

"Yes," he said, remembering his purpose. "Well, no—not yet. But…"

At this, he looked around the room nervously and lowered his voice to a conspiratorial whisper.

"She means to make *the change,* and I don't think I can stop her."

"She intends to infect herself with the blood plague?" I asked.

He nodded. "We have struggled, of course, but I am hopeful that my prayers will soon be answered. This season might be better. Jacqueline says she cannot wait and that she will starve before spring's first sprouts. I think she would hold out longer, if she could. I fear her wavering faith in God has already damned her."

I frowned. "What is it you need from me, Pierre?"

"Could you speak with her? Convince her that with all the horrors you've seen, that becoming a vampire is not the answer? If I sent her 'round to your clinic tomorrow, you would see her, wouldn't you?" The pleading in Pierre's tone bothered me, even though it was a story I'd heard a hundred times before.

"If it is her soul you worry after, perhaps it is a priest you should seek counsel from," I replied.

"I've already tried that. She will not go. Please, Doctor," he said.

I sighed. "Why would she listen to me, if not her own husband?"

"You know more about vampires than anyone. You help people. You're a woman of the church," he urged, leaning forward over the table.

I balked. "A woman of the church?"

"Yes," he said slowly, blinking in confusion. "The acts of charity, the way you help people even when they cannot pay."

"That doesn't make me a woman of the church," I chuckled darkly. "Far from it."

His face fell and he leaned back. Motivated by regret and empathy, I reached for his hand.

"Send your wife," I said softly. "Tomorrow. I will talk to her. But I will only be honest with her, and you must accept that if her mind is set, there won't be anything I can do."

Grateful, he clasped my hands. "Thank you, Doctor Van Helsing. God bless you for trying to save her. There is nothing worse than eternal damnation."

Reflecting on the horrors of my life that had fractured my own relationship with the divine, I frowned.

"Yes," I whispered, more to myself than to him. "There is."

2

RAFAEL

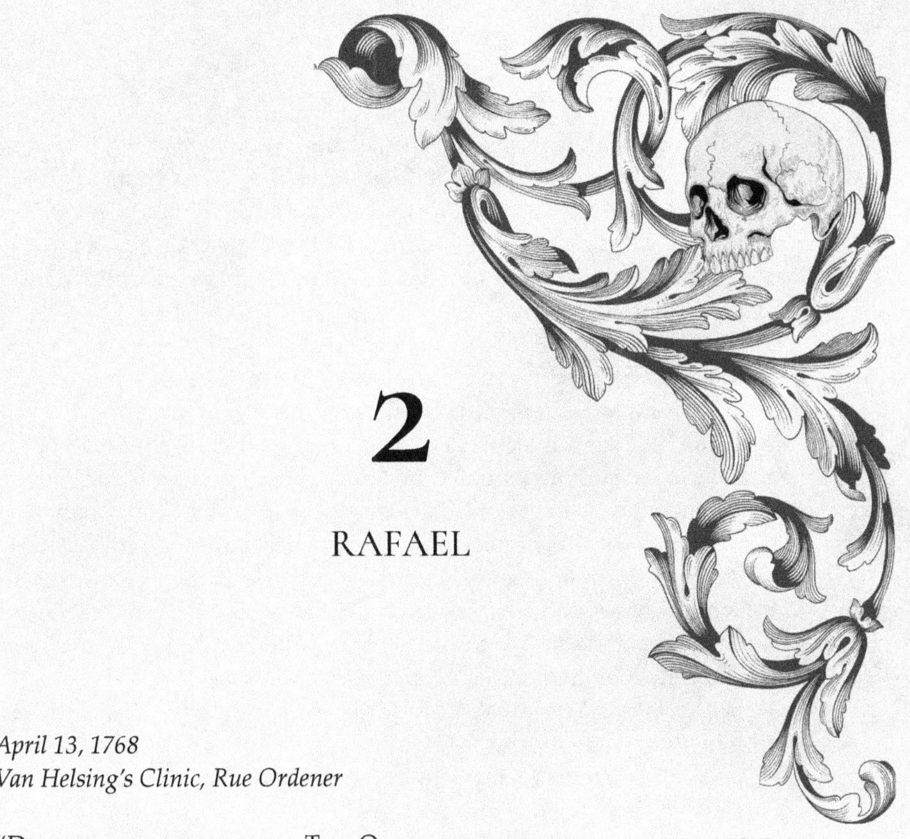

April 13, 1768
Van Helsing's Clinic, Rue Ordener

"Do you think anyone in The Order would mind if we just broke in and had a little taste?" asked the first man.

The second man chuckled. "I tell you, with a lady like that, I'd want more than a little taste. That damn doctor is a whole fucking meal."

The first man laughed himself into a coughing fit, then spit a wad of phlegm onto the street.

"Did they tell you what we were watching for? Or are we just supposed to sit here all night freezing our balls off, waiting for some filthy *sanguisuge* to show up and hex her into making the beast with two backs?"

"*Dieu,* I could do with a bit of that kind of magic, eh? Simply knock on that door, call upon the devil, and entice her to lift her skirts for me," the first man continued.

This time, the second man smacked the first upside his head, sending the fool into another coughing fit.

"That's enough, Pascal," the second man said. "*Merde,* anyone would think you'd never bedded a woman before. We're to watch the lady physician and notify The Order if any curious-looking vampires are lurking about. Not those newly turned ones, but one that looks *different,* remember? And if we happen to overhear anything that might be considered *treasonous* to His Majesty or to The Order or to us humans, we're to let them know, as well."

"Right, right. That masked man—Derais—was clear enough on that point. Now, why would he wear a damn mask if he's just going to give us his name? Crazy old sod," the man called Pascal replied. "You know, Hubert, The Order gives me the creeps, and I'm tired and cold. What if we just knock off and get a quick drink? I'd be much more alert with a bit of wine in my blood."

"Focus, man! These bloodsuckers are crafty, and if you're not paying attention, one will slip by you before you can blink," Hubert warned.

The words wrought an ironic laugh from me, but in my current animal form, it came out as a muffled hiss, too soft and small for these mortals to hear. I longed to shift into a more predatory form and rip out their throats for the things they said about Mina—*my Mina*—but that would only alert The Order that I was as predictable as I seemed to have become. I still had much to learn about my foe and killing these men would get me no closer to my end. Besides, Mina disliked when I killed, and if I was to win her back, I would at least *try* to stem my murderous urges. These men, however, were making it a Herculean trial.

Patience, Rafael. Patience! If either of them attempts to harm Mina, I will act. Until then, I must wait and watch.

I yawned and stretched my soft, leathery wings, then folded them back against my body. I twisted around to better see the front door to Mina's clinic, where I'd approached her earlier in the evening. I shouldn't have done it, but I couldn't help myself. The last time I'd seen her—or rather, the last time I'd let her see me—she'd been bound and gagged on the floor of a cave outside Gévaudan. Those abominations of my bloodline, the so-called *beasts of blood,* had abducted her and her human companion. I was forced to reveal myself to her in my wolf form to help my werewolf whelp Charlotte take on the vampire soldiers.

How Mina had looked at me then. Shock, horror, fear, recognition. *Longing,* I dared hope. Still, I would not have chosen that particular moment to confirm what I could assume were her suspicions: I was alive. I was alone. And I was in France.

And so was the blood plague—the curse that could destroy the world.

My family's curse. *My curse.*

These men The Order hired, Pascal and Hubert, stilled as they saw what I'd sensed minutes before—Mina returning from the humble tavern at the end of her street. The closer she drew to her clinic and to my disreputable group's hiding place, the louder my blood sang—calling to her. If I'd been born with a beating heart, it would have pounded in my chest, but as ever, all I felt was a vague sense of need that lessened the nearer she was to me.

She walked with purpose, but she'd always walked that way. Mina had been driven by purpose from the time I'd first met her at the tender age of sixteen, and it was comforting to see that she hadn't lost whatever it was that drove her forward.

"You walk as if your legs can't bear not to run," I used to tease. *"Women are meant to be slow, graceful creatures. Amble a little, for fuck's sake."*

I remembered how her beautiful sapphire eyes would widen when I spoke profanity to her, and it brought forth another chuckle. *How I've missed laughing in amusement.*

A man spilled out of the tavern—not drunk, but tall, thin, and weak— and hailed Mina. As he jogged to catch up to her, instinct propelled my bat wings forward and I fluttered closer, taking up a perch on the underside of a thatch roof nearby. Pascal and Hubert still leaned with forced casualness against the decrepit building at the end of the road, but I could tell they watched Mina intently.

"Please, Pierre," Mina said. "I've already told you. I will do what I can for your wife, but if you truly wish me to impress upon her the danger you believe her immortal soul is in, you will need to find someone else."

"But her soul is in danger," the man insisted.

Mina pinched the bridge of her nose—a gesture I recognized as the summoning of reserves of patience.

"Her life is in danger, Pierre," she said. "The blood plague might not be the most ideal solution to the predicament of hunger, but scores of others have found peace with it."

"Doctor, that's blasphemous," Pierre whispered.

Mina was unmoved. "Your wife's soul is not my concern. But I can tell her about the plague's effect on the body. If that's not the answer you're looking for, then I'm afraid I won't be much help to you."

She turned back to her clinic. The man called Pierre stood in the street for a moment more, then walked back to the tavern muttering to himself. I watched Mina enter and lock the door behind her. She lit a candle and collected several sheaves of paper from the desk, then disappeared into the back to climb the staircase up to her living quarters. Accepting that I would not—at least, for the time being—drain every drop of blood from Pascal and Hubert and leave their withered bodies in the gutter, I abandoned my perch and flew around the back of the building to the narrow alley that ran the length of the block. I'd stashed my clothes in a stack of empty crates before shifting to wait for Mina, but even as I thought about turning back into my human form, I reconsidered.

I needed to talk to her—to convince her to join me...to *help* me. She had been so cross earlier, and as much as I enjoyed riling her and watching the heated blood of frustration pulse through her exquisite body, I didn't think she would take kindly to a second attempt at contact so soon. She needed time, and while I didn't have a lot of time to offer her, I could give her a day to accept that I'd come back.

I am here for you, my Mina.

From my refuse-strewn alley hiding place, I looked up at the glow from her candle moving between rooms. She entered her bedchamber and after a time, the golden halo of light in her rooms went dark.

Did she think of me before she fell asleep? Surely, she would be expecting me to return. Impatience needled me. It was peculiar to have learned so many harsh lessons in the art of patience considering I'd lived longer than most and would remain even after humanity had turned to dust. Mina always brought that out in me. A restlessness that I had once termed ennui, yet she had referred to as stifled passion.

Passion. I wanted it with her. I wanted to once more visit pleasure upon her body and taste the overwhelming lust for life she carried in her blood. It had been so long—too long since I'd had anything that made me feel truly alive. Blood that didn't taste bitter. Sex that didn't fill me with shame, guilt, anger. Conversation that didn't bore me beyond measure. Existence without Mina had been unbearable, but I'd been resigned to it for the last twenty years to protect her…no, that wasn't quite true…to allow her to live, perhaps. I'd wanted to give her a chance to savor the delights of humanity instead of shackling herself to a world of pain and suffering and death. Tenacious as she was, I'd had to be rather *forceful* in severing our attachment and ruining our dream of a future together, so I understood her reasons for loathing me on sight.

Still, my need for her was almost crippling. As I'd never been any good at denying myself the mere morsels of perverse pleasure I could have and too often reveled in my own trappings of sin, I relented.

Just to look—not to touch.

Closing my eyes and letting go of my corporeal form, I turned into mist. Shifting into a formless cloud took a great toll on my energy and would leave me temporarily weakened when I returned to my body—I would need to feed tonight—but I didn't care about that now. The memory of Mina's body in my arms earlier still burned my icy, dead skin. As I floated up to her window, I briefly considered that my actions were invasive, aggressive, and disrespectful…*should I simply turn around and leave her tonight?*

An older memory flashed. She was eighteen. Fresh, young, sweet, determined to change the world. Dark brown curls splayed across the pillow, wide sapphire eyes glazed with sweet contentment, and her ivory skin made rosy by our lovemaking. Her soft, round curves felt so good beneath me, as if her beautiful body was the promise of new life itself. I

was cold, deathless, wintry Hades, and she was my Persephone—
blooming with pleasure from my touch.

*"Come for me, Lady Persephone, and bring spring to my heart," I'd
commanded.* She'd laughed at me then—laughed at a Prince of Wallachia!
—and almost refused to obey. Thankfully, her desire for me had been too
great, and she'd come apart around me.

I was so lost in thought I almost missed the soft shuffling sounds of Pascal
and Hubert creeping down the alley toward me. *What are these fools up to?*

"All I'm saying is, how do we know she doesn't have a *sanguisuge* up
there with her? I say we just climb up and take a little peek just to make
sure." Pascal snickered.

"You are the most disgusting, shameful ass," Hubert hissed. "But I'm
not about to let you get an eyeful of that pretty doctor all by yourself."

It appeared that my decision had been made for me. I would not visit
Mina tonight. I fantasized about eviscerating the men but forced myself to
focus on my plans. Perhaps I could simply lead the men away, giving
Mina some peace to rest unbothered for the night.

I swirled down to Pascal and Hubert and called forth one of my other
abilities—an ancient form of mesmerism. I *suggested* to both men that they
follow a stray dog for a few hours, convincing them that it might be the
Beast of Gévaudan. When they caught sight of the animal across the alley,
they took off after it with abandon.

Satisfied that Mina was safe from all prying eyes but my own, I
allowed myself the small pleasure of drifting up to her bedroom window.
Inside, she slept, snoring delicately and murmuring to her dream companions. What I wouldn't give to explore her mind in those moments.

The night air started to warm, and I knew sunrise would soon be upon
me. It was time to return home. I shifted into my wolf form, gathered my
clothes up in my jaws, and kept to the shadows until I arrived at the edge
of the city. Once I found the main road heading north, I took off with
supernatural speed. My great claws dug into the damp earth, sending up
showers of mud and leaves with every footfall. I inhaled deeply, using my
lupine senses to paint a picture of the farmlands around me as they gave
way to the towering trees of encroaching forest.

I followed the Seine northwest from Paris, winding through silvery
green woods, until I arrived on the outskirts of Rouen. I departed from the
main road and climbed to the top of a small hill, on which sat the crumbling ruin of a once-grand feudal castle, *le Château du Diable.* Built during
the eleventh century and destroyed during the Hundred Years' War, it had
long since gained a reputation as a damned, haunted place, which caused
the locals to avoid it entirely.

It was utterly perfect for my needs.

After the assassination of my father, I channeled my grief into the only remaining pursuit—finding my cruelly abandoned true love. *My soulmate, if I'd had a soul.* The moment I received word of Mina settling in Paris, I set my plan to action. My land agent found the property between Rouen and Paris and quietly prepared the castle for future habitation.

The charming ruins were shored up to prevent further decay, but still retained the appearance of an unlivable monument to evil. A crew of loyal workers dug down around the foundations and built an underground abode suited to my uncommon needs. I was glad to have a home here, where I could continue to work on my family's curse and keep a watchful eye on Mina.

I climbed the slick stone walls of the high tower, which would be an impossible feat for any human. The only door into my home was at the very top, disguised beneath a massive granite slab, affording me another layer of protection against any human invaders. Only a very old, very strong vampire would have the strength to move the stone and gain entrance.

I pushed the stone away as if it were a simple wooden door and jumped inside. The six-story drop to the floor was another precaution—I didn't require stairs, and anyone who made their way past the stone door would certainly fall to his death.

The interior of the tower appeared empty and ruined, but that was just for appearances. The only item inside the round chamber was a rusted wrought-iron brazier that stuck out about a foot from the wall. I pulled on the piece of metal and waited for the muted clanking sound that indicated the hidden passageway was shifting into place. My engineers had been particularly clever in designing the antechambers of my home and the mechanism still delighted me.

A small stone staircase appeared in the floor, which led down to my suite of rooms. Rather than the dark, gothic structure above, my rooms below had an altogether different feeling. I longed to leave behind the miasma of death and decay, so every hallway and room was built with pale, glittering marble floors and white and gold silken wall coverings. The ceilings bore elaborate frescoes of bluebird skies with puffy white clouds, whirling around a painted gilt sun. With the candles and fireplaces lit, I could imagine it was a day out in the sunshine. If this was as close to heaven as I could get, so be it.

As soon as I reached the bottom of the stairs, I shifted into human form. My bare feet padded silently along the plush blue and gold carpets that stretched the entire length of the hallway, winding deeper underground to my bedchamber.

I paused in front of the massive wooden doors carved with scenes from the Hades and Persephone myth, reaching out to stroke one long clawed finger across the smooth face of my Queen of Spring.

Soon, Mina.

Sighing, I pushed the doors open into my grand bedchamber—not filled with dirt, death, and a coffin, as the peasant rumors suggested—but a room dedicated to the beauty and awe of the night. A floor to ceiling mural of the night sky, set with stars and heavenly bodies welcomed me, as did the dark navy blue—nearly black—curtains adorning my massive four poster bed. My dressing room and bathing room led off this main chamber with doors set into the celestial mural disguised as constellations.

I considered ringing for a bath, but given all the transforming I'd done this evening, I needed to feed more than anything. Rather than disturb my manservant, Guillaume, I went to the small armoire near my bed and pulled out one of the crystal bottles filled with blood. This had come from one of my last victims near Gévaudan—a merchant with a penchant for brutality against his wife, mistress, and young daughter. His blood tasted as rotten as he'd been when he was alive, but the memories of his death were that much more satisfying. *God, how he'd screamed!*

I licked the last of the blood from the bottle and set it aside. Exhaustion crept through my veins, and I barely made it to my bed before sleep took me, and as ever, I dreamed of Mina.

3

MINA

April 15, 1768
Van Helsing's Clinic, Rue Ordener

THE INSISTENT BANGING AT MY BACK DOOR DISTURBED ME MORE THAN IT should have. Since the sun was only just beginning to set, I knew it wouldn't be *him*—or any of my vampire patients—but I'd been on edge for the last two days since he'd shown up.

Heart pounding, I went around back to see who was too wary or nefarious to come in through the front door to my clinic.

"Charlotte!" I exhaled, relief washing over me.

"My darling doctor," she trilled, pushing her way into the back storeroom, arms loaded with baskets of bread, cheese, and vegetables. She set them on my worktable and brushed the crumbs from the mossy green silk of her gown, set off with pink silk rosettes.

"I brought a basket of meat pies, as well—*merde*, where did I put it? I might have left it in my carriage. One short moment and I'll just pop out to check…" the distracted comtesse mumbled as she rifled through her parcels. Before she could leave, an enormous broad-shouldered French officer with striking green eyes and a queue of dark brown hair lumbered into the room, ducking as he filled—and exceeded—my doorway.

"Antoine, *chéri*, did I leave—?"

He looked at her, pushed a linen-covered basket in her hands, and swept her up in a passionate kiss. Once the Comtesse de Brionne was flushed and panting, he tipped his hat to me, winked at his dizzy fiancée, and departed without a word.

Charlotte stared dreamily after the handsome, threatening mountain of a man for long enough that I was forced to clear my throat to regain her attention.

"Sincerest apologies, Mina—you know how it is with sweet Antoine. I would suggest that perhaps my lustful attentions have been exacerbated by my werewolf turning, but frankly, I was always an avid enjoyer of bed sport so that hardly seems like a hypothesis worth investigating. Now, as I said, these baskets have more food this week because we had that horrible late snow and I'm worried about people having enough to eat. I fear the more *les Dames Dangereuses* tries to help, the worse the circumstances seem, don't you? I know you'll ensure this all gets to those who need it most. I don't blame the poor for distrusting us aristocrats, but I daresay it makes it difficult to offer aid when they won't take it," she said, filling the quiet of my clinic with a stream of effusive kindness. Once she had organized the baskets on my table, she finally turned and fixed a penetrating stare on me.

"What?" I chirped, unsettled. "Why do you regard me so?"

She tilted her head at me in a way that reminded me of a curious dog, and I huffed a nervous laugh.

"Have you given any thought to my words the other day?" she asked.

I swallowed. She had come to my clinic earlier this week and revealed she suspected my connection with the Beast of Gévaudan, or "the man in black," as she called him. She hadn't threatened me—rather, she wanted to help me and offered the warning that if she had worked out our historical attachment, The Order would, as well. I hadn't admitted anything to her then, but after Rafael had turned up on my doorstep, I knew it was only a matter of time before she sniffed him out —literally.

I cleared my throat and fiddled with one of the linen cloths covering the basket of meat pies.

"Your suspicions are correct," I said quietly.

Charlotte's lovely face betrayed nothing, but she took my hand and guided me to the chairs that sat in front of the fireplace.

"Tell me," she coaxed.

I sighed. "I haven't seen him in twenty years, Charlotte—not until that evening outside Grandrieu." Emotions tangled in my throat, making it difficult for me to continue.

"Who is he?" she asked.

"What will you tell The Order?" I inquired. "I do not want them to know. Forgive me, *mon amie,* but I do not trust them."

She nodded, sadness blooming on her face. "My loyalty is to you, Wilhelmina. Do not forget, beyond being my very dear friend, you saved my life and the lives of the people I love. As such, I must warn you things within The Order have become very dire indeed. The recent religious fervor led by the bastard Derais has driven the men into a frenzy of hate against the supernatural set. Daphne, Étienne, Antoine, and I are doing what we can to help soothe tempers and keep the peace, but more and more *les Dames Dangereuses* are being edged out of the conversation. Trust between us and The Order has fractured, but no one has yet made the first move. Of course I won't say anything to them. However, I must impress upon you the gravity of their concern. You should know The Order suspects the man in black of a great number of horrific deeds. While I don't trust The Order much these days, I'm still determining the veracity of their suspicions against him. But…if you say you have not seen him for twenty years, I would caution you to seriously consider your loyalty to someone you might not know anymore."

I opened my mouth to say more, but at that moment the bell above my door jangled and a young woman called out for me.

"Dr. Van Helsing?"

I smiled apologetically at Charlotte and hurried into the front room of the clinic. A gaunt young woman stood in the doorway, wringing her hands nervously. She was pretty—or had been, before suffering the starvation that hollowed out her face to a mere skin-covered skull. My heart squeezed at the sight.

"You must be Jacqueline," I began. "Your husband, Pierre, came to talk with me the other night. I expected you yesterday."

"My apologies," she said with a wobbly curtsy. "I was unwell."

I nodded, unsure of what to say that might alleviate some of her anxiety.

"Please, take a seat," I offered, gesturing at a chair along the wall. "I'll be with you in just a moment."

She did as she was instructed, and I went to make my apologies to Charlotte, but when I entered my back room, I discovered that she'd left. On the table with the baskets of food was a small scrap of parchment with a note.

Tell me when you're ready. I'll be here. Be careful.

XO,

Charlotte

P.S. Come to dine this evening! You simply must help me with wedding preparations.

Guilt drifted through me like wisps of smoke from an extinguished candle. I tried to ignore the rueful wash of relief I felt at being able to keep my secrets for a little while longer, even as I sensed the sands of time slipping through the hourglass of my life.

Shaking myself back to my professional demeanor, I stuffed the note in my pocket and smoothed my hands down the soft blue wool of my skirts.

"Jacqueline," I said, returning to the front of the clinic. "Tell me what's been happening at home. How are you faring?"

She smiled at me for a moment, but it slipped from her face with the first tears that spilled from her eyes.

"We cannot endure," she whispered through soft sobs. "Pierre has too little work, and even with me taking in more mending and laundry, it is not enough to put food on the table."

I allowed her some time to cry, awkwardly clutching her hand. When she sniffled a bit and seemed to recover some, I fetched her a glass of water and one of the meat pies Charlotte had brought. Jacqueline's eyes widened at the sight of the food.

"No, Doctor, I cannot—it's too much!"

I tutted and shoved the warm pastry into her hands. "I'll send you with some more for Pierre, as well. You must try to eat something but do so slowly. Small bites, or you will retch. You mustn't overtax your body."

Tentatively, she nibbled a corner of the pie and closed her eyes in bliss. Her tears continued to fall, and I contemplated my next words.

"Pierre told me you were considering infecting yourself with the blood plague," I said. "And he wished for me to talk you out of it because he fears for your immortal soul."

She turned watery eyes on me. "We cannot live on the charity of our neighborhood doctor forever. Blood is plentiful. Bread and money are not."

I'd heard the same story from nearly every poor commoner who'd come through my door over the last few years. The people of France were desperate, and relief was far from their horizons. Some—too many, truly— had made the impossible decision to protect their souls and the possibility of Heaven's mercy rather than agree to turn themselves into vampires. At the beginning of the epidemic, scores had died much faster than the plague could travel. Then, thousands began to face starvation, crippling poverty, and despair and refused to turn the other cheek. They found relatives, friends—even vampires for hire—to infect themselves with the blood plague. I did what I could to stem the tide of confusion, hunger, and misery sweeping across France by educating with as much as I knew, which was paltry. *Insufficient.* For every person I helped, ten more were beyond my help. Too often I felt like Sisyphus, forever rolling the same stone up the same mountain, unable to make any real progress. Or perhaps I was Pandora…doomed to live in a Hell of my own making for succumbing to the sin of curiosity.

For welcoming the devil into my bed…the same devil who would unleash this plague upon the world.

"I am not a priest, Jacqueline," I said with more bitterness than I intended. "I cannot speculate about what happens to our souls when we are infected with the blood plague. I cannot say if it is a punishment from God or a temptation sent to test our faith. What I can say with certainty is that every answer you believe the blood plague offers is equal to yet one more hardship. It is not the flawless solution you wish it to be. You will give up the sunlight. You must subsist on blood, but murder is still a crime, and it takes years of practice to learn how to control yourself when you feed. And what happens if you cannot find someone to feed on? Blood whores are expensive—as is their right—and there are still too few farm animals to subsist on, thanks to the poor crop yields. This is all to say nothing of the fact that King Louis is reluctant to offer any legal or economic protections for vampire-kind, despite the efforts of the vampire emissary and The Order. From a lawful, legal stance, you would be considered less than human and unprotected. Vulnerable."

Defeat leeched into Jacqueline's expression as she took another bite of the meat pie.

"If it is your decision, however, I will not stop you. I am only here to ensure that people make the decisions that they believe are best. I would encourage you to find a supportive maker—one who has at least been a vampire for a few years and can help guide your journey. Someone you trust," I said.

She finished the meat pie and licked the crumbs from her fingers. After taking a large drink of water, she stared hard at the ground between her feet.

"What about…" she paused, embarrassed. "Doctor, can vampires have children?"

Pain—hot and sharp—erupted in my chest. I swallowed the emotions trying to claw their way up my throat. Anxiously, I removed my spectacles and examined them for phantom smudges in a clumsy effort to avoid looking into Jacqueline's expectant eyes.

"Vampires and humans cannot reproduce," I replied, my voice wavering. "But two vampires may have children. It is extremely difficult but not impossible."

Jacqueline sniffed and wiped the lingering tears from her cheeks.

"Pierre would never agree to the change," she said forlornly. "And I desperately want a babe of my own."

"It is worth considering that vampire babes are exceedingly rare and grow up much differently than humans," I admitted.

"Have you met any?" she asked.

I winced seeing the hope on her face. A wave of despair washed over me, threatening to drown me in melancholy.

"Yes," I answered. "I have."

I counseled Jacqueline as best I could for the next half hour but couldn't be sure what she would decide. I hoped Pierre would support her regardless of her decision. After stuffing bread, cheese, and more meat pies into her arms and sending her on her way, I returned to my ever-waiting research in my back room. I'd been trying to understand the plague itself—why it behaved the way that it did, how it existed inside the human body, and if it could be cured. I knew other physicians working for The Order were performing some of the same work, but I had insight they did not.

I knew where it came from and how it all began.

Memories surfaced, unbidden and unwanted. I was sixteen, traveling southeast from Amsterdam through Vienna and onward with my father, the first Dr. Van Helsing—eminent surgeon, anatomist, physician, and scientist. To this day, I didn't know how I was able to convince him to take me along on his travels, lecturing and meeting with royalty and the intellectual elite. Mother had wanted me to stay at home and practice the domestic arts to find a good marriage, but I couldn't bear the thought of being sold off like some prize pig at a market of old, dull, ugly men. After months of begging, my father had relented. Looking back, I think he hadn't wanted me to marry any of the fools my mother favored. He'd convinced her that he might find a suitable match in the wealthy houses he'd frequent upon his travels.

If only they'd known then. If only I had known then.

I'd had an affinity for languages and for science, and becoming an impromptu apprentice to my father's work had been the most wonderful dream. That was what I'd wanted out of life—not to become an idle broodmare spreading my legs at the whims of my future husband's desires.

Things had been ideal until we'd entered the Hungarian city of Buda. After one of Papa's lectures, we'd been approached by a young man working for the illustrious House of Dracul, a royal house from the nearby province of Wallachia. I remembered the invitation all too well.

"Will you come to dine at my master's townhouse here in Buda? He and his family would dearly love to make your acquaintance, Doctor."

"My daughter and I would be honored," Papa had said.

Thus began the most fateful evening of my life.

Deep into my ruminating, I realized I'd been staring at the same page of notes for almost an hour. Night would soon fall, and now that I knew Rafael was somewhere in the area, I was worried about him trying to approach me again and putting both our lives in jeopardy. I enjoyed a fair amount of latitude from the operations of The Order, and I certainly didn't want to test their boundaries—or their patience.

I blew out a breath and rubbed the headache forming between my brows. *Dieu, I am tired.* I knew I had more work to do, but I owed Charlotte a visit to help her prepare for her upcoming wedding. There was also the possibility that I felt a gnawing sense of guilt at keeping secrets from her, considering I counted her as one of my best friends. As a foreigner, friends were hard to come by and even harder to keep.

Would it be so bad if Charlotte and Daphne knew? Would they condemn me for the sins of my past—my weakness of character in the face of the devil himself? Surely, they couldn't fault me for falling in love with the wrong man—not that he was a man.

But he certainly felt like one in my arms.

On the other hand, the blood plague is the thing that Daphne works so hard to rectify in France, and Charlotte was turned without her consent. Rafael is at fault for both.

As am I.

I winced as the realization condensed in my mind, like clouds blotting out the sun, but I was too much of a coward to tell them everything.

I won't risk losing their friendship...yet. Eventually, I will. Eventually, I will have to. Just not tonight.

I put on my second-best gown, an amethyst silk confection embroidered with blue flowers and trailing green vines, and pinned my curls up as best I could without a lady's maid. Charlotte and Daphne never minded my reluctance to abide by the same rules and fashions as the court, but if I didn't at least make an effort, Charlotte would spend half the evening trying to convince me to let her buy me a new wardrobe. Not that she pitied me, exactly, but she insisted the boring parties at Versailles were made more interesting with my attendance, despite my wallflower tendencies and inability to stomach champagne.

I pulled on my thick wool cloak, locked my apartment and my clinic, and made my way to the busy street where I could hire a fiacre to drive me to Charlotte's impressive estate. No sooner had I entered the dim carriage than a pair of fierce hands grabbed me and roughly pushed me back against the seat. Before I could scream, another hand came up to my face, stifling the sound and cutting off air.

Panic raced through me, and I lashed out, kicking at my attacker. I experienced a moment of triumph when I felt my boot connect with soft flesh and bone and heard a gruff curse, but the hand around my face tightened and my victory was short lived. Darkness beyond that of the encroaching night pulled at my senses, and I felt myself slip into the depths of unconsciousness.

4

RAFAEL

I sensed trouble before I was fully awake, but that didn't stop me from launching myself out of bed, shifting into my wolf form, and bolting across the countryside toward her. Even after twenty years, hundreds of miles, and lifetimes separating us, I felt her distress like a spider sensing the vibrations of flies caught in its web. Tremors of panic delicately thrummed along threads of silk that seemed to be affixed directly to my absent heart.

Fear. Anger. Not anger…outrage. Confusion. Disgust.

I struggled to concentrate—to focus on her feelings enough to determine what was happening to her and what shape these dangers would take—but as ever, I couldn't think clearly when it came to Mina. Rage built in me with every strike of my paws upon the earth, and fear for her fragile, mortal body gnawed at me. More memories surfaced as I ran, but this time they carried an ache of a different kind.

Let me make you, Mina, my love. Allow me to turn you so we won't ever be separated by time, I'd begged. Her eyes were a sharp blue that night, like a chunk of sea ice that had been worn by ocean currents into a deadly point.

Not until I know more, she had said. *I love you, Rafael, truly, I do. But I must understand what this curse holds for you. What it could mean for me, too.*

I'd railed at her, then, and stormed from the bedchamber. Ever practical, ever calculating, ever mindful Mina, who would always put knowledge and science and thought ahead of every feeling. Mina, whom I'd said loved reason more than she loved me.

I chuckled to myself now but had been devastated at the time. *What a fool I'd been.* I was so in love with her, I expected her to act as I would have—to throw everything away and dive headfirst into endless nights of ceaseless sexual pleasure and the power of consuming another human's precious life-force. She wouldn't, though. She couldn't. She was Mina, and for me to ask anything else of her…to ask her to be anything other than what she was, was utterly idiotic.

It had taken me years to learn that particular lesson.

No matter. I was back for her now, and it was up to me to convince her that I wasn't the devil she'd left behind. I was an entirely different demon now, and one who would spend however long atoning for all my mistakes.

She must believe me about the blood plague. When I speak with her, she must *believe me.*

Well, I'd have to find her first.

Onward I raced, faster and faster. Paris finally came into view. I reached out with my senses as soon as I drew near, hoping to find her in the jungle of scents and sounds all clamoring for my attention.

My mental connection to Mina flickered, and a spear of icy fear staked me in place. She wasn't dead—she couldn't be. It would certainly *feel* different. She felt…asleep. Unconscious, perhaps. An involuntary snarl slipped between my bared teeth. If I couldn't find her by sensing her, I would have to use my other skills to locate her.

I shifted to my bat form and flew to Rue Ordener. Her clinic was dark, as was her apartment above. I flew to the back alley, shifted to my human form, and donned the hidden stash of clothing I kept nearby. Nothing grand—simple black breeches, hose, a shirt, waistcoat, and jacket. Shifting was certainly useful, but ungainly when one was transforming in and around crowds of people.

I sniffed around for Pascal and Hubert, but their scents had faded some. Where had they gone? Unease built in me. I walked around to the front of her clinic and caught her scent, along with horse, leather, and wood—a fiacre. Where would she take a hired carriage at this time of night?

Two options came to mind. Either the estate of vampire Duchesse Daphne or the estate of Comtesse Charlotte de Brionne, the werewolf of my somewhat accidental making. Both women worked within The Order, were mated to a vampire and a werewolf (respectively), and had the kind of power that politicians and priests dreamed of. They loved Mina fiercely, which suited me fine, but they were formidable enemies if crossed, and I suspected they had more than one reason to distrust me.

I'd need to be on my guard and tread carefully.

Still, perhaps I could find Mina before she arrived at either *château*—if she arrived. The thought sent another spike of heated anger through me, and when I loosened my clenched fist, rivulets of blood dripped from the indentations my claws had made. I took a deep breath and forced myself calm as the tiny wounds healed.

I reached out again with my senses, detecting Mina's fading scent. Within moments, I was able to pinpoint its direction, and I took off at a rapid clip. After an hour of winding through the streets of Paris, I finally sensed I was nearing my destination.

At the end of a small lane, I spotted the dilapidated fiacre. Behind the small carriage sprawled a grim-looking cemetery, complete with overgrown graves and crumbling tombs. It was obvious the dead here didn't have many mourners to honor their memory.

As I approached the fiacre, I heard the labored grunting of two men wrestling with a weight between them. Willing myself calm again, I approached, only to see my old friends Pascal and Hubert struggling to lift an unconscious Mina down from the door of the carriage. I scanned the area again, trying to determine where they would take her in such a forgotten place. If they were trying to violate her—my claws lengthened at the thought—it seemed rather out of the way for them when they could have had her in the fiacre. *Unless they already have…*

"Gentlemen," I said smoothly. "It appears you need some help."

"Fuck off," Hubert grumbled. "This doesn't concern you."

"Be on your way, Monsieur. We don't need your help," Pascal huffed.

I chuckled—the deep, monstrous sound echoing in the night.

"You misunderstand me," I rumbled, fangs and claws lengthening. "It appears you *will need* some help."

I launched myself at Hubert, the closest man. Before his shock could register, I sank my claws into his neck and twisted his head from his shoulders. His body fell to the ground with a soft thump, and the wet sounds of blood leeching from his decapitated head. The elegant scent of copper and salt drifted up from the pile of human at my feet, making me nearly feral with hunger and violence.

An ear-piercing shriek split the night, and Pascal dropped Mina and stumbled backward. He recovered and bolted toward one of the old mausoleums, which struck me as odd until I saw the faint flicker of candlelight glowing from the cracks in the door. *A hideout of some sort?*

I caught up to him easily and lifted him by the throat. He whimpered and kicked, and I felt the frenzied beat of his pulse beneath my fingertips.

"Tell me," I soothed, compelling the truth from his lips and ignoring the siren song of fresh blood. "You watched Mina for The Order. What were you doing with her this evening?"

"They wanted her," he choked out.

"Yes," I grinned, displaying my infamous dual sets of fangs. "Don't we all?"

His eyes widened in fear and surprise. "It's…it's you! The Beast! The Master of all Vampires! The devil himself!"

"Enchanté," I said, inclining my head slightly. "Do call me Rafael." I allowed my human face to transform into a demonic shape, sprouting horns, a forked tongue, and wholly black eyes with red pinprick pupils.

Pascal squeezed his eyes shut and pissed himself.

"Why did The Order want Mina?" I repeated, in a deep voice that sounded like a legion of angry demons.

"They're looking for you," he whispered. "They think she knows more than she's telling. They wanted her in for questioning. Please don't kill me!"

"Questioning?" I echoed, concern knitting my brows. "What kind of questioning?"

Pascal pressed his lips together, but I couldn't tell if it was from fear of me or fear of The Order.

"What kind of questioning?" I boomed, infusing the command with more compulsion.

His eyes snapped to mine, and I let my demon visage melt away until I looked human again.

"They plan to question her as a witch," he finally said.

A witch. Mina was no more a witch than I was a demon. The Order would torture and murder her to get to me. Either they had become more desperate and dangerous than I'd realized, or their fear of the blood plague had introduced madness into their ranks. I'd known about The Order for years but had let them operate as they willed, especially after the Duchesse de Duras had joined and been turned. She and her mate, the recently made Duc Étienne de Noailles—who was, himself, a vampire and the vampire emissary to King Louis XV—had been fighting what I knew could only be a losing battle. Rights for vampire-kind. Peaceful coexistence between the vampire poor and the human aristocracy. *Absolutely ridiculous.*

Clearly, The Order had moved faster into cowardice, suspicion, and panic than I had anticipated. I knew what would come next. The systematic removal of every vampire they could get their hands on, along with their allies.

Pascal flailed limply, reminding me that I still held him by the throat. I quirked a brow at him.

"Were they all agreed on this course of action?"

"All but *les DD.* They could not be told," he said.

"Ah yes, *les Dames Dangereuses.* How could they not know? Don't their numbers outweigh the men of The Order by now?"

I'd asked the question rhetorically more than anything, but the look of confusion on Pascal's face told me he wouldn't be much more help.

"Well," I said brightly. "Pascal, I'm delighted to offer you two options this evening. I can either drain your entire body of blood and leave your withered corpse under a tree for the crows, *or* I can turn you and offer you the gift of immortality for the price of entering my service."

Tears slipped down Pascal's cheeks. "You know what The Order has planned for *les sanguisuges,*" he whispered. "I am damned either way."

I tutted. "*Tsk,* Pascal, *mon ami,* we are all damned. Some of us simply face judgment day a bit later than others. Which will it be?"

A strangled sob rose from his throat. "I will not risk my immortal soul to delay the death of my body."

"So be it," I replied, sinking my fangs into his throat. The need for blood surpassed all other thoughts and emotions—it had been too long since I'd fed. Unlike many of the newer vampires, I could survive on smaller amounts of blood, but when I used my abilities more frequently, I required more. Changing shape, in particular, was quite draining. Already, I felt strength and power returning to me, drugging me in the way it always had and always would. If only humans understood how precious blood truly was—this sticky, honeyed liquid that animated bones and flesh—they might not consider the blood plague as the shameful alternative to starvation. It was worth more than ten thousand loaves and fish.

Foolish humans.

I drank until I felt Pascal's life-force ebb away, then collected his and Hubert's bodies. I felt a pang of something…disgust? No. Pity, perhaps, at adding yet more lives to my tally of sins. Or perhaps it was regret for Pascal's misplaced loyalty and misguided piety. Either way, instead of tossing the bodies into the undergrowth for the animals to find, I located a rusted shovel leaning against one of the tombstones and dug makeshift, shallow graves for both men. It was too bad The Order had involved these poor human fools, and it was too bad they had come for my Mina.

I heard the faint rustling of silk fabric and soft moans emanating from near the fiacre, and I rushed over to find Mina coming to. She was murmuring something insensible, but I didn't see evidence of a head wound. I picked her up and carried her back inside the fiacre, and her head lolled limply against my shoulder, her glasses dangling haphazardly from one ear. Intrigued and somewhat concerned, I inhaled at the crook of her neck and detected a faint bitter scent carried along in her blood —laudanum.

Pascal and Hubert had evidently needed to drug her to ensure she was compliant and cooperative for The Order's brutal questioning. The knowledge reawakened the rage in me, and I fought to tamp it back down.

From my experiences with forms of opium, I knew she would need a safe place to sleep off the soporific effects of the drug. I was reluctant to return her to her home since The Order would likely send more thugs 'round to kidnap her again once they learned of Pascal and Hubert's fates.

I could attempt to take her to Charlotte's home, or Daphne's, but I was uncertain about how they would receive me. Additionally, I wasn't certain about their level of involvement with The Order's new and dangerous tactic. I believed what Pascal had told me, but I found it hard to believe that both women had been completely unaware of such an evil plot brewing from within their midst.

That left me with one option. I could bring her to my home, *le Château du Diable*, to recover. She would be furious upon waking, which could put my greater plans in jeopardy, but since I didn't trust The Order to leave her home in peace and I didn't trust *les DD* because they operated within The Order, I didn't have much of a choice.

Merde.

I found a stale-smelling blanket beneath the seat of the fiacre and tucked her in as best I could. Then I climbed out onto the seat of the small carriage and picked up the reins. It would have been faster for me to turn into my wolf form and carry her across the countryside, but I didn't want to risk being seen and I wasn't certain I'd be able to hold onto her very well when she was in this drug-induced stupor. The threat of sunrise loomed.

I was grateful for the cloak I'd stolen from Hubert's body, since it allowed me to hide the blood smeared across my face, neck, and hands. I should have washed after burying the men, but I hadn't thought I would have time. Hopefully, I could clean up when I arrived home…before Mina truly awoke.

I urged the horse faster across the countryside, racing against the dawn. By the time my château came into view, the sky was already a worrying shade of lilac. I pulled up short, jumped from the driver's seat, and pulled Mina from the fiacre. With a growl and the tearing of fabric, I shifted into an enormous bat creature, stretched my massive leathery wings, and gingerly lifted her into the air. It was during times like these I found my secret front entrance a troublesome feature, but having the door hidden at the top of the highest tower was the best form of security.

Only slightly more inconvenient was the fact that it was at this moment Mina regained consciousness.

5

MINA

April 16, 1768
Château du Diable

SOMETHING IS WRONG.

My stomach lurched with the movement of my body, but I felt as if I were underwater, moving slowly through icy currents. My mind was at odds with the rest of me, utterly blissful in a sleepy stupor I couldn't seem to climb my way out of.

What is happening to me?

I felt a strange pressure around my chest, as if my stays had grown too small. Had I laced them too tight when I dressed for my evening? Was I at Charlotte's château? Where was she? Where was I?

Confusion clouded my mind, but instead of panicking, I grasped for it like a thick blanket and wrapped it tighter around myself. Everything felt off-kilter, but so delicious.

I heard the rush of wind in my ears and a lilting giggle, which I realized had slipped from my lips.

Why am I laughing?

I cracked one eye open, expecting to find myself at home in bed, rousing from some curious late-night dream. Or perhaps I was at Charlotte's home, tucked into one of her guest room beds after having one too many glasses of champagne with dinner.

No, that's not right. I hate champagne.

Still, nothing could have prepared me for the sight I beheld.

I stared up at an enormous creature—so massive and terrifying, it looked like Hell had spat it out for being too much a horror. Half bat, half demon, it held me in its huge claws, carrying me through the air on tattered, leathery wings. Fear unlike anything I'd experienced seized me, and I opened my mouth to scream. Oddly, a hysterical laugh pierced the night instead of a shriek, and the hell-beast looked down at me. *Is that blood on its face? Is it going to eat me?*

The idea seemed so preposterous. *Have I survived all that I have to be eaten by a giant devil bat?* What a bizarre end for a doctor trying to unlock the secrets of the blood plague. Instead of feeling what would be a normal surge of terror, I could only feel…relief. *At last, the weight of obligation, responsibility, and guilt will be lifted. It is only too bad that I am here alone, and no one will know my fate.*

More laughter bubbled up from within me, until tears streamed down my cheeks, and I gasped for air. Suddenly, I found it very hard to breathe, as if my lungs would not obey the needs of my body.

The monster holding me swooped downward, and we entered a dark, crumbling stone tower at the top of a forlorn and forgotten castle. The pressure on my chest eased some, and I found myself in a heap of confused limbs on a cold stone floor. Darkness pressed in, making it impossible for me to see. From my left, I heard an ominous and nause-ating popping, squelching noise—much like the sound of bones breaking beneath flesh—but it stopped almost as soon as it had started.

Silence descended, which felt infinitely more terrifying.

"Mina," came a voice. I knew it, as if from a dream.

I scrambled to my feet but was too unsteady. I pitched forward but found myself encased in arms like bands of iron, which lifted me from the ground and carried me from the darkness of the cold tower.

My stomach rolled with the movement, and I squeezed my eyes shut to steady my equilibrium. I heard us move softly down a long hallway, entering door after door until we reached some place warm and quiet.

I heard the soft crackle of a fire in a hearth as cold but gentle hands unpinned my gown and loosened my stays. When I was down to my chemise and stockings, I felt myself being lifted again and tucked into a soft bed layered with fur and velvet blankets. Warmth seeped into my limbs and tugged at my senses, pulling me back toward the abyss of sleep.

Curiosity had me opening my eyes to look for the hell-beast from my nightmares, but in the barest glow of firelight, I only saw a man standing before me.

He was terrifying and beautiful, with long black hair, the chiseled cheekbones and patrician nose of royalty, and obsidian eyes that made me think of forbidding caves at the bottom of the deep ocean. Cold, fathomless, incomprehensible—but not empty. Filled with horrors and mysteries. His features were neutral—his expression impassive, and I realized that his entire mouth and face was covered with blood and filth. Something distant in my mind suggested that it probably wasn't his own.

Everything about the man was familiar and yet alien to me. Even as my body responded and my arms reached for him, my heart pounded a warning in my chest. I was prey to this predator, but that didn't dampen the echo of my body's need for him.

Rafael.

Sleep and the drug that whispered through my veins wrapped me tighter and I slumped back onto the pillows, but I kept my gaze on the dark man standing there, staring at me in the flickering golden glow spilling from the hearth. I wanted to ask him questions, but when I opened my mouth through the syrup of fatigue, only one phrase oozed forth.

"You came back for me."

He did not react, and it occurred to me that I might not have spoken at all. It was then that sleep finally claimed me, and I remembered no more.

FEVERED VISIONS HAUNTED MY SLEEP. SOME FELT LIKE MEMORIES. SOME FELT like nightmares, and I mourned my ability to distinguish between the two. One image surfaced again and again—Rafael covered in blood.

Queasiness swirled through my stomach, and I moaned through parched lips. I kicked the damp, sweat-soaked sheets off and blinked in the near darkness. I was in the same room as before, but this time I was alone. A small table next to the bed held my spectacles and a porcelain ewer of water, an empty goblet, and a shallow bowl of some thin, savory broth.

I sat up against the pillows, put on my spectacles, and poured myself some water. *Where am I? Where is Rafael? I didn't dream of him again, did I? How long have I been here? What happened?*

The more I came into consciousness, the faster the questions raced through my mind. Panic started to build in my chest, and it took a great feat of strength to prevent it from taking control of me. I sipped the cool water and inhaled slowly to calm myself.

Before I could dwell too much on my troubling circumstances, there was a soft knock on the bedchamber door.

"Yes," I rasped, my voice hoarse from thirst and disuse.

I'd expected a servant to enter, but Rafael stepped into the room. My heart seized in my chest and my breath caught, as it did every time I looked at him. Rather than his customary all-black suit, he was clad in a loose, white linen shirt, soft leather breeches, and a floor-length red silk dressing gown, open and trailing behind him like a royal robe. The gold embroidered dragons of his family crest glittered in the low firelight, making them look almost alive.

He padded into the room on bare feet and came to sit at the foot of the bed. I shifted slightly, pulling away from the all-too-intimate move.

He noted my discomfort and smiled.

"I'm glad to find you awake, little Mina," he soothed in his deep baritone. Seeing the obvious wariness on my face, he continued. "You have nothing to fear from me."

I sipped at my water and narrowed my eyes.

"That remains to be seen, Rafael."

He tutted and leaned down onto his side, propped up on one elbow.

"It's twice now that I've saved your life. Still, you recoil from me. Is it from our past, I wonder? Or something else?" He grinned at me, the scant light glinting off his lethal fangs. Beneath his teasing, I sensed something sad in his words, but my mind felt too fuzzy for me to explore it properly.

I gripped the water goblet tighter in my hands. I knew he could sense my emotions—not that it would take a vampire's keen senses to perceive my distress—and I didn't want to give him any more of an edge than he already possessed.

"What happened?" I asked tightly. "How did I come to be here—wherever *here* is?"

I wasn't sure what I expected, certainly not a straight answer or the bold truth of what happened. Rafael had been a spoiled young man and had enjoyed teasing me too much when we were younger. He loved playing mind games and speaking in riddles, and he had the patience of eternity to frustrate anyone unlucky enough to get drawn into a verbal battle. Sitting across from him now, I felt like a mouse staring down a rather large, rather hungry alley cat.

"Mina," he purred. "You are still overcoming the effects of the drug you were given. You're weak…tired…cold."

On the last word, his gaze dropped from my face to my nipples visible from beneath my worn cotton chemise. Despite the dim light in the bedchamber and the blackness of his eyes, I recognized the shimmer of lust. Self-conscious, I tugged the thick coverlet up to my neck.

"Yes," I lied, not chilled in the slightest. "It's frigid in here."

He quirked one sharp black brow at me, then waved his hand at the waning embers in the fireplace. With a soft word in an unrecognizable language, the flames roared to life.

My eyes widened. "Not a side effect of the blood plague?" I questioned. "Is this from the curse? Or have you been studying witchcraft?"

"Perhaps I made a deal with the devil, and he took whatever was left of my pitiful soul after all," he quipped drily. "In exchange for a wealth of varied dark powers."

I glared.

He laughed again and rose from the bed, his lean muscles flexing like a lithe jungle cat.

"Later, Mina. For now, you need rest and food and drink. Restore your body and then I will give you the answers that will satisfy your mind." The low timbre of his voice and the heat in his eyes set my skin aflame.

I sipped at the water again to try to cool my temperament.

"Whose blood was it?" I asked suddenly.

He was quiet for a moment. Then, "Why?"

I was glad that he didn't pretend to misunderstand.

"I want to know," I answered. "Are they still alive?"

He tilted his head at me in a curious way, as if observing a specimen in a bell jar.

"Not on this plane of existence, no. Why do you want to know?"

I narrowed my eyes. "I don't want to be responsible for any more deaths."

"You are not."

"Let me judge that for myself," I replied. "Whose blood was it?"

"Are you so bored and righteous that you must assume the guilt for things which you do not control? I am flattered by your self-flagellation for my sins, Mina—it shows you still care." He chuckled.

I couldn't be sure if he was teasing to get a rise out of me or if it was because he didn't want to tell me. Twenty years ago, back at the very beginning, I would have taken the bait—blushing and stammering and protesting that I didn't care for him. *I don't care about you*, I would have said. *You're nothing more than a scientific curiosity to me and a patient of my father. You aren't even human.*

How cold I'd been then.

And you're so much warmer now, came the sarcastic answering thought. And yet, I wouldn't admit to him that I still cared.

"The blood plague leeches across the continent because of your family's curse," I said coolly. "Your father tasked my father with finding the solution. He failed...*we* failed. So yes, as much as it is your fault that the plague escaped the confines of your ancestral home, it is equally my family's fault that it has not been stopped. *My fault*, Rafael. Every vampire and every death can be laid at my feet because of what my father and I could not do. Tell me whose blood it was."

I folded my arms across my chest, waiting for him to answer me. Our eyes locked across the bed in a stalemate of iron wills. A lesser person would see Rafael's stoic expression as halcyon as a marble bust, but I recognized the subtle changes that I'd long ago memorized. The dilation of his pupils, the slight flare of a nostril, the barest twitch of his lips...*frustration*. Exasperation. Annoyance. Hunger.

"Two men," he finally said. "Shall I tell you about their deaths, sweet Mina, so that you can comfort yourself while you pray for our forgiveness?"

Two men.

"Oh no," I whispered, realization dawning. I should have expected this outcome. *What a fool I'd been!* "Not Pascal and Hubert?"

Rafael's eyes widened almost imperceptibly, and he sat back on the bed.

"You knew them?" he asked, somewhat accusatory. "You knew these men were the ones watching you, salivating over you and your body... slaves of The Order." His last words came out with remarkable venom.

It offended me that he thought I was so clumsy and weak as to not notice two such stooges haunting my clinic and my apartment for weeks.

"Of course I knew them," I bit back. "Not only do I have eyes of my own, but I'm the only doctor around for this world of monsters you created. Every vampire who came in through my clinic told me the clods were skulking around, reeking of sweat and drink and The Order's dusty robes."

I swallowed my satisfaction when I caught a glint of sheepishness in Rafael's eyes. It was not enough to keep my anger at bay.

"You don't know what you've done," I muttered.

"I saved your life," he said sharply. "Those *clods* kidnapped you, drugged you with a truly inappropriate amount of laudanum, and had every intention of delivering you to The Order for questioning."

That caught my attention. "Questioning?"

"For witchcraft," he said, leveling me with an intense gaze. "Because they would use you to get to me."

"You lie! That cannot be true," I argued. "I've been an ally for The Order. Yes, I knew they wanted to watch me to see if you'd come around, but they wouldn't..."

"Wouldn't they?" Rafael snapped as he surged to his feet. "How much do you know about The Order, Mina? How much have your friends Charlotte and Daphne told you? How much do *they* know? It wasn't too long ago that The Order was aiding the church in its hunt for witches. They're still bribing, murdering, exploiting, punishing, and torturing people."

I stared at him quizzically. "And what has your family been doing for eons?"

The specter of rage flitted across his face but was gone quickly.

"That was a long time ago," he gritted out.

"Yes, well, it was long ago that The Order hunted witches," I replied, getting out of bed to pace the room in agitation. "What do you care about The Order when you can easily hide from them—outrun them—outmatch them in every way? And why did you come here if you knew they would hunt you? Is it for sport? Is it because you're bored with your life in Wallachia and your treasure trove of women and your damn castle? Is it because you're punishing me by spreading the blood plague—infecting everyone in the country that I've come to love and call my home?"

I flung each question at him like a weapon, becoming angrier by the second. He stood by the fireplace, arm braced above the mantle, staring into the flames but tensing with every barb I hurled. Other than that, he did not react.

"Damn it, Rafael, why did you really kill Pascal and Hubert?"

Finally, his composure cracked, and he moved to me in a blur of brilliant supernatural speed. He grabbed me by the shoulders and pushed me harshly against the wall next to the bed. His grip was firm, but not tight enough to be painful. A startled gasp parted my lips, and his dark gaze snagged on the movement. His eyes turned solid black with pupils of red, like rubies set in onyx pools.

"Because," he growled. "They came for you. They dared to lay their hands on you. They hurt you to get to me. I should have made them suffer, Mina. God, I wanted to. I wanted to invade their minds and spear them with a thousand unique agonies until they begged me for the release of death. I should have broken a bone for every impure thought they had about you. I should have ripped out an organ for every vile word they said against you. I could have given them so much pain, Mina—you'll never know how much."

Horror—and shamefully, excitement—rendered me speechless. A tear slipped down my cheek, catching on the glass of my spectacle. I released a silent, shaky breath, then opened my mouth hesitantly, unsure of what to say.

"I killed them because they came for you, Mina," Rafael repeated, his demonic eyes never straying from my lips as he bent to kiss me. "And you are *mine*."

His mouth descended to mine, and the moment our lips met, twenty years of betrayal, pain, loneliness, regret, and longing surged forth. Before I could access the logical part of my brain and know enough to stop this foolishness, I clung to him, sliding my hands to the nape of his neck to pull him closer.

When we'd been young together—or *younger*—our kisses had been tentative, exploratory, sweet. He always touched me as if he was afraid to break me, despite having the years of practice learning the value of his own supernatural strength.

That innocent hesitation was gone now. In its place was sheer power, monstrous hunger, and desperate need. His soft lips moved over mine while his tongue sought entry—plundering as if he wanted to consume my very soul. When I sucked at his roving tongue, I felt his deep growl of pleasure more than I heard it, vibrating from his chest as he pressed his body into mine. His arousal hardened against my stomach, unleashing a storm of desire.

I wanted him. I needed him.

I hated him.

6

RAFAEL

April 16, 1768
Château du Diable

GODS ABOVE AND DEMONS BELOW, SHE TASTED PERFECT. SHE WAS EVERY RAY of sunshine I'd missed in my life of darkness. She was everything I loved about humans—promise and curiosity and hope. If I'd been born with a heart, it would have beaten only for her. She was my world, my past, my future…*my redemption.*

I pushed her harder into the wall, loving the way her body felt beneath mine. Her thin chemise was so threadbare it might not have existed as a layer between us, and the thought drove me almost feral with lust, so great was my need to claim her.

Mina. My Mina.

Her tongue swept mine, lightly grazing my fangs. The feeling was like a bolt of lightning, making my hard cock ache. The pain of my need was almost too much to bear, but I would take this torture over anything—everything—in the world.

My hands moved of their own will, sliding down her shoulders to caress her breasts through the soft fabric of the chemise. When my thumb found the peaked, pebbled nipple of her left breast, she whimpered, and the delicate sound of pleasure nearly unmanned me.

She arched against me like a bow being pulled taut. My hand drifted down, seeking the hem of her chemise. When I lifted it to slide one cool palm up the heated skin of her thigh and round hip, her eyes flew open.

Despite the lust in her gaze and the scent of her arousal, I sensed her sudden shock and regret.

The ache of my unspent desire was chased by the acute agony of shame, remorse, and despair that for her, this was a mistake. It was not surprising then, when she put her hands to my chest and pushed me away —gently but firmly.

"No, Rafael," she huffed, but I was already across the room. "We cannot do this. I will not do this. I am not yours—not anymore."

Anger flared, white hot. *You will always be mine,* I wanted to say. Instead, I bowed my head.

"As you wish, Doctor. Forgive me for…taking liberties. I will not touch you again until you ask."

"I shall not ask," she grumbled, allowing the last of her lust to dissipate like fog chased by the sunlight of her anger. "I'm not here to be some kind of royal consort while you wreak havoc on all of Europe, only to go back to your throne and sire some selfish, monstrous heir."

Sadness bloomed in my chest, but I deserved her anger.

"I will send a maid in shortly," I said, barely keeping the bitterness from my tone. "She will help you bathe and dress and break your fast. You are still recovering from the drug, but unfortunately, The Order's actions have forced my timeline and we have much to discuss."

Her eyebrows arched.

"I can take care of myself," she protested. "I know how to manage the sickness from opium. I do not need you, or your maid, or your hospitality. I should like to return home."

I sighed in irritation. "While you are not a prisoner here, you would require my help to leave this fortress and daylight is upon us. I must rest. After that, I will say my peace and then the decision will be yours."

"Decision?" she echoed, her curiosity piqued.

"For now, we are safe here," I said, ignoring her question. "My servants are at your disposal. They will attend to your needs if you simply name them."

Something like guilt flashed across her face.

"Rafael, I…" she swallowed. "I'm sorry for…" she gestured vaguely toward the wall. "—for *participating.*"

I smirked. "Do not apologize to the devil for indulging in sin."

She bit her bottom lip, chagrined. I tried to ignore the desire to bite her bottom lip for her. I inclined my head once more and headed for the door, ringing for the maid as I left.

I could not look back.

I had stationed Mina in a guest bedchamber, but every room beneath the castle was fully equipped to address any manner of need. Just now, I wanted distance from her—from the desire I still fought and the petty hurts her words had inflicted. At least now I had a more accurate idea of what she thought of me after twenty years.

I knew she would be wounded given how we'd left things—how I'd left things. As easy as it was for me to forgive her anger, it gutted me that she believed what everyone else seemed to believe—that I was the one to let loose the blood plague and inflict my family's curse upon the world.

It was so easy for everyone to believe the worst of me, the selfish second son of Wallachia's royal family. The wastrel, the rogue, the spare. *The devil.* Only lately had I stopped believing those things of myself, so I supposed it would take Mina and the rest of the world time to catch up.

Unfortunately, it was time I didn't have.

Yet, I could wait an afternoon. The events of the previous few evenings hadn't left me much time to sleep, and after using my powers gratuitously, I needed time to restore my energy. Having drained Pascal, I didn't yet require more blood, but I didn't want the hunger to strike and shorten my temper any further with Mina. What I was about to do required great patience. As a preventative measure, I entered my library and went to the sideboard with several crystal decanters of blood and spirits. Longing for warmth in the absence of Mina's body, I mixed myself a drink of blood and *ţuică*, the potent alcohol from my homeland. The older I got, the harder it was for me to become intoxicated, but it certainly wasn't for lack of trying. Regenerative abilities had disadvantages, but most newly turned vampires wouldn't know that until a few decades into their eternities.

The heady mix of blood and alcohol burned as it went down, settling like brimstone in my gut. Rather than returning to one of the bedrooms to lie down for a spell, I sat in the plush velvet armchair that faced the polished stone fireplace. With a thought and a word, the waiting logs began to burn, and I settled back into the chair, willing dreamless sleep to come.

When I woke, I was sure I'd only dozed for a few moments, but the carriage clock on the mantle indicated otherwise. It had been several hours, and the sun would soon be setting. I hoped Mina had also rested and eaten, but I wondered if that was likely given her stubborn streak. She *would* refuse any comforts I offered out of a misplaced sense of petulant independence. I knew she could take care of herself—she obviously had for the past twenty years—but as my guest, it was my job to take care of her.

As your guest and your future wife, came the whisper of hope from the space where my heart should have been. *Hmm. Perhaps. Perhaps not,* came the answer from my logical mind.

I roused myself and washed, then changed into a fresh shirt, breeches, and banyan. Rather than the red and gold of my family's house, I opted for a deep sapphire velvet, partly because I wished for something warm and comforting, and partly because the blue reminded me of Mina's eyes. I strolled down the hall in mink-lined slippers and paused outside her door. I'd long ago sworn not to use my abilities to spy on her or invade her privacy, which included compelling her, reading her thoughts, or using my supernatural senses to pry into her solitude, but the conversation between Mina and my servant carried loudly enough that I didn't need to betray that promise.

"He's owned it for ten years, mademoiselle, but hasn't been living here all that time," the servant said.

"Ten years! He's been in France that whole time?" Mina exclaimed.

The servant sounded anxious. "As I said, he hasn't spent all his time here. He travels extensively. He's only been in residence primarily for the last year or so, I think. Truly, it's hard to know. We don't always see him when he is here. We simply do our day-to-day duties on the off chance that he'll arrive."

I could practically hear the wheels turning in Mina's head.

"That must frustrate you," she replied.

"On the contrary, mademoiselle, he is a most generous employer. Ever thoughtful, never abusive. I don't believe a word of the stories the other villagers say," the servant replied earnestly.

Satisfaction shined through me, if only for a moment. I'd plucked this young girl from a particularly vile marquis's household, along with her two younger brothers. I paid my servants handsomely and treated them better than I would have treated my own family, knowing what it was for them to serve a monster. At times, when melancholy seized me, I often wondered if my servants would be the closest I would ever get to a family of my own.

Chasing the ensuing storm from my mind, I squared my shoulders and knocked. The servant rushed to open it, and I entered to find Mina bathed and dressed in the gown of pale lemon silk I'd secured for her. With her beauty and the bright blue of her eyes, she looked like the sun. My chest tightened at the sight.

"You look exquisite," I murmured. "I hope you were able to eat and rest in my absence."

"Yes, thank you," she replied politely, if a little cold. "The gown is very fine."

The servant girl smiled, curtsied, and left us to our simmering tension.

Mina wrung her hands together and paced next to the bed. Twice she tugged her spectacles from her face and cleaned them, then replaced them atop her pert nose. Despite her anxiety, I was pleased to see she had recovered much from the near overdose of laudanum and our...*encounter.*

"I don't often wear light colors," she said nervously. "I like them, but they're so impractical for me as a physician—especially for vampires. The stains are terrible, you see, when one's life is ruled by blood."

I raised a brow, my nervousness melting with her amusing observation.

"Yes," I said with a grin. "I know."

She blushed when she realized what she'd said and who she'd said it to.

"I'm sorry, I didn't mean..."

I tilted my head as she swore under her breath and forced a brittle smile.

"Mina," I began, coming slowly to stand next to her. "Be easy, please. Too many people in this world fear and despise me, and it would be a tragedy if you became one of them. I'm sorry for earlier and I meant what I said. There are a great many things I need to tell you and after that, it will be your decision to determine your fate—and mine."

Her lovely eyes widened, and she blew out a breath, steeling herself for something unpleasant.

"Very well," she said. "I am ready."

I chuckled. "Not here. I have something else I'd like to show you, and it will make the telling somewhat more bearable."

I held out my arm for her, and she hesitated.

"Please, Mina," I implored. "Just trust me a little longer."

Nodding, she wrapped her hand around my arm, and warmth bloomed beneath her touch. I smiled gratefully and led her back down the hallway.

As we passed room after room, her little gasps of delight at my home pleased me. We paused quietly so she could admire the palatial library, the frescoed ballroom, and the Roman-styled baths—the gallery of my favorite paintings and sculptures accumulated throughout my travels. She stared in confusion and envy at my laboratory, filled with state-of-the art equipment and volumes of scientific literature from cultures around the world.

I urged her on until we arrived at my chosen destination, my favorite room in the castle apart from the library. We descended two flights of marble steps into a candlelit alcove facing two massive oak doors carved with reliefs of Persephone in the Underworld.

Releasing her hand, I opened the doors and ushered her in. The first thing one sensed when entering this part of the castle was the warm air, thick with humidity. The second thing was the peculiar fragrance—

warring scents of damp earth, a thousand varieties of perfumed flowers, rot and decay of old vegetation, and everywhere *life*. Then, as one's eyes adjusted to the low golden glow of the candlelit space, one could truly appreciate the wonder.

Mina stepped forward and turned in a slow circle.

"Rafael," she whispered. "It's like stepping into a jungle from a storybook! How is this possible?"

"Welcome to my sunken greenhouse," I said, pleased that she appreciated my favorite marvel. "The glass windows above us are hidden in the grounds around the estate and difficult for those above to see, but they let in enough light during the daytime for the plants to grow. I've collected most of these as seeds or cuttings from my travels and have longed for a place to nurture them. Plants, you see, when tended properly, can thrive for almost as long as I can. It's harder to keep and care for pets when their lifespans are but the blink of an eye for me."

She faced me, something like pity on her face. Ignoring it and the twinge of emotion it elicited in me, I continued.

"The ponds on either side contain several varieties of fish and frogs, and insects do much of the pollination. Those over there are the largest lily pads in the world," I explained, pointing to the massive leaves floating atop shallow black water.

Mina strolled along the marble paths, smiling in wonder. The tropical air condensed in small droplets on her glasses, and she took them off absently to clean them. "It's extraordinary," she whispered. "How does it stay so warm in here? I don't see any fireplaces."

"They are below us," I replied. "Stacks of bricks and tiles are heated much like they were in Roman bathhouses. The tiles beneath us bring the heat up, and it spreads out through the marble and rises upward. The sunlight during the daytime helps to heat the space, but of course, I only come here at night. My staff light the candelabras along the walls in the evening for me."

We walked beneath delicate trailing vines, hanging mosses, and fragrant tropical flowers until we reached a small grotto with a waterfall set back against the wall. A small table and two chairs sat in the middle of the grotto and spread before us was a sumptuous picnic.

Mina sat dutifully and waited as I poured her a cup of herbal tea—her preference from years ago. I poured some for myself and offered her a plate of sandwiches and almond cakes, as well as a crystal bowl of vibrant tropical fruits.

"Astonishing," she murmured, selecting a sliced mango.

Overhead, something flitted close to her hair, and she startled.

"Apologies for the behavior of my bats," I chuckled. "They can be rather greedy, but you needn't worry. These fellows only eat fruit."

I tossed a banana off to the side to entertain them and turned back to Mina, who was eyeing me with what I assumed were a million questions in her mind.

"Ask away," I said.

She scrunched up her face, pointedly searching for a place to begin.

"Botany, Rafael? Truly?"

"Mina, of all the things you could ask, you cast doubt upon my secret hobby?" Amusement sparkled in my tone, like bubbles in champagne.

She sipped her tea. "Never in my life would I have thought that you would find fascination in one of the sciences."

"You wound me, my dear. I am not the same vampire I was all those years ago, hiding from my tutors and cheating my way through exams. Besides, it was your father who sparked my interest in the subject," I said.

"Papa?" she asked, eyebrows lifting. "How?"

I sighed. "Mina, here is as good as place as any to tell you what I must."

Sensing my trepidation, she placed a hand on my arm. "Despite our past, Rafael, I am here to listen."

I took a deep breath and began.

7
RAFAEL

April 16, 1768
Château du Diable

"When you and your father came to our townhome in Buda that evening, neither of you could know what kind of an effect it would have on our family. My father had heard of your father's reputation—and now, the great Doctor Van Helsing was in our part of the world? If anyone could have found an end to our ancient curse, it would have been him. What my father didn't count on, however, was you," I said.

"Me?" Mina echoed, her brows knitting together.

I nodded. "When it was agreed that you and your father would come to our ancestral home in Wallachia to help find a cure, we all believed it would only be a matter of time before the good doctor found what we needed and the both of you would be on your way. You were just a girl, then—a young, annoying, impetuous sixteen. No one paid much attention to you, Mina."

She snorted. "And these are the words of a gentleman."

I grinned in response. "I never claimed to be a gentleman, and I was always a terrible prince."

"Pray, continue delighting me with these flattering memories," she quipped.

"For the two and a half years that you stayed with us, my father grew to suspect my *attachment* to you. At the time, it meant little because Laszlo was set to replace my father as heir to the throne of Wallachia, and I was free to be the spoiled monster I was, indulging every whim of sin and vice. My father frowned upon my flirtation with you but knew that stopping it would only increase my ardor," I explained. "But then the unthinkable happened."

Mina placed her teacup onto the table with shaking hands.

"We fell in love," she murmured.

I nodded once, swallowing around the lump of emotion in my throat.

"You were eighteen then. Your father—while making great strides in understanding the blood plague—was no closer to finding a cure than any of the others had come. He discovered so much about it, but when he couldn't explain to my father *why* only my family would be born with the curse and every other sufferer simply had to be bitten, my father lost faith."

"Yes," Mina nodded, shuddering with the awful memories. "I remember the argument they had. I half expected your father to impale mine and leave him to rot on that horrible castle's battlements."

I frowned. "I won't pretend that didn't cross his mind."

Squeezing her eyes shut, Mina blew out a breath laced with disappointment.

"My father accomplished a great many things in his life," she said. "But on his deathbed, the unanswered riddle of the blood plague was all he spoke of."

I froze. "His deathbed? Mina, when...?"

She waved away my concern. "Long ago, Rafael."

I swallowed. "I'm so sorry. I didn't know."

She lifted a shoulder in forced casualness, but I sensed the air between us thickening with grief.

"It was a natural death," she said. "Given the horrors we've seen in this world, I think that's something we can at least take comfort in."

Realization dawned. "That is why you were able to study," I said. "He didn't want you to when he was alive, but with his death, you must have found a way."

"My mother's passing preceded his by a few short months. I think his broken heart played a factor in his decline, as was his desire to be with my mother in Heaven. I was lucky to grow up without much family. My parents left me with their modest estate and a comfortable annuity. That, along with my father's reputation, was nearly enough to earn my place at the university in Padua," she said quietly.

I couldn't contain my shock. "They allowed a woman to study?"

She turned a disapproving gaze on me. "Don't be ridiculous. I bound my breasts and attended as a man. Wilhelmina is very close to Wilhelm, you see, and rather easy to forge on the necessary documents. By the time

I earned my degree and made my way to Paris, most people who truly needed my services were willing to overlook the inconvenience of my gender."

I barked a laugh and sat back, enjoying the swell of pride and admiration I felt for her.

She misinterpreted my laughter and sniffed in affront.

"I would never allow my sex to get in the way of a first-rate medical education," she said haughtily.

"I cannot, for one moment, believe how stupid and blind the other students and faculty must have been to not recognize your feminine charms," I said.

She smiled at that, warming me more than the thick tropical air of the greenhouse.

"Rafael, while I appreciate all that you're telling me, not much of it is new information. I knew your father disliked and distrusted me; I knew you were a spoiled wastrel who I fell in love with, anyway; I knew your father and mine had a falling out. What you haven't told me, however, is what happened the night we were supposed to elope," she remarked. Then, there was a delicate tightening of her jaw and her eyes narrowed. "And why you betrayed me."

"Yes, my dear, I'm coming to that. When I proposed to you that night, I couldn't believe that you would dare to say yes. Knowing what it meant for you...knowing what it meant for me...what it would mean for us. When I planned our elopement, I thought I'd accounted for every eventuality, except, of course, for my brother Laszlo's disappearance."

Shock startled a gasp from Mina. "Wait, he disappeared the same night? I didn't hear of his absence until the following year. Why didn't you tell me?"

I shook my head. "I didn't have time, Mina. I was in the stables, preparing for our departure when I found out. The stable master told me he'd caught Laszlo saddling our fastest horse the evening before. He gave me the letter Laszlo had left for our father."

"What did it say?" Mina asked.

"Laszlo had fallen in love," I answered. "The girl was one of my mother's French maids."

Mina's brow furrowed. "French maids...not Marguerite?"

I nodded. "The very same."

"She was very beautiful," Mina remembered. "But Laszlo was always so serious. I can't believe he was ruled by his passion enough to run away with a maid."

"We all underestimated him," I admitted. "But as it is said, *'Smooth runs the water where the brook is deep.'* Nevertheless, he alone noticed me making plans for us and beat me to it. His letter to my father said as much. He and Marguerite were leaving to start a life together, and it was useless for my father to pursue them. He had no interest in the throne and felt that I deserved a share of the responsibility of our family's weighty history."

Mina plucked another slice of mango from the fruit bowl, and I watched her take a bite and lick the juice from her fingers. My cock hardened immediately, and I gripped my chair, struggling to keep my thoughts on my confession.

"I took the letter to my father immediately," I choked out, nearly drowning in my desire. "And what a fool I was to do so. Upon reading it, he flew into a rage, sending men after Laszlo and demanding to know about the elopement Laszlo had mentioned. *Our* elopement, Mina. He told me he was disowning and disinheriting Laszlo and that I would be taking his place. If I refused—if I went ahead with our elopement—he would hunt us down and kill you."

Mina froze at that, dropping the fruit onto her plate.

"He wouldn't," she breathed, incredulous. "I know your father never cared for me, but he wouldn't resort to murder."

I laughed. "My father was almost four-hundred years old by then. He had been on and off the throne of Wallachia several times—each time seized through war and violent bargains. He alone started the false rumors that my brother had the penchant for impaling people, all to spread the fear that would help our family maintain control of Wallachia. It was my father who enjoyed torturing prisoners. Vlad—*Laszlo*, as he always was to me—never tortured or killed anyone unjustly off the field of battle."

"Why didn't you tell me any of this before?" Mina asked, astonished.

"Because most of that happened before I was born. I was a late addition to my father's house. I wasn't born until 1701, long after my father had given up the hope of a second son. He and Laszlo came from a different time—one where brutality and fierce religious devotion reigned. I was more *Age of Enlightenment* than they were, much to my father's disappointment."

"You told me it was rude to ask a vampire his age," Mina said. "But you never told me you were that much younger than your father and brother."

"My point in telling you all of this is not to trouble you with my family's wretched history. The only reason I did not meet you the night we were meant to elope was because I believed my father's vow. If I didn't step in and take Laszlo's place, he would kill you and, I suspect, your father. I couldn't let that happen. I planned to bide my time and wait for things to settle, then hunt down Laszlo and force him to come back and make peace with Father," I continued, rubbing at the ache building in my chest. The pain of revisiting those memories warred with the impulse to lay everything bare before her.

Mina stood abruptly, tears gathering in her eyes.

"I waited that night," she exclaimed, her voice echoing off the glass and stone walls. "I waited for you to come and take me away. I waited for us to start a life together, Rafael. I would have walked through Hell for you. Why couldn't you simply tell me?"

"Don't you understand? I didn't want you to walk through Hell for me. I wanted you to have sunlight and flowers and *life*. Even if that meant life without me," I said quietly. "I knew you would take on the world to be with me, so I did the only thing I could think to do."

"You slept with another woman," she said bitterly.

"No!" I grabbed her arm and pulled her to me, holding her fiercely against my chest. "No, I didn't. I told the stable boy to *tell* you he'd caught me with another woman. I wouldn't touch another woman for years after that."

Mina was as still as a statue in my arms.

"I went back to Amsterdam the very next day, forced to endure my mother trotting suitor after suitor in front of me in a desperate attempt to marry me off and put an end to my incessant wheedling to attend university," Mina said. "Father continued to travel more and more after that. He still sought answers for the blood plague, and so he kept watch for news of your family."

"I'm sorry," I confessed, knowing the words meant little in the face of her pain.

"It is done," she acknowledged, the hurt still evident in her voice. "I am glad you told me."

The soft trickle of the waterfall was the only sound for several minutes as I gathered the courage to finish.

"I did as my father asked. I stayed to learn how to rule. His rage at Laszlo never cooled, and for a long time, I didn't hear anything that would give me a clue as to my brother's whereabouts." My words became a whisper of lingering grief and emotion strangled my voice. "I was left alone with my father, without Laszlo to buffer our fractured relationship. My father hated me and resented that I was the one left to carry his legacy. Our remaining years together were..." I faltered. *Brutal. Unkind.* "...difficult."

Before she could say or do anything that would diminish my resolve, I carried on.

"And then while I was away, traveling back from the Ottoman Empire,

I received the news that my father was assassinated. He died as cruelly as he lived, and I barely escaped the ensuing political chaos. I went into hiding for a time, traveling under different identities. Soon, I had word of a mysterious disease—the blood plague—cropping up in the eastern part of France. I suspected Laszlo had something to do with it, or the men my father had sent after him who'd never returned. I set out after him. More and more cases were popping up, and it wasn't long after that the rumors took on a life of their own. Unfortunately, I still seem to be at the heart of them, even though I've been trying to stop the spread of the plague."

Mina's jaw dropped. "What? You have? How?"

"Your father inspired my interest in botany. I've been using his notes to try and find a cure myself. I enjoy the study of plants, but I wouldn't have come to it if I hadn't been seeking a cure for the destruction my family's curse has caused," I admitted.

Appearing bewildered and overwhelmed, Mina sat back down, rubbing at the spot between her brows.

"Why does The Order believe you are to blame?" she asked. "Why are they hunting you, Rafael?"

"Truthfully, I do not know. I can only guess Laszlo's disappearance and my father's death have left me the sole heir to that particular mantle," I said. "And there is some truth to that. If I'd sought my brother sooner, perhaps this would have been in my power to prevent. Besides, my reputation for being a young rogue that led to the moniker "Devil" surely helped the rumors spread. Only now, I'm far worse than a wastrel and a cad—they all see me as Lucifer himself."

We were silent for a time, listening to the fluttering of the bats and the steady symphony of frogs and insects heralding a new day.

"Sunrise is upon us," I said, surprised that I'd lost track of time.

"So," Mina began slowly. "Your father is gone. Your throne is gone. You've been here hunting Laszlo and trying to stop the blood plague, all while The Order nips at your heels. Where do I fit in?"

I stared at her, perplexed.

"*Where do you fit in?* Mina, yes, I am here to right my family's wrongs, but I am also here for you. I've never stopped loving you, my brilliant doctor, and it's the promise of a future with you that has inspired me to do better for this world. I hoped to have more time…to be further along in my search for the truth and the cure, but The Order's actions have forced me to show my hand sooner than I wished."

I reached for her, but she pulled away, rising to her feet.

"And with all of this—with twenty years of absence between us—I'm simply supposed to take you at your word? To trust you? We don't even know each other anymore, Rafael. I didn't know any of this! You had no idea my father had passed. You don't know what I've been through over the last two decades! You think that coming here, weaving this tale of woe —true or not—and remembering my favorite tea blend is enough to wash away the grief, the betrayal, the time?" Mina whirled around the grotto, tears shining in her eyes.

"I have nothing *but* time. My love for you has not changed. Twenty years is nothing to me," I insisted.

"It is to me!" she shouted. "You could have written, you could have sent for me, you could have shared some of this precious knowledge. We could have spent some of those years working together, looking for Laszlo, trying to find a cure. But instead, you selfishly sat in waiting, allowing me to think the worst of you because—why? You weren't ready? Your greenhouse was still being built? You didn't yet possess the answers that would make it impossible for me to refuse you?"

She shook her head in disbelief.

"All this time I've been atoning for what I thought were your sins, and now you tell me they are Laszlo's? What am I to do with this information, Rafael? I forced my heart to heal from you long ago, secure in the knowledge that you didn't care. You were happy with your father's legacy and a family curse that leeched from the confines of your horrible castle."

Stunned into silence, I could only watch as the tempest of her righteous anger dashed any hopes of our future together.

"I spent twenty years believing it was my fault. *I* wasn't enough for you. You allegedly fell into the arms of another woman because I wasn't enough…I wasn't a princess, I wasn't immortal, I wasn't a vampire, I wasn't worldly enough, I wasn't wealthy or charming or glamorous. I was the simple human daughter of a human scientist—the scientist who had failed you. That's why I believed it."

She shook her head again, and the motion gutted me to my rotten, black core.

"It wasn't that I thought the worst of you all these years, Rafael. It's that I thought the worst of *me.*"

8

MINA

April 17, 1768
Château du Diable

MY WORDS WERE LIKE CANNON FIRE IN THE SOFTNESS OF RAFAEL'S underground jungle. Suddenly, the warm, damp closeness of this tropical atmosphere felt all too suffocating, and I was desperate for fresh, cool air. Rafael had gone still and silent, and part of me wondered if he'd heard my words at all. I turned from him, hurrying toward the massive oak doors that would lead me away from here. *Away from him.*

I climbed the stairs and strode down the main hallway, my mind a tangle of conflicting emotions. I wanted to be outside in the cold sunshine, or back in my clinic, or sitting in Charlotte's parlor at *Château de Ruisseau Magdelaine*, laughing at scandalous stories of her love life before Antoine. I wanted to be anywhere but here, where I felt the walls pressing in on me and the weight of expectation like a millstone around my neck. Aimlessly, I drifted down the hallway until I found myself standing in the doorway of Rafael's laboratory.

I stepped inside, my curiosity overpowering my need for mindless escape. Floor to ceiling bookshelves lined one wall, while the other held countless glass specimen jars filled with all manner of flora and fauna. A great table stood in the middle of the room, covered with scientific equipment—some of which I'd never seen before. My gaze snagged on a beautiful brass compound microscope at the center of the table. Next to it lay an open book—Rafael's observations.

Without thinking, I bent over the book and read some of his tightly scrawled notes. It seemed he'd been experimenting with the effects of garlic and wolfsbane on two types of vampire blood, his own and a turned vampire. I shifted my attention to the microscope.

Dieu, but I wanted one. They were incredible instruments that many of the brightest minds were using and improving upon, but they were too expensive for me to purchase. I leaned forward to peer into the eyepiece.

I gasped. Based on the appearance of the specimen, I wagered it was a blood sample, but I'd never seen blood like this before. The power of magnification made the cells enormous to my eyes.

"It is a new model," came a deep voice at the door. I froze, embarrassed about being caught but too entranced by what I was seeing. "The magnification is one hundred times what the human eye can perceive."

"It is truly remarkable," I murmured, afraid to meet his gaze.

"What do you think of my observations?" he asked, leafing through the pages in his notebook.

Is that…nervousness in his voice?

Finally, I looked up. I did not possess the ability to lie easily.

"The experiments with garlic and wolfsbane have been done," I said. "They are nothing more than folk cures. They do not affect the disease."

"Yes," he nodded, looking oddly chagrined. "Yes, I'd read that."

"Why did you try to replicate the experiment?"

Rafael shifted, avoiding my eyes. "I thought, perhaps, if I tried with different types of blood, it might yield different results."

I nodded, impressed. "That is a sound hypothesis. What did you discover?"

"The results were the same," he answered in a deflated tone.

"Ah, but you learned something in the process, didn't you?" I encouraged. "And your manner of testing is smart. Why should we expect that the results of different treatments should be the same on your blood over the blood of a turned vampire? Much differentiates your abilities from theirs. It would make sense that you would react to stimuli in different ways."

Pride flashed in Rafael's face but evaporated quickly. In its place settled his mask of cool indifference.

I chewed at my bottom lip, embarrassed by my earlier outburst and rejection of his hopes. I didn't want to be at odds with him, and I didn't wish for us to go back to the way we'd been—separated by so many things. I wanted him near. I wanted to believe what he'd told me. But I needed time to reconcile twenty years of disbeliefs. How could I make him understand? How could I ask him for patience when he'd waited so long already? What could I say to ease my own anxiety?

"You have a very fine laboratory," I offered stupidly.

"Thank you, Doctor."

Ah, so we're back to Doctor. I cringed.

"Rafael, I am sorry for my outburst. My anger tells me that the wounds I claimed to have healed long ago were not so smartly healed. I reacted… badly," I apologized.

He tilted his head to study me, but the mask did not waver.

"You must be wanting to return home," he said distantly. "I'm certain your friends will be worried."

His manner sickened my heart—it seemed he was not the only one with the capacity to cause pain.

"No, but…well, yes, I'm sure they are. Do you think they are safe?" I wondered.

He lifted one shoulder in nonchalance. "If you trust them, then I do."

"That's a non-answer," I shot back.

He pursed his lips, and I found myself staring at his perfectly formed mouth.

"Mina, if you do not wish for me to pursue you, I will keep my affections to myself. But I'm afraid I must ask you for help. I need to find Laszlo, and I want to help end this blood plague. I have failed on both accounts thus far. As you said, The Order is closing in on me and I don't have people I can trust. I need your keen mind and the skills of your friends."

His tone was pleading, but his handsome face betrayed none of the emotion contained within him.

I sighed. "Well, if it was The Order who tried to take me, I suppose I'm already in danger."

Rafael grabbed my hand in one of his supernaturally quick moves. His eyes bored into mine with the intensity that frightened and excited the primal parts of me.

"Mina," he rumbled, his low voice barely more than a growl. "I won't let anything happen to you. I would ruin this world without a thought to keep you safe—even if you do not wish to be mine."

Yes, yes! My body arched toward him, spurred by its magnetic attraction to the man I'd long considered my mate. My traitorous mind halted the move but couldn't stop me from closing my eyes and tilting my lips up to his for the kiss I knew would come.

The kiss I'd told him I didn't want. *Mina, you wretched liar.*

I felt the air between us change as he leaned forward, but the kiss never arrived. In an instant, he was across the room at the doorway again.

"Follow me," he said, turning away. "I'll ensure you're safely returned to Charlotte's home."

Every silent step he took down the hall was another crack in my already bleeding heart.

"You'll forgive me if I don't come with you," Rafael said stiffly. It was well after sunrise, but it was impossible to tell given the depth of his underground abode.

Guilt and frustration gnawed at me as he led me through the labyrinth of hallways and tunnels on our way back to the empty, crumbling tower.

"Rafael," I started, unsure of what I was planning to say. "I'm sorry for earlier. Truly."

He did not stop or look back. "Yes. So you've said."

"You must understand," I tried again, reaching for his arm. "I need time to think about everything you said to me. There were a great many revelations in your words—twenty years of my belief in untruths and half-truths that I will have to come to terms with. I am sorry for what you endured in that time—for your father, for the loss of your home, for the arduous road ahead of you. I am sorry for our miserable separation and two decades of heart-wrenching loneliness. I felt those things too. I do not pretend that my life has been easy in the wake of your abandonment, but I have crafted it into something of my own."

Finally, he paused. We reached the threshold of the tower, some sixty feet below the hidden entrance to his castle. He turned to face me, his expression dark and forbidding.

I forced myself to continue. "When I thought that you were responsible for the blood plague—the only disease my father truly failed to understand—I thought it was my calling. My punishment for falling short of expectations, my family's expectations, your father's expectations, your expectations. I threw myself into this work because I felt like I owed it to everyone. Finding out so much of that is wrong has left me...*unmoored*, in a way. I care for you, Rafael. I always have. I always will. But I have been alone so long, you must at least give me leave to find my own way through this."

He raised his hand to caress my cheek but did not touch me. His fingertips hovered for a moment, and his lips parted on a breath.

"Mina..." he whispered.

I moved to lean into the touch, but he pulled his hand away, jaw flexing tightly. Whatever he'd been about to say died in the space between us. He reached for a wrought-iron candelabra sticking out of the wall and wrenched it back. There was a series of loud groans and clicks and a small stone staircase unfolded out of the wall, winding its way up the tower to a small round door hidden in the ceiling.

Rafael stepped back, letting his hand fall to his side.

"There is a windlass at the top of this tower that will help you descend. My coachman is waiting to assist you, and then he will take you on to Charlotte's. I will await your decision about Laszlo and my work on the plague, but please make haste. I fear for the safety of France, as well as for you. Trust me when I say The Order is a powerful and unfortunate enemy," he said, his words clipped.

I wanted to say goodbye. I wanted to say countless things. But before my thoughts could take form, Rafael inclined his head in a tense bow and strode back down the hallway from whence we'd come.

Feeling chastised and raw with emotion, I blew out a shuddering breath and began the long climb up the stairs. The farther away I moved, the worse I felt. I regretted some of my words, but not all of them, and Rafael's reaction shamed me and made me feel the worst kind of guilt at hurting him. Then, thoughts of anger would surface at my shame—could he really expect me to fall into his arms after twenty years and countless lies between us? Never mind the fact that we'd shared that kiss...*Mon Dieu, that kiss.*

I licked my lips at the memory.

He'd tasted so much better than I remembered. I couldn't count the number of times I'd dreamed of such kisses. And the way he looked at me as if I were the only woman in the world, like Eve stepping in the garden to meet Adam. No, not Adam...Someone more primal. One of the old gods.

Hades.

Memories came hard and fast then, and my knees nearly buckled with the remembered pleasure of making love. Rafael had thought himself Hades ...dark, forbidding, cold, and immortal. He'd called me his Persephone and told me I'd bloomed at his touch. I was so young, so naive, so much like spring to his hellish winter.

How much I loved him. *How angry I am at him.* What kind of life was he imagining for us? We would be parted by time or some unnatural death. I would age, gathering wrinkles and aches, and he would simply *be.* Trapped like an insect in amber.

I wouldn't pretend the idea of the transformation hadn't crossed my mind. In all my work and research, I'd considered making the change. But each time, I would think of the warmth of the summer sun and the vibrance of a rainbow after a thunderstorm and reject the idea of living without those wonders. Certainly, the night held its charms, but I wanted it all. Sun, moon, stars. Day and night. Spring and winter.

Myself…and Rafael.

I'd reached the top of the staircase and cast one long, dizzying look back down. Then, steeling my courage for what I knew lay ahead, I pushed open the trap door and stepped into the chilly April morning.

AFTER THE SOMEWHAT AWKWARD DESCENT WITH THE WINDLASS AND NO SMALL amount of complaining on my part, I found myself facing Rafael's impressive carriage. Four sleek, black horses, so perfectly matched they could have been two sets of twins, stamped impatiently in front of the large black conveyance. A footman helped me inside, and I frowned at the beautiful interior. Deep, plush seats covered in red velvet and satin cushions spoke to Rafael's early years as a tempting rake. I didn't want to consider how many women he'd had in this carriage.

Thick fur blankets and a small basket of almond cakes sat on the empty seat, needling me with even more guilt. He'd obviously ensured I would have every comfort, even if I treated him abominably. As much as I felt like I didn't deserve such kindness, I wouldn't want to snub him any more than I already had, so I sat back, wrapped myself in the cozy blankets, and nibbled at the sweet pastries.

The carriage lurched forward, and I leaned back against the cushions. My mind swirled with the chaos of the previous evenings, making it hard for me to focus long enough to examine my feelings. Emotions clashed and my heart pounded, but I suspected some of that had to do with what I knew would come when I showed up at Charlotte's château. I was certain Charlotte and Daphne hadn't been involved in my kidnapping, but I was even more worried The Order had managed to plot and carry out a mission without their knowledge. That meant there was a chance *les DD* had underestimated the old fools.

I took a deep breath and closed my eyes. There was nothing I could do until I arrived, and though I had no idea what I would say to her, I trusted she would at least hear me out when I explained everything. At least, I hoped.

The gentle rocking of the carriage soothed me, as did the small charcoal heater tucked beneath the cushions, and it wasn't long before I drifted off. I awoke sometime later with the sensation of the carriage slowing and noticed that the light filtering in through the curtains had brightened to a silvery cold afternoon. When we finally stopped, the driver climbed down and opened the door for me.

I wondered what Rafael's servants thought of him, and of me—if they'd heard us arguing and thought badly of me for it. I started to say something to the driver but thought better of it. It was just as well, as I was knocked off my feet by the most horrific-looking wolf creature that anyone could imagine. It was as if a normal wolf had mated with a demon, with long gangly limbs, massive jaws, enormous claws, and murderous red eyes. I would have screamed if I didn't already know this particular beast.

"Comtesse," I huffed. "Forgive me for my impertinence, but in this form, you are rather weighty. Would you be so kind as to get off me?"

The terrifying beast whined and licked my face, upsetting my spectacles. Then, with a horrendous bark, she sat back on her haunches. I got up and brushed myself off, frowning at the huge tears her claws had made down the front of my lovely lemon-yellow gown.

"*Merde*," I swore. "This was a new gown, Charlotte, and I rather liked it."

She whined at me again, then trotted off toward the front of her ostentatious, yet stunning, estate. Once we entered the grand foyer, she shifted shape—a gruesome process that I was completely entranced by. Her lupine snarls of pain became human bellows as she turned back into the beautiful chestnut-haired comtesse I knew and loved.

Once in human form, she ran to me and threw her arms around my neck, holding me in an impossibly tight embrace.

"Oh, Mina!" she cried, tears spilling down her cheeks. "We were so worried! We've all been out searching for you! We knew something was wrong, but we couldn't figure out what happened or where you went! Where have you been, my friend? What has happened? Are you well?"

"Yes, Charlotte, I'm well. I will tell you everything, *chérie*, but...don't you think it might be easier to have this conversation with a few more..." I waved vaguely at her nudity. "...layers?"

She sniffled and wiped her tears, then giggled.

"Of course, Mina! Our attitudes toward clothing in my household have become rather lax since Antoine and I have grown accustomed to shifting. Don't worry—I did speak with the household staff about it at length." At that moment, a young maid rushed forward with an exquisite dressing gown of shimmering pink satin. Charlotte donned the gown and led me upstairs.

"Daphne and Étienne will be along later this evening. We organized search parties, you see. Antoine and I took the day shifts, and Daphne and Étienne took the night shifts. We were able to follow part of your trail, but..." she grew quiet, then offered me an anxious smile. "Well, we can all discuss things when everyone arrives. Let's get changed, and I'll have lunch laid out in the dining room. I've had some gowns tailored for you—

don't look at me like that, Mina, this is as much for my benefit as it is yours—and they're in the lilac guest room down the hall, where you usually stay. I've taken the liberty of having some of your things brought here. Nothing special, just some of your books, notebooks, toiletries, and your doctor's valise. Anything to make you more comfortable here, *chérie.* Daphne left a notice on your clinic door and informed your neighbors that you would be taking a short holiday away to visit family in the country. Hopefully, we can get to the bottom of things soon and you won't have to take too much time away from your patients. Mina, darling, is this all too overwhelming? I'm *so* sorry—listen to me, prattling on when you've been through God-knows-what trauma. Are you simply exhausted? Do you need to rest first?"

Charlotte capped this loving tirade with another fierce hug and a soft kiss on my cheek.

"Thank you, Charlotte," I replied. "No, I am well. I wouldn't say no to lunch and a clean dress, but I'm ready to tell you everything."

9

MINA

April 17, 1768
Château de Ruisseau Magdelaine

CHARLOTTE WAS EAGER TO HEAR MY STORY BUT INSISTED I TAKE SOME TIME TO rest, bathe, and put on one of the new gowns she'd had made for me. Even though I avoided spirits most of the time, she persuaded me to take a snifter of brandy into the large copper bathtub the servants had set in front of the fireplace in my guest room.

"It's the best way to warm up," she'd said with a wink. "Now, off you go, and take your time. It's hours still before Daphne and Étienne will awake. I'm sure Antoine will return any moment now, and you can tell us all you need to."

I swirled my fingers lazily through the steamy lavender-scented water, sipping at the brandy. Charlotte had been right. Warmth settled in the pit of my stomach and stretched through my limbs as I sat thinking.

Had I been unfair to Rafael? Had he been unfair to me? Most likely we'd both been a bit unfair to each other. I didn't know what I wanted to say to Charlotte about him—about my feelings for him now…after everything. I didn't think I knew the truth of my feelings myself. *Dieu, I am sounding more and more like some overly romantic French woman. Pull yourself together, Mina!*

The cognac started to sour in my stomach, and I remembered I'd only eaten a few almond cakes, some of Rafael's exotic fruit, and thin broth over the last couple of days. Delicious smells wafted up from the kitchens

—baking bread, freshly brewing coffee, and roasting meat. Though Charlotte and her fiancé were werewolves and could subsist entirely on raw meat, they'd both had rather epicurean tastes in their human lives and continued to eat their favorite dishes with gusto. They employed a larger kitchen staff than almost any other household outside of Versailles.

Stepping out of the bath, I picked up the lovely garments that had been laid out. Rather than the formal court dress that Charlotte often preferred for herself, she'd selected a more modest design without the wide *panniers* that were fashionable evening wear. I pulled on the clean chemise and soft woolen stockings, then layered the quilted stays and fine linen petticoats. The bodice and skirts of the outer gown were a shimmering lilac velvet with silver flowers embroidered throughout. It was beautiful—certainly finer than anything I had in my closet. *Almost* as fine as the lemon silk gown now lying ruined upon the floor.

I dressed myself without the help of a lady's maid, and I was eminently more grateful that Charlotte had taken my status and profession into consideration when ordering the gowns. I pinned up my long, dark hair, replaced my spectacles, and made my way downstairs—only slightly unsteady from the heady warmth of the cognac.

I found Charlotte in the dining hall, dressed in a stunning gown of rose-colored silk with ivory bows.

"Mina, you look absolutely lovely. Do you feel a touch restored?" she asked, gesturing to the seat across from her.

"Yes, Charlotte, thank you. Has Antoine returned?" I replied, taking my seat.

She nodded. "He arrived home not too long ago," she said. "He is resting for now. It's been a long few days for all of us."

I frowned. "I'm sorry my absence has been so troublesome for so many of my friends."

"Hush, Mina, don't be ridiculous! We're *family*. We'd all go to the ends of the earth for you, *chérie*. Now, are you hungry? You must be. Me, I am simply famished! I had the chef prepare enough food to satisfy an army."

With a wave of her hand, her servants brought forth silver platter after silver platter covered in delights to tempt even my humble palate. I tucked in to cuts of ham, savory pies, roasted fowl and fish, poached eggs, bread, pastries, cheeses, and two decanters of wine. Charlotte was satisfied that I had an appetite—she watched me like a hawk.

After we both finished platefuls of food, she led me to the front parlor and sat me in front of the fireplace in the most comfortable chair. We took a moment to settle in as the coffee and sherry was poured, and then she looked at me with the intensity of a cat eyeing a canary.

"Now," she urged. "Start wherever it pleases you."

I swallowed, suddenly nervous.

"It is difficult for me to know where to begin," I said. "So I think I will start with the events of the other night, when I was supposed to come here."

Charlotte refilled my coffee cup and hers, and I continued.

"Did you know The Order sent men to watch me?" I asked.

Shock flashed in her eyes, followed by instant anger.

"What? No! They wouldn't...how could they...without Daphne's and my permission! They know you are protected!" Her claws grew, lethal and sharp, until she took a breath to calm herself. "I'm so sorry, Mina! Daphne and I should have expected them to do something reprehensible. These men watching you—what happened with them?"

"After weeks of watching and following me, something changed. The night I was meant to come see you, they kidnapped me, drugged me with *far* too much laudanum, and shoved me in a carriage. They were taking me to the cemetery, Charlotte—the secret entrance to The Order."

Charlotte's eyes widened, and she pursed her lips.

"Monsters!" she spat. "We will make sure they pay. How did you escape?"

"Certainly not under my power," I said.

Charlotte understood immediately.

"The man in black?" she asked.

I nodded. "Rafael. Former—rightful—Prince of Wallachia."

"A prince!" Charlotte exclaimed. "Well done, Mina."

Ignoring her teasing grin, I continued.

"Rafael followed us and killed both men," I said bluntly. I didn't want to think about it too much, or the guilt would wash over me in a tidal wave. "He took me to his castle outside Rouen so I could recover from the laudanum. He said I would not be safe back at my clinic. According to one of the men, Pascal, The Order sent for me so they might question me about Rafael's whereabouts." My anger and betrayal laced the words with venom.

"Question you?" Charlotte's brows narrowed.

"As a witch," I said coldly.

"No," she breathed. "They wouldn't! Torturing witches has been banned for years! Even with the men in The Order becoming more polarized against the supernatural cause, such measures would mean they'd been hiding more from *les DD* than Daphne and I realized." She paled at the thought. "Could Rafael be mistaken?"

I shook my head. "One of his unique powers is the ability to...*compel* the truth from people. It would have been impossible for Pascal to lie."

Her eyes snapped to mine. "Do you trust him?"

"In this, I think so. I don't know what other motivation he would have to lie to me about it. You told me yourself The Order has been moving farther away from Daphne and Étienne's influence. They have been holding back the tide of brutality against vampires, but we all knew it was only a matter of time before their strength would be overwhelmed by the power of hate."

Charlotte stood and paced in front of the fireplace, anger rippling over her skin and making her eyes flash lupine gold and red.

"Even knowing that, it appears The Order has made the first move," she murmured, oddly calm. Without warning, she picked up a small vase from the mantle, studied it for a moment, and then heaved it against the wall with a fierce roar. The vase exploded into a cloud of porcelain dust.

"*Chérie*," she said, kneeling at my feet. "I'm so deeply sorry. I should have prevented this. I'm overwhelmed by my rage and regret. I swear to you, dear one, their transgressions will not go unpunished."

"Do not berate yourself for the sins of others," I said, grasping her hands in mine. "That is a lesson I'm working to unlearn myself."

She smiled, wiped a tear from her cheek, and sat back down on the chaise across from me.

"There's more," I said, sipping my coffee to gather courage. "It is about the blood plague."

At that moment, Antoine stepped into the room with a soft knock on the doorframe. He looked more at ease than the last time I'd seen him. He was dressed in a loose cotton shirt and soft buckskin breeches, and his wavy brown hair hung loosely about his shoulders. With the moon-shaped scar across his temple and his slightly crooked nose, he reminded me of Ares, the god of war, but his temperament was infinitely more patient.

His eyes flickered over the smashed vase and then back to Charlotte, who shrugged by way of apology. He dropped a soft kiss on her forehead before bowing low to me.

"Doctor," he rumbled. "I'm most relieved to find you well."

"And you," I said. "You have my thanks and my apologies for suffering my misadventures."

"Darling, did you eat? There's plenty of food in the dining room if you'd like," Charlotte offered. Her tone was melancholy and distracted, and my gut twisted at the thought that she was blaming herself for what The Order had done.

Antoine inclined his head, studying me with his emerald eyes.

"It can wait, *l'amour*. I have a feeling the good doctor is about to tell us something rather important."

They both fixed me with a stare that made me want to squirm.

"You make me nervous—both of you! Stop looking at me like I'm a specimen to be studied. I said I would tell you, and I shall," I snapped.

They waited.

"The blood plague originated from Rafael's family," I said. "It began as an ancient curse upon his household and his family line. *Cursed to walk the earth forever for one's sins, drinking the blood of the damned,* that sort of thing. No one remembers much about the exact beginning or circumstances, which have been lost to time. What has lingered—up until quite recently—was the responsibility of the family to contain the curse. They did not turn others outside their family—it is forbidden and taboo. They are permitted to turn their mate during their wedding so they can continue their lineage. The offspring of those unions, while extremely rare, are born vampires. So far, they have been the only vampires *born* and not *made.* They're unlike any turned vampires you'll meet, possessing unique abilities beyond heightened senses and strength. They grow ever more powerful as they age, but the mantle of madness waits for the ones who live too long."

Antoine sat on a chaise opposite me, which looked amusingly small beneath his large frame. Charlotte sat next to him, clasping his hand.

"My father and I were brought to Wallachia to help find a cure for the family—the House of Dracul. There were two sons, Laszlo and Rafael. Laszlo was heir to the throne, but he fled to be with the woman he loved—a maid from their household. His father disinherited him and forced Rafael to take his place. It was around this time that the blood plague first escaped the confines of their castle."

"It was not Rafael's doing?" Charlotte asked, unable to hide her surprise and disbelief.

"Not according to him," I replied. "No, that is unfair of me...I do not believe he lies about this. He does not know exactly who is responsible, but he has come to France to find his brother and determine if he is the source. He wishes to help."

Antoine's brows shot up. "Help? How?"

Strangely, revealing Rafael's secret passion for botany felt like revealing something too intimate.

"Rafael has been searching for his brother and for a cure, just as I have. He knows The Order hunts him. He knew The Order had men watching me. He loathes The Order and does not trust them, and after the events of the other night, I'm not ashamed to say I trust them even less than I did before."

I looked pointedly at Charlotte.

"Daphne and I have been cautious about how much we revealed to The Order of *les DD's* activities. I regret the amount of time and energy

I've given to them thus far, but trust that from now on, everything changes. As soon as Daphne and Étienne arrive, we'll figure out what our next move shall be," she insisted.

Antoine's face darkened. "Whatever we do next, we must proceed with caution. The Order still has the ear of the king, which makes defying them akin to treason."

Charlotte nodded. "This betrayal truly is horrible news. Both the vampires and the human peasants are already at their breaking point. If tensions increase, I fear an outright war. If only we knew more about what The Order knows and plans… It seems *les DD* will be embarking on our most dangerous missions yet."

Worry swirled in my stomach. For so long, I'd refused to join my friends in their secret organization because I thought myself separate, somehow. Neutral. It seemed I would be taking a stand after all.

"Mina," Charlotte said lightly. "Is there anything else?"

She pinned me to my chair with a knowing look. I swallowed, the lump in my throat full of emotion.

"Ah, I do believe I'll have some lunch after all," Antoine offered awkwardly. He tipped Charlotte's face up to his and kissed her softly on the lips. Her cheeks flushed pink.

"Go easy on her," he murmured as he left the room.

His departure made me feel uncomfortably exposed, and I folded my arms across my chest.

"Long ago, Rafael and I were in love," I finally admitted. "We had plans to elope, but the night we were meant to leave, Laszlo's absence was discovered."

Charlotte sat forward on the edge of her seat, eyes wide in surprise.

"At the time, I wasn't aware of Laszlo's disappearance. That night, I was told that Rafael had been found in bed with another woman. I was devastated and angry, and because of his reputation, I believed it—too readily, perhaps. When I told my father, he was furious. He packed me up and sent me back to Amsterdam the very next day. My mother considered that the end of my ambitions for becoming a physician and tried for ages after that to marry me off. It was fortunate that she gave up after a while." Memories tightened my chest and tears threatened.

"After she and my father died, I had the time and freedom to pursue my career. I would hear occasional things about Rafael's family, but nothing substantial. I nursed a broken heart for a long time—years. Then news of the blood plague reached me, and I knew something had gone wrong in the House of Dracul."

"Oh, Mina," Charlotte breathed. "I'm so sorry. I could *kill* him for what he did to you!"

I shook my head, and the tears started to spill. I dashed them away with the back of my hand, but they would not stop flowing.

"I knew it was him in the cave outside Gévaudan, Charlotte—I realized he'd been the one to turn you. I'm so sorry, my friend. I have failed you!"

Charlotte rushed over and threw her arms around me.

"Hush, Mina! You have *not* failed me. I might not have chosen this fate, but it is mine alone. And without this curse, I would not have the gifts that allowed me to save Antoine. It is not your fault!"

Her kindness only made me cry harder. "Yes, it's my fault. My father and I should have found a way to cure the plague before it could spread. I should have gone after Rafael when I first heard about the blood plague outside Wallachia, but I didn't. And I should have told you about him sooner."

She wiped my tears on her handkerchief and clasped my hands.

"You're telling me now, Mina. These things are hard things to bear alone, and it grieves me that you have had to hold them within yourself for all this time. Rafael is certainly a villain for his behavior and what he put you through. To say nothing of turning me into some sort of hellish wolf monster with a taste for flesh," she added wryly.

"He came for me the other night," I said. "And again when The Order tried to take me. The things he told me, Charlotte…I don't know what to believe anymore. I don't know what to think."

"What do you mean?"

"He said he has returned for me. He's loved me all this time. He revealed that the night we were meant to elope, his father found out about Laszlo and forced Rafael to stay…that if Rafael tried to run away with me, his father would come after us and kill me," I blubbered. "Rafael says that in order to protect me, he had the servants lie about him sleeping with another woman—that he wasn't untrue to me that night."

"Oh, what rot," Charlotte scoffed. "That's it, Mina—I am going to cut off his head."

"He has been in France for almost ten years—just outside of Rouen. He has been looking for Laszlo and trying to find a cure for the plague on his own, and…" I swallowed nervously. "Waiting for the right time to make himself known to me in the hopes that we could finally be together."

Embarrassed with the display of far more emotions than I normally allowed, I buried my face in my hands and waited for my dear friend to pass judgment. The only sounds in the room were the soft crackle of the fire in the hearth and the steady tick of the clock on the mantle. After what felt like an eternity, I peeked at Charlotte through my fingers. Her face was a curious mixture of anger, confusion, and sympathy.

"Charlotte?"

"I can't decide if I want to cut off his head or bring him here and watch him grovel until you two can run off and rut like wild animals. Possibly both, but not in that order," she grumbled.

I couldn't help but laugh, the relief feeling like sunlight after a storm. I should have known that she would stand by my side.

"I feel the same way," I said with a watery smile. "But it doesn't matter now, because I rebuffed his advances and yelled at him for making me believe the worst over the last twenty years."

"Rightly so," Charlotte chirped. "What did he expect after so long with no word? That you'd simply open your legs and let him in?"

"You mean, *open my arms*?"

"Oh no, darling," she said. "I definitely meant *legs*."

I felt my face turn as red as a beetroot.

"What happened then?" she prompted.

"Well, he went cold on me. I fear I've really hurt him," I answered.

"*Good.* He can have a taste of his own medicine," she sniffed. "Was that the end of your time together?"

I sighed. "He asked me to help him find Laszlo and to continue looking for a cure for the plague. He seemed concerned that The Order is now after him so aggressively that it puts me in danger."

"Yes, that *is* a problem," Charlotte replied, her brows knitting in the familiar way that meant she was working out a particularly difficult challenge. Then, noting the anxious look on my face, she patted my knee.

"Don't worry, Mina. We're not going to let anything happen to you. We *might* let something happen to Rafael for this mess, but it wouldn't be death or anything so permanent—just possible maiming."

I chuckled. "He is powerful, Charlotte, but maiming would be as permanent for him as it would be for any vampire or human."

"Would it? Pity. And I suppose if you two reconciled, you'd want the use of all his appendages," she nodded. "Well, thank you for telling me all of this, Mina. I know it wasn't easy. But please believe me when I say that you won't have to bear these burdens alone anymore. When Daphne arrives this evening, we'll figure out a solution and damn *anyone* who gets in our way."

10

RAFAEL

I waited in the gloomy corner of *La Sirène*, drumming my fingers in annoyance on the filthy wooden table. In the twenty years between my failed elopement with Mina and now, I'd courted patience and had worked to curb the brash appetites that earned me the nickname "Devil" in my younger days, but in the last few weeks, I found patience eluding me once again.

I had all the time in the world, but the people around me did not. Time had become one more enemy for me to plot against

I was here because of a rumor and a begrudging lead—compelled through force from my last feed. The drunk fool had been harassing a blood whore down by the docks, and I was happy to remove him from her presence. Under the influence of my will, he told me to come here and wait for the ancient captain of a Hell-borne nightmare ship, the *Blood Bane*. According to a few sailors and soldiers, rumor had it the ship was crewed entirely by vampires—a fanciful notion, considering none of them could be on deck during the day, but I wasn't here to test the veracity of their legends. As the tales went, in their lifetimes, they'd been corsairs for King Louis XIV's vendetta against the English and the Dutch, but had turned pirate after the disappointing Treaty of Utrecht. When the blood plague arrived in France in 1748, those remaining leapt at the chance to pillage with near invincibility for the rest of their days. The hard, grizzled crew reconvened under the brutal captain, Lucien the Bloodless—so called because of his cold demeanor, supernatural condition, voracious appetite, and unwillingness to waste a drop of the life-giving liquid. They say he never let a single captive live.

One wonders how the tales were told.

After gathering up the shattered remains of my absent heart left in Mina's wake, I went back to work—playing out one of my recent leads in the hopes that it would bring me to Laszlo. If it was true that Lucien was the first vampire turned here twenty years ago, I had a lot of questions for him regarding his maker.

The tavern was cold, damp, and sparsely populated, mostly with men whose true loyalty was to the drink and none other. The very atmosphere of the place felt like purgatory—one had the sense of being enshrined in a fog of stillness and despair. It was nearly midnight when the bell above the door jingled—not a welcoming sound, but simply the herald of something else foreboding. The man who entered could have been a beggar by the looks of him, but I knew he was the one I'd come for.

Long, gray hair clung to his scalp and fell in greasy braids down his back. His pale beard matched, except for the rust-colored mustache that could have been the filth of old blood. It was possible that his stained, tattered clothes were more grime than fabric. His keen and all-seeing eyes, however, were the lightest shade of blue—so bright they almost looked white. It was somewhat unnerving being pinned by his icy gaze, and I wondered if that was the main reason for his nickname.

It was no surprise to me when he came to my table instead of approaching the bar.

"I heard you were looking for me," he said in a rough voice that sounded like low waves on a gravel beach.

"Captain," I greeted, smiling enough to show him my dual sets of fangs. "I'm honored to make your acquaintance. Won't you join me for a drink?"

The lines on the old man's face spoke of a hard and dangerous life, but his expression betrayed nothing as he sat across from me. I gestured for the barkeep to bring us a round of whatever they served around these parts.

"You aren't the first to come for me," he said, shrewd eyes assessing me. "But I expect you might be the only one who lives through the experience. *Might.*"

I ignored the threat and inclined my head. "If you can call this life," I retorted.

A glint of surprise flashed in his eyes. "What else would you call it?"

"Where I am from, we call it a curse."

"Only the self-righteous would call immortality a curse," he snarled. "For those of us who lived human lives scraping barely enough existence from the boots of everyone above us, immortality is yet another means to an end."

"What end is that?" I asked.

He shrugged. "Survival."

Two tankards of foul-smelling ale landed in front of us, practically thrown by a nervous tavern maid. I saw a hint of sadness tug at my companion's features and laughed.

"So, you have been a vampire long enough to understand one of the varied costs of *survival*—the inability to drown one's loneliness and sorrows in spirits." I raised my mug to him. "To you, Captain, and your health."

He nodded at me, downed the entire tankard at once, and grimaced.

"You're not here on behalf of the English, the Dutch, or the French," he rumbled. "So, you're not here to try and hang us for piracy. It's been some time since we've been out to sea—long enough that our ship is probably more barnacle than timber, which makes me think this ain't some ill-advised revenge scheme. And I'm sure you aren't foolhardy enough to set out just to test the legend of the 'damned and damning Lucien the Blood-less.' Why are you here, then, old master?"

"I'm looking for someone," I answered.

"I thought you were looking for me," he said wryly.

"I'm here for your maker," I replied. "Perhaps you might point me to the vampire who turned you."

A condescending laugh scraped up through his chest and spilled forth from his lips.

"That *would* be telling," he said. "I'm no rat. A man's maker is his own business."

"Normally, I would agree with you," I said, leaning back in my chair. "And truly, I'm loath to pry into any man's personal affairs. But I'm afraid it's rather important."

"As is my honor," he replied.

"Come now," I soothed. "Honor is a luxury men like us cannot afford."

"Perhaps our honor is all we have," he argued.

I tilted my head. Without looking, I sensed that the remaining tavern patrons had left their seats and were shuffling toward the door. Four more grizzled, grim sailors stepped into the room, forming a barricade against the front door. The tavern maid and the barkeep scurried away into a back room, keenly aware of impending trouble.

I swirled the ale in the bottom of my tankard as two more men filed in, blocking off the back door that led to the adjacent docks.

"You say honor is all you have, and yet you think to ambush me with ten men?" I tutted.

"T'ain't an ambush, old master," the captain replied. "Just a precaution. We don't like strangers coming around here asking questions they ought not be asking."

"Captain." I sighed. "I have enjoyed our small chat, and I have afforded you the respect I think a man like you deserves. My patience, however, has its limits, so I'll ask you politely once more. Will you tell me who your maker was?"

The old man grinned at me, his yellowed fangs lengthening with the challenge.

"I will not."

His men stepped forward on hesitant, yet loyal, feet.

"Alas, I'd hoped to keep this friendly," I said, downing the rest of the bitter ale. "It's too bad. I rather liked the idea of a crew of vampire pirates marauding around the sea, plundering unsuspecting ships in the middle of the night. I'll try to spare some of you."

The two sailors on my right and left sides lunged at once, seizing both of my arms. They hauled me up while another vampire smashed one of the chairs, plucked one of the sharp legs from the pile of splintered wood, and drove it into my chest. I grunted with the force of it, and it hurt like the devil, but it was almost worth the pain to watch their faces fall when the realization dawned that I wasn't expiring like some commonly turned vampire. In shock, the men at my sides loosened their grip, and I shoved them back.

With a deep growl, I pulled the stake from my chest and the wound began to knit together almost immediately. Captain Lucien gaped at me, confusion and fear playing at the lines on his weathered face.

"You see, Captain, for a vampire to die by wooden stake, he must be stabbed through the heart, a condition which affects turned vampires. Those of us who were born with this affliction never had hearts to begin with. All you've really done here is annoy me and ruin a perfectly good shirt," I said, exploding into my monstrous wolf form. I grabbed the nearest vampire and ripped his body in half, then tossed the pieces across the room. I snagged the other at my left, closed my jaws around his neck and wrenched his head from his shoulders, spitting it at Captain Lucien's feet. The other vampires fled through the front door, screaming all the way.

I pinned the captain with a steely gaze and shifted back into my human form. My clothes hung in tatters about me, and the black, viscous blood from his dead men dripped from my hands and face. Captain Lucien stared at me for a beat, then reached for the sword at his hip. Before he could draw, however, I forced him back into his chair with the sheer force of my will and compelled him to answer my questions.

"Who was your maker?" I snarled, power thrumming through my words. I wasn't surprised to feel resistance from him—he struck me as a man with a strong will.

"I don't know," he spit through clenched teeth.

Hm. Something between a lie and the truth. I had one more way of finding the information I'd come for, but it was a last resort.

Again, I compelled him, infusing my words with as much power as I could.

"Who was your maker?" I shouted.

His face twisted in rage as his lips formed the words.

"A girl," he choked out. "That's all I know."

A girl. Could he mean Marguerite? There was only one way for me to be certain, and it was something I dreaded. Keeping Lucien immobile with my will, I sank my fangs into his neck and drank.

Drinking from other vampires was taboo for a reason—it was damn near poison and would make one horribly ill. I'd even seen young, newly turned vampires die from it when the bloodlust seized them in a feeding frenzy. As an older, naturally born vampire, it would weaken me temporarily but not enough to stop me. The benefit of taking such a risk was that I would be able to taste for the captain's bloodline and determine if it was indeed Laszlo who turned him.

Beneath the warm, coppery tang of blood was something vaguely familiar…not my bloodline, but perhaps a degree or two removed… possibly someone Laszlo had turned. It could have been Marguerite. *Interesting.* I spit the rest of the foul liquid onto the floor and pushed Lucien back down into his chair. Dazed, he clutched at the wound on his neck that oozed thick, black blood.

"Not to worry, Captain," I said. "I didn't take enough to end your interesting, immortal life. As I said, I rather enjoy the idea of a roving crew of vampire pirates. It feels like something my father would have approved of, and I'm nothing if not sentimental. Now, if you'd be so kind, I'll relieve you of your greatcoat. I don't want to scandalize that fetching tavern maid."

Trance-like, he shucked his filthy coat and handed it to me with a glazed look in his eyes and a slack expression. I pulled it on and released my hold on him. He shook his head to clear it and regarded me with murder in his odd, pale eyes. I waited a moment to see if he would try for his sword once more, but when he did not, I inclined my head and wrapped the coat tightly around my bloodied, naked body.

"It's been a pleasure, Captain Lucien," I muttered to him as I strode out the front door.

Once outside, I walked down the docks to the end of the pier, trying to collect my thoughts and calm my predatory instincts. I inhaled the cold, salty air, heavy with the brine of the ocean and the smoke from nearby fires. The gentle lapping of the water on the timber piles and the soft rush of the waves crashing on the nearby rocks helped to soothe me and temper my anger.

The dark part of me wanted to kill the old captain and his crew for daring to challenge me, but that would likely attract attention and wouldn't serve any purpose other than soothing my frustrations. If I was honest with myself, the only way I wanted to vent those emotions was to chase Mina down, tear her clothes from her lush curves and bury myself inside her—reminding her of all the ways I could bring her pleasure and all the reasons we belonged together. Unfortunately, I'd rushed into telling her everything, and I'd consider myself lucky if I hadn't lost her for good.

Hell, what a mess. I wasn't any closer to finding Laszlo, I'd scared Mina off, and with every move, I sensed The Order closing in. I knew they'd hear of what transpired with Captain Lucien—the bastards had ears everywhere—but it was a risk I'd had to take. Moving in the shadows the last few years hadn't worked, so perhaps it was time to take some bigger chances.

As you did with Mina? The cruel thought snaked through my mind. I didn't regret telling her everything, but I berated myself for pushing her and forcing her to accept it before she had time to think on things. I would give her that time. I wouldn't—*couldn't*—risk losing her again. I needed to be patient—the one thing I struggled with when it came to Mina. *No matter.* I'd waited years to reunite with her and had a lifetime of loneliness before that. She was worth the time and my patience. She was worth everything.

And in the meantime, I would find Laszlo. My traitorous brother had a lot to answer for. Pulling the collar of the greatcoat up to hide some of the blood smeared across my face, I ducked my head down and made my way back through the darkened streets of the port city.

As I wound between the narrow alleys, I heard a scuffle that gave me pause. Outside a tavern, a couple was cloaked in darkness—a young woman's tearful pleading and the older man's rough words informed me that the tryst had less to do with pleasure than power. The thought sickened me, and my fangs lengthened reflexively.

Ah, well. I need to feed this evening, anyway.

I approached the couple quietly, scenting fear and panic on the wind. It stirred my hunger and my bloodlust.

"Good evening," I murmured.

"Fuck off," the man grunted, not bothering to face me in lieu of caging the woman against a slimy, moss-covered wall.

Suddenly, the frustration, tension, anger, and passion for vengeance collided in me. I seized the man by his collar and whirled him around.

"I've never understood the type of man who can so easily torment another human for pleasure," I said. "But I think I will enjoy tormenting you." Then, to the woman, I said: "Take your leave, Mademoiselle."

She ran without a second glance.

"Who the fuck do you think you are?" the man growled. "You'll pay for that."

His fist flew clumsily, but because of our intimate proximity, it managed to connect with my cheek. The brief flash of pain excited me, and I grinned at him.

"Remove your clothing," I instructed, forcing him with my will. Alarm lit in the man's eyes, but he did as I commanded. When he was naked and shivering from the frigid sea air, I released my hold on him.

"How does it feel to be so vulnerable?" I asked, pushing him back against the cold brick wall. "To be in the thrall of another being so much more powerful than you?"

"What the fuck are you?" he hissed, and I recognized the acrid scent of urine. The bastard had pissed himself. "Are you the devil?"

"Yes," I rumbled, infusing my answer with the terror of Hell's legions. I felt the man's heartbeat stutter beneath my fingers, and I wasted no more time. I sank my fangs into his neck and drank deeply. The smooth, salty, coppery liquid ignited in my mouth, and I felt strength and energy returning to me. When I sensed his body dying and his soul departing, I dropped his lifeless form onto the ground. I cast Captain Lucien's coat over the dead man, then donned my prey's clothes. They were too large for my lean form, but they would be good enough for now. Hoisting the man easily over my shoulder, I hurried back to the docks and threw him in the black water. His blood had restored me, and his flesh would nourish the creatures in Poseidon's realm.

"You walked a dark path in life," I said. "May your death serve a greater purpose."

"A fine sentiment from a creature born upon a dark path," came a soft voice behind me.

I whirled around, poised to strike at whoever had managed to sneak up on me. I couldn't remember a time when that had happened before—always hearing, smelling, sensing better than others. My shock intensified, however, when I stared into a pair of dark brown eyes that I knew all too well.

"Ah, so here you are. Hello, Marguerite," I murmured.

11

MINA

April 23, 1768
Cimetière des Innocents

"I DO NOT THINK THIS IS A GOOD IDEA," I SAID TO DAPHNE AS SHE ADJUSTED her black domino mask over her face.

The beautiful blonde duchesse peered at me with her piercing violet eyes and offered a sympathetic smile. Her vampire fangs glinted in the spare light of the moon peeking through the carriage windows.

"I know, *chérie*, but it cannot be helped. We must know what The Order knows. So far, they think Charlotte and I are ignorant about their activities regarding your abduction, and we must keep it that way to protect you. Would you feel comforted if we went over our plan once more?" she asked, placing her hands in mine.

"No," I muttered grimly. "But we should go over the plan again, anyway."

Charlotte fidgeted with the clasp on her jewel-encrusted *chatelaine*—a lovely broach she wore at her waist that featured several secret compartments. Hiding places, I knew, where she kept tools of her trade: a garrote, capsules of poisons and drugs, various keys, and God knew what else. She struggled to pin it to her bodice, and Daphne leaned forward to help.

"Daphne and I will attend the meeting in a few minutes," Charlotte offered. "So that we may learn what they know and keep up the appearance of our ignorance. Antoine and Étienne, who don't often attend the meetings, will wait here in the carriage to ensure your safety. The Order would hardly expect you to be right outside! We'll insist we don't know where you are and haven't heard from you, of course. We'll discuss our current missions in the hope that we can figure out more of what The Order plans to do about you and Rafael. After the meeting, we'll go back to my *château*, have several large glasses of wine and some excellent food, and formulate a plan of attack for *les DD*."

"You just want to skip to the wine part," Daphne teased, finally fastening the *chatelaine* to the bright blue silk of Charlotte's skirts.

"How dare you!" Charlotte responded with mock affront. "I'll have you know I would prefer to skip to the food, too. I'm positively ravenous. Let's hope these pompous windbags don't drone on for too long. I may just shift and eat some of them."

I smiled at the cousins' lighthearted attempts to cheer me, but reality settled back in too quickly. Before I could say anything more, Antoine and Étienne knocked softly on the carriage door and tugged it open.

"Our patrol of the area turned up nothing. No villains or beasties anywhere near," Antoine rumbled, rocking the carriage slightly as he lifted his massive form in to sit next to Charlotte.

"Well, except for those inside this carriage," Étienne said with a grin. "Daphne, *mon amour*. You look radiant. Must you waste such a lovely gown on those dusty old prats?"

She dropped a chaste kiss on the vampire rake's knuckles.

"Yes, *chéri*, but you're welcome to help me out of it when we return home," she said with a wink.

Charlotte groaned and rolled her eyes, while I averted my gaze. I could hear Étienne's seductive chuckle and was unprepared for the wave of guilt and jealousy that washed over me. How many times had I dreamt of Rafael and I teasing each other in the same way? Had I ruined my chances for any romantic future with him?

What future? My thoughts demanded insistently. *The future where you cannot be together because of who he is—what he is—and who you are? Not only does a lowly physician have no place with a prince, but a human has no fate with a vampire who will walk the earth for eternity.*

The reflections soured my stomach, adding to the anxiety I already felt about Daphne and Charlotte meeting with The Order and pretending like nothing was different. It was dark enough in the carriage that I had to strain my eyes to see them, but I could make out their silhouettes by the light of the moon. They were checking their weaponry—daggers sheathed in leather garters, pistols stuffed in the pockets of their *panniers*, garrotes disguised as bracelets, and stiletto knives hidden in their elaborate coiffures. Despite my concern and love for my friends, I knew they were more than capable of taking care of themselves.

Once they were satisfied with their armaments, they kissed their mates goodbye and squeezed my hands in comfort.

"All will be well, Mina," Charlotte said as they alit from the carriage. "You'll see."

"We promise nothing bad will happen to you," Daphne insisted. "And nothing bad will happen to us, either."

"Absolutely," Charlotte agreed. Then, throwing a mischievous grin over her shoulder, she added, "But if anything does, rest assured Daphne and I will disembowel the lot of them and feast on their entrails."

"Hush, my love—I'm already hungry," Antoine growled. "Be safe."

"We will," Charlotte replied. She fixed Antoine with an intense stare. "Protect her, darling. At all costs."

He nodded firmly, eyes fierce.

With that, they left, trudging through the mud from the late-April rain. I watched as they wound their way through the long-forgotten graves until they reached a mausoleum at the back of the cemetery. Daphne pulled on the heavy door, and flickering golden candlelight spilled across the ground for an instant as they entered The Order's secret entrance. Darkness quickly followed as they disappeared into the tomb and closed the door behind them.

"I hope they will be well," I whispered.

"Don't worry, Doctor," Antoine said, his deep voice vibrating throughout the carriage interior. "Charlotte is my maker. I'll be able to sense if she's in trouble. Besides, The Order has no reason to suspect they know about your attempted kidnapping."

"Antoine is right, *mon amie*. I would wager The Order will imply you were abducted by Rafael and use that to try and force *les DD* to bolster their efforts in hunting him down. Without the tortured testimony of Pascal, there's nothing that would connect those two men to The Order," Étienne added.

"At this point, do you believe they would listen to reason?" I asked. "Perhaps it would be in everyone's best interest if Rafael and I were to come before them and explain the situation."

Antoine scoffed and Étienne tutted gently.

"No, Doctor. I don't know that truth has much to do with anything at this point. Trust me as one who has been hunted—and nearly murdered— by The Order before. When this man, Derais, started spouting his poison about vampires being the spawn of Hell and threatening the law and order of France, the wealthy, fearful fools heeded his words. We all see the tension building between the classes. If the aristocrats have an enemy to turn their ire against, they'll do so to gain support and keep the out-of-balance status quo. When it comes to these men, I'm afraid to say if their minds are determined by fear, and I believe they are, their course has already been set," Étienne replied.

I knew he was right, but I was still disappointed by the truth of his words. I tried to distract myself from the chaos of my mind, but my thoughts continued to return to Rafael, The Order, and the past twenty years. I chewed at my bottom lip. I needed to focus on a problem. Whenever I became sad or distracted at home, I typically turned to my work.

"Antoine," I said suddenly, shattering the silence that had descended inside the carriage. "What did you mean about your connection to your maker?"

"Just that," he replied. "Despite my love for Charlotte, this connection between us only grew after she turned me. No matter where she is, I can sense strong emotions from her. Anger, frustration, fear, joy. I feel it almost as if it were my own."

"And you, Étienne? Do you share the same connection with Daphne?" I wondered.

"Not nearly as strong, but yes. I believe most vampires feel such a tie to those who drink of their blood. A way to keep track of one's blood offspring, I suppose."

I heard the rustle of fabric in the darkness and suspected he'd shrugged.

"How interesting," I said absently. My mind immediately returned to Rafael, and I wondered what it would be like to feel so connected to him. What it would have been like for him to sense my emotions for the past twenty years—all the loneliness, hurt, emptiness, fear, frustration, and tender joys I'd collected in my life. He might have sensed them from his hidden world, perhaps while he slept and dreamed during the day. Would it have made a difference? Would he have come for me? Part of me was seized with a powerful melancholy, despondent at the thought that he'd been so close and still hadn't sent word of his presence or motives, and the other part of me felt a pervasive sadness that he, too, had been alone in that time, unable to reach out.

"I can practically hear your mind racing, Doctor," Antoine said. "What do you wish to know?"

"How long does such a connection last, I wonder? Does it lessen or intensify over time?"

"I was only recently turned," he answered. "But I don't feel much of a change in it now than I did before. I am getting better at managing the entirety of another person's emotions, but I suppose I feel them the same way."

"The same for me," Étienne said.

"Forgive me for my bluntness, but how many people have you turned?" I asked the vampire.

"Only Daphne," he replied. "Before her, I couldn't fathom spending eternity with another person. In a momentary lapse of judgment brought on by the loneliness of my early vampire days, I offered to turn my half-sisters—they were wee things when I was a new vampire—but they refused."

"Your Rafael," Antoine inquired, shifting to better face me. "Has he turned many?"

Shame, guilt, and anxiety rose in my chest. How much could I tell these men? Certainly, I trusted them, but how could they understand my complicated history with the man everyone believed would be the downfall of humanity?

"Truthfully, I do not know," I answered honestly. "But when we—Papa and I—were at their home, it was forbidden for them to turn anyone outside of their family. Only the partners who married into the family would be turned. It was their great penance, they told us, to live for eternity with this curse and to remain isolated from the world and the people they wanted and needed."

"Honor can only take you so far," Étienne said. "The preceding generations must have been driven mad with such cruel fates."

"As I understand it, many were," I said.

"Poor devils," Antoine muttered. "That is great penance indeed."

"Many believe their crimes warranted such measures. And after knowing the head of that house, I think I can understand why," I said quietly.

Antoine froze then, stilling the carriage with his movements. Before I could ask, he and Étienne were on alert, charging the air with tension like the lightning that precedes the heavy thunder of violence.

"Something is wrong," he growled. "Panic, fear—I can practically taste it."

"Should we intervene?" I asked, fear lacing through my body.

"No," Étienne practically shouted. "We must trust them. We promised to stay here with you and keep you safe. I'll stay here with Mina, Antoine. If you shift and move around to those trees behind the mausoleum, you might be able to hear what's going on underground."

Antoine was already shucking his heavy coat and pulling off his boots. I was grateful for the darkness, but I slammed my eyes shut for good measure. Étienne chuckled.

"Are you not a doctor? I'm certain you've seen him in the flesh," he teased, but there was an undercurrent of unease in his voice that I did not care for.

"I am!" I insisted. "But I am not examining him right now, and I don't fancy peeking at my best friend's fiancé."

The carriage lurched as Antoine exited, and I heard the nauseating sounds of bones breaking beneath flesh and tortured groans that morphed into lupine whimpers. He'd transformed into his wolf form.

"I think your modesty is safe," Étienne murmured. "He's gone."

I opened my eyes again but needn't have bothered. The moon had moved behind a copse of trees, blacking out everything I'd scarcely been able to see before. It should have felt unnerving to be in utter darkness across from such a lethal predator, but I felt a strange comfort with these men. I'd saved both of their lives before, and I knew they were men of honor—they would lay down their lives to ensure my safety.

For a few moments, the only sounds I heard were the rustle of the bitter wind through the trees and the occasional hoot of an owl. The silence only served to exacerbate my anxiety.

"Some people say owls are ill omens," I whispered nervously. "But I've never found that. I think they're wonderful creatures, cloaked in night and keeping vermin in check. They aren't harming anyone, and yet superstitious fools will kill them because they think that will keep death at bay."

"People will do anything to keep death at bay," Étienne said distantly.

I cringed. He might've been thinking of his turning or of the lives he'd ended in order to feed himself. I hadn't meant to offend him.

"I'm sorry," I said. "I didn't mean…"

"Worry not, dear doctor," he interrupted. "It only piques my curiosity that you speak of owls in the way that I wish people spoke of vampires. Cloaked in night, keeping vermin in check."

"Humans are *not* vermin," I insisted. "And many of you do harm people, whether intentionally or not. The blood plague turns you into parasites who must absorb the blood of another, and too often your kind kills the providing host."

"Yes," he agreed. "That is unfortunate. Not all makers are equipped with the knowledge to help their whelps understand when to stop drinking. And certainly, there must be consent between both parties. Daphne and I have been trying to build a program of education from Versailles, but our efforts are failing. It seems the king is more interested in eradication than education."

His last words were sharp with frustration, and I wasn't certain if it was because of his fear for Daphne and Charlotte or if it was because his work as an emissary was proving to be nearly impossible. Likely both.

Antoine suddenly crashed through the carriage door, back in his human form and entirely naked. I shut my eyes again.

"They're coming," he huffed, tugging his pants on. "Charlotte and

Daphne are coming back. They're unharmed but upset. Worried. Something has gone wrong."

No sooner had he pulled his shirt over his broad, muscular chest than the comtesse and duchesse stumbled into the carriage. The moon had moved from behind the trees, caressing their faces with a pale, pearl-like glow. There was fear in their eyes.

"Home," Charlotte shouted at her driver. "Immediately."

Daphne wedged herself next to Étienne, then leaned forward and grasped my hands.

"There is a problem," she said.

Dread pooled in my gut, swirling furiously like Charybdis before Odysseus.

"What?" I asked on a breath.

Charlotte perched on the edge of the seat next to me and put her arm around my shoulders.

"The Order has Rafael's brother."

12

RAFAEL

April 23, 1768
Dunkirk

"Perhaps I believe you. Then again, you haven't given me much reason to," I growled at the woman sitting across from me. She tilted her head, her shrewd eyes assessing.

"Why should I lie? I had no reason to approach you. I could have stayed in hiding, watching you flail and falter as you hunted us." She sneered, her shapely cherubic lips tilting up at the corners. It was an unfortunate characteristic of Marguerite's exceptional beauty that disdain and sarcasm intensified her attractiveness. When she'd been a maid in my father's household, I'd wondered if she exacerbated every ill temperament to show her face in its most attractive light.

"Hunting isn't quite what I was doing," I replied. "And I was close enough before you revealed yourself to me. It would have been a matter of time before I discovered you and Laszlo's whereabouts."

Her brown eyes twinkled beneath long sweeps of dark lashes, and she lifted one pale shoulder in an artful shrug. Everything about her felt predatory and calculating, like a viper waiting to strike.

"Perhaps," she murmured, echoing my earlier word. We stared at each other for a long while, her slender fingers drumming lightly on the lacquered table in their townhouse.

When she had approached me at the docks, she'd been dressed in a silk gown of deep sea green—beautiful and lavish, certainly, but some years out of fashion. She persuaded me to accompany her to their town-house, which was in a nicer part of town overlooking the ocean but protected from the chilly storms that raged in the winter. Not that either of them would be bothered by the cold or damp.

The townhouse was well appointed, and I suspected Laszlo had brought enough money with him when they eloped to keep Marguerite in style, but given that our father had disinherited him, I wondered how long that money had lasted. Was that Marguerite's game? The money had run out, and so she'd tired of her immortal companion.

"Why would The Order come for him? They seem to want *me* in connection with the arrival of the blood plague," I asked. "And how did they find you here when I only just discovered you myself?"

"Maybe you're not as clever as you think." She smiled. "And I suspect they're after your entire line—everyone in the Dracul family is at fault for the blood plague."

I narrowed my eyes. "It's Laszlo who ran from his responsibilities and let loose the curse upon the world. I've been trying to fix things for the past twenty years—at *great* personal cost."

"What do you know of responsibility?" she hissed. "You forget, I worked in your house long enough to see you squander money and title and kinship on satisfying your pleasure. Long before that *girl* came along. You encouraged your wanton reputation and strained the ties between your family, pushing Laszlo away and saddling him with the entirety of a kingdom he never wanted to begin with."

"He wanted it before *you* came along! And you turned his head, feeding him God knows what lies, all so he would whisk you away from your life in service." I snarled. "You were greedy and manipulative then, and you're just as bad now. If he is with The Order, it's probably because you betrayed him so you wouldn't be tied to the penniless, nameless, first-born son of a disgraced family."

Cold anger rolled off her in waves, giving her the appearance of a vengeful Amphitrite.

"Believe me or don't," she bit out. "But I'm telling you he was taken by men four days ago. I know they worked for The Order because I over-heard them as they carted him away."

"How did you overhear them? How did they manage to take him? He would have been able to break any bonds and escape. Why didn't he?"

"I was coming home from my modiste when I saw them. I hid, natu-rally. They drugged him with an injection of quicksilver," she answered.

My lip curled in disgust. "You hid while your maker—the purported love of your life—was taken away, likely to be tortured or murdered."

"If they'd taken me, too, I wouldn't have been able to solicit your help in getting him back," she said grimly. "As much as it pains me to admit, I need your assistance, Rafael."

"You didn't seek me out, Marguerite. You waited until I was practically at your doorstep. What have you been doing since he was taken? Awaiting final measurements for your new gowns?" I shot back.

"I knew you were in France," she said coolly. "I was making preparations to find you, but instead, you turned up here asking after that fool pirate."

"You lie too easily," I hissed. This woman had seduced my only brother and taken him from me—ruining more than our lives. It was because of her I'd had to abandon Mina to stay and take Laszlo's place. It was her actions that set this whole course in motion, and I suspected she'd schemed all of it from the very beginning. I couldn't understand or believe that Laszlo loved her truly and madly, as I loved Mina. Marguerite was beautiful, but cold, distant, and dangerous.

"Dismiss me if you must, but you know something is wrong. If you'd been a better brother and had maintained your connection to him, you would have sensed it already," she sneered.

Her words cut straight to my heart—to the guilt that lingered there over the fracturing of my family. Over the past twenty years of tense silence between us and the unspoken understanding that neither had the temerity to seek the other out.

"Besides." She arched her brow. "He is obviously not here. Do you believe I have him bound and gagged somewhere? The most powerful vampire in a thousand years—restrained by his newly turned wife?"

Wife. *Wife.* So, they had married in secret after all. I didn't know why it bothered me so much. It made sense that they would marry—he was too proud to keep her as some false consort. She would have demanded it. Still, the word needled me for everything it meant. Laszlo and Marguerite had had their twenty years of love while I'd had to give up everything—*everything*—to take his place under Father's cruel eye.

I glared at Marguerite, suddenly feeling drained from the long, frustrating evening. Dawn wasn't far off, and both of us would need to rest. I blew out a breath.

"Very well, Marguerite. I'll play along. The Order has Laszlo. What do you want to do about it?" I rubbed at my temples. It couldn't be true, could it? It must be another of her lies.

She looked at me like I was an imbecile.

"I want you to go get him. Return him to me, obviously," she spat. "I want you to stop cowering in the shadows—the both of you—and seize the power that lay carelessly at your fingertips. Go to The Order, wherever those bastards are hiding out, break down that door, and drain every single one of those old fools for daring to challenge your mighty legacy. You have the strength, the power, the wisdom, and cunning to do it, Rafael, so stop bleating like some wounded animal and remember who you are." She stepped forward, grabbing me by the shoulders and shaking me with each word. "Remember *what* you are. You are a Dracul! You are a Hell-cursed monster who has walked more nights than most men could dream."

I was stunned into silence, my eyebrows lifting at her sudden passion.

She gestured wildly around her. "You possess abilities that Lucifer himself would envy and would have used to lay waste to Heaven's self-righteous legions. If you won't be responsible for your kingdom or your failings, be responsible for your brother," she pleaded, collapsing into a chair under the weight of exhaustion, or perhaps defeat. Her steely eyes met mine, imploring and shimmering with unshed tears. "Go, Rafael, and bring him back to me."

I stared, angry but oddly inspired by Marguerite's tirade. What could she want from this endeavor? Could she really love him? Was this how she won him over—by charming him and flattering him and making him feel like he was so much more than a pawn in my father's political games? Was he really in the hands of The Order? If so, how could that have happened? Sudden anxiety gnawed at me—was it possible she was telling the truth?

She shook her head, sighing heavily, and rose to her feet. When she spoke, I could hear the fatigue and exasperation in her tone.

"Sunrise approaches. There is a guest room downstairs. The servants have all been dismissed, but I'm sure it will still be comfortable, even if it's a bit dusty and stale. Rest here today, if you wish." She inclined her head in a curt nod and left the room in a swirl of deep sea green silk.

Weariness dragged at my limbs as I found my way downstairs, shuffling toward the small guest room. Marguerite had been right—the room hadn't been aired out in years and the dust and cobwebs were thick throughout. I didn't particularly care, except that it made me wonder how long ago it truly was that the money had run out. Perhaps longer than I'd originally thought.

I shook the dusty blankets out and climbed into the soft bed. *Laszlo, Laszlo. Why her? Why at that moment?*

And then, as exhaustion pulled me into sleep, I thought of Mina.

I awoke hours later, just as the sun was setting. I trudged back upstairs, hoping to borrow some of Laszlo's clothes to replace the ill-fitting ones I'd stolen from last night's meal. I didn't see or hear anything from Marguerite, but it was possible she was still sleeping. I decided to wait and amused myself by perusing their home.

They hadn't bothered to keep a kitchen but had instead turned the space into a small painting studio and gallery. Oil paints and watercolors littered the rough wooden table in the middle of the room, along with brushes and sheaves of paper with painting studies and sketches. Someone was a talented artist, and it grieved me immeasurably to not know whether it was Marguerite or Laszlo.

I continued my tour, rifling through an office—nothing out of the ordinary, except that it seemed Laszlo had made some rather poor investments. I sneered. *Was Marguerite lying? Had Laszlo simply left here and ventured across the sea to escape her disdain?*

Something about that didn't feel quite right, though, and I pushed the thought aside. I was driving myself mad with the possibilities of my brother's fate. It would be best if I could simply find him and ask him about the past twenty years. *Would he even tell me the truth?*

Having finished my explorations, I realized it had been nearly an hour since I'd risen, and night had fallen. I didn't know Marguerite's habits, but I decided if I were to play her knight in shining armor and rescue my brother from his captors in this farcical tale, I could at least demand the use of some of his clothes so I could travel home comfortably.

I crept upstairs to their bedroom and found myself facing a single locked door at the top of the landing. I knocked and waited, but no sounds spilled forth. *That's interesting.*

After another minute, my anxiety flared, and I kicked the door in, tensing as it shattered into an explosion of sticks and splinters. The room was empty, the bed undisturbed. It was tidy, as if it had been used recently, but obviously not last night. Where had she gone? Had she slipped out to hunt while I slept?

Unease threaded through me as I scanned the room, looking for signs of anyone anything. When had she left? And why?

"Marguerite?" I called out. I listened for the creak of floorboards, the rustle of fabric, the rattle of the cold sea breeze through an open window but heard nothing. The silence blanketing the townhouse felt unnervingly lifeless.

Despite my dislike of my brother's *wife*—even the thought made me growl—I worried that something had happened to her in the daytime while I'd slept downstairs. I had no firm evidence or reason to believe foul play, except decades of intuition and the knowledge that if it was indeed The Order playing these games, they would stop at nothing and had every resource at their disposal.

Above all, I needed to return to Paris. I found Laszlo's wardrobe and pulled out a smart black waistcoat and breeches, along with a worn linen shirt and a fine wool overcoat. The garments fit me better than my dinner's, but still not as well as my own. It didn't matter. I only needed them to wear until I reached the outskirts of the city, and then I could shift into my wolf form and run the rest of the way.

I left the townhouse, still scanning for any sign of Marguerite. Not even her scent lingered here, which confused me more than anything. It was almost as if I'd been with a ghost, and no trace of her remained after our encounter. While I didn't believe that, there was a part of me that clung to my earlier unease.

I walked casually through the city, trying to avoid notice and pacing myself to reach the outskirts in good time. Fortunately, no one paid attention to me. In this frustrated, heightened state, death would surely meet anyone who attempted to delay me. But finally, mercifully, I crossed the road at the bottom of a hill, and the farmlands gave way to green fields and budding forests. The winter had delayed the onset of spring, but I marveled at how nature demanded new life.

The roads were empty, but to be safe, I hiked a bit to a small glade of trees to shift into my wolf form. Picking up Laszlo's borrowed clothes in my lupine jaws, I took off heading south, hoping to reach Paris in two days' time. At a full run, if I only stopped for sunrise and didn't pause to feed, I could just make it, but I would be weak when I arrived. It was a chance I would have to take.

My paws dug into the wet earth, flinging mud around me as I ran through the trees. At this speed, it would be difficult for humans to see me, and I could only hope my luck would hold.

Onward I raced, not daring to stop until the sky began to lighten and the stars faded from view. I bolted for a cave in a nearby hill where I could rest for the day, and then as soon as the sun set, I was off again. Perhaps it was my exhaustion and hunger that drove me so quickly, or perhaps it was my worry for Mina, or the whispering doubts I had about Laszlo and Marguerite's fates—either way, I reached the countryside outside of Paris just before the sun started to rise on the second morning. During the entire journey, I'd wondered about my next steps...where I would go, what I would do, how I would verify Marguerite's story, and I'd come to one dreaded but somehow inevitable conclusion.

My paws crunched along the gravel drive up to the grand entrance of the stately château, and before I could shift and knock, the massive door flew open. I faced a bristling, irate brunette with flashing, red-gold lupine eyes.

"Well!" The Comtesse de Brionne huffed. "It's about time you arrived."

13

MINA

From my guest room in Charlotte's château, I heard a commotion in the front hall, which I expected to be news from the remaining agents in *les DD*. After we'd returned from Daphne and Charlotte's meeting with The Order, they'd spent the following nights planning and sending messages to their agents, desperate to gather word of anything that could help us determine our next move.

The Order had abducted Laszlo. They were keeping him in a locked room underground, drugged with quicksilver and nearly feral from hunger. Daphne and Charlotte both reported a peculiar sensation when they entered the mausoleum, something they'd never felt before. They asked me if I knew of any supernatural repellants other than the false folk cures, garlic and wolfsbane, but I knew of none. They described a feeling of illness and terror but could not explain its origin. I had no doubt The Order had something nefarious up their sleeves if they'd been able to keep a powerful old vampire like Laszlo incapacitated.

Laszlo. I knew they would not feed him, and it was possible—difficult, yes, but possible—for a vampire to starve to death. The Order was holding him for questioning, likely torturing him for information on the where-abouts of Rafael, unaware or uncaring that Rafael was innocent of their accusations. Perhaps Laszlo was responsible for the blood plague, but I couldn't find it in my heart to believe that was true. The Order would execute him, Daphne had said, if he couldn't prove useful.

One fewer vampire, they'd said, clearly drawing a line in the sand. It was a wonder Daphne and Charlotte had made it out of the meeting alive. Well, undead.

My thoughts turned to Rafael. Where was he? Where had he gone? Was he safe? Did he know about his brother?

And then, my traitorous heart thudded in my chest. *Does he still want me after I turned him away?*

I tugged the wool wrap around my shoulders, cold despite the slow warming of the April days. Winter had clung too long to France, but finally we'd had a couple of scant sunny days that felt like spring forcing its way through.

Another servant hurried down the hall and knocked at my door.

"Doctor," she whispered. "I think you'll want to come see this."

Usually, when people said that it meant a visceral appointment for me. Collecting my medical bag, I frowned down at my spring-inspired gown of cream decorated with a riot of tiny flowers. Charlotte had picked the fabric for me, and while I'd balked at the impracticality of it for my line of work, I couldn't help but feel delightful cheer when I put the gown on.

"Do I have time to change beforehand?" I asked the young housemaid.

"No, mademoiselle. But I don't think you'll want to, anyway," she added cryptically.

I furrowed my brow.

"Why?"

She beckoned me into the hallway and nearly pushed me toward the main staircase. When I peered down into the grand foyer, I understood the commotion.

Rafael stood in the middle of the marble floor, completely naked aside from the mud and traces of dried blood around his mouth. Charlotte stood in front him, chattering animatedly, oblivious to his unclothed state. Two servants waited patiently at the edge of the hall, poised to offer whatever their mistress required. At present, I thought that should be clothes, but that seemed to be the least of anyone else's worries. I fought to stem the annoyance I felt at everyone else having a full view of Rafael's *endowments.*

I couldn't help but allow myself a thorough look. If only for scientific purposes, I told myself. How had the vampire changed since I'd last let my eyes rove over his beautiful body—twenty years ago and yet yesterday?

He hadn't.

His lean muscles—honed through years of a soldier's training and a predator's hunting practice—flexed beneath moon-pale skin. A dusting of soft, dark hair sprayed across his chest and tapered down his abdomen. I blushed when I looked lower, embarrassed to be staring at a man I no longer claimed. Lifting my gaze back up, I noticed the tension in his shoulders as he crossed his arms over his chest and the hard lines of his jaw. His eyes were locked on Charlotte's, and they flashed with restrained anger and powerful promises. He wasn't threatening her, but he wasn't pleased with what she was telling him. A loose lock of his black hair fell forward across his brow, and as he pushed it away, his arm drew back from his chest enough that I saw what made my heart nearly stop beating.

A recent wound of fresh pink skin, directly over his absent heart. It was a rough wound that was still healing, which meant not only had someone staked him, but the fight had been a struggle for him, as well. *He is not dead,* my mind cried. *But he could be dead.* That was the hardest part about immortal beings—the fact that you could rely on their immortality...until you couldn't. The fear that followed stopped me in my tracks. Panic clawed at me, hot and sharp, until the room started to spin, and air became thick. From below, Rafael's gaze flew to mine.

In less than an instant, he was at my side.

"Mina," he murmured, smooth and low, like a bow being pulled across a cello. The comfort of my name on his lips pulled me from the brink of fainting.

"What are you doing here?" I asked, my voice hoarser than I wanted it to be.

His eyes narrowed.

"You are pale...and weak," he said, by way of an answer. "You have not been eating. Or sleeping."

"I have been busy," I huffed, pushing him away from me. "I don't need a nursemaid, Rafael. Especially one who has his own troubles." I gestured to the healing wound on his chest. It looked much worse up close—the skin around it puckering and raw.

He did not smile. "Busy? Too busy to take care of yourself?"

By that point, Charlotte had climbed the stairs and regarded us with a mixture of annoyance and excitement. She practically vibrated with her struggle to keep both contained.

"She has been refusing almost every tempting morsel I've sent up to her," she chastised. "Including almond cakes!"

Rafael's eyes widened, and he turned an accusatory gaze back to me.

"And all day long I hear her pacing about in the house, stomping from room to room. She says she's busy with her work on the blood plague and our plans, but if you ask me, it's but one thing," Charlotte continued, apparently set on revealing every ounce of my emotional distress over the last few days.

"Traitor," I muttered.

"One thing?" Rafael echoed.

"Yes, I think she's lovesick," Charlotte stated matter-of-factly. I'd never thought ill of my friend, even before I knew her so well, but in that moment, I wished for the world's strongest muzzle. I groaned inwardly. Attempting to change the subject to anything that wasn't an exercise in torturous mortification, I coughed.

"Charlotte, have you been formally introduced?"

She tilted her head at me and stifled a giggle.

"No, but we're very well acquainted. We are connected by blood, after all."

"I didn't mean…" I blushed again, embarrassed. "I know *that*. I just meant, have you had a proper introduction? You've been calling him *the man in black* since you met."

She laughed. "Please, Doctor, do introduce me to your—*ahem*—dear friend. Prince Rafael, is it? How would you prefer to be addressed, Your Highness?"

Rafael tried valiantly to cover his smirk, and I wished the ground would open and swallow me whole.

"Prince to a seized principality, Comtesse, and traveling discreetly. Rafael is fine," he said.

"Oh, certainly he is," Charlotte teased, winking at me. I scowled at Rafael's throaty chuckle and snatched the velvet dressing gown that she'd been carrying, thrusting it into Rafael's arms.

"Here," I hissed. "Charlotte, do you have a room for him?"

Her eyes glittered with mischief. "Why, the Rose room—right next to yours, of course."

A garbled noise between a squeak and a curse slipped from my lips. Charlotte finally took pity on me as she turned to Rafael and curtsied politely.

"Rafael, I bid you welcome. As morning is nearly upon us, I'm sure you'd like to bathe, feed, and rest before we discuss our plans. I'll send a bath up for you at once, and in your room, you'll find a sideboard with spirits and fresh blood. Please don't hesitate to ring for anything at all, and I shall see you in the evening. Mina, *chérie*." She smiled at me as she turned down the hallway. "Do be careful."

Rafael shrugged on the banyan and opened the door to the large guest room. The windows had been blacked out and long, dawn pink curtains hung in front of them, giving the room a fresh yet cozy feeling. The spring evening had become chilly, and a small fire crackled in the white marble hearth. Rafael strode in and surveyed the room, nodding appreciatively.

"It's not as grand as you're used to," I said anxiously, strangely defensive despite Charlotte's palatial château. "It's not a castle. But Charlotte keeps a warm and welcoming home."

"I've spent far more days in far worse places than châteaus and castles," he said softly, exhaling a little and rolling his shoulders. Weariness flowed off him like water. "This is the warmest welcome I've had in a long time, and one I deserve far less."

Anyone else would be surprised by Charlotte's willingness to overlook some of Rafael's faults, especially considering he had turned her into a werewolf without her consent. I hadn't had the chance to ask him if it had been intentional or an accident.

The atmosphere seemed to thicken with the tension of the last few days, and our stilted goodbye before that. I'd spent countless hours thinking about him—his words and his kiss. It had driven me to distraction and frustrated me beyond measure. I'd thought I'd moved on from him after twenty years of separation, but the last two weeks had proven me wrong. With a grudging acceptance, I was forced to acknowledge my feelings were as strong as ever for the vampire who'd long ago shattered my heart.

Not that it would—or could—change anything.

I watched him silently, running his long, pale fingers over the heavy brocade curtains. His demeanor was diminished, so unlike the bold, brash vampire I knew years ago and even unlike the passionate, dangerous man who'd showed up at the threshold of my clinic. Something had happened in the last few days.

"How—how are you?" I tried. It was a stupid question, but my anxiety had the better of me and I'd never been eloquent enough to drip honeyed words like a courtier.

He turned to me, dark eyes filled with emotion, on the precipice of saying something when one of Charlotte's housemaids interrupted us, bringing in the large copper bathtub. In the ensuing parade of servants who came through to fill the tub with piping hot water, I slipped out and stepped back into my bedchamber.

Rafael would want privacy, but I was far too restless to sleep. I undressed down to my chemise and unpinned my long, brown locks, running a fine bone comb through them. I should try to return to the library to do some more research, but the thought of Rafael being under the same roof was almost too much to bear. As much as I knew how sleep would elude me, focusing on research would be even more futile.

My reflection in the mirror stared back at me, looking pale and drawn.

I frowned, rubbing at the wrinkle between my eyebrows. Perhaps Charlotte and Rafael were right, and I needed some food and rest. I pulled on
my dressing gown to head to the kitchens for something to eat when there
was a firm knock on my door.

I might have pretended it was Charlotte or one of the maids, but
inside, I knew who it was. There was only one person it *could* be.

"Rafael," I whispered, opening my door.

He stood clad in the same deep red banyan as before, cinched tightly at
his waist. The thin triangle of pale skin below his throat showed he wasn't
wearing anything underneath. I swallowed—my mouth suddenly dry.

He looked somewhat restored, and I suspected he'd fed as well as
bathed. His damp hair hung just above his shoulders, loose and wild,
making him look every inch the foreign prince he truly was.

"We were interrupted earlier," he said. "My apologies."

I nodded, unsure of what to say.

"I'm glad to find you here," he said after a few moments. "Safe with
your friends."

"You found your way here too," I said quietly. "Though I suspect you
realize the circumstances are rather unfortunate."

"Laszlo," he acknowledged.

"I'm so sorry, Rafael."

He stepped into the room, closing the door behind him.

"I don't want to talk about Laszlo, Mina." His gaze was like fire, blistering in its intensity.

"What do you want to talk about?" I asked automatically, suddenly
breathless. I took a step back, and he followed me into the room, tracking
me like a predator. My heart pounded in excitement, and heat dropped
low from my stomach, as if I'd swallowed a hot coal.

"Why aren't you eating? Or sleeping?" he asked.

I paused. "I told you."

"No," he said, taking another step toward me. "You lied to me."

"I have been busy," I insisted.

One more step forward—a hair's breadth away.

"Do you know what I think, Mina?"

He raised a hand to my cheek but stopped just shy of touching me.

"I think you were distracted. Perhaps you were thinking of me as
much as I was thinking of you."

I closed my eyes, somehow both ready—and not—for the kiss that I
prayed would come. Seconds ticked by on the mantel clock and the fire
crackled in the hearth—the only sounds other than our breathing. When I
opened my eyes, Rafael was looking down at me with a thousand

unknowable thoughts flashing in his gaze. He stood there, frozen like a marble statue.

"Mina," he whispered. "I promised you before. I will not touch you until you ask."

I closed my eyes, knowing I would regret everything. Fearing even more that I would regret nothing. *Damn us both.*

"Rafael," I begged, more breath than sound. "Kiss me."

Instantly, his lips were on mine. His kiss was soft at first—restrained. Tentative. The gentleness of it brought tears to my eyes, and I felt them spill over as he sucked at my bottom lip, wordlessly seeking entry. I opened my mouth to plunder his, sweeping across his tongue in lush strokes, goading him into *more.* More passion, more fire, more heat. More Rafael. I sighed in contentment at the familiar taste of him—the bite of some sweet spirit, the faint savory tang of blood, and the delectable warmth that was all Rafael.

My hands came up to tangle in his hair, and he growled appreciatively, guiding me back toward the bed. Without thinking, I slipped my hands down his face, his neck, and across his shoulders, pushing his dressing gown down and letting it slide to the floor. His lean muscles flexed beneath his pearl white skin, and light blue veins traced paths across his arms, shoulders, chest, and abdomen. He looked exactly as he had twenty years ago, when I was so in love with him I was prepared to throw everything away so we might be together. That included my family, my future, and even my mortality—a secret I hadn't shared with him back then.

"Mina," he said, low and lush. "May I undress you?"

His eyes had melted into solid pools of black, and his pupils flashed red. He was keeping an iron grip on his control, even more so than when we'd been young and every intimacy had been full of hesitation and care. Despite his devilish reputation, he'd treated me then like something precious and breakable. Now, however, it stirred a thread of ire in me.

"That was the point of all this," I huffed, trying to untie my dressing gown in haste. His cool hands stilled on top of mine.

"You wanted me to stop before," he pointed out.

"Yes, but not *forever.*" I yanked at the knot, tightening it in my frustrated attempt to loosen it. "I was angry with you, Rafael. I am *still* angry with you. Frankly, I am angry with me too."

"If you are so angry, why do you want this? Why do you want this if you are not mine? If I am not yours?"

"Because, you fool, I will always want you. I will want you when I hate you, I will want you when I am angry with you, I will want you even if I married another man tomorrow and gave him six children," I snapped. I abandoned the knotted tie of my dressing gown, close to tears, and dangerously close to destroying my ardor.

Rafael seized my robe and pulled me tightly to him, challenge flashing in his black and red eyes.

"Do not speak of other men to me, Mina," he snarled. "Even hypothetical ones."

I snapped my mouth shut, feeling guilty for goading him, but the deep, dark, wicked part of me thrilled at the primal side of him. Excitement skittered across my skin, tightening my nipples and igniting the inferno in my blood. He traced his hand down the swell of my hip and slipped his finger beneath the belt of my robe.

"Allow me," he rumbled, slicing the knot with one sharp nail. The robe fell open, and he dropped to his knees. Catching my eye with a heated glance, he arched a brow.

"I kneel to no one but you," he said.

He lifted my chemise with one hand, the other tracing a feather-light patch up my leg, from my ankle, to my calf, to my thigh, and finally to the dark thatch of hair between my legs. He leaned forward, his warm breath tickling the sensitive skin of my groin and paused for a moment.

"Tell me again that you want this," he said, the rough edge to his voice the only sign that his cool temperament was wavering.

"Please, Rafael," I whispered, abandoning every logical thought in my head. "Tonight, I am yours."

14

MINA

April 26, 1768
Château de Ruisseau Magdelaine

He lingered a moment, exhaled softly, then leaned forward to drop kisses up the insides of my thighs. I squirmed in anticipation, twining my fingers in his lush, dark waves, gently urging him higher. I might as well have tried to move a mountain for all the good it did me.

Sensing my frustration, Rafael chuckled, then dragged one finger along the seam of my sex, pressing gently at the apex of my pleasure. My knees almost gave out from the shock of the sensation. He let go of the hem of my chemise, and I tugged it up over my head, not wanting anything else between us. Just as he was about to set his mouth to my sex, he sat back on his heels and stared up at me.

"My Mina," he whispered reverently, running his hands through his hair. "Even with eternity, I could never get used to the sight of you. My goddess of spring, Persephone—you are the most beautiful creature I've ever seen."

A blush bloomed across my cheeks and chest at his worship, but I didn't have time to reply. With vampire speed, he rushed forward and wrapped his hands around my ass, pulling my sex to his lips. Devouring me with lips and teeth and tongue, he left no part of me untasted or unloved. His fangs grazed the peak of my pleasure, sending a jolt of prickling pleasure through my entire body. Faster and faster he licked, working me into a panting puddle of sexual need. When I was nearing the crest of that impending *petite mort,* Rafael slipped his finger inside me, being careful to retract his claws. I desperately ached for release, but as I was about to come apart, he withdrew and sat back on his heels.

I growled a string of curses I'd never used before and gripped his hair by the roots while he chuckled mischievously.

"I will not leave you wanting, Mina. This helps your pleasure to build. I've waited twenty years for this—I'm going to make up for every night we spent apart." His voice vibrated over my skin and sparked lust along every nerve.

He stood and hoisted me up, carrying me over to the bed. Even with the coolness of his skin, I felt fire pulsing through him and sensed the wildness he fought to contain. God, how I wanted him to let it loose.

After laying me gently on the bed, his hands mapped my body with maddeningly delicate touches. When his fingertips ghosted my full, aching breasts, his fangs lengthened with desirous reflex. In the dim light of the fire, his black and red eyes glittered hungrily, but it wasn't for blood.

He crawled up my body, lightly scoring his fangs across my overheated skin—not enough to draw blood, but enough to coax torturous sensations in my most intimate places. Desire pooled between my legs and my core clenched in anticipation.

"Rafael," I gasped, feeling his claw circle the bud of my pleasure once more. It was a lit match in a keg of black powder, bringing me closer to the edge than I'd been before. I squeezed my eyes shut, arching my hips and grinding against his fingers.

"Open your eyes," he demanded, his voice scraping out around his fangs. It was rough—bordering on violent. His control started to fray as he palmed my breast with one hand, never relenting the maddening slow circles his fingers traced on my sex. When I didn't immediately acquiesce, he growled, pinching my nipple and slipping two fingers inside me.

"Look at me, Mina," he snarled. "I will see you come with your eyes open. I will know every flicker of passion in your gaze—will swallow every sigh when you fall to pieces at my touch." His voice was deep and captivating, making it impossible to disobey. I beheld him playing my body like some beautiful instrument, the sight both exquisite and damning. *I was lost for him.* Heat built like an inferno, and again I chased it, begging him with moans and sighs to end my agony.

Again, he pulled back. This time, my frustration summoned tears. As I opened my mouth to shout at him and curse him back to Hell, he placed a gentle but firm hand at my neck and laid his body atop mine. His erection pressed hard against my sex—the friction against my clit making me feral.

His deep, sensual laughter sounded through me.

"Yes, my goddess. Finally, you are as wild for me as I am for you." His demonic eyes shone with possessive heat, and I saw flames reflected in them. "I see how you look at me when I fight back the demons beneath my skin. I smell your excitement—hear your racing heart when I growl and bite and give chase. I'm going to make you scream, Mina, and remind you of just what a beast I am."

His lips descended to mine again but gone was every pretense of hesitation and sweetness. He nipped at my lips and thrust his tongue into my mouth with another chest-deep growl. Finally, his knee came up between my legs and nudged them apart, and with one swift, satisfying thrust, his slid into my slick, desperate channel. For one precious heartbeat, we stared at each other, frozen in time, understanding that this had been inevitable, and there was no going back from it. My wanton body demanded the release he'd joyfully denied me, and I wrapped my hands around his ass to pull him deeper still.

"More, Rafael," I pleaded. "Give me what you promised." I arched my back, seeking the delicious friction between our bodies.

Finally, blessedly, he began to move, starting slowly and building in speed and ferocity.

"Everything," he grunted, matching his thrusts with the timing of his words. "You have everything of mine, my goddess. You are everything. I will give everything and anything to please you. I will destroy everything that would keep you from me. I will give you pleasure and pain if you wish it and take only what you offer. You are mine, Mina. *Mine. Mine. Mine.*"

The darkness and dangerous threats in his words sent such passion through me, I was afraid to examine it closely. Lightning arced across every fiber of my body, drawing me forward to heights of pleasure I'd never known before—even with Rafael. Heat built to a firestorm—like a slumbering giant of a volcano awakening after millennia of being forgotten. Flames devoured me to the brink of combustion, and just when I felt like I'd burn down everything around me, pleasure seized me. My orgasm erupted with a shuddering scream and distant ringing in my ears. Rafael followed me over the edge, letting out a savage roar and sinking his fangs into the tender flesh of my breast. The sudden jolt of pain sent a second orgasm rocketing through me, and I clung to him, riding out the waves of alien contentment as my body reveled in the feeling of being joined to him—with him.

We laid there—time forgotten—as we came back to ourselves. Rafael propped himself up and looked down at me, marble-like biceps flexing.

"Are you well, Goddess?" he asked, black eyes intense. *Searching for regret.*

I smiled and reached up to tuck one wavy black lock behind his ear.

"I am, *Devil*, though I'm certain we've woken the entire household, and I don't know if I'll ever be able to face them again. Are you well?" I whispered.

He flopped down next to me and pulled me into his arms, tucking my head against his chest. With a kiss on my forehead, he swaddled our entwined bodies in the soft blankets we'd discarded in our lovemaking.

"You are my waking dream, Mina, and here you are in my arms. Of course I'm well."

Thoughts began to circle as sleep pulled at me. *What will happen next? Where has Rafael been? What does this mean for us? What does it mean for me? What do I want it to mean?*

Rafael pressed a finger into the furrow of my brow.

"I can practically hear you panicking in here," he said with a wry smile. "What's the trouble?"

"I'm not panicking," I protested. "I'm worrying. There's a difference."

He chuckled. "I don't suppose I could convince you to leave the worrying until we wake later tonight."

"If only it were that easy," I sighed. "The real world outside beckons, Rafael, despite my desire to keep it at bay."

One cool hand slipped down to caress my hip and give my ass a firm squeeze. Heat sparked in my belly again, a soft breath on passion's waning embers.

"Fuck the real world, Goddess," he whispered in my ear. One finger slid around to stroke the slick seam of my sex again, and my desire rekindled. "Stay with me among the stars for a little while longer."

His cock hardened against my thigh, and my exhaustion evaporated. With twenty years of heartbreak and denial between us, I supposed my cold tomorrow could wait for a few hours more.

MUCH, *MUCH* LATER, I WOKE TO THE SOUNDS OF VOICES CARRYING UP FROM downstairs. I felt around in the darkness, expecting—hoping—to find Rafael's cool body next to mine, but did not. I wanted to ignore the disappointment that bloomed in my chest given that we'd made no promises to each other, and despite our words in the heat of passion, I had no idea where we stood. Our attraction to each other given our past was undeniable, and it would have been absurd to pretend to misunderstand his feelings for me, but that didn't change my trepidation or our circumstances. It was absurd to even consider entertaining the idea of a future when everything was so uncertain.

The voices downstairs grew louder, prompting me to kick the covers off and dress quickly. I wasn't sure what the commotion was, but given the tone of the voices, I suspected it was serious. I pinned my hair up beneath a lace cap and made for the door, only to step hard into a solid wall of man and stumble backward.

"Easy, Goddess," Rafael said, pulling me upright. "That's twice that you've run into me. I'm beginning to wonder if it's not some ruse to capture my attention."

I bristled at his charm, still put out by waking up alone after…whatever it was that we shared.

"Well, it's not my fault you lurk outside the door of every space I occupy," I said snidely. "Perhaps it's *your* attempt to have an excuse to lay your hands on me and save me from a tumble."

His lips were at my ear in an instant. "Believe me, Mina, I don't need an excuse to lay my hands on you. Simply permission." With those devastating words, he pressed a soft kiss to my neck and held out his arm for me. "Shall we?"

I cleared my throat and willed the blush from my cheeks, hesitating before taking his arm. We made our way down the stairs together, heading toward the collection of voices emanating from Charlotte's formal dining room. The massive doors were slightly ajar, but I knocked in case the conversation was something Rafael and I weren't meant to hear. Charlotte poked her head through the gap in the door and grinned knowingly.

"Well! I certainly wondered if we'd see either of you this evening. I hope you got some rest," she teased, emphasizing *rest* as if she knew we'd done anything but.

Rafael's stoic face betrayed nothing, but I saw the flash of heat in his eyes.

"What's going on in there, Charlotte?" I asked. "It sounds like you've got an entire army of excited women in there."

"I do!" she grinned. "Won't you join us? Daphne and I are convening *les DD* to discuss what we know and plan what to do about The Order."

"And Laszlo?" Rafael asked quietly.

Charlotte nodded—her lips drawn in a tight line. She pulled open the door and waved us in.

I'd seen Charlotte's dining room decked out for countless dinner parties, holidays, and balls, and it was always impressive. Nothing, however, could have prepared me for the sight this evening. Two dozen women sat around the large table, sipping wine and nibbling on a variety of hors d'oeuvres while they chatted amiably. I recognized many of them

—unlike meetings with The Order, none of these women wore masks in each other's company. Daphne sat at one end of the table, giggling through a conversation with one of Étienne's half-sisters, Josephine, famed madam of the illustrious *Maison des Nymphes*. Étienne sat on Josephine's other side, and next to him were two other women from the brothel. Across from them was the well-known Italian opera singer, Signora Russo. Antoine sat away from the table against the back wall, watching but not a part of any ongoing conversation. His eyes tracked a couple of aristocratic women I didn't know with guarded interest. Several at the table were bourgeoisie, but many looked to be peasants and commoners. Based on the number of wine glasses filled with blood, I estimated about half of them were vampires.

Rafael stilled beside me, making me wonder if he was nervous. It seemed silly to even suggest such a thing, given his status and raw supernatural power, but his face reflected a careful neutrality and his posture took on the appearance of forced casualness.

"No one is going to attack you," I whispered in his ear. "Be easy, Rafael. Many of these women are my friends."

"Your friends, Mina—not mine," he replied. "Given our history and the rumors circulating, I wouldn't be surprised if that gave them even more of a reason to despise me."

Charlotte's small smile widened, and I knew she'd heard our exchange. I clamped my mouth shut to keep from giving any more away.

"*Mesdames*," she announced. Every conversation quieted and heads turned to face her. A few curious gazes lit on Rafael, and I tensed—preparing for what, I don't know.

"Thank you so much for journeying into the chilly night to discuss our incredibly troubling and precarious situation," Charlotte said, her voice echoing through the large room. "Daphne, do you want to catch everyone up?"

Daphne stood. "As you are all undoubtedly aware, our aims have been slowly diverging from that of The Order over the past year. You're all familiar with Derais—his rather sudden and fervent religious devotion that's swaying the minds of the other men in The Order. The emissary and I have been working to bring King Louis to our cause for some time now, but our efforts have faltered. In the wake of Madame Pompadour's tragic death, it seems His Majesty has turned away from Pompadour's more liberal influences and found solace in the conservative members of the aristocracy, notably those in the church and the older courtiers in The Order, including Derais. As such, The Order has reached the height of their power thus far—their selfish tendrils have snaked their way throughout every influential structure in France. Now, they fear no one.

They've already started to move against those they perceive as a threat to their power."

"Vampires," hissed someone.

"Women." Josephine chuckled.

"The bourgeois," another chimed in. "And the poor."

"Immigrants, foreigners, and minorities," Signora Russo said with a sniff.

"The backward fools in The Order are the minority," Antoine muttered from the back of the room. Everyone quieted, turning to look at him. "But they are the powerful minority."

Charlotte cleared her throat.

"All of the above," she agreed.

Daphne's mouth thinned to a tight line, and her jaw flexed. I knew she was frustrated that her work in The Order had come to naught. She'd once told me that despite her wealth, title, and connections, the only thing that would matter in the end was how she could help the people of France. *"King Louis is my cousin. If I can't convince him to consider embracing vampirekind, then I fear our cause is already lost."* Now that The Order had the ear of the king, they would boldly focus on what I always expected their true aims would be—further consolidating power within their own ranks. The Order wouldn't have to pretend to care about anyone but themselves. Rafael's words from weeks ago echoed in my mind. *How much do you know about The Order, Mina? How much have your friends Charlotte and Daphne told you? How much do they know?*

"As such," Daphne continued, silencing the whispers and chatter that had begun to circulate. "We have decided to *unofficially* sever our ties with The Order."

"They won't stand for that!" Signora Russo interjected. "Those *bastardi* will never allow you—us—to form our own group without their misguided oversight."

"Right you are, Signora," Charlotte chirped. "Which is why we're not going to tell them…at least, for now."

"What do you mean?" one of the other courtiers asked.

"It would be irresponsible for us to launch a coup without an immaculate plan and several well-thought-out backup plans. The Order will be dangerous enemies, and we want to know what they're planning every step of the way. If they believe we are beneath their notice and beneath their control, it will give us the opportunity to destroy them utterly when we make our move," Daphne said, fangs lengthening and eyes flashing.

"Daphne and I will continue to attend their summons. We will all carry on with our current assignments with one notable exception—any information relayed to them as part of intelligence work will be somewhat altered. We will only tell them what is required for our ruse to continue, but it will not be enough for them to gain an edge. All assignments regarding blackmail, intimidation, assassination, or such will be put on hold until Daphne and I can regroup and evaluate the targets in question," Charlotte added.

"But what about the blood plague?" one of the vampires from the brothel asked. "What are we going to do about that? And vampire rights? If The Order has truly turned against us, when can we expect the stakings to start?"

"Honestly, I'm surprised they haven't started already," Josephine grumbled.

"Haven't they?" Étienne hissed sourly.

"But why all of a sudden?" another woman asked.

"Yes," the vampire from the brothel agreed. "What has changed so much that we've all been summoned tonight?"

Daphne held up her hand for quiet.

"Please," she said. "I think now is a good time for me to introduce our special guest this evening. Ladies, I present to you Prince Rafael of House Dracul of Wallachia, also known as the Beast of Gévaudan—and allegedly the devil who unleashed the blood plague upon us."

Every pair of eyes locked on Rafael, who inclined his head politely. His bland expression covered what I knew was a storm of emotions—notably anger, frustration, and barely restrained tension.

"Good evening, ladies," he murmured with a decadent smile. "I'm honored to have found sanctuary in your ranks."

15

RAFAEL

April 26, 1768
Château de Ruisseau Magdelaine

So, Duchesse Daphne had not been quite as forgiving or welcoming as Charlotte. I would press her on the matter another time—perhaps when my life and the lives of my remaining family were not in jeopardy.

I didn't think any of these women would be taken in by charm, but I would offer it nonetheless—if only so that Mina wouldn't look upon me and regret our time together. As irascible as I felt, I didn't think alienating a group of dangerous, bloodthirsty women was a sensible first step toward a future with Mina.

"Thank you, Duchesse. And thank you, Comtesse de Brionne, for allowing me to remain here given everything that has happened," I said.

Charlotte smiled and nodded, encouraging me to continue.

"Assembled members of *les DD*, I will not lower myself to address every salacious rumor you've undoubtedly heard of me or my family. I believe you're all too intelligent to be taken in given how well you understand the value of information and the power of misguided and ill-used gossip. I am here before you to plead my case, humbly asking for help, and offering what truths I can," I said.

One of the young bourgeois women piped up. "Some mighty accusations lay at your feet, Your Highness. Why should we trust you? Who vouches for you?"

"I do!" Charlotte insisted angrily, standing quickly and almost knocking her chair over. "Françoise, you little minx, who are you to question my judgment when I've known you for years and you've only just spent your first six months with *les DD?*"

"We all love you, Charlotte, but you *did* marry a man who summoned a demon and murdered several people in his quest to win Daphne's heart. Why shouldn't we question your judgment?" Françoise replied.

Charlotte's mouth hung open for a moment before it snapped shut, putting me in mind of an irate fish. Her eyes glowed with lupine power as her anger condensed.

"None of us knew what he was truly capable of," Daphne interjected, casting a warning glance at Charlotte. She winced slightly as she said, "Though, she has a point, *chérie.*"

From the back of the room, Antoine growled low and quiet.

"Yes," I said, trying again for peace. "Of course, none of you know me well enough to say that my intentions are…"

"I vouch for him," Mina interrupted. Until now, she'd been silent. Always watching. Always waiting. Always calculating.

"Doctor?" the madam—Josephine, I thought she was called—looked at Mina questioningly.

"I am not a member of *les DD,*" Mina said, removing her spectacles to clean them with her handkerchief. "And I am not a vampire. But most of you know me. And if you do not know me, you know of me. I do not stand with The Order. I stand for myself—for what I believe is right. I have known Rafael a long time, and I know he speaks the truth. Please, Rafael, continue."

If I'd had one, my heart would've beat right out of my chest at Mina's forthright declaration. I could not—would not—let her down. *Yet you do not deserve her,* ferocious doubt whispered to me. I brushed the thought aside for the time being.

"I did not bring the blood plague to France," I said. "And I cannot say for certain who did, but I have been hunting for the answers for a long time. I am close to the truth, but in my search, I've come up against a problem that I alone cannot solve. I believe The Order has taken my brother."

"Taken? What do you mean, taken?" Signora Russo asked.

"Kidnapped, abducted, removed by force!" Charlotte snapped, still upset at having her judgment questioned. "Do try to keep up, Signora."

The opera singer glared at Charlotte, and I fought to keep from grinning.

"It's true," Daphne admitted. "Charlotte and I saw him. The Order has abducted the disinherited Prince Laszlo and intends to try him for the genocide of French people. They are holding him responsible for the origin of the blood plague."

"Is he responsible?" Josephine asked.

Silence descended and I felt the weight of every gaze in the room. I pursed my lips, still unsure how much I trusted these women. Without their aid, I wouldn't be able to recover Laszlo, but that didn't mean I was ready to divulge the full weight of my family's history and my suspicions about the genesis of the plague.

"I'm not quite sure," I admitted. An honest answer, but not the full truth.

I was met with sighs of frustration and hisses of disapproval. Mina squeezed my arm, but I wasn't sure if it was for comfort or from the pressure to say more.

"As I said, I've been trying to track down the source. Days ago, I was led to a vampire up north who was as close to my original bloodline as I've gotten, but it wasn't enough for me to determine the true source of the infection," I explained.

"If we're to believe the blood plague comes from your family, why should it matter if it comes from you or your brother? You are complicit, if not directly responsible. This is your curse. You should be held accountable," Françoise said acidly. "Perhaps we should deliver you to The Order and let them figure out what to do with you as punishment. Then *we* can get on with finding a cure and cleaning up the mess you and your brother left."

Several of the vampires in the room hissed at her. Charlotte tensed, glaring in her direction. I noticed Mina cringe, perhaps hearing her words to me from weeks ago.

"Not all of us are so desperate for a cure," Daphne pointed out. "But one should be available, if some so choose. I believe Mina's work will deliver one to us—it is only a matter of time." Then, she turned back to me. "Rest assured, we will not be delivering you to The Order, Rafael."

She must have seen the relief flit across my face because she continued.

"But Françoise raises some excellent points. What can you offer us as proof of your intentions and willingness to serve the people of France beyond your own obvious loyalty?" Her strange violet eyes flicked to Mina, then back at me. Her meaning was clear.

I straightened, trying to ignore the slights at my honor.

"It is true that this is my family's curse and my responsibility regardless of how it escaped the confines of my ancestral home. Since I first received word of it in France, I have stopped at nothing to find out how it arrived here. My family and I have been trying to find a cure for longer than any of you have been alive. Dr. Van Helsing can attest to that. For generations, we have hunted dead end after dead end—if you'll pardon the pun—trying every scientific potion, folk cure, religious relic, holy man, prayer, counter curse, exorcism, and more. Nothing has worked for us, but that doesn't mean I will stop searching for an end," I explained.

Daphne's eyes found mine across the table, and she smiled encouragingly. Perhaps she wouldn't be so hard to win over. Françoise, however, would not be dissuaded. She opened her mouth to speak, the frown on her lips deepening, but I cut her off.

"What none of you have yet to grasp is that this didn't start out as an epidemic or an illness for us. My family has been living with this curse— and it is that, *a curse*—for thousands of years. We have borne the brunt of this penance for sins so long ago forgotten, the gods to whom we beg forgiveness have become the dust and whispers of memory. We have seen more death, suffering, and midnights than you can fathom."

The younger vampires in the room looked away at that—likely too afraid to confront the true meaning of eternity as I spoke of it.

"And yet, there is hope," I said, looking at Mina. These words were more for her than anyone here. "There will always be hope. Hope is the universal virtue that unites humanity, even when it feeds on greed, despair, pride, ignorance, and corruption. There is hope for the future. As much depravity and evil as humans are capable of, they are capable of equal measures of kindness, compassion, and beauty. It is true that I am loyal to one in particular here, but that is because to me—after everything I have seen in all my years—she embodies the best of humanity. I will protect it for her."

No one moved, nor spoke a word. Mina's clear blue gaze was glassy with emotion, but too many at once for me to fully understand. After a few minutes of awkward silence, the sound of a tearful sniff shattered the quiet.

Charlotte waved her hand airily as tears tracked down her cheeks.

"Oh Rafael, that was so beautiful," she blubbered. "Mina, *honestly*."

A few people chuckled. Antoine stiffened and threw me a dark look.

"I don't know that I can offer you more proof than that," I said.

I looked up at Daphne again, and she grinned, showing me her full fangs. With a wink, she stood.

"Well said, Rafael," she said. "I, for one, am convinced. I will not speak for all the women assembled here tonight, but you will have my support and whatever resources I can provide." She gestured to the two empty seats at the massive dining table. Mina and I crossed the room silently and sat as we were bid.

"*Mesdames,*" Daphne continued. "Now, the fact of the matter remains —The Order has Rafael's brother in their clutches. Regardless of who brought the plague down upon France, I think it is safe to say we cannot allow The Order's warped sense of justice to dictate what happens to anyone anymore—let alone a foreign prince who may be innocent."

"We don't know that," Françoise mumbled.

"We don't know that he's guilty, either, Françoise! *Mon Dieu,* how you test me sometimes. Do you need another glass of wine or a cream puff? Anything to make your manner more tolerable while we discuss these very difficult things?" Charlotte groaned.

Françoise narrowed her eyes at the exasperated Comtesse and begrudgingly plucked an eclair from the tower of sweets in the center of the table.

Josephine cleared her throat. "Duchesse, Comtesse, I take it you both have come up with a plan?"

"Well, *of course* we have," Charlotte said with an effusive smile.

Daphne frowned.

"We have *most* of a plan," Charlotte corrected.

Daphne chewed on her lip, her needle-like fangs coming down nearly to her chin.

"Some of a plan?" Charlotte queried. Then, after a beat— "Very well. We have *an idea!*"

Noises of disappointment and frustration erupted in the room as the news settled over the group. If the two most senior agents had been unable to formulate some course of action, I hated to think what that would mean for our chances of success. For *my* chance of success—and Laszlo's life.

"If everyone would please calm down," Daphne shouted. "We can tell you what we know, and what we want to do. Then, it will be up to us—all of us—to determine how to proceed. This isn't a lost cause, but moving against The Order will require craft and cunning unlike we've ever had to muster thus far. It will take all of us working together."

Somewhat mollified, the ladies sat back in their chairs and waited expectantly.

"If anyone here is not set in our task or this new plan of action, I would ask that you excuse yourself now. You'll be in no danger from the rest of us, but I know what we're asking, and we don't ask it lightly. You all have your own lives, and the road ahead is rife with danger. If you wish to bow out, do so now, *mes amies,*" Charlotte offered, looking pointedly at Françoise. The younger woman shrugged and reached for another eclair.

"I don't have any particular loyalty for His Highness," Signora Russo declared. "But I have loyalty to you, *miei amici.* If we are to bring down the bastards in The Order, I'm all in for a bit of fun."

When no one else spoke up or moved for the door, Mina's fingers slowly threaded through mine beneath the table. She didn't risk a glance in my direction, but the corner of her beautiful lips lifted ever so slightly, and it was enough to cheer me from my melancholy.

"We're not going after The Order just yet," Daphne said, the relief evident in her tone. I wasn't certain if she had expected her recruits to abandon her in her hour of need because she doubted them, or herself. Either way, it was comforting that she'd been proven wrong, and this band of delightful, dangerous women agreed to help me rescue Laszlo.

"We are, however, going to break into the mausoleum and—ahem —*reacquire* Rafael's long-lost brother," Charlotte finished.

"It will require many of you using your laudable feminine wiles to keep the dusty prats entertained—*distracted*—for an evening," Daphne said.

"And how are we going to do that?" Josephine asked.

A wicked grin split Charlotte's face as she looked at her. "Dearest Josephine, I am *so* glad you asked."

THE MEETING CARRIED ON INTO THE SMALL HOURS OF THE NIGHT, WHEN purpling skies and the faint trills of birdsong heralded the approach of dawn. Due to the rampant exhaustion plaguing the assemblage and the necessities of the supernatural set, our meeting was adjourned before all the final details had been worked out.

I had to hand it to *les DD*—their plan was simple, bold, and brash. Of course, that meant there were about a thousand ways that it could, and probably would, go spectacularly wrong.

After bidding the other guests a good morning, I walked Mina to the door of her guest suite. She hadn't slept more than a few hours in the last couple of days, and likely less than that before my arrival. I cursed myself for keeping her up yesterday when I should have been encouraging her to rest. The dark hollows beneath her eyes gave her a somewhat frayed look around the edges, tugging at my absent heartstrings.

She paused at the threshold of her bedchamber, just long enough for me to make my decision. As she turned to me with what was certainly a "good morning" on her lips, I picked her up and carried her into my own guest room.

"Rafael," she gasped. "What are you doing?"

"Was Charlotte correct earlier when she said you hadn't been eating or sleeping lately? Were you going to lie down and rest the moment I left? Or were you going to stay up, pacing your room, flipping through your medical texts, and trying to come up with some solution to the mystery of the blood plague that you hadn't considered before?" I inquired, plopping her down on my bed.

She blinked at me, the lie taking form in her mouth.

"No—never mind," I said. "Mina, why did you allow me to take so much from you? You need rest, nourishment."

I bent to remove her slippers. She pulled away at first, frowning at me.

"I can take care of myself, Rafael," she said petulantly. "I have been doing so for ages before you came back into my life. In fact, I've gotten quite good at it."

"Yes, you're so good at it that you've completely forgotten how to address your human body's needs," I tutted, grabbing her feet once more.

"I'm a doctor, for God's sake! I know how to address my *human body's* needs," she gritted out, but allowed me to tug her slippers off and massage the arches of her feet.

"I know you do," I admitted, sliding my hands up her calves to untie her stockings and slip them down over her toes. I swallowed the burning lust building in me—as much as I desired her again, I wanted to care for her more.

"Why are you doing this?" she whispered, staring at my fingers on her legs.

"Because, Mina, I know you are strong and smart and capable, but if any of your stress or insomnia has been due to my unceremonious return to your life, I wish to help make amends. I want you to be well," I said, quietly untying her skirts and reaching up to unpin her bodice. "I *need* you to be well."

She swallowed once and, after a moment, nodded. I continued my ministrations, desperately trying to ignore the ache growing in my cock as I undressed her. Gods above and demons below, she was beautiful.

"Do you think it will work?" she murmured when I'd gotten her down to her cotton chemise.

"I don't know," I admitted. "But we will try."

I removed her spectacles and placed them on the bedside table, then reached up to unpin her glossy locks from her coiffure. They were like silk in my hands. I threaded my fingers through her hair and gently rubbed her scalp, and a soft sigh of pleasure spilled from her lips.

"Did you mean it?" she asked.

"Yes," I replied, not bothering to ask what she meant. "You are what gives me hope. You are the hope of everything for me, Mina. A future without you would be the worst kind of Hell—but I will endure it if you still do not wish to be mine."

The words were bitter and wrong leaving my mouth, but I had to say them. Perhaps one day I would believe them. Then again, perhaps there would be hope for us yet.

Hope.

She sighed again, that soft smile tugging at her lips once more. Scooting back against the pillows, she slid her feet beneath the sheets and I tucked her in under the thick velvet coverlet. By the time I leaned down to brush a kiss to her forehead, she had fallen asleep.

"Rest well, Mina, my love," I whispered. "Tomorrow night, everything changes."

16

MINA

April 27, 1768
Château de Ruisseau Magdelaine

WHEN THE MASSIVE GRANDFATHER CLOCK DOWNSTAIRS CHIMED SIX, IT WAS A struggle for me to pull myself from the grip of sleep—and Rafael. As much as I hated to admit it, he'd been right about the fact that I was exhausted…mentally, physically, emotionally, and spiritually worn down. The rest had done me a world of good, and I woke up famished.

Rafael's strong arms encircled me like a chilly cage, one around my waist and one beneath my shoulders. His eyes were closed, but I doubted if he was truly sleeping. All the time we'd known each other, I hadn't known him to sleep much even after we'd made love. Instead, he'd hold me close, rub my back, and tell me stories of his childhood. Sometimes he'd sing to me in his native tongue, his deep, rich voice so soothing, I would swear he could cast spells like lullabies.

"Good evening, Mina," he murmured without opening his eyes. "I'm glad you slept well."

"Did you sleep at all?" I asked, reluctant to move.

"Enough," he replied. His eyes opened slowly, dark and warm and fathomless. They were like portals to some decadent circle of Hell, and I shivered with fear and desire.

"I wish I understood that aspect of the blood plague," I said. "How you can exist with the barest amount of sleep and such small requirements to feed. It seems so many other vampires require a full day's rest and at least a pint of blood per day to keep going. You only seem to need more when you shift form or use other abilities."

"My brother needs even less," he said, tucking one of my stray curls behind my ear. "And he is so much more powerful than me. I often wondered if it was because of his age, or because our mother was a newly turned vampire when she fell pregnant with him. She was much older when I was conceived."

I'd considered the line of thinking in my research. Well, my father had initially, and I'd picked up the thread after his death. Something about a born vampire made one markedly more powerful than a turned one, and it seemed that the closer one was to the true Dracul curse lineage, the more intense those powers were. Perhaps it was due to proximity to the first cursed members of the clan, and over the years, the strength of the curse waned as its effects became diluted through the blood of others.

"I've met so few vampire women who were able to conceive, and yet your mother had two. Yet another medical mystery," I said idly. Rafael tensed, and I regretted my words immediately.

"I have mourned the hope that I would ever have my own children. I know how hard it is for vampires to reproduce. I never believed I would have the opportunity," he said, the sadness apparent in his voice. "Besides, the life I live doesn't exactly make me father material."

"I think you'd make an exceptional father," I said, strangely defensive.

"Did you never want babes of your own?" he asked, stilling beneath my exploratory hands.

"No," I admitted. "I admire mothers, and I like children, but I always enjoyed my freedom. I feel too much like a mother to my work to want the responsibility. I suppose you think me selfish, though, for thinking more highly of my profession than of my biological abilities."

"Certainly not," he replied. "The impact you've had on countless lives could never be seen as selfish when it is as much of a sacrifice as it is. You never put yourself first, Mina, even when you should, logically."

I smirked. Charlotte had said similar things to me over the course of our friendship, but I always brushed them off.

"I don't find it logical to weigh my life as more important than the lives of others," I said.

"It is to me," he said softly, pulling me in for a searing kiss. When he pulled away, he swallowed thickly and caressed my cheek. "Mina, when this is all over, do you think…"

His words were cut off by a knock at the bedroom door, and the frustration in his eyes was powerful. I couldn't be sure if I was devastated or relieved that he hadn't managed to say whatever it was.

"Monsieur, Mademoiselle, dinner is being served in the dining room," one of the housekeepers said through the door. "My lady requests your presence."

The faintest flicker of hope on Rafael's face evaporated, replaced by his seductive, charming grin. I wondered if I'd imagined the expression.

"Yes, thank you," he told the housekeeper. "We'll be along shortly."

Rafael was already sliding out of bed, and my cheeks heated at the sight of his naked body. *Dieu*, he was beautiful.

Throwing a saucy glance over his shoulder as he tugged his breeches on, he offered, "It'll keep."

I frowned, certain that whatever it was, it had been important. I started to protest, but there was another knock at the door. Annoyed by yet another interruption, I stomped over to answer it.

"Oh, Mina!" Daphne exclaimed, tugging me into the hall before I could express my surprise.

"What are you doing?" I huffed. "I was just about to get dressed!"

"Excellent. I have something special for you to wear this evening, given what we're all about to undertake," Daphne said. "Don't worry. I rather think you'll enjoy this. It's incredibly practical."

She led me back to my guest room and gestured at the pile of black laying on the bed.

"Daphne." I blinked in confusion. "You're certain that's for me? That looks more like something Rafael would wear."

"Don't dismiss it just yet. Both Charlotte and I have worn breeches before, and they can be remarkably liberating. She still tends to prefer gowns, but I've always rather loved the feeling of breeches on my legs."

Atop the black buckskin breeches lay a soft, black chemise and black leather waistcoat that was positively bedecked with pockets.

"Daphne, these are *men's* clothes," I scoffed. "Why are you and Charlotte forever trying to dress me in things that are not my preference? If it isn't bloody ballgowns, it's breeches."

I hadn't told Daphne or Charlotte—or anyone, except Rafael—that I'd dressed as a man for the entirety of my medical education. Those clothes had been baggy, shapeless, and brown and had hidden me from the eyes of every disinterested student and every pompous professor. Memories flooded back; binding my breasts every morning, sneaking baths in a nearby pond at midnight, hiding everything from everyone for two difficult years.

The thick black cloak and the black tricorne hat on the edge of the bed were at least sensible, but decidedly more masculine than I would have liked. When I picked them up and turned back to Daphne to further complain, the lightness in her expression was gone.

"Mina, tonight is one of the most dangerous missions we've ever undertaken. You've already been kidnapped once before, despite having some of the most powerful friends in France. If Rafael hadn't found you... I shudder to think what The Order would have done. It's clear to me that they will stop at nothing to get what they want and I...I feel quite betrayed. I'm so sorry, *ma chère amie*. I fear it's our friendship that has put you in jeopardy, and I cannot forgive myself for that. Especially after everything you did for Étienne and me—and Charlotte, of course," she said, diminished beneath the weight of her memories. She turned fierce eyes upon me, and they glittered with supernatural, predatory power.

"Nothing will happen to you tonight," she insisted. "We are all watching out for you and ready to protect you, but you're the only one who can help Laszlo if he's been injured or drugged—or worse. You're not an agent, it's true, but you're smart and strong and brave. These clothes are simply another layer of protection. You're less likely to be recognized dressed as a man, and if you are, these garments are equipped with various means of protection."

"I won't use weapons, Daphne," I frowned. "I appreciate what you're offering, but it goes against everything I believe in as a physician. I only want to heal people—not take lives."

A wry smile quirked the corner of her lips up.

"I thought you might say that," she said, crossing the room to empty the pockets of the waistcoat. "And so, I have provided you with many non-violent and non-lethal alternatives."

She pulled a series of vials from one pocket. "These are fairly standard. Deadly nightshade, hemlock, various concentrations of opium, and quicksilver, just in case The Order has hired vampire guards. I'm certain you remember how harmful mercury can be to blood plague sufferers. The amount here isn't enough to kill, but it's enough to make one rather ill."

She reached into another of the waistcoat's pockets. "Here we have three small wooden stakes and two small daggers—evenly balanced for throwing, but without the practice, you might just want to hold onto them. Now, don't look at me like that, Mina, these aren't just for stabbing. Should you find yourself bound, they can be quite handy in cutting ropes. In the other pouch here, there's a garrote, my personal favorite, you know, because you can strangle someone without killing them. I know you already know how to render a person unconscious thanks to your thorough medical knowledge, but these options will help."

From yet another pocket, she produced the smallest flintlock pistol I'd ever seen. "This beauty is a new design. Small caliber, short range. If you don't want to kill anyone with it, I trust you know where to aim. Bullets, wadding, and gunpowder are in the pocket just to the left of it. Now, in this last pocket, I've created something of a miniature doctor's kit for you.

Plenty of healing salves—your own recipes, of course—clean linen bandages, forceps, tweezers, a magnifying glass, scalpel. If there are other things you find you'll need in an emergency, do let me know and I'll have them added to any future clothing."

I ran my hands over the waistcoat, stunned into impressed silence.

"You thought of everything," I said, embarrassed by the tears that gathered in my eyes.

Daphne grinned. "I tried to. Charlotte did too. We were positively unhinged when we'd heard you were taken. I tried to think of everything you'd need so that it doesn't happen again."

I nodded and pulled away, but the memory of Pascal and Hubert overpowering me in the carriage made me feel weak and vulnerable. I raged at the thought. I'd always been confident in my intelligence and my abilities, but compared with my immortal friends, I was merely a liability. Daphne seemed to sense my apprehension because she offered a determined smile.

"We'll all be there together tonight," she insisted. "And I suppose if all else fails, just shout as loudly as possible."

She'd meant the words as a comfort, but the shame of them was a festering wound to my pride. Not wanting to offend her, I returned her smile. "Because a ferocious pack of werewolves and vampires will rush to my aid?"

"Of course! But truthfully, I think Rafael will be at your side before the scream even leaves your lips," Daphne said, a curious fear flickering in her violet eyes. "And may God have mercy on the poor soul who threatened you."

"I have known him too long," I said quietly, reassuring myself as much as Daphne. "I do not fear Rafael."

The terror in her eyes surprised me, given how powerful both she and Étienne were.

"I know, *chérie*. But you are the only one who does not."

We were still for a beat, the heavy confession thick between us. Then, in an instant, her defenses were back up, and she smiled at me, dispelling some of the anxiety in the air.

"Hurry and dress. Charlotte had the chef prepare all your favorites tonight." She chuckled. "She believes if we're heading into battle, at least we'll do so well-fed." She popped off the bed with more energy than I would have thought possible, given the gravity of what we had ahead of us.

In the wake of Daphne's exodus, the room felt strangely quiet, and it allowed me time to reflect.

I regarded the unusual garments on the bed while considering how strange my life had become over the last month. Mere weeks ago, I was resigned to my quiet existence—if one could call being a vampire physi-cian *quiet*—working, studying, researching, and finding sips of happiness at teas and dinner parties with my supernatural friends. It would be untrue of me to say that I'd been completely fulfilled…that I hadn't been touched by loneliness, or the longing that comes from the heartbreak of your first love, your first *true* love, but I'd found my kind of contentment. Satisfaction. I had a purpose, and that suited me. Perhaps I'd been too frightened, too numb to hope for anything more. Yet in the last few weeks, my entire existence had been upended. There had been a distressing number of outbursts and tears and reawakened *feelings* that my very recent past self would have scoffed at.

For the first time in years, I didn't have a plan. I didn't know what my next days or nights would bring. I didn't know the intimate structure of the hours of my tomorrow—exactly when I would wake, what I would eat, which patients I would visit, which medicines I would craft, which experiments I would attempt. Rafael's presence in my life had reintro-duced chaos like only he could, and while that gnawed at the edges of my anxiety, I found myself thrilled by it. Did that mean I was ready to move beyond our past? I couldn't be sure. If I were being truthful, I didn't want to consider what our lovemaking meant for us—for me. For now, I could enjoy how his touch brought my body back to life as if from some wintry hibernation, and I wanted to leave it at that. No heavy discussions of our past devastations, our present circumstances, or our impossible future—just pleasure, plain and simple.

Even if there is nothing simple about it, my treacherous heart insisted.

I turned back to the clothes and obediently began to dress. The soft, supple buckskin of the breeches was snug on my legs and felt entirely alien compared to the heavy wool and silk skirts I was used to, but not altogether unpleasant. I appreciated the freedom of movement, though even I could see that despite the well-cut fit of masculine clothes, the shape of them on my body looked positively indecent. I assumed the thick cloak would help hide me in the gathering night, as would the hat if I pulled it low over my brow.

Sorting through the waistcoat pockets again to familiarize myself with the contents of my mercenary accessories, I grimaced at the more lethal items. Daphne included them for my protection, and I was grateful for her concern, but the thought of using them on anyone turned my stomach. The small travel kit of medical accessories could prove useful, though, and my heart swelled at her thought to include them.

Tying back my long, dark hair, I grabbed the cloak and hat from the bed and made my way to the dining room. Étienne was seated at the end of the table, sipping blood from a crystal goblet. He smiled when I entered the room.

"Well?" he asked, gesturing to my new clothes. "How do they feel?"

I blushed. "Oddly freeing, if a little uncomfortable. I feel rather scandalous."

"Excellent," he returned, his smile widening. "Sometimes it's good to be a little scandalous."

Daphne entered then and whispered something to him. He nodded and winked at me, then left. As Daphne came around the table, I saw that she, too, wore men's clothing. The form-fitting breeches, blousy shirt, waistcoat, and cravat looked stylish on her, and it made me even more self-conscious.

She approached me and placed a hand on my shoulder.

"You look very fine," she said. "Almost a proper gentleman."

"The clothes look odd on me," I muttered. "But they are well made."

Daphne tilted her head. "The clothes suit you," she countered. "But I don't think it is merely the clothes. Over the last few weeks, you've had a certain air—a glow, almost. Charlotte teases you about not eating or sleeping, so I know it has nothing to do with your health."

She brushed a loose strand of hair from my cheek and smiled fondly.

"If it were anyone else, I would say it was love."

I blanched. "That's preposterous."

The smile slipped from her lips, but her eyes carried the sparkle of mirth.

"Of course," she said. "Perhaps it's simply the exertion and excitement of the last few days."

"It must be," I answered, glaring, wishing to be anywhere but beneath those intense, amethyst-colored eyes.

"It would be absurd to suggest that you'd found love within mere weeks with the man who broke your heart twenty years ago, who was *not* the villain you believed him to be, and who has come back to claim you once more," she continued. "You're much too sensible to fall for his charms again. Humans and vampires make difficult pairings if you do not wish for immortality. You know that, of course. He is handsome and honorable, I believe, but his past...well, you know. Some women have a hard time settling down with rogues, even if they are reformed. Still, he would make a fine match for any supernatural woman."

The thought of Rafael with another woman kicked bile up into my throat, and I swallowed the instinctive swell of anger with force.

"He would, of course," I said with a tight smile. "A fine match for a supernatural woman. Clearly anyone but me." The words came out bitter and dripping with misery. *Of course I don't deserve him. I'm just some lowly human.*

"Oh?" Her sharp gaze pinned me in place, seeing through my lie. Mercifully, she carried on as if I hadn't said the words. "I've never known you to be interested in marriage or immortality," she said airily, walking back to her seat at the end of the table and picking up Étienne's abandoned glass of blood. "I suppose you worry a husband would force you to stop working and that marriage would be terribly dull. And that immortality comes with too many sacrifices and too few benefits."

I didn't say it, but Daphne had put her fingers on two precise reasons why I'd been so afraid to consider a future with Rafael. I pursed my lips, wishing this exchange would end.

She sighed as she sat down. "It would be untrue of me to say I didn't miss a warm, sunny afternoon now and then. The hum of birdsong and insects in a summer meadow. The glitter of sunlight on freshly fallen snow. The dazzling blue of a cloudless sky."

I wasn't particularly attuned to the natural world, but every time I had considered immortality, I shied away from it like a coward.

"Of course," I said. "Your world is marked by blood and darkness and death."

"So it is," she agreed, with a knowing smile. "But so is yours."

I opened my mouth to argue, but upon reflection, realized that she was right. Even if I wasn't a vampire, I'd kept to a supernatural schedule for so long, I couldn't remember the last time I'd seen a sunny afternoon. And in my profession, blood and death were as common as they were to any vampire. It was an odd realization and one that gave me pause.

"On the other hand," she said, violet eyes fixed on the red swirling in her glass. "There is beauty to be found everywhere, and supernatural senses have much to offer. Sometimes, when it is truly quiet in the small hours of the night, I could swear I hear the stars singing."

A floorboard creaked behind me, and Daphne's gaze rose above my shoulder.

"Rafael," she said, her sly smile returning. "I do hope you haven't been waiting there long."

Dread pooled in my stomach. I prayed he hadn't heard our conversation, but from the fiery look in his eyes, it was obvious he had.

Merde.

17

RAFAEL

April 27, 1768
Château de Ruisseau Magdelaine

WHEN I ENTERED THE DINING ROOM, TWO THINGS BECAME EXCRUCIATINGLY clear to me. The first was that Mina was wearing breeches. *Gods above and demons below, this must be some sort of test.* The second was that I suspected Daphne had known I was outside the dining room and expected me to hear every word of their conversation.

Nursing the gaping wound where my heart would have been made it a touch easier to try to ignore the discomfort of my hard cock pressing against my breeches. I couldn't help but stare, taking in the way the supple buckskin caressed her round ass and shapely legs as my hands had done a day ago. The men's clothing showed off every curve of her body in a way that made my mouth go bone dry. I felt my eyes darken to black and red and my fangs lengthened, startling me with the ferocity of my desire. Altogether inconvenient given Mina had just confessed she thought I'd make a better husband for someone else.

"Rafael," she said, her voice pitched high with panic.

"I'll just go see where Charlotte is," Daphne said, downing the last of her blood and hurrying from the room. Mina's gaze cut to the retreating duchess—also clad in men's attire—as if she would rescue her from the looming storm of my anger.

The door closed quietly behind her, but the sound was like cannon fire in the tense silence that stretched between us.

"What Daphne said…I didn't mean…" Mina fumbled over the words.

Frustration pulled my nerves taut. Maybe it had been naïve of me, but after the intimacy we'd shared, I'd sensed a change in her. A softening. I dared to hope it meant we'd be able to work through some of the things that parted us, but I'd been fooling myself. How could I have expected her to leave behind a past that she felt defined her? She'd told me herself. Following my false betrayal, she'd forged a life of ambition and solitude. I didn't fault her for that, but it was devastating that my absent heart had become entangled in a mere physical distraction for her. Despite that, I would be with Mina in any way she would allow—even if it meant never having her completely. That heavy knowledge made me the world's greatest fool.

Pain took root in my chest and seemed to wind throughout my body, irritating me like thorns beneath my skin. The pitying expression on Mina's face cut worse than a thousand harsh words. I stalked to the end of the table where Daphne had left the decanter of blood and poured myself a glass.

"Be easy, Mina," I said, draining the glass and pouring myself another. I had to get a handle on myself—on the raging emotions warring in my head. With the smooth, salty tang sliding down my throat, my ire lessened, and I felt my eyes shift back to normal. I sighed, strangely fatigued given that I'd slept and fed more in the last day than I had in the previous week.

"You promised me you wouldn't invade my mind—my privacy," she said quietly.

I cocked a brow. "I did not invade your mind or betray your privacy. I was merely answering a summons. I was unfortunate enough to overhear what I suspect the duchess wanted me to hear."

Mina tilted her head, confused. "What do you mean? Daphne wouldn't do that. She wouldn't purposely…"

"Wouldn't she?" I snapped. "To protect you, I suspect, from me."

"I don't need protection from you," she replied.

I rushed forward in a blur of supernatural speed, pushing her back into the heavy wooden door.

"Are you so certain?" I growled. "Perhaps she is right. Perhaps the rumors are true. Maybe I am a hedonistic rake—selfish and bent on serving my needs. A murderer and a devil, summoning demons and using hellish magic to torment humans while I infect the world with my cursed plague. Is that what you think of me? Is that what you think I have always been—what I've become? Is that why I am only good enough to warm your bed?"

Her heart pounded in her chest, but I could tell it was from excitement, not fear. I dropped one arm to her waist and swept my fingers from her leather-clad hip to her ass and lifted my knee to part her legs. Her blue eyes widened, and a gasp of pleasure escaped her lips, testing my restraint.

"Perhaps you do need protection from me, Mina. You already know how I want you—what I would do to get you. Maybe the devil in me that bays for your sex will one day bay for your blood. It seems even your friends mistrust me—fear me—and they have no idea what I can do. I could make you my willing slave, Mina. I could mesmerize you, compel you to strip for me, force you to your knees to suck my cock until I said stop. I could have you bouncing naked on my lap, your breasts in my hands and your perfect little clit stroking my shaft and even then, I could invade your mind and keep your release at bay. Could you imagine that, my Persephone? Endless days and nights of sex without an orgasm, all because I might have a torturous whim."

Fire sparked in her gaze, and her cheeks grew pink. Her breath came in panting huffs and her lust made me wild. I pressed my knee higher into her groin and felt the damp heat pooling between her legs. I grinned wickedly, my fangs long and sharp.

"I can smell your desire, little goddess, and it tells me I wouldn't even need to ask. I wouldn't need to compel you. I could just take it." I leaned forward and licked from her collarbone up to her delicious throat. The tips of my fangs grazed her skin, sending shocks of pleasure along my nerves —exquisite torment.

"I could take it like I could take your life, beloved. One slip of my fangs and I could bring you to Death, taking away your sunshine and your summer afternoons. I could turn you against your will and tie you to me for eternity. Perhaps I'm tired of waiting for your forgiveness. Perhaps I'm still the spoiled, selfish, reckless prince. Perhaps I will change my mind and give up caring for the hope of humanity because you are the only human worth saving, and you despise me."

I shifted my knee, and she moaned slightly, her eyes clouding with emotion.

"I don't," she whispered. "I don't despise you." Her breath was coming quickly, ragged and raw.

"You do," I said, resigned. "You may like what I can do with your body, but you do not want me, Mina. After everything, you have found your own path, and it is not through the underworld with me."

I pressed a lingering kiss to her throat, loving the feel of her pulse beneath my lips.

My thoughts clanged and crashed and rattled through my skull. I wanted her with a need so powerful, it dwarfed every thought. Every emotion. Every ancient, eternal piece of me.

I could take much from you, love, but I won't. No matter what, I will give you what you desire. If you consented to be mine, I would burn this world down and rebuild it stone by stone, brick by brick to suit your tastes. If I had a heart, I would cut it out and give it to you, if you wished to possess it. If you wanted the end of every vampire on earth, I would stake them all without a thought.

Words I could not—would not—say anymore.

A tear slipped down her cheek, and I reached up to wipe it away.

"If your wish is that I give you up—well and truly—I will leave you to your peace and never darken your doorstep again."

I didn't tell her it would kill me to do so.

She swallowed, intent on saying the words that would probably damn me to an eternity of misery.

"I..."

The door swung open with a loud thud, smashing into the opposite wall. I briefly entertained the idea of ripping out the throat of the person who'd done it.

Merde, does no one knock in this household?

A young woman stood in the doorway, bloody, bedraggled, and panting. She choked out a sob and looked around wildly. Mina pushed off the wall and hurried over to her.

"Charlotte!" the young woman yelled. "Where is Charlotte? I have news for her."

Charlotte rushed into the room behind the woman, a whirlwind of dark purple skirts and the acrid scent of fear.

"Nanette! What has happened? Are you injured?" Charlotte gently pushed the woman down into a chair and motioned to Mina to look her over.

"No, I am fine. This blood is not mine," Nanette replied. "I escaped. But I was there—at the graveyard. I was watching from the trees. The vampire Laszlo is not alone. The Order has another, but it is a woman."

"What do you mean?" Daphne asked, coming into the room with Étienne and Antoine on her heels. "They have a woman? You are certain she is a vampire? Is she with The Order or have they captured her?"

Fear and apprehension whispered through me.

"She is a vampire. At first it looked like she was with them—she was yelling at two masked men as they walked toward the mausoleum, but something happened," Nanette said, pausing to take a sip of the water that Mina offered.

"What happened?" Charlotte pressed.

"I couldn't see exactly. The woman said something that upset the men she was with, and the argument escalated. One of the men attacked her, and even with her vampire strength, they overpowered her and dragged her into the mausoleum by force. It was awful. After that, I thought the coast was clear. I climbed down from my hiding spot, but one of their hired thugs must have spotted me leaving, because he chased me around the graveyard. When he caught up with me, we tussled, but I broke free and managed to lose him a few streets later."

Mina dabbed a clean cloth across a small cut on Nanette's eyebrow, but that appeared to be the worst of her injuries. Charlotte and Daphne exchanged a look.

"Did you recognize the woman?" Daphne asked.

Nanette shook her head. "Never seen her before. She was pretty, though. Dark hair, dark well-made gown. She was definitely French."

"We must find out who this woman is. If The Order is starting to round up vampires off the street, we're in serious trouble," Charlotte said grimly.

"That doesn't make any sense," Daphne argued. "They wouldn't choose any vampire at random. Our first action must be to find out who this mystery vampire is and what The Order wants with her."

A heavy sense of foreboding weighed on me when I answered.

"She is Marguerite. She is Laszlo's wife."

Everyone turned to regard me.

"How do you know?" Charlotte asked.

"That's a rather vague description for you to be so certain," Daphne said.

"I hadn't seen Marguerite in twenty years before this past week," I said, fighting my annoyance at the interfering duchesse. "Laszlo's trail led me to Dunkirk up north. When I was there questioning one of the older vampires about his maker, Marguerite appeared."

"What did she say?" Mina asked, focused on me now that Nanette was somewhat recovered.

"She asked me for help. She told me Laszlo had been taken by The Order and she asked me to get him back," I said. "I stayed at their meager townhouse to shelter from the day, but when I awoke the next evening, Marguerite was gone. Vanished without a trace. I still have not determined how much I trust her...or her story."

"Why didn't you bring this news to us sooner?" Charlotte demanded. They were the first words of frustration I'd heard from her, and it grieved me to wonder if I'd lost my only other ally.

"I couldn't be sure that she was involved," I replied evenly. "And forgive me, but I do not answer to you or your organization."

"Why do you suspect she is involved?" Mina asked.

"How much do you remember about Marguerite, Mina?" I scoffed.

"She was a selfish, entitled human with her sights set on my brother and when she got what she wanted from him, she threw him to The Order. Probably told them he was the cause of the blood plague."

"Why?"

"Perhaps she is tired of him. Perhaps it is about money. Without Laszlo, she will inherit whatever my father left him."

"But your father disowned Laszlo," Mina argued, her brow furrowing in confusion.

I laughed bitterly. "True. But if there's one thing my family has never had much use for, it's wills. It might seem strange to you, but when you expect to live forever, you don't really think about leaving your worldly belongings behind. After my father was assassinated, I discovered he'd never officially disinherited Laszlo. As the eldest son and heir, he inherited what's left of my father's holdings, but no one has been able to find him to give him his settlement. And naturally, if Laszlo dies, the assets that have been moldering away in various banks and vaults in Hungary will pass to his wife."

"Would Marguerite know that? If you only discovered it after your father's death, how would she know that she stood to gain anything?" Charlotte pointed out.

"That much is unclear. But as far as I know, no one communicated with Laszlo after he ran away. There was no request for formal abdication— Hell, no one even knew where to find him to tell him Father had been murdered." I tried to explain things with forced casualness but talking about my family meant *thinking* about my family, and that always brought me to a dark mood. I didn't hate my father, exactly, but he'd been distant from my earliest memory. Laszlo was the favorite—the true heir—and I was the unexpected, unwanted extra. My wretched behavior in my younger days was the only escape I had, but it further drove the wedge between my father and me. Even after Laszlo's betrayal, there was never any gratitude at my willingness to step up and take over—just resentment that Father was left with the unacceptable spare to continue his brutal legacy. When he was killed, I grieved not for him, but for the relationship I always wished we might have had.

"So," Daphne hedged. "We continue with our original plan. Only this time, Rafael, you will be responsible for Marguerite, as well. If she is a prisoner, she is to return with us. If she is in league with The Order…"

"If she is responsible for Laszlo's kidnapping, I will kill her," I growled.

"We don't know that she is," Mina said anxiously. "She could have been in trouble at the cemetery."

"Ah, Mina, always looking for the best in people—even when there is very little to be found," I said, still angry beneath my teasing smile. "So delightfully human."

She straightened and glared. "Better than being a cynical old bloodsucker."

Everyone turned expectant eyes on me, waiting to gauge my reaction and probably expecting me to fly into some monstrous rage. I was almost sorry to disappoint them.

I laughed heartily at her insult and was rewarded with the slightest smile on her lips.

"Guilty as charged," I admitted. Then, with more gravity, I added, "But I'll be surprised if Marguerite isn't the one orchestrating Laszlo's kidnapping in an effort to regain her freedom and any lingering wealth she feels entitled to."

"Forgive the impertinence," Charlotte interjected. "But is there any lingering wealth? If you were on the wrong end of a coup, I assume most of your holdings have been seized. I would expect Marguerite would draw the same conclusions."

"We're not returning to Wallachia for any crown jewels or royal residences, but yes, there is a considerable fortune that my brother is owed. As I said, it is unclear whether he or Marguerite are aware of that fact," I replied.

Daphne nodded. "Knowing your sister-in-law, how do you think we should proceed?"

"As you said. Carry on with your original plan. I'll deal with Marguerite," I said.

Everyone seemed to agree, but there was palpable unease in the room now that we had another variable to consider. As the room emptied and we each steeled ourselves for the next steps, Mina stayed me with a hand on my arm.

"You cannot kill her," Mina insisted. "Rafael, you must promise me. You don't know what she's been through, and you don't know that she's at fault. You go into this with your own prejudice, and it will end badly for everyone."

Anger and hurt made me peevish, my brittle temper snapping.

"Why do you care? You don't know her, Mina, any more than you know Laszlo. She might be the cause of the blood plague—of all that suffering you've been fighting to hold back. You should be begging me to put an end to her and free the world from the curse of the plague. Your life would be so much simpler then, wouldn't it?"

The last thought was one I'd meant to keep to myself, but it was out now, souring the air between us.

"And anyway, she isn't your family nor your responsibility. You can carry on with your part of the plan and then, when this is over, we can all move on."

"What are you talking about? Move on?" Mina narrowed her eyes.

"It's what you want, isn't it? You've been clear with me from the beginning—you made your life and it's better without me in it. I can respect that, Mina. We can leave what we've enjoyed behind, and you can return to your clinic and your research," I said.

"Damn it, Rafael, would you stop trying to determine my life for me?" she shouted.

Anger made her face cold and storm clouds gathered in her sky blue eyes. Her jaw clenched as she faced me, fierce and frustrated. I took an involuntary step back.

"Ever since our failed elopement, you've been deciding on our course of action without talking to me about it. You alone decided to stay and take up your family's mantle when Laszlo left. You forced me from your world after inviting me in, left me in bleak silence for twenty years, then determined you would come back, and we would have a future...without ever stopping to wonder if that's what I wanted. You expect it to be easy, for me to be pliant—you expect that because I still have feelings for you and desire you, that it erases all the pain and hurt and memories? That my feelings for you solve all the problems that live between us? And when I don't immediately uproot everything I've built over the last two decades, you determine it must be because I want nothing to do with you and I do not care for you, and all I want is your body?"

She advanced on me, jabbing her finger in my chest with each crushing point.

"You admit I am smart and capable, and yet you won't even do me the courtesy of letting me make my own decisions. You make them for me under the guise of love because you are too afraid of what I will say and do if you let me have my choices," she spat. "Still the spoiled young prince! You, Rafael, are too afraid of hard work. You don't want the arguments, the responsibility for your actions, or the ownership of the pain you knowingly caused me. You want to move forward without paying the price. You want a future with me without healing our past. You want to find the cause of the blood plague so you can prove it's not your fault. You want to blame Marguerite for your brother's departure from your life without stopping to consider if your poisonous father or your youthful indiscretions had a hand in it. You want to absolve me of the responsibility of having to say no to you and risk breaking your heart when you wouldn't afford me that consideration from the beginning."

"I..." I opened my mouth to argue, but she held up her hand.

"I am not finished!" she continued. "You want me to agree to be with you forever without admitting that it would require a sacrifice on my part —that if I *don't* want to make that sacrifice, it must mean I don't love you enough. You are drawing conclusions without examining all the evidence before you, which I can promise you will always lead you to the wrong answers. You say you are a scientist now, Rafael—a botanist. What evidence do you have to make these theories? And what right do you have to make any kind of choice in my stead?"

God, she was magnificent. Her eyes were blue fire, and the pink flush of outrage colored her cheeks. She was like a sunrise in her rage and I loved her all the more, even as she cut me to ribbons.

"Then what?" I asked, my voice low. "What is it that you want from me? If not my love, my protection, my hope…what?"

She closed her eyes and exhaled.

"Time," she answered. "The one thing you have more of than anyone, Rafael. Just *time*."

18

MINA

April 27, 1768
Château de Ruisseau Magdelaine

THE DAMNED FOOL STARED AT ME, TOO STUNNED TO REPLY. BEYOND frustrated, beyond exasperated, and more fatigued than I'd been in a long while, I stepped back and turned toward the door.

"You could do me the honor of allowing me some time to work through these events. You had twenty years to think and plot and wait. I had *nothing*, Rafael. Nothing! No word from you, very little news of your family, no support while I mourned the loss of our relationship and the deaths of my parents, no rationale for your decisions—nothing. You showed up in Gévaudan a few months ago and approached me mere weeks ago. It's rather a lot to take in, and it's been incredibly difficult. Since you have all the time in the world, perhaps you'd lend me some," I said.

The words came out harsher than I intended, but I was hurt by his actions. I could understand if he was losing patience with me given that he'd waited twenty years to confess everything, but he failed to grasp that this was all still new for me. I was tired of feeling pressure from him to move on, and I was tired of feeling *less than* my supernatural friends because I was simply human. My pride smarted at being coddled by Daphne and Charlotte for this all-important mission, and I was done with people trying to manage me *for my own good*. I'd had enough of that with my mother, God rest her soul.

Well, no longer. Perhaps it was the breeches that gave me the courage I needed, or perhaps I'd simply reached my breaking point. Whatever it was, I would no longer stand for it.

Rafael's dark eyes softened, and his gaze fell. A lock of raven hair draped over his forehead, reminding me of him as a young, well, *younger* rake. My fingers itched to tuck it back behind his ear, to place my warm palm against his cool cheek and kiss the downturned corners of his beautiful lips, but I didn't. My need to touch him—to be near him was almost overpowering, but this time I was listening to my head, not my heart.

Rather than sit in the path of temptation, I left Rafael to his thoughts and headed for the front hall. With everything we had ahead of us tonight, it was time for me to regain my focus.

Charlotte, Daphne, Étienne, and Antoine entered the hall shortly after I did. The air in the room was heavy with anticipation—even Charlotte was quiet and introspective. Each of us was dressed similarly, in snug black breeches, black shirts, black waistcoats, black hats, and black cloaks. At a great enough distance in the black of the night, it would be difficult for any human to tell us apart. Vampires, however, were another story. I hoped The Order didn't employ too many—it could prove tricky for our work this evening.

The grandfather clock in the hall struck eleven, and Rafael emerged from the dining room. I avoided looking at him, partly because I wanted to keep my mind clear and partly because tendrils of guilt whispered through me at my outburst. Had I been too hard on him? *No.* No! If he was upset with me for speaking my mind, that was his problem—not mine.

Daphne cleared her throat. "Is everyone feeling well? Are we all together?"

Silent agreement all around.

"Good. To the carriage, then. Charlotte, Antoine, we shall see you soon. Good luck and be safe." Daphne patted Charlotte on the shoulder and threw Antoine a determined glance. Without another word, there was a nauseating explosion of flesh rending and fur and claws knitting together, and the two massive wolf creatures that had been Charlotte and Antoine raced out the front door in the direction of the cemetery.

"I think, perhaps, I might be more useful flying alongside the carriage," Rafael said quietly. "I'll keep an eye on things from above."

I shuddered, remembering the massive bat demon I'd seen him become in my opium haze.

"As you wish," Daphne said with a shrug.

I turned to him uneasily, but he didn't spare me a glance as he walked down the front steps. In the blink of an eye, he'd shifted into a small, normal looking bat. *Rather cute*, I thought.

Daphne's eyes widened a bit at the transformation, and I remembered she'd only seen Charlotte and Antoine shift before. But she kept her thoughts to herself and blew Étienne a kiss as he perched atop the carriage in the driver's seat. Daphne and I climbed inside. Étienne uttered a gentle command to the horses, and we lurched forward. Rafael had flitted off into the night, but I sensed his presence nearby.

Even in the ink-dark interior of the carriage, I knew Daphne was staring at me. As the carriage trundled on, shafts of light from the full moon outside filtered in through the windows and I noted her pensive expression.

I suspected she'd heard everything Rafael and I had argued about inside. In a household full of supernatural beings, the walls had ears—and claws.

"What?" I snapped.

"I didn't say anything," she said defensively.

"I can feel you staring at me," I argued. "Out with it, Duchesse."

She sighed. "You seemed very angry with him."

"Did you bait him?" I asked.

I could see moonlight glinting off her fangs as she smiled—answer enough.

"Why?" I asked, anger rising. "Things between us are complicated enough. I don't need your help to muddy the waters any further. Is it because you dislike him? Hate him for what he is—what he has done?"

"No."

Genuine shock stuttered through me.

"Good," I said. "Because you shouldn't. You said it yourself. He is honorable. Perhaps he had a difficult past, but who hasn't?"

"I do not hold anyone's past against them, Mina." The chill in her tone reminded me that she, too, had been through enough trials to last the rest of her immortal life, and yet here she was, barreling into more.

"Are you aiming to drive a wedge between us because you don't approve?"

"Certainly not. That would be absurd," she laughed.

Irritation climbed up my spine. "Then why?"

Another sigh—softer this time. "I was simply trying to feel you out. And him."

"It is no affair of yours," I said tartly.

"You're right," she agreed. Then, more gently, "Mina, I will be honest with you. Before Étienne and I realized how powerful our love for each other was, it took an act of near Herculean willpower for either of us to entertain the idea of a future together. We loved each other by then, of course, but neither of us wanted to acknowledge it and accept what it would mean. It was no small thing for me to declare myself to him and to likewise accept him. Beyond the vast differences in our worlds—our lives—we faced more than simply prejudice. And I paid the highest price for my love of Étienne—my mortality. But I have never looked back or wished for a different choice."

I fidgeted, uncomfortable with the emotions Daphne laid bare before me.

"Love is sacrifice, Mina, or it is nothing. It is not always easy. But when your soul calls so strongly to another, the alternative is worse than death. If you hadn't come to us and made us realize that a future together was possible, we would have carried on living dull half-lives, lonely and pining for each other. It was your intervention that helped us find our way in the dark."

I nodded.

"And so you think to do the same for me?" I asked, understanding dawning. "You try to—what is the expression—set a cat among the pigeons? Stir things up so we can get over our past and be together."

"I wouldn't presume to tell you what to do," she said. "But I will give you the intelligence I have collected."

I waited.

"Rafael loves you, Mina. He loves you so fiercely, I fear what he would do if something were to happen to you. End the world, I think," she continued. The gravity of her tone told me she wasn't exaggerating.

"He has told me as much," I admitted. I didn't tell her that his words frightened me—not because I feared him, but because I feared I couldn't match his passion. *Me. Cold, calculating, logical Mina.* Of course I loved him. I never stopped loving him, even when I hated him. It wasn't enough.

"You don't doubt his devotion to you," Daphne said, face illuminating ghostly white in a shaft of moonlight as the carriage turned down the cobblestone street blocks away from the cemetery. "Is it that you doubt your devotion to him?"

I didn't answer. She couldn't know what it had been like the last twenty years—the loneliness, the grief, the rage. The cold kept those fires of misery at bay. I found comfort in the cold because feeling anything else was too much pain.

"You love each other," Daphne insisted, gentle but firm.

"It has been a long time," I said, "since I have allowed myself the luxury of that thought."

"The fact that it holds true means something. If you still love him after all these years, after the awful things he did, that is a powerful kind of love."

More likely, it meant that I was warped. I'd clung to the memory of our love even when Rafael abandoned me for his family and his kingdom. Clung to the hope like a beaten dog returning to its abusive master. And then, miraculously, when the pain and hurt from that betrayal had become too much, I'd found the cold within me. It had been so easy—too easy—to shut everything else out. I didn't want to tell Daphne that, or Charlotte or Rafael, for that matter. I couldn't admit that I was afraid of what love looked like after spending so long being comfortable in the cold.

I struggled against the lump in my throat. Humiliating tears pooled in my eyes, and I dashed them away before they could fall.

"It is not enough." Even with more time, could I forgive him? Even with all the apologies and declarations and penance, if he somehow surpassed my unforgiving nature and we could move on, he was still immortal and I was human. With everything between us—our past and the reality of time itself—love wouldn't be enough. *I wouldn't be enough.*

Daphne cocked her head as the carriage slowed.

"Perhaps not now. But it's a start."

The inside of the carriage suddenly seemed too small—too warm. The pressure of expectation weighed on me, boxing me in. Why did everyone expect me to simply move on? To simply *be fine*? To forgive and forget and throw myself headfirst into a relationship with a man I loved and hated in equal measure. To give up everything I'd worked for and start anew. It was bad enough Rafael was here, waiting and hoping and *expecting*, and now Daphne and Charlotte had thrown their lot in with him. It left me no room to breathe, no space to think.

I lunged for the door, worried I would heave my guts up all over her fine upholstery. As soon as I threw open the door and gulped the steadying, cool breaths, I heard her final statement on the matter.

"Mina," she said, low and stern, as if she'd plucked the very thought from my mind. "*You* are enough. It is why he has come for you after all these years. It is why we fight tonight. It is why we will all die to protect you."

Just as Charlotte had said. Just as Rafael had said. But I couldn't escape the truth—tonight, I was a liability. I wasn't the master healer in her clinic, the bold woman breaking the rules of a top university to acquire the best education, the preeminent supernatural physician sought out by kings and foreign courts and vampires worldwide. I was simply the human who needed protecting. I wanted to scream.

I frowned and jumped down from the carriage. It had rained lightly throughout the day, leaving mud puddles glinting with moonlight in the carriage ruts. Étienne had driven past the cemetery to an overgrown, tree-lined lane to park the carriage as we waited for word from Charlotte and Antoine's patrol.

Étienne jumped down to help Daphne emerge from the carriage, and I grimaced at the sounds of their tender kisses behind me.

"I may not have vampire hearing, but that is loud enough for human ears," I complained.

Étienne chuckled and came to stand beside me. Daphne was occupied taking various weapons out of the box at the back of the carriage, and Rafael, it seemed, was still off surveying us from some aerial perch. While we waited, Étienne nudged me with his shoulder, as affectionately as a brother.

"She's right, you know," he said softly, casting his eyes to his mate. Daphne was oblivious to us, checking the powder and shot in the twin flintlock pistols she wore in a harness around her waist.

"I swear upon all that is holy and unholy, Étienne, if you say anything else to me about the conversations that were meant to be private *or* my… situation…with Rafael, I will fill your veins with quicksilver and leave you writhing on the floor," I warned. A headache of annoyance had begun to build between my eyebrows.

He laughed again and held up his hands in defeat. We waited another few minutes in companionable silence.

"Do you know how he learned his other abilities?" Étienne asked quietly. "I have learned only the simplest illusions. Yet he seems to ooze power."

"I don't even know what all his abilities are," I admitted. "Suffice it to say that the ones I do know of are truly horrifying."

"One wonders why he needs *les DD* to help him retrieve his brother," Daphne said casually as she came to stand beside us.

"Perhaps it is because of your dazzling company," came that rich voice from the disembodied night around us.

Rafael materialized from the shadows.

"No, that is a very good question," I said. "Why can't you simply go in and take him?"

"I suspect the cell where Laszlo is being kept is warded with some holy power, or spell," Rafael said.

"How could you know that?" Étienne asked. "Have you been inside?"

Rafael shook his head. "No, but it would take something very powerful indeed to contain my brother. Very powerful and very, very bad."

Anxiety swept through me like winds across a field, caressing my nerves and tightening my muscles.

"How powerful is he if he managed to be captured?" Étienne wondered.

"That's what truly worries me. Either he is wounded and unwell, or whatever means they have for subduing supernatural beings is straight from the depths of Hell. Either way, it's unlikely that I would be able to save him alone—even with my *gifts*."

The wind began to whip up, colder than I'd expected. I tugged the thick wool cloak tighter around me, wishing for the fire in my study or a hot bath. The air smelled of damp earth and fresh rain, and I smiled despite myself.

"What's so amusing?" Rafael all but whispered, coming to stand on my other side.

I tensed, trying to forget everything Daphne had said on the ride over here. That familiar millstone of expectation pulling me down. The self-doubt and comforting cold. The fear of being a liability—useless. *Less than.*

"That scent," I replied after a moment. "I think I like it more than flowers. The wet mud after the rain—it means the promise of spring. It is the scent of hope to me."

He inhaled deeply. The moonlight on his face was a soft blue caress, highlighting parts and throwing others in shadow. His ancient vampire eyes glowed faintly, giving him an ethereal appearance. With his stunning, cold beauty, he might have been a haughty angel.

He remained in profile, standing next to me a few feet away. Whether it was because he wanted to respect my space after my tirade or because he dwelt in his own melancholy, I didn't know.

"You will be fine tonight," he said. "In there." He nodded toward the mausoleum.

My temper flared. "I know," I snapped. "Everyone here is on the lookout for me. Everyone will protect me. Weak, human Mina will be watched over and cared for."

"No," he said firmly, turning to me. "Not because of us. Because of you. You were right, Mina. You are strong, and smart, and capable. You are all you need. You will be fine because…you will be fine."

Daphne and Étienne had wandered away from the carriage, drawn toward a stand of trees a short distance away.

"I'm sorry for how I behaved earlier," he said. "For how I have behaved this whole time. You have every right to your anger and frustration. For all my immortality, I struggle with patience when it comes to you. You sunk tenterhooks into my soul long ago, and my single-mindedness in pursuit of yours has consumed me. I've told you I would give you anything, so I will give you what you ask—time. After tonight, I will wait for your summons. I won't come to you until you are ready."

I blinked. I hadn't expected him to agree so easily, given how hard he'd been fighting for me. It was what I wanted, wasn't it? I found myself nodding to him, heard myself thanking him, but something dark and despondent snaked through my chest.

I didn't have much time to examine the thoughts swirling through my mind because at that moment, two massive Hell-touched wolves bounded in from the trees where Daphne and Étienne had been skulking.

"No patrols?" Daphne asked.

Charlotte barked.

"Very well. That's…unexpected."

"Do you think it's a trap?" Étienne whispered.

"Likely," Rafael said, lifting a shoulder casually. He didn't seem particularly concerned, but Daphne tensed, scanning the area as if she could detect some unseen threat. Her hands went to the pistols strapped at her sides.

"What choice do we have?" I asked.

"Change of plans. Charlotte, you and Antoine stay out here on guard. Étienne, Rafael, and I will go in first. Mina, I don't know what we're walking into but…I'm sorry. You'll have to wait in the carriage."

"What?" I almost shouted. "Absolutely not. If Laszlo is hurt, time may be of the essence. You might not be able to move him. I'm going with you."

"It's too risky," Daphne said. "I'm sorry. But something feels…off. They tried to come for you once, Mina, I won't let them grab you again."

I made an outraged sputter, looking to Étienne and Charlotte for help. Étienne winced and refused to meet my eyes, rubbing the back of his neck with his hand. Charlotte merely whined and licked my land.

"If Mina wants to come, she comes," Rafael growled. He took a step toward Daphne, and Étienne tensed, hand on the wooden daggers at his waist.

"Please, Mina," Daphne begged, frowning. "We need to get moving. We don't have much time."

"Fine," I gritted out. "But we are going to have a *serious* discussion about boundaries and friendship when you return."

I stomped back to the carriage, disgusted by my petulance and embarrassed by my mortality. I couldn't face Rafael as they all turned toward the cemetery, easily vaulting the eight-foot iron fence. I watched them dart among the headstones until they came to that wretched mausoleum entrance of The Order's subterranean hideout. With a sharp tug and a metallic groan, the door swung open, and I watched with frothing anxiety as the living darkness in the tomb swallowed them entirely.

19
RAFAEL

April 27, 1768
Cimetière des Innocents

OF COURSE, IT WOULD BE A TRAP. HOW GOOD OF A TRAP, THOUGH, REMAINED to be seen. Tearing my lingering focus from Mina's well-deserved sulk in the carriage, I reached out with my senses as Daphne, Étienne, and I descended into the yawning gloom of the mausoleum. We climbed down a staircase until we reached the dank hallway below, which reeked of wet rot, old sweat, and greasy smoke from tallow candles. I paused at the foot of the stairs, uneasy.

"What is it?" Daphne whispered.

"Beyond the hallway," I said, puzzled. "I can't sense anything."

"So?" Étienne prodded.

"I can't hear anyone through the walls," I explained. "I can't smell the blood of any living thing or touch the consciousness of anyone."

"We're beneath a graveyard," Étienne retorted. "Why would you?"

"Because," I said impatiently. "That means no one is here. *No one.* Not just guards or prisoners, but rats, insects, and every other cold wriggling thing that makes the deep earth its home."

"How is that possible?" Daphne asked, taking half a step forward.

"It isn't," I said. "It means this *is* a trap. It means there is some kind of dark magic at work here that affects my abilities. It means that beyond this hallway, every other supernatural gift I possess is effectively useless."

"That settles it," Daphne replied. "We're turning back. I'm not risking our safety. Tomorrow, we'll regroup and come up with a different plan."

"Are you certain?" I asked. "If you're not prepared to carry on…"

"We'll come back, Rafael," Étienne insisted.

"If you wish," I said, affecting an air of disappointment. My inability to sense Laszlo worried me more than I cared to admit, and I was reluctant to leave without getting some idea of what The Order had planned for him. Resentment gnawed at me. I didn't want to be here; I wanted to be holed up in my castle with Mina. The sooner I could put an end to this mystery, the better.

"Then we should return to the carriage," I said.

I sensed the relief flowing from Daphne and Étienne, and could only hope they would forgive me for what I was about to do. We walked silently back up toward the mausoleum entrance. The moment they exited into the moonlit graveyard, I slammed the tomb door closed behind them and barred it with one of the tall candelabras inside.

"What the devil do you think you're doing?" Étienne shouted, banging against the iron door.

"Go back to the carriage and keep Mina safe," I replied. "It's better for everyone if I face this alone."

"We're not leaving you here," Daphne hissed. "Mina will have my head!"

Étienne swore beneath his breath, and by the sound of it, heaved his body into the door. The metal clanged and groaned. I knew the door wouldn't keep them out for long, which meant time was of the essence. There were several soft metallic clicks—Daphne loading her pistols in the dark. I hurried back down the stairs in case she tried to shoot her way through the barrier.

I moved forward swiftly and silently. With every step, I reached out again and again with my supernatural senses, hoping I'd been wrong— that I wasn't stumbling blindly into Death's waiting embrace. Each time, I felt the same thing—a void of feeling, sensation. As if I was coming to a precipice and was about to tumble off the edge of a map.

The corridor ended in a large door, cast in something like iron, but… not. It was much thicker than the one in the graveyard above and while this one felt like it had been fashioned recently, the material it was hewn from felt ancient and rare. I placed my hand against it and recoiled almost immediately. The cold that leeched from it was unearthly and *wrong*.

This strange material must be some kind of prison door. Now, I was certain Laszlo was inside. I only prayed he was alive.

The massive door swung open easily, as if it had been waiting for me to arrive. Every instinct screamed at me to stop—go back—go no further, but I silenced them. I was here for answers—and for my brother.

I entered a large underground study with a great table in the center. Aside from the stacked bookshelves lining the walls, there were maps of Paris and charts of Europe, all covered with cryptic codes and pins. Curiosity needled me. What was The Order's master plan? Was it truly as simple as eliminating every vampire and maintaining their consolidation of power? Who would be the scapegoat for their evil deeds when all the vampires had been wiped off the map?

Suspecting Laszlo would be somewhere further underground, I reached out again with my supernatural senses and found them severely diminished, as though wandering through an empty void. If there was a secret dungeon underground, it would be well hidden. Searching for any kind of clue, I noted a conspicuous lack of dust in front of one of the bookshelves lining the wall. Running my hands along the edge of it, I found a catch and pulled. The bookshelf creaked forward, revealing a hidden archway leading even further into the darkness.

The floor was damp stone, and I heard the faint drip of water below. Despite my muted senses, at the edge of my awareness was something dim—familiar. A soft, shuddering breath and a wracking cough split the silence and I raced down the stone steps.

"Laszlo!" I hissed. "Is that you, brother?"

"My god…Rafael? Is that you?" His voice was weak and hoarse, and icy rage settled in my gut when I realized he had to have been starved and badly beaten to sound so diminished.

The small circular room was lined with seven cells. All were empty, save one. I rushed forward and gripped the bars, then pulled back as if burned.

"The bars," Laszlo huffed. "They are the same as the door."

"What is it?" I asked.

Laszlo had been sitting in the back corner of his otherwise empty cell. He struggled to stand and shuffled forward to clasp my arms through the bars.

My stomach dropped. Laszlo had once been so tall, strong, and handsome, taking all the best parts of our parents without the weak chin and sloping shoulders the other side was prone to. But here before me, he had wasted away to a skeletal corpse. Skin stretched over his bones and his long, black hair hung in greasy threads over his forehead. Fresh cuts, purpling bruises, and open festering wounds indicated he'd been tortured extensively, but hadn't been able to heal.

"How is this possible?" I muttered. "You can't have been here so long.

How have you not healed? Why have you not ended these fools with a thought?"

Laszlo shook his head with great effort. "They know things, Rafael. They know enough to keep me in this weakened state. The inner door and the bars of my cell interfere with my abilities, as I'm sure you learned."

"We must hurry, Laszlo. Who holds the keys to your cell?" I asked, darting around. I scanned every surface for a keyring or latch that would open the cell door but saw nothing. "And where are they keeping Marguerite?"

"Marguerite is here?" Laszlo asked, stunned. "When? How?"

"You didn't know? The traitorous bitch! I knew something was off. I went to Dunkirk to find you and she approached me there, took me to your townhouse and spun me some tapestry of falsehoods about you being taken against your will by The Order. But how could they have found you? How could they have subdued you?"

A crash echoed from above. I hoped it wasn't The Order coming to ensnare us all in their wretched net. I paused in my hunt for the key to Laszlo's cell to brace myself for my enemy, who I could hear running down the stairs above me.

A blonde head poked around the doorframe, and a sigh of relief whooshed out of me.

"I'll have you know Étienne and I are *very* put out, Rafael," Daphne grumbled. "This is a horribly ill-advised idea, and if we get into trouble down here, it's entirely your fault." She inclined her head at Laszlo and smiled. "Your Highness."

He eyed me questioningly.

"It's a very long story," I answered. I looked back at Daphne. "Étienne? Mina?"

She waved my concern away. "The only reason I'm down here is because I convinced them to wait in the carriage while I came down to fetch you." Her eyes sparkled when she added, "And I don't fancy being in your shoes when Mina gets a hold of you. I don't think I've ever heard her use that language."

I winced. "Best for us to hurry, then. I'm looking for the key to this cell."

"Oh, damn the key, Rafael, let me see if I can pick the lock."

She produced a small roll of leather with half a dozen thin, metal picks of varying size and shape. As she knelt before the lock, I came back to Laszlo.

"What happened? And where is everyone tonight?" I wanted to know.

"We were wondering why they would leave you unguarded. Do you know when they will return?" Daphne asked.

After a few tense moments, there was a soft, metallic click and Daphne let out a triumphant laugh. She yanked the door back, hissing when she touched the metal, and Laszlo fell forward into my arms. He stumbled, nearly dragging me down with him.

"Just give me a moment," he wheezed. "I haven't much strength left."

"Rafael, we will need to carry him! We must get out of here before The Order returns," Daphne pressed.

A piercing sense of foreboding sliced through me just as I picked up the sounds of a struggle above me. Daphne whirled around; her face drained of color.

"Étienne!" she screamed.

She ran for the door in a blur of speed but staggered back just as she reached it. Two young vampires marched in, carrying the unconscious emissary between them. There was a mighty gash on his head spilling thick, black blood, but he was otherwise unharmed. The vampires tossed him in one of the cells. Before the enraged duchesse could launch herself at her love's captors, Marguerite appeared in the stairwell behind them.

"Easy, Duchesse," she warned. "I wouldn't want anything to happen to your friend here."

Terror gripped my body, almost swallowing me into oblivion. Marguerite tugged Mina forward, bound, gagged, and bleeding from her nose. She kicked furiously at Marguerite, connecting with a satisfying *thwack*. Marguerite grunted and dropped Mina to the ground, where she landed with a sickening crack. She stilled, but I could still hear the beat of her heart—alive, but unconscious. I made to run toward her, but bands of iron wrapped around my waist and held me in place—*Laszlo*.

Stunned, confused, I turned to him. "Laszlo! What are you doing?"

His thin lips cracked on a sad smile.

"I'm sorry, Rafael—truly I am. But they said it was you or us."

I stared, uncomprehending. He couldn't be—*couldn't be*—betraying me again. Not after all this time. Not after everything I went through to find him. To come here and release him.

"Unhand me, you absolute clod! Do you have any idea who I am?" The outraged bellows of Charlotte's voice drifted through the staircase next, followed by the roar of rage coming from Antoine.

"Yes, Comtesse de Brionne," said a soft voice that sent chills down my spine. "But I'm afraid titles don't impress the likes of us very much."

"I wasn't talking about my title," she snarled. "I meant that the moment I get out of here, I'm going to rip your throat out with my teeth and spill your insides with my claws."

Several more vampires trudged in. Charlotte was utterly nude beneath what looked like a borrowed cloak, her wrists and ankles shackled in the same peculiar metal as the cells and the inner door. Antoine, pinned between four vampires, was led in behind her, similarly bound. The vampires shoved them into the cell next to Daphne and Étienne, closed the doors, and marched back out of the room. In their wake, a cloaked, masked figure emerged. He was tall and lean, with silvery hair and the sloped shoulders of idle aristocracy. He reeked of expensive perfume that could not hide the stink of rancid hair pomade, sweat, and cognac.

"Monsieur Derais," Charlotte chuckled darkly. "I know you're not intelligent enough to try to carry out some villainous plan all on your own. Where, pray tell, are your compatriots?"

The gentleman sneered. "How like you, Comtesse, to swiftly come to the wrong conclusion. We are not the ones plotting a coup."

"*Mon Dieu*, have you been drinking? What the Hell are you on about? No, you know what? I do not care. Simply release my friends and I, and I shall endeavor to forget this whole misunderstanding happened," she said airily.

I had to hand it to her—she was putting on a spectacular performance of the entitled aristocrat, given I could scent her fear.

"What is this all about, Derais?" Daphne cut in. She'd cleaned Étienne's wound and was wrapping it with a strip of clean linen from some secret pocket.

Monsieur Derais seemed to have some ounce of respect or fear for the duchesse, because he frowned apologetically as he approached her cell.

"His Majesty wants someone brought to justice for the blood plague. He believes the growing restlessness of the commoners can be...*redirected*...toward a shared enemy. We know the plague hails from the Dracul curse, and frankly, we don't care who initially brought it over the border. We will present the king with both brothers and have him try them publicly for execution. Crimes against humanity—and the crown," Derais said matter-of-factly.

Laszlo turned to him, shock written on his gaunt face.

"You said we would go free! My wife and I—we could return to Dunkirk after we brought Rafael to you! It was promised!"

"You fool," I snarled, shoving Laszlo to the ground. "You believed the word of these cowardly maniacs?"

"I'm sorry," Laszlo mumbled, his voice a strangled sob. "I just wanted to return home with Marguerite. They ambushed me in Dunkirk. After days of torture, they sent word to her and offered the bargain. If we could bring you out from hiding, they would let us go."

Derais whirled on Laszlo, a cruel smile lighting his face. "You don't expect us to let you continue roaming our country, poisoning everything with your vile infection. You and your blasphemous family and wretched blood offspring will burn on earth before burning in Hell. The Order will see to it. *I* will see to it. You and all your kind will be punished."

"You have done more to poison this country than vampires ever did," Daphne growled. "I regret that I was blind to your true aims for so long. I only hoped to steer you toward a more moderate and peaceful existence between human and vampire alike."

Crouching to better meet her furious gaze, Derais sneered and spat through the bars of her cell. "Filthy *sanguisuges!* There was never going to be a peaceful existence between vampires and humans. Vampires are an abomination—a crime against God. We will cleanse your kind from our country just as God cleansed the wicked from the Earth with the great flood."

From his cell, Antoine stretched out his long legs and grunted. "Sounds pretty blasphemous to me."

"Right you are, *mon cher.* Derais, you cannot simply hold us here. Daphne and I have the protection of the king. He would be furious if he found out you were holding us without just cause," Charlotte pointed out.

Derais rose and crossed back to stand above Mina, then tried to shift her with his foot. Rage ignited in my blood, first white hot, then fathomless black.

"You will *not* touch her," I snarled, my voice coming out like a demon's. Derais raised a supercilious eyebrow, challenging me.

"You think the king can save you? You were breaking in to release our prisoner, who represents the greatest threat to mankind. I think His Majesty would find that was cause enough," Derais replied.

Mina began to rouse herself with a groan, clutching at her head.

"Doctor, so glad you could join us," Derais offered, malice sparking in his gaze. "As much as we have enjoyed your services, I'm afraid they are no longer required. We won't need doctors for supernatural threats after we manage to eliminate them entirely."

He tugged a pistol from his waistcoat pocket and hauled Mina up from the floor by her hair. I reached deep into myself to transform, to mesmerize—anything—but was entirely impotent. *Almost human.* At her yelp of pain, I screamed in abject horror.

"Derais!" I shouted. "Stop! I will give you anything—do anything. Please do not hurt her. She is innocent. She is human. She is *good.*" The words caught in my throat, and I hated myself for the begging in my tone, but I would do it for her every time. "Please."

Derais looked at me for a moment—considering.

"No," Mina whispered, looking at me. "Rafael, no. I...I'm sorry. For everything. I just...thought we would have more time to figure things out, but...I love you."

Tears of blood leaked from my eyes, and the more I wanted to scream and rage and unleash brutal violence, the weaker I felt.

"I will not say goodbye to you again, Mina," I said. "Derais, please. I will serve you. I will help destroy your enemies. I will give you wealth, land, armies…*Anything.*"

The pause of deliberation was enough for a breath of hope. In one swift move, Mina stamped hard on Derais's foot. He screamed, dropping the pistol and releasing Mina's hair. She leapt up and ran for the door, taking the stairs two at a time.

Derais shrieked at Laszlo. "Go after her, Dracul, and I *might* spare you and your wife."

"No, Laszlo! Brother, please!" I shouted, launching myself at Derais.

But Laszlo was off like a shot, hobbling up the stairs after Mina. I had Derais in my hands, but I felt the sharp edge of a blade at the back of my neck. Marguerite stood behind me, holding a short sword.

"Let him go, Rafael," she said, her voice trembling. "He cannot grant us safe passage if he is dead."

Blind rage gripped me as Derais smiled. I knew Marguerite would behead me with one stroke if I so much as breathed wrong. Seething, I let go of Derais and stepped back slowly.

"Hear me now," I growled at him. "There is no place on earth you can hide that I will not find you. I have visited torment on lesser men than you for lesser injustices, so believe me when I say that you, Derais, will reap what you sow. I will have you begging for death when I've only just begun with you."

A flicker of fear passed over the older man's face, and he swallowed but stood and squared his shoulders.

"Powerful words from a powerless vampire." He sneered. "Step back, Dracul, into that cell there. Yes—those bars that feel so strange to you? That's Judas silver."

I would have said it was impossible, but my inability to access any of my powers proved it was true. Even now, I could feel my supernatural strength siphoning off, draining every-so-slightly, like a trickle of water from a cracked pitcher.

"What's Judas silver?" Charlotte asked, uneasy.

"Surely, you remember the story," Derais scoffed. "Judas betrayed Jesus to the Romans for thirty pieces of silver—blood money that led to the death of our Lord and Savior. Even if you and your kind are sinners for succumbing to the temptation of the blood plague's power, I'm certain you recall how well that played out for humanity's greatest traitor."

"*Mon Dieu*, Daphne, I forgot how melodramatic Derais could be,"

Charlotte droned, rolling her eyes. "Look, if you're going to execute us, just get it over with. I don't need the torture of Bible study before I die."

Daphne snickered and Étienne stirred in her lap. She stroked his bloodied hair idly, no doubt trying to comfort him and quell her fear.

Derais's face twisted in anger, but he continued.

"Well, what happened to those thirty pieces of ill-gotten silver? Cursed, they were. Tainted. They left the mark of evil on everyone and everything they touched. They disappeared from legend for a few hundred years, only to resurface during the Crusades. When people slowly realized what they were, they were collected and kept in a lead vault in the holy land. The Order formed sometime after that, and then the blood plague came to France, and my holy brothers agreed the ultimate test of the silver's effects would be to pit it against the greatest, most powerful threat to our world—the House of Dracul."

He paced, seething in righteousness as I slumped to the floor. The more he spoke, the wilder the gleam in his eye became and the more rabid his tone. Flecks of spit flew from his lips as he continued his tirade.

"I secured the unholy treasure myself this past year at great personal cost, but it was worth it. Now, we finally have a means to eliminate every supernatural creature from the face of the earth. Once we had the cursed silver, it was almost *too* easy to find ways to use it—to smelt it down, mix it with other metals, and turn it into powerful weapons against blasphemous threats."

"You are mad, Derais," I growled. I tried to fight the rising nausea and weakness snaking through my body. "You and your Order are twisted. If you wish to protect humanity from its greatest threat, you should start by hanging yourself."

Derais crossed the room and closed the cell door, locking me into Laszlo's old cell. Placing the keys in his front pockets, he gestured to the door and motioned for Marguerite to leave. She flicked one glance back at me, regret written on her face.

"I'm sorry, Rafael," she whispered. "But Laszlo is all I have."

I wanted to hurl an insult at her, to scream and rage and wrap my hands around her delicate neck, but the sound of Mina's screams split the night, and my horror froze me in place.

20

MINA

April 27, 1768
Cimetière des Innocents

FASTER AND FASTER I RAN, SWERVING BETWEEN TREES AND DODGING SHRUBS and puddles. Laszlo had come staggering out of the mausoleum, obviously weakened from his imprisonment. Otherwise, I would have already been caught—or dead.

He gained ground ever so slowly, and I knew I had to do something to gain the advantage. But the farther we got from The Order's headquarters, the more he seemed to recover, as if his strength was slowly finding its way back to his tormented bones. Sheer terror had me in its thrall, and I couldn't think—couldn't puzzle my way out of this one.

"Doctor, please!" he called from behind me, closer than I would have liked. "Please, you must understand! I don't want to hurt you! I just need to do as they say, and they'll let Marguerite and I go!"

I wouldn't be able to hide from him, and I couldn't outrun him for long, but that meant my only recourse was to stand and fight.

Impossible. Even weakened, Laszlo was probably stronger and more powerful than Rafael, and it was only a matter of time before he caught up with me and hauled me back to The Order for my execution.

I stumbled on the root of a large tree and nearly went down, but as I twisted to right, I heard the faint clink of glass from my waistcoat. *The vials in my medical kit. The pockets! The weapons!* Realization slammed into me as I hurdled a low shrub—Charlotte and Daphne had given me everything I needed to defend myself; I simply had to find the right time and place to use it.

I groped blindly through the pockets, trying to remember which ones held what. I plucked the vial of quicksilver and a small wooden stake from my waistcoat, held them out, and then slowed to prepare for my final stand.

Laszlo was almost upon me, but he stopped after seeing the items in my hands. I knew they wouldn't be enough to kill him, but if he was still weak, they would be enough to delay him considerably. I brandished them before me.

"Let me go, Laszlo," I warned, desperately trying to catch my breath.

He shook his head slowly.

"You know I cannot do that," he said. "If I don't take you back, they will kill Marguerite."

"If you take me back, they will kill me," I pleaded. "And they will not let you go, Laszlo. You will take me to them, and they will kill you, anyway, and Marguerite. They will kill my friends. And they will kill Rafael."

My voice broke on his name.

"I have to try," he choked out. "I must try for Marguerite. She has been through so much. I cannot leave her there with them."

"You are damned either way," I said. "But if we work together, there might be a way to save us all."

"How?"

I sighed, hating myself for advocating the death of anyone, no matter how evil. "We could take them down *together*."

He stepped toward me. "What do you mean?"

I backed up. "You and Rafael are more powerful than all The Order put together. The two of you could go through those men like a hot knife through butter."

Laszlo huffed a laugh. "Surely you saw the vile things their witchcraft does to vampires. With that, we're weaker than human. Besides, killing them would only prove the humans right about us. The Order would be martyrs, and we would be the monsters everyone already suspects we are. There would be no doubt in anyone's minds."

He had a point, but I wasn't ready to give up. Pain throbbed in my ankle, and I wouldn't be able to outrun him. I had to try to reason with him.

"So we tell everyone the truth about The Order. How they've lied and stolen and controlled all along. Make everyone see them as the power-hungry manipulators they truly are."

He slowed, considering. From the tree above us, an owl hooted softly.

We both tilted our heads toward the sound. I desperately wanted to believe it wasn't an ill omen—that they were watching over us, offering hope. *Hope.*

"Please, Laszlo," I begged, playing every card in my hand. "I've spent the last twenty years hating Rafael for abandoning me and serving penance for his mistakes. Now that he's come back into my life, I'm not ready to have it all end before we can set things right. Frankly, I'm not even ready to forgive him. I love him, but I just…need more time. We all need more time."

Turning his gaze from the owl to the fallen tree at his side, he scrubbed his hands across his face, and he sat down hard.

"It was never supposed to happen," he said, his voice drifting absently on a gentle wind.

I waited, still palming the quicksilver and wooden stake in case he decided our parlay was at an end.

After a beat, I asked, "What wasn't supposed to happen?"

His dark eyes—so much like Rafael's, yet weary and sad—lifted to mine.

"Marguerite was pregnant when we fled Wallachia," he said.

The news hit me like the shock of cold from winter's first frost.

"But—that's impossible. Humans and vampires cannot reproduce," I argued.

"Yes, that's what we've believed all along. My ancestors and now the modern vampire…it simply does not happen. And yet, Marguerite grew with my child while we made our home in Dunkirk."

Logic compelled me to ask the impertinent question.

"You're certain it was yours?"

A dark, rasping chuckle issued from his chest.

"I wasn't at first, but when the pregnancy began to show signs of the curse, it became evident. I had not planned on eloping, but when she told me about the babe, everything in my life became clear. I would not allow my child to live in this world of darkness. I would not allow my father to corrupt the only good thing in my life. So I did the only thing I could think to do I packed up as much as I could without drawing notice, and we ran."

I watched Laszlo as he spoke, the despair plain on his face and in the set of his shoulders. He ran his fingers through a patch of damp grass at his feet, and I tried not to stare at his long, lethal claws trailing through the dew.

"We traveled around for a while, trying to hide from the men my father sent after us, but eventually I had to kill them. We couldn't keep running. We went north as far as we could, but she was so weak then. We stopped at Dunkirk to shelter and rest for a while—she was so ill. I had to turn her then, you see. She would not have survived the birth of the child if it was, in fact, a blood drinker."

I considered going to sit on the log next to him but thought better of it. Instead, I crouched where I was, ready to jump up at the slightest twitch of his movement. The owl above us had fallen silent, as if sensing the heaviness of our conversation.

"Marguerite's condition during the turning left her weak, and even when she completed the transformation, she was weaker than most vampires. But she survived—that was all that mattered to me. And the babe in her belly continued to grow, unharmed by her change of state. When my daughter was born, nothing in the world had prepared me for how much I would love—could love—another being. I'd loved my parents, but feared them, and I'd loved Rafael, but we had grown apart after our childhood. Marguerite was the first person who made me believe I was more than a monster or some ancestral obligation. And then she gave me the one thing that I'd never felt worthy of having—a love so pure, I would have done anything to keep it. To protect it."

"A family trait," I offered.

A sad smile tugged at the corners of his lips. Thinner than Rafael's lips, but the same shape.

Rafael. Hold on, Rafael.

"For a few years, we existed in bliss. We were living meagerly, but one of Marguerite's sisters came to stay with us to help care for our daughter. Lucy. My little Lucy, sweet starlight of my life."

He gasped out a painful sob, and a tear of blood spilled down his cheek.

"I should have seen it coming. Could have prevented it if I'd been smarter or faster. But it was an accident, my little Lucy biting her aunt. She nearly drained her—too young to know how to stop in the grip of a blood frenzy. When Marguerite found her sister, almost dead, and Lucy at her throat, she panicked."

Pieces started to fall into place. "Marguerite turned her sister, rather than let her die."

"It was forbidden," Laszlo said. "It is forbidden for any of the Dracul family to turn another, except for our mates. It was a way to ensure the curse was contained to our family."

"What happened to Lucy?"

"Marguerite's sister did not take to the turning well. It was painful and messy. When she awoke as a vampire, it was...*wrong*. She was wrong—broken. I don't know what happened, if it was because she was the first outsider to undergo the change, or perhaps because Marguerite was weak when she tried to turn her. Whatever it was…she awoke angry—and hungry. In her wrath, she killed Lucy and nearly killed Marguerite. She fled into the countryside before I returned home. I have not seen or heard from her since, but we looked. How we looked! After burying Lucy and caring for Marguerite during her recovery, my grief was too heavy for me to consider vengeance."

My heart broke at Laszlo's confession, for the loss of his daughter and the near loss of his mate—his wife. The blood plague hadn't come to France because of a malicious, corrupt vampire nor his greedy, selfish wife —it had simply been an accident. A true tragedy, brought about by terror and confusion and grief. I felt sick.

"I'm sorry," I whispered, unacknowledged tears falling down my own cheeks. "I cannot fathom the depths of your loss."

He nodded. "It does not get easier, even with time," he said. "Time does not heal wounds, as they say. In my experience, time simply earns us more wounds so that we cannot focus on the pain of one for too long."

"Time grants us perspective," I said. "But that is all."

Laszlo offered a half smile and opened his mouth to say something, but a distant crash echoed through the woods. He was up before I could blink, panic glittering in his eyes.

"It is Derais!" he hissed.

"They will stop at nothing, Laszlo. Even if you give me to them, you and Marguerite do not stand a chance. Then, they will come for every vampire in France. It will be genocide!"

Desperation and anger warred in his expression.

"Please, Laszlo! I have spent my life trying to help your kind. Do not let my work be in vain. Do not let your brother pay for the shattered dream of your family—it was no more his fault than Lucy's."

He took the words like a blow, wincing as they landed.

"Dracul!" came Derais's shouts. "Dracul, you better have my prize in your filthy claws, or I will remove your pretty wife's head."

Enraged, Laszlo roared into the night. The sound was horrifying and hellish, filled with anger and pain and torment.

"Run," he commanded, the sound guttural and inhuman. His form began to shift, bones breaking and sinew snapping and skin ripping away from his body. For a moment, I stood there and watched, transfixed by the shapeshifting. In a heartbeat, he had finished, and I couldn't help the scream that climbed its way up from the pit of my stomach.

Where Laszlo's gaunt, sagging human form had stood now appeared a true monster from the lowest, most nightmarish circle of Hell. He looked like the devil himself, with spindly, garish sets of fangs—his eyes, black puddles of darkness that glowed with a faint red light. Massive bat wings sprouted from the upper body of a creature that was a demonic shadow of the wolf creature Rafael could become. A thick, scaly tail whipped around his powerful legs and long, razor sharp claws erupted from his fingers and toes.

Run, he said again, this time in my mind.

I didn't need to be told again. I took off, weaving through the trees until I came to the low wall on the opposite side of the cemetery. I crouched behind a massive oak tree with the cemetery at my back. The moonlight dappled silver on the ground, and I heard Derais's threatening shouts at Marguerite and Laszlo.

Given that he'd just shifted into an eight-foot-tall monster, Laszlo seemed to be healing more quickly than I'd expected. I didn't know what he intended to do, but I wasn't prepared to question it just yet.

Derais stormed into the clearing where Lazlo and I had been. He dragged Marguerite behind him and threw her to the ground—her head making a sickening crack against the fallen tree. Laszlo roared and rushed to her side. She struggled to rise and reached for him.

"You had her! You had her and you let her go!" Derais screamed. "You filthy beasts, we should have slaughtered you where we found you."

Laszlo picked Marguerite up from the ground, shielding her with his enormous wings. I watched in horror as Derais slipped the pistol from his pocket and aimed at Laszlo's back.

"No!" I shouted, rushing forward. Anger and horror propelled me forward, and no small amount of stupidity. "Please! Don't kill them!"

Laszlo whirled around, a low growl spilling from his throat.

"Please," I begged Derais again. "Just let them go!"

Confused, still enraged, Derais turned to me. "My dear Doctor, why the Hell should I? They're abominations—they should all be wiped off the face of the Earth."

"They're not," I insisted. He turned the pistol on me, and I froze. "They're cursed, as you say. But the plague was not their fault—it was an accident, and they have suffered enough. They did not come here with malice in their hearts. If you do believe in God and divine justice, you must also believe in penance and forgiveness. The Draculs have been paying penance for longer than any of us have been alive. Leave them, Derais. Let them go home. Let them live."

For one heartbreaking moment, I thought he would listen. But Derais hissed out a breath, madness clouding his eyes.

"The Order is the right hand of God, and I am acting on his behalf."

The shot cracked the silence of the night in the same instant that Derais screamed. I staggered back with the force of being hit but didn't understand how. Laszlo had Derais by the throat, and Marguerite was slumped on the ground, sobbing those strange vampire tears of blood. Slowly, cold seeped through me, and it became difficult to draw breath.

How strange.

A phantom pain throbbed in my chest and at last, I looked down to see a sticky wetness spreading down my new waistcoat.

Understanding dawned.

"I've been shot," I huffed, stunned. I took a step forward, then my legs failed, and I crumpled onto the damp ground.

There was a strange rushing in my ears, and I was suddenly exhausted.

Mina.

It was Laszlo in my mind again.

Mina, you have been shot in the heart with a powerful bullet—one made from Judas silver. You are dying. Do you wish for me to save you?

I opened my eyes, unprepared for the shock of seeing Laszlo's demon form looming above me.

"Save me? From death?" My voice was strangely distant.

Yes. You asked for time. Do you still wish for it? I can give it to you—all the time in the world. I can turn you, Mina, if you wish.

"But the sunshine..." I said thickly. I didn't want a life without sunshine. No, that wasn't right. I didn't want a life without Rafael. I didn't want to die without Rafael. Curiously, Daphne's words drifted through my mind. *Sometimes, when it is truly quiet in the small hours of the night, I could swear I have heard the stars singing.* She was right—my life had always circled blood and death and darkness. Even without Rafael in it, that was where I took comfort. It was never the lightness of a summer afternoon or a lemon-yellow gown. The darkness in my life was mine—it was me. It wasn't because of Rafael. He was the only thing that brought me true joy and passion, and who gave me the ability to value life as much as I did. And with remarkable clarity, I knew my answer.

Yes, Laszlo. Give me more time. Give me darkness. Give me a chance at a future with Rafael.

The terrifying demon nodded once and bent his head to my neck. He raised his wrist above my lips and sliced his arm open with one long, sharp claw, and black liquid copper slid over my tongue and down my throat. Then he bent his head, and his lethal fangs found my throat—his claws digging into the bullet wound in my chest at the same time. I would have screamed from the agony, but my vocal cords no longer worked. Eternities of pain crashed through my body, igniting every nerve in a symphony of suffering, and then a cold, silent darkness descended, and I knew no more.

21

RAFAEL

April 28, 1768
Cimetière des Innocents

"Rafael, stop trying to wrench those bars apart; they're not going to move," Charlotte called to me from across the dungeon. "We have to come up with another plan."

"Damn it, why can't I pick this bloody lock?" Daphne shouted, discarding her fourth bent hairpin onto the floor.

I ignored the lot of them and heaved my shoulder against the hinges in the door, near feral with desperation to get to Mina. To keep me sane, I fantasized about all the ways I would torture each surviving member of The Order and punish Laszlo and Marguerite for betraying me.

The insistent throb of pain in my head and spreading weakness in my limbs sang the Judas silver's song. Each time I flung myself at the bars, the pain echoed louder and louder, but I wouldn't—couldn't—sit in this pit and do *nothing*.

Noises drifted down from the stairwell, and I scented blood. When I realized whose blood, I collapsed to the floor, screaming.

To my horror, Laszlo filled the doorway, covered in blood. Marguerite leaned on his shoulder, and in his arms, he carried *her*.

My reason for existing.

But it was wrong—she was wrong. Her beautiful throat—the one that I'd lavished kisses upon and drawn laughter from—was ravaged. There was a gaping wound in her chest, right above her heart. *Her heart*, which no longer beat.

Daphne and Charlotte screamed as they saw the lifeless body of their friend hanging limp in the arms of a naked, bloody Laszlo.

"I am going to kill you, Laszlo!" I screamed. "I am going to rip you apart! What have you done? What have you done to my Mina?"

Tears of hot blood streamed down my face as I shouted and sobbed.

Marguerite pulled something from her skirts and came to my cell door.

"I gave her time," Laszlo said.

"What the fuck does that mean?" I choked out.

"She asked me for more time, brother, and so I turned her."

The room went silent and began to spin.

"Derais shot her in the heart with a Judas silver bullet," Marguerite said softly. She brandished the key and slipped it in the lock. "She was dying, Rafael. Laszlo offered to turn her, and she agreed."

For one shocking moment, there was only the faint sound of water dripping somewhere above.

"She—she is turning?" I whispered, not believing it. "I don't believe you! What have you done to her? Where is Derais? I'm going to end you all!"

My screams of rage had turned to sobs as I stared at the family who had betrayed me.

"Forgive us," whispered Marguerite. "If you must have vengeance, visit it upon me. Laszlo wanted no part in this. He only wanted to protect me. He could not save Mina from Derais…from the bullet. He could only turn her. Forgive him. *Forgive him.*"

For once, I did not sense any treachery from her. I felt only grief. Lifting my eyes to Laszlo, I saw the same look of regret and haunted sadness.

Could it be? *My Mina—turning.* Her summers and her sunshine, my spring goddess. My Persephone, doomed to a life of darkness and death.

The cell door swung open, and I pushed Marguerite aside to go to Laszlo. He gingerly handed Mina's limp body to me. I cradled her in my arms. In the distance, I heard Marguerite unlocking the doors of Charlotte and Daphne's cells. They came to stand at my side.

"If she is turning, we will need a safe place for her to heal and be reborn," Marguerite said.

"Where is Derais?" Charlotte asked sharply.

"In pieces too small to be found," Laszlo replied.

Daphne and Charlotte exchanged a look.

"Well, I expect neither of our homes will be particularly safe after tonight. Once The Order returns and finds Laszlo and Marguerite gone and Derais…erm, *indisposed*…they will come for us, and they know where to find us," Charlotte said.

"Where can we go?" Étienne asked. "I don't want to risk my sisters' safety by hiding out with them."

"My home," I said. "You may stay at my home. It is outside Rouen."

Daphne nodded. "We are grateful, Rafael."

"And us?" Laszlo asked.

"You must come. We have much to discuss," I replied. My voice sounded hollow.

He nodded and reached for Marguerite's hand. We filed silently up the stairs, exiting through the mausoleum. The deep indigo of the night sky was beginning to lighten to a soft pewter as we made our way toward Daphne's hidden carriage. Once outside the influence of the Judas silver, Charlotte and Antoine shifted to their wolf forms to run alongside the carriage. Étienne and Laszlo perched atop the driver's seat, while Marguerite, Daphne and I carried Mina between us in the carriage.

The ride was an exercise in patience. Every bump and shake of the carriage jostled Mina's body and sent fresh spikes of fear through me—what if Laszlo had been too late? What if Mina didn't react well to the blood plague? Would the effect of that poisonous bullet prevent her from turning, or turn her into something else entirely? What if she regretted her choice?

What if she found she had eternity waiting for her, and even then, decided it was not enough time to heal from the pain I'd caused her? She'd chosen life after death…but what if she didn't choose me?

By the time my ruined castle came into view, I was deep in my melancholy and the sun was almost at the horizon. I hadn't been this close to the sunrise in a long time, and it was almost impossible not to admire the soft oranges and pinks and dusky purples of the sky.

"Cutting it a bit close, brother," Laszlo grunted, coming down from the driver's seat.

Charlotte and Antoine padded up next to us and shifted back to human form.

"Well, this is charming, but you seem to be missing a roof, Rafael," Charlotte observed.

"The entrance is at the top of the tower. Laszlo and I will shift and fly you all up. I'll take Mina first, and then come back for the rest of you," I said, not bothering to wait for their acknowledgement. I exploded into my large bat form and picked up Mina's body in my claws. Behind me, I heard Laszlo change as well, and saw him grab Charlotte and Marguerite in his beastly hands.

We entered the tower, and I summoned Guillaume, explaining everything as quickly as I could. Though I was loathe to do it, I handed Mina's cold, still body to him and leapt back up the tower to pick up Daphne and Étienne. Laszlo was on my heels with Antoine in his claws just as the first rays of sunlight crested the horizon. I threw the stone door in place just in time. Exhausted beyond words, I led our group through the halls of my home, assigning them guest rooms as we went. I instructed the household staff to bring blood and fresh meat to everyone, as well as draw hot baths.

"Rest for the day, my friends," I said. "We will dine together after sundown. Then, I will be happy to show you the rest of my home. Please be comfortable here. If you should need anything, my staff will gladly attend to you."

I bowed stiffly and headed on swift feet to the guest room where I'd had Guillaume bring Mina. Already, the maids had come in and removed her bloodied clothing and changed her into a simple cotton chemise. She was tucked into the large bed while one of the maids stoked the fire in the fireplace. The young girl wasn't surprised to see me arrive, but merely rose and inclined her head.

"I've made her as comfortable as possible," she said forlornly. "But her wounds…"

"She will recover," I said. "She is cursed now."

The maid's eyes widened, and she nodded quickly, then hurried from the room.

Exhausted, depleted, I came to the side of the bed and fell to my knees. Here, alone, I let my despair and fear wash over me as I clasped her hand.

"I never wanted this for you, Mina," I whispered, bloody tears coming hot and fast. "I never wanted you to have to leave your world behind for me. How I have tainted you and your future—all because I could not bear to be apart from you. All because I was afraid of hurting you. And no matter how much I wanted to protect you, you still ended up here. Forgive me, my love. Please forgive me. I will spend the rest of eternity earning your forgiveness, even if you wish to banish me from your sight. I will give you all the time in the world to come back to me. But please, Mina…please come back to me."

Her breathing had stilled, her limbs lay stiff and cold—a sign that her mortal body was dying. Even as I hoped the transformation would go well and she would recover quickly, I still mourned the death of her human self. It was the Mina I'd fallen in love with, the Mina I'd dreamed of marrying, the Mina whose blue eyes turned silver like a storm at sea when she was angry. The Mina who loved little almond cakes and small bouquets of yellow daisies, even though she would never admit such small romantic gestures delighted her. The Mina who fought harder than everyone for what was right. The Mina who had the strength for others when they fell to weakness. Ever logical, ever curious, ever questioning, ever loyal and loving Mina.

I wasn't sure how long I stayed there on my knees at her bed. It felt like a few moments and an eternity at the same time. Eventually, Charlotte came in—somewhat rested and restored, and damp from a bath. She told me to sleep and feed, which I refused until she insisted that Mina wouldn't want me to deteriorate at her bedside when nothing could be done.

"Besides," she said. "If she wakes, I hardly think you'll want to greet her looking like *that*. Do have yourself a bath, Rafael."

She crawled into the bed on Mina's other side and withdrew a romance novel from her skirts. She began reading out loud as if Mina was awake, even though I was sure she knew Mina would have been too embarrassed to read something so salacious.

Despite my melancholy, the ghost of a smile played about my lips, and I allowed Charlotte some time to grieve for the woman that we both loved. I expected Daphne would be along in time, as well, which gave me a measure of comfort while I dragged myself into my bedchamber. There was a bath waiting for me and two large decanters of blood, which I devoured. The Judas silver had leeched much of my strength, and the blood helped to restore some of it, as would a few hours of rest.

Sending a silent prayer to my long-abandoned gods for Mina's health, I quickly washed and slipped beneath the covers. It wasn't long before sleep wrapped me in its drugging embrace and pulled me under.

I woke to the sounds of bare feet padding toward my bedroom door. Before the knock came, I threw on my banyan and rushed to yank the door open. Daphne stumbled back a step, startled.

"She—she's awake," she said.

Without another word, I ran to the guest room where I heard Charlotte chattering excitedly and soft, rasping laughter from Mina.

Mina.

She was sitting up in bed, her long dark hair thrown over her shoulder and her blue eyes sparkling. She looked a touch pale and drawn, but considering she'd come back from the precipice of Death, she looked remarkably well.

The relief I felt staggered me, stealing my strength almost as much as the cell of Judas silver. I gripped the door frame and took a steadying breath, determined not to collapse and come apart. Charlotte looked up and saw me, and fortunately had the good grace not to tease me at that moment.

"We'll talk later," she promised Mina, winking at me as she and

Daphne left the room. In the silence that followed, I could only stare, unsure if I was dreaming or if this was truly happening.

MINA

THE SENSATIONS THAT ASSAULTED ME WERE INTENSE ENOUGH TO BE PAINFUL. The sounds and smells and uncomfortable awareness of thoughts from everyone in the household pressed against my consciousness until I wanted to claw my brain from my skull. Slowly, my new form became accustomed to the riot of stimuli, and with effort, I found a place of quiet stillness in my mind. It was falling asleep in a dark cave, then suddenly waking up in the middle of the busiest square in Paris.

Once the shock wore off, I was left with the waning embers of hope and the gnawing doubts about what had befallen Rafael and my friends back inside The Order's mausoleum.

Some strange, new instinct had me closing my eyes and stepping out from the quiet place in my mind and reaching out—listening. I heard people moving in the household. I heard birdsong in the world above me, the soft sounds of wind across the grass, and the burbling of a distant stream tripping its way over river stones. I found myself open to vast amounts of sensory information, and if I was careful and mindful, I could home in on one being at a time. It wasn't like reading another person's mind, but if I focused hard enough, I could perceive the shape and feeling of an individual's thoughts. In this household, it was a heady mixture of fear, love, relief, and worry. When my mind drifted to Rafael, the sense of his grief, shame, and regret broke my heart, but the persistent pulse of love from him was a soothing balm.

Most of the vampire turnings I'd seen, as well as Charlotte and Antoine's werewolf turning, had taken place over the course of days— weeks, in some cases. And yet, mine had taken place over the course of a few hours. It could have been from the strength of Laszlo's blood and his proximity to the curse, but I wasn't certain. I'd need to speak with him— and soon.

RAFAEL

Mina tilted her head—a soft smile appearing on her lips.

"You are not dreaming," she murmured.

I froze.

"You can—read minds," I said slowly.

"I can...sense...thoughts," she replied, her brow furrowing. "It is strange. I feel very strange, Rafael. Everything is more intense."

"You're alive. You survived death and the turning," I stated, stunned.

"Yes," she acknowledged, softly.

Emotions surged and I stumbled, gripping the door frame for strength.

"I thought you were dead," I choked out.

She tilted her head, considering. "Technically, I was," she replied. "And now I am...not. It's a very odd thing." Her eyebrows pinched together. "When this is over, I will need to update my notes and my medical texts. I fear I got a few things wrong in my understanding of supernatural anatomy." She held up her formerly human hand and stared at it as she grew long, lethally sharp claws.

Her logical assessment of the miracle of her rebirth unlocked me, and I smiled.

"It will be like this for a few days as your body learns to adjust to your supernatural senses," I said softly. I crossed the room to sit next to the bed in the chair Daphne had occupied.

Mina reached for a pitcher of water on the nightstand and a pewter cup.

"Allow me," I offered, pouring her a drink. I tried not to stare at her—to evaluate what else was different about her supernatural form from her human one. She seemed the same, if a little worn out and on edge.

"It is not what I expected," she blurted out, massaging the place between her brows that usually held her tension.

I bit my lip, trying to keep from peppering her with questions or launching my body at hers and covering her skin in worshipful kisses.

"Oh?" was all I replied. "What did you expect?" *Why didn't you want me to turn you?* The traitorous, selfish thought whined in my ear like a mosquito of self-doubt.

She sighed, pursing her lips. After a moment, she began.

"It's not that I never considered turning, Rafael. Of course I did—for you. But that was years ago, and I spent the rest of my life convincing myself that I didn't need to become supernatural to prove that I had value—that I was worth something. At first, after you sent me away, I wanted to be enough for you. And then, when I had soothed some of my hurt, I wanted to be enough for myself." She reached for a small glass of blood on the nightstand that had been kept warm by the low flame of a candle. Curiously, she sniffed at it, lifted it to her lips, and drank greedily. When she was finished, her eyebrows lifted in surprise. "Fascinating!"

"Mina, you have always been enough for me. You have always been worth more than ten of me—a thousand of me, even. When I sent you away, I thought I was protecting you from my father's wrath. I never considered that I was protecting myself from the pain I feared I would feel when we were separated by time. Perhaps I didn't want to approach you to find a solution together because part of me believed it was futile, since you did not want to turn. For that, I am sorry—I will never stop apologizing for getting things so wrong." I stood to refill the glass of blood from a crystal decanter.

"My anger at you has protected me, as well, Rafael. But when I was lying there on the ground, feeling my life ebb away, there was peace and… clarity. I held onto my anger because it was a shield. Yet the only thing it protected me from was finding happiness and closure without you. I think, on some level, I didn't want to heal from our wounds because it would mean having to let you go. And even though we have been apart for the last twenty years, I think I have always lived my life alongside yours. Keeping to a nightly schedule, immersing myself in work benefiting vampires and vampirekind, forming relationships with supernatural people…the proximity to blood, death, and darkness…it has been my life even without you. I was never one for spring flowers and sunshine. I would have always found the night—and found you in it, waiting for me. The threads of my entire being have been interwoven with yours from the beginning."

I was speechless—devastating grief and overwhelming hope warring in me like the forces of nature building a hurricane. I opened my mouth to speak, but she pressed a gentle finger to my lips.

"When I was dying, I wanted more time, but not for me. For you. We spent so long apart, and I couldn't believe things were over now that we'd found our way back to each other. I realized I still wanted the same things I always wanted, but for the first time ever, I could see you standing next to me in my dreams of the future. I want the happiness being with you gives me. I want the joy and love we forged years ago. I want the life we dreamed of back when we were too young and naïve to know the cruelties the world had in store for us."

I sucked in a breath.

"What are you saying?" My chest ached with longing to hear the words from her lips—words I'd dreamt of every night since we separated years ago.

"I love you, Rafael. I cheated Death to be with you. I defied the laws of nature to stay on earth and claim you as my own. I have carved out my place in the darkness so that together, we can be our own light."

I closed my eyes and leaned forward, touching my forehead to hers. I threaded my fingers through her hair and thanked the gods—every one I could name—for answering my pleas.

"Mina, my goddess, my Persephone, has finally come to the Underworld."

"Rafael, my devil, my wintry Hades…I have always been here." A tear slipped down her cheek—not blood, but a soft, glowing silver.

I pressed my lips to hers, so softly, fearing this was all a dream that would fade away with the dying light of sundown. The gentle kiss deepened, and she laced her fingers behind my neck, pulling me down to cover her body. Her soft, pink tongue licked at the seam of my lips, igniting volcanic lust buried in me. The leash of my holy restraint snapped. I pulled back quickly, the question hovering on my lips.

"Mina, are you certain—do you feel well enough to…"

Blue fire sparked in her eyes and in answer, she ripped my clothes from my body with a flick of her wrist.

22

MINA

April 28, 1768
Château du Diable

I WAS STARTLED BY THE SHARPNESS OF MY CLAWS AND THE STRENGTH IN MY fingers—I'd need to be careful. Unused to this odd supernatural body and its new, inner workings, I pulled away slightly, intimidated and hesitant.

Rafael smiled softly and straddled me, tugging the chemise up over my head.

"Say it again, Mina," he purred, his eyes liquid pools of jet.

"I love you," I murmured, feeling more contentment than I had in the past twenty years. Perhaps even longer.

He closed his eyes for the briefest moment, then lowered his body to mine and buried his face in my neck.

"If I heard those words from you every day until the end of time, it would not be enough," he said.

The soft brush of his lips on my collarbone sent a ripple of fire through me, and I arched toward his luscious mouth. I felt him smile against the skin on my neck, and his tongue slid out—licking and exploring my jawline and my earlobe. Every feeling was so intense, as if my nerves had doubled, and my brain struggled to keep up with the delicious torture from the lightest touches. He dropped kisses on my cheeks, forehead, eyelids and chin before my need urged me to yank his mouth to mine and plunder it thoroughly.

The slickness of his tongue tangling with mine sent heat spiraling straight to my core. My nipples tightened, and I felt painful pressure in my gums as fangs lengthened in my mouth. I pulled back, my hands flying to my teeth. Rafael and Laszlo had two sets of fangs, more than other turned vampires, but I had…*Mon Dieu.* All my teeth had become fangs. Embarrassment and confusion battled against my lust, but Rafael dropped back on the bed as if he had all the time in the world. Perhaps we did.

"It's all right, my darling," he said, stroking one firm hand up my arm. "That's perfectly normal. It will take you some time to get used to them. Do not fear them and do not be ashamed of them. Every vampire's fangs are different. Yours are beautiful—dangerous and lethal. Impossibly erotic."

I nodded, running my tongue across the sharp points. His red pupils flared with the movement, and he crawled forward again, predatory and excited.

"Would you like to continue? Or would you prefer we waited until you've had more time to adjust to your new form?"

I didn't even pause to consider the question. I offered an encouraging smile and beckoned him closer. When he'd wrapped me in his arms again, I rolled him over and pinned his hands above his head, emboldened by the way he'd looked at me with my new, disconcerting teeth. For the first time ever, I had no trouble pinning him to the bed. My strength matched —and possibly surpassed—his own. The thrill in his eyes and the wild grin on his lips was a heady rush of power, and I found myself drinking it in greedily.

I slid my hands down his pale, muscled chest, tickling the soft, dark hair beneath his belly button and nestling his hard cock. I leaned down to twirl my tongue around his nipples and loved every muscle in his stomach that tightened, every harsh breath he sucked in, every filthy word he hissed when I trailed my lips and tongue and claws lower.

When I wrapped my fingers around his impressive length, he bowed off the bed and snarled at me.

"Mina," he groaned. "Please."

Tentatively, I licked the smooth skin underneath. A litany of words in a language I didn't recognize exploded from him in a bestial growl. I couldn't help but chuckle, reveling in this newfound sense of power and control.

"I wonder how much you held back from me because you were afraid of damaging my human body," I said idly, taking him into my mouth completely. I sucked gently, swirling my tongue from the base of him to the salty tip. He almost came up off the bed, but I pushed him back down.

"Gods above, please," he growled. "You are killing me. I need you, Mina."

"Did you?" I asked, encircling him with my hands.

"Yes," he almost sobbed. "I had to. I couldn't—I didn't want to hurt you."

"Hm," I replied, curiosity peaked. I released him and straddled his hips, positioning my ready heat above him. His gaze flew to mine, his fangs glinting in the candlelight. I'd seen him in the throes of passion before, but never like this—he was a wild animal straining at the end of a tether. It would only take one word to set him free.

"Don't," I said, surprised at the tone of command in my voice. "Don't hold back this time."

The leash snapped—the beast was free. He grabbed my hips, sliding his thumbs forward to gently part my sex and dip his fingers in the wetness between my legs. He slipped one finger to the apex of my pleasure. I tilted my head back and moaned in satisfaction, and the sound made him feral.

He thrust up into me, filling me, fitting like something that had been missing for a long time. We stilled for a moment, and then he began moving, slowly at first, then faster and harder as he lost himself in the primal pleasure of it. As the heat at my core spun out through my body, Rafael pushed me back down on the bed, rolling me to my side. His hands found my breasts, and he pinched my nipples, then snaked one hand back down to rub tight circles on the bud of pleasure that threatened to ignite my entire body. Faster his fingers worked, harder and harder he thrust, until all the years of longing and need and hope and love condensed into one perfect moment of absolute, earth-shattering joy, and I came apart around him. He was quick to follow me over the precipice, growling an animal *"Mine!"* as he sank his fangs into my neck and shuddered with release.

I collapsed back against him, then turned around to offer him a satisfied kiss. The curious expression on his face made me pause.

"Mina, your eyes," he whispered. "They're silver."

"What?"

He reached toward the nightstand and pulled a small mirror from the drawer. Just as his eyes filled with black and red, mine appeared filled with silver, with glowing moonstone-colored pupils in the center.

"Interesting," I murmured. "I've never seen a transformation like this before."

"Nor I," he said. "They're beautiful, darling. They suit you."

"You haven't? Doesn't that worry you?" I asked, unease threading through me.

His dark chuckle vibrated through me as he pulled me against his naked body.

"No. Hours ago, my only worry was confronting eternity without you. Given what we know about Charlotte and Antoine's turning—how the plague changed with them—it does not surprise me that it would change again in you. You are the strongest person I know. Laszlo's blood is the most powerful supernatural blood on earth. You died with a Judas silver bullet in your heart. All these factors could explain why you are...*different.*"

"I shall have to perform some experiments," I said, feeling apprehensive.

Rafael kissed my forehead and I felt a wave of love pulse from him.

Hm, I could get used to this. Well, I supposed I'd have to. I nuzzled against Rafael's strong chest and wrapped my limbs around his body. A vague awareness of another presence alerted me of the incoming intrusion just before the knock sounded on the door.

"Why is it every time I get you in bed, the world outside beckons insistently?" he complained.

"Probably because the only time we make love is when we're facing earthly peril," I said wryly. "Perhaps you should work on the timing of your romantic overtures."

I stood somewhat unsteadily, my legs unused to their new strength and speed. I wobbled over to the chair where the blue silk dressing gown had been placed and shrugged it on. When I turned around, Rafael was already dressed in his customary crimson banyan with gold dragon embroidery.

"It's like watching a little fawn find its legs for the first time," he smirked. "Adorable."

I narrowed my eyes and stuck my tongue out at him like a petulant child.

He rushed to me with supernatural speed, pinning me against the wall. Caged between his arms, lust ignited in me again.

"Be careful with that tongue, goddess," he growled through lengthening fangs. "I have plans for it later."

I laughed and pushed past him, making my way to the door. I felt the tug of a ghostly thread of connection and knew exactly who was standing on the other side of the door.

"Laszlo," I greeted, offering him a small smile.

He looked much recovered after being kept in The Order's dungeon. He had obviously found rest, nourishment, and a bath—his hollow cheeks had filled in some, and his lips had a touch of color. His long black hair hung down his back in a thick braid and he wore a bright green banyan with a gold dragon, similar to Rafael's. Now that he was free from the horror and filth of his dim cell, it was easy to see the similarities between the brothers. They shared the same aquiline nose, the same faintly almond-shaped eyes, and the same shaped lips. But where Rafael's eyes were almost black, Laszlo's were a warmer brown with delicate rings of green in his irises.

He bowed formally, and I waved the gesture away. I opened the door and waited for him to enter. Rafael frowned and sat in a plush chair next to the fireplace.

"Come in. I know we have much to discuss," I said.

His gaze flicked to Rafael.

"Would you prefer we were alone?" I asked.

"Absolutely not, Mina," Rafael said. "The last time I left the two of you together, things didn't end very well for you. I'm staying."

Laszlo winced slightly but nodded.

"As you wish, brother," he said. His voice was warm and rich, unlike the despondent roughness from the previous evening. He walked to the fireplace and sat in the chair next to Rafael, leaving me the remaining seat on his left. Before sitting down, I picked up the glass of blood from the nightstand and drank deeply. My new, vicious thirst was somewhat mollified.

"Can I offer you some refreshment?" I asked.

"I would be honored," he said.

"Thank you for granting my request," I said quietly, handing him a glass. "For turning me. I know you are forbidden from turning anyone who isn't your mate, and I want you to know the sacrifice is not lost on me."

Rafael was silent, assessing us.

"I have wanted to turn others," Laszlo admitted, swirling the dark red liquid in his glass. "Marguerite is not the first woman I've loved. I've lived lifetimes longer than even Rafael, and no matter what they say, it never gets easier to watch the humans in your life wither and die. But I've never broken that rule. I have never turned anyone except for her. And I did so out of sheer desperation." His eyes cut to Rafael, the silent question on his face.

Rafael shook his head. "Never. I kill and drain when necessary, but I have never turned another. I would have turned Mina had she asked."

The edge in his voice drew my attention, but there was no animosity in his expression.

Laszlo tilted his head to regard me.

"I knew you were something special, Doctor—even before I offered you the choice. You spent your entire human life trying to help my kind and solve problems that were not yours. You atoned for mistakes you never made. You speak of my sacrifice, but it is you who has lived as a martyr to our curse." He drained the glass and stood to place the empty crystal on the mantel. "And make no mistake—it *is* a curse. You will have Rafael to coax your happiness through eternity, but you must be prepared for the loneliness of time."

"All of my friends have been turned," I replied. "I felt more lonesome as the last lingering human in our group. It grieved me to think of aging while they remained trapped in amber—looking down on my slow decay with pity."

Laszlo shook his head slowly. "I speak not of company, though that is part of it. When you have been alive for hundreds and hundreds of years, young one—only then will you understand. You will see the world change in ways you are not prepared for. It is a sad thing to look around you and feel as ancient as naught but the mountains. The older you get, the harder it becomes to...*understand* people, places, things. You become a living relic —ancient and sacred. Something meant to be enshrined in a tomb, not walking around, witnessing the relentless march of days."

I was stunned, overcome by the gravity of his words.

"I pray you retain this zeal you have for life, Doctor. This passion! Do anything—*anything*—to keep it. Do not fall victim to the melancholy of millennia when you cease to feel rapture at the miracles of the world. The growth of a tree. The birth of a human baby. The moon and the tides. The true curse we bear is not that we must live like parasites, surviving on the blood of others. The curse is that we must exist with more loneliness than anyone can bear over countless lifetimes."

I nodded, my emotions caught in my throat.

"You had gifts before you were turned, Doctor: kindness, intelligence, compassion, strength, loyalty. These gifts are better than anything you could have gained from your turning—though I suspect those will reveal themselves to you in time. Respect the rules of our curse. Honor your gifts. And do not forget to keep the candle of your humanity lit."

He came to stand before me, then kneeled to take my hands in his. The smile on his face was small and heartbreakingly sad. I wondered if he'd had a full smile since the death of his daughter.

"You will do many great things. Trust in yourself. Trust your instincts. Let the blood tell you what it wants you to know. I have the utmost faith in you, Doctor Wilhelmina Van Helsing."

I blinked back tears—the same strange silver ones that I'd cried before.

"Marguerite is recovering," he said, turning to Rafael. "We thank you for your hospitality, brother. I know you have no reason to offer it. We will not stay here overlong."

The shadow of disappointment crossed Rafael's face, but he lifted a shoulder in forced nonchalance.

"You will do as you please," he said. "But we should all agree upon what needs to be done about The Order. If everyone is feeling up to it, I will have sustenance brought to the greenhouse and we can discuss the matter there."

Laszlo's brows hitched up. "The greenhouse?"

If Rafael had been capable of blushing, he would have been as red as a beet.

"Yes, I...well, I'd like to show it to you. I think you'd appreciate it," he stammered. The boyish need for approval from his big brother made him seem so human, the sweetness of it almost shattered me.

Laszlo nodded appreciatively.

"I am certain I would," he said, walking back to the door. "I'll rouse Marguerite and we'll await your summons."

Rafael threw me a glare as his older brother closed the door behind him, but I flung myself at him before he could deny his embarrassment.

23

MINA

April 28, 1768
Château du Diable

I WAS COMFORTED TO SEE EVERYONE RECOVERED WHEN WE GATHERED IN FRONT of the greenhouse. The mood was subdued, but there was a palpable sense of relief. Étienne had given me a brotherly once-over, checking to make sure the gaping wound in my chest and my savaged throat had completely healed. Once he was satisfied, he began telling me all the best places to get good blood—even *virgin* blood—which I knew had peculiar healing properties. Antoine, for his part, materialized before me and threw his arms around me for quite possibly the most unexpected embrace of my life. Even Charlotte looked at him as if he'd grown a second head for a moment, then some understanding seemed to dawn on her, and she patted his back gently.

"I'm glad you're alive. Er, undead," he said. "I was—am—unprepared to lose another…friend."

Charlotte had told me about the loss of his sister and nephew—it had been one of the things that set their love story in motion.

"Thank you, Antoine," I said, touched by his admission. I'd wanted siblings when I was a child, and it seemed that now, throughout every-thing we'd endured together, I'd found them.

"Yes, yes, we're all glad Mina isn't worm food," Charlotte scoffed. "Darling, have you tested out your abilities yet? Can you change shape? Do you subsist on blood, or meat, as well? Can you fly like Rafael?"

"I don't know," I admitted. "I am becoming aware of some gifts. Others feel…possible, but I haven't tested anything yet."

"Yes, well, you have time," Rafael encouraged.

"Perhaps," Daphne said, warning in her tone. "The Order will strike again, hard and fast. We need to come up with a new plan."

Charlotte suddenly noticed the carved wooden door in front of us and the beautiful reliefs of Hades and Persephone.

"Rafael," she said, intrigued. "Is that…Mina?" Now that she said it, the resemblance was impossible not to notice.

He coughed.

"I don't believe it!" she shrieked, laughing. "Honestly, Mina, it's so romantic I could die all over again. Antoine, my love, why haven't *you* ever had a door carved with my likeness as a goddess?"

Rafael covered a smirk and opened the doors, once again revealing the exquisite underground greenhouse. The gasps and whispers of appreciation added a little bounce to his step, and I was glad for my friends—as mismatched as we were.

In the back of the greenhouse, tucked beneath several massive tropical trees, sat a large circular table. It had been set with pitchers of blood for the vampires and dishes of raw meat for Charlotte and Antoine. The sun had only just set, and the warm sherbet of the sky cast the entire space in a delicate pink and purple glow. Two maids set about lighting candles and torches along the walls. We all sat down around the table for our bizarre little dinner party.

Rafael offered me a glass of blood, but Charlotte's raw steak smelled equally enticing. I reached out to pluck a cube of meat from her plate and sampled it—*heavenly.* She raised a brow at me, and I shrugged. Yet another new trait for me to log.

Daphne downed her glass and stood.

"As I said, they will come for us again. They will not stop, but they will not be stupid, either. The way I see it, we have two choices. We can eliminate the threat or try to turn the king against them. He's the only person with power over them," she said.

Laszlo chuckled. "With the greatest respect, Duchesse, The Order has existed in some form long before your king. They will spring up again whether he agrees with their politics or methods—or not."

"I agree," Rafael said. "Laszlo and I have left them alone for long enough, and they came for both of us. They came through all of you to get to us. It is time for them to understand who they're dealing with."

"Does that mean impaling?" Charlotte whispered to Marguerite.

Marguerite paled and scooted closer to Laszlo.

"The Draculs are right," said Antoine. "I never wish for violence, but we cannot risk them coming for any of us again."

"Mina, your judgment has weight here," Étienne said over the low din of conversation. "Laszlo and Marguerite suffered terribly at their hands, but your human life was effectively ended by their cruelty."

Charlotte turned to me. "Darling, I know you didn't want to get involved with them before. I know you never trusted them. But I also know how you feel about killing. If you wish for us to find another path, I will stand with you."

All seven sets of eyes fell upon me, but for once, the weight of expectation didn't feel like an impossibly heavy yoke around my neck. Charlotte was right—I didn't want the killing. I wanted humans to have as much of a chance at life as vampires did. I feared a future with Rafael and me on the run—like Laszlo and Marguerite. I didn't want to hide away from the world, constantly looking over my shoulder for threats. I considered the people around this table—the pain The Order had caused them, directly and indirectly. I wanted futures for my friends as much as I wanted my own. I knew what my answer would be.

"It should be swift. Quick, clean kills. If we are to do this, it must be thorough—we must find everyone in their network. We should act when they are all together, otherwise word could travel and some of them might slink off to hide away in their little holes," I said decisively.

Daphne's eyes widened in surprise, but Charlotte grinned fiercely and patted my hand.

"Fortunately, *mes amis*, I happen to know exactly when that will be," Charlotte said.

OVER THE NEXT FEW WEEKS, WE REMAINED AT RAFAEL'S HOME, FALLING INTO A kind of routine. Daphne, Rafael, Antoine, Marguerite, and Étienne began to sketch out a rough plan, while I worked with Charlotte and Laszlo in the evenings to connect with my new supernatural gifts. Laszlo helped me learn the basics of blocking out or shielding the persistent mental connection to others and taught me ways to focus that strength to mesmerize and control. The idea of controlling another person turned my stomach, but he said it was important for me to learn both the reach and limitations of my power.

Rafael *did* enjoy when we retired, and he allowed me to bend his mind to my will. Actually, we'd both enjoyed that rather thoroughly.

As the May days marched on and the nights warmed up, finally shaking off the long, cold spring thaw, we drew nearer to the evening we'd planned for our final mission with The Order. The mood in the house was thick with tension.

One evening, to escape Daphne's incessant pacing and Antoine's worrisome brooding, Charlotte and I went outside to the grounds above the castle for a bit of fresh air. We wandered through the secluded forest nearby and when we came to the edge of a clearing, she shucked her gown and tossed it to the side.

"Now," she began. "The key to shifting forms is to find that place within yourself. It is your inner animal—your inner beast. You must call it forth. Allow your human shape to fall away. Do not fear the pain. It is uncomfortable, but brief."

With that, she shifted into her wolf form, exploding in a blur of skin and fur and bones. When she was done, she tilted her head back for an unearthly, horrific howl. Then, she sat on her haunches and watched me expectantly.

"I don't think I have an inner beast," I said.

Charlotte growled and laid down.

You do too. Now, hurry up—I want to go for a run.

The benefit to my mental connection was being able to communicate with her when she was unable to speak.

"Very well," I agreed, laughing. "I'll summon forth my animal self—if only for the sake of science."

I closed my eyes. I stilled my thoughts, allowing the rise and fall of my breath to calm the ever-present power simmering beneath my skin. I thought about werewolves and bats and demons—everything I'd seen in my work with supernatural creatures. I turned inward and searched. The deeper I went, the darker things became, as if I'd stepped into Rafael's Underworld and found myself amongst the monsters. There, at the edge of my consciousness, knelt something...*primal*. I reached for it, stroked it, and imagined picking it up and throwing it over my shoulders like a cloak.

Pain exploded in my body. Wrenching, scraping, splitting, breaking, burning pain, and then just as suddenly as it started, it stopped. I stood, uncertain of what to expect. When I opened my eyes, the first thing I saw was Charlotte cowering, tail tucked between her legs.

Mina? She tentatively pushed against my consciousness.

That was incredibly unpleasant, I answered.

I looked down at my limbs and suddenly understood her fear. I hadn't shifted into a wolf or a small bat—I'd shifted into the eight-foot-tall bat demon that Laszlo had turned into when he bit me. But that meant...

Yes! I rolled my shoulder muscles and felt them—massive leathery wings. I flexed them tentatively and spread them open, then took an experimental leap from the ground. I soared through the air.

Stop showing off, Charlotte challenged. *Is that all you can do?*

I landed back on the ground with a thud. Stilling my mind again, reaching for that inner place, I shifted once more. This time, the pain wasn't quite so bad, but I heard myself howling when the transformation finished.

That's more like it, Charlotte said, wagging her tail. I looked down and beheld giant paws tipped with long claws—a wolf form.

Hold on, I bid her. *I want to try one more thing.*

This time, when I centered myself, I went back to my inner darkness. I let go of my thoughts and expectations, focusing instead on that raw, primal power. As I neared it, I could sense the pulse of it; ancient, dark, patient. I extended my thoughts to it and let it take root.

No pain this time. Simply...*quiet.* I lost track of my physical sensations. When I came to my outer awareness again, Charlotte was calling for me.

Mina! Where have you gone?

I am here, I answered.

She turned to me, trying to track my scent on the wind.

What are you? she asked.

I don't know, I replied. I saw the grass below me and drifted low to the ground. As I neared it, the grass began to wilt away, recoiling into the soil. All that was left behind was a faint silver sheen. Charlotte noticed and whined.

I can see you—faintly. Like a soft, silver cloud, she said. *But I don't know what you are. It's wreaking havoc on my lupine senses.*

I stared at the fallow ground that I'd touched.

Charlotte, I think—I think I am Death.

HOURS LATER, WE RETURNED TO OUR ROOMS JUST AS THE SUN WAS RISING. I'd told my companions about my strange new abilities, anxiously waiting for fear and disgust. Instead, they comforted me and offered me blood and raw meat to restore my depleted strength.

"It must be from the Judas silver," Rafael said. "It would explain the eyes, the tears... Brother, have you ever seen anything like this? Or heard of it happening?"

Laszlo shook his head. "Rafael and I can turn into mist, but it's just that—mist. Closer to weather than anything else."

Étienne chuckled. "Simply marvelous. The only one of us that has a real problem killing anything has become the embodiment of Death. I suppose that's one way Fate will stop you from taking advantage of these *gifts*, Mina."

"You know," Daphne hedged. "This does present us with an opportunity. Of course, it's probably too dangerous to even consider given how little we know about this ability."

I knew exactly what she was about to say—I'd considered it myself.

"I'll do it," I said.

"Do what?" Rafael asked, concern in his tone. "What are you talking about?"

"I'll go into the mausoleum alone," I said. "If The Order are all assembled, I can eliminate them with one fell swoop. None of you need to risk putting yourselves in jeopardy again, given how we know the Judas silver affects you."

"Absolutely not!" Rafael insisted, rising from his chair. "We have no idea what will happen if you try this on humans, and we know even less about how you will react to the Judas silver door when you're down there. If the worst happens in either instance, you will be down there *alone* and at their mercy. And I think we all know just how *merciful* The Order can be. I'm sorry, Mina, but you've already died once at their hands—I will not let that happen again."

"Rafael's right," Charlotte added, placing her hand on my arm. "It's too dangerous."

"I appreciate your concern," I said. "But it's my decision to make."

"Mina, please," Rafael beseeched. The pleading in his tone shook the foundations of my resolve, but I knew what I had to do to keep my friends safe. What I had the power to do.

"If it makes you feel better, you can come with me and wait outside in the cemetery," I offered. "If something goes awry, you can swoop in and rip out as many throats as you like. As it stands, I am the only one who can go in alone and do what needs to be done."

"You don't know that," Rafael argued.

"The bullet," Antoine said suddenly. "Laszlo, what happened to the bullet from Mina's chest?"

"I ripped it from her and threw it on the ground in the woods," he said. "I wasn't sure if she would be able to turn with it lodged in her heart."

"What if we retrieved it?" Antoine asked. "And used it to see if the Judas silver affected her as it does the rest of us?"

"It's not a bad idea," Daphne agreed. "Mina, Rafael, what say you? If we manage to find the bullet and it doesn't affect Mina's abilities to shift, then she goes in alone. We will be there, of course, right outside in case something goes wrong."

"No," Rafael said firmly.

"Yes," I agreed. "Rafael, you must give me a chance. Just once, let me be the one to protect you. Almost all my life I've been surrounded by powerful, supernatural beings and I've always been the weak one—the one to watch out for, to keep an eye on. Now that things are different, let me try to be the strong one for a change."

"You have *always* been the strong one," Rafael insisted, but I heard an undertone of defeat in his voice. "But I know you, Mina, and I know how fruitless it is to try and stand in your way when your mind is made up. I will stand by your decision, even if I do not like it—or agree with it."

I squeezed his hand. "Thank you."

"It's daylight now, but as soon as the sun goes down, we'll send someone to retrieve the bullet," Daphne said.

"I'll go," Marguerite volunteered. "I know where we were in the woods when the doctor was turned. Besides, it was mine and Laszlo's actions that brought us to this place—we are far in your debt."

Daphne nodded. "Very well. We could use a report, as well, to see if anything has changed around The Order's headquarters over the last few weeks. You will not go alone, Marguerite. Étienne will go with you."

Étienne grinned at her and saluted.

"Good. Well, I'm sure we're all exhausted. Let's adjourn for the morning and get some rest," Charlotte suggested.

I blew out a breath. My explorations with my abilities had sapped both my physical and mental strength, and by the time Rafael and I made our way to his bedchamber, I was nearly asleep on my feet. Blessedly, he helped me undress, slipped a clean chemise over my head and tucked me into bed.

I watched as he pulled his shirt and breeches off and slipped into bed naked. The crease in his brow and the tight set of his mouth was enough for me to roll over and lay my hand on his chest.

"Do not be cross with me, Rafael," I said.

"I'm not cross," he argued. "I'm worried."

"You are both," I replied. "Would you love me as much if I were simpering and biddable?"

He wrapped strong arms around me and pulled me into his embrace.

"I would love you in every way, in every world, in every afterlife," he sighed. "But that doesn't mean it is easy for me to let you walk into danger."

I yawned and his hands drifted to my low back, caressing and stroking.

"I understand," I said. "But you will be there. You can always save me if things start to go awry."

He chuckled and the sound hummed through my very bones. The sensation soothed me deeper into sleep, and I almost missed his final words as I drifted off.

"Mina, you've never needed me to save you, but I will always be there to try, anyway."

24

RAFAEL

May 20, 1768
Château du Diable

I woke some hours later with Mina's lush, shapely ass cradling my insistent erection. As much as I wanted her—needed to feel that connection between us—she needed sleep. She was still learning what her new abilities demanded from her body. I thought back to my youth, when my abilities had begun to manifest and stifled a laugh. What a terror I'd been.

Mina shifted back against me, and I tensed, desire building in my body.

No, I chided myself. *Let her rest.*

She sighed in her sleep and arched against me, lightly rubbing her breasts against my arm. I fought against the onslaught of wild heat that raged in me, desperate to think of anything but burying myself in her and claiming her again. *Mine. After everything, she is mine.* She moved again, her soft skin pressing against the hard ridge of my cock, and when I bit back a groan, I heard a soft explosion of laughter.

"Torturous minx," I growled. "How long have you been awake?"

"Long enough to enjoy a little torment," she chuckled, rolling over to face me. She leaned forward and captured my mouth in a passionate kiss, sucking my lower lip between her fangs. The friction was like a jolt of lightning.

I moaned into her mouth and reached between her legs, slipping one finger through her wet heat. I shuddered when her hand snaked down to encircle me, then she angled her hips to slide me inside of her.

I swore—ready to die from the perfection of it. Of her. Of us together. I pushed myself up over her, nudging her legs apart and thrusting into her again. Her soft moans grew louder, and I wondered if I'd ever heard anything so beautiful.

"No matter what happens," she said, wrapping her legs around my waist to grant me deeper access. "I will always be yours, Rafael. You will always be mine."

"Mine," I grunted, already so close to release. I reached down between our legs to stroke that sensitive spot above our joining. She bowed up off the bed and I seized the opportunity to bend down and capture her right nipple in my mouth. When I gently sucked and then grazed the underside of her breast with my fangs, I felt her pleasure draw up and shatter, and she screamed as she came apart. I followed her over the edge, thrusting into her, swearing against gods and demons alike that I would destroy anything that challenged me for her.

"I love you," she whispered, placing a hand against my cheek.

I touched my forehead to hers and kissed her again, softly. As if I could bottle this moment and cherish it forever.

"I love you," I replied. "I have always loved you, Mina. I will die loving you."

She smiled at that. "Hopefully not too soon."

I chuckled, drawing her into my arms again.

A few moments later, there was a soft knock on the door.

"My lord," Guillaume said from the hall. "The lady Marguerite and the emissary have returned."

That familiar pit of worry opened inside me again, but I told him we would join them shortly.

"We should go," Mina said, rising to dress. "I'm anxious to have this done with."

I nodded, unsure of what to say. I'd had some of her clothes brought into my wardrobe, and I watched as she adeptly laced her stays, tied on her skirts, and pinned her bodice in place. The gown she'd selected was one of my favorites—an ethereally soft midnight blue velvet, embroidered with stars in glittering silver thread.

She caught me staring as I stumbled into my black shirt and breeches.

"Fitting for the queen of the underworld, no?" she teased.

I grinned. "I shall endeavor to be worthy of you, Your Highness."

We finished dressing and made our way to my laboratory, where I'd told everyone to gather. I had enough equipment here to allow Mina to test whatever she wished and had several supernatural remedies on hand, just in case.

Charlotte lifted a brow as we entered.

"I do hope you're taking some time to actually *rest*," she said. "Though by the look of things, I'm not so sure about that."

Étienne laughed. "I'm sure we all remember what our early days after turning are like. Once you recover and grow accustomed to things, then the *hunger* sets in—in more ways than one." He winked, and Daphne rolled her eyes.

Laszlo and Marguerite entered, clutching a small lead box. Marguerite placed it onto the main worktable in the center of the room and grimaced.

"It was where we expected to find it," she said. "Nothing seems different about the area itself, but as we made our way back, we overheard a couple of vampire guards keeping watch over the cemetery."

"Were you seen?" I demanded.

Étienne laughed again. "How insulting! I may not be as old as you, but have some respect for me compared to a couple of freshly turned mercenaries. We were all but invisible to them."

"What did you hear from the guards?" Charlotte asked.

"Our homes are being watched. The Order has been hunting the agents of *les DD* that they know of, but it sounds like your warning letters arrived in time and they've all gone to ground. With no one to question and none of their leads playing out, they are forced to sit and wait for us to make our move," Étienne replied.

"They will be waiting for us," Marguerite said, a warning in her tone.

"What do they know of Mina?" Daphne asked.

Marguerite shook her head. "Nothing. When The Order arrived back at the mausoleum that night, they discovered Laszlo's and my cell empty and Derais's blood in the woods. They believe we turned on Derais and fled with Rafael, but they don't know anything about Mina. They are watching her clinic, but they don't know the extent of her involvement."

"Good," Mina said. "That will at least give me the element of surprise."

We all stared as she reached forward to pick up the box. When she opened it, everyone took an involuntary step back—the poisonous feeling of the Judas silver bullet repulsed us all.

All but Mina.

She tipped the bullet into her hand and stroked it, then held it up to her face to get a better look.

Antoine paled, and Charlotte clapped a hand over her mouth.

"What do you feel?" I asked, my voice a breath above a whisper.

Mina stared at the lump of silver in her palm, warped where it had met her vital human organs. She narrowed her eyes and glared at it, and we all watched in astonishment as the ball began to melt into a puddle of liquid metal in her bare hand.

"I feel—*kinship*," she replied in a strange voice. The silver liquid pulsed and flexed, moving around her hand as she willed it with some secret power. She closed her eyes, and then the silver was absorbed into her skin. When she opened her eyes, they were that same silver with moonstone-colored pupils. She smiled—but of all the ways I'd seen Mina smile, I'd never seen her look like this.

"I'm ready," she said, her voice sounding distant and ethereal.

Daphne raised her brows and cleared her throat. I would have sworn I heard a tremor of fear in her voice, but I might have imagined it. "Well, we have a few things left to do," she hedged. "Charlotte, let's send our messages to the remaining agents of *les DD*. Étienne, you send word to our staff and Charlotte's that they're not to return to our homes over the next few days—we don't know what will happen, and I don't want any of them getting caught up in The Order's collateral damage if something goes wrong."

"Send your messages," Mina said in that strange, otherworldly voice. "But The Order convenes tonight, does it not?"

"Yes, but we weren't planning on going in until they meet next week," Charlotte said, staring at Mina with a mixture of admiration and horror.

"I will go tonight," Mina said.

Daphne and Charlotte exchanged a look.

"If you're certain…" Daphne began.

"Yes," Mina replied. "Come on horseback, or in a carriage, if you wish. I'm going to fly."

She turned to me, her strange silver eyes glittering in the low light of the laboratory. She smiled again, but this time it was closer to a true Mina smile. She closed her eyes for a moment, and then when she opened them, her eyes were back to their normal sapphire blue.

"Care to join me?" she asked, as if nothing bizarre had happened.

"You must be joking," I replied—too unsteadily. "What the Hell was that?"

"I'm not entirely sure," she said. "But I don't feel any ill effects from the silver."

"Mina…" I began, but she held up a hand to stay me.

"Rafael, yes. You and I will run a barrage of experiments on my abilities when this is over. However, we face a more pressing threat. I'm going to deal with that first. Are you coming?"

The silence that fell over our companions was tense, as if everything hinged upon my ability to allow Mina to lead us into battle. *Mina, my*

Mina. The one person I'd fought so hard to protect, and the one person who needed my protection the least—even before she'd been turned into a supernatural creature with god-like powers. *Goddess.* I sighed, swallowing the shredded remains of my pride, and inclined my head.

"Lead the way, Persephone."

W E STOOD AT THE CRUMBLING EDGE OF THE HIGH TOWER, FACING SOUTHEAST toward Paris. Charlotte and Antoine prepared to shift, tying their clothes in a bundle around their shoulders. Daphne, Marguerite, and Étienne would be on horseback, which was less conspicuous than a carriage, but would also save their energy from having to run the distance. Laszlo, Mina, and I would fly.

The sun had set, turning the night sky the same soft midnight blue as Mina's gown. As Laszlo and I began to disrobe prior to shifting, she eyed us anxiously.

"I'd hate for you to ruin that gown when you look so fetching in it," I purred, hoping to ease some of her nerves. "Laszlo will turn around, so you needn't worry about him."

For once, my brother's raspy chuckle split the silence.

"As lovely as you are, Doctor, trust that I only have eyes for my beloved Marguerite." He bundled his clothes and tied them to his waist, then turned to face the opposite direction.

Satisfied, Mina undressed in haste. When she was down to her stays, I stepped over to help her unlace them.

"Everything is going to be okay," I said in her ear. "We'll all be there together. Trust your instincts. They've served you well thus far."

She nodded, then twisted back to give me a perfunctory kiss on the lips.

Fear and anxiety fought to take hold, but I refused to let Mina sense them from me. As much as I hated to stand aside and let her take on The Order alone, I knew she could do it.

"Ready?" I asked when she'd finished undressing.

She offered a tight smile.

"As I'll ever be."

MINA

When the pain of the transformation ebbed, I looked around. The sight of two massive, hellish wolf creatures and two—no, *three*—enormous bat demons would have shocked even the most unshakeable person. A bubble of manic laughter burst in my chest, coming out as a warped growl from behind my fangs.

The Judas silver pulsed in my blood, whispering to me to do terrible things. *Betray. Punish. Kill.* When I'd first encountered it inside Rafael's laboratory, I'd sensed it immediately. It wasn't repellant to me as it was to the others. Rather, it seemed to call to me...coaxing, enticing, seducing. I could feel it sliding through my body along my muscles and bones, tempting me to unleash power I'd only recently become acquainted with. *Very well.* I would use it. I would let it feed me to bring down The Order— to help me ensure they would be stopped from their dangerous campaign against the sufferers of the blood plague. And then, I would purge the haunting silver power from my body and bury it in a place where no one could find it again.

I stretched out my wings and kicked off the ground, soaring high into the night sky. The air cooled as I ascended, and the wind buffeted me mercilessly until I found a warm air current that propelled me forward. I felt Laszlo and Rafael at my sides as we careened over the treetops, and I allowed myself a few moments of joy at the novelty of this new feat. I was flying! Despite the strange and sometimes uncomfortable feelings my new abilities gave me, this felt like a true miracle.

As I sped on, I saw the distant shapes of Charlotte and Antoine below me, running all out through the woods. Daphne, Marguerite, and Étienne were on their heels, their horses kicking up a fine mist of soft earth and gravel in their wake. We traveled faster than I'd ever believed possible, spurred on by our collective desire to protect ourselves, our friends. Our people.

When the suburbs outside Paris came into view and we closed in on the little forgotten cemetery, my stomach clenched at the thought of what I was about to do—what I was prepared to do. I'd never willingly ended a life before, and here I was, cozying up to the idea of taking out two dozen men. I considered the fact that they believed they were doing what was right for the people of France, that many of them had families, that not all of them were perhaps...*evil.* Knowing these things, doubt rooted in my gut, despite the hissing, brutal encouragements from the Judas silver slithering between my nerves.

We touched down in the small, wooded area just outside the cemetery. My heart pounded with the memories of running from Laszlo and Derais —the pain and fear of my death and turning. Within minutes, Charlotte and Antoine arrived at our chosen rendezvous and split off to survey the area around the cemetery, looking for threats. Daphne, Étienne, and Marguerite raced in and dismounted, then tied their exhausted horses to a nearby tree.

Rafael, Laszlo, and I dressed in silence as I reached out to Charlotte. Our mental connection had proven the strongest—aside from mine with Rafael—and it was easy for us to communicate without me having to break through mental barriers to read her mind. She sent me a comforting wave of reassurance.

I turned to Rafael. His beautiful face was impassive, but I could see the angst sparking in his eyes. Without a word, I pressed my lips to his, infusing the kiss with as much love as I dared. I needed him to understand that I would come back to him…that I would always come back to him. This wasn't goodbye.

Taking one final breath of resolve, I smoothed my hands down my lovely midnight gown and walked into the cemetery. Behind me and around me, I felt gentle brushes of strength, hope, and gratitude. It helped to settle my stomach and calm my raging nerves. It temporarily tamed the vicious bloodlust the Judas silver inspired.

When I reached the mausoleum, I paused at the door and listened. Beneath me, I heard muted voices arguing, snarling, deriding each other. The men of The Order were here, convening below. As I opened the heavy door to descend into the tomb, a wave of surprised rage emanated from the forest.

It seemed The Order's vampire mercenary guards had shown up. Before I could drop my hand from the door and turn to help, Rafael sent a pulse of reassurance to me.

We will be fine. Go, my love. Finish this.

In the distance, I heard a horrifying, unearthly scream, followed by a wet, crunching sound, and then eerie silence. More screams, then—but not from Rafael or my friends.

Another wave of ease, this time from Charlotte.

All is well. Go, Mina! We have your back.

I rolled my shoulders, threw open the door, and descended into the black maw of the tomb.

25

MINA

May 20, 1768
Cimetière des Innocents

I walked down the stairs, listening for clear threads of the conversation from the members below.

"No sign of them! How can that be? They cannot have fallen off the face of the earth!"

"Unbelievable. If His Majesty would only allow us more resources, we'd be able to cast a wider net and broaden our search."

"His Majesty doesn't *officially* endorse anything we do, and I doubt he would condone the hunt of one of his cousins."

"It's not my incompetence that led us here. Whose idea was it to allow the women to join? I swear, they're more of a curse than the damn blood plague."

I considered shifting then but felt one last bubble of hope lift in my chest that maybe, *maybe*, there was another way.

When I reached the inner door at the end of the hallway, the silver in my veins vibrated with energy at the proximity to the silver inside the door. I willed it calm for the moment, then knocked firmly. The men on the other side stilled.

The door opened a fraction, and a man with salt and pepper hair and a black domino mask looked me over. Surprise and recognition lit in his brown eyes, and I thought I remembered him from the last ball I'd attended at Versailles, but I couldn't be sure. He waited expectantly—eyes wide.

"Good evening," I said. "I'm here to negotiate with you."

Laughter deepened the wrinkles around his forehead and mouth, and the hollow sound filled me with a white-hot stab of anger.

"Well, I suppose we should hear you out," he replied. "Do come in, Doctor."

I entered the room and beheld the disapproving sneers beneath two dozen domino masks. I'd seen more than a few of these men before and knew they kept their masks merely for the sake of tradition.

A second man approached and smiled, offering me a seat at the large round table in the middle of the room. Gradually, each man came to the table and sat down, at least indicating a willingness to listen. I considered that a positive sign.

"Gentlemen," I began. "You know me—you know who I am. I'm here to negotiate on behalf of a few individuals: the House of Dracul, the Comtesse de Brionne, Captain Antoine de Valle, the Vampire Emissary and his wife, the duchesse—"

"Yes," the second man interrupted. "We are aware of the identities your friends. Get to the point. What is it you're requesting, and what is it you're offering?"

"I'm requesting the full cessation of your campaign against the sufferers of the blood plague; the vampires. I'm requesting the protection of my friends and their families. And I'm requesting the absolute and total dissolution of the shadow dealings of The Order," I said in a cool, even tone. "For this, you will be allowed to leave here with your lives. You will be allowed to return to your families...and bask in the sunlight."

Laughter erupted around the table. I waited with waning patience for their response.

The second man spoke again.

"You cannot be serious," he replied.

"Respectfully, I am not known for my sense of humor," I shot back. "I'm afraid you must decide now. Renounce this foolish campaign and fight for peaceful coexistence or suffer the consequences of your actions."

The first man flicked his gaze to two younger men waiting against the walls. They moved toward the door, barring anyone from leaving—attempting to barricade me inside.

"*Respectfully,*" the man scoffed. "We are charged with protecting our king and our people. You come in here attempting to parlay with us to allow our country to fall under the ruin of some foreign bloodsucker? How utterly idiotic. You haven't even come with anything worth bartering—our *sanguisuge* dogs are outside right now, sniffing your lot out. They're armed with something very special, Doctor. Perhaps you've seen its effects on that wretched Dracul filth."

My heart pounded. I looked around the room, making eye contact with each of these self-righteous men. Gently, I pressed against their minds, hoping to find something…*anything*. A crack in their resolve. The faintest tendril of self-doubt. Willingness to change.

Despair took hold of me when I came up empty.

I stood from the table, and one of the men behind me moved away from the door to put his heavy hand on my shoulder, trying to force me back into my chair. I turned around, finding the man's gaze in the gloom.

"Do not touch me again," I warned.

Yes, hello, the silver whispered in my blood. *Have you come to threaten me?*

"We know more than you think, Van Helsing," the second man continued. "We know you're the younger Dracul's little whore. We know of your father's failure to find a cure for the disease. We know your hellcat friends are plotting to infiltrate and dismantle our Order from within. We have the weapons we need to take them out and end the line of bastard monsters in its entirety. God works through us, and we are fit to damn you all to the fires of Hell."

"I've never been a particularly religious woman," I answered. "But I do know there is no God here. You serve your own aims, and your actions are guided by fear and greed. It is not too late to change. Simply say the words, and I will spare you."

Again, riotous laughter filled the dark little space.

"I've heard enough of your madness," the man said, waving a hand in dismissal. "Take her below. At least we can use her as bait to trap that bastard Dracul and his filthy brother. Send out word to the bloodsuckers —we move against the homes of the comtesse and the duchesse tonight. Burn everything. No survivors."

The man at my back moved forward, reaching for my shoulder again.

My heartbeat drumming a war cry in my ears, I closed my eyes and let the silver take hold. Pain fractured my bones and flesh apart, but only for an instant. In one breath, I was sitting at the table, having a calmly insulting conversation. In the next breath, I was without form, a shapeless silver mist, driven by the need to protect. *Hunt. Kill.*

Amid the exclamations of surprise, I slid up my aggressor's extended arm…corrupting, breaking, poisoning. I watched as he screamed—a bloodcurdling sound—and collapsed to the ground as his heart sizzled in his chest. *Dead.* I went to the next man by the door, slithered down his open mouth, took root in his stomach and exploded outward in splinters of cursed silver.

Shrieks and terrified shouts echoed off the damp stone walls as I drifted through each man at the table, still searching for those dim threads of hope, still finding nothing but rage and hatred. The scent of scorched flesh and fresh blood and shredded skin permeated the room as I worked, ending life after life. At last, I came to the man who'd spoken so cruelly to me.

I shifted back to my human form, suddenly naked, but altogether uncaring.

"Holy Mary, Mother of God," the man screamed, falling to his knees in prayer. "Protect me with your divine mercy. Save me from this unclean spirit—this demon from Hell!"

"You know," I said, stepping forward to haul the man up by his throat. "I would have been happy as a simple vampire. I would have turned to be with the man I love. We would have lived together happily, working toward finding a cure. Hoping that in that time, hearts and minds would change. But it was you who changed everything. Your hatred and fear took on a life of its own, and because of that, Derais ended my human life. I died with a Judas silver bullet lodged in my heart and came back as what you see before you. Maybe you think I am an abomination—perhaps I am. But this…"

I summoned the Judas silver from my blood, and we watched as it pooled into the palm of my hand, rising through my skin.

"This was by your hand," I murmured. I squeezed my hand closed, pressing the silver into a small lump.

"Anything," the man whispered, tears running down his cheeks. "I will give you anything to let me live. Money. Power. Influence!"

I sighed, letting my mouth full of fangs lengthen.

"All I ever wanted was peace," I said forlornly. "But instead, you brought me war."

I sank my teeth into his throat, drinking until I felt his pulse still and his soul depart. Letting his body fall to the floor, I stepped back to survey the damage. The gory carnage turned my stomach, and I immediately retched. Numbly, I climbed back up the stairs, scanning the dark corridor for the faint glow of moonlight.

As I stepped onto the grassy earth outside of the mausoleum entrance, I fell to the ground. Heaving sobs wracked my body, and I screamed— agonized by the destruction I'd wrought. I was dimly aware of a pair of strong arms grabbing me, holding me steady, encircling me with faint waves of comfort, hope, love, gratitude.

Time ticked by, and I felt the individual presences of my friends—my family—standing close to me. Charlotte draped a soft woolen cloak over my shoulders and eventually, I peeled my face away from Rafael's damp shirt.

No one spoke.

"It is done," I muttered. "The Order is no more."

Daphne nodded, rubbing a hand down my back.

"I'm so sorry," she whispered. "I'm sorry for what you've endured."

"I will spend my eternity wondering if it was the right thing to do," I replied, my voice oddly calm.

"Oh, it was, darling, it was!" Charlotte insisted, throwing her arms around me. "You've done more for the people of France than all of us. And you've protected us all—you've done what none of us could have accomplished."

I looked up into her warm brown eyes, finally noticing the blood caked to her face. I whirled around, taking in the blood on *everyone*. Faces, hands, and clothes were shredded, bloody messes.

"I take it that was The Order's mercenary gang?" I asked.

Awkward silence descended, along with a tension I recognized as reluctance for them to tell me the truth. To avoid worrying me.

Antoine shuffled at the back.

"Not really much of a gang now," he rumbled. "Just a collection of spare parts."

Charlotte threw an exasperated look at him, but he simply shrugged.

"They came out of nowhere, really," she defended. "Caught us by surprise. And you know what they say about surprising a predator."

"I'm sorry I wasn't there," I replied. "I should have sensed them coming."

"You had more important things to do," Rafael said. "And we had it covered. You're not the only one with special gifts."

Étienne spat in the dirt behind Daphne.

"You weren't kidding, Rafael," he coughed. "Vampires taste *terrible*."

"I told you not to swallow," Laszlo said.

Suddenly, Charlotte erupted with laughter. For the briefest moment, everyone looked at her in horror.

"I'm so sorry—do forgive me. I know it's inappropriate, but that's simply the filthiest thing I've heard Laszlo say."

"I didn't mean it like *that*," he insisted.

Charlotte laughed even harder. Then, surprisingly, Marguerite joined in, covering a ladylike giggle with her blood-soaked hands. Étienne started up, and then Daphne, until everyone was in a collective bout of hysterics. Eventually, the absurdity of it hit me, and I joined in.

Rafael squeezed my hand, sending a wave of assurance through me.

When at last we recovered, I jerked my head back toward the mausoleum.

"I wanted to burn it," I said. "But I didn't know if there was anything down there that you thought was worth saving, Daphne."

She tilted her head for a moment, considering. "We can always come back for the Judas silver. As to the rest...I think it's time for a fresh start, wouldn't you say, Charlotte?"

"Oh, most definitely. Antoine, darling, you're so good with fire. Would you do the honors?" she asked, handing her mate a flint.

Antoine disappeared into the tomb for a few moments, and we heard the soft hiss and crackle of flames, followed by the acrid scent of smoke curling up from the mouth of the tomb. Antoine returned a minute later, looking a shade paler than before. He caught my eye and nodded—an acknowledgment of the devastation I'd wrought.

"For heaven's sake, I'm starving, and Daphne and I don't have any staff right now—we sent them all on holiday until we could get things sorted out with The Order. Rafael, darling, be a dear and have us over for a little longer, would you?" Charlotte asked, attempting to pin her wild brown curls back into her coiffure, and failing.

Rafael chuckled, the sound tugging at my scarred heart.

"What say you, Mina? Are you ready to go?" he asked.

Overcome with exhaustion, grief, and the sudden desire for an hours-long bath, I nodded.

"As I'll ever be. Take me home," I said, allowing him to help me to my feet.

We walked away from the mausoleum, pausing once to turn back as the flames expanded, licking the sides of the tomb. I was struck by the image—thinking it looked like the mouth of Hell. In some ways, I suppose it was.

Charlotte and Antoine shifted into their wolf forms and bounded off, followed by Daphne and Étienne on horseback. Laszlo opted to ride with Marguerite this time, so they set forth on a much slower course, leaving Rafael and me at the back.

"Are you well?" he asked.

"No." I shook my head. "But perhaps with time, I will be."

"I will be here with you. I will help you every step of the way," he said. "And now, at last, time is on our side."

I gazed up into his dark eyes, so full of hope and the promise of love for years to come, and for the first time in years, I felt like he was right.

I pulled him down for a tender kiss, and we prepared to shift together.

"Ready?" he asked, shooting me an encouraging smile.

I grinned back at him. A bit damaged, perhaps, but ready to begin healing—as we were, together.

"As I'll ever be."

EPILOGUE
MINA

October 31, 1768
Château du Diable

"For the life of me, I'll never understand why you didn't want a spring wedding," Charlotte opined, staring out the windows at the driving rain. "This weather is absolutely ghastly! It's one thing to have a nighttime wedding—I mean, obviously—but why not in the spring with all the flowers blooming? Or in the summer, when the temperature is more pleasant for all our human friends?"

"You'll see," I said with a smile. "It's a bit of a surprise. It was Rafael's idea, actually."

Daphne paused her ministrations with my hair, holding one errant curl aloft.

"Rafael helped plan the wedding?" she asked, stunned.

"In truth, he planned the entire thing," I admitted, a little chagrined.

"I don't believe it." Charlotte chuckled. "Are we all going to strip naked for a blood orgy and impale some priests for entertainment?"

"Laugh all you want," I smirked. "But he was most insistent. I suppose I didn't help matters by complaining every time he asked for my opinion on fabrics, flowers, or the guest list. He has such a romantic streak in him, I feel a bit guilty about not doing more."

Truthfully, it had taken me some time to recover mentally after the events of the previous May, and the weeks after the downfall of The Order had been busy and dark. We were relieved to not have to worry about the safety of our friends for the time being, but no one knew what would happen when King Louis learned about The Order's demise. The court had covered up the news of the aristocrats' deaths by blaming a random vampire gang for the violence, though the gossip from my bourgeois and commoner patients was that no one truly believed any of the stories coming out of Versailles.

For a time, we all were content to lie low and see how the dust settled. I'd gone back to the graveyard to recover the remains of the Judas silver and had it tucked away in a vault in Rafael's—*our*—home. Charlotte and Daphne continued to lead *les DD* in the efforts to undo much of The Order's more nefarious deeds, and they worked diligently to right a great many wrongs. It would be a long road for all of us.

And then, as the days wore on and we found a new sort of normal, I realized how lucky I'd been—how lucky *we* were—to have this second chance. Admitting as much to Rafael had resulted in a bout of fevered lovemaking that ended with a marriage proposal. Not content to wait another moment, he'd begged for my hand in the throes of bliss and came apart beneath me when I'd said yes. From that evening onward, he was a whirlwind of loving motivation—determined for us to marry as soon as possible and with as much fanfare as I'd allow.

I'd stalwartly refused to let Rafael hire servants for me, especially to dress me for a wedding. It felt too intimate to have strangers come in and gawk at the fiancée of the devilish Beast of Gévaudan. By way of compromise, he enlisted Charlotte and Daphne to help, and they were only too happy with the arrangement.

Charlotte came to admire Daphne's handiwork and wiped a tear from her eye.

"Is it that bad?" I teased.

"I'll have you know I practiced this style for a month!" Daphne replied.

Charlotte sniffed and smiled. "She did! You should have seen it. Every lady's maid from her household and mine walked around with the same coiffure for weeks."

Daphne grinned and pulled me up from the chair, twirling me around to stand before the large mirror in the bedroom.

Though I wasn't prone to vanity, I couldn't help the catch in my breath when I saw my reflection. Daphne had swept my dark curls up into a beautiful twist on top of my head, allowing a few loose strands to frame my face. She'd pinned dozens of tiny, jeweled flowers in, which made my head sparkle beneath the candlelight.

Charlotte had overseen the design of the wedding gown, and it was sheer perfection—elegant yet simple. The fitted bodice and flared, flowing skirts were the lightest shade of blue, like the color of sky seen through a wispy cloud. Small flowers were embroidered across the bodice and hem in shining silver thread.

For a moment, no one said anything.

"You look like a queen," Charlotte finally blubbered, fanning her face to keep the tears from streaking her makeup.

Daphne grasped my hands and squeezed.

"She *is* a queen," she said, her voice thick with emotion.

"I look…" I struggled to find the right words that would encompass my joy and gratitude, the love for my friends, and the astonishment I felt at looking so splendid. "…pretty."

"Pretty?" Charlotte shrieked. "Mina, *chérie*, you look well beyond pretty. You look enchanting, gorgeous, stunning, angelic—like perfection itself. It's no wonder Rafael's loved you for twenty years."

I bit my lip to keep my emotions contained.

"I love you both," I murmured. "Truly."

Daphne and Charlotte threw their arms around me, and we held the embrace until Guillaume's light knock broke the emotional silence.

"The guests are seated and waiting," he said.

"Are you ready?" Daphne whispered.

I nodded. "As I'll ever be."

Guillaume led us down the hall toward the sunken greenhouse and paused, waiting for my nod. With a steadying breath, I gripped Charlotte's and Daphne's hands, and Guillaume threw open the door.

Getting married in the greenhouse had been Rafael's idea, and though I'd had my doubts about the practicality of it, I didn't have the heart to relay them to him. I merely let him plan and plot, and now laughed at how wrong I'd been to doubt him.

The greenhouse was positively aglow with candlelight, and flowers trailed along every surface of the marble pathway. It looked like an enchanted fairy garden from a children's storybook. A string quartet played heartbreakingly beautiful music off to the side, and rain delicately tapped on the glass ceiling while wedding guests murmured quietly to each other. I closed my eyes to memorize the sound. It was one of the most wonderful things I'd ever heard.

Daphne and Charlotte kissed my cheeks and found their seats with Étienne, Antoine, Laszlo, and Marguerite. I scanned the room and saw all *les DD* agents were in attendance, along with a few of my better-known patients. Rafael stepped into the aisle ahead of me, and when our gazes met, the world fell away.

"Oh," he breathed, shock freezing him in place.

"Is that all you can say?" I whispered, teasing. "Oh?"

The spell rooting him in place broke, and he smiled more broadly than I'd ever seen. The wave of love and joy I felt from him was almost enough to drown me.

"You're the most exquisite creature I've ever seen, Mina. You look ravishing," he rumbled, his eyes flooding with the black and red of his desire.

A suit of black silk hugged his body perfectly, with delicate touches of silver embroidery that matched the details on my gown. His black hair was tied back and though his face was a mask of calm happiness, beneath the peaceful expression I sensed the wildness of his emotions—excitement, impatience, hunger, lust, and a flicker of annoyance that he couldn't lift my skirts and take me right here. I loved him even more for the duality.

His cool hand slipped into mine, and he gestured at the altar built in front of the waterfall where we'd first sat together. I gazed up into his dark eyes, happier than I'd ever been.

"Are you ready, Rafael?" I asked.

He winked and led me forward over the flower-strewn path.

"As I'll ever be."

BONUS EPILOGUE
MINA

February 6, 1769
Venice

"IF THAT MAN LOOKS AT YOU ONE MORE TIME, I'LL TAKE GREAT PLEASURE IN plucking his eyes from his skull," Rafael grumbled, glaring at the scientist sitting in the front row of the lecture hall.

I turned to see who had drawn my new husband's ire and swallowed a laugh—Signore Bianchi was in his seventies and likely squinting through cataracts.

"You have nothing to worry about, my love," I soothed. "I can assure you his interest is purely academic."

"Mina, you think every man's interest in you is *purely academic*. You don't see what I see—the heat in their eyes as their unworthy gazes slide over your body. The interest sparking in their faces when they listen to you speak. Even when they know I'm here with you, they cannot keep their lustful thoughts hidden," he growled. "My fangs ache to rip out their throats and offer their blood to you as tribute, my goddess."

A heady swirl of violent desire made my focus waver, but I cleared my throat and adjusted the tight neckline on my modest gown. As much as I loved carving out my place in the scientific communities across Europe, part of me longed to be done with the lecture circuit—to simply spend my evenings in bed with my dark prince, learning all the ways we could find amusement in each other's arms. With each stuffy academic event, I felt more guilt at dragging Rafael along when we were supposed to be on our honeymoon trip around the world.

"I appreciate you attending tonight's lecture, but you've heard the material a hundred times already—you must be bored. Why don't you go explore the city, or take in an opera? I'm sure the Carnivale fêtes would prove most diverting."

"If you think I'd rather spend my evenings carousing with a lot of sweaty, drunken revelers instead of watching you deliver hour-long talks on the metaphysical properties of supernatural blood types...clearly you are mistaking me with the man I was twenty years ago," he smirked. His hand snaked around my waist as I collected stacks of notes and illustrations.

"Besides, when you speak passionately about your work, your cheeks flush and you nibble on that delicious bottom lip. It is *unbearably* erotic. It makes me think of all the things I'm going to do to you as soon as we get back to our rooms..."

A gruff cough interrupted us.

"Doctor Van Helsing, your research is *most* inspiring," the older scientist said. He bowed stiffly and I worried that he might topple right over, so I reached forward to help him.

"Signore Bianchi, thank you," I said. "It's an honor to make your acquaintance. I enjoyed your book on foraminifera and have read it many times. May I present my husband, Rafael of House Dracul? Darling, Signore Bianchi helped persuade the academy to invite me to speak."

Rafael inclined his head, offering a lethal smile.

"Thank you, Signore, for arranging this evening on my wife's lecture tour. Your correspondence has brought her much joy and it is, of course, my life's pursuit to keep her happy," he charmed. "I hear your cabinet of curiosities is unparalleled in this part of the world. At some point, I would dearly love to see it."

Signore Bianchi preened and smoothed a gnarled hand over the vanishing forest of gray hair atop his head.

"I do boast a very comprehensive specimen collection," he said, warming to the attention. "I should be delighted to invite the two of you to visit me in Rimini. I wonder—would you be willing to donate to my ever-growing collection?"

Confusion drew my brows up. I felt Rafael stiffen next to me.

"Donate, Signore?" I asked. "I'm afraid my husband and I don't have many specimens. A botany lab of some note, but nothing that would interest a collector like you."

"Well, ah, I'm most interested in samples of your blood—the both of you," Signore Bianchi replied. "The both of you are rather rare specimens yourselves. You should both be examined. Studied! The blood of an elder Dracul must have such interesting properties. A true prize for any collector."

Nausea rolled through my gut as the realization solidified. I hadn't been invited here to discuss my research or my life's work—I'd been invited here because of our reputations as mere scientific oddities. Staring into the older man's expectant face, I allowed myself a gentle push against his consciousness. *Interest. Curiosity. Greed. Disgust.*

My heart sank.

"I'm afraid that's quite impossible," I heard myself say. "The research my husband and I do on the blood plague is…well, we prefer to keep it *in house*, so to speak. I do thank you for your interest, and for the invitation to lecture this evening."

Lip curling in displeasure, Signore Bianchi stepped forward to argue— to insist, no doubt. Before my curt retort had time to fully form on my tongue, Rafael moved in front of him.

"I suggest you find the exit, Signore, or the only blood sampled tonight will be yours," he growled, flashing a threatening amount of fang.

The older man paled and wisely determined not to press his luck. He hurried over to a knot of older men, hissing whispers of outrage.

"I take it the late reception of sherry and coffee is no longer on offer," I mumbled, gathering the last of my notes and books. I was keen to distract myself from the blooming disappointment growing like a parasite in my chest. Rafael seethed at my elbow, barely containing his rage as we made our way from the academy lecture hall and into the winding streets near the Piazza San Marco.

The narrow alleys along the canals were choked with tourists for Carnivale, and while their boisterous joy lightened my mood somewhat, it was clear Rafael didn't share my amusement. Guilt threaded through me —all his life he'd been an outsider, a *thing* to be feared and reviled, and despite the inroads he'd made recovering his reputation over the last few months, people still thought of him as a monster. A *creature.*

He was a lost prince to a fallen kingdom, and my academic work had put him in the path of yet another insult tonight.

When we reached the sprawling piazza, revelers in masquerade finery crowded around market stalls selling wine and sweets, cheap trinkets, and garish masks. Musicians and theater troupes drew small crowds, and my sharp supernatural eyes caught several young pickpockets weaving through the unsuspecting groups, lifting purses from oblivious marks.

"Would you like a gelato before we head back to our rooms, Rafael?" I offered, hoping to assuage some of my guilt. "My treat, since you've been such a patient, supportive husband allowing me my academic pursuits on our honeymoon."

He grunted and frowned, but led me over to a vendor selling the delicious confection. *Oh yes, he was definitely upset.*

I dug through the pockets of my red brocade gown, fishing for my coin purse, but Rafael sighed and insisted on paying. Anxiety almost curdled the iced cream in my hands at his sour temperament.

"That was meant to be my peace offering," I said quietly as we found the darkened edge of the square. Torches and braziers guttered with flickering orange light, but neither my vampire lover nor I needed it to see our way along the canals.

We ate our treats in silence for a few moments, until finally, Rafael regarded me with arched brows.

"Peace offering?" he echoed. I watched as his tongue swiped a lick of the swiftly melting lemon cream and something low in my belly clenched.

"Yes, I..." My voice was a touch breathless, and I swallowed. *Focus, Mina.* "I'm sorry for what Signore Bianchi said. For how he treated us —*you*. But that's not all...I'm sorry for taking away from our time together for all these silly lectures and society events. It's far from fair, but I just... well, I hadn't been asked—*allowed*, really—to lecture much before but after I turned and we got married, the invitations poured in, and I felt a bit like the belle of the ball."

The last of the gelato eaten, Rafael crumpled the paper cup and tossed it into the nearest brazier. A devastating smile tugged at the corners of his mouth. With excruciating slowness, he drew a finger across my lower lip to wipe an errant drop of cream, then sucked it off his finger. Lust exploded in my veins—far from a slowly stoked fire, much closer to a destructive volcanic eruption.

"And I've never been the belle of the ball before, you see? Not that it matters, but...Oh, I'm rambling," I squeaked out, still staring at his delicious mouth, my thoughts a dizzying jumble of embarrassment and desire.

"Have you finished?" he asked patiently, slowly forcing me back me against a wall.

I nodded, my breath coming in excited pants.

"You have nothing to apologize for, my darling. Every time I have the privilege of watching you teach others about your work, I fall in love with you all over again. You are brilliant, and it grieves me that you haven't had every opportunity before now. If this was all you wanted to do with your supernatural life, I would happily consent to follow you everywhere just so I could carry your books and ink your quills..." he pressed his hard length against my belly and nipped at my earlobe. I whimpered. "And feast on your divine cunt while the pathetic scientists and physicians who scorned you go back to their sad, lonely laboratories and stroke themselves over the pretty doctor they cannot have."

I was going to go mad with the force of my sexual need. My heavy breasts and peaked nipples strained beneath the bodice of my suddenly too-tight gown and desire soaked my underskirts. Rafael chuckled, grinding against me and ghosting kisses up my neck. *Dieu, if he is quick, I will have him right here.*

"I don't need you to make amends, my love," he whispered against my heated skin. "I need you to *scream.*"

My knees buckled and pressure built in my gums as my monstrous fangs lengthened. My blood burned in my veins—I needed Rafael with a dangerous ferocity, and I knew just how to unlock his demonic side.

"Make me," I challenged, reaching for the falls of his tight black breeches.

He pulled back slightly, his eyes a flood of black and red possessiveness.

"What?" he growled.

"Your hearing is impeccable, husband," I taunted. "Is it comprehension you lack? If you want me to scream, you'll have to make me."

The lust in his gaze sharpened to a knife point, stripping me bare of my bravado. I watched several expressions dance across his face as he fought to control the wicked things he kept leashed out of consideration for me. But I knew who I married—who I cleaved my eternity to.

"Do you understand what you're asking for, my Mina?" he ground out, anxiously flexing his trembling hands on my waist.

I nodded. "I do."

He closed his eyes and shuddered against me; a desperate moan wrenched from his lips. When he opened them, there was an unhinged excitement glowing in his gaze.

"Should you wish me to stop, you'll need to say *almond cake.* Agreed?" he rasped.

"Agreed. Touch me, Rafael, before I go mad with want," I begged, leaning forward for a kiss. Before my lips could make contact, he pulled back and threw me over his shoulder. I shrieked as he ran down the darkened canal at supernatural speed until he reached a small private dock. He set me down with heartbreaking care, gesturing to a sleek black gondola bobbing in the water ahead.

"Surprise," he murmured, tugging my hand toward the impressive watercraft. A small cabin sat perched in the center of the boat—a *felze,* I thought they were called.

Confusion stole some of my passion away, and I turned to him quizzically.

"Are we going somewhere?" I asked.

"Well, we can go anywhere we want. I had it made for you, my love. Come, let me show you," he said.

"You bought me a boat?" I replied, stunned. "Rafael, the expense!"

He waved away my concern and helped me step down into the beautiful gondola. Intricate carvings decorated the bow and plump pillows studded the seats. As he led me forward, he pulled up the rope tying us to the dock and with a swift motion, poled us into a wider part of the lagoon. Once we neared a small island a short distance away, he abandoned the oar and opened the door of the cabin. Inside was a plush bed—just big enough for two—with a navy blue silk coverlet and an avalanche of pillows. Candlelight flickered from small sconces along the walls, and a tray of sandwiches, sweets, and two full decanters of blood sat against a bench in front of an open window.

"Oh, Rafael," I breathed. "This is wonderful. How unbearably romantic!"

When I turned to thank him, I gasped at the hunger in his eyes. His fangs lengthened over his lower lip in a predatory smile, and he backed me into the cabin until I stumbled backwards onto the bed. With brutal efficiency, he sliced through my gown, stays and chemise with his lethal claws, baring my naked body to the cool night air and his scorching gaze. The heat of desire that had cooled to a slow simmer came blazing back.

"How does this all stop?" he rasped, divesting himself of his jacket, waistcoat, breeches and shirt in frenzied haste.

"Almond cake," I replied obediently.

"Good girl," he said with a nod.

Pushing me onto my back, he crawled forward, covering my body with his. With a snap of his fingers and an unfamiliar word, the door and the window slammed shut, extinguishing all but one of the candles. In its guttering light, shadows danced across Rafael's handsome face, making his beauty all the more sinister. Reaching beneath the mountain of pillows, he extracted several lengths of black silk cord.

"I've always fantasized about tying you up, my Mina," he said, the hitch in his voice the only sign he was at the precipice of control. "When we were apart all those years, I stroked myself often over the same visions —binding your glorious body to my bed and visiting unending pleasures upon you until you agreed to be mine—until you relented and realized how perfect and horrifying my devotion is."

His hands shook as he tied my wrists to the headboard, and then with a wicked grin, tied my ankles to the bedposts, splaying my body shamelessly wide for his roving attentions. Once he was satisfied with the gentle but firm bindings, he sat back on his heels. His erection bobbed between us and he ran one hand along it, leisurely stroking as his eyes bored into mine. Liquid desire pooled between my legs and I swore.

For the first time, I began to worry that I'd bitten off more than I could chew.

RAFAEL

Mina. Mine. Mine. Mine. Mine. Mine. Mine. Mine. Mine. Mine. Mine. Mine. Mine. Mine. Mine. Mina.

MINA

"Rafael," I pleaded.

"That doesn't sound like a scream to me," he snarled.

With a growl, he lunged forward, capturing one peaked nipple in his mouth and running the smooth backs of his claws over the other, sending lightning bolts of pleasure across my nerves. As he laved my breasts with his tongue and pricked the sensitive points with his claws, I couldn't fight the reflexive need to grind my hips upward, seeking his hard cock.

"Poor little Mina," he drawled, lowering a hand to cup my heated sex. "We've only just begun and already this sweet cunt is dripping for me." One fingertip slipped through the slick seam and mercilessly circled the tight bud of my pleasure. I bucked against his hand, seeking more—more, until he relented and slipped one, then two fingers inside me. His deep groans melted into growls as he worked me to a fevered pitch.

"Yes, yes, my love—oh, Rafael, I'm going to come. I'm so close!" I keened.

Mina. The word echoed through my head. *Mina. You will not. You have not yet screamed prettily enough for me.*

I grunted a curse and bucked harder, determined to seize the pleasure that dangled from my husband's tantalizing fingers.

As I felt the sharp edge of bliss near, I started to cry out—only to be silenced by Rafael's voracious mouth on mine.

That is not the scream I want, he said in my head.

I'm going to come—you cannot stop me, I shot back, shuddering against him, sucking at his tongue and lips in a wild frenzy.

Just as the orgasm started to crest, cold enveloped me, as though I'd been dunked in a glacial sea. My pleasure faded away and I stared up at Rafael—shocked.

The devilish glint in his eyes told me what I needed to know. Suddenly, I remembered his threats to me once in Charlotte's home:

"I could have you bouncing naked on my lap, your breasts in my hands and your perfect little clit stroking my shaft and even then, I could invade your mind and keep your release at bay. Could you imagine that, my Persephone? Endless days and nights of sex without an orgasm, all because I might have a torturous whim."

Understanding dawned and I beheld satisfaction on Rafael's face as he realized I'd connected the dots. I opened my mouth to rage at him, my lust warring with my anger, but then I remembered he'd given me the key to this all at the very beginning. *Almond cake.* I could say it—give in to his torment and beg him to release my pleasure. He would, I knew. He would make me come a thousand times if I asked—if I ended our game. A perverse delight sparked in my chest, my stubbornness and pride winning out for the moment.

"Do you have something to say, my beloved?" he asked softly, circling my nipple with one claw.

"Yes," I replied on a gasp. His eyes met mine expectantly. "Is that all?"

With a wicked chuckle and no other preamble, he dove between my legs, covering my sex with his mouth and sucking my clit with fierce abandon. Bright pleasure sheared through my thoughts again—a symphony of sensation. Fangs grazing my slick lips, he plunged two fingers inside my heated channel, curling them against the hidden spot where pleasure lay. A denied orgasm started to rise from the ashes of the previous one, closing in on me in haste.

"Yes, my love. *More.* I need more," I begged.

I know what you need, he said in my head, not pausing in his onslaught of sexual worship. The thought came with graphic visions of what was to come, along with phantom sensations of being filled—stretched—to the point of devastating rapture. This time, the combination of his mesmeric powers and his expert tongue and fingers brought me screaming to the start of another orgasm and suddenly...

Cold.

A void where ecstasy should have been.

Rafael sat back once more, licking my wetness from his claws and glaring at me in challenge. Precum dripped from his hard cock and a muscle ticked in his jaw—the only signs that gave me the sense that he was just as desperate as I was.

I considered ripping through the bonds and attacking him out of pulsing fury and lust, or sobbing out my safety words to end my aching torment. Both felt like defeat to me, and I would not be so easily defeated.

I would beat him at this game.

Closing my eyes against the silver tears that threatened, I centered myself and reached for the darkness that knelt in me, always at the ready.

Rafael, I called to him through our mental connection. *Do you not wish to claim my body? To sink into me? To fill me utterly with your very essence? Do you not long to sear my needy cunt with your heat? I need you, my love. I am yours.*

The words were my siren song to him, accompanied by my own phantom touches along his ears, neck, abdomen, and straining erection. An unwilling groan rumbled from his chest and his mouth dropped open, on the cusp of uttering our safety words. His breathing stuttered as he watched me writhe against my silken bonds.

"Mina," he rasped, running his fingers through his hair. "I fear I started a game I no longer have the strength to finish."

He quickly reached down to untie the ropes on my ankles and wrists, sowing fevered kisses up my skin.

"Forgive me for indulging my demons too much," he begged, notching the slick head of his cock at my quivering entrance.

"Perhaps I enjoy your demons," I laughed, shifting into my massive demon form. Curling horns, broad bat wings, and a long, pointed tail erupted from my blue-grey body as I changed into my favorite she-devil shape—the stuff of nightmares. Startled, Rafael rolled to the side as I burst through the door of the cabin and shot into the sky. A cry of anguish rose from the deck of the gondola, followed by the sound of splintering wood. I hoped he hadn't destroyed our lovely boat in his frustration.

It wasn't long before he'd caught up to me, his expansive wings powering him through the night sky toward me.

Torturous minx, he laughed. *Once again, you run from me! I should've kept you tied to my bed.*

Grinning back at the bat-like monster pursuing me, I dipped low over the lagoon and skimmed my claws through the black water. I loved Rafael's demon form—glossy black wings, a thick, barbed tail, claws twice the length of his vampiric fingers. If I'd become the stuff of nightmares, he was something out of my darkest dreams. He gained on me inch by inch, until he was close enough to seize me by my tail. The move pulled us both off balance and we tumbled out of the sky, rolling together onto a beach of silty gray sand along the small island nearby.

When we stilled, Rafael pinned me beneath him and inhaled deeply at the crook of my neck. His long, forked tongue snaked out, tracing the outer shell of my ear. I shivered against him as it caressed a path south, swirling over my breasts and dipping low between my legs. He rumbled with pleasure at my whimper when his tongue speared me and rolled through my pussy in a torturously slow twist. When he had me squirming beneath him, he pulled his tongue back into his fanged maw with an obscenely wet *pop.*

Do you want to continue this game, wife? Rafael asked, his thick length a heated brand between us. In this demon form, his cock was red veined with black, and I was desperate to see it sliding between my blue-gray lips.

Have your demons had enough, husband? I responded, hooking one clawed foot behind his ass and positioning him at my entrance, still slick with arousal. His tail snaked up to my breasts, rubbing at the sensitive peaked points.

He nodded, bending down to kiss me with tenderness unbecoming of his monstrous form.

Sometimes, my demons forget I have the keys to Heaven right here, he purred, sliding into me on a growl from us both. The drawn-out foreplay had us both in a frenzy, sensations heightened to the apex of pleasure. Every slow stroke of his cock, every pricking of his claws, every shuddering grunt of desperation stoked the fires hotter and hotter, until his movements stuttered, and his rhythm began to falter.

I don't think I can hold back much longer, my love, Rafael groaned, his thoughts coming through in a rough crackle of oncoming need. Reaching between us, he pressed the flat of his thumb against my over-sensitive clit, and pleasure arced from the touch like lightning finding metal.

Nor I, I moaned, bearing down on his pistoning hips. As the orgasm wound its tendrils through my nerves, I clutched at Rafael, sinking my claws into his back and wrapping my tail around his thigh.

Come with me, my beautiful doctor. My wife. My Mina, he gasped, sinking his teeth into my neck as pleasure rocked through him. His bliss gave way to my own, and I followed him over the edge—my monstrous screams fracturing the night like an orgy of demons.

Collapsing on top of me, I felt Rafael smile against my shoulder.

"How beautifully you screamed for me," he huffed, as we shifted back to our human forms. "It will live in my memories for years to come."

I sighed in satisfaction, staring up into star-studded sky. Soft silver clouds scraped across the fat, round moon, casting our naked forms in a pale gold-tinged glow. My hands drifted over Rafael's smooth, cool skin in reverence. As beautiful as my dark prince was, I found his primal demon form equally compelling.

"Let's head back to the gondola. I could use some refreshment and a bite of something sweet before we continue our...diversions," I said, placing a chaste kiss on his nose.

"Anything you desire," he replied, lifting me into his arms. "What sort of refreshment did you have in mind?"

Almond cake.

ABOUT THE AUTHOR

Lily Riley is a romance novelist currently focused on books that feature a little bit of cheek and a lot of steam.

Her *Vampires in Versailles* series begins with *The Assassin and the Libertine*, continues with *The Agent and the Outlaw,* and ends with *The Doctor and the Devil.*

When Lily isn't writing about dreamy, supernatural beings in 18th century France, she enjoys sipping champagne, eating cake, and dancing naked by the light of the full moon.

To sign up for her newsletter or read more about her upcoming projects, visit: www.authorlilyriley.com